ONE DOOR AWAY FROM HEAVEN

Also by Dean Koontz from Headline Feature

From the Corner of his Eye
False Memory
Seize the Night
Fear Nothing
Sole Survivor
Intensity
Dark Rivers of the Heart
Mr Murder
Dragon Tears
Hideaway
Cold Fire
The Bad Place
Midnight
Lightning
Watchers
Ticktock
Strange Highways
Demon Seed
Icebound
Winter Moon
The Funhouse
The Face of Fear
The Mask
Shadowfires
The Eyes of Darkness
The Servants of Twilight
The Door to December
The Key to Midnight
The House of Thunder
Phantoms
Whispers
Shattered
Chase
Twilight Eyes
The Voice of the Night
Strangers
Darkness Comes
The Vision
Night Chills

ONE DOOR AWAY FROM HEAVEN

Dean Koontz

HEADLINE
FEATURE

First published in Great Britain in 2001 by
HEADLINE BOOK PUBLISHING

A HEADLINE FEATURE book

10 9 8 7 6 5 4 3 2 1

British Library Cataloguing in Publication Data

Koontz, Dean R., 1945–
    One door away from heaven
    1. Suspense fiction
    I. Title
    813.5'4[F]

ISBN 0 7472 7072 4 (hardback)
ISBN 0 7472 7075 9 (trade paperback)

Typeset by Palimpsest Book Production Limited,
Polmont, Stirlingshire
Printed and bound in Great Britain by
Mackays of Chatham plc, Chatham, Kent

HEADLINE BOOK PUBLISHING
A division of Hodder Headline
338 Euston Road
London NW1 3BH

www.headline.co.uk
www.hodderheadline.com

This book is dedicated to Irwyn Applebaum, who has encouraged me 'to take the train out there where the trains don't usually go,' and whose character as both a publisher and a man has restored my lost faith in the publishing industry, or business, or folly, or whatever else it might accurately be called.

And:

To Tracy Devine, my editor, who never panics when, far past my deadline, I want to take yet more time to do draft number forty before turning in the script, whose editorial eye has twenty-ten vision, who is graciousness personified, who makes every phase of the work a delight – and who will think that this dedication is too effusive and in need of cutting. Well, this time she's wrong.

Humor is emotional chaos remembered in tranquility.
 —James Thurber

Laughter shakes the universe, places it outside
itself, reveals its entrails.
 —Octavio Paz

Why does man kill? He kills for food. And not only
food: frequently, there must be a beverage.
 —Woody Allen

In the end, everything is a gag.
 —Charlie Chaplin

Unextinguished laughter shakes the skies.
 —Homer, *The Iliad*

Funny had better be sad somewhere.
 —Jerry Lewis

1

The world is full of broken people. Splints, casts, miracle drugs, and time can't mend fractured hearts, wounded minds, torn spirits.

Currently, sunshine was Micky Bellsong's medication of choice, and southern California in late August was an apothecary with a deep supply of this prescription.

Tuesday afternoon, wearing a bikini and oiled for broiling, Micky reclined in a lounge chair in her aunt Geneva's backyard. The nylon webbing was a nausea-inducing shade of green, and it sagged, too, and the aluminum joints creaked as though the lawn furniture were far older than Micky, who was only twenty-eight, but who sometimes felt ancient.

Her aunt, from whom fate had stolen everything except a reliable sense of humor, referred to the yard as 'the garden.' That would be the rosebush.

The property was wider than it was deep, to allow the full length of the house trailer to face the street. Instead of a lawn with trees, a narrow covered patio shaded the front entrance. Here in the back, a strip of grass extended from one side of the lot to the other, but it provided a scant twelve feet of turf between the door and the rear fence. The grass flourished because Geneva watered it regularly with a hose.

The rosebush, however, responded perversely to tender care.

In spite of ample sunshine, water, and plant food, in spite of the regular aeration of its roots and periodic treatment with measured doses of insecticide, the bush remained as scraggly and as blighted as any specimen watered with venom and fed pure sulfur in the satanic gardens of Hell.

Face to the sun, eyes closed, striving to empty her mind of all thought, yet troubled by insistent memories, Micky had been cooking for half an hour when a small sweet voice asked, 'Are you suicidal?'

She turned her head toward the speaker and saw a girl of nine or ten standing at the low, sagging picket fence that separated this trailer space from the one to the west. Sun glare veiled the kid's features.

'Skin cancer kills,' the girl explained.

'So does vitamin D deficiency.'

'Not likely.'

'Your bones get soft.'

'Rickets. I know. But you can get vitamin D in tuna, eggs, and dairy products. That's better than too much sun.'

Closing her eyes again, turning her face to the deadly blazing heavens, Micky said, 'Well, I don't intend to live forever.'

'Why not?'

'Maybe you haven't noticed, but nobody does.'

'I probably will,' the girl declared.

'How's that work?'

'A little extraterrestrial DNA.'

'Yeah, right. You're part alien.'

'Not yet. I have to make contact first.'

Micky opened her eyes again and squinted at the ET wannabe. 'You've been watching too many reruns of *The X Files*, kid.'

'I've only got until my next birthday, and then all bets are off.' The girl moved along the swooning fence to a point where it had entirely collapsed. She clattered across the flattened section of pickets and approached Micky. 'Do you believe in life after death?'

'I'm not sure I believe in life *before* death,' Micky said.

'I knew you were suicidal.'

'I'm not suicidal. I'm just a wiseass.'

Even after stepping off the splintered fence staves onto the grass, the girl moved awkwardly. 'We're renting next door. We just moved in. My name's Leilani.'

As Leilani drew closer, Micky saw that she wore a complicated steel brace on her left leg, from the ankle to above the knee.

'Isn't that an Hawaiian name?' Micky asked.

'My mother's a little nuts about all things Hawaiian.'

Leilani wore khaki shorts. Her right leg was fine, but in the cradle of steel and padding, her left leg appeared to be mal-formed.

'In fact,' Leilani continued, 'old Sinsemilla – that's my mother – is a little nuts, period.'

'Sinsemilla? That's a . . .'

'Type of marijuana. Maybe she was Cindy Sue or Barbara way back in the Jurassic period, but she's called herself Sinsemilla as long as I've known her.' Leilani settled into a hideous orange-and-blue chair as decrepit as Micky's bile-green lounge. 'This lawn furniture sucks.'

'Someone gave it to Aunt Geneva for nothing.'

'She ought to've been paid to take it. Anyway, they put old Sinsemilla in an institution once and shot like fifty or a hundred thousand volts of electricity through her brain, but it didn't help.'

'You shouldn't make up stuff like that about your own mother.'

Leilani shrugged. 'It's the truth. I couldn't make up anything as weird as what is. In fact, they blasted her brain several times. Probably, if they'd done it just once more, old Sinsemilla would've developed a taste for electricity. Now she'd be sticking her finger in a socket about ten times a day. She's an addictive personality, but she means well.'

Although the sky was a furnace grate, although Micky was slick with coconut-scented lotion and sweat, she'd grown all but oblivious of the sun. 'How old are you, kid?'

'Nine. But I'm precocious. What's your name?'

'Micky.'

'That's a name for a boy or a mouse. So it's probably Michelle. Most women your age are named Michelle or Heather or Courtney.'

'My age?'

'No offense intended.'

'It's Michelina.'

Leilani wrinkled her nose. 'Too precious.'

'Michelina Bellsong.'

'No wonder you're suicidal.'

'Therefore – Micky.'

'I'm Klonk.'

'You're what?'

'Leilani Klonk.'

Micky cocked her head and frowned skeptically. 'I'm not sure I should believe anything you tell me.'

'Sometimes names are destiny. Look at you. Two pretty names, and you're as gorgeous as a model – except for all the sweat and your face puffy with a hangover.'

'Thanks. I guess.'

'Me, on the other hand – I've got one pretty name followed by a clinker like Klonk. Half of me is sort of pretty—'

'You're *very* pretty,' Micky assured her.

This was true. Golden hair. Eyes as blue as gentian petals. The clarity of Leilani's features promised that hers was not the transient beauty of childhood, but an enduring quality.

'Half of me,' Leilani conceded, 'might turn heads one day, but that's balanced by the fact that I'm a mutant.'

'You're not a mutant.'

The girl stamped her left foot on the ground, causing the leg brace to rattle softly. She raised her left hand, which proved to be deformed: The little finger and the ring finger were fused into a single misshapen digit that was connected by a thick web of tissue to a gnarled and stubby middle finger.

Until now, Micky hadn't noticed this deformity. 'Everyone's got imperfections,' she said.

'This isn't like having a big schnoz. I'm either a mutant or a cripple, and I refuse to be a cripple. People pity cripples, but they're afraid of mutants.'

'You want people to be afraid of you?'

'Fear implies respect,' Leilani said.

'So far, you're not registering high on my terror meter.'

'Give me time. You've got a great body.'

Disconcerted to hear such a thing from a child, Micky covered her discomfort with self-deprecation: 'Yeah, well, by nature I'm a huge pudding. I've got to work hard to stay like this.'

'No you don't. You were born perfect, and you've got one of those metabolisms tuned like a space-shuttle gyroscope. You could eat half a cow and drink a keg of beer every day, and your butt would actually tighten up a notch.'

Micky couldn't remember the last time that she'd been rendered speechless by anyone, but with this girl, she was nearly befuddled into silence. 'How would you know?'

'I can tell,' Leilani assured her. 'You don't run, you don't power walk—'

'I work out.'

'Oh? When was your last workout?'

'Yesterday,' Micky lied.

'Yeah,' said Leilani, 'and I was out waltzing all night.' She stamped her left foot again, rattling her leg brace. 'Having a great metabolism is nothing to be ashamed about. It's not like laziness or anything.'

'Thanks for your approval.'

'Your boobs are real, aren't they?'

'Girl, you are an amazing piece of work.'

'Thanks. They must be real. Even the best implants don't look that natural. Unless there's major improvement in implant technology, my best hope is to develop good boobs. You can be a mutant and still attract men if you've got great boobs. That's been my observation, anyway. Men can be lovely creatures, but in some ways, they're pathetically predictable.'

'You're nine, huh?'

'My birthday was February twenty-eighth. That was Ash Wednesday this year. Do you believe in fasting and penitence?'

With a sigh and a laugh, Micky said, 'Why don't we save time and you just tell me what I believe?'

'Probably not much of anything,' Leilani said, without a pause. 'Except in having fun and getting through the day.'

Micky was left speechless not by the child's acute perception but by hearing the truth put so bluntly, especially as this was a truth that she had long avoided contemplating.

'Nothing wrong with having fun,' said Leilani. 'One of the things I believe, if you want to know, is that we're here to enjoy life.' She shook her head. 'Amazing. Men must be all over you.'

'Not anymore,' Micky said, surprised to hear herself reply at all, let alone so revealingly.

A lopsided smile tugged at the right corner of the girl's mouth, and unmistakable merriment enlivened her blue eyes. 'Now don't you wish you could see me as a mutant?'

'What?'

'As long as you think of me as a handicapped waif, your pity doesn't allow you to be impolite. On the other hand, if you could see me as a weird and possibly dangerous mutant, you'd tell me none of this is my business, and you'd hustle me back to my own yard.'

'You're looking more like a mutant all the time.'

Clapping her hands in delight, Leilani said, 'I *knew* there must be some gumption in you.' She rose from her chair with a hitch and pointed across the backyard. 'What's that thing?'

'A rosebush.'

'No, really.'

'Really. It's a rosebush.'

'No roses.'

'The potential's there.'

'Hardly any leaves.'

'Lots of thorns, though,' Micky noted.

Squinching her face, Leilani said, 'I bet it pulls up its roots late at night and creeps around the neighborhood, eating stray cats.'

'Lock your doors.'

'We don't have cats.' Leilani blinked. 'Oh.' She grinned. 'Good one.' She hooked her right hand into an imitation of a claw, raked the air, and hissed.

'What did you mean when you said "all bets are off"?'

'When did I say that?' Leilani asked disingenuously.

'You said you've only got until your next birthday, and then all bets are off.'

'Oh, the alien-contact thing.'

Although that wasn't an answer, she turned away from Micky and crossed the lawn in a steel-stiffened gait.

Micky leaned forward from the angled back of the lounge chair. 'Leilani?'

'I say a lot of stuff. Not all of it means anything.' At the gap in the broken fence, the girl stopped and turned. 'Say, Michelina Bellsong, did I ask whether you believe in life after death?'

'And I was a wiseass.'

'Yeah, I remember now.'

'So . . . do *you?*' Micky asked.

'Do I what?'

'Believe in life after death?'

Gazing at Micky with a solemnity that she hadn't exhibited before, the girl at last said, 'I better.'

As she negotiated the fallen pickets and crossed the neglected sun-browned lawn next door, the faint click-and-squeak of her leg brace faded until it could have been mistaken for the language of industrious insects hard at work in the hot, dry air.

For a while after the girl had gone into the neighboring house trailer, Micky sat forward in the lounge chair, staring at the door through which she had disappeared.

Leilani was a pretty package of charm, intelligence, and cocky attitude that masked an aching vulnerability. But while remembered moments of their encounter now brought a smile to Micky, she was also left with a vague uneasiness. Like a quick dark fish, some disturbing half-glimpsed truth had seemed to dart beneath the surface of their conversation, though it eluded her net.

The liquid-thick heat of the late August sun pooled around Micky. She felt as though she were floating in a hot bath.

The scent of recently mown grass saturated the still air: the intoxicating essence of summer.

In the distance rose the lulling rumble-hum of freeway traffic, a not unpleasant drone that might be mistaken for the rhythmic susurration of the sea.

She should have grown drowsy, at least lethargic, but her mind hummed more busily than the traffic, and her body grew stiff with a tension that the sun couldn't cook from her.

Although it seemed unrelated to Leilani Klonk, Micky recalled something that her aunt Geneva had said only the previous evening, over dinner . . . .

'Change isn't easy, Micky. Changing the way you live means changing how you think. Changing how you think means changing what you believe about life. That's hard, sweetie. When we make our own misery, we sometimes cling to it even when we want so bad to change, because the misery is something we know. The misery is comfortable.'

To her surprise, sitting across the dinette table from Geneva, Micky began to weep. No racking sobs. Discreet, this weeping. The plate of homemade lasagna blurred in front of her, and hot tears slid down her cheeks. She kept her fork in motion throughout this silent salty storm, loath to acknowledge what was happening to her.

She hadn't cried since childhood. She'd thought that she was beyond tears, too tough for self-pity and too hardened to be moved by the plight of anyone else. With grim determination, angry with herself for this weakness, she continued eating even though her throat grew so thick with emotion that she had difficulty swallowing.

Geneva, who knew her niece's stoic nature, nevertheless didn't seem surprised by the tears. She didn't comment on them, because she surely knew that consolation wouldn't be welcome.

By the time Micky's vision cleared and her plate was clean, she was able to say, 'I can do what I need to do. I can get where I want to go, no matter how hard it is.'

Geneva added one thought before changing the subject: 'It's also true that sometimes – not often, but once in a great while – your life can change for the better in one moment of grace, almost a sort of miracle. Something so powerful can happen, someone so special come along, some precious understanding descend on you so unexpectedly that it just pivots you in a new direction, changes you forever. Girl, I'd give everything I have if that could happen for you.'

To stave off more tears, Micky said, 'That's sweet, Aunt Gen, but everything you have doesn't amount to squat.'

Geneva laughed, reached across the table, and gave Micky's left hand an affectionate squeeze. 'That's true enough, honey. But I've still got about half a squat more than *you* do.'

Strangely, here in the sunshine, less than a day later, Micky couldn't stop thinking about the transforming moment of grace that Geneva had wished for her. She didn't believe in miracles, neither the supernatural sort that involved guardian angels and the radiant hand of God revealed nor the merely statistical variety that might present her with a winning lottery ticket.

Yet she had the curious and unsettling sensation of movement within, of a turning in her heart and mind, toward a new point on the compass.

'Just indigestion,' she murmured with self-derision, because she knew that she was the same shiftless, screwed-up woman who had come to Geneva a week ago with two suitcases full of clothes, an '81 Chevrolet Camaro that whiffered and wheezed worse than a pneumonic horse, and a past that wound like chains around her.

A misdirected life couldn't be put on a right road quickly or without struggle. For all of Geneva's appealing talk of a miraculous moment of transformation, nothing had happened to pivot Micky toward grace.

Nevertheless, for reasons that she could not understand, every aspect of this day – the spangled sunshine, the heat, the rumble of the distant freeway traffic, the fragrances of cut grass and sweat-soured coconut oil, three yellow butterflies as bright as gift-box bows – suddenly seemed full of meaning, mystery, and moment.

2

In a faint and inconstant breeze, waves stir through the lush meadow. At this lonely hour, in this strange place, a boy can easily imagine that monsters swim ceaselessly through the moon-silvered sea of grass that shimmers out there beyond the trees.

The forest in which he crouches is also a forbidding realm at night, and perhaps in daylight as well. Fear has been his companion for the past hour, as he's traveled twisting trails through exotic underbrush, beneath interlaced boughs that have provided only an occasional brief glimpse of the night sky.

Predators on the wooden highways overhead might be stalking him, leaping gracefully limb to limb, as silent and as merciless as the cold stars beneath which they prowl. Or perhaps without warning, a hideous tunneling *something*, all teeth and appetite, will explode out of the forest floor under his feet, biting him in half or swallowing him whole.

A vivid imagination has always been his refuge. Tonight it is his curse.

Before him, past this final line of trees, the meadow waits. Waits. Too bright under the fat moon. Deceptively peaceful.

He suspects this is a killing ground. He doubts that he will reach the next stand of trees alive.

Sheltering against a weathered outcropping of rock, he wishes desperately that his mother were with him. But she will never be at his side again in this life.

An hour ago, he witnessed her murder.

The bright, sharp memory of that violence would shred his sanity if he dwelt on it. For the sake of survival, he must forget, at least for now, that particular terror, that unbearable loss.

Huddled in the hostile night, he hears himself making miserable sounds. His mother always told him that he was a brave boy; but no brave boy surrenders this easily to his misery.

Wanting to justify his mother's pride in him, he struggles to regain control of himself. Later, if he lives, he'll have a lifetime for anguish, loss, and loneliness.

Gradually he finds strength not in the memory of her murder, not in a thirst for vengeance or justice, but in the memory of her love, her toughness, her steely resolution. His wretched sobbing subsides.

Silence.

The darkness of the woods.

The meadow waiting under the moon.

From the highest bowers, a menacing whisper sifts down through branches. Maybe it is nothing more than a breeze that has found an open door in the attic of the forest.

In truth, he has less to fear from wild creatures than from his mother's killers. He has no doubt that they still pursue him.

They should have caught him long ago. This territory, however, is as unknown to them as it is to him.

And perhaps his mother's spirit watches over him.

Even if she's here in the night, unseen at his side, he can't rely on her. He has no guardian but himself, no hope other than his wits and courage.

Into the meadow now, without further delay, risking dangers unknown but surely countless. A ripe grassy scent overlays the more subtle smell of rich, raw soil.

The land slopes down to the west. The earth is soft, and the grass is easily trampled. When he pauses to look back, even the pale moonlamp is bright enough to reveal the route he followed.

He has no choice but to forge on.

If he ever dreamed, he could convince himself that he's in a dream now, that this landscape seems strange because it exists only in his mind, that regardless of how long or how fast he runs, he'll never arrive at a destination, but will race perpetually through alternating stretches of moon-dazzled meadow and bristling blind-dark forest.

In fact, he has no idea where he's going. He's not familiar with this land. Civilization might lie within reach, but more likely than not, he's plunging deeper into a vast wilderness.

In his peripheral vision, he repeatedly glimpses movement: ghostly stalkers flanking him. Each time that he looks more directly, he sees only tall grass trembling in the breeze. Yet these phantom outrunners frighten him, and breath by ragged breath, he becomes increasingly convinced that he won't live to reach the next growth of trees.

At the mere thought of survival, guilt churns a bitter butter in his blood. He has no right to live when everyone else perished.

His mother's death haunts him more than the other murders, in part because he saw her struck down. He heard the screams of the others, but by the time he found them, they were dead, and their steaming remains were so grisly that he could not make an emotional connection between the loved ones he had known and those hideous cadavers.

Now, from moonlight into darkling forest once more. The meadow behind him. The tangled maze of brush and bramble ahead.

Against all odds, he's still alive.

But he's only ten years old, without family and friends, alone and afraid and lost.

3

Noah Farrel was sitting in his parked Chevy, minding someone else's business, when the windshield imploded.

Noshing on a cream-filled snack cake, contentedly plastering a fresh coat of fat on his artery walls, he suddenly found himself holding a half-eaten treat rendered crunchier but inedible by sprinkles of gummy-prickly safety glass.

Even as Noah dropped the ruined cake, the front passenger's-side window shattered under the impact of a tire iron.

He bolted from the car through the driver's door, looked across the roof, and confronted a man mountain with a shaved head and a nose ring. The Chevy stood in an open space midway between massive Indian laurels, and though it wasn't shaded by the trees, it was sixty or eighty feet from the nearest streetlamp and thus in gloom; however, the glow of the Chevy's interior lights allowed Noah to see the window-basher. The guy grinned and winked.

Movement to Noah's left drew his attention. A few feet away, another demolition expert swung a sledgehammer at a head-light.

This steroid-inflated gentleman wore sneakers, pink workout pants with a drawstring waist, and a black T-shirt. The impressive mass of bone in his brow surely weighed more than the five-pound sledge that he swung, and his upper lip was nearly as long as his ponytail.

Even as the last of the cracked plastic and the shattered glass from the headlamp rang and rattled against the pavement, the human Good & Plenty slammed the hammer against the hood of the car

Simultaneously, the guy with the polished head and the decorated nostril used the lug-wrench end of the tire iron to break out the rear window on the passenger's side, perhaps because he'd been offended by his reflection.

The noise grew hellish. Prone to headaches these days, Noah wanted nothing more than quiet and a pair of aspirin.

'Excuse me,' he said to the bargain-basement Thor as the hammer arced high over the hood again, and he leaned into the car through the open door to pluck the key from the ignition.

His house key was on the same ring. When he finally got home, by whatever means, he didn't want to discover that these behemoths were hosting a World Wrestling Federation beer party in his bungalow.

On the passenger's seat lay the digital camera that contained photos of the philandering husband entering the house across the street and being greeted at the door by his lover. If Noah reached for the camera, he'd no doubt be left with a hand full of bones as shattered as the windshield.

Pocketing his keys, he walked away, past modest ranch-style houses with neatly trimmed lawns and shrubs, where moon-silvered trees stood whisperless in the warm still air.

Behind him, underlying the steady rhythmic crash of the hammer, the tire iron took up a syncopated beat, tattooing the Chevy fenders and trunk lid.

Here on the perimeter of a respectable residential neighborhood in Anaheim, the home of Disneyland, scenes from *A Clockwork Orange* weren't reenacted every day. Nevertheless, made fearful by too much television news, the residents proved more cautious than curious. No one ventured outside to discover the reason for the fracas.

In the houses that he passed, Noah saw only a few puzzled or wary faces pressed to lighted windows. None of them was Mickey, Minnie, Donald, or Goofy.

When he glanced back, he noticed a Lincoln Navigator pulling away from the curb across the street, no doubt containing associates of the creative pair who were making modern art out of his car. Every ten or twelve steps, he checked on the SUV, and always it drifted slowly along in his wake, pacing him.

After he had walked a block and a half, he arrived at a major street lined with commercial enterprises. Many businesses were closed now, at 9:20 on a Tuesday night.

The Chevy-smashing shivaree continued unabated, but distance and intervening layers of laurel branches filtered cacophony into a muted clump-and-crackle.

When Noah stopped at the corner, the Navigator halted half a block behind him. The driver waited to see which way he would go.

In the small of his back, holstered under his Hawaiian shirt, Noah carried a revolver. He didn't think he would need the weapon. Nevertheless, he had no plans to remake it into a plowshare.

He turned right and, within another block and a half, arrived at a tavern. Here he might not be able to obtain aspirin, but ice-cold Dos Equis would be available.

When it came to health care, he wasn't a fanatic about specific remedies.

The long bar lay to the right of the door. In a row down the center of the room, each of eight plank-top tables bore a candle in an amber-glass holder.

Fewer than half the stools and chairs were occupied. Several guys and one woman wore cowboy hats, as though they had been abducted and then displaced in space or time by meddling extraterrestrials.

The concrete floor, painted ruby-red, appeared to have been mopped at least a couple times since Christmas, and underlying the stale-beer smell was a faint scent of disinfectant. If the place had cockroaches, they would probably be small enough that Noah might just be able to wrestle them into submission.

Along the left wall were high-backed wooden booths with seats padded in red leatherette, a few unoccupied. He settled into the booth farthest from the door.

He ordered a beer from a waitress who had evidently sewn herself into her faded, peg-legged blue jeans and red checkered shirt. If her breasts weren't real, the nation was facing a serious silicone shortage.

'You want a glass?' she asked.

'The bottle's probably cleaner.'

'Has to be,' she agreed as she headed for the bar.

While Alan Jackson filled the jukebox with a melancholy lament about loneliness, Noah fished the automobile-club card out of his wallet. He unclipped the phone from his belt and called the twenty-four-hour help-line number.

The woman who assisted him sounded like his aunt Lilly, his old man's sister, whom he hadn't seen in fifteen years, but her voice had no sentimental effect on him. Lilly had shot Noah's dad in the head, killing him, and had wounded Noah himself – once in the left shoulder, once in the right thigh – when he was sixteen, thereby squelching any affection he might have felt toward her.

'The tires will probably be slashed,' he told the auto-club woman, 'so send a flatbed instead of a standard tow truck.' He gave her the address where the car could be found and also the name of the dealership to which it should be delivered. 'Tomorrow morning's soon enough. Better not send anyone out there until the Beagle Boys have hammered themselves into exhaustion.'

'Who?'

'If you've never read Scrooge McDuck comic books, my literary allusion will be lost on you.'

Arriving just then with a Dos Equis, the cowgirl waitress said, 'When I was seventeen, I applied for a character job at Disneyland, but they turned me down.'

Pressing END on his phone, Noah frowned. 'Character job?'

'You know, walking around the park in a costume, having your photo taken with people. I wanted to be Minnie Mouse or at least maybe Snow White, but I was too busty.'

'Minnie's pretty flat-chested.'

'Yeah, well, she's a mouse.'

'Good point,' Noah said.

'And their idea was that Snow White – she ought to look virginal. I don't know why.'

'Maybe because if Snow was as sexy as you, people would start to wonder what she might've been up to with those seven dwarves – which isn't a Disney sort of thought.'

She brightened. 'Hey, you probably got something there.' Then her sigh vented volumes of disappointment. 'I sure did want to be Minnie.'

'Dreams die hard.'

'They really do.'

'You'd have made a fine Minnie.'

'You think so?'

He smiled. 'Lucky Mickey.'

'You're sweet.'

'My aunt Lilly didn't think so. She shot me.'

'Ah, gee, I wouldn't take it personal,' said the waitress. 'Every-body's family's screwed up these days.' She continued on her rounds.

From the jukebox, a mournful Garth Brooks followed Alan Jackson, and the brims of all the Stetsons at the bar dipped as though in sad commiseration. When the Dixie Chicks followed Brooks, the Stetsons bobbed happily.

Noah had finished half the beer, straight from the bottle, when a slab of beef – marinated in hair oil and spicy cologne, wearing black jeans and a LOVE IS THE ANSWER T-shirt – slipped into the booth, across the table from him. 'Do you have a death wish?'

'Are you planning to grant it?' Noah asked.

'Not me. I'm a pacifist.' A meticulously detailed tattoo of a rattlesnake twined around the pacifist's right arm, its fangs bared on the back of his hand, its eyes bright with hatred. 'But you ought to realize that running surveillance on a man as powerful as Congressman Sharmer is substantially stupid.'

'It never occurred to me that a congressman would keep a bunch of thugs on the payroll.'

'Who *else* would he keep on the payroll?'

'I guess I'm not in Kansas anymore.'

'Hell, Dorothy, where you are, they shoot little dogs like Toto for sport. And girls like you are stomped flat if you don't stay out of the way.'

'The country's Founding Fathers would be so proud.'

The stranger's eyes, previously as empty as a sociopath's heart, filled with suspicion. 'What're you – some political nut? I thought you were just a sad-ass gumshoe grubbing a few bucks by peeping in people's bedrooms.'

'I need more than a few right now. How much did your Navigator cost?' Noah asked.

'You couldn't afford one.'

'I've got good credit.'

The pacifist laughed knowingly. When the waitress approached, he waved her away. Then he produced a small waxy bag and dropped it on the table.

Noah drew comfort from the beer.

Repeatedly clenching and relaxing his right hand, as though he were troubled by joint stiffness after long hours of punching babies and nuns, the pacifist said, 'The congressman isn't unreasonable. By taking his wife as a client, you declared that you were his enemy. But he's such a good man, he wants to make you his friend.'

'What a Christian.'

'Let's not start name-calling.' Each time the politician's man flexed his fist, the fanged mouth widened on the tattoo snake. 'At least take a look at his peace offering.'

The bag was folded and sealed. Noah peeled back the tape, opened the flap, and half extracted a wad of hundred-dollar bills.

'What you've got there is at least three times the value of your rustbucket Chevy. Plus the cost of the camera you left on the front seat.'

'Still not the price of a Navigator,' Noah observed.

'We're not negotiating, Sherlock.'

'I don't see the strings.'

'There's only one. You wait a few days, then you tell the wife you followed the congressman all over, but the only time he ever slung his willy out of his pants was when he needed to take a leak.'

'What about when he was screwing the country?'

'You don't sound like a guy who wants to be friends.'

'I've never been much good at relationships . . . but I'm willing to try.'

'I'm sure glad to hear that. Frankly, I've been worried about you. In the movies, private eyes are always so incorruptible, they'd rather have their teeth kicked out than betray a client.'

'I never go to the movies.'

Pointing to the small bag as Noah tucked the cash into it once more, the pacifist said, 'Don't you realize what that is?'

'A payoff.'

'I mean the bag. It's an *airsickness* bag.' His grin faded. 'What – you never saw one before?'

'I never travel.'

'The congressman has a nice sense of humor.'

'He's hysterical.' Noah shoved the bag into a pants pocket.

'He's saying money's nothing but vomit to him.'

'He's quite the philosopher.'

'You know what he's got that's better than money?'

'Certainly not wit.'

'Power. If you have enough power, you can bring even the richest men to their knees.'

'Who said that originally? Thomas Jefferson? Abe Lincoln?'

The bagman cocked his head and wagged one finger at Noah. 'You have an anger problem, don't you?'

'Absolutely. I don't have enough of it anymore.'

'What you need is to join the Circle of Friends.'

'Sounds like Quakers.'

'It's an organization the congressman founded. That's where he made a name for himself, before politics – helping troubled youth, turning their lives around.'

'I'm thirty-three,' Noah said.

'The Circle serves all age groups now. It really works. You learn there may be a million questions in life but only one answer—'

'Which you're wearing,' Noah guessed, pointing at the guy's LOVE IS THE ANSWER T-shirt.

'Love yourself, love your brothers and sisters, love nature.'

'This kind of thing always starts with "love yourself."'

'It has to. You can't love others until you love yourself. I was sixteen when I joined the Circle, seven years ago. A wickedly messed-up kid. Selling drugs, doing drugs, violent just for the thrill of it, mixed up in a dead-end gang. But I got turned around.'

'Now you're in a gang with a future.'

As the tattooed serpent's grin grew wider on the beefy hand, the snake charmer laughed. 'I like you, Farrel.'

'Everybody does.'

'You might not approve of the congressman's methods, but he's got a vision for this country that could bring us all together.'

'The ends justify the means, huh?'

'See, there's that anger again.'

Noah finished his beer. 'Guys like you and the congressman used to hide behind Jesus. Now it's psychology and self-esteem.'

'Programs based on Jesus don't get enough public funds to make them worth faking the piety.' He slid out of the booth and rose to his feet. 'You wouldn't do something stupid like take the money and then not deliver, would you? You're really going to shaft his wife?'

Noah shrugged. 'I never liked her anyway.'

'She's a juiceless bitch, isn't she?'

'Dry as a cracker.'

'But she sure does give the man major class and respectability. Now you go out there and do the right thing, okay?'

Noah raised his eyebrows. 'What? You mean . . . you want me to give this bag of money to the cops and press charges against the congressman?'

This time, the pacifist didn't smile. 'Guess I should have said do the *smart* thing.'

'Just clarifying,' Noah assured him.

'You could clarify yourself right into a casket.'

With the coils of his soul exposed for all to see, the bagman, sans bag, swaggered toward the front of the tavern.

On their barstools and chairs, the cowboys turned, and with their glares they herded him toward the door. If they had been genuine riders of the purple sage instead of computer-networking specialists or real-estate salesmen, one of them might have whupped his ass just as a matter of principle.

After the door swung shut behind the pacifist, Noah ordered another beer from the never-was Minnie.

When she returned with a dew-beaded bottle of Dos Equis, the waitress said, 'Was that guy a stoolie or something?'

'Something.'

'And you're a cop.'

'Used to be. Is it that obvious?'

'Yeah. And you're wearing an Hawaiian shirt. Plainclothes cops like Hawaiian shirts, 'cause you can hide a gun under them.'

'Well,' he lied, 'I'm not hiding anything under this one except a yellowed undershirt I should've thrown away five years ago.'

'My dad liked Hawaiian shirts.'

'Your dad's a cop?'

'Till they killed him.'

'Sorry to hear that.'

'I'm Francene, named after the ZZ Top song.'

'Why do a lot of cops from back then like ZZ Top?' he wondered.

'Maybe it was an antidote to all that crap the Eagles sang.'

He smiled. 'I think you've got something there, Francene.'

'My shift's over at eleven.'

'You're a temptation,' he admitted. 'But I'm married.'

Glancing at his hands, seeing no rings, she said, 'Married to what?'

'Now that's a hard question.'

'Maybe not so hard if you're honest with yourself.'

Noah had been so taken with her body and her beauty that until now he hadn't seen the kindness in her eyes.

'Could be self-pity,' he said, naming his bride.

'Not you,' she disagreed, as though she knew him well. 'Anger's more like it.'

'What's the name of this bar – Firewater and Philosophy?'

'After you listen to country music all day, every day, you start seeing everyone as a three-minute story.'

Sincerely, he said, 'Damn, you would have been a funny Minnie.'

'You're probably just like my dad. You have this kind of pride. Honor, he called it. But these days, honor is for suckers, and that makes you angry.'

He stared up at her, searching for a reply and finding none. In addition to her kindness, he had become aware of a melancholy in her that he couldn't bear to see. 'That guy over there's signaling for a waitress.'

She continued to hold Noah's gaze as she said, 'Well, if you ever get divorced, you know where I work.'

He watched her walk away. Then between long swallows, he studied his beer as though it meant something.

Later, when he had only an empty bottle to study, Noah left Francene a tip larger than the total of his two-beer check.

Outside, an upwash of urban glow overlaid a yellow stain on the blackness of the lower sky. High above, unsullied, hung a polished-silver moon. In the deep pure black above the lunar curve, a few stars looked clean, so far from Earth.

He walked eastward, through the warm gusts of wind stirred

21

by traffic, alert for any indication that he was under surveillance.

No one followed him, not even at a distance.

Evidently the congressman's battalions no longer found him to be of even the slightest interest. His apparent cowardice and the alacrity with which he had betrayed his client confirmed for them that he was, by the current definition, a good citizen.

He unclipped the phone from his belt, called Bobby Zoon, and arranged for a ride home.

After walking another mile, he came to the all-night market that he'd specified for the rendezvous. Bobby's Honda was parked next to a collection bin for Salvation Army thrift shops.

When Noah got into the front passenger's seat, Bobby – twenty, skinny, with a scraggly chin beard and the slightly vacant look of a long-term Ecstasy user – was behind the steering wheel, picking his nose.

Noah grimaced. 'You're disgusting.'

'What?' Bobby asked, genuinely surprised by the insult, even though his index finger was still wedged in his right nostril.

'At least I didn't catch you playing with yourself. Let's get out of here.'

'That was cool back there,' Bobby said as he started the engine. 'Absolutely arctic.'

'Cool? You idiot, I liked that car.'

'Your Chevy? It was a piece of crap.'

'Yeah, but it was *my* piece of crap.'

'Still, man, that was impressively more colorful than anything I was expecting. We got more than we needed.'

'Yeah,' Noah acknowledged without enthusiasm.

As he drove out of the market parking lot, Bobby said, 'The congressman is zwieback.'

'He's what?'

'Toast done twice.'

'Where do you get this stuff?'

'What stuff?' Bobby asked.

'This zwieback crap.'

'I'm always working on a screenplay in my head. In film school, they teach you everything's material, and *this* sure is.'

'Hell is spending eternity as the hero in a Bobby Zoon flick.'

With an earnestness that could be achieved only by a boy-man with a wispy goatee and the conviction that movies are life, Bobby said, 'You're not the hero. *My* part's the male lead. You're in the Sandra Bullock role.'

4

Down through the high forest to lower terrain, from night-kissed ridges into night-smothered valleys, out of the trees into a broad planted field, the motherless boy hurries. He follows the crop rows to a rail fence.

He is amazed to be alive. He doesn't dare to hope that he has lost his pursuers. They are out there, still searching, cunning and indefatigable.

The fence, old and in need of repair, clatters as he climbs across it. When he drops to the lane beyond, he crouches motionless until he is sure that the noise has drawn no one's attention.

Previously scattered clouds, as woolly as sheep, have been herded together around the shepherd moon.

In this darker night, several structures loom, all humble and yet mysterious. A barn, a stable, outbuildings. With haste, he passes among them.

The lowing of cows and the soft whickering of horses aren't responses to his intrusion. These sounds are as natural a part of the night as the musky smell of animals and the not altogether unpleasant scent of straw-riddled manure.

Beyond the hard-packed barnyard earth lies a recently mown lawn. A concrete birdbath. Beds of roses. An abandoned bicycle on its side. A grape arbor is entwined with vines, clothed with leaves, hung with fruit.

Through the tunnel of the arbor, and then across more grass, he approaches the farmhouse. At the back porch, brick steps lead up to a weathered plank floor. He creaks and scrapes to the door, which opens for him.

He hesitates on the threshold, troubled by both the risk that he's taking and the crime he's intending to commit. His mother has raised him with strong values; but if he's to survive this night, he will have to steal.

Furthermore, he is reluctant to put these people – whoever they may be – at risk. If the killers track him to this place while he's still inside, they won't spare anyone. They have no mercy, and they dare not leave witnesses.

Yet if he doesn't seek help here, he'll have to visit the next farmhouse, or the one after the next. He is exhausted, afraid, still lost, and in need of a plan. He's got to stop running long enough to think.

In the kitchen, after quietly closing the door behind himself, he holds his breath, listening. The house is silent. Evidently, his small noises haven't awakened anyone.

Cupboard to cupboard, drawer to drawer, he searches until he discovers candles and matches, which he considers but discards. At last, a flashlight.

He needs several items, and a quick but cautious tour of the lower floor convinces him that he will have to go upstairs to find those necessities.

At the foot of the steps, he's paralyzed by dread. Perhaps the killers are already here. Upstairs. Waiting in the dark, waiting for him to find them. *Surprise.*

Ridiculous. They aren't the type to play games. They're vicious and efficient. If they were here now, he'd already be dead.

He feels small, weak, alone, doomed. He feels foolish, too, for continuing to hesitate even when reason tells him that he has nothing to fear other than getting caught by the people who live here.

Finally, he starts up toward the second floor. The stairs softly protest. As he ascends, he stays close to the wall, where the treads are less noisy.

At the top is a short hallway. Four doors.

The first door opens on a bathroom. The second leads to a bedroom; hooding the flashlight to dim and more tightly focus the beam, he enters.

A man and a woman lie in the bed, sleeping soundly. They snore in counterpoint: he an oboe with a split reed; she a whistling flute.

On a dresser, in a small decorative tray: coins and a man's

wallet. In the wallet, the boy finds one ten-dollar bill, two fives, four ones.

These are not rich people, and he feels guilty about taking their money. One day, if he lives long enough, he will return to this house and repay his debt.

He wants the coins, too, but he doesn't touch them. In his nervousness, he's likely to jingle or drop them, rousing the farmer and his wife.

The man grumbles, turns on his side . . . but doesn't wake.

Retreating quickly and silently from the bedroom, the boy sees movement in the hall, a pair of shining eyes, a flash of teeth in the hooded beam of light. He almost cries out in alarm.

A dog. Black and white. Shaggy.

He has a way with dogs, and this one is no exception. It nuzzles him and then, panting happily, leads him along the hallway to another door that stands ajar.

Perhaps the dog came from this room. Now it glances back at its new friend, grins, wags its tail, and slips across the threshold as fluidly as a supernatural familiar ready to assist with some magical enterprise.

Affixed to the door is a stainless-steel plaque with laser-cut letters: STARSHIP COMMAND CENTER, *Captain Curtis Hammond.*

Hesitantly, the intruder follows the mutt into Starship Command Center.

This is a boy's room, papered with large monster-movie posters. Display shelves are cluttered with collections of science-fiction action figures and models of ornate but improbable spaceships. In one corner a life-size plastic model of a human skeleton hangs from a metal stand, grinning as if death is great fun.

Perhaps signifying the beginning of a shift in the obsessions of the resident, a single poster of Britney Spears also adorns one wall. With her deep cleavage, bared belly, and aggressive sparkling smile, she's powerfully intriguing – but also nearly as scary as any of the snarling, carnivorous antagonists of the horror films.

The young intruder looks away from the pop star, confused by his feelings, surprised that he possesses the capacity for any emotions other than fear and grief, considering the ordeal he has so recently endured.

Under the Britney Spears poster, in a tangle of sheets, sprawled facedown in bed, his head turned to one side, lies Curtis Hammond, commander of this vessel, who sleeps on, unaware that the sanctity of his starship bridge has been violated. He might be eleven or even twelve, but he's somewhat small for his age, about the size of the night visitor who stands over him.

Curtis Hammond is a source of bitter envy, not because he has found peace in sleep, but because he is not orphaned, is not alone. For a moment, the young intruder's envy curdles into a hatred so thick and poisonous that he feels compelled to lash out, to hammer the dreaming boy and diminish this intolerable pain by sharing it.

Although trembling with the pressure of his misplaced rage, he doesn't vent it, but leaves Curtis untouched. The hatred subsides as quickly as it flourished, and the grief that was briefly drowned by this fierce animosity now reappears like a gray winter beach from beneath an ebbing tide.

On the nightstand, in front of a clock radio, lie several coins and a used Band-Aid with a blot of dried blood on the gauze pad. This isn't much blood, but the intruder has recently seen so much violence that he shudders. He does not touch the coins.

Accompanied by dog snuffles and a flurry of fur, the motherless boy moves stealthily to the closet. The door is ajar. He opens it wider. With the flashlight beam, he shops for clothes.

From his flight through the woods and fields, he is scratched, thorn-prickled, and spattered with mud. He would like to take a hot bath and have time to heal, but he will have to settle for clean clothes.

The dog watches, head cocked, looking every bit as puzzled as it ought to be.

Throughout the theft of shirt, jeans, socks, and shoes, Curtis Hammond sleeps as soundly as though a spell has been cast upon him. Were he a genuine starship captain, his crew might fall prey to brain-eating aliens or his vessel might spiral into the gravitational vortex of a black hole while he dreamed of Britney Spears.

Not a brain-eating alien but feeling as though he himself is in the thrall of black-hole gravity, the intruder returns quietly to the open bedroom door, the dog remaining by his side.

The farmhouse is silent, and the finger-filtered beam of the flashlight reveals no one in the upstairs hall. Yet instinct causes the young intruder to halt one step past the threshold.

Something isn't right, the silence *too* deep. Perhaps Curtis's parents have awakened.

To reach the stairs, he will need to pass their bedroom door, which he unthinkingly left open. If the farmer and his wife have been roused from sleep, they will probably remember that their door was closed when they retired for the night.

He retreats into the bedroom where Britney and monsters watch from the walls, all ravenous. Switches off the flashlight. Holds his breath.

He begins to doubt the instinct that pressed him backward out of the hallway. Then he realizes that the dog's swishing tail, which had been softly lashing his legs, has suddenly gone still. The animal has also stopped panting.

Dim gray rectangles float in the dark: curtained windows. He crosses the room toward them, struggling to recall the placement of furniture, hoping to avoid raising a clatter.

After he puts down the extinguished flashlight, as he pulls the curtains aside, plastic rings scrape and click softly along a brass rod, as though the hanging skeleton, animated by sorcery, is flexing its bony fingers in the gloom.

Curtis Hammond mutters, wrestles briefly with his sheets, but doesn't wake.

A thumb-turn lock frees the window. Gingerly, the intruder raises the lower sash. He slips out of the house, onto the front-porch roof, and glances back.

The dog looms at the open window, forepaws on the sill, as if it will abandon its master in favor of this new friend and a night of adventure.

'Stay,' whispers the motherless boy.

In a crouch, he crosses the roof to the brink. When he looks back again, the mutt whines beseechingly but doesn't follow.

The boy is athletic, agile. The leap from the porch roof is a challenge easily met. He lands on the lawn with bent knees, drops, rolls through cold dew, through the sweet crisp scent of grass that bursts from the crushed blades under him, and scrambles at once to his feet.

A dirt lane, flanked by fenced meadows and oiled to control dust, leads to a public road about two hundred yards to the west.

Hurrying, he has covered less than half that distance when he hears the dog bark far behind him.

Lights blaze, blink, and blaze again behind the windows of the Hammond place, a strobing chaos, as though the farmhouse has become a carnival funhouse awhirl with bright flickering spooks.

With the lights come screams, soul-searing even at a distance, not just shouts of alarm, but shrieks of terror, wails of anguish. The most piercing squeals seem less like human sounds than like the panicked cries of pigs catching sight of the abattoir master's gleaming blade, although these also are surely human, the wretched plaints of the tortured Hammonds in their last moments on this earth.

The killers had been even closer on his trail than he'd feared.

What he sensed, stepping into that upstairs hallway, hadn't been the farmer and wife, awakened and suspicious. These are the same hunters who brutally murdered his family, come down through the mountains to the back door of the Hammond house.

Racing away into the night, trying to outrun the screams and the guilt that they drill into him, the boy gasps for breath, and the cool air is rough in his raw throat. His heart like a horse's hooves kicks, kicks against the stable of his ribs.

The prisoner moon escapes the dungeon clouds, and the oiled lane under the boy's swift feet glistens with the reflected glow.

By the time he nears the public road, he can no longer hear the terrible cries, only his explosive breathing. Turning, he sees lights steady in every window of the house, and he knows that the killers are searching for him in attic, closets, cellar.

More black than white, its coat a perfect camouflage against the moon-dappled oil, the dog sprints out of the night. It takes refuge at the boy's side, pressing against his legs as it looks back toward the Hammond place.

The dog's flanks shudder, striking sympathetic shivers in the boy. Punctuating its panting are pitiful whimpers of fear, but the boy dares not surrender to his desire to sit in the lane beside the dog and cry in chorus with it.

Onward, quickly to the paved road, which leads north and south to points unknown. Either direction will most likely bring him to the same hard death.

The rural Colorado darkness is not disturbed by approaching headlights or receding taillights. When he holds his breath, he hears only stillness and the panting dog, not the growl of an approaching engine.

He tries to shoo away the dog, but it will not be shooed. It has cast its fortune with his.

Reluctant to be responsible even for this animal, but resigned to – and even somewhat grateful for – its companionship, he turns left, south, because a hill lies to the north. He doesn't think he has the stamina to take that long incline at a run.

On his right, a meadow bank grows, then looms, as the two-lane blacktop descends, while on his left, tall sentinel pines rise at the verge of the road, saluting the moon with their higher branches. The *slap-slap-slap* of his sneakers echoes between the bank and the trees, *slap-slap-slap*, a spoor of sound that sooner or later will draw his pursuers.

Once more he glances back, but only once, because he sees the pulse of flames in the east, throbbing in the dark, and he knows that the Hammond place has been set ablaze. Reduced to blackened bones and ashes, the bodies of the dead will offer fewer clues to the true identity of the killers.

A curve in the road and more trees screen him from sight of the fire, and when he entirely rounds the bend, he sees a truck stopped on the shoulder of the highway. Headlights doused in favor of the parking lights, this vehicle stands with engine idling, grumbling softly like some hulking beast that has been ridden hard and is half asleep on its feet.

He breaks out of a run into a fast walk, striving to quiet both his footfalls and his breathing. Taking its cue from him, the dog slows to a trot, then lowers its head and *slinks* forward at his side, more like a cat than like a canine.

The cargo bed of the truck has a canvas roof and walls. It's open at the back except for a low tailgate.

As he reaches the rear bumper, feeling dangerously exposed in the ruddy glow of the parking lights, the boy hears voices. Men in easy conversation.

Cautiously he looks forward along the driver's side of the truck, sees no one, and moves to the passenger's side. Two men stand toward the front of the vehicle, their backs to the highway, facing the woods. Lambent moonlight spangles an arc of urine.

He doesn't want to endanger these people. If he stays here, they might be dead even before they empty their bladders: a longer rest stop than they had planned. Yet he'll never elude his pursuers if he remains on foot.

The tailgate is hinged at the bottom. Two latch bolts fix it at the top.

He quietly slips the bolt on the right, holds the gate with one hand as he moves to the left, slips that bolt, too, and lowers the barrier, which is well oiled and rattle-free. He could have stepped onto the bumper and swung over the gate, but his four-legged friend wouldn't have been able to climb after him.

Understanding his new master's intent, the dog springs into the cargo bed of the truck, landing so lightly among its contents that even the low rhythmic wheeze of the idling engine provides sufficient screening sound.

The boy follows his spry companion into this tented blackness.

Pulling the tailgate up from the inside is an awkward job, but with determination, he succeeds. He slides one bolt into its hasp, then engages the other, as outside the two men break into laughter.

Behind the truck, the highway remains deserted. The parallel median lines, yellow in daylight, appear white under the influence of the frost-pale moon, and the boy can't help but think of them as twin fuses along which terror will come, hissing and smoking, to a sudden detonation.

Hurry, he urges the men, as if by willpower alone he can move them. *Hurry*.

Groping blindly, he discovers that the truck is loaded in part with a great many blankets, some rolled and strapped singly, others bundled in bales and tied with sisal twine. His right hand finds smooth leather, the distinctive curve of a cantle, the slope of a seat, pommel, fork, and horn: a saddle.

The driver and his partner return to the cab of the truck. One door slams, then the other.

More saddles are braced among the blankets, some as smooth as the first, but others enhanced with ornate hand-tooled designs that, to the boy's questioning fingertips, speak of parades, horse shows, and rodeos. Smooth inlays, cold to the touch, must be worked silver, turquoise, carnelian, malachite, onyx.

The driver pops the hand brake. As the vehicle angles off the shoulder and onto the pavement, the tires cast loose stones that rattle like dice into the darkness.

The truck rolls southwest into the night, with the twin fuses on the blacktop raveling longer in its wake, and utility poles, carrying electric and telephone wires, seem to march like soldiers toward a battleground beyond the horizon.

Among mounds of blankets and saddlery, swathed in the cozy odors of felt and sheepskin and fine leather and saddle soap – and not least of all in the curiously comforting, secondhand scent of horses – the motherless boy and the ragtag dog huddle together. They are bonded by grievous loss and by a sharp instinct for survival, traveling into an unknown land, toward an unknowable future.

5

Wednesday, after a fruitless day of job-seeking, Micky Bellsong returned to the trailer park, where much of the meager landscaping drooped wearily under the scorching sun and the rest appeared to be withered beyond recovery. The raging tornadoes that routinely sought vulnerable trailer parks across the plains states were unknown here in southern California, but summer heat made these blighted streets miserable enough until the next earthquake could do a tornado's work.

Aunt Geneva's aged house trailer looked like a giant oven built for the roasting of whole cows, in multiples. Perhaps a malevolent sun god lived in the metal walls, for the air immediately around the place shimmered as if with the spirits of attending demons.

Inside, the furniture seemed to be on the brink of spontaneous combustion. The sliding windows were open to admit a draft, but the August day declined the invitation to provide a breeze.

In her tiny bedroom, Micky kicked off her toe-pinching high heels. She stripped out of her cheap cotton suit and pantyhose.

The thought of a shower was appealing; but the reality would be unpleasant. The cramped bathroom had only a small window, and in this heat, the roiling steam wouldn't properly vent.

She slipped into white shorts and a sleeveless Chinese-red blouse. In the mirror on the back of the bedroom door, she looked better than she felt.

At one time, she'd been proud of her beauty. Now she wondered why she had taken so much pride in something that required no effort, no slightest sacrifice.

Over the past year, with as much mulish resistance as the most obstinate creature ever to pull a plow, Micky had drawn herself to the unpleasant conclusion that her life to date had been wasted and that she was solely to blame for what she had become. The anger that she'd once directed at others had been turned upon herself.

Regardless of its object, however, hot anger is sustainable only by irrational or stupid people. Micky was neither. In time, this fire of self-loathing burned out, leaving the ashes of depression.

Depression passed, too. Lately she had made her way from day to day in a curious and fragile state of expectancy.

After giving her good looks, fate had never again been generous. Consequently, Micky wasn't able to identify a reason for this almost sweet anticipation. Defensively, she tempered it with wariness.

Nevertheless, during the week that she'd been staying with Aunt Gen, she awakened each morning with the conviction that change was coming and that it would be a change for the better.

Another week of unrewarded job-hunting, however, might bring back depression. Also, more than once during the day, she'd been troubled by a new version of her former rage; this sullen resentment wasn't as hot as her anger had been in the past, but it had the potential to quicken. The long day of rejection left her weary in body, mind, and spirit. And her emotional unsteadiness scared her.

Barefoot, she went into the kitchen, where Geneva was preparing dinner. A small electric fan, set on the kitchen floor, churned the hot air with less cooling effect than might be produced by a wooden spoon stirring the contents of a bubbling soup pot.

Because of the criminal stupidity and stupid criminality of California's elected officials, the state had suffered electricity shortages early in the summer, and in an overreaction to the crisis had piled up surpluses of power at grossly high prices. Utility rates had soared. Geneva couldn't afford to use the air conditioning.

As Aunt Gen sprinkled Parmesan cheese over a bowl of cold pasta salad, she served up a smile that could have charmed the snake of Eden into a mood of benign companionship. Gen's once golden hair was pale blond now, streaked with gray. Yet because she'd grown plump with age, her face was smooth; coppery freckles and lively green eyes testified to the abiding presence of the young girl thriving in the sixty-year-old woman. 'Micky, sweetie, did you have a good day?'

'Sucky day, Aunt Gen.'

'That's a word I never know whether to be embarrassed about.'

'I didn't realize anyone got embarrassed about anything anymore. In this case, it just means "as bad as a sucking chest wound."'

'Ah. Then I'm not embarrassed, just slightly sickened. Why don't you get a glass of cold lemonade, honey? I made fresh.'

'What I really need is a beer.'

'There's also beer. Your uncle Vernon liked two icy beers more evenings than not.'

Aunt Gen didn't drink beer. Vernon had been dead for eighteen years. Still, Geneva kept his favorite brand in the refrigerator, and if no one drank it, she periodically replaced it with new stock when its freshness date had passed.

Although conceding the game to Death, she remained determined not to let Death also take sweet memories and long-kept traditions in addition to his prize of flesh.

Micky popped open a can of Budweiser. 'They think the economy's going down the drain.'

'Who does, dear?'

'Everyone I talked to about a job.'

Having set the pasta salad on the dinette table, Geneva began slicing roasted chicken breasts for sandwiches. 'Those people are just pessimists. The economy's always going down the drain for some folks, but it's a warm bath for others. You'll find work, sweetie.'

The beer provided icy solace. 'How do you stay so upbeat?'

Focused on the chicken, Geneva said, 'Easy. I just look around.'

Micky looked around. 'Sorry, Aunt Gen, but all I see is a poky little trailer kitchen so old the gloss is worn off the Formica.'

'Then you don't know how to look yet, honey. There's a dish of pickles, some olives, a bowl of potato salad, a tray of cheese, and other stuff in the fridge. Would you put everything on the table?'

Extracting the cheese tray from the refrigerator, Micky said, 'Are you cooking for a cellblock full of condemned men or something?'

Geneva set a platter of sliced chicken on the table. 'Didn't you notice – we have three place settings this evening?'

'A dinner guest?'

A knock answered the question. The back door stood open to facilitate air circulation, so Leilani Klonk rapped on the jamb.

'Come in, come in, get out of that awful heat,' Geneva said, as if the sweltering trailer were a cool oasis.

Backlit by the westering sun, wearing khaki shorts and a white T-shirt with a small green heart embroidered on the left breast, Leilani entered in a rattle and clatter of steely leg brace, though she had climbed the three back steps with no noise.

This had been worse than a sucky day. The language necessary to describe Micky's job search in its full dreadfulness would not merely have embarrassed Aunt Geneva; it would have shocked and appalled her. Therefore, at the arrival of the disabled girl, Micky was surprised to feel the same buoying expectation that had kept her from drowning in self-pity since she'd moved in here.

'Mrs. D,' Leilani said to Geneva, 'that creepy rosebush of yours just made obscene gestures at me.'

Geneva smiled. 'If there was an altercation, dear, I'm sure you started it.'

With the thumb on her deformed hand, Leilani gestured toward Geneva, and said to Micky, 'She's an original. Where'd you find her?'

'She's my father's sister, so she was part of the deal.'

'Bonus points,' said Leilani. 'Your dad must be great.'

'Why would you think so?'

'His sister's cool.'

Micky said, 'He abandoned my mother and me when I was three.'

'That's tough. But *my* useless dad skipped the day I was born.'

'I didn't know we were in a rotten-dad contest.'

'At least my real dad isn't a murderer like my current *pseudo*father – or as far as I know, he isn't. Is your dad a murderer?'

'I lose again. He's just a selfish pig.'

'Mrs. D, you don't mind she calls your brother a selfish pig?'

'Sadly, dear, it's true.'

'So you aren't just bonus points, Mrs. D. You're like this terrific prize that turned up in a box of rancid old Cracker Jack.'

Geneva beamed. 'That's so sweet, Leilani. Would you like some fresh lemonade?'

Indicating the can of Budweiser on the table, the girl said, 'If beer's good enough for Micky, it's good enough for me.'

Geneva poured lemonade. 'Pretend it's Budweiser.'

To Micky, Leilani said, 'She thinks I'm a child.'

'You *are* a child.'

'Depends on your definition of *child*.'

'Anyone twelve or younger.'

'Oh, that's sad. You resorted to an arbitrary number. That reveals a shallow capacity for independent thought and analysis.'

'Okay,' said Micky, 'then try this one on for size. You're a child because you don't yet have boobs.'

Leilani winced. 'Unfair. You *know* that's one of my sore points.'

'No sore points. No points at all,' Mickey observed. 'Flat as a slice of the Swiss cheese on that platter.'

'Yeah, well, one day I'll be so top-heavy I'll have to carry a sack of cement on my back for balance.'

To Micky, Aunt Gen said, 'Isn't she something?'

'She's an absolute, no-doubt-about-it, fine young mutant.'

'Dinner's ready,' Geneva announced. 'Cold salads and sandwich fixings. Not very fancy, but right for the weather.'

'Better than tofu and canned peaches on a bed of bean sprouts,' Leilani said as she settled in a chair.

'What wouldn't be?' Geneva wondered.

'Oh, lots of things. Old Sinsemilla may be a lousy mother, but she can take pride in being an equally lousy cook.'

Switching off the overhead lights to save money and to avoid adding heat to the kitchen, Geneva said, 'We'll use candles later.'

Now, at seven o'clock, the summer-evening sun was red-gold and still so fierce at the open window that the shadows, which draped but didn't cool the kitchen, were no darker than lavender and umber.

Seated, bowing her head, Geneva offered a succinct but heartfelt prayer: 'Thank you, God, for providing us with all we need and for giving us the grace to be satisfied with what we have.'

'I've got trouble with the *satisfied* part,' Leilani said.

Micky reached across the dinette table, and the girl responded without hesitation: They slapped palms in a modified high-five.

'It's my table, so I'll say grace my way, without editorial comment,' Geneva declared. 'And when I'm drinking pina coladas on a palm-shaded terrace in Heaven, what will they be serving in Hell?'

'Probably this lemonade,' said Leilani.

Spooning pasta salad onto her plate, Micky said, 'So, Leilani, you and Aunt Gen have been hanging out?'

'Most of the day, yeah. Mrs. D is teaching me all about sex.'

'Girl, don't say such things!' Geneva admonished. 'Someone will believe you. We were playing five-hundred rummy.'

'I would have let her win,' said Leilani, 'out of courtesy and respect for her advanced age, but before I had a chance, she won by cheating.'

'Aunt Gen always cheats,' Micky confirmed.

'Good thing we weren't playing Russian roulette,' Leilani said. 'My brains would be all over the kitchen.'

'I don't cheat.' Gen's sly look was worthy of a Mafia accountant testifying before a congressional committee. 'I just employ advanced and complex techniques.'

'When you notice those pina coladas are garnished with live, poisonous centipedes,' Micky warned, 'maybe you'll realize your palm-shaded terrace isn't in Heaven.'

Aunt Gen used a paper napkin to blot her brow. 'Don't flatter yourself that I'm sweating with guilt. It's the heat.'

Leilani said, 'This is great potato salad, Mrs. D.'

'Thank you. Are you sure your mother wouldn't like to join us?'

'No. She's wasted on crack cocaine and hallucinogenic mushrooms. The only way old Sinsemilla could get here is crawl, and if she tried to eat anything in her condition, she'd just puke it up.'

Geneva frowned at Micky, and Micky shrugged. She didn't know whether these tales of Sinsemilla's debauchery were truth or fantasy, although she suspected wild exaggeration. Tough talk and wisecracks could be a cover for low self-esteem. From childhood at least through adolescence, Micky herself had been familiar with that strategy.

'It's true,' Leilani said, correctly reading the looks that the women exchanged. 'We've only lived beside you three days. Give old Sinsemilla a little time, and you'll see.'

'Drugs do terrible damage,' Aunt Gen said with sudden solemnity. 'I was in love with this man in Chicago once . . . .'

'Aunt Gen,' Micky cautioned.

Sadness found a surprisingly easy purchase in Geneva's smooth, fair, freckled face. 'He was so handsome, so sensitive—'

Sighing, Micky got up to retrieve a second beer from the refrigerator.

'—but he was on the needle,' Geneva said. 'Heroin. A loser in everyone's eyes but mine. I just knew he could be redeemed.'

'That's monumentally romantic, Mrs. D, but as my mother's proved with numerous doper boyfriends, it always ends badly with junkies.'

'Not in this case,' said Geneva. 'I saved him.'

'You did? How?'

'Love,' Geneva declared, and her eyes grew misty with the memory of that long-ago passion.

Popping open a Budweiser, Micky returned to her chair. 'Aunt Gen, this sensitive junkie from Chicago . . . wasn't he Frank Sinatra?'

'Seriously?' Leilani's eyes widened. Her hand paused with a forkful of pasta halfway between plate and mouth. 'The dead singer?'

'He wasn't dead then,' Geneva assured the girl. 'He hadn't even begun to lose his hair yet.'

'The compassionate young woman who saved him from the needle,' Micky pressed, 'was she you, Aunt Gen . . . or was she Kim Novak?'

Geneva's face puckered in puzzlement. 'I was attractive in my day, but I was never in Kim Novak's league.'

'Aunt Gen, you're thinking of *The Man with the Golden Arm*. Frank Sinatra, Kim Novak. It hit theaters sometime in the 1950s.'

Geneva's puzzlement dissolved into a smile. 'You're absolutely right, dear. I never had a romantic relationship with Sinatra, though if he'd ever come around, I'm not sure I could have resisted him.'

Returning the untouched forkful of pasta salad to her plate, Leilani looked to Micky for an explanation.

Enjoying the girl's perplexity, Micky shrugged. 'I'm not sure I could have resisted him, either.'

'Oh, for goodness' sake, stop teasing the child,' Geneva said. 'You'll have to forgive me, Leilani. I've had these memory problems now and then, ever since I was shot in the head. A few wires got scrambled up here' – she tapped her right temple – 'and sometimes old movies seem as real to me as my own past.'

'Could I have more lemonade?' Leilani asked.

'Of course, dear.' Geneva poured from a glass pitcher that dripped icy condensation.

Micky watched their guest take a long drink. 'Don't try to fool me, mutant girl. You're not so cool that you can roll with *that* one.'

Putting down the lemonade, Leilani relented: 'Oh, all right. I'll bite. When were you shot in the head, Mrs. D?'

'This July third, just passed, made eighteen years.'

'Aunt Gen and Uncle Vernon owned a little corner grocery,' Micky explained, 'which is like being targets in a shooting gallery if it's on the *wrong* corner.'

'The day before the July Fourth holiday,' Geneva said, 'you sell lots of lunchmeats and beer. It's mostly a cash business.'

'And someone wanted the cash,' Leilani guessed.

'He was a perfect gentleman about it,' Geneva recalled.

'Except for the shooting.'

'Well, yes, except for that,' Geneva agreed. 'But he came up to the cash register with this lovely smile. Well dressed, soft-spoken. He says, "I'd be really grateful if you'd give me the money in the register, and please don't forget the large bills under the drawer."'

Leilani squinted with righteous indignation. 'So you refused to give it to him.'

'Heavens, no, dear. We emptied the register and all but thanked him for sparing us the trouble of paying income tax on it.'

'And he shot you anyway?'

'He shot my Vernon twice, and apparently then he shot me.'

'Apparently?'

'I remember him shooting Vernon. I wish I didn't, but I do.'

Earlier, sadness had cast a gray shadow across Geneva's face at the counterfeit memory of her anguish-filled love affair with a heroin junkie; but now a flush of happiness pinked her features, and she smiled. 'Vernon was a wonderful man, as sweet as honey in the comb.'

Micky reached for her aunt's hand. 'I loved him, too, Aunt Gen.'

To Leilani, Geneva said, 'I miss him so much, even after all these years, but I can't cry over him anymore, because every memory, even that awful day, reminds me of how sweet he was, how loving.'

'My brother, Lukipela – he was like that.' In spite of this tribute to her brother, Leilani was not inspired to match Geneva's smile. Instead, the girl's cocky cheerfulness melted into melancholy. Her clear eyes clouded toward a more troubled shade of blue.

For a moment, Micky perceived in their young visitor a quality that chilled her because it was like a view of the darker ravines of her own interior landscape: a glimpse of reckless anger, despair, a brief revelation of a sense of worthlessness that the girl would deny but that from personal experience Micky recognized too well.

No sooner had Leilani's defenses cracked than they mended. Her eyes glazed with emotion at the mention of her brother, but now they focused. Her gaze rose from her deformed hand to smiling Geneva, and she smiled, too. 'Mrs. D, you said *apparently* the gunman shot you.'

'Well, I know he shot me, of course, but I have no memory of it. I remember him shooting Vernon, and then the next thing I knew, I was waking up in the hospital, disoriented, more than four days later.'

'The bullet didn't actually penetrate her head,' Micky said.

'Too hard,' Geneva declared proudly.

'Luck,' Micky clarified. 'The angle of the shot was severe. The slug literally ricocheted off her skull, fracturing it, and furrowed through her scalp.'

'So, Mrs. D, how did your wires get scrambled?' Leilani asked, tapping her head.

'It was a depressed fracture,' said Geneva. 'Bone chips in the brain. A blood clot.'

'They opened Aunt Gen's head as though it were a can of beans.'

'Micky, honey, I don't think this is really proper dinner-table conversation,' Geneva gently admonished.

'Oh, I've heard much worse at our house,' Leilani assured them. 'Old Sinsemilla fancies herself an artist with a camera, and she has this artistic compulsion to take pictures of road kill when we're traveling. At dinner sometimes she likes to talk about what she saw squashed on the highway that day. And my pseudofather—'

'That would be the murderer,' Micky interrupted without a wink or a smirk, as though she'd never think to question the outrageous family portrait that the girl was painting for them.

'Yeah, Dr. Doom,' Leilani confirmed.

'Never let him adopt you,' Micky said. 'Even Leilani Klonk is preferable to Leilani Doom.'

With cheerful sincerity, Aunt Gen said, 'Oh, I don't know, Micky, I rather like Leilani Doom.'

As though it were the most natural thing to do, the girl picked up Micky's fresh can of Budweiser and, instead of drinking from it, rolled it back and forth across her brow, cooling her forehead.

'Dr. Doom isn't his real name, of course. It's what I call him behind his back. Sometimes at dinner, he likes to talk about people he's killed – the way they looked when they died, their last words, if they cried, whether they peed themselves, all sorts of kinky stuff.'

The girl put down the beer – on the far side of her plate, out of Micky's reach. Her manner was casual, but her motive was nonetheless clear. She had appointed herself guardian of Micky's sobriety.

'Maybe,' Leilani continued, 'you think that would be interesting conversation, even if sort of gross, but let me tell you, it loses its charm pretty quick.'

'What's your pseudofather's real name?' Geneva asked.

Before Leilani could reply, Micky suggested, 'Hannibal Lecter.'

'To some people, his name's scarier than Lecter's. I'm sure you've heard of him. Preston Maddoc.'

'What an impressive name,' Geneva said. 'Like a Supreme Court justice or a senator, or someone grand.'

Leilani said, 'He comes from a family of Ivy League academic snots. Nobody in that crowd has a regular first name. They're worse about names than old Sinsemilla. They're all Hudson,

Lombard, Trevor or Kingsley, Wycliffe, Crispin. You'd grow old and die trying to find a Jim or Bob among them. Dr. Doom's parents were professors – history, literature – so his middle name is Claudius. Preston Claudius Maddoc.'

'I've never heard of him,' Micky said.

Leilani appeared to be surprised. 'Don't you read newspapers?'

'I stopped reading them when they stopped carrying news,' said Geneva. 'They're all opinion now, front page to last.'

'He's been all over television,' Leilani said.

Geneva shook her miswired head. 'I don't watch anything on TV except old movies.'

'I just don't *like* news,' Micky explained. 'It's mostly bad, and when it isn't bad, it's mostly lies.'

'Ah.' Leilani's eyes widened 'You're the twelve percenters.'

'The what?'

'Every time the newspaper or TV people take a poll, no matter what the question, twelve percent of the public has no opinion. You could ask them if a group of mad scientists ought to be allowed to create a new species of human beings crossed with crocodiles, and twelve percent would have no opinion.'

'I'd be opposed,' said Geneva, brandishing a carrot stick.

'Me, too,' Micky agreed.

'Some human beings are mean enough without crocodile blood in their veins,' Geneva said.

'What about alligators?' Micky asked her aunt.

'Opposed,' Geneva responded with firm resolve.

'What about human beings crossed with wildly poisonous vipers?' Micky proposed.

'Not if I have anything to say about it,' Geneva promised.

'Okay, then what about human beings crossed with puppy dogs?'

Geneva brightened. 'Now you're talking.'

To Leilani, Micky said, 'So I guess we're not twelve percenters, after all. We have lots of opinions, and we're proud of them.'

Grinning, Leilani bit into a crisp dill pickle. 'I really like you, Micky B. You, too, Mrs. D.'

'And we like you, sweetheart,' Geneva assured her.

'Only one of you was shot in the head,' Leilani said, 'but you've both got scrambled wiring – for the most part in a nice way.'

'You're a master of the gracious compliment,' Micky said.

'And so smart,' Aunt Gen said proudly, as if the girl were her daughter. 'Micky, did you know she's got an IQ of one eighty-six?'

'I thought it would be at least one ninety,' Micky replied.

'The day of the test,' Leilani said, 'I had chocolate ice cream for breakfast. If I'd had oatmeal, I might've scored six or eight points higher. Sinsemilla's not a boffo mom when it comes to keeping the fridge stocked. So I took the test through a sugar rush and a major post-sugar crash. Not that I'm making excuses or complaining. I'm lucky there was ice cream and not just marijuana brownies. Heck, I'm lucky I'm not dead and buried in some unmarked grave, with worms making passionate worm love inside my empty skull – or taken away in an extraterrestrial starship, like Lukipela, and hauled off to some godforsaken alien planet where there's nothing worth watching on TV and the only flavor of ice cream is chunky cockroach with crushed-glass sprinkles.'

'So now,' said Micky, 'in addition to your perpetually wasted tofu-peaches-bean-sprouts mother and your murderous stepfather, we're to believe you had a brother who was abducted by aliens.'

'That's the current story,' Leilani said, 'and we're sticking to it. Strange lights in the sky, pale green levitation beams that suck you right out of your shoes and up into the mother ship, little gray men with big heads and enormous eyes – the whole package. Mrs. D, may I have one of those radishes that looks like a rose?'

'Of course, dear.' Geneva slid the dish of garnishes across the table.

Laughing softly, shaking her head, Micky said, 'Kiddo, you've pushed this Addams Family routine one step too far. I don't buy the alien abduction for a second.'

'Frankly,' Leilani said, 'neither do I. But the alternative is too hideous to consider, so I just suspend my disbelief.'

'What alternative?'

'If Lukipela isn't on an alien planet, then he's somewhere else, and wherever that somewhere might be, you can bet it's not warm, clean, with good potato salad and great chicken sandwiches.'

For an instant, in the girl's lustrous blue eyes, behind the twin mirror images of the window and its burden of smoldering summer-evening light, behind the smoky reflections of the layered kitchen shadows, something seemed to turn with horrid laziness, like a body twisting slowly, slowly back and forth at the end of a hangman's noose. Leilani looked away almost at once, and yet on the strength of a single Budweiser, Micky imagined that she had glimpsed a soul suspended over an abyss.

6

Like the supernatural sylph of folklore, who inhabited the air, she approached along the hallway as though not quite touching the floor, tall and slim, wearing a platinum-gray silk suit, as graceful as a quiver of light.

Constance Veronica Tavenall-Sharmer, wife of the media-revered congressman who disbursed payoffs in airsickness bags, had been born from the headwaters of the human gene pool, before the river flowed out of Eden and became polluted with the tributaries of a fallen world. Her hair wasn't merely blond but the rich shade of pure-gold coins, fitting for a descendant of an old-money family that earned its fortune in banking and brokerage. Matte-satin skin. Features that would, if carved in stone, earn their sculptor the highest accolades and also immortality, if you measure immortality by mere centuries and expect to find it in museums. Her willow-leaf eyes were as green as spring and as cool as the layered shade deep in a grove of trees.

When he'd met her two weeks ago, Noah Farrel had disliked this woman on first sight, strictly as a matter of principle. Born to wealth and blessed with great beauty, she would skate through life with a smile, warm in even the most bitter wind, describing graceful arabesques upon her flashing blades, while all around her people perished in the cold and fell through the ice that, though solid under her, was treacherously thin for them.

By the time Mrs. Sharmer had left his office at the end of that first meeting, Noah's determination to dislike her had given way to admiration. She wore her beauty with humility, but more impressively, she kept her pedigree in her purse and never flashed it, as did so many others of her economic station.

At forty, she was only seven years older than Noah. Another

woman this beautiful would inspire his sexual interest – even an octogenarian kept youthful by a vile diet of monkey glands. By this third meeting, however, he regarded her as he might have regarded a sister: with the desire only to protect her and earn her approval.

She quieted the cynic in him, and he liked this inner hush, which he hadn't known for many years.

When she arrived at the open door of the presidential suite where Noah stood, she offered her hand; if younger and more foolish, he might have kissed it. Instead, they shook. Her grip was firm.

Her voice wasn't full of money, no disdain or evidence of tutor-shaped enunciation, but rich with quiet self-possession and faraway music. 'How are you this evening, Mr. Farrel?'

'Just wondering how I ever took pleasure in this line of work.'

'The cloak-and-dagger aspect ought to be fun, and the sleuthing. I've always loved the Rex Stout mysteries.'

'Yeah, but it never quite makes up for always being the bearer of bad news.' He stepped back from the door to let her enter.

The presidential suite was hers, not because she had booked the use of it, but because she owned the hotel. She was directly engaged in all her business enterprises; if her husband were having her followed, this early-evening visit wouldn't raise his suspicions.

'Is bad news what you always bring?' she asked as Noah closed the door and followed her into the suite.

'Often enough that it seems like always.'

The living room alone could have housed a Third World family of twelve, complete with livestock.

'Then why not do something else?' she asked.

'They'll never let me be a cop again, but my mind doesn't have a reset button. If I can't be a cop, I'll be a make-believe cop, like what I am now, and if someday I can't do this . . . Well, then . . .'

When he trailed off, she finished for him: 'Then screw it.'

Noah smiled. This was one reason he liked her. Class and style without pretension. 'Exactly.'

The suite featured contemporary decor. The honey-toned, bird's-eye maple entertainment center, with ebony accents, was a modified obelisk, not gracefully tapered like a standard obelisk, but of chunky proportions. The open doors revealed a large TV screen.

Instead of seeking chairs, they remained standing for the show.

A single lamp glowed. Like a jury of ghosts, ranks of shadows gathered in the room.

Earlier Noah had loaded the tape in the VCR. Now he pushed PLAY on the remote control.

On screen: the residential street in Anaheim. The camera tilted down from a height, focusing on the house of the congressman's lover.

'That's a severe angle,' Mrs. Sharmer said. 'Where were you?'

'I'm not shooting this. My associate is at an attic window of the place across the street. We made financial arrangements with the owner. It's item number seven on your final bill.'

The camera pulled back and angled down even more severely to reveal Noah's Chevrolet parked at the curb: battered but beloved steed, still ready to race when this had been shot, subsequently rendered into spare parts by a machine knacker.

'That's my car,' he explained. 'I'm behind the wheel.'

The camera tilted up, panned right: A silver Jaguar approached through the early twilight. The car stopped at the paramour's house, a tall man got out of the passenger's door, and the Jaguar drove away.

Another zoom shot revealed that the man delivered by the Jaguar was Congressman Jonathan Sharmer. His handsome profile was ideal for stone monuments in a heroic age, though by his actions he had proved that he possessed neither the heart nor the soul to match his face.

Arrogance issued from him as holy light might radiate from the apparition of a saint, and he stood facing the street, head raised as though he were admiring the palette of the twilight sky.

'Because he keeps tabs on you, he's been on to me from the start, but he doesn't know that I know that *he* knows. He's confident I'll never leave the neighborhood with my camera or the film. Playing with me. He isn't aware of my associate in the attic.'

Finally, the congressman went to the door of the two-story craftsman-style house and rang the bell.

A maximum-zoom shot captured the young brunette who answered the bell. In skintight shorts and a tube top stretched so extravagantly that it might kill bystanders if it snapped, she was temptation packaged for easy access.

'Her name's Karla Rhymes,' Noah reported. 'When she worked as a dancer, she called herself Tiffany Tush.'

'Not a ballerina, I assume.'

'She performed at a club called Planet Pussycat.'

On the threshold, Karla and the politician embraced. Even in the fading light of dusk, and further obscured by the shade of the porch roof, their long kiss could not be mistaken for platonic affection.

'She's on the payroll of your husband's charitable foundation.'

'The Circle of Friends.'

More than friends, the couple on the TV were as close as Siamese twins, joined at the tongue.

'She gets eighty-six thousand a year,' Noah said.

The video had been silent. When the kiss ended, sound was added: Jonathan Sharmer and his charity-funded squeeze engaged in something less than sparkling romantic conversation.

'Did this Farrel asshole really show up, Jonny?'

'Don't look directly. The old Chevy across the street.'

'The scabby little pervert can't even afford a real car.'

'My guys will junk it. He better have a bus pass for backup.'

'I bet he's giving himself a hand job right now, watching us.'

'I love your nasty mouth.'

Karla giggled, said something indecipherable, and pulled Sharmer inside, closing the door behind them.

Constance Tavenall – no doubt soon to cleanse herself of the name Sharmer – stared at the TV. She had married the congressman five years ago, before the first of his three successful political campaigns. By creating the Circle of Friends, he wove an image as a compassionate thinker with innovative approaches to social problems, while marriage to this woman lent him class, respectability. For a husband utterly lacking in character, such a spouse was the moral equivalent of arm candy, meant to dazzle the cognoscenti, not with her beauty, but with her sterling reputation, making it less likely that Sharmer would be the object of suspicion or the subject of close scrutiny.

Considering that all this had just now become incontestably clear to Constance, her composure was remarkable. The crudeness of what she heard failed to fire a blush in her. If she harbored anger, she hid it well. Instead, a barely perceptible yet awful sadness manifested as a faint glister in her eyes.

'A highly efficient directional microphone was synchronized with the camera,' Noah explained. 'We've added a soundtrack only where we've got conversation that'll ruin him.'

'A stripper. Such a cliche.' Even in the thread of quiet sorrow that this tape spun around her, she found a thin filament of humor, the irony that is the mother-of-all in human relationships. 'Jonathan cultivates an image of hip sophistication. The press see themselves in him. They'd forgive him anything, even murder, but they'll turn savage now because the cliche of this will embarrass them.'

The tape went silent again as a perfectly executed time dissolve brought the viewer from twilight to full night on the same street.

'We're using a camera and special film with exceptional ability to record clear images in a minimum of light.'

Noah half expected to hear ominous music building toward the assault on the Chevy. Once in a while, Bobby Zoon couldn't resist indulging in the techniques that he was learning in film school.

The first time that he'd worked for Noah, the kid had delivered a handsomely shot and effectively edited ten-minute piece showing a software designer trading diskettes containing his employer's most precious product secrets in return for a suitcase full of cash. The tape began with a title card that announced *A Film by Robert Zoon*, and Bobby was crushed when Noah insisted that he remove his credit.

In the Sharmer case, Bobby didn't catch the jolly approach of the Beagle Boys with their sledgehammer and tire iron. He focused on Karla's house, on the lighted window of an upstairs bedroom, where the gap between the half-closed drapes tantalized with the prospect of an image suitable for the front page of the sleaziest tabloid.

Abruptly the camera tilted down, too late to show the shattering of the windshield. Documented, however, were the bashing of the side window, Noah's eruption from the Chevy, and the gleeful capering of the two brightly costumed behemoths who obviously had learned all the wrong lessons from the morning cartoon programs that had been the sole source of moral education during their formative years.

'No doubt,' Noah said, 'they were once troubled youths rescued from a life of mischief, and rehabilitated by the Circle of Friends. I expected to be spotted and warned off, but I thought the approach, however it came, would be a lot more discreet than this.'

'Jonathan likes walking the edge. Risk excites him.'

As proof of what Constance Tavenall had just said, the videotape cut from the Chevy to the soft light at the bedroom window across the street. The drapes had been pulled aside. Karla Rhymes stood at the pane, as though showcased: visible above the waist, nude. Jonathan Sharmer, also nude, loomed behind her, hands on her bare shoulders.

Sound returned to the tape. Over a background crash-and-clatter of Chevy-bashing, the directional microphone captured the laughter and most of the running commentary between Karla and the congressman as they enjoyed the spectacle in the street below.

The violence aroused them. Jonathan's hands slid from Karla's shoulders to her breasts. Soon he was joined with her, from behind.

Earlier, the congressman had admired Karla's 'nasty mouth.' Now he proved that he himself could not have had a dirtier mouth if he'd spent the past few years licking the streets of Washington, D.C. He called the woman obscene names, heaped verbal abuse on her, and she seemed to thrill to every vicious and demeaning thing he said.

Noah pressed STOP on the remote control. 'There's only more of the same.' He took the videotape from the VCR and put it in a Neiman Marcus shopping bag that he'd brought. 'I've given you two more copies, plus cassettes of all the raw footage before we edited it.'

'What a perfectly appropriate word – *raw*.'

'I've kept copies in case anything happens to yours.'

'I'm not afraid of him.'

'I never imagined you were. More news – Karla's house was bought with Circle of Friends money. Half a million disguised as a research grant. Her own nonprofit corporation holds title to the property.'

'They're all such selfless do-gooders.' Constance Tavenall's voice was crisp with sarcasm but remarkably free of bitterness.

'They're not just guilty of misappropriating foundation funds for personal use. Circle of Friends receives millions in government grants, so they're in violation of numerous other federal statutes.'

'You have the corroborating evidence?'

He nodded. 'It's all in the Neiman Marcus bag.' He hesitated, but then decided that this woman's exceptional strength matched the congressman's weakness. She didn't have to be coddled. 'Karla Rhymes isn't his only mistress. There's one in New York, one in Washington. Circle of Friends indirectly purchased their residences, too.'

'That's in the bag? Then you've completely destroyed him, Mr. Farrel.'

'My pleasure.'

'He underestimated you. And I regret to admit, when I came to you, my expectations weren't terribly high, either.'

In their initial meeting, she acknowledged that she would have preferred a large detective agency or a private security firm with nationwide reach. She suspected, however, that all those operations did business, from time to time, with individual politicians and with the major political parties. She was concerned that the one she chose would have an existing relationship with her husband or with a friend of his in Congress, and that they might see more long-term profit in betraying her than in serving her honestly and well.

'No offense taken,' Noah said. 'No sane person ought to have confidence in a guy whose business address is also his apartment – and the whole shebang in three rooms above a palm-reader's office.'

She had settled in a chair at a nearby writing desk. Opening her small purse, extracting a checkbook, she asked, 'So why're you there? And why isn't your operation bigger?'

'Have you ever seen a really good dog act, Ms. Tavenall?'

Tweaked by puzzlement, her classic features had a pixie charm. 'Excuse me?'

'When I was a little kid, I saw a fantastic performing-dog act. This golden retriever did all these astonishingly clever tricks. When I saw what potential dogs possess, how smart they *can* be, I wondered why they're mostly happy to hang out doing dumb dog stuff. It's the silly kind of thing a little kid can get to wondering about. Twenty years later, I saw another dog act, and I realized that in the meantime life had taught me the answer to the mystery. Dogs have talent . . . but no ambition.'

Her puzzlement passed to pained compassion, and Noah knew

that she had read the text and subtext of his remark: not more than was true about him, but more than he intended to reveal. 'You're no dog, Mr. Farrel.'

'Maybe I'm not,' he said, although the word *maybe* issued from him without conscious intention, 'but my level of ambition is about that of an old basset hound on a hot summer afternoon.'

'Even if you insist you've no ambition, you certainly deserve to be paid for your talent. May I see that final bill you mentioned?'

He retrieved the invoice from the Neiman Marcus tote, and with it the airsickness bag still packed full of hundred-dollar bills.

'What's this?' she asked.

'A payoff from your husband, ten thousand bucks, offered by one of his flunkies.'

'Payoff for what?'

'Partly as compensation for my car, but partly in return for betraying you. Along with the videotapes, I've included a nota-rized affidavit describing the man who gave me the money and recounting our conversation in detail.'

'I've got more than enough to destroy Jonathan without this. Keep his bribe as a bonus. There's a nice irony in that.'

'I wouldn't feel clean with his money in my pocket. I'll be satisfied with payment of that invoice.'

Her pen paused on the downswing of the *l* in *Farrel*, and when she raised her head to look at Noah, her smile was as subtly expressive as an underlining flourish by a master of restrained calligraphy. 'Mr. Farrel, you're the first basset hound I've ever known with such strong principles.'

'Well, maybe I've padded your bill to make up for not keeping that ten thousand,' he said, though he had done nothing of the sort, and though he knew that she was not for an instant disposed to take seriously his suggestion of dishonesty.

He was dismayed by his inability to accept her compliment with grace, and he wondered – though not with any analytic passion – why he felt obliged to slander himself.

Shaking her head, gentle amusement still written on her face, she returned her attention to the checkbook.

From the woman's demeanor and a quality of mystery in her smile, Noah suspected that she understood him better than he knew himself. This suspicion didn't inspire contemplation, and he busied himself switching off the TV and closing the doors on the entertainment center while she finished writing the check.

While Noah watched her from the doorway, Constance Tavenall left the presidential suite, carrying the congressman's doom in the Neiman Marcus bag. The weight of her husband's betrayals didn't pull the lady's plumb-bob spine even one millimeter out of true. Like a sylph she had come; and after she turned the corner at the far end of the hallway, disappearing into the elevator alcove, the path that she had followed seemed to be charged with some supernatural energy, as the aura of an elemental spirit might linger after its visitation.

While the red and then the purple dust of twilight settled, Noah remained in the three-bedroom suite, roaming room to room, gazing out of a series of windows at the millions of points of light that blossomed across the peopled plains and hills, the shimmering dazzle of an electric garden. Although some loved this place as though it were Eden re-created, everything here was inferior to the original Garden in all ways but one: If you counted snakes an asset, then not merely a single serpent lurked within this foliage, but a wealth of vipers, all schooled in the knowledge of darkness, well practiced in deception.

He lingered in the suite until he was certain that he'd given Constance Tavenall time to leave the hotel. In case one of the congressman's minions coiled in a car outside, waiting to follow the woman, Noah must avoid being seen.

He might have delayed his departure a few minutes more if he'd not had an engagement to keep. Visiting hours at the Haven of the Lonesome and the Long Forgotten were drawing toward a close, and a damaged angel waited there for him.

7

So her brother was on Mars, her hapless mother was on dope, and her stepfather was on a murderous rampage. Leilani's eccentric tales were acceptable conversation over dinner in an asylum; but in spite of how looney life could sometimes be here in Casa Geneva, and though the relentless August heat withered common sense and wilted reason, Micky decided that they were setting a new standard for irrationality in this trailer where genteel daffiness and screwball self-delusion had heretofore been the closest they had come to madness.

'So who did your stepfather kill?' she asked nevertheless, playing Leilani's curious game if for no reason other than it was more amusing than talking about a miserable day of job-hunting.

'Yes, dear, who did he whack?' Aunt Gen asked with bright-eyed interest. Perhaps her occasional confusion of real-life experiences with the fantasies of the cinema had prepared her to relate to the girl's Hitchcockian-Spielbergian biography with less skepticism than the narrative aroused in Micky.

Without hesitation, Leilani said, 'Four elderly women, three elderly men, a thirty-year-old mother of two, a rich gay-nightclub owner in San Francisco, a seventeen-year-old high-school football star in Iowa – and a six-year-old boy in a wheelchair not far from here, in a town called Tustin.'

The specificity of the answer was disconcerting. Leilani's words struck a bell in Micky's mind, and she recognized the sound as the ring of truth.

Yesterday in the backyard, when Micky admonished the girl not to invent unkind stories about her mother, Leilani had said, *I couldn't make up anything as weird as what is.*

But a stepfather who had committed eleven murders? Who killed elderly women? And a little boy in a wheelchair?

Even as instinct argued that she was hearing the clear ring of truth, reason insisted it was the reverberant gong of sheer fantasy.

'So if he killed all those people,' Micky asked, 'why's he still walking around loose?'

'It's a wonderment, isn't it?' the girl said.

'More than a wonderment. It's impossible.'

'Dr. Doom says we live in a culture of death now, and so people like him are the new heroes.'

'What does that mean?'

'I don't explain the doctor,' Leilani said. 'I just quote him.'

'He sounds like a perfectly dreadful man,' Aunt Gen said, as though Leilani had accused Maddoc of nothing worse than habitually breaking wind and being rude to nuns.

'If I were you, I wouldn't invite him to dinner. By the way, he doesn't know I'm here. He wouldn't allow this. But he's out tonight.'

'I'd rather invite Satan than him,' said Geneva. 'You're welcome here anytime, Leilani, but he better stay on his side of the fence.'

'He will. He doesn't like people much, unless they're dead. He isn't likely to chat you up across the backyard fence. But if you do run into him, don't call him Preston or Maddoc. These days he looks a lot different, and he travels under the name Jordan – "call me Jorry" – Banks. If you use his real name, he'll know I've ratted on him.'

'I won't be talking to him,' said Geneva. 'After what I've just heard, I'd as soon smack him as look at him.'

Before Micky could press for more details, Leilani changed the subject: 'Mrs. D, did the cops catch the guy who robbed your store?'

Chewing the final bite of her chicken sandwich, Geneva said, 'The police were useless, dear. I had to track him down myself.'

'That's so completely radical!' In the gathering shadows that darkened but didn't cool the kitchen, in the scarlet light of the retiring sun, Leilani's face shone as much with enchantment as with a patina of perspiration. In spite of her genius IQ, her street smarts, and her well-polished wise-ass attitude, the girl retained some of the gullibility of a child. 'But how'd you do what the cops couldn't?'

As Micky struck a match to light the three candles in the center of the table, Aunt Gen said, 'Trained detectives can't compete with a wronged woman if she's determined, spunky, and has a hard edge.'

'Spunky though you are,' Micky said as the second candle cloned the flame on her match, 'I suspect you're thinking about Ashley Judd or Sharon Stone, or maybe Pam Grier.'

Leaning across the dinette table, whispering dramatically to Leilani, Geneva said, 'I located the bastard in New Orleans.'

'You've never been to New Orleans,' Micky affectionately reminded her.

Frowning, Geneva said, 'Maybe it was Las Vegas.'

Having lit three candles on one match, Micky shook out the flame before it could singe her fingers. 'This isn't real memory, Aunt Gen It's movie memory again.'

'Is it?' Geneva still leaned forward. The slow unsynchronized throbbing of the candle flames cast an undulant glow across her face, brightening her eyes but failing to dispel the shadow of confusion in which she sat. 'But, sweetie, I remember so clearly . . . the wonderful satisfaction of shooting him.'

'You don't own a gun, Aunt Gen.'

'That's right. I don't own a gun.' Geneva's sudden smile was more radiant than the candlelight. 'Now that I think about it, the man who was shot in New Orleans – he was Alec Baldwin.'

'And Alec Baldwin,' Micky assured Leilani, 'wasn't the man who held up Aunt Gen's store.'

'Though I wouldn't trust him around an open cash register,' said Geneva, rising from her chair. 'Alec Baldwin is a more believable villain than hero.'

Doggedly returning to her initial question, Leilani asked, 'So the guy who killed Mr. D – was he caught?'

'No,' Micky said. 'Cops haven't had one lead in eighteen years.'

'That reeks.'

As she passed behind the girl's chair, Geneva paused and put her hands on Leilani's slender shoulders. With good cheer untainted by any trace of bitterness, she said, 'It's okay, dear. If the man who shot my Vernon isn't already roasting in Hell, he will be soon.'

'I'm not sure I believe Hell exists,' the girl replied with the gravity of one who has given the matter considerable thought during the lonely hours of the night.

'Well, of course it does, sweetheart. What would the world be like without toilets?'

Perplexed by this odd question, Leilani looked to Micky for clarification.

Micky shrugged.

'An afterlife without Hell,' Aunt Gen explained, 'would be as polluted and unendurable as a world without toilets.' She kissed the top of the girl's head. 'And now I myself am off to have a nice sit-down with Nature.'

As Geneva left the kitchen, disappeared into the short dark hallway, and closed the bathroom door behind her, Leilani and Micky stared at each other across the dinette table. For languid seconds in the time-distorting August heat, they were as silent as the trinity of flames bright upon the smokeless wicks between them.

Finally, Micky said, 'If you want to establish yourself as an eccentric around this place, you've got your work cut out for you.'

'The competition is pretty stiff,' Leilani acknowledged.

'So your stepfather's a murderer.'

'It could be worse, I guess,' the girl said with a calculated jauntiness. 'He could be a bad dresser. A weaselly enough attorney can find a justification for virtually any murder, but there's no excuse for a tacky wardrobe.'

'Does he dress well?'

'He has a certain style. At least one isn't mortified to be seen in his company.'

'Even though he kills old ladies and boys in wheelchairs?'

'Only one boy in a wheelchair, as far as I know.'

Beyond the window, the wounded day left an arterial stain across the western sky, pulling over itself a shroud of gold and of purple.

When Micky rose to clear away the dinner dishes, Leilani pushed her chair back from the table and started to get up.

'Relax.' Micky switched on the light above the sink. 'I can handle it.'

'I'm not a cripple.'

'Don't be so sensitive. You *are* a guest, and we don't charge guests for dinner or make them work it off.'

Ignoring her, the girl plucked a roll of plastic wrap from a counter and began to cover the serving bowls, which were half full.

Rinsing the dishes and the flatware, stacking them in the sink to be washed later, Micky said, 'The logical assumption is that all this talk of the killer stepfather is just a vivid imagination at work, merely an attempt to add some dark glamor to the image of Ms. Leilani Klonk, flamboyant young mutant eccentric.'

'That would be a *wrong* assumption.'

'Just a bunch of hooey—'

'I live in a hooey-free zone.'

'—but a bunch of hooey that maybe has a second and more serious purpose,' Micky suggested.

Returning the potato salad to the refrigerator, Leilani said, 'What – you think I'm talking in riddles?'

Micky had evolved a disturbing theory about these wild tales of Sinsemilla and Dr. Doom. If she stated her suspicions directly, however, she would risk driving Leilani to further evasion. For reasons that she hadn't yet found time to analyze, she wanted to provide the girl with whatever help was needed if indeed help was being sought.

Instead of making eye contact, avoiding any approach that might seem like an inquisition, Micky continued rinsing dishes as she said, 'Not riddles exactly. Sometimes there are things we can't easily talk about, so we talk *around* them.'

Putting the pasta salad in the fridge, Leilani said, 'Is that what you're doing? Talking *around* what you really want to talk about? And I'm – what? – supposed to guess the true subject?'

'No, no.' Micky hesitated. 'Well, yes, that *is* what I'm doing. But I meant maybe *you're* talking around something when you tell these tall tales about Dr. Doom murdering boys in wheelchairs.'

From the corner of her eye, Micky was aware that the girl had stopped working and had turned to face her. 'Help me here, Michelina Bellsong. This little chat of ours is making me dizzy. What is it you think I'm talking around?'

'I don't have any idea what you're talking around,' Micky lied. 'That's for you to tell me . . . when you're ready.'

'How long have you been living with Mrs. D?'

'What's that matter? A week.'

'One week, and already you're a master of hugely befuddling conversation. Oh, I'd love to hear what a chinfest between the two of you is like when I'm not here to provide some rationality.'

'*You* provide rationality?' Micky rinsed the last of the dishes. 'Just when was the last time you actually ate tofu and canned peaches on a bed of bean sprouts?'

'I never eat it,' Leilani said. 'The last time old Sinsemilla *served* it was Monday. So come on, tell me, what do you think I'm talking around? You brought it up, so you must suspect something.'

Micky was flummoxed that her amateur psychology was proving to be no more successful than would have been a little amateur nuclear-reactor engineering or a session of brain surgery with kitchen utensils.

Drying her hands on a dishtowel, she turned to the girl. 'I don't have any suspicions. I'm just saying, if you want to talk about anything instead of just around it, I'm here.'

'Oh, Lord.' Although the sparkle in Leilani's eyes might have been read as something other than merriment, the mirth in her voice was unmistakable: 'You think I'm making up stories about Dr. Doom killing people because I'm too fearful or too ashamed to bring myself to talk about what he *really* does, and what you think maybe he *really* does is have his sweaty, greasy, drooling, lustful way with me.'

Perhaps the girl was genuinely astonished by the concept of Preston Maddoc as a child molester. Or perhaps this was nothing more than a pretense of amusement, to cover her discomfort at how close Micky had come to the truth.

The only thing trickier than an amateur using a psychologist's techniques was an amateur trying to interpret a patient's responses. If this *had* been nuclear-reactor engineering, Micky would already have been reduced to a cloud of radioactive dust.

Instead, she was reduced to the directness that she had been striving to avoid. 'Does he?' she asked Leilani.

Picking up Micky's second can of Budweiser from the table, the girl said, 'There's at least a million reasons why that's an absurd idea.'

'Give me one.'

'Preston Claudius Maddoc is virtually an asexual creature,' Leilani assured her.

'There's no such thing.'

'What about the amoeba?'

Micky understood this special girl well enough to know that the mysteries of her heart were many, that the answers to them could be learned only by earning her complete trust, and that her trust could be gained only by respecting her, by accepting her highly ornamental eccentricities, which included playing her baroque conversational games. In that spirit, Micky said, 'I'm not sure amoebas are asexual.'

'Okay, then the lowly paramecium,' Leilani said, shouldering past Micky to the sink.

'I don't even know what a paramecium is.'

'Good grief, didn't you go to school?'

'I went, but I didn't listen much. Besides, you aren't studying amoebas and parameciums in fourth grade.'

'I'm not in fourth grade,' Leilani said, pouring the warm beer into the sink. 'We're twenty-first-century Gypsies, searching for the stairway to the stars, never staying in one place long enough to put down a single rootlet. I'm homeschooled, currently learning at a twelfth-grade level.' The beer, foaming in the drain basket, produced a malty perfume that at once masked the faint smell of the hot wax from the candles on the table. 'Dr. Doom is my teacher, on paper, but the fact is I'm self-taught. The word for it is *autodidact*. I'm an autodidact and a good one, because I'll kick my own ass if I don't learn, which is a sight to see with this leg brace.' As though to prove how tough she was, Leilani crumpled the empty beer can in her good hand. 'Anyway, Dr. Doom might have been an okay professor when he worked at the university, but I can't rely on him to educate me now, because it's impossible to concentrate on your lessons when your teacher has his hand up your skirt.'

This time, Micky resisted being charmed. 'That's not funny, Leilani.'

Staring at the partially crushed can in her small fist, avoiding eye contact, the girl said, 'Well, I'll admit it's not as amusing as a good dumb-blonde joke, which I enjoy even though I'm a blonde myself, and it isn't a fraction as hilarious as a highly convincing puddle of plastic vomit, and there's no chance whatsoever I'd be making light of the subject if I were actually being molested.' She opened the cabinet door under the sink and tossed the can into the trash receptacle. 'But the fact is that Dr. Doom would never touch me even if he were *that* kind of pervert, because he pities me the way you would pity a truck-smashed dog all mangled but still alive on the highway, and he finds my deformities so disgusting that if he dared to kiss me on the cheek, he'd probably puke up his guts.'

In spite of the girl's jocular tone, her words were wasps, and the truth in them appeared to sting her, sharp as venom.

Sympathy cinched Micky's heart, but for a moment she was unable to think of something to say that wouldn't be the *wrong* thing.

Even more loquacious than usual, talking faster, as though the briefest interruption in the flow of words might dam the stream forever, leaving her parched and mute and defenseless, Leilani filled the narrow silence left by Micky's hesitation: 'As long back as I can remember, old Preston has touched me only twice, and I don't mean dirty-old-man-going-to-jail touching. Just ordinary touching. Both times, so much blood drained out of the poor dear's face, he looked like one of the walking dead – though I've got to admit he smelled better than your average corpse.'

'Stop,' Micky said, dismayed to hear the word come out with a harsh edge. Then more softly: 'Just stop.'

Leilani looked up at last, her lovely face unreadable, as free of all emotional tension as the countenance of the most serene bronze Buddha.

Perhaps the girl mistakenly believed that every secret of her soul was written on her features, or perhaps she saw more in Micky's face than she cared to see. She switched off the light above the sink, returning them to the silken gloom and the suety glow of the candle flames.

'Are you never serious?' Micky asked. 'Are you always making with the wisecracks, the patter?'

'I'm *always* serious, but I'm always laughing inside, too.'

'Laughing at what?'

'Haven't you ever stopped and looked around, Michelina Bellsong? Life. It's one long comedy.'

They stood but three feet apart, face-to-face, and in spite of Micky's compassionate intentions, a peculiar quality of confrontation had crept into their exchange.

'I don't get your attitude.'

'Oh, Micky B, you get it, all right. You're a smartie just like me. There's always too much going on in your head, just like in mine. You sort of hide it, but I can see.'

'You know what I think?' Micky asked.

'I know what you think and *why*. You think Dr. Doom diddles little girls, because that's what experience has taught you to think. I feel bad about that, Micky B, about whatever you went through.'

Word by word, the girl quieted almost to a whisper, yet her soft voice had the power to hammer open a door in Micky's heart, a door that had for a long time been kept locked, barred, and bolted. Beyond lay feelings tumultuous and unresolved, emotions so powerful that the mere recognition of them, after long denial, knocked the breath out of her.

'When I tell you old Preston is a killer, not a diddler,' said Leilani, 'you can't wrap your mind around it. I know why you can't, too, and that's all right.'

Slam the door. Throw shut the locks, the bars, the bolts. Before the girl could say more, Micky turned away from the threshold of those unwanted memories, found her breath and voice: 'That's not what I was going to say. What I think is you're *afraid* to stop laughing—'

'Scared shitless,' Leilani agreed.

Unprepared for the girl's admission, Micky stumbled a few words further. '—because you . . . because if . . .'

'I know all the becauses. No need to list them.'

Sometime during the two days she'd known Leilani, Micky arrived, as though by whirlwind, in a strange territory. She'd been journeying through a land of mirrors that initially appeared to be as baffling and as unreal as a funhouse, and yet repeatedly she had encountered reflections of herself so excruciatingly precise in their details and of such explicit depth that she turned away from them in revulsion or in anger, or in fear. The clear-eyed, steel-supported girl, larky and lurching, seemed at first to be a fabulist whose flamboyant fantasies rivaled Dorothy's dreams of Oz; however, Micky could get no glimpse of yellow bricks on this road, and here, now, in the lingering sour scent of warm beer, in this small kitchen where only a trinity of candle flames held back the insistent sinuous shadows, with the sudden sound of a toilet flushing elsewhere in the trailer, she was stricken by the terrible perception that under Leilani's mismatched feet had never been anything other than the rough track of reality.

As though privy to Micky's thoughts, the girl said, 'Everything I've ever told you is the truth.'

Outside: a shriek.

Micky looked to the open window, where the last murky glow of the drowning twilight radiated weak purple beams through black tides of incoming night.

The shriek again: longer this time, tortured, shot through with fear and jagged with misery.

'Old Sinsemilla,' said Leilani.

8

Less than twenty-four hours after the close call in Colorado, with the house fire and the hideous screams still vivid in memory, the motherless boy relaxes behind the steering wheel of a new Ford Explorer, while the harlequin dog sits erect beside him in the passenger's seat, listening to a radio program of classic Western tunes – at the moment, 'Ghost Riders in the Sky' – as they sail through the Utah night, four feet above the highway.

Sometimes, from the side windows, depending on the encroaching landscape, they are able to see the starry sky, low near the horizon, but nothing of the greater vault above, where ghost riders would be likely to gallop. The windshield provides a view only of another – and unoccupied – Explorer ahead, plus the underside of the vehicles on the upper platform of this double-deck automobile carrier.

In the late afternoon, they had boarded the auto transport in the immense parking lot of a busy truck stop near Provo, while the driver lingered over a slice of pie in the diner. The door of one of the Explorers opened for the boy, and he quickly slipped inside.

The dog had continued to be an instinctive conspirator, huddling quietly with his master, below the windows, until the pie-powered trucker returned and they ventured out upon the road again. Even then, in daylight, they had slouched low, to avoid being seen by passing motorists who might signal the driver about his stowaways.

With some of the money taken from the Hammond farmhouse, the famished boy had purchased two cheeseburgers at the truck stop. Soon after the truck began to roll, he'd eaten one sandwich and fed the other, in pieces, to the mutt.

He had been less generous with the small bag of potato chips.

They were crisp and so delicious that he groaned with pleasure while eating them.

This apparently had been an exotic treat to the dog, as well. When first given a chip, he turned the morsel on his tongue, as though puzzled by the texture or the taste, warily tested the edibility of the offering, then crunched the salty delicacy with exaggerated movements of his jaws. The hound likewise had savored each of three additional tidbits that his young master was conned into sharing, instead of wolfing them down.

The boy had drunk bottled water from the container, but this had proved more difficult for the dog, resulting in splashed upholstery and wet fur. In the console between the seats were molded-plastic cupholders, and when the boy filled one of these with water, his companion lapped it up efficiently.

Since decamping from the Colorado mountains, they had journeyed wherever a series of convenient rides had taken them.

For now, they travel without a destination, vagabonds but not carefree.

The killers are exceptionally well trained in stalking, using both their natural skills and electronic support, so resourceful and cunning that they are likely to track down their quarry no matter how successful the boy might be at quickly putting miles between himself and them. Although distance won't foil his enemies, time is his ally. The longer he eludes that savage crew, the fainter his trail becomes – or at least this is what he believes. Every hour of survival will bring him closer to ultimate freedom, and each new sunrise will allow a slight diminishment of his fear.

Now, in the Utah night, he sits boldly in the Explorer and sings along with the catchy music on the radio, having pretty much learned the repeating chorus and also each verse as he first heard it. Ghost riders in the sky. Can there be such things?

Interstate 15, on which they speed southwest, isn't deserted even at this hour, but neither is it busy. Beyond the wide median strip, traffic races northeast toward Salt Lake City, with what seems like angry energy, as knights might thunder toward a joust, lances of light piercing the high-desert darkness. In these nearer southbound lanes, cars overtake the auto transport and, from time to time, large trucks pass, as well.

The digital readout on the radio, powered by the car's battery, emits a glow, but the faint radiance is insufficient to illuminate the boy or to draw the attention of any motorist rocketing by at seventy or eighty miles per hour. He's not concerned about being seen, only about losing the comforting music when the battery eventually dies.

Cozy in the dark SUV, in the embracing scent of new leather and the comforting smell of the damp but drying dog, he isn't much interested in those passing travelers. He's peripherally aware of them only because of their roaring engines and their wind wakes, which buffet the transport.

'Ghost Riders in the Sky' is followed by 'Cool Water,' a song about a thirst-plagued cowboy and his horse as they cross burning desert sands. After 'Cool Water' comes a spate of advertisements, nothing to sing along with.

When the boy looks out the window in the driver's door, he sees a familiar vehicle streaking past, faster than ever it had gone when he and the dog had ridden in the back of it among horse blankets and saddles. The white cab features a spotlight rack on the roof. Black canvas walls enclose the cargo bed. This appears to be the truck that had been parked along the lonely country road near the Hammond place, less than twenty-four hours ago.

Of course, that vehicle hadn't been unique. Hundreds like it must be in use on ranches across the West.

Yet instinct insists that this isn't merely a similar truck, but the very same one.

He and the dog had abandoned that wheeled sanctuary shortly after dawn, west of Grand Junction, when the driver and his associate stopped to refuel and grab breakfast.

This auto carrier is their third rolling refuge since dawn, three rides during a day in which they have ricocheted across Utah with the unpredictability of a pinball. After all this time and considering the haphazard nature of their journey, the likelihood of a chance encounter with the saddlery-laden truck is small, though it isn't beyond the realm of possibility.

A coincidence, however, is frequently a glimpse of a pattern otherwise hidden. His heart tells him indisputably what his mind resists: This is no random event, but part of the elaborate design in a tapestry, and at the center of the design is he himself, caught and murdered.

The brow of the cab gleams as white as skull bone. One loose corner of black canvas flaps like the Reaper's robe. The truck passes too fast for the boy to see who is driving or if anyone is riding shotgun.

Supposing he had glimpsed two men wearing cowboy hats, he still couldn't have been sure that they were the same people who had driven him out of the mountains and west through Grand Junction. He has never seen their faces clearly.

Even if he could have identified them, they might no longer be innocent horsemen transporting ornate saddles to a rodeo or a show arena. They might have become part of the net that is closing around him, straining the dry sea of the desert for the sole survivor of the massacre in Colorado.

Now they are gone into the night, either unaware that they have passed within feet of him – or alert to his presence and planning to capture him at a roadblock ahead.

The dog curls on the passenger's seat and lies with his chin on the console, eyes glimmering with the reflected light of the radio readout.

Stroking the mutt's head, rubbing behind one of the floppy ears and then behind the other, the frightened boy takes comfort from the silken coat and the warmth of his friend, successfully repressing a fit of the shivers, though unable entirely to banish an inner chill.

He is the most-wanted fugitive in the fabled West, surely the most desperately sought runaway in the entire country, from sea to shining sea. A mighty power is set hard against him, and ruthless hunters swarm the night.

A melodic voice arises from the radio, recounting the story of a lonesome cowpoke and his girlfriend in faraway Texas, but the boy is no longer in the mood to sing along.

9

Banshees, shrikes tearing at their impaled prey, coyote packs in the heat of the hunt, werewolves in the misery of the moon could not have produced more chilling cries than those that caused Leilani to say, 'Old Sinsemilla,' and that drew Micky to the open back door of the trailer.

To the door and through it, down three concrete-block steps, onto the lawn in the last magenta murk of twilight, Micky proceeded with caution. Her wariness didn't halt her altogether, because she was certain that someone in terrible pain needed immediate help.

In the yard next door, beyond the sagging picket fence, a white-robed figure thrashed in the gloaming, as though ablaze and frantic to douse the flames. Not a single tongue of fire could be seen.

Micky crazily thought of killer bees, which might also have caused the shrieking figure to perform these frenzied gyrations. With the sun down, however, this was not an hour for bees, not even though the baked earth still radiated stored heat. Besides, the air wasn't vibrating with the hum of an angry swarm.

Micky glanced back at the trailer, where Leilani stood in the open doorway, silhouetted against faint candleglow.

'I haven't had dessert yet,' the girl said, and she retreated out of sight.

The apparition in the dark yard next door stopped squealing, but in a silence as disconcerting as the cries had been, it continued to turn, to writhe, to flail at the air. Its diaphanous white robe billowed and whirled as though this were a manic ghost that had no patience for the eerie but tedious pace of a traditional haunting.

When she reached the swagging fence, Micky could see that the tormented spirit was of this earth, not visiting from Beyond. Pale and willowy, the woman spun and swooned and jerked erect and spun again, barefoot in the crisp dead grass.

She didn't seem to be in physical pain, after all. She might have been working off excess energy in a frenetic freestyle dance, but she might just as likely have been suffering some type of spasmodic fit.

She wore a silk or nainsook full-length slip with elaborate embroidery and ribbon lace on the wide shoulder straps and bodice, as well as on the deep flounce that hemmed the skirt. The garment appeared not merely old-fashioned but antique, not feminine in a liberated contemporary let's-have-hot-sex style, but feminine in a frilly post-Victorian sense, and Micky imagined that it had been packed away in someone's attic trunk for decades.

Exhaling explosively, inhaling in great ragged gasps, the woman flung herself toward exhaustion, whether by fit or fandango.

'Are you all right?' Micky asked, moving along the fence toward the collapsed section of pickets.

Apparently neither as a reply nor as an expression of physical pain, the dancing woman let out a pathetic whimper, the fearful sound that a miserable dog might make in a cage at the animal pound.

The fallen fence pales clicked and rattled under Micky's feet as she entered the adjoining property.

Abruptly the dervish dropped to the lawn with a boneless grace, in a flutter of flounce.

Micky hurried to her, knelt at her side. 'What's wrong? Are you all right?'

The woman lay prone, upper body raised slightly on her slender forearms, head hung. Her face was an inch or two from the ground and hidden by glossy cascades of hair that appeared to be white in the crosslight of the moon and the fading purple dusk, but that probably matched Leilani's shade of blond. Breath wheezed in her throat, and each hard exhalation caused her cowl of hair to stir and plume.

After a hesitation, Micky put a consoling hand on her shoulder, but Mrs. Maddoc didn't respond to the touch any more than she had reacted to her name or to a question. Tremors quaked through her.

Remaining at the stricken woman's side, Micky looked across

the fence and saw Geneva at the back door of the trailer, standing on the top step, watching. Leilani remained inside.

Reliably off-center, Aunt Gen waved gaily, as though the trailer were an ocean liner about to steam out of port on a long holiday.

Micky wasn't surprised to find herself returning the wave. After a week with Geneva, she'd already absorbed a measure of her aunt's attitude toward the bad news and the sorrier turns of life that fate delivered. Gen met misfortune not simply with stoic resignation, but with a sort of amused embrace; she refused to dwell on or even to lament adversities, and she remained determined instead to receive them as though they were disguised blessings from which unexpected benefits would arise in time. Part of Micky figured this approach to hardship and calamity worked best if you'd been shot in the head and if you confused sentimental cinema with reality, but another part of her, the newly evolving Micky, found not only solace but inspiration in this Gen Zen. This evolving Micky returned her aunt's wave.

Geneva waved again, more exuberantly, but before Micky could become involved in an Abbott and Costello routine involving gestures instead of banter, the fallen woman at her side whimpered pitiably, more than once this time. Her thin cold plaints melted into a moan of abject misery, and the moan quickly dissolved into weeping – not the genteel tears of a melancholy maiden, but wretched racking sobs.

'What's wrong? What can I do?' Micky worried, although she no longer expected a coherent reply or even any response whatsoever.

At the Maddocs' rented mobile home, drapery-filtered lamplight glowed dark sour orange, less welcoming than the baleful fire in a menacing jack-o'-lantern. The draperies were shut tight, and no one watched from any window. Beyond the open back door lay a deserted kitchen dimly revealed by the face of an illuminated wall clock.

If Preston Maddoc, alias Dr. Doom, was at home, his disinterest in his wife's extreme distress couldn't have been more complete.

Micky squeezed the woman's shoulder reassuringly. Although she believed it was the fabrication of Leilani's pyrotechnic imagination, she used the only name that she knew: 'Sinsemilla?'

Whip-quick, the woman snapped her head up, blond tresses

lashing the air. Her face, half revealed in the gloom, drew taut with shock; the startled eyes flared so wide that white shone around the full circumference of each iris.

She threw off Micky's hand and scooted backward in the grass. A last sob clogged her throat, and when she tried to swallow it, the thick cry resurged, although not as a sob anymore, but as a snarl.

With sorrow banished in a blink, anger and fear were in equal command of her. *'You don't own me!'*

'Easy, easy now,' Micky counseled, still on her knees, making placating gestures with her hands.

'You can't control me with a name!'

'I was only trying to—'

Fury fired her rant, which grew hotter by the word: 'Witch with a broomstick up your ass, witch bitch, diabolist, hag, flying down out of the moon with my name on your tongue, think you can spellcast me with a shrewd guess of a name, but *that's* not going to happen, no one's the boss of me or ever will be, not by magic or money, not with force or doctors or laws or sweet talk, nobody EVER the boss of me!'

In response to this wild irrationality, with the potential for violence implicit in this woman's nuclear-hot anger, Micky realized that only silence and retreat made sense. Rocking knee to knee in the prickly grass, she edged backward.

Evidently inflamed by this movement even though it represented a clear concession, Sinsemilla spun to her feet with such agitation that she seemed to *flail* herself erect: skirt flounce churning around her legs, hair tossing like the deadly locks of an enraged Medusa. In her furious ascension, she stirred up an acrid cloud of dust and a powder of dead grass pulverized by a summer of hammering sun.

Through clenched teeth that squeezed each sibilant into a hiss, she said, 'Hag of a witch bitch, sorcerer's seed, you don't scare me!'

Having risen from her knees as Sinsemilla whirled upright, Micky sidled toward the fence, reluctant to turn her back on this neighbor from the wrong side of Hell.

A thieving cloud pocketed the silver-coin moon. At the western horizon, as the last livid blister of light drained off the heel of night, Micky glimpsed enough of a resemblance between this crazed woman and Leilani to be convinced against her will that they were mother and daughter.

When brittle wood cracked and she felt a picket underfoot, she knew that she'd found the passage in the fence. She wanted to glance down, afraid the pickets might trip her, but she kept her attention on her unpredictable neighbor.

Sinsemilla seemed to shed her anger as suddenly as she'd grown it. She adjusted the shoulder straps on her full-length slip, and then seized the roomy skirt in both hands and shook it as if casting off bits of dry grass. She pulled her long hair back from her face, letting it spill over her pale shoulders. Arching her spine, rolling her head, spreading her arms, the woman stretched as languorously as a sleeper waking from a delicious dream.

At what she judged to be a safe distance, perhaps ten feet past the fence, Micky stopped to watch Leilani's mother, half mesmerized by her bizarre performance.

From her back door, Aunt Gen said, 'Micky dear, we're putting dessert on the table, so don't be long,' and she went inside.

Repenting its larceny, the cloud surrendered the stolen moon, and Sinsemilla raised her slender arms toward the sky as though the lunar light inspired joy. Face tilted to bask in the silvery rays, she turned slowly in place, and then sidestepped in a circle. Soon she began to dance light-footedly, in a graceful swooping manner, as though keeping time to a slow waltz that only she could hear, with her face raised to the moon as if it were an admiring prince who held her in his arms.

Brief trills of laughter escaped Sinsemilla. Not brittle and mad laughter, as Micky might have expected. This was a girlish merriment, sweet and musical, almost shy.

In a minute, the laughter trailed away, and the waltz spun to a conclusion. The woman allowed her invisible partner to escort her to the back-door steps, upon which she sat in a swirl of ruffled embroidery, as a schoolgirl in another age might have been returned to one of the chairs around the dance floor at a cotillion.

Oblivious of Micky, Sinsemilla sat, elbows propped on her knees, chin cupped in the heels of her hands, gazing at the starry sky. She seemed to be a young girl dreamily fantasizing about true romance or filled with wonder as she contemplated the immensity of creation.

Then her fingers fanned across her face. She hung her head. The new round of weeping was subdued, inexpressibly melancholy, so quiet that the lament drifted to Micky as might the voice of a real ghost: the faint sound of a soul trapped in the narrow emptiness between the surface membranes of this world and the next.

Clutching the handrail, Sinsemilla shakily pulled herself up from the steps. She went inside, into the clock light and shadows of her kitchen, and the jack-o'-lantern glow beyond.

Micky scrubbed at her knees with the palms of her hands, rubbing off the prickly blades of dead grass that had stuck to her skin.

The pooled heat of August, like broth in a cannibal's pot, still cooked a thin perspiration from her, and the calm night had no breath to cool the summer soup.

Although the flesh might simmer, the mind had a thermostat of its own. The chill that shivered through Micky seemed cold enough to freeze droplets of sweat into beads of ice upon her brow.

Leilani is as good as dead.

She rejected that unnerving thought as soon as it pierced her. She, too, had grown up in a wretched family, abandoned by her father, left to the care of a cruel mother incapable of love, abused both psychologically and physically – and yet she had survived. Leilani's situation was no better but no worse than Micky's had been, only different. Hardship strengthens those it doesn't break, and already, at nine, Leilani was clearly unbreakable.

Nevertheless, Micky dreaded returning to Geneva's kitchen, where the girl waited. If Sinsemilla in all her baroque detail was not a fabrication, then what of the murderous stepfather, Dr. Doom, and his eleven victims?

Yesterday, in this yard, as Micky had broiled on the lounge chair, amused and a little disoriented by her first encounter with the self-proclaimed dangerous mutant, Leilani had said several peculiar things. Now one of them echoed in memory. The girl had asked if Micky believed in life after death, and when Micky returned the question, the girl's simple reply had been, *I better.*

At the time, the answer seemed odd, although not particularly dark with meaning. In retrospect, those two words carried a heavier load than any of the freight trains that Micky had imagined escaping on when, as she lay sleepless in another time and place, they had rolled past in the night with a rhythmic clatter and a fine mournful whistle.

Here, now, the hot August darkness. The moon. The stars and the mysteries beyond. No getaway train for Leilani, and perhaps none for Micky herself.

Do you believe in life after death?

I better.

Four elderly women, three elderly men, a thirty-year-old mother of two . . . a six-year-old boy in a wheelchair . . .

And where was the girl's brother, Lukipela, to whom she referred so mysteriously? Was he Preston Maddoc's twelfth victim?

Do you believe in life after death?

I better.

'Dear God,' Micky whispered, 'what am I going to do?'

10

Eighteen-wheelers loaded with everything from spools of abb to zymometers, reefer semis hauling ice cream or meat, cheese or frozen dinners, flatbeds laden with concrete pipe and construction steel and railroad ties, automobile transports, slat-sided trailers carrying livestock, tankers full of gasoline, chemicals: Scores of mammoth rigs, headlights doused but cab-roof lights and marker lights colorfully aglow, encircle the pump islands in much the way that nibbling stegosaurs and grazing brontosauruses and packs of hunting theropods had eons ago circled too close to the treacherous bogs that swallowed them by the thousands, by the millions. Rumbling-growling-wheezing-panting, each big truck waits for its communion with the nozzle, feeding on two hundred million years of bog distillations.

This is how the motherless boy understands the current theory of bitumen deposits in general and petroleum deposits in particular, as put forth locally in everything from textbooks to the Internet. Yet even though he finds the idea of dinosaurs-to-diesel-fuel silly enough to have first been expounded by Daffy Duck or another Looney Toons star, he is excited by the spectacle of all these cool trucks congregating at rank upon rank of pumps, in a great dazzle and rumble and fumy reek here in the middle of an otherwise dark, silent, and nearly scent-free desert.

From his hiding place in the Explorer on the lower deck of the car transport, he watches as purposeful men and women busily tend to their rigs, some of them colorful figures in hand-tooled boots and Stetsons, in studded and embroidered denim jackets, many in T-shirts emblazoned with the names of automotive products, snack foods, beers, and country-and-western bars from Omaha to Santa Fe, to Abilene, to Houston, to Reno, to Denver.

Disinterested in the bustle, not stirred – as the boy is – by the romance of travel and the mystery of exotic places embodied in these superhighway Gypsies, the dog is curled compactly on the passenger's seat, lightly dozing.

Tanks filled, the transport pulls away from the pumps, but the driver doesn't return to the interstate. Instead, he steers his rig into an immense parking lot, apparently intending to stop either for dinner or a rest.

This is the largest truck stop the boy has seen, complete with a sprawling motel, motor-home park, diner, gift shop, and according to one highway sign glimpsed earlier, a 'full range of services,' whatever that might encompass. He has never been to a carnival, but he imagines that the excitement he feels about this place must be akin to the thrill of being on an attraction-packed midway.

Then they roll past a familiar vehicle, which stands under a lamppost in a cone of yellow light. It's smaller than the giant rigs parked side by side on the blacktop. White cab, black canvas walls. The saddlery truck from Colorado.

A moment ago, he'd been eager to investigate this place. Now he wants only to move on – and quickly.

The transport swings into a wide space between two huge trucks.

Air brakes squeal and sigh. The rumbling engine stops. After the twin teams of Explorers stir slightly in their traces, like sleeping horses briefly roused from dreams of sweet pastures, the silence that settles is deeper than any the boy has heard since the high meadows of Colorado.

As the puddle of black-and-white fur on the passenger's seat becomes unmistakably a dog once more, rising to check out their new circumstances, the boy says worriedly, 'We've got to keep moving.'

In one sense, the nearness of those searching for him doesn't matter. The likelihood of his being apprehended within the next few minutes would be just as great if he were a thousand miles from here. His mother has often told him that if you're clever, cunning, and bold, you can hide in plain sight as confidently as in the most remote and well-disguised bolt-hole. Neither geography nor distance is the key to survival: Only time matters. The longer he stays free and hidden, the less likely that he will ever be found.

Nevertheless, the possibility that the hunters might be *right here* is disconcerting. Their nearness makes him nervous, and when he's nervous, he's less likely to be clever or cunning, or bold; and they will find him, *know* him, whether he's in plain sight or hiding in a cave a thousand feet from sunlight.

Hesitantly, he eases open the driver's door and slips out of the SUV onto the bed of the transport.

He listens. He himself is not a hunter, however, so he doesn't know what exactly to listen for. The action at the pump islands is a faraway grumble. Muffled country music, oscillating between faint and fainter, seasons the night with enchantment, the land-locked Western equivalent of a siren's irresistible song drifting across a night-shrouded sea with a promise of wonder and companionship.

The ramped bed of the auto transport isn't much wider than the Explorer, too narrow to allow the dog to land safely in a leap from the driver's seat, which he now occupies. If in fact he had jumped from the porch roof at the Hammond farmhouse, surely the mutt can clear the truck entirely, avoiding the vertical supports between the decks of the open cargo trailer, and spring directly to the parking lot; however, if he possesses the agility to accomplish this feat, he doesn't possess the confidence. Peering down from his perch, the dog cocks his head left, then right, makes a pathetic sound of anxiety, stifles the whine as though he recognizes the need for stealth, and stares beseechingly at his master.

The boy lifts the dog out of the Explorer, as earlier he had lifted him up and in, not without considerable contortion. He teeters but keeps his balance and puts his shaggy burden down on the floor of the transport.

As the boy eases shut the door of the Explorer, the mongrel pads toward the back of the auto carrier, following the ramped bed. He is waiting immediately behind the truck when his master arrives.

The ears are pricked, the head lifted, the nose twitching. The fluffy tail, usually a proud plume, is held low.

Although domesticated, this animal nevertheless remains to some degree a hunter, as the boy is not, and he has the instincts of a survivor. His wariness must be taken seriously. Evidently, something in the night smells threatening or at least suspicious.

Currently, no vehicles are either entering or leaving the lot. No truckers are in sight across the acres of blacktop.

Although a couple hundred people are nearby, this place in this moment of time seems as lonely as any crater on the moon.

From the west, out of the desert, arises a light breeze, warm but not hot, carrying the silicate scent of sand and the faint alkaline fragrance of the hardy plants that grow in parched lands.

The boy is reminded of home, which he will most likely never see again. A pleasant nostalgia wells within him, too quickly swells into a gush of homesickness, inevitably reminding him of the terrible loss of his family, and suddenly he sways as though physically battered by the flood of grief that storms through his heart.

Later. Tears are for later. Survival comes first. He can almost hear his mother's spirit urging him to control himself and to leave the grieving for safer times.

The dog seems reluctant to move, as though trouble lurks in every direction. His tail lowers further, wrapping partly around his right hind leg.

The motel and the diner lay out of sight to the east, beyond the ranks of parked vehicles, marked by the fiery glow of red neon. The boy sets off in that direction.

The mutt is gradually becoming his master's psychic brother as well as his only friend. He shakes off his hesitancy and trots at the boy's side.

'Good pup,' the boy whispers.

They pass behind eight semis and are at the back of a ninth when a low growl from the dog halts the boy. Even if the animal's sudden anxiety hadn't been strong enough to feel, the nearest of the tall pole lamps provides sufficient sour yellow light to reveal the animal's raised hackles.

The dog peers at something in the oily black gloom under the big truck. Instead of growling again, he glances up at the boy and mewls entreatingly.

Trusting the wisdom of his brother-becoming, the boy drops to his knees, braces one hand against the trailer, and squints into the pooled darkness. He can see nothing in the murk between the parallel sets of tires.

Then movement catches his eye, not immediately under the rig but along the side of it, in the lamplit passageway between this vehicle and the next. A pair of cowboy boots, blue jeans tucked in the tops: Someone is walking beside the trailer, approaching the back where the boy kneels.

Most likely this is an ordinary driver, unaware of the boyhunt that is being conducted discreetly but with great resources and urgency across the West. He's probably returning from a late dinner, with a thermos full of fresh coffee, ready to hit the road again.

Another pair of boots follows the first. Two men, not just one. Neither talks, both move purposefully.

Maybe ordinary drivers, maybe not.

The young fugitive drops flat to the pavement and slips under the trailer, and the dog crawls beside him into hiding. They huddle together, turning their heads to watch the passing boots, and the boy is oddly excited because this is a situation encountered in all the adventure stories that he loves.

Admittedly, the character of his excitement is different from what he feels when he experiences such exploits vicariously, through the pages of books. Young heroes of adventure stories from *Treasure Island* to *The Amber Spyglass*, are never eviscerated, decapitated, torn limb from limb, and immolated – which is a possible fate that he envisions for himself too clearly to embrace fully the traditional boys'-book spirit of derring-do. His excitement has a nervous edge sharper than anything Huckleberry Finn was required to feel, a darker quality. He's a boy nonetheless, and he's virtually programmed by nature to be thrilled by events that test his pluck, his fortitude, and his wits.

The two men reach the back of the trailer, where they pause, evidently surveying the parking lot, perhaps not quite able to recall where they left their rig. They remain silent, as though listening for the telltale sounds that only born hunters can perceive and properly interpret.

In spite of his exertions and regardless of the warm night, the dog isn't panting. He lies motionless against his master's side.

Good pup.

Instrument of nostalgia, scented with desert fragrances that remind the boy of home, the breeze is also a broom to the blacktop, sweeping along puffs of dust, spidery twists of dry desert grass, and scraps of litter. With a soft rustle, a loosely crumpled wad of paper twirls lazily across the pavement and comes to rest against the toe of one of the boots. The parking-lot light is bright enough that from a distance of a few feet, the boy can see this is debris with value: a five-dollar bill.

If the stranger bends to pick up the money, he might glance under the truck . . . .

No. Even if the man drops to one knee, instead of simply bending down, his head will be well above the bottom of the trailer. He won't inadvertently get a glimpse of a boy-shape-dog-shape cowering in the shadows cast by the rig.

After trembling against the boot toe, the five-dollar bill blows free . . . and twirls under the truck.

In the gloom, the boy loses track of the money. He's focused intently on the cowboy boots.

Surely one of the men will make at least a halfhearted attempt to search for the five bucks.

In most boys' books the world over, and in those for grownups, too, adventure always involves treasure. This globe rotates on a spindle of gold. A peglegged, parrot-petting pirate said exactly that, in one tale or another.

Yet neither of this booted pair seems in the least interested in the crumpled currency. Still without speaking a word to each other, they move on, away from the truck.

The possibility that neither of them noticed the money is slim. By their disinterest in the five dollars, they have revealed their true nature. They are engaged in an urgent search for something more important than treasure, and they won't be distracted.

The two men walk westward from the back of the semi – in the general direction of the automobile transport.

The boy and his companion crawl forward, farther under the trailer, toward the cab, and then they slip out of shelter, into the open space between this rig and the next, where they had first glimpsed the cowboy boots.

Evidently having snatched a small treasure from the teeth of the desert breeze, the dog holds the five-dollar bill in his mouth.

'Good pup.'

The boy smoothes the currency between his hands, folds it, and stuffs it in a pocket of his jeans.

Their meager financial resources won't carry them far, and they can't expect to find money in the wind whenever they need it. For the time being, however, they are spared the humiliation of committing another larceny.

Maybe dogs aren't capable of feeling humiliated. The boy's never had a dog before. He knows their nature only from movies, books, and a few casual encounters.

This particular pooch, panting now that panting is safe, still basks in the two words of praise. He is a scamp, a rascally fun-loving creature that lives by the simple rules of wild things.

In becoming brothers, they will change each other. The dog might become as easily humiliated and as fearfully aware of ever-looming death as his master is, which would be sad. And the boy figures that during their desperate, lonely, and probably long flight for freedom, he himself will have to guard against becoming too much like a dog, wild and given to rash action.

Without shame, the mutt squats and urinates on the blacktop.

The boy promises himself that public toileting is a behavior he will never adopt, regardless of how wild the dog might otherwise inspire him to be.

Better move.

The two silent men who had headed toward the auto transport won't be the only searchers prowling the night.

Skulking among the trucks, staying as much as possible out of the open lanes of the parking lot, the alert dog ever at his side, he chooses an indirect route, as if making his way through a maze, toward the promise of the red neon.

Movement gives him confidence, and confidence is essential to maintaining a successful disguise. Besides, motion is commotion, which has value as camouflage. More of his mother's wisdom.

Being among people is helpful, too. A crowd distracts the enemy – not much but sometimes enough to matter – and provides a screening effect behind which a fugitive can, with luck, pass undetected.

The truck lot adjoins a separate parking area for cars. Here, the boy is more exposed than he was among the big rigs.

He moves faster and more boldly, striking out directly toward the 'full range of services,' which are provided in a complex of structures farther back from the highway than the service islands and fuel pumps.

Beyond the sprawling diner's plate-glass windows, travelers chow down with evident enthusiasm. The sight of them reminds the boy how much time has passed since he ate a cold cheeseburger in the Explorer.

The dog whines with hunger.

Out of the warm night into the pleasantly cool restaurant, into eddying tides of appetizing aromas that instantly render him ravenous, the boy realizes he is grinning as widely as the dog.

The dog, not the grin, draws the attention of a uniformed woman standing at a lectern labeled HOSTESS. She's petite, pretty, speaks with a comic drawl, but is as formidable as a prison-camp guard when she assumes a blocking stance directly in his path. 'Honeylamb, I'll admit this here's not a five-star establishment, but we still say no to barefoot bozos and all four-legged kind, regardless of how cute they are.'

The boy is neither barefoot nor a clown, and so after a brief confusion, he realizes she's talking about the dog. By bursting into the restaurant with the animal at his side, he's drawn attention to himself when he can least afford to do so.

'Sorry, ma'am,' he apologizes.

Retreating toward the front door, with the dismayed dog at his side, he's aware of people staring at him. A smiling waitress. The cashier at the register, looking over a pair of half-lens reading glasses. A customer paying his check.

None of these people appears to be suspicious of him, and none seems likely to be one of the relentless trackers on his trail. Fortunately, this blunder will not be the death of him.

Outside once more, he tells the dog to sit. The pooch settles obediently beside the diner door. The boy hunkers in front of the mutt, pets him, scratches behind his ears, and says, 'You wait right here. I'll be back. With food.'

A man looms over them – tall, with a glossy black beard, wearing a green cap with the words DRIVING MACHINE in yellow letters above the bill – not the customer who was at the cash register, but another who's on his way into the restaurant. 'That's sure a fine tailwagger you have there,' the driving machine says, and the dog obligingly swishes his tail, sweeping the pavement on which he sits. 'Got a name?'

'Curtis Hammond,' he replies without hesitation, using the name of the boy whose clothes he wears, but at once wonders if this is a wise choice.

Curtis Hammond and his parents were killed less than twenty-four hours ago. If by now the Colorado authorities have realized that the fire at the farmhouse was arson, and if autopsies have revealed that the three victims were savagely assaulted, perhaps tortured, all dead before the fire was set, then the names of the murdered have surely been heard widely on news broadcasts.

With no apparent recognition of the name, the bearded trucker, who may be only what he appears to be, but who may also be Death with facial hair, says, 'Curtis Hammond. That's a powerfully peculiar name for a dog.'

'Oh. Yeah. My dog,' the boy says, feeling stupid and dismally incompetent at this passing-for-nobody-special business. He hasn't given a thought to naming his four-legged companion, because he's known that eventually, when he bonds better with the animal, he'll arrive at not just any name, but at the *exactly right* one. With no time to wait for better bonding, scratching the dog under the chin, he takes inspiration from a movie: 'The name's Old Yeller.'

Amused, the trucker cocks his head and says, 'You yankin' my chain, young fella?'

'No, sir. Why would I?'

'And what's the logic, callin' this beauty Old Yeller, when there's not one yellow hair from nose to tail tip?'

Abashed at his nervous bumbling in the face of this man's easy and nonthreatening conversation, the boy tries to recover from his foolish gaff. 'Well, sir, color doesn't have anything to do with it. We like the name just because this here is the best old dog in the world, just exactly like Old Yeller in the movie.'

'Not exactly like,' the driving machine disagrees. 'Old Yeller was a male. This lovely black-and-white lady here must get a mite confused from time to time, bein' called a male name and a color she isn't.'

The boy hasn't previously given much thought to the gender of the dog. *Stupid, stupid, stupid.*

He remembers his mother's counsel that in order to pass for

someone you're not, you must have confidence, confidence above all else, because self-consciousness and self-doubt fade the disguise. He must not allow himself to be rattled by the trucker's latest observation.

'Oh, we don't think of it as just a male name or a female name,' the boy explains, still nervous but pleased by his growing fluency, which improves when he keeps his attention on the pooch instead of looking up at the trucker. 'Any dog could be a Yeller.'

'Evidently so. I think I'll buy me a girl cat and call her Mr. Rover.'

No meanness is evident in this tall, somewhat portly man, no suspicion or calculation in his twinkling blue eyes. He looks like Santa Claus with a dye job.

Nevertheless, standing erect, the boy wishes the trucker would go away, but he can't think of a thing to say to make him leave.

'Where's your folks, son?' the man asks.

'I'm with my dad. He's inside getting takeout, so we can eat on the road. They won't let our dog in, you know.'

Frowning, surveying the activity at the service islands and the contrasting quiet of the acres of parked vehicles, the trucker says, 'You shouldn't stray from right here, son. There's all kinds of people in the world, and some you don't want to meet at night in a lonely corner of a parkin' lot.'

'Sure, I know about their kind.'

The dog sits up straighter and pricks her ears, as if to say that she, too, is well informed about such fiends.

Smiling, reaching down to stroke the lovely lady's head, the trucker says, 'I guess you'll be all right with Old Yeller here to take a chunk of meat out of anyone who might try to do you wrong.'

'She's real protective,' the boy assures him.

'Just don't you stray from here,' the driving machine warns. He tugs on the bill of his green cap, the way a polite cowboy in the movies will sometimes tug on the brim of his Stetson, an abbreviated tipping of the hat, meant as a sign of respect to ladies and other upstanding citizens, and at last he goes inside.

The boy watches through the glass door and the windows as the hostess greets the trucker and escorts him to a table. Fortunately, he is seated with his back toward the entrance. With his cap still on, he appears to be at once enthralled by the offerings on the tall, two-fold menu.

To the faithful canine, the boy says, 'Stay here, girl. I'll be back soon.'

She chuffs softly, as though she understands.

Out in the vast parking area, where cones of dirty yellow light alternate with funnels of shadow, there's no sign of the two silent men who wouldn't stoop to pick up five dollars.

Sooner or later, they'll come back here, run a search through the diner, around the motel, and wherever else their suspicion draws them, even if they've searched those places before. And if not those same two men, then two others. Or four. Or ten. Or legions.

Better move.

11

Generous slices of homemade apple pie. Simple white plates bought at Sears. Yellow plastic place mats from Wal-Mart. The homey glow of three unscented candles that had been acquired with twenty-one others in an economy pack at a discount hardware store.

This humble scene at Geneva's kitchen table was a fresh breeze of reality, clearing away the lingering mists of unreason that the chaotic encounter with Sinsemilla had left in Micky's head. Indeed, the contrast between Geneva polishing each already-clean dessert fork on a dishtowel before placing it on the table and Sinsemilla waltzing with the moon was less like a mere refreshing breeze than like sudden immersion in an arctic sea.

How peculiar the world had grown if now life with Aunt Gen had become the sterling standard of normalcy.

'Coffee?' Geneva inquired.

'Uh, yeah.'

'Hot or iced?'

'Hot. But spike it,' Micky said.

'Spike it with what, dear?'

'Brandy and milk,' Micky said, and at once Leilani, who was not drinking coffee, suggested, 'Milk,' speaking in her capacity as self-appointed temperance enforcer on assignment to Michelina Bellsong.

'Brandy and milk and milk,' Aunt Gen noted, taking the order for Micky's complex spike as she poured the coffee.

'Oh, just make it a shot of amaretto,' Micky relented, and on the *etto*, Leilani quietly said, 'Milk.'

Ordinarily, nothing made Micky bristle with anger or triggered her stubbornness more quickly than being told she couldn't have what she wanted, unless it was being told that her choices in life hadn't been the best, unless it was being told that she would screw up the rest of her life if she wasn't careful, unless it was being told that she had an alcohol problem or an attitude problem, or a problem with motivation, or with men. In the recent past, Leilani's well-meaning murmured insistence on milk would have jammed down the detonation plunger, not on all these issues, but on enough of them to have assured an explosion of respectable magnitude.

During the past year, however, Micky had spent a great many hours in late-night self-analysis, if only because her circumstances had given her so much time for contemplation that she couldn't avoid shining a light into a few of the rooms in her heart. Until then, she had long resisted such explorations, perhaps out of fear that she'd find a haunted house within herself, occupied by everything from mere ghosts to hobgoblins, with monsters of a singular nature crouched behind doors from the attic to the subcellar. She'd found a few monsters, all right, but she'd been more disturbed by the discovery that in the mansion of her soul, a greater number of rooms than not were unfurnished spaces, dusty and unheated. Since childhood, her defenses against a cruel life had been anger and stubbornness. She'd seen herself as the lone defender of the castle, ceaselessly prowling the ramparts, at war with the world. But a constant state of battle readiness had held off friends as well as enemies, and in fact it had prevented her from experiencing the fullness of life, which might have filled those vacant rooms with good memories to balance the bad that cluttered other chambers.

As a matter of emotional survival, she had recently been making an effort to keep her anger sheathed and to let her stubbornness rest in its scabbard. Now she said, 'Just milk, Aunt Gen.'

This evening wasn't about Micky Bellsong, anyway, not about what she wanted or whether she was self-destructive, or whether she would be able to pull her life out of the fire into which she herself had cast it. This evening had become all about Leilani Klonk, if it had not actually been about the girl from the start, and Micky had never in her memory been less focused on her own interests or needs – or resentments.

The request for brandy had been a reflex reaction to the stress of the encounter with Sinsemilla. Over the years, alcohol had become a reliable part of her arsenal, as useful for keeping life at bay as were anger and pigheadedness. Too useful.

Returning to her chair, Geneva said, 'So, Micky, will we all be getting together for a neighborly barbecue anytime soon?'

'The woman is either nuts or higher than a Navajo shaman with a one-pound-a-day peyote habit.'

Poking her pie with a fork, Leilani said, 'It's both, actually. Though not peyote. Like I told you – tonight it's crack cocaine and hallucinogenic mushrooms, much enhanced by old Sinsemilla's patented brand of lunatic charm.'

Micky had no appetite. She left the pie untouched. 'She really was in an institution once, wasn't she?'

'I told you yesterday. They shot like six hundred thousand volts of electricity through her head—'

'You said fifty or a hundred thousand.'

'Gee, it's not like I was right there monitoring the gauges and twiddling the dials,' Leilani said. 'You've got to allow me a *little* literary license.'

'Where was she institutionalized?'

'We lived in San Francisco then.'

'When?'

'Over two years ago. I was seven going on eight.'

'Who did you live with while she was hospitalized?'

'Dr. Doom. They've been together four and a half years now. See, there's even kismet for crackpots. Anyway, the headshrinkers shot like *nine* hundred thousand volts through old Sinsemilla's noggin, unless you want to nitpick my figures, and it didn't help her any way whatsoever, though the feedback of lunacy from her brain probably blew out power-company transformers all over the Bay Area. Great pie, Mrs. D!'

'Thank you, dear. It's a Martha Stewart recipe. Not that she gave it to me personally. I took it down from her TV show.'

Micky said, 'Leilani, for God's sake, is your mother always like that – the way I just saw her?'

'No, no. Sometimes she's simply impossible.'

'This isn't funny, Leilani.'

'You're wrong. It's hilarious.'

'The woman is a menace.'

'To be fair,' Leilani said, forking pie into her mouth as she talked, 'my dear *mater* isn't always drugged out of her mind the way you just saw her. She saves that for special evenings – birthdays, anniversaries, when the moon is in the seventh house, when Jupiter is aligned with Mars, that kind of thing. Most of the time, she's satisfied with tokin' on a joint, keeping a nice light buzz, maybe floating on a Quaalude. She even goes clean and straight some days, though that's when the depression sets in.'

Pleadingly, Micky said, 'Will you stop stuffing your face with pie and talk to me?'

'I can talk around the pie, even if it isn't polite. I haven't belched all evening, so I ought to have some etiquette points to my credit. I'm not going to miss out on one bite of this. Old Sinsemilla couldn't bake up anything this good if her life depended on it – not that she's ever likely to face a pie-or-die threat.'

'What sort of baking does your mother do?' Geneva asked.

'She made an earthworm pie once,' Leilani said. 'That was when she was deep in a passionate natural-foods phase that stretched the definition of *natural* to include things like chocolate-covered ants, pickled slugs, and crushed-insect protein. The earthworm pie sort of put an end to all that. I'm absolutely sure it wasn't a Martha Stewart recipe.'

Micky finished her coffee in long swallows, as though she had forgotten it wasn't spiked, and though she most definitely didn't need a caffeine jolt. Her hands were shaking. The cup rattled against the saucer when she put it down.

'Leilani, you can't go on living with her.'

'With who?'

'Old Sinsemilla. Who else? She's psychotic. As they say when they commit people to the psychiatric ward against their will – she's a danger to herself and others.'

'To herself, for sure,' Leilani agreed. 'Not really to others.'

'She was a danger to *me* in the yard, all that screaming about hag of a witch bitch and spellcasting and not being the boss of her.'

Geneva had risen from her chair to fetch the pot from the Mr. Coffee machine. She poured a refill for Micky. 'Maybe it'll settle your nerves, dear.'

With no pie left on her plate, Leilani put down her fork. 'Old Sinsemilla *scared* you, that's all. She can be as scary as Bela

Lugosi and Boris Karloff and Big Bird all rolled into one, but she's not dangerous. At least as long as my *pseudo*father keeps her supplied with drugs. She might be a terror if she ever went into withdrawal.'

Freshening her own coffee, Geneva said, 'I don't find Big Bird scary, dear, just unnerving.'

'Oh, Mrs. D, I disagree. People dressing up in big weird animal suits where you can't see their faces – that's scarier than sleeping with a nuclear bomb under your bed. You have to figure people like that have real *issues* to resolve.'

'Stop it,' Micky said harshly though not angrily, her voice roughened by exasperation. 'Just, please, stop it.'

Leilani pretended puzzlement. 'Stop what?'

'You know very well what I mean. Stop all this avoidance. Talk to me, *deal* with this situation.'

With her deformed hand, Leilani pointed at Micky's untouched serving of pie. 'Are you going to eat that?'

Micky pulled the plate closer to herself. 'I'll trade pie for a serious discussion.'

'We've been *having* a serious discussion.'

'There's half a pie left,' Geneva offered cheerily.

'I'd love a piece, thanks,' Leilani said.

'The half that's left is off-limits,' Micky declared. 'The only pie in play is my piece.'

'Nonsense, Micky,' Geneva said. 'Tomorrow I can bake another apple pie all for you.'

As Geneva rose from the table, Micky said, 'Aunt Gen, sit down. This isn't about pie.'

'It is from *my* perspective,' said Leilani.

'Listen, kid, you can't come around here, doing your dangerous-young-mutant act, worming your way—'

Grimacing, Leilani said, 'Worming?'

'*Worming* your way into . . .' Micky fell silent, surprised by what she had been about to say.

'Into your spleen?' Leilani suggested.

For longer than she could remember, Micky hadn't allowed herself to be emotionally affected by anyone to any significant degree.

Leaning across the table as though earnestly determined to

help Micky find the elusive word, Leilani said, 'Into your gall bladder?'

Caring was dangerous. Caring made you vulnerable. Stay up on the high ramparts, safe behind the battlements.

Geneva said, 'Kidneys?'

'Worming your way into our hearts,' Micky continued, because saying *our* instead of *my* seemed to share the risk and to leave her less exposed, 'and then expect us not to care when we see the danger you're in.'

Still armored in drollery, with a full bandolier of cheerful banter, Leilani said, 'I never thought of myself as heartworm, but I guess it's a perfectly respectable parasite. Anyway, I assure you with all seriousness – if that's what it takes to get the pie – that my mother isn't a danger to me. I've lived with her ever since she popped me out of the oven, and I've still got all my limbs, or at least the same odd arrangement I was born with. She's pathetic, old Sinsemilla, not fearsome. Anyway, she *is* my mother, and when you're a nine-year-old girl, even an unusually smart one with a gift for gab, you can't just pack your bags, walk out, find a good apartment, get a high-paying job in software design, and be tooling around in your new Corvette by Thursday. I'm sort of stuck with her, if you see what I mean, and I know how to cope with that.'

'Child Protective Services—'

'Well-meaning but useless,' Leilani interrupted. She seemed to be speaking from experience. 'Anyway, the *last* thing I want is for old Sinsemilla to be put back in the nuthouse for a refresher course in ear-to-ear electrocution, because that'll leave me alone with my pseudofather.'

Micky shook her head. 'They wouldn't leave you in the care of your mother's boyfriend.'

'When I call him my pseudofather, I'm indulging in wishful thinking. He's my legal stepfather. He married old Sinsemilla four years ago, when I was five going on six. I wasn't reading anywhere near at a college level then, but I understood the implications, anyway. It was an amazing wedding, let me tell you, though there wasn't a carved-ice swan. Do you like carved-ice swans, Mrs. D?'

Geneva said, 'I've never seen one, dear.'

'Neither have I. But the idea appeals to me. And so right after he married Sinsemilla, he said that even though he hadn't actually adopted me and Lukipela, we should start using his last name, but I still use the Klonk I was born with. You've got to be mad to be Maddoc – that's what Luki and I used to say.'

Here came that unsettling shift in the girl's eyes, like a sudden muddy tide washing through clean water, an uncharacteristic despair that even candlelight was sufficiently bright to reveal.

In spite of the news about the marriage, Micky clung to the hope that her newfound desire to act as – so to speak – her sister's keeper could be fulfilled at least to some small extent. 'Whether he's your legal stepfather or not, the proper authorities will—'

'The proper authorities didn't nail the guy who killed Mrs. D's husband,' Leilani said. 'She had to track Alec Baldwin to New Orleans and blow him away herself.'

'With great satisfaction,' Geneva noted, raising her coffee cup as if in a toast to the liberating power of vengeance.

For once, no sparkle of humor enlivened Leilani's blue eyes, no thinnest paring of a wry smile curled either corner of her mouth, and no sportive note informed her voice as she met Micky's stare with a piercing directness, and said almost in a whisper, 'When you were such a pretty little girl and bad people took things from you that you never-ever wanted to give, the proper authorities weren't there for you even once, were they, Michelina?'

Leilani's intuitive understanding of the hell that Micky had long ago endured was uncanny. The empathy in those blue eyes rocked her and left her with the certain sense that the most closely guarded truths about herself had been exposed, ugly secrets around which she had constructed impregnable vaults of shame. And though she had never expected to speak to another human being about those years of ordeal and humiliation, although until this moment she would have angrily denied ever being *anyone's* victim, she didn't feel wounded by this exposure, as she would have expected, didn't feel mortified or in the least diminished, but felt instead as if a painfully constricting knot had at last come loose inside her, and realized that sympathy, as this girl had shown it to her, did not have to contain any element of condescension.

'Were they ever there?' Leilani asked again.

Not trusting herself to speak, Micky shook her head, which was the first admission she had ever made of the painful past on which her life was built. She slid her guarded dessert, untouched, in front of Leilani.

Geneva was the only one to bring tears to the table, and she blew her nose noisily in a Kleenex. Of course, she might be flashing back to some tender moment she believed that she'd shared with Clark Gable or Jimmy Stewart, or William Holden, but Micky sensed that her aunt was fully in the thrall of this moment and in the firm grip of the real.

Micky said, 'It's hard to make up anything as weird as what *is*.'

'Yeah, I heard that somewhere,' Leilani replied, picking up her fork.

'He is a murderer – isn't he? – just as your mother turned out to be the way you said she was.'

Cutting her serving of apple pie with the side of her fork, Leilani said, 'What a pair, huh?'

'But eleven people? How could he—'

'No offense, Micky, but the story of Dr. Doom and his multiple homicides is a dreary tale, more tedious than titillating, and it can only bring this lovely evening to a new low. It's already been dragged pretty low, thanks to old Sinsemilla's performance. If you really want to know about Preston Claudius Maddoc, kissing cousin to the Grim Reaper, try reading the news. He hasn't been on the front pages for a while, but the whole strange story is out there if you want to look it up. As for me, I'd rather eat pie, talk about pie, philosophize about pie, and just in general spend the rest of the evening in a pie kind of mood.'

'Yeah, I can see why you'd want to do that. But you've got to know one question I can't avoid asking.'

'Sure, I know,' the girl said, lowering her gaze to her plate, but hesitating with her fork poised over the pie.

In a miserable voice, Aunt Gen said, 'It's never this bad in the movies.'

And Micky said to Leilani, 'Did he kill your brother, Lukipela?'

'Yes.'

12

Inside the restaurant, which must have the capacity to seat at least three hundred, the boy, without dog, glides past the distracted hostess.

Quickly glancing around as he moves, he notices only a few children here and there, all with their families. He'd been hoping for more kids, lots of kids, so he won't be so easy to spot if the wrong people come looking.

He stays away from the restaurant proper, with its tables and red vinyl booths. Instead he goes directly to the lunch counter, where customers occupy fewer than half the stools.

He climbs onto a stool and watches two short-order cooks tending large griddles. They're frying bacon, hamburger patties, eggs, and mounds of crispy hash browns glistening with oil.

As if there's already something of the dog's heart twined with his own, the boy finds his mouth filled with saliva, and he swallows hard to keep from drooling.

'What can I do ya for, big guy?' a counter waitress inquires.

She's a fantastically large person, nearly as round as she is tall: bosoms the size of goose-down pillows, fine hulking shoulders, a neck made to burst restraining collars, and the proud chins of a fattened bull. Her uniform features short sleeves, and her exposed arms are as big as those of a bodybuilder, although without muscle definition – immense, smooth, pink. As if to provide the illusion of height and to balance her spherical body, she boasts a colossal mass of lustrous auburn hair, twisted and braided and flared and folded into an amazing work of architecture, high at the top of which is pinned a little yellow-and-white uniform cap that could be easily mistaken for a resting butterfly.

The boy marvels, wondering what being this woman would

be like, whether she always feels as great and powerful as she looks, rhino-powerful, or whether sometimes she feels as weak and frightened as any lesser person. Surely not. She is majestic. She is magnificent, beautiful. She can live by her own rules, do as she wishes, and the world will treat her with awe, with the respect that she deserves.

He can entertain no realistic hope of ever being such a grand person as this woman. With his weak will and unreliable wits, he's barely able to be poor Curtis Hammond. And yet he tries. He says, 'My name's Curtis, and my dad sent me in for some grub to go.'

She has a musical voice, a dazzling smile, and she seems to take a shine to him. 'Well, Curtis, my name's Donella, 'cause my dad was Don and my mom was Ella – and I think what we serve here is a few notches above plain grub.'

'It sure smells fantastic.' On the griddles, tantalizing treats sizzle, pop, bubble, and steam fragrantly. 'Boy, I've never seen a place like this.'

'Really? You don't look like you've been raised in a box.'

He blinks, thinking furiously, striving to comprehend what she has suggested, but he can't avoid the question: 'Were *you*?'

'Were I what?'

'Raised in a box?'

Donella wrinkles her nose. This is virtually the only part of her face that she *can* wrinkle, because everything else is gloriously full, round, smooth, and too firmly packed even to dimple. 'Curtis, you disappoint me. I thought you were a good boy, a nice boy, not a smart aleck.'

Oh, Lord, he's put his foot wrong again, stepped in a pile of doo-doo, figuratively speaking, but he can't understand what he's done to offend and can't imagine how to get himself admitted to her good graces once more. He dare not call undue attention to himself, not with so many murderous hunters looking for someone his size, and he absolutely must obtain food for himself and for Old Yeller, who is depending on him, but Donella controls his access to the grub, or to whatever you call it when it's a few notches above plain grub.

'I *am* a nice boy,' he assures her. 'My mother was always proud of me.'

Donella's stern expression softens slightly, though she still won't give the enchanting smile with which she first greeted him.

Speaking his heart seems the best way to make amends. 'You're so fabulous, so beautiful, so magnificent, Ms. Donella.'

Even his compliment fails to pump the air back into her deflated smile. In fact her soft pink features suddenly appear stone-hard, and cold enough to bring an early end to summer across the entire North American continent. 'Don't you mock me, Curtis.'

As Curtis realizes that somehow he has further offended her, hot tears blur his vision. 'I only want you to like me,' he pleads.

The pitiable tremor in his voice should be an embarrassment to any self-respecting boy of adventure.

Of course, he isn't adventuring at the moment. He's socializing, which is immeasurably more difficult than engaging in dangerous exploits and heroic deeds.

He's rapidly losing confidence. Lacking adequate self-assurance, no fugitive can maintain a credible deception. Perfect poise is the key to survival. Mom always said so, and Mom knew her stuff.

Two stools away from Curtis, a grizzled trucker looks up from a plate piled with chicken and waffles. 'Donella, don't be too hard on the kid. He didn't mean nothing by what he said. Nothing like you think. Can't you see he's not quite right?'

A fly line of panic casts a hook into the boy's heart, and he clutches the edge of the counter to avoid reeling off the stool. He thinks for a moment that they see through him, recognize him as the most-wanted fish for which so many nets have been cast.

'You hush your mouth, Burt Hooper,' says the majestic Donella. 'A man who wears bib overalls and long johns instead of proper pants and a shirt isn't a reliable judge of who's not quite right.'

Burt Hooper takes this upbraiding without offense, cackles with amusement, and says, 'If I got to choose between comfort and being a sex object, I'll choose comfort every time.'

'Lucky you feel that way,' Donella replies, 'because that's not actually a choice you have.'

Through a blur of tears, the boy sees the glorious smile once more, a smile as radiant as that of a goddess.

Donella says, 'Curtis, I'm sorry I snapped at you.'

Trying to regain control of his emotions, but still blubbering a little, he says, 'I don't know why I offended you, ma'am. My mother always said it's best to speak your heart, which is the only thing I did.'

'I realize that now, sugar. I didn't first see you're . . . one of those rare folks with a pure soul.'

'So then . . . do you think I'm "not quite right"?' he asks, fiercely gripping the edge of the counter, still half afraid that they are beginning to recognize him for the fugitive he is.

'No, Curtis. I just think you're too sweet for this world.'

Her statement both reassures and strangely disconcerts the boy, so he makes another effort at compliment, speaking with sincerity and emotion that cannot be misconstrued as anything else: 'You really are beautiful, Ms. Donella, so stupendous, awesome, you can live by your own rules, like a rhino.'

Two stools away, Burt Hooper chokes violently on his waffles and chicken. His fork clatters against his plate as he grabs his glass of Pepsi. Sputtering, with cola foaming from his nostrils, face turning as red and mottled as a boiled lobster, he at last clears his throat of food only to fill it with laughter, making such a spectacle of himself that it's evident he would be a lousy fugitive.

Perhaps the trucker has just now remembered a particularly funny joke. His unrestrained hilarity is nonetheless rude, distracting Curtis and Donella from their mutual apologies.

The divine Donella glares at Burt with the expression of a perturbed rhino, lacking only the threat of a large pointed horn to make the comparison perfect.

In the same way that a clatter of laughter had knocked its way through the last of Burt's choking, so now a rattle of words raps out of him between guffaws: 'Oh, damn . . . I'm splat . . . in the middle . . . of *Forrest Gump*!'

The boy is puzzled. 'I know that movie.'

'Never you mind, Curtis,' Donella says. 'We're no more splat in the middle of *Forrest Gump* than we are in the middle of *Godzilla*.'

'I sure hope not, ma'am. That was one mean lizard.'

Burt is spluttering again, half choking, even though his throat was clear a moment ago, and his deteriorating condition causes the boy concern. The trucker seems on the brink of a medical emergency.

Donella declares, 'If anyone around here has a box of chocolates for a brain, then he's sitting in front of a plate of chicken and waffles.'

'That's you, Mr. Hooper,' Curtis observes. Then he understands. 'Oh.' The trucker's tears of laughter are this poor afflicted man's way of dealing with his loneliness, his disability, his pain. 'I'm sorry, sir.' The boy feels deep sympathy for this truck-driving Gump, and he regrets being so insensitive as to have thought that Burt Hooper was simply rude. 'I'd help you if I could.'

Although the trucker looks vastly amused, this is, of course, purely sham amusement to cover his embarrassment at his own shortcomings. '*You* help *me*? How?'

'If I could, I'd make you normal just like Ms. Donella and me.'

The intellectually disadvantaged trucker is so deeply touched by this expression of concern that he swivels on his stool, putting his back to Curtis, and struggles to master his emotions. Although to all appearances, Burt Hooper is striving to quell a fit of giddiness, the boy now knows that this is like the laughter of a secretly forlorn clown: genuine if you listen with just your ears, but sadly fraudulent if you listen with your heart.

Exhibiting rhinoscerosian contempt for Mr. Hooper, Donella turns away from him. 'Don't you pay any mind to him, Curtis. He's had every opportunity to be normal his whole life, but he's always chosen to be just the sorry soul he is.'

This baffles the boy because he's been under the impression that a Gump has no choice but to be a Gump, as nature made him.

'Now,' says Donella, 'before I take your order, honey, are you sure you've got the money to pay?'

From a pocket of his jeans, he extracts a crumpled wad of currency, including the remaining proceeds from the Hammond larceny and the five bucks that the dog snatched from the breeze in the parking lot.

'Why, you are indeed a gentleman of means,' says Donella. 'You just put it away for now, and pay the cashier when you leave.'

'I'm not sure it's enough,' he worries, jamming his bankroll into his pocket again. 'I need two bottles of water, a cheeseburger for my dad, a cheeseburger for me, potato chips, and probably two cheeseburgers for Old Yeller.'

'Old Yeller would be your dog?'

He beams, for he and the waitress are clearly connecting now. 'That's exactly right.'

'No sense paying big bucks for cheeseburgers when your dog will like something else better,' Donella advises.

'What's that?'

'I'll have the cook grill up a couple meat patties, rare, and mix them with some plain cooked rice and a little gravy. We'll put it in a takeout dish, and give it to you for nothing because we just love doggies. Your pooch will think he's died and gone to Heaven.'

The boy almost corrects her on two counts. First, Old Yeller in this case is a she, not a he. Second, the dog surely knows what Heaven's like and won't confuse paradise with a good dinner.

He raises neither issue. Bad guys are looking for him. He's been too long in this one spot. Motion is commotion.

'Thank you, Ms. Donella. You're as wonderful as I just knew you were when I first saw you.'

Surprising the boy, she affectionately squeezes his right hand. 'Whenever people think they're smarter than you, Curtis, just you remember what I'm going to tell you.' She leans across the counter as far as her fabulous bulk will allow, bringing her face closer to his, and she whispers these teaberry-scented words: 'You're a better *person* than any of them.'

Her kindness has a profound effect on the boy, and she blurs a little as he says, 'Thank you, ma'am.'

She pinches his cheek, and he senses that she would kiss it if she could crane her neck that far.

As a desperate but relatively unseasoned fugitive, he has been largely successful at adventuring, and now he's hopeful that he'll learn to be good at socializing, too, which is vitally important if he is to pass as an ordinary boy under the name Curtis Hammond or any other.

His confidence is restored.

The loud drumming of fear with which he has lived for the past twenty-four hours has subsided to a faint rataplan of less-exhausting anxiety.

He has found hope. Hope that he will survive. Hope that he will discover a place where he belongs and where he feels at home.

Now, if he can find a toilet, all will be right with the world.

He asks Donella if there's a toilet nearby, and as she writes up his takeout order on a small notepad, she explains that it's more polite to say *restroom*.

When Curtis clarifies that he doesn't need to rest, but rather that he urgently needs to relieve himself, this explanation touches off another emotional reaction from Burt Hooper, which appears to be laughter, but which is probably something more psychologically complex, as before.

Anyway, the toilet – the *restroom* – is within sight from the lunch counter, at the end of a long hallway. Even poor Mr. Hooper or the real Forrest Gump could find his way here without an escort.

The facilities are extensive and fascinating, featuring seven stalls, a bank of five urinals from which arises the cedar scent of disinfectant cakes, six sinks with a built-in liquid-soap dispenser at each, and two paper-towel dispensers. A pair of wall-mounted hot-air dryers activate when you hold your hands under them, although these machines aren't smart enough to withhold their heat when your hands are dry.

The vending machine is smarter than the hand dryers. It offers pocket combs, nail clippers, disposable lighters, and more exotic items that the boy can't identify, but it knows whether or not you've fed coins to it. When he pulls a lever without paying, the machine won't give him a packet of Trojans, whatever they might be.

When he realizes that he's the only occupant of the restroom, he seizes the opportunity and runs from stall to stall, pushing all the flush levers in quick succession. The overlapping swish-and-glug of seven toilets strikes him as hilarious, and the combined flow demand causes plumbing to rattle in the walls. Cool.

After he relieves himself, as he's washing his hands with enough liquid soap to fill the sink with glittering foamy masses of suds, he looks in the streaked mirror and sees a boy who will be all right, given enough time, a boy who will find his way and come to terms with his losses, a boy who will not only live but also flourish.

He decides to continue being Curtis Hammond. Thus far no one has connected the name to the murdered family in Colorado. And since he's grown comfortable with this identity, why change?

He dries his hands thoroughly on paper towels, but then holds them under one of the hot-air blowers, just for the kick of tricking the machine.

Refreshed, hurrying along the corridor between the restrooms and the restaurant, Curtis comes to a sudden halt when he spots two men standing out there at the lunch counter, talking to Burt Hooper. They are tall, made taller by their Stetsons. Both wear their blue jeans tucked into their cowboy boots.

Donella appears to be arguing with Mr. Hooper, probably trying to get him to shut his trap, but poor Mr. Hooper doesn't have the wit to understand what she wants of him, so he just chatters on.

When the trucker points toward the restrooms, the cowboys look up and see Curtis a little past the midpoint of the hall. They stare at him, and he returns their stares.

Maybe they aren't sure if he's his mother's son or some other woman's child. Maybe he could fake them out, pass for an ordinary baseball-loving, school-hating ten-year-old boy whose interests are limited entirely to down-to-earth stuff like TV wrestling, video games, dinosaurs, and serial-flushing public toilets.

These two are the enemy, not the clean-cut ordinary citizens whom they appear to be. No doubt about it. They radiate the telltale intensity: in their stance, in their demeanor. In their eyes.

They will see through him, perhaps not immediately, but soon, and if they get their hands on him, he will be dead for sure.

As one, the two cowboys start toward Curtis.

13

'Intergalactic spacecraft, alien abductions, an extraterrestrial base hidden on the dark side of the moon, supersecret human and alien crossbreeding programs, saucer-eyed gray aliens who can walk through walls and levitate and play concert-quality clarinet with their butts – Preston Maddoc believes in all of it, and more,' Leilani reported.

The power failed. They were conversing by candlelight, but the clock on the oven blinked off, and at the far end of the adjacent living room, a ginger-jar lamp with a rose damask shade went dark with a pink wink. The aged refrigerator choked like a terminal patient on life-support machinery, denied a desperately needed mechanical respirator; the compressor motor rattled and expired.

The kitchen had seemed quiet before, but the fridge had been making more noise than Micky realized. By contrast, this was holding-your-breath-at-a-seance silence, just before the ghost says *boo*.

Micky found herself staring up expectantly at the ceiling, and she realized that the timing of the power outage, just as Leilani was talking about UFOs, had given her the crazy notion that they had suffered a blackout not because of California's ongoing crisis, but because a pulsing, whirling disc craft from a far nebula was hovering over Geneva's motor home, casting a power pall just like alien ships always did in the movies. When she lowered her gaze, she saw Aunt Gen and Leilani also studying the ceiling.

In this deep quiet, Micky gradually became aware of the whispery sputter-sizzle of burning candle wicks, a sound as faint as the memory of a long-ago serpent's hiss.

Gen sighed. 'Rolling blackout. Third World inconvenience with the warm regards of the governor. Not supposed to have them at night, only in high-demand hours. Maybe it's just an *ordinary* screw-up.'

'I can live without power as long as I've got pie,' Leilani said, but she still hadn't forked up a mouthful of her second piece.

'So Dr. Doom is a UFO nut,' Micky pressed.

'He's a broad-spectrum, three-hundred-sixty-degree, inside-out, all-the-way-around, perfect, true, and *complete* nut. UFOs are only one of his interests. But since marrying old Sinsemilla, he's pretty much dedicated his life to the saucer circuit. He has this honking big motor home, and we travel all around the country, to the sites of famous close encounters, from Roswell, New Mexico, to Phlegm Falls, Iowa, wherever the aliens are supposed to have been in the past, we go hoping they'll show up again. And when there's a new sighting or a new abduction story, we haul ass for the place, wherever it is, so maybe we'll get there while the action is still hot. The only reason we're renting next door for a week is because the motor home is in the shop for an overhaul, and Dr. Doom won't stay in a hotel or motel because he thinks they're all just breeding grounds for legionnaire's disease and that gross flesh-eating bacteria, whatever it's called.'

'You mean you'll be gone in a week?' Aunt Gen asked. A web of worry strung spokes and spirals at the corners of her eyes

'More like a few days,' Leilani said. 'We just spent July in Roswell, actually, because it was July 1947 when an alien starship pilot, evidently drunk or asleep at the joystick, crashed his saucer into the desert. Dr. Doom thinks ETs are more likely to visit a site at the same time of year they visited it before, I guess sort of the way college students go to Fort Lauderdale every spring break. And isn't it amazing, really, how often these weird little gray guys are supposed to have totaled one of their gazillion-dollar, galaxy-crossing SUVs? If they ever decide to conquer Earth, I don't think we've got much to worry about. What we're dealing with here is Darth Vader with lots of Larry, Curly, and Moe blood in his veins.'

Micky had figured to let the girl wind down, but the longer that Leilani circled the subject of her brother's fate, the more tightly wound she seemed to become. 'Okay, what's the point? What's all this UFO stuff have to do with Lukipela?'

After a hesitation, Leilani said, 'Dr. Doom says he's had this vision that we'll both be healed by extraterrestrials.'

'Healed?' Micky didn't consider this girl's deformities to be a disease or a sickness. In fact, Leilani's self-assurance, her wit, and her indomitable spirit made it hard to think of her as disabled, even now when her left hand rested on the table, obviously misshapen in the otherwise forgiving glow of the three candles.

'Luki was born with a wickedly malformed pelvis, Tinkertoy hip joints built with monkey logic, a right femur shorter than the left, and some bone fusion in his right foot. Sinsemilla has this theory that hallucinogens during pregnancy give the baby psychic powers.'

The night heat couldn't bake the chill from Micky's bones. In memory she saw the fury-tightened face of the woman in the frilly slip, and moonlight painting points on the teeth in her snarl.

'What do you think of that theory, Mrs. D?' Leilani asked with little of her usual humor, but with a quiet note of long-throttled anger in her voice.

'Sucky,' Aunt Gen said.

Leilani smiled wanly. 'Sucky. We're still waiting for the day when I'm able to foretell next week's winning lottery numbers, start fires with the power of my mind, and teleport to Paris for lunch.'

Micky said, 'Some of your brother's problems . . . It sounds like surgery could have helped at least a little.'

'Oh, Mother's far too terribly smart to put any faith in Western medicine. She relied on crystal harmonics, chanting, herbal remedies, and a lot of poultices that would give any urine-soaked, puke-covered wino competition for the worst smell outside of a Calcutta sewer.'

Micky had finished her second cup of coffee. She couldn't recall drinking it. She got up to pour a refill. She felt helpless, and she needed to keep her hands busy, because if her hands weren't occupied, her anger might overwhelm her. She wanted to lash out at someone on Leilani's behalf, take a hard satisfying swing, but there was no one here to punch. Yet if she went next door to knock some sense into Sinsemilla, and even if the psychotic moon dancer didn't kill her, she wouldn't improve the girl's situation, only make it worse.

Standing at the counter in the near dark, pouring coffee with the care of a blind woman, Micky said, 'So this nutball is driving you and Luki around looking for aliens with healing hands.'

'Healing technology,' Leilani corrected. 'An alien species, having mastered interstellar travel and the problem of toileting neatly at faster-than-light speeds, is sure to be able to take the wrinkles out of this body or pop me into a brand new body identical to this one but with no imperfections. Anyway, that's the plan we've been operating on for about four years now.'

'Leilani, honey, you're not going back there,' Geneva declared. 'We're not going to let you go back to them. Are we, Micky?'

Perhaps the only good thing about the unextinguishable anger that had charred Micky's life was that it also burned from her all illusions. She didn't entertain fantasies derived from the movies or from any other source. Aunt Gen might for a moment see herself as Ingrid Bergman or Doris Day, capable of rescuing an imperiled waif with just a dazzling smile and a righteous speech – and stirring music in the background – but Micky saw clearly the hopelessness of this situation. On the other hand, if only hopelessness was the result, perhaps the burning away of illusions wasn't so desirable, after all.

Micky sat at the table again. 'Where did Lukipela disappear?'

Leilani looked toward the kitchen window but seemed to be gazing at something far away in time and at a considerable distance beyond the California darkness. 'Montana. This place in the mountains.'

'How long ago?'

'Nine months. The nineteenth of November. Luki's birthday was the twentieth. He would have been ten years old. In the vision that the old doom doctor had, the one where he claimed he saw us being healed by ETs – it was supposed to happen before we were ten. Each of us would be made whole, he promised Sinsemilla, before we were ten.'

'"Strange lights in the sky,"' Micky quoted, '"pale green levitation beams that suck you right out of your shoes and up into the mother ship."'

'I didn't see any of that myself. It's what I was told happened to Luki.'

'Told?' Aunt Gen asked. 'Who told you, dear?'

'My pseudofather. Late that afternoon, he parked the motor home in a roadside lay-by. Not a campground. Not even a real rest stop with bathrooms or a picnic table, or anything. Just this lonely wide area along the shoulder of the road. Forest all around. He said we'd go on to a motor-home park later. First, he wanted to visit this special site, a couple miles away, where some guy named Carver or Carter claimed to've been abducted by purple squids from Jupiter or something, three years before. I figured he'd drag us all along, as usual, but once he unhitched the SUV that we tow behind the motor home, he only wanted to take Luki.'

The girl grew silent.

Micky didn't press for further details. She needed to know what came next, but she didn't entirely want to hear it.

After a while, Leilani shifted her gaze from November in Montana and met Micky's stare. 'I knew then what was happening. I tried to go along with them, but he . . . Preston wouldn't let me. And Sinsemilla . . . she held me back.' A ghost drifted along the corridors of the girl's memory, a small spirit with Tinkertoy hips and one leg shorter than the other, and Micky could almost see the shape of this apparition haunting those blue eyes. 'I remember Lukipela walking to the SUV, clomping along with his one built-up shoe, his leg stiff, rolling his hips in that funny way he did. And then . . . as they drove away . . . Luki looked back at me. His face was blurred a little because the window was dirty. I think he waved.'

14

Perched happily on his stool at the lunch counter, poor dumb Burt Hooper knows that he himself is a truck driver and knows that he himself is eating chicken and waffles, but he doesn't know that he himself is a total Forrest Gump, good-hearted but a Gump nonetheless. Well-meaning, Mr. Hooper points toward the hallway that leads to the restrooms.

As one, the two cowboys start toward Curtis.

Donella calls to them, but even she, in her majestic immensity, can't restrain them by word alone.

To Curtis's right lies a pivot-hinged door with an inset oval of glass. The porthole is too high to provide a view to him, so he pushes through the door without knowing what lies beyond.

He's in a large commercial kitchen with a white-ceramic-tile floor. Banks of large ovens, cooktops, refrigerators, sinks, and preparation tables, all stainless steel, gleaming and lustrous, provide him with a maze of work aisles along which a stooping-crouching-scuttling boy might be able to escape.

Not every delicacy is prepared by the two short-order cooks out front. The kitchen staff is large and busy. No one appears interested in Curtis when he enters.

Oven to oven, past a ten-foot-long cooktop, past an array of deep fryers full of roiling hot oil, around the end of a long prep table, Curtis hurries into a narrow work aisle with loosely thatched rubber mats on the floor. He stays low, hoping to get out of sight before the two cowboys arrive. He avoids collisions with the staff, squeezing around them, dodging left, right, but they're no longer disinterested in him.

'Hey, kid.'

'What're you doin' here, boy?'

'*¡Tener cuidado, muchacho!*'
'Watch it, watch it!'
'*¡Loco mocoso!*'

He's just entering the next aisle, one layer deeper into the huge kitchen, when he hears the two cowboys arrive. There's no mistaking their entrance for anything else. With the arrogance and the blood hunger of Gestapos, they *slam* through the swinging door, their boot heels clopping hard against the tile floor.

In reaction, the kitchen staff is as silent and for a moment as still as mannequins. No one demands to know who these brash intruders are, or makes a clatter of pots that might draw attention, probably because everyone fears that these two are federal immigration agents, rousting illegal aliens – of which there's no doubt one present – and that they will hassle even properly documented workers if they're in a belligerent mood.

By their very presence, however, the cowboys have won allies for Curtis. As the crouching boy progresses by hitch and twitch through the kitchen, cooks and bakers and salad-makers and dishwashers ease out of his way, facilitate his passage, use their bodies to further block the cowboys' view of him, and direct him with subtle gestures toward what he assumes will be a rear exit.

He's scared, mouth suddenly bitter with the taste of what might be his mortality, lungs cinched tight enough to make each breath a labor, heart rapping with woodpecker frenzy – and yet he is acutely aware of the delicious aromas of roasting chicken, baking ham, frying potatoes. Fear doesn't entirely trump hunger, and though the flood of saliva is bitter, it fails to diminish his appetite.

Noises in his wake suggest that the killers are trying to track him. Contentious voices quickly arise as the kitchen staff, realizing that these two cowboys have no law-enforcement credentials, object to their intrusion.

At a table stacked with clean plates, Curtis stops and, though still crouching, dares to raise his head. He peers between two towers of dishes, and sees one of his pursuers about fifteen feet away.

The hunter has a handsome, potentially genial face. If he were to smile instead of glower, put on a mask of kindness, the kitchen staff might warm at once to him and point him toward his quarry.

But although Curtis is sometimes fooled by appearances, he's perceptive enough to see that this is a man whose face gives out at every pore the homicidal toxins in which his brain now marinates. Pressing sweet peach juice from a handful of dried pits would be easier than squeezing one drop of pity from this hunter's heart, and mercy would more likely be wrung from any stone.

As he moves along the salad-prep aisle, the grim cowboy looks left and right, shoving aside the men and women in his way as if they are mere furniture. His partner isn't immediately behind him, and might be approaching by a different route.

The restaurant employees are protesting less, maybe because the hunters' steely indifference to every objection and their cold-eyed persistence is too intimidating to resist. You see guys like this on the TV news, shooting up shopping centers or office buildings because of a wife's decision to file for divorce, because they've lost a job, or just because. Yet with discreet nods and gestures, the workers continue to shepherd Curtis toward escape.

In a half squat, shambling side to side and using his swinging arms for counterbalance, just as a frightened monkey might scamper, the boy turns a corner at a long butcher block and encounters a cook who's gazing out across the enormous kitchen, wide-eyed, watching the hunters. The white-uniformed cook might be an angel, considering that he holds a plastic-wrapped bundle of hot dogs, which he has just taken from the open cooler behind him.

A crash rocks the room, rattles cookware. Someone slamming through the swinging door from the restroom hallway. Following the cowboys. More hard and hurried footfalls on the tile floor. Voices. Then shouting. 'FBI! FBI! Freeze, freeze, freeze!'

Curtis clutches at the hot dogs. Startled, the man lets go of the bundle. Having claimed the meaty treasure, Curtis scuttles past the cook, bound for freedom and a makeshift dinner, surprised by the arrival of the FBI, but not in the least heartened by this unexpected development.

When it rains, it pours, his mother had said. She never claimed that the thought was original with her. Universal truths often find expression in universal cliches. *When it rains, it pours, and when it pours, the river runs wild, and suddenly we're caught up in a flood. But when we're in a flood, we don't panic, do we, baby boy?* And he always knew the answer to that one: *No, we never panic.* And she would say,

Why don't we panic in the flood? And he would say, *Because we're too busy swimming!*

Behind him, elsewhere in the kitchen, dishes clatter-shatter on the floor, and a soup pot or somesuch bounces *bong-bong-bong* across the tiles. Spoons or forks, or butter knives, spill in quantity, ringing off stainless-steel and ceramic surfaces with a sound like the bells that might announce a demonic holiday.

Then gunfire.

15

The coffee had simmered long enough to turn slightly bitter. By the time she sampled her third cup, Micky didn't mind the edge that the brew acquired. In fact, Leilani's story stirred in Micky a long simmering bitterness to which the coffee was a perfect accompaniment.

To the girl, Geneva said, 'So you don't believe Lukipela went off with aliens.'

'I pretend to,' Leilani said quietly. 'Around Dr. Doom, I play along with his story, all agog over Luki coming back to us one day – a year from now, two years – in a new body. It's safer that way.'

Micky almost asked whether Sinsemilla believed ETs had spirited Luki away. Then she realized that the woman she'd encountered earlier would not only accept such a story but might as easily be convinced that Luki and the compassionate spacemen were sending her subliminal messages in reruns of *Seinfeld*, in the advertising copy on boxes of cornflakes, or in the patterns made by flocks of birds in flight.

Leilani took the first bite from her second serving of pie. She chewed longer than cooked apples warranted, gazing at her plate, as though puzzling over a change in the texture of the dessert.

'Why would he kill a helpless child?' Geneva asked.

'It's what he does. Like the postman delivers the mail. Like a baker makes bread.' Leilani shrugged. 'Read about him. You'll see.'

'You haven't gone to the police,' Micky said.

'I'm just a kid.'

'They listen to kids,' Geneva advised.

Micky knew from experience that this was not reliably the case.

'Anyway,' she said, 'whether they believe you or not, they sure won't swallow your stepfather's story about extraterrestrial healers.'

'It's not a story they'll hear from him. He says the ETs don't want publicity. This isn't just alien modesty. They're dead serious about it. He says if we tell anyone about them, they'll never bring Luki back. They have big plans for elevating human civilization to a level that merits Earth's inclusion in a Galactic Congress – sometimes he calls it the Parliament of Planets – and those plans will take time to carry out. While they're busy doing lots of mysterious good works behind the scenes, saving us from nuclear war and the embarrassment of chronic dandruff, they don't want a bunch of ignorant rubes poking around, searching for them in certain mountains in Montana and other places they like to hang out. So we're supposed to talk about the ETs only among ourselves. Sinsemilla totally buys into this.'

'When he has to explain where Luki's gone, what'll he say?' Geneva wondered.

'First of all, there's nobody who'd notice or think to ask. We're always on the move, rambling around the country. No permanent neighbors. No friends, just people we meet on the road, like at a campground for an evening, and we never see them again. Sinsemilla long ago chopped loose her family. Before I was born. I haven't met any of them, don't know where they are. She never speaks about them, except once in a while she says what an intolerant and uptight bunch of poop vents they were – though, as you might expect, she uses more-colorful language. One of my pacts with God is that I won't be as foul-mouthed as my mother, and in return for all my self-discipline, He'll give her as long as she needs to explain her moral choices once she dies and finds herself standing at judgment. I'm not sure that God, even though He's God with all His resources, realizes what He's gotten himself into by agreeing to *those* terms.'

The girl forked up another mouthful of pie, and again she chewed with a stoic expression that suggested she was eating broccoli, not with clear distaste, but with the indifference of nutritional duty.

Geneva said, 'Well, if it's the police asking after Luki—'

'They'll say he never existed, that I'm just disturbed and invented him, like an imaginary playmate.'

'They can't get away with that, dear.'

'Sure they can. Even before Dr. Doom, Sinsemilla was footloose. She says we lived in Santa Fe, San Francisco, Monterey, Telluride, Taos, Las Vegas, Lake Tahoe, Tucson, and Coeur d'Alene before Dr. Doom. I remember some places, but I was too little to have memories of them all. A few months here, a few there. She was with different men, too, some doing drugs, selling, all looking for a big easy score of one kind or another, all the move-along type, because if they didn't move along, the local cops would've provided each of 'em with a room and a boyfriend. Anyway, who knows where any of those guys are now or whether they'd remember Luki – or admit to remembering him.'

'Birth certificates,' Micky suggested. 'That would be proof. Where were you born? Where was Luki born?'

Another bite of pie. More joyless chewing. 'I don't know.'

'You don't know where you were born?'

'Sinsemilla says the Fates can't find you to snip your thread and end your life if they don't know where you were born, and they won't know if you can never speak of the place, so then you'll live forever. And she doesn't believe in doctors, hospitals. She says we were born at home, wherever home was then. At best . . . maybe a midwife. I'd be beyond amazed if our births were ever registered anywhere.'

The bitter coffee had grown cool. Micky sipped it anyway. She was afraid that if she didn't drink it, she'd fetch the brandy and drink that instead, regardless of Leilani's objections. Alcohol never soothed her rage. She'd become a drinker because booze inflamed the anger, and for so long she'd *cherished* her anger. Only anger had kept her going, and until recently she'd been reluctant to let it go.

'You've got your father's name,' Geneva said hopefully. 'If he could be found . . .'

'I'm not sure Lukipela's dad and mine are the same. Sinsemilla's never said. She might not know herself. Luki and I have the same last name, but that doesn't mean anything. It's not actually our father's name. She's never told us his name. She's got this thing about names. She says they're magical. Knowing someone's name gives you power over him, and keeping your own name secret gives you more power still.'

Witch with a broomstick up your ass, witch bitch, diabolist, hag, flying down out of the moon with my name on your tongue, think you can spellcast me with a shrewd guess of a name . . .

Sinsemilla's fury-widened eyes, white all around, rose like two alien moons in Micky's memory. She shuddered.

Leilani said, 'She just calls him Klonk because she claims that was the noise he made if you rapped him on the head. She hates him a lot, which is maybe why she hates me and Luki a little, too. And Luki more than me, for some reason.'

In spite of all that she knew about Sinsemilla Maddoc, Geneva cringed from this charge against the woman. 'Leilani, sweetie, even though she's a deeply disturbed person, she's still your mother, and in her own way, she loves you very much.' Aunt Gen was childless, not by choice. The love she'd never been able to spend on a daughter or a son hadn't diminished in value over time, but had grown into a wealth of feeling that she now paid out to everyone she knew. 'No mother can ever truly hate her child, dear. No mother anywhere.'

Micky wished, not for the first time, that she had been Geneva's daughter. How different her life would have been: so free of anger and self-destructive impulses.

Meeting Micky's eyes, Geneva read the love in them, and smiled, but then seemed to read something else as well, something that helped her to understand the depth of her naivete on this matter. Her smile faltered, faded, vanished. 'No mother anywhere,' she repeated softly, but to Micky this time. 'That's what I've always thought. If I'd ever realized differently, I wouldn't have just . . . stood by.'

Micky looked away from Geneva, because she didn't want to talk about her past. Not here, not now. This was about Leilani Klonk, not about Michelina Bellsong. Leilani was only nine, and in spite of what she'd been through, she wasn't screwed up yet; she was tough, smart; she had a *chance*, a future, even if at the moment it seemed to hang by a gossamer thread; she didn't have a thousand stupid choices to live down. In this girl, Micky saw the hope of a good, clean life full of purpose – which she couldn't quite yet see clearly in herself.

Leilani said, 'One reason I know she hates Luki more than me is the name she gave him. She says she called me Leilani, which means "heavenly flower," because maybe . . . maybe people will think of me as more than just a pathetic cripple. That's old Sinsemilla at the peak of her motherly concern. But she says she knew Luki for what he was even before he popped out of her. Lukipela is Hawaiian for "Lucifer".'

Appalled, Geneva looked as though she might bring to the table the brandy that Micky had thus far resisted, though strictly for her own fortification.

'Photographs,' Micky said. 'Pictures of you and Luki. That would be proof he wasn't just your imaginary brother.'

'They destroyed all the pictures of him. Because when he comes back with the aliens, he'll be completely fit. If anybody ever saw pictures of him with deformities, they'd know it *had* to be aliens who made him right. Then the jig would be up for our friends, the ETs. They'd be so busy dodging alien hunters that they wouldn't be able to lift up human civilization and get us into the Parliament of Planets, with all the cool Welcome Wagon gifts and valuable discount coupons that come with membership. Sinsemilla also buys that one. Probably because she wants to. Anyway, I hid two snapshots of Luki, but they found them. Now the only place I can see his face is in my mind. But I take time every day to concentrate on his face, on remembering it, keeping the details sharp, especially his smile. I'm never going to let his face fade away. I'm never going to forget the way he looked.' The girl's voice grew softer but also more penetrating, as air finds its way into places from which water is kept out. 'He can't have been here ten years and suffered like he did, and then just be gone as if he never lived. That's not right. Hell if it is. *Hell* if it is. Someone's got to remember, you know. Someone.'

Realizing the full horror of the girl's situation, Aunt Gen was reduced to stunned silence and to at least a temporary emotional paralysis. All her life, until now, Geneva Davis had always found exactly the right consoling words for any situation, had known when she could smooth your hackled heart just by lovingly smoothing your hair, quell your fear with a cuddle and a kiss on the brow.

Micky was scared as she hadn't been scared in fifteen years or longer. She felt enslaved once more to fate, to chance, to dangerous men, as helpless as she had been throughout a childhood lived under the threat of those same forces. She could think of no way to rescue Leilani, just as she had never been able to save herself, and this impotence suggested that she might never find the wit, the courage, and the determination to accomplish the far more difficult task of redeeming her own screwed-up life.

Solemnly, Leilani finished the second piece of pie, solemnly, as though she were eating it not to satisfy her own need or desire, but as though she were eating it on behalf of he who could not share this table with them, eating it in the name of a boy with a wickedly malformed pelvis and Tinkertoy hips, a boy who clomped along bravely in one built-up shoe, a brother who had probably liked apple pie and whose memory must be fed in his enduring absence.

A butterfly flutter of light, a sibilant sputter, a serpent of smoke rising lazily from the black stump of a dead wick: One of the three candles burned out, and darkness eagerly pulled its chair a little closer to the table.

16

Gunfire but also frankfurters. Hunters loom, but the chaos provides cover. Hostility is all around, but hope of escape lies ahead.

Even in the darkest moments, light exists if you have the faith to see it. Fear is a poison produced by the mind, and courage is the antidote stored always ready in the soul. In misfortune lies the seed of future triumph. They have no hope who have no belief in the intelligent design of all things, but those who see meaning in every day will live in joy. Confronted in battle by a superior foe, you will find that a kick to the sex organs is generally effective.

Those sagacities and uncounted others are from *Mother's Big Book of Street-Smart Advice for the Hunted and the Would-Be Chameleon*. This isn't a published work, of course, although in the boy's mind, he can see those pages as clearly as the pages of any real book that he's ever read, chapter after chapter of hard-won wisdom. His mom had been first of all his mom, but she'd also been a universally admired symbol of resistance to oppression, an advocate of freedom, whose teachings – both her philosophy and her practical survival advice – had been passed from believer to believer, much the way that folk tales were preserved through centuries by being told and retold in the glow of campfire and hearth light.

Curtis hopes that he won't have to kick anyone in the sex organs, but he's prepared to do whatever is required to survive. By nature, he's more of a dreamer than he is a schemer, more poet than warrior, though he's admittedly hard-pressed to see anything *either* poetic or warriorlike about clutching a package of frankfurters to his chest, scampering like a monkey, and retreating pell-mell from the battle that has broken out behind him.

Around and under more prep tables, past tall cabinets with open shelves full of stacked dishes, taking cover behind hulking culinary equipment of unknown purpose, Curtis moves indirectly but steadily into the end of the kitchen toward which the workers had initially seemed to be directing him.

None of the employees any longer offers guidance. They're too busy diving for cover, belly-crawling like soldiers seeking shelter in an unexpected firefight, and saying their prayers, each of them determined to protect the precious bottom that his mama once talcumed so lovingly.

In addition to the sharp crack of gunfire, Curtis hears lead slugs ricocheting with a whistle or with a cymbal-like *ping* off range hoods and off other metal surfaces, slamming – *thwack!* – into wood or plaster, puncturing full soup pots with a flat *bonk* and drilling empty pots with a hollow reverberant *pong*. Shot dinnerware explodes in noisy disharmonious chords; bullet-plucked metal racks produce jarring arpeggios; from a severed refrigeration line, a toxic mist of rapidly evaporating coolant hisses like a displeased audience at a symphony of talentless musicians; and perhaps he's able to call forth his poetic side in the midst of warfare, after all.

The FBI doesn't as a matter of habit open negotiations with gun-play, which means the cowboys must have initiated hostilities. And the two men wouldn't resort to violence so immediately if they weren't certain that these Bureau agents know them for who they really are.

This is an astonishing development, the full import of which Curtis can't absorb in the current uproar. If federal authorities have become aware of the dark forces that pursue this motherless boy, then they are aware of the boy himself, and if they can recognize the hunters, they must be able to recognize the boy, as well.

Curtis had thought he was being pursued by a platoon. Perhaps it is instead an army. And the enemies of his enemies are not always his friends, certainly not in this case.

He rounds the end of another work aisle and finds an employee sitting on the floor, wedged into the corner formed by banks of tall cabinets. The kitchen worker is apparently paralyzed by panic.

With his knees drawn up to his chest, the guy's trying to make himself as small as possible, to avoid ricochets and stray bullets. He's wearing a large stainless-steel colander as though it's a hat, holding it in place with both hands, his face entirely concealed, evidently because he thinks this will provide some protection against a head shot.

Elsewhere in the kitchen, a man screams. Maybe he's been shot. Curtis has never heard the cry made by a gunshot victim. This is a hideous squeal of agony. He has heard cries like this before, too often. It's difficult to believe that a mere bullet wound could be the cause of such horrendous, tortured shrieks.

The terror-polished eyes of the man in the colander can be seen through the pattern of small drain holes, and when he speaks fluent Vietnamese, he can be heard in spite of his metal hood: *'We're all going to die.'*

Responding in Vietnamese, Curtis passes along some of his mom's wisdom, which he hopes will give comfort: *'In misfortune lies the seed of future triumph.'*

This isn't the smoothest socializing the boy has done to date, but the terrified worker overreacts to this well-meant if less than completely appropriate advice: *'Maniac! Crazy boy!'*

Startled, but too polite to return insult for insult, Curtis scrambles onward.

The anguished screams are to the boy's blood as vinegar to milk, and although a thunderous fusillade halts the screaming, it doesn't as quickly halt the curdling. He's losing his appetite for the hot dogs, but he holds fiercely to them, anyway, because he knows from long experience that hunger can quickly return in the wake of even nauseating fear. The heart may heal slowly, but the mind is resilient and the body ever needy.

Besides, he's got Old Yeller to think about. *Good pup. I'm coming, pup.*

The roar of the long barrage has left his ears ringing. Yet in the aftermath, Curtis is able to hear people shouting, a couple men cursing, a woman shakily reciting the Hail Mary prayer over and over. The character of all their voices suggests that the battle isn't over and perhaps isn't going to be brief; there's no relief in even one voice among them – only stark anxiety, urgency, wariness.

Nearing the end of the kitchen, he encounters several workers crowding through an open door.

He considers following them before he realizes that they're entering a walk-in cooler, apparently with the intention of pulling shut the insulated steel door. This might be a bulletproof refuge, or the next-best thing.

Curtis doesn't want a refuge. He wants to find an escape hatch. And quickly.

Another door. Beyond it lies a small storeroom, approximately eight feet wide and ten feet long, with a door at the farther end. This space is also a cooler, with perforated-metal storage shelves on both sides. The shelves hold half-gallon plastic containers of orange juice, grapefruit juice, apple juice, milk, also cartons of eggs, blocks of cheese . . . .

He grabs the handle on a container of orange juice, making a mental note to return to Utah someday – assuming he ever gets out of the state alive – to make restitution for this and for the hot dogs. He's sincere in his intention to pay for what he takes, but nevertheless he feels like a criminal.

Putting all his hopes on the door at the end of this cooler, Curtis discovers that it opens into a larger and warmer receiving room stacked with those supplies that don't need refrigeration. Cartons of napkins, toilet tissue, cleaning fluids, floor wax.

Logically, a receiving room should open to the outdoors, to a loading dock or to a parking lot, and beyond the next door, he finds logic rewarded. A warm breeze, free of kitchen odors and the smell of gunfire, leaps at him, like a playful dog, and tosses his hair.

He turns right on the dimly lighted dock and sprints to the end. Four concrete steps lead down to another blacktop parking lot, which is only half as well lighted as those he's seen previously.

Most of the vehicles back here probably belong to employees of the restaurant, the service station, the motel, and the associated enterprises. Pickup trucks are favored over cars, and the few SUVs have a desert-scorched, sand-abraided, brush-scratched look acquired by more arduous use than trips to the supermarket.

With the container of Florida's finest in one hand, the package of hot dogs firmly in the other, Curtis dashes between two SUVs, frantic to get out of sight before the FBI agents, the hunters in cowboy disguise, possibly the juice police, and maybe frankfurter enforcement officers all descend on him at once, blasting away.

Just as he plunges into the shadows between the vehicles, he hears shouting, people running – suddenly so *close*.

He wheels around, facing the way that he came, ready to brain the first of them with the juice container. The hot dogs are useless as a weapon. His mother's self-defense instructions never involved sausages of any kind. After the juice, all he can count on is kicking their sex organs.

Two, three, five men burst past the front of the parallel SUVs, a formidable pack of husky specimens, all wearing either black vests or black windbreakers with the letters FBI blazing in white across their chests and backs. Two carry shotguns; the others have handguns. They are prepared, pumped, pissed – and so intently focused on the rear entrance to the restaurant that not one of them catches sight of Curtis as they race past. They leave him untouched, and still in possession of his dangerous jug of orange juice and his pathetic wieners.

Sucking in great lungfuls of the astringent desert air, giving it back hotter than he receives it, the boy weaves westward, using the employees' vehicles for cover. He's not sure where he should go, but he's eager to put some distance between himself and this complex of buildings.

He rounds the tailgate of a Dodge pickup, hurrying into a new aisle, and here the loyal dog is waiting, a black shape splashed with a few whorls of white, like tossed-off scarves of moonlight floating on the night-stained surface of a pond. She is alert, ears pricked, drawn not by the frankfurters but by an awareness of her master's predicament.

Good pup. Let's get out of here.

She whips around – no older than she is yellow – and trots away, not at a full run, but at a pace that the boy can match. Trusting her sharper senses, assuming she won't lead them straight into any associates of the cowboys who might be – surely are – in the vicinity, or into another posse of FBI agents bristling with weapons, Curtis follows her.

17

To everyone but Noah Farrel, the Haven of the Lonesome and the Long Forgotten was known as Cielo Vista Care Home. The real name of the establishment promised a view of Heaven but provided something more like a glimpse of Purgatory.

He wasn't entirely sure why he had given the place another – and so maudlin – name by which he usually thought of it. Life otherwise had entirely purged him of sentimentality, although he would admit to an ever-dwindling but not yet eradicated capacity for romanticism.

Not that anything about the care home was romantic, other than its Spanish architecture and lattice-shaded sidewalks draped with yellow and purple bougainvillea. In spite of those inviting arbors, no one would come here in search of love or chivalrous adventure.

Throughout the institution, the floors – gray vinyl speckled with peach and turquoise – were immaculate. Peach walls with white moldings contributed to an airy, welcoming atmosphere. Cleanliness and cheery colors, however, proved insufficient to con Noah into a holiday mood.

This was a private establishment with a dedicated, friendly staff. Noah appreciated their professionalism, but their smiles and greetings seemed false, not because he doubted their sincerity, but because he himself found it hard to raise a genuine smile in this place, and because he arrived under such a weight of guilt that his heart was too compressed to contain the more expansive emotions.

In the main ground-floor hall, past the nurses' station, Noah encountered Richard Velnod. Richard preferred to be called Rickster, the affectionate nickname that his dad had given him.

Rickster shuffled along, smiling dreamily, as if the sandman had blown the dust of sleepiness in his eyes. With his thick neck, heavy rounded shoulders, and short arms and legs, he brought to mind characters of fantasy and fairy lore, though always a benign version: a kindly troll or perhaps a good-hearted kobold on his way to watch over – rather than torment – coal miners in deep dangerous tunnels.

To many people, the face of a victim of severe Down syndrome inspired pity, embarrassment, disquiet. Instead, each time Noah saw this boy – twenty-six but to some degree a boy forever – he was pierced by an awareness of the bond of imperfection that all the sons and daughters of this world share without exception, and by gratitude that the worst of his own imperfections were within his ability to make right if he could find the willpower to deal with them.

'Does the little orange lady like the dark out?' Rickster asked.

'What little orange lady would that be?' Noah asked.

Rickster's hands were cupped together as though they concealed a treasure that he was bearing as a gift to throne or altar.

When Noah leaned close to have a look, Rickster's hands parted hesitantly; a wary oyster, jealous of its precious pearl, might have opened its shell to feed in this guarded fashion. In the palm of the lower hand crawled a ladybug, orange carapace like a polished bead.

'She sort of flies a little.' Rickster quickly closed his hands. 'I'll put her loose.' He glanced at the new-fallen night beyond a nearby window. 'Maybe she's scared. Out in the dark, I mean.'

'I know ladybugs,' Noah said. 'They all love the night.'

'You sure? The sky goes away in the dark, and everything gets so big. I don't want her scared.'

In Rickster's soft features, as well as in his earnest eyes, were a profound natural kindness that he hadn't needed to learn by example and an innocence that could not be corrupted, which required that his concern for the insect be addressed seriously.

'Birds are something ladybugs worry about, you know.'

''Cause birds eat bugs.'

'Exactly right. But a lot of birds go to roost at night and stay there till morning. Your little orange lady is safer in the dark.'

Rickster's sloped brow, his flat nose, and the heavy lines of his face seemed best suited for morose expressions, yet his smile was broad and winning. 'I put a lot of things loose, you know?'

'I know.'

Flies, ants. Moths weary from battling window glass or fat from feasting on wool. Wriggling spiders. Tiny pill bugs curled as tightly as threatened armadillos. All these and more had been rescued by this child-man, taken out of Cielo Vista, and set free.

Once, when an outlaw mouse scurried from room to room and along hallways, eluding a comic posse of janitors and nurses, Rickster knelt and extended a hand to it. As though sensing the spirit of St. Francis reborn, the frightened fugitive scampered directly to him, onto his palm, up his arm, finally to a stop on his slumped shoulder. To the delight and applause of the staff and residents, he walked outside and released the trembling creature on the rear lawn, where it dashed out of sight into a bed of red and coral-pink impatiens.

As it was no doubt a domestic mouse, favoring hearth over field, the beastie had most likely hidden among the flowers only until its terror passed. By nightfall it would have found a way back into the heated and cat-free sanctuary of the care home.

From these rescues, Noah inferred that Rickster considered residence in Cielo Vista, in spite of its caring staff and comforts, to be an unnatural condition for any form of life.

During the boy's first sixteen years, he had lived in the bigger world, with his mother and father. They had been killed by a drunk driver on the Pacific Coast Highway: Only ten minutes from home, they suddenly found themselves even closer than ten minutes to paradise.

Rickster's uncle, executor of the estate, was also guardian of the boy. An embarrassment to his relatives, Rickster was dispatched to Cielo Vista. He arrived shy, scared, without protest. A week later, he became the benefactor to bugs, emancipator of mice.

'I put loose a lady like this once before, twice maybe, but those were daylight.'

Suspecting that Rickster might be a little afraid of the night, Noah said, 'Do you want me to take her outside and turn her free?'

'No thanks. I want to see her go. I'll put her on the roses. She'll like them.'

With hands cupped protectively and held near his heart, he shuffled toward the lobby and the front entrance.

Noah's feet felt as heavily iron-shod as Rickster's appeared to be, but he tried not to shuffle the rest of the way to Laura's room.

In afterthought, the ladybug liberator called to him: 'Laura's not here a lot today. Gone off in one of those places she goes.'

Noah stopped, dismayed. 'Which one?'

Without looking back, the boy said, 'The one that's sad.'

At the end of the hall, her room was small but not cramped, and nothing about it cried *hospital* or whispered *sanitarium*. The faux-Persian rug, though inexpensive, lent grace and warmth to the space: jewel-sharp, jewel-dark colors, like a pirate's treasure of sapphires spilled among emeralds, scattered with rubies. The furnishings were not typical institutional Formica-and-case-steel items, but maple stained and finished to the color and glimmer of Cabernet.

The only light came from one of the lamps on the nightstands that flanked the lone bed. Laura didn't share quarters, because she didn't possess the capacity to socialize to the extent that the care home required of a roommate.

Barefoot, wearing white cotton pants and a pink blouse, she lay on the bed, atop the rumpled chenille spread, head upon a pillow, her back to the door and to the lamp, her face in shadow. She didn't stir when he entered or acknowledge his presence when he rounded the bed and stood gazing down at her.

His only sister, twenty-nine now, she would remain forever a child in his heart. When she was twelve, he'd lost her. Until then, she'd been a radiance, the one brightness in a family that otherwise lived in shadow and fed on darkness.

Beautiful at twelve, still half beautiful, she lay on her left side, presenting only her right profile, which was unmarked by the violence that had changed her life. The unrevealed half of her face, pressed into the pillow, was the phantom-of-the-opera hemisphere, its battered bone structure held together by cords of scar tissue.

Although the finest restorative surgeon couldn't have rebuilt her beauty, the worst of the horror might have been smoothed out of her crushed features and a plain profile constructed from the ruins. Insurance companies, however, decline to pay for expensive plastic surgery when the patient also suffers serious brain damage that allows little self-awareness and no hope of a normal life.

As Rickster had warned, Laura was in one of her private places. Oblivious of everything around her, she stared raptly into some other world of memory or fantasy, as though watching a drama unfold for an audience of one.

Other days, she might lie here smiling, eyes shining with amusement, occasionally issuing a soft murmur of delight. But now she had gone to the sad place, the second-worst of the unknown lands in which her roaming spirit seemed to travel. Dampness darkened the pillowcase under her head, her cheek was wet, pendent salty jewels quivered on her lashes, and fresh tears shimmered in her brown eyes.

Noah spoke her name, but as he expected, Laura didn't respond.

He touched her brow. She didn't twitch or even so much as blink in response.

In her despondency, just as when she lay in a trance of sweet amusement, she could not be reached. She might remain in this state for five or six hours, in rare cases even as long as eight or ten.

When not cataleptic, she could dress and feed herself, though she appeared mildly bemused, as if not entirely sure what she was doing or why she was doing it. In that more common condition, Laura now and then answered to her name, although usually she appeared not to know who she was – or to care.

She seldom spoke, and never recognized Noah. If she possessed any memory whatsoever of the days when she'd been whole, her shattered recollections were scattered across the darkscape of her mind in fragments so minuscule that she could no more easily piece them together than she could gather from the beach all the tiny chips of broken seashells, worn to polished flakes by ages of relentless tides, and reassemble them into their original architectures.

Noah settled into the armchair, from which he was able to see her dreamlit gaze, the periodic blink of her eyelids, and the slow steady flow of tears.

As difficult as it was to watch over her when she lay in this trance of despair, Noah was grateful that she hadn't descended into the more disturbing realm where she sometimes became lost. In that even less hospitable place, her tearless eyes filled with horror, and sharp fear carved ugly lines in the lovely half of her face.

'Profit from this case will buy another six months here,' Noah told her. 'So now we have the first half of next year covered.'

Providing for Laura was the reason that he worked, the reason that he lived in a low-rent apartment, drove a rustbucket, never traveled, and bought his clothes at warehouse-clubs. Providing for Laura was, in fact, the reason that he lived at all.

If he had acted responsibly all those years ago, when she was twelve and he was sixteen, if he'd had the courage to turn against his contemptible family and to do the right thing, his sister would not have been beaten and left for dead. Her life wouldn't now be a long series of waking dreams and nightmares punctuated by spells of bewildered placidity.

'You'd like Constance Tavenall,' he said. 'If you'd had a chance to grow up, I think you'd have been a lot like her.'

When he visited Laura, he talked to her at length. Whether in a trance like this or more alert, she never responded, never appeared to comprehend a sentence of his monologue. And yet he held forth until drained of words, often until his throat grew dry and hot.

He remained convinced that on a deep mysterious level, against all evidence to the contrary, he was making a connection with her. His stubborn persistence through the years had been motivated by something more desperate than hope, by a faith that sometimes seemed foolish to him but that he never abandoned. He needed to believe that God existed, that He cherished Laura, that He would not allow her to suffer in the misery of absolute isolation, that He permitted Noah's voice and the meaning of his words to reach Laura's cloistered heart, thus providing her comfort.

To carry the burden of each day and to keep breathing under the weight of every night, Noah Farrel held fast to the idea that this service to Laura might eventually redeem him. The hope of atonement was the only nourishment that his soul received, and the possibility of redemption watered the desert of his heart.

Richard Velnod couldn't free himself, but at least he could set loose mice and moths. Noah could free neither himself nor his sister, and could take satisfaction only from the possibility that his voice, like a rag rubbing soot from a window, might facilitate the passage of a thin but precious light into the darkness where she dwelt.

18

Hurrying out of the employee parking lot, dangerously exposed on an open field of blacktop, circling the truck-stop complex, and into the civilian car park where no big rigs are allowed, the boy thinks he hears sporadic gunfire. He can't be sure. His explosive breathing and the slap of his sneakers on the pavement mask other noises; the desert breeze breaks over him, and in the shells of his ears, this stir of air fosters the dry sound of a long-dead sea.

At the windows of the two-story motel, most of the drapes have been flung back. Curious, worried lodgers peer out in search of the source of the tumult.

Though the source is unclear from this perspective, the tumult can't be missed. Fleeing customers are jammed in the bottleneck at the restaurant's front door, not in danger of trampling one another like agitated fans at a soccer match or like music-mad celebrity-besotted attendees at a rock concert, but surely suffering tromped toes and elbow-poked ribs aplenty. The tangled escapees ravel out of the restaurant like a spring-loaded joke snake erupting from a trick can labeled PEANUTS. Released, they run alone or in pairs, or in families, toward their vehicles, some glancing back in fear as more gunfire – Curtis hears it for sure this time – erupts, muffled but unmistakable, from the depths of the building.

Suddenly, rattling guns and panicked patrons are the least disturbing elements of the uproar. Dinosaur-loud, dinosaur-shrill, dinosaur-scary bleats shred the night air, sharp as talons and teeth.

With repeated blasts of its air horn to clear the way, a semi roars down the exit ramp from the interstate, straight toward the service area. The driver is flashing his headlights, too, signaling that he's got a runaway eighteen-wheeler under his butt.

Some of the station's huge storage tanks hold diesel fuel, which is combustible but not highly explosive, although other tanks contain gasoline, which is without doubt a valid ticket to an apocalypse. If the hurtling truck slams into the pumps and sheers them off as though they were fence pickets, the explosions should convince locals in a ten-mile radius that Almighty God, in His more easily disappointed Old Testament persona, has finally seen too much of human sin and is angrily stomping out His creations with giant fiery boots.

Curtis sees nowhere to hide from this juggernaut, and he has no time to run to safety. He's not at serious risk of being flattened by the speeding truck, because it would have to plow through too many service-station pumps and barricades of parked vehicles to reach him. Billowing balls of fire, arcing jets of burning gasoline, airborne flaming debris, and a bullet-fast barrage of shrapnel are more likely to be what the coroner will certify as the cause of his death.

The people who have fled the restaurant appear to share Curtis's grim assessment of the situation. All but a few of them freeze at the sight of the runaway semi, riveted by the impending disaster.

Engine screaming, klaxons shrieking, lights flashing as though with the fury of dragon eyes, the Peterbilt roars through an empty service bay, between islands of pumps. Station attendants, truckers, and on-foot motorists scatter before it. For them, certain death is instantly transformed into a terrific story to tell the grandkids someday, because the big truck doesn't clip even one pump, doesn't barrel into any of the vehicles hooked to the hoses and guzzling from the nozzles, but flies out from under the long service-bay canopy and angles toward the buildings, downshifting with a hack and grind of protesting gear teeth.

The plosive squeal of air brakes, recklessly applied so late, reveals the driver not as a man at the mercy of an out-of-control machine, after all, but as a drunk or a lunatic. The tires suddenly churn up clouds of pale blue smoke and appear to stutter on the pavement. The Peterbilt sways, seems certain to jackknife and roll. Bursts of noise erupt from the brakes, and a series of hard yelps issues from the abused tires, as the driver judiciously pumps the pedal instead of standing on it.

An alligator of tread strips away from one wheel and lashes across the pavement, snapping like a whipping tail.

The dog whimpers.

So does Curtis.

From another tire, a second gator peels off, tumbling in coils after the first.

A tire blows, the trailer bounces, the stacks bark as loud as a mortar lobbing hundred-millimeter rounds toward enemy positions, another tire blows. An air line ruptures and pressure falls and the brakes automatically lock, so the truck skates like a pig on ice, with a lot more squeal than grace, though the biggest prize hog ever judged couldn't have weighed a fraction of the tonnage at which this behemoth tips the scales. In a reek of scorched rubber, with one last attenuated grunt of protesting gears, it shudders to a halt in front of the motel, next to the restaurant, still upright, hissing and rumbling, smoking and steaming.

With a whimper, the dog squats and pees.

Curtis successfully resists the urge to water the pavement, too, but he counts himself fortunate to have used the restroom only a short while ago.

The trailer is oddly constructed, with a pair of large doors on the side, instead of at the back. An instant after the semi comes to a full stop, these doors slide open, and men in riot gear jump out of the rig, not staggering and bewildered, as they ought to be, but instantly balanced and oriented, as though they have been delivered with all the gentle consideration that might have been accorded a truckload of eggs.

At least thirty men, dressed in black, debark from the trailer: not merely a SWAT team, not even a SWAT squad, but more accurately a SWAT platoon. Shiny black riot helmets. Shatterproof acrylic face shields feature built-in microphones to allow continuous strategic coordination of every man in the force. Kevlar vests. Utility belts festooned with spare magazines of ammunition, dump pouches, cans of Mace, Tasers, stun grenades, handcuffs. Automatic pistols are holstered at their hips, but they arrive with more powerful weapons in hand.

They are here to kick ass.

Perhaps Curtis's ass, among others.

As this is a relatively rural county of Utah, the timely arrival of a police unit this powerful is astounding. Not even a major city, with a fat budget and crime-busting mayor, could turn out a force of this size and sophistication on just a five-minute notice, and Curtis doubts that even five minutes have passed since the first shots were fired in the kitchen.

Even as the troops are pouring out of the trailer, a helmetless man throws open the passenger's-side door on the truck cab and jumps to the pavement. Although he was riding shotgun position beside the driver, he's the only member of this contingent who's not carrying either a pistol-grip twelve gauge or an Uzi. He's wearing a headset with an extension arm that puts the penny-size microphone two inches in front of his lips, and though the other platoon members bear no identifying legends or insignia, this man is wearing a dark blue or black windbreaker with white letters that *don't* stand for Free Beer on Ice.

From at least a score of movies, Curtis has learned that the Bureau possesses the resources to mount an operation like this in the Utah boondocks as easily as in Manhattan – although not with a mere five-minute warning. They've obviously been tracking the hunters who have been tracking Curtis and his family. Consequently, they must know the entire story; and although it must seem improbable to them, they clearly have developed sufficient evidence to overcome all their doubts.

If the Bureau knows what those two cowboys are up to, and if it understands how many others are combing this part of the West in close coordination with the cowboys, then these FBI agents must also know the identity of their quarry: which is one small boy. Curtis. Standing here in plain sight. Perhaps ten yards from them. Under a parking-lot arc lamp.

Can you say *sitting duck*?

Rooted to the blacktop by terror, temporarily as immovable as an oak tree knotted to the earth, Curtis expects to be immediately riddled with bullets or, alternately, to be Maced, Tasered, clubbed, handcuffed for interrogation, and at some *later* date, at his captors' leisure, riddled extensively.

Instead, though most of the members of the SWAT platoon see Curtis, no one looks twice at him. Scant seconds after storming out of the semi, they're forming up and hurrying toward the restaurant and the front of the motel.

So they don't know everything, after all. Even the Bureau can make mistakes. The ghost of J. Edgar Hoover must be throwing fits somewhere in the night nearby, struggling to work up enough ectoplasm to produce a credible apparition and point at least a few of the SWAT agents toward Curtis.

As one, the customers exiting the building had been paralyzed in midflight by the arrival of this scowling strike force. Now, also as one, they spin into motion, scattering toward their vehicles, eager to clear out of the battle zone.

On all sides of Curtis, remote-released locks electronically disengage with sharp double-beep signals, like a pack of miniature dachshunds whose tails have been trod upon in rapid succession.

Old Yeller either reacts to this serenade of bleats or to an instinctive realization that time to escape is fast ticking away. The truck stop is a hot zone; they need a ride out to a more comfortable place where the heat isn't blistering. She turns in a four-legged pirouette, with enough grace to qualify her for the New York City Ballet, considering her options as she rotates. Then she sprints around the front of a nearby Honda and out of sight.

Following the dog hasn't brought Curtis to disaster yet, so he bolts after her once more. As he races down an aisle of parked cars and other civilian vehicles, he catches up with Old Yeller and comes upon a Windchaser motor home at the very moment when two loud beeps blare from it. The headlights flash, flash again, as though a vehicle this enormous could not be located at night without identifying pyrotechnics.

At once the mutt skids to a stop, and so does Curtis. They look at each other, at the door, at each other again, executing as fast a double take as ever did Asta the dog and his master, the detective Nick Charles, in those old Thin Man movies.

The owners of the Windchaser aren't in sight, but they must be nearby to be able to trigger the lock by remote control. They're most likely fast approaching from the other side of the vehicle.

This isn't the ideal ride, but Curtis isn't likely to luck into a cushy berth on another automobile transport any more than he's likely to escape on a flying carpet with a magic lamp and a helpful genie.

Besides, there's no time to pick and choose. As those SWAT agents help their more conventional brethren deal with the cowboys and secure the restaurant, they will hear about the kid who was the object of the chase, and they will remember the boy standing in the parking lot, clutching a half-gallon container of orange juice and a package of frankfurters, with a dog at his side.

Then: big trouble.

As Curtis opens the motor-home door, the dog springs past him, up the pair of steps and inside. He follows, pulling the door shut behind them, staying low to avoid being seen through the windshield.

The cockpit, with two large seats, is to his right, a lounge area to the left. All lies in shadow, but through windows along the sides of the vehicle and through a series of small skylights, enough yellow light from the parking lot penetrates to allow Curtis to move quickly toward the back of the motor home, although he feels his way with outstretched hands to guard against surprises.

Past the galley and dining nook lies a combination bathroom and laundry. The dog's panting acquires a hollow note in this confined space.

Hiding in the tiny toilet enclosure is out of the question. The owners just came from the restaurant, and maybe they finished their dinner before the hullabaloo. One of them is likely to hit the john soon after they hit the road.

Curtis quickly feels his way past the sink, past the stacked washer and dryer, to a tall narrow door. A shallow closet. It's apparently packed as full and chaotically as a maniac's mind, and as he senses and then feels unseen masses of road-life paraphernalia beginning slowly to slide toward him, he jams the door shut again, to hold back the avalanche before it gains unstoppable momentum.

At the front of the vehicle, the door opens, and the first things through it are the excited voices of a man and a woman.

Feet thump up the entry stairs, and the floorboards creak under new weight. Lamps come on in the forward lounge, and a gray wash of secondhand light spills all the way to Curtis.

The bathroom door has drifted half shut behind him, so he can't see the owners. They can't see him either. Yet.

Before one of them comes back here to take a leak, Curtis opens the last door and steps into more gloom untouched by the feeble light in the bathroom. To his left, two rectangular windows glimmer dimly, like switched-off TV screens with a lingering phosphorescence, though the tint is faintly yellow.

Up front, the two voices are louder, more excited. The engine starts. Before either of the owners takes a bathroom break, they are intent on getting away from flying bullets.

No longer panting, the dog slips past Curtis, brushing his leg. Evidently the dark room holds nothing threatening that her keener senses can detect.

He crosses the threshold and eases the door shut behind him.

Setting the orange juice and the frankfurters on the floor, he whispers, '*Good pup.*' He hopes that Old Yeller will understand this to be an admonition against eating the sausages.

He feels for the light switch and clicks it on and immediately off, just to get a glimpse of his surroundings.

The room is small. One queen-size bed with a minimum of walk-around space. Built-in nightstands, a corner TV cabinet. A pair of sliding mirrored doors probably conceal a wardrobe jammed full of too many clothes to allow a boy and a dog to shelter among the shirts and shoes.

Of course, this is a little cottage on wheels, not a castle. It doesn't afford as many hiding places as a titled lord's domain: no receiving rooms or studies, no secret passageways, no dungeons deep or towers high.

Coming in, he'd known the risks. What he hadn't realized, until now, was that the motor home has no back door. He must leave the same way he entered – or go out of a window.

Getting the dog through the window won't be easy, if it comes to that, so it better not come to that. Escape-with-canine isn't a feat that can be accomplished in a flash, while the startled owners stand gaping in the bedroom doorway. Old Yeller isn't a Great Dane, thank God, but she's not a Chihuahua, either, and Curtis can't simply tuck her inside his shirt and scramble through one of these less than generous windows with the agility of a caped superhero.

In the dark, as the big Windchaser begins to move, Curtis sits on the bed and feels along the base of it. Instead of a standard frame, he discovers a solid wooden platform anchored to the floor; the box springs and the mattress rest upon the platform, and even the thinnest slip of a boogeyman couldn't hide under this bed.

The motor-home horn blares. In fact the noisy night sounds like a honk-if-you-love-Jesus moment at a convention of Christian road warriors.

Curtis goes to the window, where the drapes have already been drawn aside, and peers out at the truck-stop parking lot. Cars and pickups and SUVs and a few RVs nearly as big as this one careen across the blacktop, moving recklessly and fast, in total disregard of marked lanes, as if the drivers never heard about the courtesy of the road. Everyone's hellbent on getting to the interstate, racing around and between the service islands, terrorizing the same hapless folks who only moments ago escaped death under the wheels of the runaway SWAT transport.

Over bleating horns, screeching tires, and squealing brakes, another sound flicks at the boy's ears: rhythmic and crisp, faint at first, then suddenly rhythmic and solid, like the whoosh of a sword cutting air; and then even more solid, a whoosh and a thump combined, as a blade might sound if it could slice off slabs of the night, and if the slabs could fall heavily to the blacktop. Blades, indeed, but not knives. Helicopter rotors.

Curtis finds the window latch and slides one pane aside. He thrusts his head out of the window, cranes his neck, looking for the source of the sound, as a slipstream of warm desert air cuffs his face and tosses his hair.

Big sky, black and wide. The brassy glare from sodium arc lamps under inverted-wok shades. Stars burning eternal. The motion of the Windchaser makes the moon appear to roll like a wheel.

Curtis can't see any lights in the sky that nature didn't put there, but the helicopter is growing louder by the second, no longer slicing the air but chopping it with hard blows that sound like an ax splitting cordwood. He can *feel* the rhythmic compression waves hammering first against his eardrums, then against the sensitive surfaces of his upturned eyes.

And – *chuddaboom!* – the chopper is right here, passing across the Windchaser, so *low*, maybe fifteen feet above Curtis, maybe less. This isn't a traffic-monitoring craft like the highway patrol would use, not a news chopper or even a corporate-executive eggbeater with comfortable seating for eight, but huge and black and fully armored. Bristling, fierce in every line, turbines screaming, this seems to be a military gunship, surely armed with machine guns, possibly with rockets. The shriek of the engines vibrates through the boy's skull and makes his teeth ring like an array of tuning forks. The battering downdraft *slams* him, rich with the stink of hot metal and motor oil.

The chopper roars past them, toward the complex of buildings, and in its tumultuous wake, the Windchaser accelerates. The driver is suddenly as reckless as all the others who are making a break for the interstate.

'Go, go, *go!*' Curtis urges, because the night has grown strange, and is now a great black beast with a million searching eyes. Motion is commotion, and distraction buys time, and time – not mere distance – is the key to escape, to freedom, and to being Curtis Hammond. 'Go, go, *go!*'

19

By the time that Leilani rose from the kitchen table to leave Geneva's trailer, she was ashamed of herself, and honest enough to admit to the shame, though dishonest enough to try to avoid facing up to the true cause of it.

She had talked with her mouth full of pie. She had hogged down a second piece. All right, okay, bad table manners and a little gluttony were cause for embarrassment, but neither was sufficient reason for shame, unless you were a hopeless self-dramatizer who believed every head cold was the bubonic plague and who wrote lousy weepy epic poems about hangnails and bad-hair days.

Leilani herself had written lousy weepy epic poems about lost puppies and kittens nobody wanted, but she had been six years old then, seven at most, and wretchedly jejune. *Jejune* was a word she liked a lot because it meant 'dull, insipid, juvenile, immature' – and yet it *sounded* as though it ought to mean something sophisticated and classy and smart. She liked things that weren't what they seemed to be, because too much in life was *exactly* what it seemed to be: dull, insipid, juvenile, and immature. Like her mother, for instance, like most TV shows and movies and half the actors in them – although not, of course, Haley Joel Osment, who was cute, sensitive, intelligent, charming, radiant, divine.

Micky and Mrs. D tried to delay Leilani's departure. They were afraid for her. They worried that her mother would hack her to pieces in the middle of the night or stuff cloves up her butt and stick an apple in her mouth and bake her for tomorrow's dinner – although they didn't express their concern in terms quite that graphic.

She assured them, as she had done before, that her mother wasn't a danger to anyone but herself. Sure, once they were on

139

the road again, old Sinsemilla might set the motor home on fire while cooking up rock cocaine for an evening of good smoking. But she didn't have the capacity for violence. Violence required not merely a passing madness or an enduring insanity, but also passion. If looniness could be converted into bricks of gold, old Sinsemilla would provide paving for a six-lane highway from here to Oz, but she didn't have any real passion left; drugs of infinite variety had scorched away all her passion, leaving her with nothing but dreary need.

Mrs. D and Micky were also worried about Dr. Doom. Of course he was a more serious case than old Sinsemilla because he had reservoirs of passion, and every drop of it was used to water his fascination with death. He lived in a flourishing garden of death, in love with the beauty of his black roses, with the fragrance of decay.

He also had rules that he lived by, standards that he wouldn't compromise, and procedures that must be strictly followed in all life-and-death matters. Because he had committed himself to healing Leilani one way or another by her tenth birthday, she wouldn't be in danger until the eve of that anniversary; by then, however, if she hadn't ascended in the sparkling rapture of a starship's levitation beam, Preston would 'cure' her more speedily and with a lot fewer dazzling special effects than extraterrestrials – a theatrical bunch – traditionally employed. Smothering her with a pillow or administering a lethal injection *prior* to the eve of her birthday would violate Preston's code of ethics, and he was as serious about his ethics as the most devout priest was serious about his faith.

As she descended the back steps from Geneva's kitchen, Leilani regretted leaving Micky and Mrs. D so anxious about her welfare. She enjoyed making people smile. She always hoped to leave them thinking, *What a crackerjack that girl is, what a sassy piece of work.* By *sassy*, of course, she wanted them to mean 'pert, smart, jaunty' rather than 'insolent, rude, impudent.' Walking the line between the right kind of sassy and the wrong kind was tricky, but if you pulled it off, you would never leave them thinking, *What a sad little crippled girl she is, with her little twisted leg and her little gnarled hand.* This evening, she suspected that she'd crossed the line between the wrong and the right kinds of sassy, and in fact walked out of sassy altogether, leaving them feeling more pity than delight.

The failure to achieve sassy status still wasn't the reason she was ashamed of herself, but she was getting closer to the truth, so as she crossed the dark backyard, she distracted herself with a silly joke. Pretending that the thorny tentacles of the bloomless rosebush had threatened her, she turned to confront it, formed a cross with her arms – '*Back, back!*' – and warded it off as if it were a vampire.

Leilani glanced toward Geneva's place to determine whether this performance had been well received, but scoping the audience was a mistake. Micky stood at the bottom of the steps, and Mrs. D stood above her, in the open doorway, and even in this poor light, Leilani could see that they both still looked deeply concerned. Worse than concerned. Grim. Maybe even bleak.

Another spectacular, memorable social triumph by Ms. Heavenly Flower Klonk! Invite this charmer to dinner, and she'll repay you with emotional devastation! Serve her chicken sandwiches, and she'll give you a tale of woe that might wring pity even from the chicken she's eating, were the poor fowl still alive! Extend your invitations now! Her social calendar is nearly full! Remember: Only a statistically insignificant number of her dinner companions commit suicide!

Leilani didn't glance back again. She made a point of crossing the rest of the yard and negotiating the fallen fence with as little hitching of her braced leg as possible. When she concentrated on physical performance, she could move with a degree of gracefulness and even with surprising speed for short distances.

She continued to feel ashamed of herself, not because of the dumb joke with the rosebush, but because she had rudely presumed to monitor and restrict Micky's use of alcohol. Such meddling required remorse, even though she'd been motivated by genuine concern. Micky wasn't Sinsemilla, after all. Micky could have a brandy or two and not wind up, one year later, facedown in a puddle of vomit, her nasal cartilage rotted away by cocaine, with a lush crop of hallucinogenic mushrooms growing on the surface of her brain. Micky was better than that. Yeah, sure, all right, Micky did indeed harbor the *tendency* to self-destruct through addiction. Leilani could detect that dangerous inclination more reliably than the most talented fungi-hunting pig could locate buried truffles, which wasn't a flattering comparison, although true. But Micky's tendency wouldn't cause her to wander off forever into the spooky woods where Sinsemilla lived, because Micky also owned a moral compass, which Sinsemilla either never possessed or long ago lost. So any nine-year-old smart-ass who was judgmental enough to tell Michelina Bellsong that she'd had enough to drink *ought* to be ashamed.

As she crossed the next backyard, where earlier her mother danced with the moon, Leilani admitted that her shame hadn't arisen from her rudeness regarding Micky's drinking any more than it had been caused by eating two pieces of pie. The truth – which she had promised God always to honor, but which sometimes she sidled up to when she didn't have the nerve to approach it directly – *the truth* was that her shame arose from the fact that she had spilled her guts this evening. Spilled, gushed, spewed. She'd told them everything about Sinsemilla, about Preston and the aliens, about Lukipela murdered and probably buried in the woods of Montana.

Micky and Mrs. D were nice people, caring people, and when Leilani shared the details of her situation with them, she couldn't have done them a greater disservice if she had driven a dump truck through the front wall of their house and unloaded a few tons of fresh manure in their living room. Not only was it a hideous and distressing story, *but they could do nothing to help her*. Leilani knew better than anyone that she was caught in a trap nobody could pry open for her, that to have any hope of escape, she must chew off her foot and leave the trap behind – figuratively speaking, of course – before her birthday. Spilling her guts this evening had gained her nothing, but she'd left Micky and sweet Mrs. D under a big stinky pile of bad news from which they should have been spared.

Reaching the steps on which Sinsemilla perched after the moon dance, Leilani felt tempted to glance toward Geneva's. She resisted the urge. She knew they were still watching her, but a cheery wave wouldn't buck up their spirits and send them to bed with a smile.

Sinsemilla had left the kitchen door open. Leilani went inside.

During her short walk, the electrical service had come on again. The wall clock glowed, but it displayed the wrong time.

In spite of the slender red hand sweeping sixty moments per

minute from the clock face, the flow of time seemed to have been dammed into a still pool. Saturated by silence, the house brimmed also with an unnerving expectancy, as though some bulwark were about to crack, permitting a violent flood to sweep everything away.

Dr. Doom had gone out to a movie or to dinner. Or to kill someone.

One day a would-be victim, impervious to Preston's dry charm and oily sympathy, would have a surprise ready for the doctor. Not much physical strength was required to pull a trigger.

Luck never favored Leilani, however, so she didn't assume that this would be the night when he received a heart-stopping dose of his own poison. He would return home sooner or later, smelling of one kind of death or another.

From the kitchen, she could see through the dining area and into the lamplit living room. Her mother wasn't in view, but that didn't mean she wasn't present. By this hour, old Sinsemilla would have been dragged so low by her demons and her drugs that she was less likely to be found in an armchair than hiding behind a sofa or curled in the fetal position on the floor of a closet.

As might be expected in an ancient and fully furnished mobile home available for by-the-week rental, the decor didn't rank with that in Windsor Castle. Acoustic ceiling tiles crawled with water stains from a long-ago leak, all vaguely resembling large insects. Sunlight had bleached the drapes into shades no doubt familiar to chronic depressives from their dreams; the rotting fabric sagged in greasy folds, reeking of years of cigarette smoke. Scraped, gouged, stained, patched furniture stood on an orange shag carpet that could no longer manage to be shaggy: The knotted nap was flat, all springiness crushed out of it, as if by the weight of all the hopes and dreams that people had allowed to die here over the years.

Sinsemilla wasn't in the living room.

The closet just inside the front door provided a perfect haven from the goblins that were sometimes unleashed by a double dose of blotter acid, peyote buttons, or angel dust. If Sinsemilla had taken refuge here, imaginary goblins had eaten her as neatly as a duchess might eat pudding with a spoon. Currently the closet contained only a cluster of unused wire coat hangers that jangled in the influx of air when Leilani pulled open the door.

She hated searching for her mother like this. She never knew in what condition Sinsemilla would be found.

Sometimes dear Mater came complete with a mess to clean up. Leilani could handle messes. She didn't want to make a life's work out of swabbing up puke and urine, but she could do what needed to be done without adding two half-used pieces of apple pie to the mix.

The blood was worse. There were never oceans of it; but a little blood can appear to be a lot before you've assessed the situation.

Old Sinsemilla would never intentionally kill herself. She ate no red meat, restricted her smoking solely to dope, drank ten glasses of bottled water a day to cleanse herself of toxins, took twenty-seven tablets and capsules of vitamin supplements, and spent a lot of time worrying about global warming. She had been alive for thirty-six years, she said, and she intended to hang around for fifty more or until human pollution and the sheer weight of human population caused Earth's axis to shift violently and wipe out ninety-nine percent of all life on the planet, whichever came first.

Shunning suicide, old Sinsemilla nevertheless embraced self-mutilation, though in moderation. She worked on herself no more than once a month. She always sterilized the scalpel with a candle flame and her skin with alcohol, and she made each cut only after much judicious consideration.

Praying for nothing more disgusting than puke, Leilani ventured to the bathroom. This cramped, mildew-scented space was deserted and no worse of a mess than it had been when they moved in here.

A short hall, lined with imitation wood paneling, featured three doors. Two bedrooms and a closet.

In the closet: no Mom, no puke, no blood, no hidden passageway leading to a magical kingdom where everyone was beautiful and rich and happy. Leilani didn't actually search for the passageway, but based on past experience, she made the logical assumption that it wasn't here; as a much younger girl, she had often expected to find a secret door to fantastic other lands, but she had been routinely disappointed, so she had decided that if any such door existed, *it* would have to find *her*. Besides, if this closet were the equivalent of a bus station between California and a glorious domain of fun-loving wizards, surely there would be crumpled wrappers from weird and unknown brands of candy discarded by traveling trolls or at least a pile of elf droppings, but the closet held nothing more exotic than one dead cockroach.

Two doors remained, both closed. On the right lay the small bedroom assigned to Leilani. Directly ahead was the room that her mother shared with Preston.

Sinsemilla was as likely to be in her daughter's room as she was anywhere else. She had no respect for other people's personal space and never demanded respect for her own, perhaps because with drugs she created a vast wilderness in her mind, where she enjoyed blissful solitude whenever she required it.

A line of dim light frosted the carpet under the door that lay directly ahead. No light, however, was visible under the door to the right.

This didn't mean anything, either. Sinsemilla liked to sit alone in the dark, sometimes trying to communicate with the spirit world, sometimes just talking to herself.

Leilani listened intently. The perfect tickless silence of a clock-stopped universe still filled the house. Bleeding, of course, is a quiet process.

In spite of a free-spirited tendency to be unrestrained in all things, Sinsemilla had thus far restricted her artistic scalpel work to her left arm. A six-inch-long, two-inch-wide snowflake pattern of carefully connected scars, as intricate as lacework, decorated or disfigured her forearm, depending on your taste in these matters. The smooth, almost shiny, scar tissue glowed whiter than the surrounding skin, an impressive tone-on-tone design, although the contrast became more pronounced when she tanned.

Leave the house. Sleep in the yard. Let Dr. Doom deal with the mess if there is one.

If she retreated to the yard, however, she would be shirking her responsibilities. Which was exactly what old Sinsemilla would do in a similar situation. In any predicament whatsoever, if Leilani wondered which among many courses of action was the right one and the wisest, she ultimately made her decision based on the same guiding principle: Do the opposite of what Sinsemilla would do, and there is a better chance that you'll come through all right, as well as an immeasurably higher likelihood that you'll be able to look in the mirror again without cringing.

Leilani opened the door to her room and switched on the light. Her bed was as neatly made as the ratty spread would allow, just as she'd left it. Her few personal items hadn't been disturbed. The Sinsemilla circus had not played an engagement here.

One door remained.

Her palms were damp. She blotted them on her T-shirt.

She remembered an old short story that she'd read, 'The Lady or the Tiger,' in which a man was forced to choose between two doors, with deadly consequences if he opened the wrong one. Behind *this* door waited neither a lady nor a tiger, but an altogether unique specimen. Leilani would have preferred the tiger.

Not out of morbid interest but with some degree of alarm, she'd researched self-mutilation soon after her mother became interested in it. According to psychologists, most self-mutilators were teenage girls and young women in their twenties. Sinsemilla was too old for this game. Self-mutilators frequently suffered from low self-esteem, even self-loathing. By contrast, Sinsemilla seemed to like herself enormously, most of the time, or at least when medicated, which was in fact most of the time. Of course, you had to suppose that she had originally gotten into heavy drugs not merely because 'they taste so good,' as she put it, but because of a self-destructive impulse.

Leilani's palms were still damp. She blotted them again. In spite of the August heat, her hands were cold. A bitter taste arose in her mouth, perhaps an onion blowback from Geneva's potato salad, and her tongue stuck to the roof of her mouth.

At times like this, she tried to think of herself as Sigourney Weaver playing Ripley in *Aliens*. Your hands were damp, sure, and your hands were cold, all right, and your mouth was dry, but nevertheless you had to stiffen your spine, work up some spit, open the damn door, and go in there where the beast was, and *you had to do what needed to be done*.

She blotted her hands on her shorts.

Most self-mutilators were deeply self-involved. A small number could be confidently diagnosed as narcissists, which was where old Sinsemilla and the psychologists definitely could shake hands. Mother in a merry mood often sang an ebullient mantra that she'd composed herself: 'I am a sly cat, I am a summer wind, I am birds in flight, I am the sun, I am the sea, I am *me!*' Depending on the mix of illegal substances that she consumed, when she was balancing just so on the tightrope between hyperactivity and drooling unconsciousness, she would sometimes repeat this mantra in a singsong voice, a hundred times, two hundred, until she either fell asleep or broke down sobbing and *then* fell asleep.

In three clinkless steel-assisted steps, Leilani reached the door.

Ear to the jamb. Not a sound from the other side.

Ripley usually had a big gun and a flamethrower.

Here was where Mrs. D's occasional confusion of reality and cinema would come in handy. Recalling her previous triumph over the egg-laying alien queen, Geneva would smash through the door without hesitation, and kick butt.

One more blot. You didn't want slippery hands in a slippery situation.

Sinsemilla said she cried because she was a flower in a world of thorns, because no one here could see the full beautiful spectrum of her radiance. Sometimes Leilani thought this might indeed be the reason that her mother dissolved so often in tears, which was scary because it implied a degree of delusion that made this woman more alien than the ETs that Preston eagerly pursued. *Narcissistic* seemed inadequate to describe someone who, even when caked in her own vomit and reeking of urine and babbling incoherently, believed herself to be a more delicate and exquisite flower than any hothouse orchid.

Leilani knocked on the bedroom door. Unlike her mother, she had a respect for other people's personal spaces.

Sinsemilla didn't respond to the knock.

Maybe dear Mater was fine, in spite of her performance in the backyard. Maybe she was sleeping peacefully and ought to be left to enjoy her dreams of better worlds.

Yeah, but maybe she was in trouble. Maybe this was one of those times when knowing CPR proved useful or when you wanted paramedics. If you were on the road in unknown territory, you could pull down directions to the nearest hospital from a satellite; this high-tech age was the safest time in history for perpetually wrecked freaks with a yen to travel.

She knocked again.

She wasn't sure whether she should be relieved or anxious when her mother called out to her in a fruity theatrical voice: 'Pray ye, say who knocketh upon my chamber door.'

On a few occasions, when Sinsemilla had been in one of these playacting moods, Leilani had played along with her, speaking with the fake old-English dialect, using stage gestures and exaggerated expressions, hoping that a minim of mother-daughter bonding might occur. This always proved to be a bad idea. Old Sinsemilla didn't want you to become a member of the cast; you were expected only to admire and be charmed by her performance, for this was a one-woman show. If you persisted in sharing the spotlight, the larky dialogue took a nasty turn, whereupon you found yourself the target of mean criticism and vicious obscenities delivered in the stupid phony voice of whatever Shakespearean character or figure from Arthurian legend that Sinsemilla imagined herself to be.

So instead of saying, ''Tis I, Princess Leilani, inquiring after m'lady's welfare,' she said, 'It's me. You okay?'

'Enter, enter, Maiden Leilani, and come thou quickly to thy queen's side.'

Yuck. This was going to be worse than blood and mutilation.

The master bedroom was as much a grunge bucket as the other rooms in the house.

Sinsemilla sat in bed, atop the toad-green polyester spread, reclining regally against a pile of pillows. She wore the full-length embroidered slip with flounce-trimmed skirt that she had bought last month at a flea market near Albuquerque, New Mexico, on their way to explore the alien enigmas of Roswell.

If whorehouse decor favored red light, as reputed, then this atmosphere was better suited to a prostitute than to a queen. Though both nightstand lamps were aglow, a scarlet silk blouse draped one lampshade, and a scarlet cotton blouse covered the other.

This quality of light flattered Sinsemilla. Bindles, kilos, bales, ounces, pints, and gallons of illegal substances had stolen less of her beauty than seemed either probable or fair, and as good as she looked in daylight, she was even prettier here. Although her bare feet were grass-stained and filthy, though her fine slip was rumpled and streaked with dirt, though her hair had been tossed and tangled by the moon dance, she might pass for a queen.

'What saith thee, young maiden, in the presence of Cleopatra?'

Stopping two steps inside the door, Leilani didn't suggest that an Egyptian queen who had reigned more than two thousand years ago probably had not spoken in a phony accent out of a bad production of *Camelot*. 'I was going to bed, and I just thought I'd see if you were all right.'

Waving Leilani toward her, Sinsemilla said, 'Come hither, dour peasant girl, and let thy queen acquaint thee with a work of art fair suitable for the galleries of Eden.'

Leilani had no clue to the meaning of her mother's words. From experience she knew that purposefully remaining clueless might be the wisest policy.

She advanced one more step, not out of a sense of obligation or curiosity, but because by turning away too quickly, she might invite accusations of rudeness. Her mother imposed no rules or standards on her children, gave them the freedom of her indifference; yet she was sensitive to any indication that her indifference might be repaid in kind, and she wouldn't tolerate a thankless child.

Regardless of the inconsequential nature or the questionable validity of the triggering offense, an upbraiding from old Sinsemilla could escalate into a long bout of vicious hectoring. Although Mother might not be capable of physical violence, she could do serious damage with words. Because she'd follow you anywhere, push through any door, and insist on your attention, you could find no sanctuary and had to endure her verbal battering – sometimes for hours – until she wound down or went away to get high. During the worst of these harangues, Leilani often wished that her mother would dispense with all the hateful words and throw a few punches instead.

Leaning forward from the pillows, old Sinsemilla Cleopatra spoke with a smiling insistence that Leilani knew to be a cold command: 'Come, glowering girl, come, come! Looketh upon this little beauty and wish that thou were as well made as she.'

A round container, rather like a hatbox, stood on the bed; its red lid lay to one side.

Sinsemilla had been shopping earlier, in the afternoon. With her, Preston was generous, providing money for drugs and baubles.

Maybe she had in fact bought a hat, for in her more seductive moods, she liked the glamour of berets and billycocks, panamas and turbans, cloches and calashes.

'Don't tarry, child!' the queen commanded. 'Come hither at once and lay thine eyes upon this treasure out of Eden.'

Obviously, this audience with her highness wouldn't end until the new hat – or whatever – had been properly admired.

With a mental sigh that she dared not voice, Leilani approached the bed.

As she drew closer, she noticed that the hatbox was perforated by two parallel, encircling lines of small holes. For a moment this seemed like mere decoration, and Leilani didn't deduce the function of the holes until she saw what had come in the container.

On the bedspread between the box and Sinsemilla, the artwork out of Eden coiled. Emerald-green, burnt umber, with a filigree of chrome-yellow. Sinuous body, flat head, glittering black eyes, and a flickering tongue designed for deception.

The snake turned its head to inspect its new admirer, and with no warning, it struck at Leilani as quick as an electrical current would leap across an arc between two charged poles.

20

On the highway, bound southwest toward Nevada, Curtis and Old Yeller sit on the bed, in the dark, sharing the frankfurters. Their bonding has progressed sufficiently that even in the gloom, the dog doesn't once mistake boy fingers for a permissible part of dinner.

This mutt isn't, as Curtis first thought, his brother-becoming. She is instead his sister-becoming, and that's okay, too.

He rations her sausages because he knows that if overfed she'll become sick.

All but incapable of being overfed, he consumes the remaining hot dogs once he senses that Old Yeller is just one furter from an unpleasant flowback. The sausages are cold but delicious. He would eat more if he had them. Being Curtis Hammond requires a remarkable amount of energy.

He can only imagine the daunting quantity of energy required to be Donella, the waitress whose magnificent dimensions are matched by the size of her good heart.

Reminded of Donella, he worries about her welfare. What might have happened to her among all the flying bullets? On the other hand, although she provides a convenient target, her fantastic bulk no doubt makes her more difficult to kill than are ordinary mortals.

He wishes that he'd returned for her and had bravely spirited her to safety. This is a ridiculously romantic and perhaps irrational notion. He's just a boy of comparatively little experience, and she's a grand person of great age and immeasurable wisdom. Nevertheless, he wishes he had been brave for her.

Helicopter rotors rattle the night again. Curtis tenses, half expecting gunfire to riddle the motor home, to hear the booted feet of winch-lowered SWAT officers thumping on the roof and demands for his surrender blasted on a loudspeaker. The *chudda-chudda-chudda* of air-slicing steel grows thunderous . . . but then diminishes and fades entirely away.

Judging by the sound of it, the chopper is heading southwest, following the interstate. This is not good.

Finished with the hot dogs, Curtis drinks orange juice from the container – and realizes that Old Yeller is thirsty, too.

Drawing upon the messy experience of giving the dog a drink from a bottle of water in the Explorer, he decides to search for a bowl or for something that can serve as one.

The motor home is rolling along at the speed limit or faster, and he assumes that the owners – the man and woman whose voices he heard earlier – are still in the cockpit, hashing over the excitement at the truck stop. If they're sitting at the far end of the vehicle, facing away from the bedroom, they aren't in a position to see any light that might leak under or around the door.

Curtis eases off the bed. He feels the wall beside the jamb, finds the switch.

His dark-adapted eyes sting briefly from the glare.

Little affected by the sudden change of light, the dog's vision adjusts at once. Previously lying on the bed, she now stands upon it, following Curtis's movements with curiosity, her tail wagging in expectation of either adventure or a share of the juice.

The bedroom is too small and too utilitarian for decorative bowls or for knickknacks that might be of use.

Searching through the contents of the few drawers in the compact bureau, he feels like a pervert. He's not exactly sure what perverts do, or why they do whatever it is they do, but he knows that secretly poking through other people's underwear is definitely a sign that you are a pervert, and there seems to be as much underwear in this bureau as anything else.

Flushed with embarrassment, unable to look at Old Yeller, the boy turns from the bureau and tries the top drawer on the nearest nightstand. Inside, among articles of no use to him, are a pair of white plastic jars, each four inches in diameter and three inches tall. Though small, either of these will be suitable as a dish for the dog; he will simply refill it with juice as often as the pooch requires.

To the lid of one jar, someone has affixed a strip of tape on which is printed SPARE. Curtis interprets this to mean that of the two jars, this is the one of less importance to the owners of the motor home, and so he decides to appropriate this spare in order to cause them as little inconvenience as possible.

The jar features a screw-top. When he twists off the lid, he is horrified to discover a full set of teeth inside. They grin at him, complete with pink gums, but purged of blood.

Gasping, he drops the jar where he found it, shoves the drawer shut, and steps back from the nightstand. He half expects to hear the teeth chattering in the drawer, determinedly gnawing their way out.

He has seen movies about serial killers. These human monsters collect souvenirs of their kills. Some keep severed heads in the refrigerator or preserve their victims' eyes in jars of formaldehyde. Others make garments from the skin of those they murder, or they create mobiles with weird arrangements of dangling bones.

None of those movies or books has introduced him to a homicidal psychopath who collects teeth still firmly fixed in carved-out chunks of jawbone, gums attached. Nevertheless, though just a boy, he is sufficiently well informed about the darker side of human nature to understand what he saw in that jar.

'Serial killers,' he whispers to Old Yeller. *Serial killers.*

This concept is too complex for the dog to grasp. She lacks the cultural references to make sense of it. Her tail stops wagging, but only because she feels her brother-becoming's distress.

Curtis still must find a bowl for the orange juice, but he's not going to look in any more nightstand drawers. No way.

Otherwise, only the closet remains unexplored.

Movies and books warn that closets are problematical. The worst thing that you could dream up in a nightmare, no matter how hideous and fantastic and unlikely, might be waiting for you in a closet.

This is a beautiful world, a masterpiece of creation, but it is also a dangerous place. Villains human and inhuman and supernatural lurk in basements and in cobweb-festooned attics. In graveyards at night. In abandoned houses, in castles inhabited by people with surnames of Germanic or Slavic origin, in funeral homes, in ancient pyramids, in lonely woods, under the surface of virtually any large body of water, even also on occasion under the soap-obscured surface of a full bathtub, and of course in spaceships whether they are here on Earth or cruising distant avenues of the universe.

Right now, he'd rather explore a graveyard or a scarab-infested pyramid with mummies on the march, or the chambers of any spaceship, instead of the closet in these serial killers' motor home. He's not in an Egyptian desert, however, and he's not aboard a faster-than-light vessel beyond the Horsehead Nebula in the constellation of Orion. He's here, like it or not, and if ever he has needed to draw strength from his mother's courageous example, this is the moment.

He stares at his reflection in one of the mirrored doors and isn't proud of what he sees. Pale face. Eyes wide and shining with fear. The posture of a fright-buckled child: tensed body, hunched shoulders, head tucked down as if he expects someone to strike him.

Old Yeller turns her attention from Curtis to the closet. She issues a low growl.

Maybe something hideous *does* lurk in there. Perhaps awaiting Curtis is a discovery far more disgusting and terrifying than the teeth.

Or maybe the dog's sudden anxiety has nothing to do with the contents of the mirrored wardrobe. She might simply have absorbed Curtis's mood.

The closet door rattles. Probably just road vibration.

Resolved to live up to his mother's expectations, reminding himself of his remorse over failing to rescue Donella, determined to locate a suitable juice bowl for his thirsty dog, he grips the handle on one of the sliding doors. He draws a deep breath, clenches his teeth, and opens the closet.

As his reflection slides away from him and as the interior of the wardrobe is revealed, Curtis sighs with relief when he fails to find jars of pickled eyeballs arrayed on the one long shelf. None of the garments hanging from the rod appears to be made of human skin.

Still wary but with growing confidence, he drops to his knees to search the closet floor for anything that might be used as a bowl.

He finds only men's and women's shoes, and he's grateful that they don't contain a collection of severed feet.

A pair of men's walking shoes appear new. He takes one of these from the closet, puts it on the floor near the bed, and fills it with orange juice from the plastic jug.

Ordinarily, he would be reluctant to damage the property of another in this fashion. But serial killers don't deserve the same respect as law-abiding citizens.

Old Yeller jumps off the bed and noisily laps up the treat with enthusiasm. She doesn't hesitate or pause to consider the taste – as though she has drunk orange juice before.

Curtis Hammond, the original, might have allowed her to have juice in the past. The current Curtis Hammond suspects, however, that he and the mutt are continuing to bond and that she recognizes the taste from his recent experience of it.

A boy and his dog can form astonishing, profound connections. He knows this to be true not entirely from movies and books, but from experience with animals in the past.

Curtis is 'not quite right,' as Burt Hooper put it, and Old Yeller is neither yellow nor male, nor particularly old, but they are going to be a great team.

After refilling the shoe, he puts down the juice container and sits on the edge of the bed to watch the dog drink.

I'll take good care of you, he promises.

He is pleased by his ability to function in spite of his fear. He's also pleased by his resourcefulness.

Although they're riding the Hannibal Lecter band bus and running from a pack of terminators who have more attitude than Schwarzenegger with a bee up his ass, although they're wanted by the FBI and surely by other government agencies that have more-ominous initials and less-honorable intentions, Curtis remains optimistic about his chances of escape. The sight of his canine companion, happily drinking, draws a smile from him. He takes a moment to thank God for keeping him alive, and he thanks his mother for the survival training that so far has been an invaluable assist to God in this matter.

A siren arises in the distance. This could be a fire truck, an ambulance, a police vehicle, or a clown car. Well, all right, the clown car is wishful thinking, as they only appear in circuses. In fact, it's certain to be the police.

Old Yeller looks up from the shoe, juice dripping off her chin.

The siren quickly grows louder until it's close behind the motor home.

21

Jaws cracked wide as if unhinged, backward-hooked fangs exposed to their full wicked arc, split tongue fluttering, the serpent swam through the air with the wriggle of an eel through water, but faster than any eel, as bottle-rocket fast as a fireworks snake, launched straight at Leilani's face.

Although she juked, the viper must also have misaimed, because her reaction alone wouldn't have been quick enough to spare her from a bite. She might have imagined the thin hiss as the thwarted snake sailed past her left ear, but the lash of smooth dry scales across her cheek was real. This caressing flick, cold or not, sent chills chasing chills along her spine, with such palpable shivers that she could almost believe the hateful serpent had slipped under the collar of her T-shirt and along the small of her back.

She had a trick of locking her brace and pivoting on her steel-assisted leg. Even as she heard the hiss or dreamed it, she twisted around in time to see the 'treasure out of Eden' as it raveled in a long arc to the floor, the brighter fraction of its scales glinting like sequins in the red light.

The snake wasn't huge, between two and three feet long, about as thick as a man's index finger, but when it struck the floor and tumbled, lashing angrily, as though mistaking its own whipping coils for those of a predator, it couldn't have been scarier if it had been a massive python or a full-grown rattlesnake. After that brief moment of frenzy, the viper slithered loose of its own tangles and flowed swiftly across the squashed-shag carpet, as if it were a quickness of water following the course of a rillet. Encountering the baseboard under the window, it reeled itself into a coiled pile once more and raised its head to assess the situation, ready to strike again.

Leading with her good leg, dragging her left, long-practiced grace abandoned, hard-won dignity lost, Leilani clumped in a panicked stagger toward the hallway. Though off-balance with every step, she managed to remain upright, lurching all the way to the door, where she clutched at the knob for support.

She had to escape from the snake. Get to her bedroom. Try to barricade that door against her mother's intrusion.

Sinsemilla was highly amused. Words whooped from her on peals of laughter. 'It's not poisonous, you ninny! It's a pet-shop snake. You should've *seen* the look on your face!'

Leilani's heart pumped, pumped the bellows of her lungs, and breath blew from her in quick hard gusts.

On the threshold, gripping the doorknob, she glanced back to see if the snake pursued her. It remained coiled under the window.

Kneeling on the mattress, her mother bounced like a schoolgirl, making the springs sing and the bedrails rattle, laughing, shiny-eyed with delight over a prank well played. 'Don't be such a goof! It's just a little slippery thingy, not a monster!'

Here's the deal: If she fled to her room and barricaded the door, she still wouldn't be safe, because sooner or later she'd have to come out. To get food. To use the bathroom. They were going to be here a few more days, and if the creature was loose in the house, it could be anywhere, and once she came out of her room to go to the toilet or to get something to eat, then it could slip in her room, too, through the one-inch gap under the poorly hung door, or because Sinsemilla *let* it into her room, and then it could be waiting under Leilani's bed, *in* her bed. She'll have no sanctuary, no peace. Every place will belong to the snake; no place will belong to Leilani, no smallest place. Usually she had only a corner, a nook, a precious retreat; though Sinsemilla might invade any room without warning, Leilani could at least *pretend* her nook was a private place. But the snake won't allow even a pretense of privacy. She'll have no respite from torment, no relief from the expectation of attack, not even when Sinsemilla is asleep, because the snake is essentially sleepless. This wasn't a way Leilani could live, not a situation she could endure, this was too much, too much, *intolerable*.

Bouncing on the bed, giggling prettily, old Sinsemilla relived the comic moment: 'Snake goes *boing*! straight in the air, and Leilani goes *yikes*! just about straight in the air herself, and then she's makin' for the door like two drunk kangaroos in a three-legged sack race!'

Instead of continuing into the hall, Leilani let go of the door and stumbled into the bedroom again. Fear kept her from regaining her usual ease of movement, but also anger; she remained unbalanced by a sense of injustice that quaked through her with 1906 San Francisco intensity, rocking her from good leg to bad, rolling through her in nauseating waves.

'Cute little slippery thingy won't kill you, Leilani. Little thingy just wants what we all want, baby. Little thingy just wants love,' Sinsemilla said, drawing out *love* until it was longer than a twelve-syllable word, and she laughed with strange delight.

Poisonous or not, the snake had struck at Leilani's face, her *face*, which was the best thing she had going for her, the best thing she might *ever* have going for her, because in truth she'd probably never develop great bouncing bosoms, regardless of what she had told Micky. When she was sitting in a restaurant or somewhere, with her clatter-clank leg under a table, with her poster-child hand tucked out of sight in her lap, people looked at her face and often smiled, treated her like any other kid, with no sorrow in their eyes, no pity, because nothing in her face said *cripple*. The snake had struck at her *face*, and she didn't give a rat's ass whether it was poisonous or not, because it could have changed her life if it had gotten those fangs in her cheek or her nose. Then people would never think of her as sassy, but would always think, *What a sad little crippled girl she is, with her little twisted leg and her little gnarled hand and her snake-gnawed face and her snake-chomped nose.*

So much to lose.

She must deal with this, and fast; but nothing on the bed would be of help to her in a snake chase, snake fight. The chest of drawers contained but a few articles of clothing, nothing else, because they were living out of suitcases for the short time they were here. In fact, suitcases were open on a bench at the foot of the bed and on a straight-backed chair; neither the luggage nor the furniture suggested a strategy for this battle.

The snake still coiled near the baseboard, under the window. Luminous eyes. Head weaving as if to the music of a charmer's flute.

'Boing! Yikes!' Sinsemilla had compressed the anecdote into two words. She rollicked even to this abridged version, abusing the bed more than might have any gaggle of giddy girls at a pajama party.

Forgetting to use the brace's mechanical knee joint, swinging her caged leg from the hip, Leilani hitched and clumped toward the closet, which regrettably put the bed between her and the snake. She was convinced that the moment the slippery little reptile was out of her sight, it slithered toward her, coming at her from under the bed.

'Baby, baby,' Sinsemilla said, 'look at this, look, look. Baby, look, see, look.' She extended her hand, offering something. 'Baby, it's okay, see, baby, look.'

Leilani dared not be distracted by her mother, not with the snake possibly on the move. But Sinsemilla couldn't be ignored any more than you could ignore an asteroid the size of Texas hurtling at Earth with impact predicted for noon Friday.

Sinsemilla's left hand was clenched. She opened it to reveal a wad of bloody Kleenex that Leilani hadn't been able to see before. The crimson tissues dropped out of her grip; in the meaty part of her palm were two small wounds.

'Poor scared thingy bit me when the lights went out.'

Dark with clotted blood, the holes no longer oozed.

'Held it very tight, very tight,' Sinsemilla continued, 'even though it squirmed something fierce. Took a lot of time to work its fangs out of me. Didn't want to tear up my hand, but I didn't want to hurt thingy, either.'

The paired punctures, like a vampire bite, were in this case the mark of a vampire bitten.

'Then I held poor scared thingy a long time in the dark, the two of us here on the bed, and after a while thingy stopped squirming. We *communed*, baby, me and thingy. Oh, baby, we bonded so totally while we waited for the lights to come on. It was the coolest thing ever.'

Leilani's hard-pounding heart seemed to clunk as arrhythmically and as awkwardly as a panicked girl with one shackled leg might run.

Warped Masonite, cracked plastic glides, and a corroded track conspired to prevent her from sliding the closet door with ease. Grunting, she shoved and shook it out of her way.

'No venom, baby. Thingy has fangs but no poison. Don't wet your panties, girl, we're doing less laundry to conserve electricity.'

As in Leilani's own closet, a tubular-steel pole, approximately two inches in diameter, spanned the seven-foot width. Only a few women's blouses and men's shirts hung from it.

She glanced down at her feet. No snake.

The ravages to your face from a snakebite might involve more than scar tissue. Maybe nerve damage. Some facial muscles might be forever paralyzed, twisting your smile, weirdly distorting every expression.

The pole rested in U-shaped brackets. She lifted it up and out of the fixtures. The hangers slid off the rod, taking the clothes to the closet floor.

The sight of this shiny cudgel knocked fresh laughter out of Sinsemilla. She clapped her hands, oblivious of the bite, excited by the prospect of the entertainment to come.

Leilani would have preferred a shovel. A garden hoe. But this length of tubular steel was better than bare hands, something to keep the serpent away from her face.

Gripping the pole in her right hand as if it were a shepherd's staff, she used it to help maintain her balance as she stumped toward the foot of the bed.

Waving her hands in the air as a gospel singer waves praises to the heavens while shouting hallelujahs, Sinsemilla said, 'Oh, Lani, baby, you should *see* yourself! You look so completely St. Patrick, in a total snake-driving mood!'

Hitching clumsily but warily alongside the bed, telling herself *Calm*. Telling herself, *Get a grip*.

Leilani wasn't able to act on her own good advice. Fear and anger prevented mind and body from being properly coordinated.

If the snake had struck her face, it might have bitten her eye. It might have left her half blind.

She cracked her hip against the chunky post at the corner of the footboard, fell against the bed, but at once levered herself upright, feeling stupid, feeling clumsy, feeling as though she were the Girl from Castle Frankenstein, lacking only bolts in the neck, an early experiment that hadn't gone half as well as the creature that Karloff played.

She wanted nothing more than to hold on to whatever she had

that looked normal and worked properly. This wasn't so much to want. The twisted leg, the deformed hand, the brain too smart for her own good: She couldn't trade those in for standard-issue parts. She hoped only to keep the strong right leg, the good right hand, the pleasing face. Pride had nothing to do with it, either. Considering all her other problems, a pleasing face wasn't just about looking good; it was about *survival*.

When she rounded the end of the bed, she saw the pet-shop terror where she had left it, stacked in scaly ringlets under the window. Evil-looking head raised. Alert.

'Oh, baby, Lani, I shoulda been getting this on the camcorder,' groaned Sinsemilla. 'We'd win big bucks on TV – that show, *America's Funniest Home Videos*.'

Face. Eyes. So much to lose. *Get out. Leave.* But they'd bring her back. And where would the snake be by then? Somewhere, anywhere, everywhere, waiting. And what if her mother took it with them when they hit the road in the motor home? In that tin can on wheels, already trapped with Preston and Sinsemilla, she'd have this third snake to worry about. There's no way to flee outside when you're cruising at sixty miles per hour.

Holding the pole in front of herself with both hands, Leilani wondered what maximum distance a snake could travel through the air when it flung itself out of a tight coil. She thought maybe she'd read that it could shoot twice its length, in this case five to six feet, which might leave her unbitten, but if this particular specimen happened to be ambitious, if it always gave that extra ten percent, like the hero of some demented children's book – *The Little Snake that Could* – then she was screwed.

Leilani didn't have a fearsome capacity for violence, maybe not any. She never fantasized about being a whole-of-limb, hard-bodied, martial-arts wunderkind. The Klonk way wasn't the way of the Ninja. The Klonk way was to ingratiate, to amuse, to charm, but while you could expect a high degree of success with this approach when you were dealing with schoolteachers and ministers and sweetly daffy pie-baking neighbors, all you would get for trying to charm a snake was your eye on the end of a fang.

'Better go, thingy, better squiggle,' Sinsemilla advised gleefully. 'Here come bad-ass Lani, and dis here girl mean bidness!'

Because any hesitation would lead to the complete collapse of Leilani's will, she had to act while desperate with fear and fierce with anger. She surprised herself when she choked out a strangled cry, part misery and part fury, as she jabbed the lance hard at the coiled target.

She pinned the thrashing serpent to the baseboard, but only for two seconds, maybe three, and then her sinuous whipping adversary flailed loose.

'Go, thingy, go, *go!*'

Jabbing, jabbing, Leilani poked the villain once more, crushed it against the baseboard, bearing on it with all her strength, trying to hurt it, cut it in half, but again it writhed free, no easier to kill than a serpent of smoke, as hard to nail down as your father's identity, as what happened to your brother, as just about anything in this screwy life, but all you could do was keep jabbing, keep trying.

As the snake slithered along the wall and under the tall chest of drawers, Sinsemilla bounced on the bed: 'Oh, trouble now, trouble with a capital S-n-a-k-e. Thingy's pissed, hidin' under the highboy, him bruised and bitter, him havin' a hissy fit, him broodin' up *bad* snaky revenge.'

Leilani hoped to see bloodstains on the baseboard – or if a snake didn't have exactly blood in it, then a smear of something else that said *mortal wounds* as clearly as a lot of good red gore would have said it. But she saw no blood, no ichor, no snake syrup of any kind.

The sawn-off circular end of the hollow tubular pole wouldn't be as effective as a sharp knife, but it would cut even tough scales and muscled coils if driven hard enough, if a lot of insistent pressure was put behind it. Her sweaty hands had slipped on the polished steel, but surely some damage had been done to the snake.

The chest of drawers stood against the wall, on four stubby legs. More than five feet high. Four feet wide. Maybe twenty inches deep. The bottom rail cleared the floor by three inches.

Snake under there somewhere. When Leilani held her breath, she could hear the angry hissing. The reverberant bottom of the lowest drawer amplified the sound in that confined space.

She'd better get a fix on the creature while it was stunned. She backed away, dropped awkwardly to her knees. Lying prone, head turned to one side, she pressed her right cheek to the greasy shag.

If Death had pockets in his robe, they smelled like this filthy carpet. Nauseating waves of righteous anger still churned Leilani, and the rotten-sour sludge of scent that pooled on the wall-to-wall gave her another reason to worry about losing her apple pie.

'Oh, listen to that snaky brain a-hummin', listen to old thingy schemin' up a scheme, like when he wants to kill him a tasty mouse.'

The silk-textured light, as red as Sinsemilla's favorite party blouse, barely brightened the nest of shadows under the chest of drawers.

Leilani was gasping, not from exhaustion – she hadn't exerted herself *that* much – but because she was worried, scared, *in a state*. As she lay squinting for a glimpse of the beast, her face only six or seven feet from the reptile's crawlspace, she breathed rapidly, noisily, through her mouth, and her tongue translated the stink of the carpet into a taste that made her gag.

Under the chest of drawers, shadows appeared to throb and turn as shadows always do when you stare hard enough at them, but the lipstick light kissed only one form among all the shifting phantom shapes. Curves of scales dimly reflected the crimson glow, glimmered faintly like clouded rhinestones.

'Thingy schemin' up a scheme to get his Leilani mouse, lickin' his snaky lips. Thingy, him be dreamin' what Lani girl gonna taste like.'

The serpent huddled all the way back against the wall, and about as far from one side of the chest of drawers as from the other.

Leilani rose to her knees again. She seized the pole with both hands and rammed it hard under the furniture, dead-on for the snake. She struck again, again, again, furiously, burning her knuckles from friction with the shag, and she could hear the critter thrashing, its body slapping loudly against the bottom of the lowest drawer.

On the bed, Sinsemilla romped, cheering one of the combatants, cursing the other, and though Leilani wasn't any longer able to make sense of her mother's words, she figured the woman's sympathies were with the thingy.

She couldn't clearly hear Sinsemilla's ranting because of the snake lashing a crazy drumbeat on the underside of the chest, because of the pole punching into the snarled coils and knocking on the baseboard and rattling against the legs of the furniture – but also because she herself was grunting like a wild beast. Her throat felt scorched. Her raw voice didn't sound like her own: wordless, thick, hideous with a primitive need that she didn't dare contemplate.

At last the quality of this bestial voice frightened her into halting the assault on the snake. It was dead, anyway. She had killed it some time ago. Under the tall chest of drawers, nothing flopped, nothing hissed.

Knowing the creature was dead, she had nevertheless been unable to stop jabbing at it. Out of control. And who did those three words bring to mind? *Out of control.* Like mother, like daughter. Leilani's accelerator had been pressed to the floorboard by fear, rather than by drugs, also by anger, but this distinction didn't matter as much to her as did the discovery that she, like Sinsemilla, could lose control of herself under the right circumstances.

Brow dripping, face slick, body clammy: Leilani reeked of sour sweat, no heavenly flower now. On her knees, shoulders hunched, head cocked, wild damp hair hanging in tangles over her face, hands still clenched with such rage that she couldn't release the pole, she made her bid for being Quasimodo reborn, only nine and a return to Notre Dame still years away.

She felt diminished, humiliated, shaken – no less afraid than she'd been a moment ago, but now for different reasons. Some serpents were more frightening than others: the specimens that didn't come in ventilated pet-shop boxes, that never slithered through any field or forest, serpents invisible that inhabited the deeper regions of your mind. Until now, she hadn't been aware that she herself provided a nest for such potent snakes of fear and anger, or that her heart could be inflamed and set racing by their sudden bite, so quickly reducing her to these spasms, these half-mad headlong frenzies, out of control.

Like a gargoyle above, Sinsemilla leaned over the footboard of the bed, her face shadowed but her head haloed by red lamplight, glittery-eyed with excitement. 'Thingy, him a hard-ass stubborn little crawly boy.'

Leilani didn't actually make sense of those words, and she was saved only because she met her mother's eyes and saw where they were focused. Not on her daughter. On the nearest end of the makeshift cudgel, just behind Leilani's two-hand grip.

The tubular-steel rod was hollow, two inches in diameter. The snake, not dead after all, seeking refuge when the battering stopped, had squirmed inside the pole. By this pipeline, it traveled unseen from beneath the chest of drawers to Leilani's exposed back, where now it slowly extruded on the floor behind her like the finished product of a snake-making machine.

Whether the serpent moved slowly because it was hurt or because it was being cautious to deceive, Leilani didn't know, didn't care. Just as the full length of it oozed from the hollow cudgel, she seized it by the tail. She knew that snakehandlers always gripped immediately under the head to immobilize the jaws, but fear for her one good hand caused her to choose the nether end.

Slick it was, wet-slick and therefore injured, but still lively enough to wriggle fiercely in a quest for freedom.

Before the snake could wind back on itself and bite her hand, Leilani shot to her feet faster than her braced leg had ever before allowed, playing cowgirl-with-lariat as she rose from the floor.

Swung like a rope, stretched long by centrifugal force that thwarted its inward-coiling efforts, the reptile parted the air with a *swoosh* louder than its hiss. She swung it twice as she stumbled two steps toward the chest of drawers, the bared fangs missing her mother's face by inches on the first revolution, and then during the third swing, the serpent met the furniture with a *crack* of skull that took all the wriggle out of it forever.

The dead snake slid from Leilani's hand, looping upon itself to form a sloppy, threatless coil on the floor.

Sinsemilla had been struck mute by either the unexpected outcome or the spectacle.

Although she could let go of the broken serpent and use the pivoting trick with her braced leg to turn her back on the scaly mess, Leilani couldn't turn away as easily from the mental image of herself in a fit of grunting, gasping, snake-killing rage and terror. Like a foxtail bramble, this hateful picture would work its way deep into the flesh of her memory, beyond the hope of excision, and prickle as long as she lived.

Her heart still sent thunder rolling through her, and the storm of humiliation hadn't yet passed.

She refused to cry. Not here. Not now. Neither fear nor anger, nor even this unwanted new knowledge of herself, could wring tears from her in front of her mother. The world didn't have enough misery in it to force her to reveal her vulnerability before Sinsemilla.

Her usual ease of movement still eluded Leilani; however, when she thought through the movement of each step before taking it, like a patient learning to walk again after spinal injury, she was able to proceed to the open bedroom door with a measure of dignity.

In the hall, a violent fit of the shakes overcame her, rattling teeth to teeth, knocking elbows against ribs, but she willed steel into her good knee and kept moving.

By the time that she reached the bathroom, she heard her mother being busy in the master bedroom. She looked back just as a pulse of icy light filled that open doorway. The flash from a camera. The snake wasn't road kill, but apparently the artist in Sinsemilla had been inspired by the grisly grace of the serpentine carcass resting on a grave cloth of orange shag.

Another pulse.

Leilani went into the bathroom, switched on the light and the fan. She closed the door and locked her mother out.

She turned on the shower, as well, but she didn't undress. Instead, she lowered the lid on the toilet and sat there.

With the hum of the fan and the noise of the running water as cover, she did what she had never done in front of her mother or Preston Maddoc. Here. Now. She wept.

22

As tasty as fresh orange juice is when lapped out of a shoe, Old Yeller nevertheless loses interest in her drink when the siren grows as loud as an air-raid warning in the immediate wake of the motor home. Curtis's concern becomes her concern, too, and she watches him, ears pricked, body tensed, ready to follow his lead.

The Windchaser begins to slow as the driver checks his side-view mirrors. Even serial killers who keep collections of victims' teeth at bedside for nostalgic examination will evidently pull over without hesitation for the highway patrol.

When the police cruiser sweeps past and rockets away into the night, the motor home gains speed once more, but Old Yeller doesn't return to her juice. As long as Curtis remains uneasy, the dog will stay on guard, as well.

First the helicopter tracking the highway toward Nevada and now this patrol car following: These are signs and portents of trouble ahead. Though he may be dead, J. Edgar Hoover is no fool, and if his restless spirit guides the organization from which he so reluctantly departed, then two squads of FBI agents, and probably various other authorities, are already establishing roadblocks on the interstate both northeast and southwest of the truck stop.

Sitting on the edge of the bed once more, Curtis extracts the wadded currency from the pockets of his jeans. He smooths the bills and sorts them. Not much to sort. He counts his treasury. Not much to count.

He certainly doesn't have enough money to bribe an FBI agent, and by far the most of them can't be bribed, anyway. They aren't politicians, after all. If the National Security Agency also has operatives in the field here, which now seems likely, and possibly the CIA, as well – those guys won't sell out their country and their honor for a few wrinkled five-dollar bills. Not if movies, suspense novels, and history books can be believed. Maybe the history texts are written with political bias, and maybe some of those novelists took literary license, but you could trust most of what you saw in movies, for sure.

With his meager resources, Curtis has little hope of being able to bribe his way past even state or local authorities. He shoves the currency into his pockets once more.

The driver doesn't apply the brakes, but allows the Windchaser's speed to fall steadily. Not good, not good. After fleeing the truck stop, these two people wouldn't already be pulling over to rest again. Traffic must be clotting ahead of them.

'Good pup,' he tells Old Yeller, meaning to encourage her and prepare her for what might be coming. *Good pup. Stay close.*

As their speed continues to fall precipitously to fifty, then below forty, under thirty, as the brakes are tapped a time or two, Curtis goes to the bedroom window.

The dog follows at his heels.

Curtis slides a pane open. Wind blusters like restless bears at the bars of a cage, but this is a mildly warm and toothless zephyr.

He boosts himself against the sill. Leaning out, he squints into the wind, toward the front of the motor home.

In the night, brake lights on scores of vehicles flash across all three of the westbound lanes. More than half a mile ahead, at the top of a rise, traffic has come to a complete stop.

As the Windchaser slows steadily, Curtis slides shut the window and takes up a position at the bedroom door. The faithful dog stays at his side.

Good pup.

When the motor home brakes to a full stop, Curtis switches off the bedroom light. He waits in darkness.

More likely than not, both sociopathic owners of the Windchaser will remain in their cockpit seats for a while. They'll be studying the roadblock with acute interest, planning strategy in the event of a vehicle inspection.

At any moment, however, one of them might retreat here to the bedroom. If a search by authorities seems imminent, these tooth fetishists will try to gather up and dispose of their incriminating collection of grisly souvenirs.

The advantage of surprise will belong to Curtis, but he's not confident that surprise alone will carry the day. Either of the murderous pair up front will enjoy the greater advantages of size, strength, and psychotic disregard for his or her personal safety.

In addition to surprise, however, the boy has Old Yeller. And the dog has teeth. Curtis has teeth, too, though his aren't as big and sharp as those of the dog, and unlike his four-legged companion, he doesn't have the heart to use them.

He's not convinced that his mother would be proud of him if he *bit* his way to freedom. Fighting men and women have seldom, if ever, to his knowledge, been decorated for bravery after gnawing their way through their adversaries. Thank God, then, for his sister-becoming.

Good pup.

After the Windchaser has been stopped for a couple minutes, it eases forward a few car lengths before halting again, and Curtis uses this distraction to open the bedroom door a crack. The lever-action handle squeaks softly, as do the hinges, and the door swings outward.

He puts one eye to the inch-wide gap and studies the bathroom beyond, which separates the bedroom from the galley, lounge, and cockpit. The door at the opposite end of the bath stands less than halfway open, admitting light from the forward part of the vehicle, but he can't see much of what lies beyond it.

Staying closer than Curtis intended, the dog presses against his legs and pushes her nose to the gap between jamb and door. He hears her sniffing. Her exceptional sense of smell brings to her more information than all five human senses combined, so he doesn't nudge her out of the way.

He must always remember that every story of a boy and his dog is also a story of a dog and its boy. No such relationship can be a success without respect.

The dog's tail wags, brushing Curtis's legs, either because she catches an appealing scent or because she agrees with his assessment of the fundamental requirement of a boy-dog friendship.

Suddenly a man enters the bathroom from the front of the motor home.

In the dark bedroom, Curtis almost shuts the door in shock. He realizes just in time that the one-inch gap won't draw the man's attention as much as will the movement of the door closing.

He expects the guy to come directly to the bedroom, and he's ready to use the door as a battering ram to knock this killer off his feet. Then he and the dog will dash for freedom.

Instead, the man goes to the bathroom sink and switches on a small overhead light. Standing in profile to Curtis, he examines his face in the mirror.

Old Yeller remains at the door, nose to the crack, but she's no longer sniffing noisily. She's in stealth mode, though her tail continues to wag gently.

Although scared, Curtis is also intrigued. There's something fascinating about secretly watching strangers in their own home, even if their home is on wheels.

The man squints at the mirror. He rubs one finger over the right corner of his mouth, squints again, and seems satisfied. With two fingers, he pulls down both lower eyelids and examines his eyes – God knows for what. Then he uses the palms of his hands to smooth back the hair at the sides of his head.

Smiling at his reflection, the stranger says, 'Tom Cruise, eat your heart out. Vern Tuttle rules.'

Curtis doesn't know who Vern Tuttle may be, but Tom Cruise is, of course, an actor, a movie star, a worldwide icon. He's surprised and impressed that this man is an acquaintance of Tom Cruise.

He's heard people say that it's a small world, and this Cruise connection sure does support that contention.

Next, the man grins at his reflection. This is not an amusing grin. Even viewed in profile, it's an exaggerated, *ferocious* grin. He leans over the sink, closer to the mirror, and studies his bared teeth with unnervingly intense interest.

Curtis is disturbed but not surprised by this development. He already knows that one or both of these people are homicidal tooth fetishists.

More disturbing even than the grinning man's obsession with his teeth is the fact that otherwise he appears *entirely normal*. Pudgy, about sixty, with a full head of thick white hair, he might play a grandfather if he were ever in a major motion picture; but he would never be cast as a chainsaw-wielding maniac.

Many of the same folks who say that it's a small world have also said you can't judge a book by its cover, meaning people as well as books, and now they are proved right again.

Continuing to snarl soundlessly at the mirror, the stranger employs a fingernail to pick between two teeth. He examines whatever is now on his finger, frowns, looks closer, and finally flicks the bit of stuff into the sink.

Curtis shudders. His fevered imagination supplies numerous chilling possibilities for what was dislodged from those teeth, all related to the well-known fact that most serial killers are also cannibals.

Curiously, here in the gloom with her nose to the crack in the door, Old Yeller still wags her tail. She hasn't acquired Curtis's dread of this human monster. She seems to have an opinion of her own, to which she stubbornly clings. The boy worries about the reliability of her animal instincts.

The likely cannibal clicks off the sink light, turns, and crosses the bathroom to the small cubicle that contains the toilet. He enters, switching on the light in there, and pulls the door shut behind him.

The boy's mother used to say that a wasted opportunity wasn't just a missed chance, but was a wound to your future. Miss too many opportunities, thus sustaining too many wounds, and you wouldn't have a future at all.

With one killer attending to his bodily functions and the other in the driver's seat of the Windchaser, this is an opportunity that only a disobedient, mother-ignoring boy would fail to take.

Curtis pushes open the bedroom door. *You first, girl.*

Tail wagging, the pooch pads into the bathroom – and straight toward the toilet cubicle.

No, pup, no, no! Out, pup, out!

Maybe the power of Curtis's panic is transmitted to Old Yeller along the psychic wire that links every boy to his dog, but that's unlikely because the two of them have so recently met and therefore are still in the process of becoming a fully simpatico boy-dog unit. More likely, she's gotten a better smell of the cunningly deceptive grandfatherly stranger in the toilet cubicle and now recognizes him for the monster that he is. Whether the psychic wire or a good nose is responsible, she changes direction and pads out of the bathroom into the galley.

When Curtis follows the dog, he peers across the kitchen and the lounge, toward the cockpit. The woman occupies the driver's seat, her attention devoted to the stalled traffic blocking the highway.

Curtis is relieved to see that this co-killer is encumbered by a safety harness that secures her to the command chair. She won't be able to release those restraints and clamber out of the seat in time to block the exit.

Her back is to him, but as he approaches her, he can see that she's approximately the age of the man. Her short-cropped hair glows supernaturally white.

Chastened by her near-disastrous misreading of the grand-fatherly man's character, Old Yeller proceeds waglessly and with caution, past the dining nook, paw by stealthy paw, pussyfooting as silently as any creeping cat.

As the dog arrives at the exit and as Curtis reaches over the dog toward the door handle, the woman senses them. She's snacking on something, and she looks up, chewing, expecting the man, startled to discover a boy and his dog. Surprise freezes her in mid-chew, with her hand halfway to her mouth, and in that hand is a human ear.

Curtis screams, and even when he realizes that the snack in her hand isn't a human ear, after all, but merely a large potato chip, he isn't able to stop screaming. For all he knows, she eats potato chips *with* human ears, the way other people eat them with pretzels on the side, or with peanuts, or with sour-cream dip.

Door won't open. Handle won't move. He presses, presses harder. No good. Locked, it must be locked. He rattles it up and down, up and down, insistently, to no effect.

In the driver's seat, the startled woman comes unstartled enough to speak, but the boy can't make out what she's saying because the loud rapping of his jackhammer heart renders meaningless those few words that penetrate his screaming.

Curtis and the door, willpower against matter, on the micro scale where will should win: Yet the lock holds, and still the door doesn't open for him. Magic lock, bolt fused to the striker plate by a sorcerer's spell, it resists his muscle and his mind.

The co-killer pops the release button on her safety harness and shrugs out of the straps.

Oh, Lord, there's just one door, the sucker's magically locked, all his tricks are thwarted, and he's trapped in this claustrophobic rolling slaughterhouse with psychotic retirees who'll eat him with chips and keep his teeth in their nightstand drawer.

Fierce as she has never been before, Old Yeller lunges toward the woman. Snarling, snapping, foaming, spitting, the dog seems to be saying, *Teeth? You want teeth? Take a look at THESE teeth, go fang-to-fang with ME, you psychotic bitch, and see how much you still like teeth when I'M done with you!*

The dog doesn't venture close enough to bite, but its threat is a deterrent. The woman at once abandons the idea of getting up from the driver's seat. She shrinks away from them, and terror twists her face into an ugly knot that is no doubt the same expression she has seen on the faces of the many victims to whom she herself has shown no mercy.

Jerked up and jammed down, the lever handle doesn't release the latch, but pulled inward, it works, revealing that it wasn't locked. No spell had been cast on the mechanism, after all. Curtis's failure to open it sooner wasn't a failure of mind or muscle, but a collapse of reason, the result of runaway fear.

Although the boy is mortified by this discovery, he's also still unable to get a grip on the tossing reins of his panic. He throws the door open, plunges down the steps, and stumbles recklessly onto the blacktop with such momentum that he crashes into the side of a Lexus stopped in the lane adjacent to the motor home.

Face to glass, nose flattened a millimeter short of fracture, he peers into the car as if into an aquarium stocked with strange fish. The fish – actually a man with a buzz cut behind the wheel, a brunette with spiky hair in the passenger's seat – stare back at him with the lidless eyes and the puckered-O mouths that he would have encountered from the finny residents of a real aquarium.

Curtis pushes away from the car and turns just as Old Yeller, no longer barking savagely, leaps out of the motor home. Grinning, wagging her tail, aware that she's the hero of the hour, she turns left and trots away with the spring of pride in her step.

The dog follows the broken white line that defines this lane of stopped traffic from the next, and the boy hurries after the dog. He's no longer screaming, but he's still sufficiently addled by fear to concede leadership temporarily to his brave companion.

He glances back into a blaze of headlights and sees the white-haired woman gazing out and down at him from behind the windshield of the Windchaser. She's half out of her seat, pulling herself up with the steering wheel, the better to see him. From here, she might be mistaken for an innocent and kindly woman – perhaps a librarian, considering that a librarian would know how easily a book of monsters could be disguised as a sweet romance novel with just a switch of the dust jackets.

A whiff of the city has come to this high desert. The warm air is bitter with the stink of exhaust fumes from the idling engines of the vehicles that are backed up from the roadblock.

Some motorists, recognizing the length of the delay ahead of them, have switched off their engines and gotten out of their cars to stretch their legs. Not all have fled the showdown at the truck stop; and as they rub the backs of their necks, roll their shoulders, arch their spines, and crack their knuckles, they ask one another what's-happening-what's-up-what's-this-all-about.

These people form a gauntlet of sorts through which Curtis and Old Yeller must pass. Twisting, dodging, the boy treats them with equal courtesy, although he knows that they may be either ministers or murderers, or murdering ministers, either saints or sinners, bank clerks or bank robbers, humble or arrogant, generous or envious, sane or quite mad. 'Excuse me, sir. Thank you, ma'am. Sorry, sir. Excuse me, ma'am. Excuse me, sir.'

Eventually, Curtis is halted by a tall man with the gray pinched face and permanently engraved wince lines of a long-term sufferer of constipation. Between a Ford van and a red Cadillac, he steps in the boy's way and places a hand on his chest. 'Whoa there, son, what's the matter, where you going?'

'Serial killers,' Curtis gasps, pointing toward the motor home, which is more than twenty vehicles behind him. 'In that Windchaser, they keep body parts in the bedroom.'

Disconcerted, the stranger drops his restraining hand, and his wince lines cut deeper into his lean face as he squints toward the sixteen-ton, motorized house of horrors.

Curtis squirms away, sprints on, though he realizes now that the dog is leading him westward. The roadblock is still a considerable distance ahead, beyond the top of the hill and not yet in sight, but this isn't the direction that they ought to be taking.

Between a Chevy pickup and a Volkswagen, a jolly-looking man with a freckled face and a clown's crop of fiery red hair snares Curtis by the shirt, nearly causing him to skid off his feet. 'Hey, hey, hey! Who're you running from, boy?'

Sensing that this guy won't be rattled by the serial-killer alert – or by much else, for that matter – Curtis resorts to the excuse that Burt Hooper, the waffle-eating trucker in Donella's restaurant, made for him earlier. He isn't sure what it means, but it got him out of trouble before, so he says, 'Sir, I'm not quite right.'

'Hell, that's no surprise to me,' the red-haired man declares, but the tail of Curtis's shirt remains twisted tightly in his fist. 'You steal something, boy?'

No rational person would suppose that a ten-year-old boy would roam the interstate, waiting for a police roadblock to stop traffic and provide an opportunity to steal from motorists. Therefore, Curtis assumes that this freckled interrogator intuits his larcenies dating all the way back to the Hammond house in Colorado. Perhaps this man is psychic and will momentarily receive clairvoyant visions of five-dollar bills and frankfurters filched during Curtis's long flight for freedom.

Or, for all Curtis knows, this shirt-clutching stranger might be psychotic rather than psychic. Loony, mad, insane. There's a lot of that going around. Dressed in sandals and baggy plaid shorts and a T-shirt that proclaims LOVE IS THE ANSWER, with his jolly freckled face, this man doesn't appear to be a lunatic, but so many things in this world aren't what they appear to be, including Curtis himself.

The dog goes straight for the shorts. No bark, no growl, no warning, in fact no evident animosity: Almost playful, she bounds forward, snatches a muzzleful of plaid, and jerks the stranger off his feet. The man cries out and lets go of Curtis, but Old Yeller isn't as quick to release the shorts. She pulls them down his legs, baring his underwear. He kicks at her, but the shorts trammel him; he fails to land a foot in fur, though unintentionally he flings off one of his sandals.

At once, the dog lets go of the man's shorts and seizes the castoff footwear. Grinning around a mouthful of sandal, she sprints westward along the broken white line, flanked by frustrated motorists in their overheating vehicles.

She's still headed in the dead-wrong direction, but Curtis races after Old Yeller because they can't turn back toward the Windchaser, not with so many altercations likely to be rejoined if they do. They can't cross the median strip and attempt to hitchhike east, either, because the traffic whizzing past in that direction will be halted by another roadblock somewhere beyond the truck stop.

Their only hope lies in the vastness of the high desert to the north of the interstate, out there where the black sky and the black land meet, where the sharper facets of quartz-rich rocks reflect the glitter of stars. Rattlesnakes, scorpions, and tarantulas will be more hospitable than the merciless pack of hunters to which the two cowboys had belonged – to which they still belong if they survived the firefight in the restaurant kitchen.

The FBI, the National Security Agency, and other legitimate authorities won't kill Curtis immediately upon identifying him, as will the cowboys and their ilk. Once he's in custody, however, he won't be allowed to go free. Not ever.

Worse: If he's in custody, those vicious hunters who killed his family – and the Hammond family, too – will sooner or later learn his whereabouts. Eventually they will get to him no matter in what deep bunker or high redoubt he's kept, regardless of how many heavily armed bodyguards are assigned to protect him.

Ahead, Old Yeller drops the sandal and turns right, between two stopped vehicles. Curtis follows. The dog lingers on the shoulder of the highway until the boy catches up with her. Then, untroubled by the possibility of capture or snakebite, frisky with the prospect of new terrain and greater excitement, tail raised like a flag, she leads the charge down the gently sloped embankment from the elevated interstate.

If Curtis could trade this particular swell adventure for a raft and a river, he would without hesitation make the swap. Instead, he lights out for the Territory, chasing the clever mutt, hurrying away from the carnival blaze of blockaded traffic and across a gradually rising wasteland of sand, scrub, shale. Weathered stone sentinels loom like the Injuns who probably stood here to watch wagon trains full of nervous settlers wending westward when the interstate had been defined not by pavement and signposts but by nothing more than landmarks, broken wagon wheels of previous failed expeditions, and the scattered bones of men and horses stripped of flesh by vultures, vermin. Curtis and Old Yeller go now where both the brave and the foolish have gone before them, in ages past: boy and dog, dog and boy, with the moon retiring behind blankets of clouds in the west and the sun still fast abed in the east, sister-becoming and her devoted brother racing north through the desert darkness, into darkness deeper still.

23

In the armchair, Noah Farrel talked past the point where he bothered to listen to himself anymore, and he kept talking until he was wrung dry of words.

On the bed, so still that the chenille spread was undisturbed, Laura remained cataleptic, curled in the fetal position. Wordless throughout her brother's monologue, she remained mute now.

This exhausted silence was the closest thing that Noah knew to peace. A few times in the past, he had in fact dozed off in this chair. The only dreamless sleep he ever experienced was the silken repose that overcame him after words had failed, after he could do nothing but share the silence of his sister.

Perhaps peace came only with acceptance.

Acceptance, however, seemed too much like resignation. Even on those evenings when he napped in the armchair, he woke with guilt reborn, his sense of injustice not worn away by dreamless rest but sharpened on the whetstone of sleep.

He had a bone to chew with Fate, and he gnawed at it even though he knew that of the two of them, Fate possessed the sharper teeth, the stronger jaws.

This evening, he didn't doze, and after a while his mind began to brim once more with unwanted thoughts. Words threatened to spill from him again, but this time they were likely to come in the form of rants of anger, self-loathing, self-pity. If *these* words filtered through the prison of the damaged brain in which Laura served her life sentence, that inner darkness wouldn't be brightened by them.

He went to the bed, leaned down to his sister, and kissed her damp cheek. If he had asked for water and had been given vinegar, it couldn't have tasted more bitter than her slow steady tears.

In the hallway, he encountered a nurse pushing a stainless-steel serving cart: a petite raven-haired brunette with the pink complexion and the twinkling blue eyes of a Nordic blonde. In her crisp white-and-peach uniform, she was as perky as a parakeet on Dexedrine. Her infectious smile might have cultured one in Noah if the dispiriting visit with Laura hadn't inoculated him against smiling for a while.

Her name was Wendy Quail. New to the staff. He'd only met her once before, but he had a cop's memory for names.

'Bad?' she asked, glancing toward Laura's room.

'Bad enough,' he admitted.

'She's been blue all day,' said Wendy Quail.

The word *blue* was so absurdly inadequate to describe the depths of Laura's misery that Noah almost managed a laugh even though a smile had eluded him. Oh, but it would have been a humorless bark of a laugh that might make this earnest little nurse want to jump off a bridge, so he held it back and simply nodded.

Wendy sighed. 'We all have our plights and pickles.'

'Our what?'

'Plights and pickles. Troubles. Some of us get 'em served one at a time on a little plate, and some of us get full servings of 'em on bigger plates, but your poor sweet sister, she got hers heaped high on a platter.'

Thinking about plates and platters of plights and pickles, Noah risked an even more inappropriate laugh than the one he'd suppressed.

'But all the troubles in the world,' said Wendy, 'have the same one answer.'

Although he could never again wear a badge, Noah carried in his mind a cop's rope of suspicion, which he now tied in a hangman's knot. 'What answer?' he asked, recalling the Circle of Friends thug with the snake tattoo on his arm and the platitude on his T-shirt.

'Ice cream, of course!' With a flourish, she plucked the lid off the insulated rectangular serving pan that stood on the cart.

Inside the server were vanilla ice-cream sundaes with chocolate sauce, toasted coconut, and crowning maraschino cherries. Wendy was bringing a bedtime treat to her trouble-plagued wards.

Recognizing the sudden hardness in Noah's demeanor, she said, 'What did you think I was going to say?'

'Love. I thought you would say love is the answer.'

Her sweet gamine face wasn't designed for ironic smiles, but she tricked one out of it anyway. 'Judging by the men I've fallen for, ice cream beats love every time.'

Finally he smiled.

'Will Laura want a sundae?' she asked.

'She's not in any condition to feed herself right now. Maybe if I helped her into in a chair and fed her myself—'

'No, no, Mr. Farrel. I'll distribute the rest of these and then see if she wants the last one. I'll feed her if I can. I love taking care of her. Taking care of all these special people . . . that's my ice cream.'

Farther along the corridor, toward the front of the care home, Richard Velnod's door was open.

Rickster, liberator of ladybugs and mice, stood in the middle of his room, in bright yellow pajamas, savoring his ice cream while gazing out the window.

'Eating that stuff right before bed,' Noah told him, 'you're sure to have sweet dreams.'

Rickster's slightly slurred voice was further numbed by the cold treat: 'You know what's a really good thing? Sundays on Wednesday.'

At first Noah didn't get it.

'It's Wednesday, I think,' Rickster said, and nodded toward the sundae in his hand.

'Oh. Yeah. Nice things when you don't expect them. That makes them even better. You're right. Here's to Sundaes on Wednesdays.'

'You turning yourself loose?' Rickster asked.

'Yeah. Yeah, I'm leaving.'

With only a wistful expression, Rickster said that being able to turn yourself loose, whenever you wanted to go, was a really good thing, too, better even than Sundaes on Wednesday.

Outside the Haven of the Lonesome and the Long Forgotten, under trellises draped with bougainvillea, Noah took deep breaths of the warm night air. On the way to his car – another rustbucket Chevy – he tried to settle his nerves.

The suspicion he'd directed at Wendy Quail had been misplaced.

Laura was safe.

In the days ahead, if any of Congressman Sharmer's Circle of Friends couldn't resist a little payback, they would come for Noah, not for his sister. Jonathan Sharmer was a thug wrapped in the robes of compassion and fairness that were the costume of preference among politicians, but he was still reliably a thug. And one of the few rules by which the criminal class lived – not counting the more psychotic street gangs – was the injunction against settling grudges by committing violence on family members who weren't in the business. Wives and children were untouchable. And sisters.

The rattletrap engine turned over on the first try. The other car had always needed coaxing. The hand-brake release worked smoothly, the gear shift didn't stick much, and the clatter-creak of the aged frame and body wasn't loud enough to interfere with conversation, supposing that he'd had anyone to talk to other than himself. Hell, it was like driving a Mercedes-Benz.

24

Brushing without toothpaste is poor dental maintenance, but the flavor of a bedtime cocktail isn't enhanced by a residue of Pepsodent.

After a mintless scrubbing of her teeth, Micky retreated to her tiny bedroom, which she'd already stocked with a plastic tumbler and an ice bucket. In the bottom drawer of her small dresser, she kept a supply of cheap lemon-flavored vodka.

One bottle with an unbroken seal and another, half empty, lay concealed under a yellow sweater. Micky wasn't hiding the booze from Geneva; her aunt knew that she enjoyed a drink before bed – and that she usually had one whether or not she enjoyed it.

Micky kept the vodka under the sweater because she didn't want to see it each time that she opened the drawer in search of something else. The sight of this stash, when she wasn't immediately in need of it, had the power to dispirit her, and even to stir a heart-darkening cloud from a sediment of shame.

Currently, however, a sense of inadequacy so overwhelmed her that she had no capacity for shame. In this chill of helplessness, familiar to her since childhood, an icy resentment sometimes formed, and from it she often generated a blinding blizzard of anger that isolated her from other people, from life, from all hope.

To avoid brooding too much about her impotence in the matter of Leilani Klonk, Micky loaded the tumbler with two shots of anesthesia, over ice. She promised herself at least a second round of the same gauge, with the hope that these double-barreled blasts would blow her into sleep before helplessness bred anger, because inevitably anger left her tossing sleepless in the sheets.

She had been drunk only once since moving in with Geneva a week ago. In fact she'd gotten through two of these seven days without any alcohol whatsoever. She wouldn't get sloppy tonight, just numb enough to stop caring about helpless girls – the one next door and the one that she herself had been not many years ago.

After stripping down to panties and a tank top, she sat in bed, atop the sheets, sipping cold lemon vodka in the warm darkness.

At the open window, the night lay breathless.

From the freeway arose the drone of traffic, ceaseless at any hour. This was a less romantic sound than the rush and rumble of the trains to which she had listened on many other nights.

Nonetheless, she could imagine that the people passing on the highway were in some cases traveling from one point of contentment to another, even from happiness to happiness, in lives with meaning, purpose, satisfaction. Certainly not all of them. Maybe not most of them. But *some* of them.

For bleak periods of her life, she'd been unable to entertain enough optimism to believe anyone might be truly happy, anywhere, anytime. Geneva said this newfound fragile hopefulness represented progress, and Micky wished this would prove true; but she might be setting herself up for disappointment. Faith in the basic rightness of the world, in the existence of meaning, required courage, because with it came the need to take responsibility for your actions – and because every act of caring exposed the heart to a potential wound.

The soft knock wasn't opportunity, but Micky said, 'Come in.'

Geneva left the door half open behind her. She sat on the edge of the bed, sideways to her niece.

The dim glow of the hallway ceiling fixture barely invaded the room. The shadows negotiated with the light instead of retreating from it.

Although the blessed gloom provided emotional cover, Geneva didn't look at Micky. She stared at the bottle on the dresser.

That piece of furniture and all else upon it remained shadowy shapes, but the bottle had a strange attraction for light, and the vodka glimmered like quicksilver.

Eventually, Geneva asked, 'What are we going to do?'

'I don't know.'

'Neither do I. But we can't just do nothing.'

'No, we can't. I've got to think.'

'I try,' Geneva said, 'but my mind spins around it till I feel like something inside my head's going to fly loose. She's so sweet.'

'She's tough, too. She knows what she can handle.'

'Oh, little mouse, what's wrong with me that I let the child go back there?'

Geneva hadn't said 'little mouse' in fifteen years or longer.

When Micky heard this pet name, her throat tightened so much that a swallow of lemony vodka seemed to thicken as she drank it. Crisp in her mouth, it became an astringent syrup as it went down.

She wasn't sure that she could speak, but after a hesitation, she found her voice: 'They'd have come for her, Aunt Gen. There's nothing we can do tonight.'

'It's true, isn't it, all that crazy stuff she told us? It's not like me and Alec Baldwin in New Orleans.'

'It's true, all right.'

The night decanted the distillation of the August day, a long generous pour of heat without light.

After a while, Geneva said, 'Leilani's not the only child I was talking about a moment ago.'

'I know.'

'Some things were said tonight, some other things suggested.'

'I wish you'd never heard them.'

'I wish I'd heard them back when I could've helped you.'

'That was all a long time ago, Aunt Gen.'

The drone of traffic now seemed like the muffled buzzing of insects, as though the interior of the earth were one great hive, crowded to capacity with a busy horde that at any moment would break through the surface and fill the air with angry wings.

'I've seen your mother go through a lot of men over the years. She's always been so . . . *restless*. I knew it wasn't a good atmosphere.'

'Let it go, Aunt Gen. I have.'

'But you haven't. You haven't let it go at all.'

'Okay, maybe not.' A dry sour laugh escaped her as she said, 'But I sure have done my best to *wash* it away,' and with vodka she tried but failed to rinse the taste of that admission from her mouth.

'Some of your mother's boyfriends . . .'

Only Aunt Gen, last of the innocents, would call them *boyfriends* – those predators, pariahs proud of their rejection of all values and obligations, motivated by the pure self-interest of parasites to whom the blood of others was the staff of life.

'I knew they were faithless, shiftless,' Geneva continued.

'Mama likes bad boys.'

'But I never dreamed that one of them would . . . that you . . .'

Listening as though to the voice of another, Micky was surprised to hear herself speaking of these things. Before Leilani, revelation had been impossible. Now it was merely excruciating. 'It wasn't just one bastard. Mom drew the type . . . not all of them, but more than one . . . and they could always smell the opportunity.'

Geneva leaned forward on the edge of the bed, shoulders hunched, as though she were on a pew, seeking a bench for her knees.

'They just looked at me,' Micky said, 'and smelled the chance. If I saw this certain smile, then I knew *they* knew what the situation was. Me scared and Mama willing not to see. The smile . . . not a wicked smile, either, like you might expect, but a half-sad smile, as if it was going to be too easy and they preferred when it wasn't easy.'

'She couldn't have known,' Geneva said, but those four words were more of a question than they were a confident assessment.

'I told her more than once. She punished me for lying. But she knew it was all true.'

Fingertips steepled toward the bridge of her nose, Geneva half hid her face in a prayer clasp, as if the shadows didn't provide enough concealment, as if she were whispering a confession into the private chapel of her cupped hands.

Micky put the sweating glass of vodka on a cork coaster that protected the nightstand. 'She valued her men more than she valued me. She always got tired of them sooner or later, and she always knew she would, sooner or later. Yet right up until the minute she decided she needed a change, until she threw each of the bastards out, she cared about me less than him, and me less than the new bastard who was coming in.'

'When did it stop – or did it ever?' Geneva asked. Her softly spoken question reverberated hollowly through the serried arches of her steepled fingers.

'When I wasn't scared anymore. When I was big enough and angry enough to *make* it stop.' Micky's hands were cold and moist from the condensation on the glass. She blotted her palms against the sheets. 'I was almost twelve when it ended.'

'I never realized,' Geneva said miserably. 'Never. I never suspected.'

'I know you didn't, Aunt Gen. I know.'

Geneva's voice wavered on *God* and broke on *fool*: 'Oh, God, what a blind stupid worthless fool I was.'

Micky swung her legs over the side of the bed, slid next to her aunt, and put an arm around her shoulders. 'No, honey. Never you, none of that. You were just a good woman, too good and far too kind to imagine such a thing.'

'Being naive is no damn excuse.' Geneva trembled. She lowered her hands from her face, wringing them so hard that in a spirit of repentance, she must have wanted to fire up the pain in her arthritic knuckles. 'Maybe I was stupid because I wanted to be stupid.'

'Listen, Aunt Gen, one of the things that kept me from going nuts all those years was you, just the way you are.'

'Not me, not bat-blind Geneva.'

'Because of you, I knew there were decent people in the world, not just the garbage my mother hung with.' Micky tried to keep her wetter emotions bottled in the cellar of her heart, safe storage that she'd successfully maintained until recently, but now the cork was pulled and apparently lost. Her vision blurred, and she heard vintage feeling wash through her words. 'I could hope . . . one day I might be decent, too. Decent like you.'

Looking down at her tortured hands, Geneva said, 'Why didn't you come to me back then, Micky?'

'Fear. Shame. I felt dirty.'

'And all these years of silence since then.'

'Not fear anymore. But . . . most days I still don't feel clean.'

'Sweetie, you're a victim, you've nothing to be ashamed about.'

'But it's there, just the same. And I think maybe . . . I was afraid if I ever talked about it, I might let go of the anger. Anger's kept me going all my life, Aunt Gen. If I let it go, what do I have then?'

'Peace,' said Geneva. She raised her head and at last made eye contact. 'Peace, and God knows you deserve it.'

Micky closed her eyes against the sight of her aunt's perfect and unconditional love, which brought her to a high cliff of emotion so steep that it scared her, and a sea of long-forbidden sentiments breaking below.

Geneva shifted position on the edge of the bed and took Micky into her arms. The great warmth of her voice was even more consoling than her embrace: 'Little mouse, you were so quick, so bright, so sweet, so full of *life*. And you still are everything you were then. None of it's lost forever. All that promise, all that hope, that love and goodness – it's still inside you. No one can take the gifts God gave you. Only you can throw them away, little mouse. Only you.'

∾ ∾ ∾

Later, after Aunt Gen had gone to her room, when Micky sat back once more upon the pillows piled against her headboard, everything had changed, and nothing had changed.

The August heat. The breathless dark. The far-bound traffic on the freeway. Leilani under her mother's roof, and her brother in a lonely grave in some Montana forest.

What had changed was hope: the hope of change, which had seemed impossible to her only yesterday, but which seemed only impossibly difficult now.

She had spoken to Geneva of things she'd never expected to speak of to anyone, and she'd found relief in revelation. For a while, in the grip of the thorny bramble that had for so long encircled it, her heart beat with less pain than usual, but the thorns still pierced her, each a terrible memory that she could never pluck free.

Drinking the melted ice in the plastic tumbler, she swore off the second double shot of vodka that earlier she'd promised herself. She couldn't as easily swear off self-destructive anger and shame, but it seemed an achievable goal to give up booze without a Twelve Step program.

She wasn't an alcoholic, after all. She didn't drink or feel the need to drink every day. Stress and self-loathing were the two bartenders who served her, and right now she felt freer of both than she'd been in years.

Hope, however, isn't all that's needed to achieve change. Hope is a hand extended, but two hands are required to be pulled out of a deep hole. The second hand was faith – the faith that her hope would be borne out; and although her hope had grown stronger, perhaps her faith had not.

No job. No prospects. No money in the bank. An '81 Camaro that still somewhat resembled a thoroughbred but performed like a worn-out plow horse.

Leilani in the house of Sinsemilla. Leilani limping ever closer to a bomb-clock birthday, ticking toward ten. One boy with Tinkertoy hips put together with monkey logic, thrown down into a lonely grave, spadefuls of raw earth cast into his eternally surprise-filled eyes, into his small mouth open in a last cry for mercy, and his body by now reduced to deformed bones . . .

Micky didn't quite realize that she was getting out of bed to pour another double shot until she was at the dresser, dropping ice cubes in the glass. After uncapping the vodka, she hesitated before pouring. But then she poured.

Courage would be required to stand up for Leilani, but Micky didn't deceive herself into thinking that she would find courage in a bottle. To form a strategy and to follow through successfully with it, she would need to be shrewd, but she was not self-deluded enough to think that vodka would make her more astute.

Instead, she told herself that now more than ever, she needed her anger, because it was her fiery wrath that tempered her and made her tough, that ensured her survival, that motivated. Drink often fueled her anger, and so she drank now in the service of Leilani.

Later, when she poured a third portion of vodka more generous than either of the previous rounds, she braced herself with the same lie once more. This wasn't really vodka for Micky. This was anger for Leilani, a necessary step toward winning freedom for the girl.

At least she knew the excuse was a lie. She supposed that her inability to fully deceive herself might eventually be her salvation. Or damnation.

The heat. The dark. From time to time the wet rattle of melting ice shifting in the bucket. And without cease, the hum of traffic on the freeway, engines stroking and tires turning: an ever-approaching burr that might be the sound of hope, but also ever receding.

25

Some days Sinsemilla stank like cabbage stew. Other days she drifted in clouds of attar of roses. Monday, she might smell like oranges; Tuesday, like St.-John's-wort and celery root; Wednesday, faintly like zinc and powdered copper; Thursday, like fruitcake, which seemed to Leilani to be the most appropriate of all her mother's fragrances.

Old Sinsemilla was a devoted practitioner of aromatherapy and a believer in purging toxins through reverse osmosis in a properly formulated hot bath. She traveled with such a spectacular omnium-gatherum of bath additives that any citizen of medieval times would have recognized her at once as an alchemist or sorcerer. Extracts, elixirs, spirits, oils, essences, quintessences, florescences, salts, concentrates, and distillations filled a glittery collection of vials and charming ornate bottles fitted in two custom-designed carrying cases, each as large as a Samsonite two-suiter, and both bags now stood bursting with potential in this rank, mildew-riddled bathroom.

Leilani knew that many intelligent, well-balanced, responsible, and especially good-smelling people practiced aromatherapy and toxin purging. Yet she shied from using the bath seasonings for the same reason that she didn't participate in *any* of her mother's eccentric interests or activities, even when some of them appeared to be fun. She feared that a single indulgence in the pleasures of Sinsemilla – for example, a luxurious bath infused with coconut oil and distilled essence of cocoa butter – would be the first step on a slippery slope of addiction and insanity. Regardless of who her father might have been, Klonk or not Klonk, she was undeniably her mother's daughter; therefore, her genes might be her destiny if she wasn't careful.

Besides, Leilani didn't *want* to purge herself of all her toxins. She was comfortable with her toxins. Her toxins, accumulated through more than nine years of living, were an integral part of her, perhaps more important to the definition of who she was than medical science yet realized. What if she purged herself of every particle of toxic substances and then woke up one morning to discover that she wasn't Leilani anymore, that she was the pope or maybe some pure and saintly girl named Hortense? She didn't have anything against the pope or saintly girls named Hortense, but more than not, she *liked* herself, warts and all, including grotesque appendages and strange nodules on the brain – so she would just have to remain *saturated* with toxins.

Instead of a bath, she took a shower. Her soap of choice – a cake of Ivory – worked well enough to scrub the snake ichor from her hands, to sluice away the sweat of the day, and to remove every trace of the salty tears that offended her more than oozing serpent guts.

Mutants do not cry. In particular, dangerous mutants. She had an image to protect.

Usually, she avoided the shower and soaked in the tub – though with nothing more fragrant than Ivory soap and sometimes with an imaginary sumo wrestler and professional assassin named Kato, with whom she devised elaborate acts of revenge on her mother and on Dr. Doom. This night, in spite of what Sinsemilla had done, Leilani wasn't in the mood to conjure up Kato.

The shower wasn't as safe as the tub. Whenever she took off her leg brace, she was hesitant to risk standing on a slippery surface.

As now, however, she sometimes showered without removing the brace. Afterward, she'd have to towel it well and use a hair dryer on the joints, but an occasional drenching wouldn't hurt it.

The grim device wasn't a standard orthopedic knee brace; those were mostly designed from formed plastic, leather straps, and elastic belts. Leilani liked to believe that this contraption had a nicely ominous, killer-cyborg quality. Made of steel, hard black rubber, and foam padding, it provided to her some of the style and sexy allure of a robot hunter who had been constructed in a laboratory in the future and sent back in time by an evil machine intelligence to track down and destroy the mother of its most effective human enemy.

After blow-drying her hair and her leg brace, the young killer cyborg wiped the steam off the mirror and studied her torso. No boobs yet. She hadn't expected any dramatic change, just perhaps vague swellings, like an attractively aligned pair of mosquito bites.

A month ago, she had read a magazine article about enlarging your breasts through the power of positive thinking. Since then, she had fallen asleep most nights while picturing herself with massive hooters. The author of the article was probably full of beans, but Leilani figured she'd sleep better if she dozed off while positively thinking herself into a C-cup instead of brooding about all the many problems in her life, which she could dwell on if she ever wanted to explore the power of *negative* thinking.

Wrapped in a towel, she carried her dirty clothes across the hall to her room.

All was quiet in the kingdom of Cleopatra. No throb of camera flash. No declaiming in a phony Old English accent.

Leilani dressed in a pair of summer-weight cotton pajamas. Midnight-blue shorts and matching short-sleeved top. On the back of the shirt, a cool yellow-and-red logo said ROSWELL, NEW MEXICO. On the front, the word STARCHILD was emblazoned in two-inch red letters.

She'd seen the pajamas on the recent tour through the saucer sites of New Mexico, and it had seemed to her that acting silly-kid excited about them would help convince Dr. Doom that she continued to believe his cockamamie story about Luki being levitated to the mother ship. *The aliens sometimes abduct people right out of bed, Preston. You told us stories like that. Well, gee, then for sure if I'm wearing these jammies, they'll know I'm ready to go, I'm pumped, I'm psyched. Maybe they'll beam me up before my birthday, bring me and Luki back together, with a new leg and new hand for the party!*

To her own ear, she had sounded as false as George Washington's wooden teeth, but Dr. Doom had heard only sincerity. He didn't know squat about kids, didn't care to learn, and he expected them to be excitable and shallow and, in general, dorky to the max.

He always bought her what she requested – the pajamas were no exception – probably because these gifts made him feel better about scheming to kill her. Leilani seldom asked for more than paperback books. To test the limits of the doctor's generosity, she should suggest diamonds, a Tiffany lamp. No matter how ingenuously she phrased the request, asking for a shotgun would probably alarm him.

Now, boldly identified as a starchild, virtually *daring* the ETs to come and get her, she picked up the first-aid kit from her dresser and returned to her mother's room.

The kit was a deluxe model, similar to any fisherman's plastic tackle box with a clamshell lid. Dr. Doom wasn't a medical doctor, but as a seasoned motor-home enthusiast, he understood the need to be prepared for minor injuries while on the road. And because Leilani understood her mother's penchant for mishap and calamity, she had added supplies to the basic kit. She kept it always near at hand.

Red blouses still draped the lamps. The scarlet light no longer fostered a brothel atmosphere; in view of recent events in this room, the feeling was now palace-of-the-Martian-king, creepy and surreal.

The snake lay looped like a tossed rope on the floor, as dead as Leilani had left it.

Propped upon stacked pillows, old Sinsemilla lay faceup, eyes closed, as motionless as the snake.

Leilani had needed the shower, the change of clothes, and time to gather the raveled ends of herself before she had been able to return here. She hadn't been Leilani Klonk when she hurried from this room. She'd been a frightened, angry, and humiliated girl, panicked into flight. She would not ever be that person again. Never. The real Leilani was back – rested, refreshed, ready to take care of business.

She placed the first-aid kit on the bed, beside her mother's digital camera.

Sinsemilla snored softly. Having crashed from her chemical high, she was planted deeper than sleep, though not as deep as coma. She'd probably lie limp and unresponsive until late morning.

Leilani timed her mother's pulse. Regular but fast. Metabolism racing to rid the body of drugs.

Although the serpent hadn't been poisonous, the bite looked wicked. The punctures were small. No blood flowed now, but much of the surrounding soft tissue was blue-black. Probably just bruises.

Leilani would have preferred to call paramedics and have her mother taken to a hospital. Sinsemilla would then, of course, be mad-dog furious for having been subjected to university-trained doctors and Western medicine, which she despised. When she returned home, she would launch a campaign of hectoring recriminations that would last hours, days, until you prayed to go deaf and considered cutting off your ears with an electric carving knife just to change the subject.

Besides, if Sinsemilla flipped out when she woke up and found herself in a hospital, her performance might earn a transfer to the psychiatric ward.

Then Leilani would be alone with Dr. Doom.

He wasn't a diddler. She'd told Micky the truth about that.

He did kill people, however, and though he wasn't a hotheaded homicidal maniac, though he was a comparatively genteel murderer, you nevertheless didn't want to be alone with him any more than you would want to be alone with Charles Manson and a chain saw.

Anyway, when the doctors learned Sinsemilla was the wife of *that* Preston Claudius Maddoc, the chances of their transferring her to a head-case ward would diminish to zero. They might send her home in a stretch limousine, perhaps with a complementary heroin lollipop.

In most cases, these circumstances – drug-soaked psycho mother, dead snake, traumatized young mutant girl – would mobilize government social workers to consider placing Leilani temporarily in foster care. Already separated from Luki forever, she would be willing to risk a foster home, but this wouldn't be handled like an ordinary case, and she wouldn't be given that opportunity.

Preston Claudius Maddoc wasn't an ordinary mortal. If anyone attempted to take his stepdaughter from him, powerful forces would spring to his defense. Like most district attorneys and police coast to coast, local authorities would probably decline to do battle with him. Short of being caught on video in the act of blowing someone's brains out, Preston Maddoc was untouchable.

Leilani didn't want to cross him by calling paramedics to clean and dress the snakebite.

If he began to think she was a troublemaker, he might decide to prepare a nice dirt bed for her, like the one he'd made for Lukipela, and put her to sleep in it immediately, instead of waiting any longer for the extraterrestrials to show up. Then for Sinsemilla's delight, the doom doctor would concoct a heartwarming story about a twinkly cute spaceship, smartly tailored alien diplomats from the Parliament of Planets, and Leilani waving goodbye with an American flag in one hand and a Fourth of July sparkler in the other as she ascended in a pale green levitation beam.

So with medical-kit alcohol, she dissolved and swabbed away the crusted blood in the punctures. She applied hydrogen per-oxide, too, which churned up a bloody foam. Then she worked sulfacetamide powder into the wounds with a small syringelike applicator.

A few times, Sinsemilla whimpered or groaned, although she never woke or attempted to pull away from Leilani.

If the fangs had reached the bone, infection would most likely develop regardless of these simple efforts to flush the wounds with antiseptics. Then, Sinsemilla might feel differently about seeing a university-trained doctor.

Meanwhile, Leilani did the best that she could with the skills she had and with the materials at her disposal. After using dabs of Neosporin to seal the sulfacetamide in the punctures, she bandaged the wound to keep it clean.

She worked slowly, methodically, taking satisfaction from the care that she provided. In spite of the Martian light and the dead snake, there was a peaceful quality to the moment that she savored for its rarity.

Even disheveled, in the dirty rumpled full-length slip with its squashed and filthy flounce, Sinsemilla was beautiful. She might indeed have been a princess once, in a previous incar-nation, during another life when she'd not been so confused and sad.

This was nice. Quiet. Placing a nonstick cotton pad over the punc-tures. Opening a roll of two-inch-wide gauze bandage. Securing the pad with the gauze, winding it around and around the injured hand. Finishing it with two strips of waterproof tape. Nice. This tender, quiet caregiving was almost a normal mother-daughter moment. It didn't matter that their roles were reversed, that the daughter was providing the mothering. Only the normality mattered. The peace. Here, now, Leilani was overcome with a pleasant if melancholy sense of what might have been – but never would be.

26

At the top of the slope, dog and boy – one panting, one gasping – halt and turn to look back toward the highway, which lies a third of a mile to the south.

If Curtis had just finished a plate of dirt for dinner, his tongue could not have felt grainier than it did now, and the plaque of dust gritting between his teeth could not have been more vile. He is unable to work up enough saliva to spit out a foul alkaline taste. Having been raised for a time on the edge of a desert more forbidding than this one, he knows that sprinting flat-out through such terrain in twenty-percent humidity, even long after sundown, is extremely debilitating. They have hardly begun to run, and already he feels parched.

On the bosom of the dark plain below, a half-mile necklace of stopped traffic, continually growing longer, twinkles diamond-bright and ruby-red. From this elevation, he can see the interdiction point to the southwest. The westbound lanes are blocked by police vehicles that form a gate, and traffic is being funneled down from three lanes to one.

North of the highway, near the roadblock, the large, armored, and perhaps armed helicopter stands in open land. The rotors aren't turning, but evidently the engines are running, since the interior is softly illuminated. From the open double-bay doors in the chopper's fuselage, sufficient light escapes to reveal men gathered alongside the craft. At this distance, it's impossible to discern whether these are additional SWAT-team units or uni-formed troops.

With a *Grrrrrrrr*, spoken and thought, Old Yeller draws Curtis's attention away from the chopper in the west to action in the east.

Two big SUVs, modified for police use, with racks of rotating red and blue emergency beacons on their roofs, sirens silent, are departing the interstate. They descend the gently sloped embankment and proceed westward across open terrain, paralleling but bypassing the halted traffic on the highway.

Curtis assumes they will continue past him, all the way to the roadblock. Instead, they slow to a stop at a point where a group of people apparently waits for them on the embankment approximately due south of him.

He hadn't noticed this gathering of tiny figures before: Eight or ten motorists have descended part of the slope from the highway. Three have flashlights, which they've used to flag down the SUVs.

Above this group, on the interstate, a larger crowd – forty or fifty strong – has formed along the shoulder, watching the activity below. They have assembled just west of the Windchaser owned by the psychotic teeth collectors.

Alerted by Curtis's warning as he'd fled the motor home, maybe other motorists investigated the Windchaser. Having found the grisly souvenirs, they have made a citizens' arrest of the geriatric serial killers and are holding them for justice.

Or maybe not.

From the roadblock, vehicle to vehicle, word might have filtered back to the effect that the authorities are searching for a young boy and a harlequin dog. A motorist – the jolly freckled man with the mop of red hair and one sandal, or perhaps the murderous retirees in the Windchaser – could then have used a cell phone or an in-car computer to report that the fugitive pair had only minutes ago created a scene on the interstate before fleeing north into the wildland.

Below, the three flashlights swivel in unison and point due north. Toward Curtis.

He's at too great a distance for those beams to expose him. And in the absence of a moon, although he stands on the ridge line, the sky is too dark to reveal him in silhouette.

Nevertheless, instinctively he crouches when the lights point toward him, making himself no taller than one of the scattered clumps of sagebrush that stipple the landscape. He puts one hand on the back of the dog's neck. Together they wait, alert.

The scale of these events and the rapidity with which they are unfolding allow for no measurable effect of willpower. Yet Curtis wishes with all his might that what appears to be happening between the motorists and the law-enforcement officers in those two SUVs is not happening. He wishes they would just continue westward, along the base of the highway embankment, until they reach the helicopter. He pictures this in his mind, envisions it vividly, and wishes, wishes, wishes.

If wishes were fishes, no hooks would be needed, no line and no rod, no reel and no patience. But wishes are merely wishes, swimming only the waters of the mind, and now one of the SUVs guns its engine, swings north, drives maybe twenty feet deeper into the desert, and brakes to a halt, facing toward Curtis.

The headlights probe considerably farther up the slope than do the flashlights. But they still reach far less than halfway toward Curtis and Old Yeller.

On the roof of the SUV, a searchlight suddenly blazes, so powerful and so tightly focused that it appears to have the substance of a sword. Motorized, the lamp moves, and each time the slicing beam finds sagebrush or a gnarled spray of withered weeds, it cuts loose twisted shadows that leap into the night. Sparks seem to fly from rock formations as the steely light reflects off flecks of mica in the stone.

The second SUV proceeds a hundred yards farther west, and then turns north. A searchlight flares on the roof, stabbing out from the jeweled hilt of red and blue emergency beacons.

Paralleling each other, these two vehicles move north, toward Curtis. They grind along slowly, sweeping the landscape ahead of them with light, hoping to spot an obviously trampled clump of weeds or deep footprints where table stone gives way to a swale of soft sand.

Sooner rather than later, they are likely to find the spoor they seek. Then they will pick up speed.

The officers in the SUVs are operating under the aegis of one legitimate law-enforcement agency or another, and they most likely are who they appear to be. There's always the chance, however, that they might instead be more of the ferocious killers who struck in Colorado and who have pursued Curtis ever since.

Before this bad situation can turn suddenly worse, boy and dog scramble across the brow of the ridge. Ahead, the land slopes down toward dark and arid realms.

Relinquishing leadership to Old Yeller, he follows her, although not as fast as she would like to lead. He skids and nearly falls on a cascade of loose shale, thrashes through an unseen cluster of knee-high sage, is snared on a low cactus, crying out involuntarily as the sharp spines prickle through the sock on his right foot and tattoo a pattern of pain on his ankle – all because he doesn't always proceed exactly in the dog's wake, but at times ranges to the left and right of her.

Trust. They are bonding: He has no doubt that their relationship is growing deeper by the day, better by the hour. Yet they are still becoming what they eventually will be to each other, not yet entirely synchronized spirit to spirit. Curtis is reluctant to commit blindly and headlong to his companion's lead until they have achieved total synergism.

Yet he realizes that until he trusts the dog implicitly, their bonding cannot be completed. Until then, they will be a boy and his dog, a dog and her boy, which is a grand thing, beautiful and true, but not as fine a relationship as that of the cross-species siblings they could become, brother and sister of the heart.

Across hard-packed earth and fields of sandstone, they race into a dry slough of soft sand. The surefooted dog at once adapts to this abrupt change in the terrain, but because Curtis is not fully attuned to his sister-becoming, he blunders after her into the waterless bog without adjusting his pace or step. He sinks to his ankles, is thrown off-balance, and topples forward, imprinting his face in the sand, fortunately quick-thinking enough to close his eyes and his mouth before making a solid but graceless impact.

Raising his face out of its concave image, snorting sand out of his nostrils, blowing a silicate frosting off his lips, blinking grains from his eyelashes, Curtis pushes up onto his knees. If his mother's spirit abides with him now, she is laughing, worried, and frustrated all at once.

Old Yeller returns to him. He thinks she's offering the usual doggy commiseration, maybe laughing at him a little, too, but then he realizes that her attention is elsewhere.

The moonless darkness baffles, but the dog is close enough for Curtis to see that she's interested in the top of the hill that they recently crossed. Raising her snout, she seeks scents that he can't apprehend. She clenches her muzzle to stop panting, pricks her ears toward whatever sound engages her.

A flux of light throbs through the air beyond the ridge line: the moving searchlight beams reflecting off the pale stone and soil as the SUVs ascend the slope.

Although Curtis can't prick his ears – one of the drawbacks of being Curtis Hammond instead of being Old Yeller – he follows the dog's example and holds his breath, the better to detect whatever noise caught her attention. At first he hears only the grumble of the SUVs . . . . Then, in the distance, a flutter of sound arises, faint but unmistakable: helicopter rotors beating the thin desert air.

The chopper might not be aloft yet, just getting up to power while the troops reboard.

Whether already airborne or not, it will be coming. Soon. And if the craft itself doesn't possess the latest electronic search-and-locate gear, the troops will. Darkness won't thwart them. They have special ways of seeing that make the night as penetrable as daylight.

Trust. Curtis has no choice now but to put his full faith in the dog. If they are to be free, they will be free only together. Whether they live or die, they will live or die as one. His destiny is hers, and her fate is inseparably twined with his. If she leads him out of this danger or if she leads him off the edge of a high cliff, so be it; even in his dying fall, he will love her, his sister-becoming.

A little moonlight nevertheless would be welcome. Rising out of the distant mountains, great wings of black clouds span the western sky, and continue to unfurl in this direction, as though a vault deep in the earth has cracked open to release a terrible presence that is spreading its dominion over all the world. A generous seasoning of stars salts the clear part of the sky, but still the desert steadily darkles, minute by minute, deeper than mere night.

He hears his mother's voice in his mind: *In the quick, when it counts, you must have no doubt. Spit out all your doubt, breathe it out, pluck it from your heart, tear it loose from your mind, throw it away, be rid of it. We weren't born into this universe to doubt. We were born to hope, to love, to live, to learn, to know joy, to have faith that our lives have meaning . . . and to find The Way.*

Banishing doubt, seizing hope with a desperation grip, Curtis swallows hard and prepares himself for an exhilarating journey.

Go, pup, he says or only thinks.

She goes.

With no hesitation, determined to make his mother proud, to be daring and courageous, the boy sprints after the dog. Being Curtis Hammond, he isn't designed for speed as well as Old Yeller is, but she matches her pace to meet his fastest sprint, leading him north into the barrens.

Through darkness he flees, all but blind, not without fear but purged of doubt, across sandstone but also sand, across loose shale, between masses of sage and weather-sculpted thrusts of rock, zigging and zagging, legs reaching for the land ahead, sneakered feet landing with assurance on terrain that had previously been treacherous, arms pump-pump-pumping like the connecting rods on the driving wheels of a locomotive, the dog often visible in front of him, but sometimes seen less than sensed, sometimes seen not at all, but always reappearing, the two of them bonding more intimately the farther they travel, spirit sewn to spirit with the strong thread of Curtis's reckless trust.

Running with this strange blind exuberance, he loses all sense of distance and time, so he doesn't know how far they have gone when the quality of the night abruptly changes, one moment marked by a worrisome air of danger and the next moment *thick* with a terrifying sense of peril. Curtis's heart, furiously drumming from the physical demands of flight, now booms also with fear. Into the night has entered a threat more ominous than that represented by the officers in the SUVs and the troops in the helicopter. Dog and therefore boy together recognize that they are no longer merely the objects of a feverish search, but again the game in a hunt, the prey of predators, for in the August gloom arise new scents-sounds-pressures-energies that raise the hackles on Old Yeller and pebble-texture the nape of Curtis's neck. Death is in the desert, striding the sand and sage, stealthy under the stars.

Drawing on reserves that he didn't know he possessed, the boy runs faster. And the dog. In harmony.

27

Snake killed, mother patched, prayers said, Leilani retired to bed in the blessed dark.

Since the age of three or four, she hadn't wanted a night-light. As a *little* little girl, she'd thought that a luminous Donald Duck or a radiant plastic Tweetie Bird would ward off hungry demons and spare her from all sorts of supernatural unpleasantness, but she had soon learned that night-lights were more likely to draw the demon than repel it.

Old Sinsemilla sometimes rambled in the most wee of the wee hours, restless because she craved drugs or because she had stuffed herself with too many drugs, or maybe just because she was a haunted woman. Though she had no respect for her children's need to sleep, she was inexplicably less inclined to wake them when the room was dark than when a plug-in cartoon character watched over them.

Scooby Doo, Buzz Lightyear, the Lion King, Mickey Mouse – they all drew Sinsemilla into their light. She'd often awakened Luki and Leilani from sound sleep to tell them bedtime stories, and she had seemed to deliver these narratives as much to Scooby or to Buzz as to her children, as though these were not molded-plastic lamps made in Taiwan, but graven images of benign gods that listened and that were moved by her tears.

Tears always punctuated the conclusions of her bedtime stories. When she told fairy tales, the classic yarns on which they were based could be recognized, although she fractured the narratives so badly that they made no sense. Snow White was likely to wind up dwarfless in a carriage that turned into a pumpkin pulled by dragons; and poor Cinderella might dance herself to death in a pair of red shoes while baking blackbirds in a pie for

Rumpelstiltskin. Loss and calamity were the lessons of her stories. Sinsemilla's versions of Mother Goose and the Brothers Grimm were deeply disturbing, but sometimes she recounted instead her true-life adventures before Lukipela and Leilani were born, which had more hair-raising effect than any tales ever written about ogres, trolls, and goblins.

So goodbye to Scooby, goodbye to Buzz, to Donald in his sailor suit – and hello, Darkness, my old friend. The only light visible was the ambient suburban glow at the open window, but it didn't penetrate the bedroom.

No slightest draft sifted through the screen, either, and the hot night was nearly as quiet as it was windless. For a while, no sound disturbed the trailer park except for the steady hum of freeway traffic, but this white noise was so constant and so familiar that you heard it only if you listened for it.

Even by the time the midnight hour had passed, the distant drone of cars and trucks had not lulled Leilani to sleep. Lying with her eyes open, staring at the ceiling, she heard the Dodge Durango pull up in front of the house.

The engine had a distinctive timbre that she would never fail to recognize. In this Durango, Luki had been taken away into the Montana mountains on that slate-gray November afternoon when she'd last seen him.

Dr. Doom didn't slam the driver's door, but closed it with such care that Leilani could barely detect the discreet sound even though her bedroom window faced the street. Wherever their travels led them, he treated their neighbors with utmost consideration.

Animals elicited his kindness, as well. Whenever he saw a stray dog, Preston always coaxed it to him, checked for a license, and then tracked down its owner if the address was on the collar, regardless of the time and effort involved. Two weeks ago, on a highway in New Mexico, he'd spotted a car-struck cat lying on the shoulder of the road, both rear legs broken, still alive. He carried a veterinary kit for such emergencies, and he tenderly administered an overdose of tranquilizer to that suffering animal. As he'd knelt on the graveled verge, watching the cat slip into sleep and then into death, he'd wept quietly.

He tipped generously in restaurants, too, and always stopped to assist a stranded motorist, and never raised his voice to anyone.

Without fail, he would help an arthritic old lady across a busy street – unless he decided to kill her instead.

Now Leilani rolled onto her right side, putting her back to the door. A single sheet covered her, and she pulled it under her chin.

She had removed her leg brace for comfort, but as usual, she had kept the apparatus in bed with her. She reached out to touch it under the sheet. The metal felt cool beneath her exploring fingers.

A few times over the years, when she'd left the brace on the floor beside her bed, she had awakened to discover that it had been moved during the night. More accurately, hidden.

No game was less amusing than find-the-brace, though Sinsemilla thought it entertaining and also professed to believe that it taught Leilani self-reliance, sharpened her wits, and reminded her that life 'throws more stones at you than buttered cornbread,' whatever that might mean.

Leilani never rebuked her mother for this cruelty, or for any other, because Sinsemilla would not tolerate a thankless child. When forced into this hateful game, she proceeded with grim determination and without comment, aware that either a harsh word or refusal to play would bring down upon her the shrillest, most accusative, and most unrelenting of her mother's upbraidings. And in the end, she would have to find the brace anyway.

Now her open window admitted the sound of Preston at the front door. The jingle of keys. The *clack* as the dead-bolt lock disengaged. The quiet scrape of metal weatherstripping against the threshold as he gently closed the door behind him.

Perhaps he would visit the kitchen for a glass of water or a late-night snack.

Drawn by the red light spilling into the hall, perhaps he would go directly to the master bedroom.

What would he make of the dead snake, the discarded closet pole, and Sinsemilla's bandaged hand?

Most likely he wouldn't stop in Leilani's room. He would respect her privacy and her need for rest.

On a daily basis, Preston treated her with the same kindness that always he exhibited toward neighbors and waitresses and animals.

On the eve of her tenth birthday, next February, if she had not yet escaped him or devised an effective defense, he would kill her with the selfsame regret and sadness that he had shown when euthanizing the crippled cat. He might even weep for her.

He traveled silently on the matted orange shag, and she didn't hear him coming through the house until he opened her door. No stop for water or a snack. No curiosity about the red glow in the master bedroom. Directly to Leilani.

Because her back was to him, she hadn't closed her eyes. A pale rectangle of hall light projected on the wall opposite the entrance, and in that image of the door stood the effigy of Preston Maddoc.

'Leilani?' he whispered. 'Are you awake?'

She remained dead-cat still and didn't reply.

As considerate as ever, lest the hallway lamp wake her, Preston entered. He soundlessly closed the door behind him.

In addition to the bed, the room contained little furniture. One nightstand. A dresser. A cane chair.

Leilani knew that Preston had moved the chair close to the bed when she heard him sit on it. The interlaced strips of cane protested when they received his weight.

For a while he was mum. The cane, which would creak and rasp with the slightest shift of his body, produced no faintest noise. He remained perfectly motionless for a minute, two minutes, three.

He must be meditating, for it was too much to hope that he had been turned to stone by one of the gods in whom he didn't believe.

Although Leilani could see nothing in the darkness and though Preston was behind her, she kept her eyes open.

She hoped he couldn't hear her thudding heart, which seemed to clump up and down and up the staircase of her ribs.

'We did a fine thing tonight,' he said at last.

Preston Maddoc's voice, an instrument of smoke and steel, could ring with conviction or express steadfast belief equally well in a murmur. Like the finest actor, he was able to project a whisper to the back wall of a theater. His voice flowed as molten and as rich as hot caramel but not as sweet, and Leilani was reminded of one of those caramel-dipped tart green apples that you could sometimes buy at a carnival. In his university classes, students had surely sat in rapt attention; and if he had ever been inclined to prey upon naive coeds, his soft yet reverberant voice would have been one of his principal tools of seduction.

He spoke now in a hushed tone, although not exactly a whisper: 'Her name was Tetsy, an unfortunate variant of Elizabeth. Her parents were well meaning. But I can't imagine what they were thinking. Not that they seem to think all that much. Both are somewhat dense, if you ask me. *Tetsy* wasn't a diminutive, but her legal name. *Tetsy* – it sounds more like a little lap dog or a cat. She must have been teased mercilessly. Oh, perhaps the name might have worked if she'd been sprightly, cute, and elfin. But of course, she wasn't any of that, poor girl.'

In Leilani's vital coils, a chill arose. She prayed that she wouldn't shiver and, by shivering, alert Preston to the fact that she was awake.

'Tetsy was twenty-four, and she'd had some good years. The world is full of people who've never known a good year.'

Starvation, disease, Leilani thought grimly.

'Starvation, disease,' Preston said, 'desperate poverty—'

War and oppression, Leilani thought.

'– war, and oppression,' Preston continued. 'This world is the only hell we need, the only hell there is.'

Leilani much preferred Sinsemilla's screwed-up fairy tales to Preston's familiar soft-spoken rant, even if, when Beauty and the Beast came to the rescue of Goldilocks, Beauty was torn to pieces by the bears, and the Beast's dark side was thrilled by the bears' savagery, motivating him to slaughter Goldilocks and to eat her kidneys, and even if the bears and the maddened Beast then joined forces with the Big Bad Wolf and launched a brutal attack on the home of three very unfortunate little pigs.

The silken voice of Preston Maddoc slipped through the darkness, as supple as a strangler's scarf: '*Leilani? Are you awake?*'

The chill at the core of her grew colder, spreading loop to loop through her bowels.

She closed her eyes and concentrated on remaining still. She thought that she heard him move on the thatched seat of the chair. Her eyes snapped open.

The cane was quiet.

'*Leilani?*'

Under the sheets, her good hand still rested on the detached brace. Earlier, the steel had felt cool to the touch. Now it was icy.

'*Are you awake?*'

She clutched the brace.

Still speaking quietly, he said, 'Tetsy had more than her share of good years, so it would have been greedy for the poor girl to want still more.'

As Preston rose from the chair, the stretched cane flexed with considerable noise, as though he had been more difficult to support than would have been any man of equal size.

'Tetsy collected miniatures. Only penguins. Ceramic penguins, glass penguins, carved wood, cast metal, all kinds.'

He eased closer to the bed. Leilani sensed him hulking over her.

'I brought one of her penguins for you.'

If she threw back the sheet, rolled off her side and up, all in one motion, she could swing the brace like a club, toward that darker place in the darkness where she imagined his face to be.

She wouldn't strike at him unless he touched her.

Looming, Preston said nothing. He must be gazing down at her, though he couldn't possibly see anything but the vaguest shape in the gloom.

He always avoided touching Leilani, as though her deformities might be contagious. Contact with her at least disturbed him and, she believed, filled him with disgust that he struggled to conceal. When the aliens failed to come, when the time finally arrived for baking a birthday cake and for buying party hats, when he *had* to touch her to kill her, he would surely wear gloves.

'I brought you one little penguin in particular because it reminds me of Luki. It's very sweet. I'll put it on your nightstand.'

A faint click. Penguin deposited.

She didn't want his souvenir, stolen from a dead girl.

As if this house had been built to defeat the laws of gravity, Preston seemed not to be standing by the bed, but to hang from the floor like a bat adapted to strange rules, wings furled and silently watchful, a suspensefully suspended presence.

Perhaps he was already wearing gloves.

She tightened her grip on the steel bludgeon.

After what seemed an interminable time, he broke this latest silence in a voice hushed by the importance of the news that he delivered: *'We burst her heart.'*

Leilani knew that he was speaking of the stranger named Tetsy, who had loved and been loved, who laughed and cried, who collected miniature animals to brighten her life, and who never expected to die at twenty-four.

'We did it without fanfare, just family. No one will know. We burst her heart, but I'm confident she felt no pain.'

How satisfying it must be to live with unshakable confidence, to know beyond doubt that your intentions are honorable, that your reasoning is always correct, that therefore the consequences of your actions, no matter how extreme, are beyond judgment.

God, take her home, Leilani thought, referring to the dead woman who had been a stranger moments ago, but to whom she herself was now forever linked through the heartless mercy of Preston Maddoc. *Take her home now where she belongs.*

With supreme confidence even in the darkness, he returned the cane chair to the spot from which he'd moved it. Surefooted, he went to the door.

If earlier the snake had spoken to Leilani, while coiled upon her mother's bed or from its refuge under the chest of drawers, this would have been its voice, not wickedly sibilant but a honeyed croon: *'I would never have caused her pain, Leilani. I'm the enemy of pain. I've devoted my life to relieving it.'*

When Preston opened the bedroom door, a ghostly portal of light appeared on the wall opposite him, as before, and his phantom form hesitated on that threshold, looking back at her. Then his shadow appeared to cross into another reality, distorting as it went, and a slab of blackness swung shut upon the exit he had taken.

Leilani wished that the shadow show represented reality and that Preston had indeed stepped out of this world and forever into another place better suited to him, perhaps a world in which everyone would be born dead and therefore could never be subjected to pain. He was but a wall or two away, however, still sharing the breath of life with her, still abiding under the same vault of stars that were, to her, filled with wonder and mystery, but that were, to him, nothing more than distant balls of fire and cataclysm.

28

Curtis hears or smells or senses tarantulas springing out of sand tunnels, swarming away from his feet, and he hears or smells or senses rattlesnakes wriggling out of his path or coiling to shake a warning at him in maraca code, frightened rodents scampering away from him and from the feeding snakes, prairie dogs bolting into their burrows, startled birds erupting into flight from nests in the hollow arms of half-dead cactuses, lizards slithering liquid-quick across sand and stone from which still radiates the stored heat of the fierce sun long set, hawks circling high above, and coyotes ranging singly and in packs far to the left and to the right of him. These things might be figments of his imagination rather than real presences perceived through a mystical sharing of the dog's keen senses, but the night *seems* to bustle with life.

Old Yeller leads him, as never Lassie led Timmy, up slopes and down, into ravines and out, fast and faster. Cactus groves are mazes of needles at night. Layers of small round stones and smaller gravel, quarried out of the original rock strata and piled into ridges by the massive moving glaciers of an ancient ice age, provide treacherous passage to more welcoming terrain.

They have put additional distance between themselves and the pair of SUVs, which continue to prowl in their wake, now more than one hill away. Once, a search flare had gone up, casting an unearthly bluish brilliance across a wide swath of the landscape, but it had been safely behind Curtis and the dog.

Initially to the rear of the SUVs but soon parallel with them, the helicopter has tacked west to east, east to west, back and forth across the field of search, proceeding steadily north by indirection. The chopper is most likely equipped with a powerful searchlight that would make the gear on the two SUVs seem like mere votive candles by comparison. Yet the craft conducts its maneuvers without this aid, from which Curtis infers that they have sophisticated electronic tracking packages aboard.

Not good.

Infrared tracking might be of only limited use to them right now, because the land itself is shedding so much stored heat from the day that the body heat of living creatures on the move will not be clearly readable against the background glare. If their computer technology is sufficiently advanced, however, good analytic software could screen out background thermals – thus revealing coyotes, dogs, and running boys.

More worrisome: If they possess open-terrain motion-detection equipment, conditions are ideal for its use, because the night is not merely windless but again dead calm. Furthermore, mule deer move in small herds, coyotes hunt in packs or on occasion singly, while a boy and his dog are by definition a twosome, presenting a unique and at once identifiable signature on the search scope.

Regardless of the resources that the FBI and the military may bring to bear, other enemies roam the desert, more dangerous than those legitimate authorities. The killers from Colorado are urgently monitoring other search scopes for the unique energy signal of the boy who would be Curtis Hammond. Their return to the game, a short time ago, was accompanied by the ominous pressure that thickens the air in advance of a thunderstorm, and by a subtle disturbance of the ether similar to the flux in electromagnetic fields that makes many animals anxious and alert in the moments before a major earthquake.

Spurred on by the boy's analysis or by her own instincts, Old Yeller picks up speed, thereby demanding more of him. Running, he has sucked in and blown out enough scorching breaths to inflate one of those giant hot-air balloons. His lips are cracked, his mouth is as dry as the arid ground under his flying feet, and his throat feels charred. Agonizing pain burns in his calves, in his thighs, but now with some effort, he begins to mask most of this discomfort. Curtis Hammond isn't the most efficient machine of bone and muscle in the world, but he isn't entirely at the mercy of his physiology, either. Pain is just electrical impulses traveling along a transmission grid of nerves, and for a while, his willpower can prevail over it.

The dog chases freedom, and Curtis chases the dog, and in time they top another hill and discover below them what appear to be salt flats. The land slopes gracefully down to form a broad valley, the length and width of which are not easily determined in the moonless murk; however, the level floor of the valley, eerily phosphorescent, offers a measure of relief from the previously oppressive darkness.

Hundreds of thousands of years ago, this was one finger of an inland sea. As the water evaporated over centuries, the dead ocean left behind this faintly luminous ghost spread shore to shore.

The self-lit land lies smooth and barren, for the salt-rich soil is inhospitable even to hardy desert scrub. Crossing it, they will be easily spotted, whether or not their many pursuers employ electronic surveillance gear.

This valley lies on a southwest-northeast axis; and but for one detail, boy and dog would follow the ridge line northeast, avoiding the risk of exposure on the open flats. The detail is a town. A town or a cluster of buildings.

Approximately forty structures of various sizes, most one or two stories high, are divided into roughly equal groups that flank a single street on the gentle slope near the base of the valley wall. They stand this side of the salt deposits, where more-accommodating soil and an underground water source support a few big shade trees.

On a blistering summer day, when shimmering snakes of heat swarm the air, writhing like flute-teased cobras, this settlement, whatever its nature, must from a distance appear to be an illusion. Even now, crisply silhouetted against the fluorescent flats beyond, these buildings rise like the unconvincing architecture in a mirage.

Darkness paves the lonely street, and not a single light gleams in any window.

On the brink of the valley, gazing down, dog and boy stand at full alert. They hold their breath. Her nose quivers. His doesn't. She pricks her ears. He can't. Simultaneously, they cock their heads, both to the right. They listen.

No crump, snap, thud, clunk, crack, bang, or whisper rises to them. The scene is at first as silent as the surface of a moon that lacks an atmosphere.

Then comes a sound, not from below, but out of the south, that might at first be mistaken for the thundering iron-shod hooves of a large posse displaced in time.

Dog and boy look to the black lowering clouds. Dog puzzled. Boy searching for ghost riders in the sky.

Of course, when the sound swiftly grows louder, it resolves into the stutter of the dreaded helicopter. The chopper is still tacking east and west across the field of search, not headed directly toward them, but it will arrive sooner than Curtis would prefer.

Side by side, neither of them any longer in the lead, boy and dog quickly descend from the valley crest toward the dark settlement. Stealth matters now as much as speed, and they no longer plunge into the night with wild abandon.

An excellent argument could be made for avoiding this place and for continuing northeast along the valley wall. In the case of both federal agents and the military, standard procedure probably requires that upon discovery these buildings must be scouted, searched, and cleared. They offer only brief concealment.

If people reside here, however, they'll distract the searchers and provide screening that will make electronic detection of Curtis a little more difficult. As always, for a fugitive, there's value in commotion.

More important, he needs to find water. With willpower, he could deny his thirst and eliminate his desire for a drink, but he wouldn't be able to prevent dehydration strictly by an act of will. Besides, Old Yeller, too thickly furred for long-distance running in this climate, is at risk of heatstroke.

On closer inspection, these houses – or whatever they are – prove to be crudely constructed. Roughly planed planks form the walls, and although they have been slopped with paint, they're splintery under Curtis's hands. No ornamentation. Even in better light, they wouldn't likely reveal the finessed details of high-quality carpentry.

Except for the six or eight immense old trees rising among and high above the structures, no landscaping is evident, no softening grass or flowers, or shrubs. These dreary shelters hulk and huddle without grace on hard bare earth.

By now slowed to a cautious pace, Curtis and Old Yeller follow a narrow passageway between two buildings. A faint scent of wood rot. The musky odor of mice nesting among chinks in the rough foundations.

The wall on their left is blank. On the right, two windows offer Curtis views into a blackness deep enough to be eternal.

Each time that he pauses to put nose to glass, he expects a pale and moldering face to materialize suddenly on the other side of the pane, eyes crimson with blood, teeth like pointed yellow staves. His brain is such a young sponge, yet it has soaked up a library of books and films, many featuring frights of one kind or another. He's been highly entertained, but perhaps he's also been too sensitized to the possibility of violent death at the hands of ghouls, poltergeists, vampires, serial killers, Mafia hit men, murderous transvestites with mother fixations, murderous kidnappers with wood chippers in their backyards, stranglers, ax maniacs, and cannibals.

As he and the dog near the end of the passageway, night birds or bats flutter overhead, darting from one eave to the other. Yeah, right. Bats or birds. Or a thousand possibilities more terrifying than rabid bats or Hitchcockian birds, every one of them feverishly eager to snatch a gob of tasty boy guts or to snack on canine brains.

Old Yeller whimpers nervously, possibly at something she smells in the night, but probably because Curtis transferred his fearfulness to her by psychic osmosis. There's a downside for the dog in boy-dog bonding if the boy is a hysteric whose mother would be embarrassed to see how easily he spooks.

'Sorry, pup.'

When they step out from between the buildings, into the street, Curtis discovers they are in a Western movie. He turns slowly in a full circle, astonished.

On both sides, the buildings front against a communal board-walk (with hitching posts) elevated to keep it out of the mud on those infrequent occasions when the street floods during a hard-pouring toad-drowner. Many structures toward the center of the town feature second-story balconies that overhang the boardwalk, providing shade on days when even the Gila monsters either hide or fry.

A general store advertising dry goods, groceries, and hardware. A combination jail and sheriff's office. A small white church with a modest steeple. Here is a combination doctor's-assayer's office, and there is a boardinghouse, and over *there* stands a saloon and gambling parlor where more than a few guns must have been drawn when too many bad poker hands were dealt in a row.

Ghost town.

Curtis's first thought is that he's standing in a genuine, for-sure, bona fide, dead-right, all-wool-and-a-yard-wide, for-a-fact-amen ghost town in which no one has set foot since twice the century has turned, where all the citizens were long ago planted in the local boot hill, and where the ornery spirits of gunslingers walk the night itching for a shootout.

Rough as they may be, however, the buildings are in considerably better condition than they would be after a century of abandonment. Even in this gloom, the paint looks fresh. The signs over the stores have not been bleached unreadable by decades of desert sun.

Then he notices what might be docent stations positioned at regular intervals along the street, in front of the hitching posts. The nearest of these is at the saloon. A pair of four-feet-high rustic posts support a tilted board to which is fixed a black acrylic plaque with text in white block letters.

In this starless and moonless dismality, he can't read much of the history of the building, even though the text is a generous size, but he can make out enough to confirm his new suspicion. Once this had been an authentic ghost town, abandoned, decaying. Now it's been restored: a historic site where visitors take self-guided tours.

At night, it remains a ghost town, when tourists aren't strolling the street and poking through the rehabilitated buildings. With no utility poles leading from the distant highway, the comforts are only those of the 19th century, and no one lives here.

Nostalgic for the Old West, Curtis would enjoy exploring these buildings with just an oil lamp, to preserve the frontier mood. He lacks a lamp, however, and the buildings must be locked at night.

A gruff remark from Old Yeller and a pawing at the boy's leg remind him that they aren't on vacation. The clatter-whump of the helicopter is gone; but the search will tack in this direction again.

Water. They've sweated out more moisture than the orange juice had contained. Dying here of dehydration, in order to be buried in boot hill with gunslingers and plugged sheriffs and dance-hall girls, is carrying nostalgia too far.

Movies reliably place public stables and a blacksmith's shop at the end of the main street of every town in the Old West. Curtis searches south and finds SMITHY'S LIVERY. Once again motion pictures prove to be a source of dependably accurate information.

Stables mean horses. Horses need shoes. Blacksmiths make shoes. Horses must have water to drink, and blacksmiths must have it both to drink and to conduct their work. Curtis recalls a scene in which a smithy, while in conversation with a town sheriff, keeps dunking red-hot horseshoes in a barrel of water; a cloud of steam roils into the air with the quenching of each shoe.

Sometimes the smithy's pump is also the public water source for residents who have no wells, but if the common font is elsewhere, the blacksmith will have his own supply. And here he does. Right out front. God bless Warner Brothers, Paramount, Universal Pictures, RKO, Republic Studios, Metro Goldwyn Mayer, and 20th Century Fox.

If the town has been restored with historical accuracy, the pump will be functional. Curtis climbs onto the foot-high wooden platform surrounding the wellhead, grips the pump handle with both hands, and works it as if it were a jack. The mechanism creaks and rasps. The piston moves easily at first, loose enough to make Curtis wonder if it's broken or if the pump isn't self-priming, but then it stiffens as fluid rises in the pipe, ascending from the same aquifer that sustains the trees, which were no doubt here before the town.

A vigorous gout abruptly gushes from the spout and splashes across the wooden deck, pouring down through the drainage slots.

The dog springs exuberantly onto the platform. She laps at the arc of spilling water, standing to the side of it, scooping liquid refreshment out of the air with her long pink tongue.

Once the pump is primed, Curtis doesn't have to work the handle as continuously as before. He steps around to the spout to fill his cupped hands, from which the dog drinks gratefully. He pumps again, once more offers the bowl of his hands to her, then drinks his fill.

As the stream from the spout diminishes, Old Yeller chases her tail through it, so Curtis jacks more water out of the ground, and the dog capers in delight.

Cool. Cool, wet, good. Goodgoodgood. Clean smell, cool smell, water smell, faint stony odor, slight taste of lime, taste of a deep place. Fur soaked, paws cool, toes cool. Paws so hot, now so cool. Shake off the water. Shakeshakeshake. Like the swimming hole near the farmhouse, splashing with Curtis all afternoon, diving and splashing, swimming after a ball, Curtis and the ball and nothing but fun all day. That was like this but even more fun then. Fur soaked again, fur soaked. Oh, look at Curtis now. Look, look. Curtis dry. Remember this game? Get Curtis. Make him wet. Get him, get him! Shakeshakeshake. Get Curtis, getgetget! Curtis laughing. Fun. Hey, get his shoe! Shoe, fun, shoe, shoe! Curtis laughing. What could be better than this, except a cat chase, except good things to eat? Shoe, shoe, SHOE!

A light suddenly flares across boy and dog, dog and boy.

Startled, Curtis looks up. The beam is bright.

Oh, Lord, he's in trouble now.

29

Seventeen years after they had healed, the bullet wound in Noah's left shoulder and the wound in his right thigh began to ache, as though he were afflicted with psychosomatic rheumatism.

Called out of bed, summoned from a bad dream into a waking nightmare, he drove south first on freeways and then on surface streets, pushing the rustbucket Chevy to its limits. Traffic was light at this hour, some streets deserted. For the most part, he ignored stop signs and speed limits, as if he were back in uniform, behind the wheel of a black-and-white.

Pain *popped* in the old gunshot wounds as if surgical stitches had just burst, when in fact they had been removed by a doctor half a lifetime ago. Noah glanced down at his shoulder, at his thigh, convinced that he would see blood seeping through his clothes, that his scars had become strange stigmata, reminders not of the love of God, but of his own guilt.

Aunt Lilly, his old man's sister, had shot the old man first, because he was the danger, pumped one round in his face at point-blank range, and then she had shot Noah twice, just because he was there, a witness. She'd said, 'I'm sorry about this, Nono,' because Nono was a pet name that some in the family had called him since he was a child, and then Lilly had opened fire.

If your entire family is engaged in a highly profitable criminal enterprise, a disagreement among relatives can occasionally involve a subject much more serious than how best to divide up grandmamma's porcelain collection when she dies without a will. Manufacturing methamphetamine in convenient tablet, capsule, liquid, and powder forms for distribution without prescription was as illegal back then as it is seventeen years later. If you're able to identify interested consumers, establish distribution, and protect your territory from competitors, meth can be as profitable as cocaine, and because there's no import risk involved, because you can cook it yourself from easily obtainable ingredients, the business is comparatively hassle-free. The family that cooks together, however, does not in this case necessarily stay together, because meth churns off floods of dirty money that can corrupt even blood relationships.

At sixteen, Noah hadn't been *in* the business, but he had been *around* it for as long as he could remember. He never actually pushed the crap, didn't distribute it or collect the cash, never did the street work. But he knew the fine points of cooking; he became a full-fledged meth chemist. And he capped up a lot of bulk flashpowder over the years, filled countless little plastic bags with capsules in street units, and topped off a lot of ozer bottles with injectable liquid, earning spending money like other kids might earn it from mowing lawns and raking leaves.

His father had plans for him, intended to groom him to run the shop one day, but not until he was finished with school, because the old man believed in the value of an education. Noah always knew that his dad was a sleazebag, and however you might describe the nature of their relationship, you would never use the word *love* with a straight face. Obligation, shared history, family duty – and in Noah's case, fear – bound them together. Yet his dad took genuine pride in Noah's skill as a cooker and in his willingness to do scut work like bagging and bottling. Funny, but even though you knew that your old man was walking slime, a cancer on humanity, you nonetheless felt a strange satisfaction when he said he was proud of you. After all, whatever else he might be, he was still your *dad*; the President of the United States was never going to say he was proud of you, and you weren't likely ever to be taken under the wing of a committed high-school coach or teacher like Denzel Washington might play in the movies, so you took your *attaboys* where you could get them.

Even as the old man, face-shot, hit the floor in a full-dead flop, and even as Aunt Lilly said, 'I'm sorry about this, Nono,' Noah ran for his life. Her first round missed him, the second tore through his shoulder, and the third chopped his thigh.

By then, however, he had reached the front door and opened it, and the thigh shot kicked him outside, onto the front porch, where he dropped and rolled down the steps as though he were a bundled rug on moving day. Lilly didn't want to come right out on the front lawn and pop him in the head, not in this quiet middle-class community, where teenagers on skateboards and neighborhood moms pushing strollers were likely to have enough civic spirit to testify in court. Instead, she took a chance that Noah would bleed to death before he could finger her for the cops, and she went out the back way, as she had come in.

Noah disappointed her, and about ten months into her thirty-year sentence, Lilly found Jesus, maybe for real or maybe just to impress the parole board. Although she'd by now done more than half her time, the board continued to weigh her devotion to her savior against the psychologists' professional opinion that she was still an evil scheming homicidal bitch.

Each year she sent Noah a Christmas card, sometimes a manger scene, sometimes Santa Claus. She always included a neat handwritten message of remorse – except in year nine of her incarceration, when she'd expressed, in language frowned upon by every known Christian denomination, the wish that she had shot him in the crotch. Although Noah was convinced that all the Freud boys, who insisted on calling themselves scientists, were priests of a religion immeasurably less rational than any established faith in the history of humanity, he passed that card along to the parole board for evaluation.

Aunt Lilly was a mean, brother-killing, nephew-wounding piece of work, but she was generally rational, which couldn't always be said for her husband, Kelvin. Everyone had called him Crankcase or Crank, for a variety of reasons. Just two months before Lilly killed the old man regarding a dispute over seven hundred thousand dollars, Kelvin had beaten Noah's sister, Laura, almost to death. Lilly had acted out of cold financial self-interest; but Crank went after Laura for reasons that even Crank himself didn't understand.

For a long time, Uncle Crank had been sampling the family's product. Even if the family's product had been apple juice, it would have been a bad idea to partake of the quantities that Uncle Crank consumed when he was in a mood to pop some meth or poke it. If you do enough methamphetamine, byproducts of phenyl-2-propanone, a chemical used in the manufacturing of the drug, begin to accumulate in your brain tissue, and if you're as dedicated to amped-up recreation as Crank had been, eventually you'll experience toxic psychosis, which is maybe less fun than being eaten alive by fire ants, though not a whole lot less.

When fuses started to blow out in Uncle Crank's brain box, he tried to soothe his suddenly anxious soul and to settle his confusion by beating the hell out of someone. That was when twelve-year-old Laura rang the doorbell. Or perhaps she had rung the doorbell five minutes before the fuses blew, and Uncle Crank had invited his niece in for one of his justly famous lemon ice cream sodas, but then he'd succumbed to these maximum-bad whimwhams. Earlier, Lilly had taken the dog for a walk, and she hadn't returned home until Uncle Crank had been pounding on Laura for a few minutes, first with his fists and then with a carved-mesquite statuette of Lady Luck that he had bought in a Las Vegas gift shop.

Lilly pulled Crank away from the girl and made him sit in an armchair. Perhaps only she could have subdued him so easily, because even during an episode of full-blown toxic psychosis, Uncle Crank was afraid of his wife.

Aunt Lilly's brother – Noah's dad – lived only a block away, and three minutes after receiving Lilly's call, he was on her doorstep. His daughter was horribly beaten, unconscious, and possibly dying, and he wanted to call an ambulance, but he understood, as did Lilly, that they had to deal with Crank first. Uncle Crank was not as much a member of the family as he was a liability by marriage; even clean and sober and in charge of his faculties, if he found himself in a jam, he might sell them out to get a reduction of the charges against him. Now, meth-wrecked, mumbling, paranoid, delusional, alternately expressing anger at his niece's imagined 'snottiness' and weeping with remorse for what he'd done to her, he was likely to ruin all of them in his first five minutes with the police – without even realizing what he was doing.

Fortunately for the family, Uncle Crank committed suicide seven minutes later.

With his patient wife's firm guidance, he wrote a heartfelt confession. *Dear Laura, I am wasted on meth and some stuff. I did not know what I was doing. I am not a bad man. I am just an awful mess. Do not blame your sweet aunt for what I done. She is a good honest woman. I want her to buy you the biggest damn teddy bear of which she can find and give it from me. Love to you, Uncle Crank.* In his derangement, he thought the note was going to be given to Laura in a get-well card.

The effort of putting these sentiments into words exhausted him, and by the time he signed his name, he phased from toxic-psychosis frenzy into a state of post-meth fatigue that meth freaks referred to as being 'amped out.' In fact he was so thoroughly amped out that he couldn't negotiate the stairs on his own and had to be supported by Lilly and by his brother-in-law on his way to the master bathroom on the second floor.

He believed that once he shaved and cleaned up, they were going to take him to a combination spa and clinic in Palm Springs, where he would undergo a Twelve Step program to cure his addiction, receive a really good daily massage, tighten up his gut with a healthier diet, and perhaps learn to play golf. While his brother-in-law balanced him with one hand to keep him from tumbling to the floor, Crank actually sat on the closed lid of the toilet and dozed – until Lilly disturbed him when she eased the barrel of the pistol into his mouth. She had put on a glove and wrapped a silk pillowcase around her arm to ensure that she wouldn't be incriminated by traces of gunpowder. Surprised, biting on the barrel, Uncle Crank opened his eyes, seemed to realize that getting a last-minute reservation at the Palm Springs spa was going to be more difficult than first thought, and then Lilly pulled the trigger.

Of the available household weapons, she had chosen the smallest caliber required to get the job done. Too much gun would result in unnecessary mess and the risk of incriminating contamination from the splash. Lilly had a good mind for criminal conspiracy. Besides, she liked a neat house.

For over twenty minutes while Crank was being prepared for Hell and was finally dispatched there, Laura had been left lying on the living-room floor, with half her once-lovely face shattered and with cerebral damage progressing, before Lilly had called paramedics.

Noah had not been present for any of this. He'd heard about it secondhand, from his father.

The old man recounted these events as he might have retold a war story from his youth, as though it had been an adventure, for God's sake, with eerily few references to the horror that his daughter had endured or to her tragic condition, but with brotherly admiration for Lilly's quick thinking under pressure. 'She is one hard-assed bitch when she needs to be, your aunt Lil. I've known men who, in a pinch, would go all female on you sooner than Lil.' His attitude seemed to be, *Hey, shit happens, it's horrible, it's sad, but that's the way the world is, there's no more justice than what we dealt out to Crank, we're all just meat in the end, so get over it and move on.* 'Live in the now,' the old man liked to say, which was psychobabble he'd heard spouted by some sociopathic self-help guru on television.

More shit happened two months later, when Aunt Lilly showed up with a far more powerful gun than the one she had used on Uncle Crank and with no concern about neatness, since the house wasn't hers. Her brother had concealed seven hundred thousand dollars in meth profits. She didn't want merely an honest accounting; she wanted him out of the business. Even the old man's appeal to sisterly mercy didn't persuade Lilly to 'go all female' on him: Only Noah merited an *I'm sorry* from her before she squeezed the trigger.

Double-shot, first certain that he was dying on the front lawn, then later in the hospital when he knew he would survive, Noah had decided that his wounds were what he deserved, punishment for failing to protect his little sister. He wasn't a bad kid, really. He wasn't a bad seed, either, not born in his father's image. His indifference to his family's criminal behavior had not been nature's fault; as the parenting experts would put it, his moral drift was the consequence of inadequate nurturing. But abed with time to think, Noah had come to understand that it was immaterial whether nature or nurture was to blame. Only he himself possessed the thread and needles to sew up his shabby life and to transform it into a suit presentable in the company of decent people. Only guilt over his sister's suffering led him to the conclusion that this difficult tailoring was essential if he was to have any future worth living.

Guilt in fact gave him the power to become his own Pygmalion, allowed him to sculpt a new Noah Farrel from the stone of the old. Guilt was his hammer; guilt was his chisel. Guilt was his bread and his inspiration.

Whenever he heard anyone declare that guilt was a destructive emotion, that a fully self-realized person had to 'get past' his guilt, he knew that he was listening to a fool. Guilt had been his soul's salvation.

Over the past seventeen years, however, he had also arrived at the realization that acceptance of guilt was not an end in itself. Truly taking responsibility for the consequences of your acts – or in his case, the consequences of his failure to act – did not lead to redemption. And until he found that door of redemption, until he opened it and crossed the threshold, the old Noah Farrel would never quite feel that he belonged inside the new man he had created; always he would feel like an impostor, unworthy and waiting to be exposed as the thoughtless boy that he had been.

The only path to redemption that seemed open to him was his sister. After enough years of paying for her care, after thousands of hours of talking to her as she lay unresponsive behind her elsewhere eyes, might a moment come at last when the door appeared before him? If ever she made eye contact with him, soul to soul, however brief, and if in that instant her expression told him that she had heard his monologues and had been comforted by them, then the threshold would lie before him, and the room beyond the door might be called *hope*.

Now, in the most unforgiving hours of the night, speeding along the streets of south Orange County, Noah was scared as he had never been before, scared worse than when he'd taken Lilly's two bullets and rolled down the front porch steps with the expectation of taking a third in the back of the head. The prospect of redemption receded from him the faster he drove, and receding with it was all hope.

When he jammed the brakes and slid the Chevy sideways into the driveway at Cielo Vista Care Home, despair overcame him at the sight of all the police units parked around the front entrance. The phone call that roused him from bed, the call that might have been a hoax or a mistake, was proved true and accurate by every pulse of red light and by every chasing shadow that leaped across the face of the building and through the bougainvillea twining the trellises.

Laura.

30

Dog dripping, boy dripping, dog grinning, boy *not* grinning, and therefore dog ceasing to grin, but both still dripping, they stand in the sudden light, Old Yeller trying to control her doggy exuberance, Curtis reminding himself to react now as a boy would react, not as a dog would react, trying to work his foot fully back into the shoe that Old Yeller had pulled half off him.

The pump creaks and groans as declining pressure allows the untended handle to settle into the full at-rest position. The flow from the iron spout quickly diminishes from a gush to a stream, to a trickle, to a dribble, to a drip.

'What the jumpin' blue blazes you doin' out here, boy?' asks the man who holds the flashlight.

Not much can be seen of this person. Largely hidden behind the glare, he shines the light in Curtis's face.

'You leave your ears in your other pants, boy?'

Curtis has just figured out that he should disregard 'the jumpin' blue blazes' from the first question in order to discover the essence of it, and now this second question baffles him.

'They full of horseshit, boy?'

'Who's "they," sir?' Curtis asks.

'Your ears,' the stranger says impatiently.

'Good Lord, no, sir.'

'That there your dog?'

'Yes, sir.'

'He be vicious?'

'She be not, sir.'

'Say what?'

'Say *she*, sir.'

'You stupid or somethin'?'

'Somethin', I guess.'

'I ain't afeared of dogs.'

'She ain't afeared of you neither, sir.'

'Don't you go tryin' to bullyrag me, boy.'

'I wouldn't even if I knew how, sir.'

'You some sassy-assed, spit-in-the-eye malefactor?'

'As far as I can understand what you might mean, sir, I don't think I am.'

Curtis is comfortable with a lot of languages, and he believes that he could conduct conversation easily in most regional dialects of English, but this one is challenging enough to rattle his self-confidence.

The stranger lowers the flashlight, focusing it on Old Yeller. 'I seen dogs sweet like this here, then you dares turn your back an' they bite off your co-jones.'

'Jones?' Curtis replies, thinking maybe they're talking about a person named Ko Jones.

With the bright beam out of his eyes, Curtis sees that this man is none other than Gabby Hayes, the greatest sidekick in the history of Western movies, and for a moment he's as delighted as he's ever been. Then he realizes this can't be Gabby, because Gabby must have died decades ago.

Frizzles of white hair, a beard like Santa's with mange, a face seamed and saddle-stitched by a lifetime of desert sun and prairie wind, a body that appears to be composed more of leathery tendons and knobby bones than of anything else: He is your typical weathered and buzzard-tough prospector, your weathered and cranky but lovable ranch hand, your weathered and comical but dependable deputy, irascible but well-meaning and weathered saloonkeeper, crotchety but tender-hearted and banjo-playing and weathered wagon-train cook. With the exception of a pair of orange-and-white Nikes that look as big as clown shoes, his outfit is totally Gabby: rumpled baggy khakis, red suspenders, a cotton shirt striped like mattress ticking; his squashed, dusty, sweat-stained cowboy hat is slightly too small for his head and is parked on his grizzled skull with such desert-rat insouciance that it looks like a growth that has been with him since birth.

'She goes after my co-jones, I'll plug her, so help me Jesus.'

Just as you would expect of any cranky citizen of the Old West, regardless of his profession, this man has a gun. It's not a revolver of the proper period, but a 9-mm pistol.

'Maybe I ain't so well-appearanced, but I sure ain't no useless codgerdick, like you might think. I'm the night caretaker for this here resurrected hellhole, and I can more than do the job.'

Although he's old, this man isn't old enough to be Gabby Hayes even if Gabby Hayes somehow could still be alive, and he isn't dead, either, so he can't be Gabby Hayes brought back to life as a flesh-eating zombie in another kind of movie altogether. Nevertheless the resemblance is so strong that he must be a descendant of Gabby's, perhaps his grandson, Gabby Hayes III. Flushed with excitement and awe, Curtis feels as humbled as he might feel in the presence of royalty.

'I can shoot me a man around the corner, by calculated ricochet, if I got to, so you keep that flea hotel in check, and don't you try to run nowheres.'

'No, sir.'

'Where is your folks, boy?'

'They is dead, sir.'

Bushy white eyebrows jump toward his hat brim. '*Dead*? You say *dead*, boy?'

'I say dead, yessir.'

'Here?' The caretaker worriedly surveys the street, as though hired guns have ridden into town to shoot down all the sheep ranchers or the homesteading farmers, or whoever the evil land barons or the greedy railroad barons currently want to have shot down. The pistol wobbles in his hand, as if it is suddenly too heavy to hold. 'Dead here on my watch? Well, ain't this just an antigodlin mess? Where is these folks of yours?'

'Colorado, sir.'

'Colorado? I thought you said they was dead here.'

'I meant they was dead in Colorado.'

The caretaker looks relieved, and the gun doesn't shake as much as it shook before. 'Then how'd you and this biscuit-eater come to be here after closin' time?'

'Runnin' for our lives, sir,' Curtis explains, because he feels that he can tell at least a portion of the truth to any descendant of Mr. Hayes.

The caretaker's wrinkle-garden face sprouts a new crop where you would have thought he had no room to plant the seeds for any more. 'You ain't tellin' me you run all the way here from Colorado?'

'Run at the start of it, sir, then hitched most of the time, and run this last piece.'

Old Yeller pants as if in confirmation.

'Who's the damn scalawags you been runnin' from?'

'Lots of scalawags, sir. Some nicer than others. I guess the nicest would be the government.'

'The gov'ment!' declares the caretaker, and his wrinkles rise like hackles, pulling his face into a surprisingly taut bristle of pure disgust. 'Tax collectors, land grabbers, nosey do-gooders more self-righteous than any Bible-poundin' preacher ever born!'

Curtis says, 'I've seen the FBI, whole SWAT teams of them, and I suspect the National Security Agency's in on this, plus one special-forces branch of the military or another, and probably more.'

'Gov'ment!' The caretaker is so beside himself with outrage that if *beside himself* could be taken literally, there would be two of him standing before Curtis. 'Rule-makin', power-crazy, know-nothin' bunch of lily-livered skunks in bald-faced shirts! A man an' his wife pays social-security tax out the ass all their life, an' she dies just two checks into retirement, an' the gov'ment keeps all she paid, greedy bastards, she ain't really got her no *account* with 'em like they tell you. So here's me gettin' one monthly check no bigger than a brush-rabbit turd, hardly enough to buy me the makin's of a good long beer piss, while Barney Colter's worthless lazy donkey-wit son, who never worked a day in his useless life, he collects *twice* what I get 'cause the gov'ment says his drug addiction's left him *emotionally disabled*. So the doped-up little slug sits on his saggy ass, scarfin' Cheez Doodles, while to make ends meet, I haul myself out here to this historical hellhole five nights a week an' listen to blowsnakes blow, waitin' to be turned into buzzard brunch when my ticker pops, an' now facin' down dangerous wild dogs what wants to chew off my co-jones. You see the idea I'm gettin' at, boy?'

'Not entirely, sir,' Curtis replies.

Because of all the excitement of trying to get Curtis's shoe and the fun of splashing in the outfall of well water, and also because Gabby's angry rant has frightened her, Old Yeller whines, squats, and pees on the pump platform.

Curtis perfectly understands her feelings about the caretaker. They have heard a lot of crankiness but not much lovableness, have been doused with buckets of crotchety talk but not with one teaspoon of tender-hearted sympathy; plus as yet there's no sign whatsoever of a banjo.

'What's wrong with your dog, boy?'

'Nothing, sir. She's just been through a lot lately.'

And here comes more trouble for dog and boy: the giant-dragonfly thrum of the huge helicopter throbbing across the desert.

The caretaker cocks his head, and Curtis half expects the man's unusually large ears to turn toward the sound like the data-gathering dishes of radio telescopes. 'Holy howlin' saints alive, that thing sounds big as Judgment Day. You mean them egg-suckin' bastards is chasin' you in *that*?'

'That and more,' Curtis confirms.

'Gov'ment must want you bad as a damn gopher snake wants to get its snout in warm gopher guts.'

'I'm not so happy to hear it put that way, sir.'

Pointing the flashlight at the ground between them, Gabby asks, 'What they want you for, boy?'

'Mostly the worse scalawags wanted my mother, and they got her, and now I'm just sort of a loose end they have to tie up.'

'What they want your mother for? Was it . . . a land thing?'

Curtis has no idea what the caretaker means by *land thing*, but the opportunity exists to make an ally of this man. So he takes a chance and replies, 'Yes, sir, it was a land thing.'

Spluttering with anger, Gabby says, 'Call me a hog an' butcher me for bacon, but don't you *ever* tell me the gov'ment ain't a land-crazy, dirt-grabbin' tyrant!'

The very thought of butchering anyone repulses Curtis; in fact, the suggestion entirely bewilders him. And he's too polite to call the caretaker a hog, even if the peculiar request was as sincere as it sounded.

Fortunately, Curtis isn't required to formulate an inoffensive response, because at once the fuming caretaker inhales a great chest-expanding breath and blows out a storm of words: 'Me and the missus, we bought us this sweet piece of land, not a nicer plot of dirt up in Paradise itself, got its own water source, got this grove of big old cottonwoods been there so long they probably has dinosaur bones a-tangled in the roots, got some good pasture with it, taken us the better part of fifteen years to pay off the blood-suckin' bank, then more years savin' to carpenter-up a little place, an' when we finally gets ready to dig us a foundation, the *gov'ment* says we can't. The *gov'ment* says this here butt-ugly, bandy-shanked stink bug what lives on the property might be *disturbed* by us movin' in, which would be what the *gov'ment* calls an ecological tragedy, because this sticky-footed, no-necked, crap-eatin' stink bug maybe exists on only a hundred twenty-two tracts of land in five Western states. So me and the missus have ourselves this sweet property we can't build on, an' no jackass ever born ain't crazy enough to buy it from us if they can't never build it, neither. But, oh, it sure do give me a special fine fuzzy-good feelin' in my heart to know *the dung-eatin', flame-fartin' stink bug is all snug and cozy and AIN'T NEVER GOIN' TO BE DISTURBED!'*

By now Old Yeller is hiding behind Curtis.

In the east, the *chop-chop-chop* of the helicopter grows louder, and this ceaseless cutting sound echoes off the hard land, back into the wounded air. Steadily, rapidly closer.

'Iffen they catch you, what they plannin' to do, boy?'

'The worse ones,' says Curtis, 'will kill me. But the government . . . most likely they'll first try to hide me someplace they think is safe, where they can interrogate me. And if the worse scalawags don't find me where the FBI's hidden me . . . well, then sooner or later the government will probably do experiments on me.'

Although his claim sounds outrageous, Curtis is describing what he genuinely believes will happen to him.

Either the caretaker hears truth resonating in the boy's voice or he is prepared to believe *any* horror story about a government that values him less than it does a stink bug. 'Experiment! On a child!'

'Yes, sir.'

Gabby doesn't need to know what type of experiments Curtis would be subjected to or what purpose they would serve. Evidently he's able to stir up endless hideous possibilities in the pot of paranoia that is ever boiling on his mental stove. 'Sure, why the blazes not, what better them dirty bastards got to do with my taxes but go torture a child? Hell's bells, them is the type what would hack you up, cook you in some rice, serve you with salsa to the damn stink bugs if they thought that might make the damn stink bugs happy.'

Beyond the eastern crest of the valley, a pale radiance blooms in the night: the reflected beams of headlamps or searchlights from the two SUVs and the helicopter. Flowering brighter by the second.

'Better move,' Curtis says, more to himself and to the dog than to the caretaker.

Gabby glares at the rising light in the east, the frizzles of his beard seeming to bristle as if enlivened by an electric current. Then he squints so intently at Curtis that his sun-toughened face crinkles and twills and crimps and puckers like the features of an Egyptian mummy engaged in a long but losing battle with eternity. 'You ain't been shovelin' horseshit, have you, boy?'

'No, sir, and my ears aren't full of it, either.'

'Then, by all that's holy and some that's not, we're gonna feed these skunks our dust. Now you stay on me like grease on Spam, you understand?'

'No, sir, I don't,' Curtis admits.

'Like green on grass, boy, like wet on water,' the caretaker explains impatiently. 'Come on!' In that quick but hitching gait familiar from his grandfather's many movies, Gabby runs past the front of Smithy's Livery toward the hotel next door.

Curtis hesitates, puzzling over how to be grease, green, and wet. He's still a little *damp* from playing at the pump, though the desert air has already more than half dried him out.

In spite of her previous reservations about the caretaker, Old Yeller trots after him. Apparently instinct tells her that her faith is well placed.

Trusting his sister-becoming and therefore Gabby, Curtis lights out after them, past the livery and onto the boardwalk in front of Bettleby's Grand Hotel. Bettleby's is a forty-foot-wide, three-story, shabby clapboard building that could no more satisfy a taste for grandness than a cow pie could satisfy when you wanted a slice of grandma's deep-dish apple.

Suddenly the *chop* of the helicopter rotors explodes into a *boom-boom-boom*, no longer muffled by the valley wall.

Curtis senses that if he looks to his right, across the street and over the roofs of buildings on the other side of town, he will see the aircraft hovering at the crest of the valley, an ominous black mass defined only by its small red and white running lights. Instead, he keeps his mind on Old Yeller, keeps his eyes fixed on Gabby and on the bobbling beam of the flashlight.

Past the hotel, tightly adjoining it, stands Jensen's Readymade, ALL DONE OUTFITS FOR LADIES AND GENTLEMEN. A hand-lettered sign in the window announces that fashions 'currently to be seen everywhere in San Francisco' are now for sale here, which makes San Francisco seem as far away as Paris.

Past Jensen's Readymade and before reaching the post office, Gabby turns left, off the boardwalk and into a narrow walkway between buildings. This passage is similar to the one by which Curtis and Old Yeller earlier entered town from the other side of the street.

The chopper approaches: an avalanche of hard rhythmic sound sliding down the valley wall.

Something else is coming, too. Something marked by a hum that Curtis feels in his teeth, that resonates in his sinuses, and by a rapidly swelling but also quickly subsiding tingle in the Haversian canals of his bones.

To counter a rising tide of fear, he reminds himself that the way to avoid panicking in a flood is to concentrate on swimming.

The wood-frame structures, crowding them on both sides, glow golden as the flashlight passes. Shadows ebb up the plank walls in advance of Gabby, flow down again in his wake, and spill across Curtis as he wades after the caretaker and the dog.

Overall the faint fumes of recently applied paint, with an underlying spice of turpentine. A whiff of dry rabbit pellets. So peculiar that a rabbit would venture in here where it might easily be trapped by predators. Tart fragrance of a discarded apple core, fresh this very day, still a human scent clinging to it. Coyote urine, aggressively bitter.

Reaching the end of the passageway, the caretaker switches off the flashlight, and the moonless dark closes over them as if they have descended into a storm cellar and pulled the door shut at their backs. Gabby halts only a step or two into the open dirt yard beyond the west side of town.

If not for the dog's guidance, Curtis would collide with the old man. Instead, he steps around him.

Gabby grabs Curtis, pulls him close, and raises his voice above the thunder of the incoming chopper. 'We goin' spang north to the barn what ain't a barn!'

Curtis figures that the barn-what-ain't-a-barn, whatever it might be, isn't far enough north to be safe. The Canadian border isn't far enough north, for that matter, nor the Arctic Circle.

Judging by the sound of it, the helicopter is putting down at the south end of town, in the vicinity of Smithy's Livery. Near the evidence of the sodden platform and the wet footprints in the dirt around the water pump.

The FBI – and the soldiers, if there are any – will be conducting a sweep south to north, the direction in which Gabby and Curtis and Old Yeller now flee. They'll be highly trained in search-and-secure procedures, and most if not all of them will be equipped with night-vision goggles.

Peripherally, to his left, Curtis becomes aware of a faint pearly radiance close to the earth. Alarmed, he glances west and sees what appears to be a low skim of mist blanketing the ground, but then he realizes he's looking out across the salt flats not from a higher perspective, as before, but from the zero elevation of the valley floor. The illusory mist is in fact the natural phosphorescence of the barren plain, the ghost of the long-dead sea.

The hard whack of chopper blades abruptly softens, accompanied by a wheezy whistle of decelerating rotation. The aircraft is on the ground.

They're coming. They'll be efficient and *fast*.

Hurrying north, Curtis is worried, but not primarily about the men in the helicopter or those in the two SUVs that are probably even now descending the valley wall. Worse enemies have arrived.

The intervening buildings foil thermal-reading and motion-detection gear. They also somewhat, but not entirely, screen the telltale energy signature that only Curtis emits.

Because of the natural fluorescence of the nearby salt fields, the night isn't as black as it was just moments ago. Curtis can see Gabby ahead, and the dog's white flags.

The caretaker doesn't run in the usual sense of the word, but progresses in the herky-jerky fashion that his presumed grandfather displayed when, in those movie moments of high jeopardy, he had said, *Dang, we better skedaddle*. This Gabby moves fast in a skedaddle, but he keeps stopping to look back, waving his gun, as if he expects to discover a villain of one kind or another looming point-blank over him every time he turns.

Curtis wants to scream *Move-move-move*, but Gabby is probably an ornery cuss who always does things his way and who won't react well to instruction.

Though the search squads must be pouring out of the helicopter, there's no light to the south, where they landed. They're conducting a natural-conditions exploration, because they believe that their high-tech gear makes darkness their friend.

In addition to the buildings, commotion screens Curtis, too, makes it more difficult for the hunters to read his special energy signature, and there's going to be plenty of commotion coming in mere seconds.

In fact, it starts with screaming. The shrieks of a grown man reduced by terror to the condition of a small child.

Gabby hitches to a halt again and squints back along the route they followed, his pistol jabbing this and that way as he seeks a threat.

Clutching the caretaker by the arm, Curtis urges him onward.

Toward the south end of town, two men are screaming. Now three or even four. How suddenly the horror struck, and how rapidly it escalates.

'*Criminy*! What's that?' Gabby wonders, his voice quaking.

Curtis tugs at him, and the caretaker starts to move again, but then the screams are punctuated by the rattle and crack of automatic-weapons fire.

'The fools blastin' at *each other*?'

'Go, go, *go*,' Curtis demands, guided now by panic that overrides all sense of diplomacy, trying to muscle the old man into motion once more.

Men being torn apart, men being gutted, men being eaten alive would scream no more chillingly than this.

In skittles and lurches, the caretaker heads north again, Curtis at his side rather than behind him, the dog preceding them, as if by some psychic perception, she knows where to find the barn-what-ain't-a-barn.

With only half the town behind them, as they arrive at another passageway between buildings, a strange light flares to their right, out in the street, framed for their view by a tunnel of plank walls. Sapphire and scintillant, as brief as fireworks, it twice pulses, the way that a luminous jellyfish propels itself through the sea. Out of the subsequent gloom, while a negative image of the pyrotechnic burst still blossoms like a black flower in Curtis's vision, a smoldering dark mass hurtles from the street into the passage, tumbling end-over-end toward them.

Spry but graceless in the manner of a marionette jerked backward on its control strings, all bony shoulders and sharp elbows and knobby knees, Gabby springs out of the way with surprising alacrity. Curtis jukes, and the dog bolts for cover.

With shot-out-of-a-cannon velocity, a stone-dead man caroms off the flanking buildings, extremities noisily flailing the palisades of the narrow passageway, as though he's the apparition in a high-speed seance, rapping out a dire warning from the Other Side. He bursts into the open and explodes past Curtis. A lightning-struck scarecrow, spat out by a raging tornado, could not have been cast off with any greater force than this, and the carcass finally comes to rest in the tattered, bristling, yet boneless posture of a cast-down cornfield guardian. The steaming stink of him, however, is indescribably worse than a scarecrow's wet straw, moldering clothes, and moth-infested flour-sack face.

On the victim's sprung chest, scorched and wrinkled but still readable, a large white *F* and a large white *I* bracket the missing, blown-out *B*.

Ornery cuss or not, arthritic or not, the grizzled caretaker recognizes big trouble when he sees it, and he finds in himself the comparatively more youthful energy and nimbleness that his famous elder had shown in earlier films like *Bells of Rosarita* and *The Arizona Kid*. He sets out spang for the barn, as if challenging the dog to a race, and Curtis hurries after him, playing the sidekick's sidekick.

Screams, anxious shouts, and gunfire echo among the buildings, and then comes an eerie sound – *priong, priong, priong, priong* – such as the stiff steel tines of a garden rake might produce if they could be plucked as easily as the strings of a fiddle.

One Curtis Hammond lies dead in Colorado, and another now runs headlong toward a grave of his own.

31

Buttons gleamed, badges flashed, buckles shone on the khaki uniforms of the cops milling outside the front door of Cielo Vista Care Home.

Martin Vasquez, general manager of this facility, stood apart from the police, beside one of the columns that supported the loggia trellis. Called from bed at a bleak hour, he had nonetheless taken time, as an expression of respect, to dress in a dark suit.

In his forties, Vasquez had the smooth face and the guileless eyes of a pious young novitiate. As he watched Noah Farrel approach, he looked as though he would have gladly traded this night's duty for vows of poverty and celibacy. 'I'm so sorry, so sick about this. If you'll come to my office, I'll try to make sense of it for you, as much as can be made.'

Noah had been a cop for only three years, but he'd been present at four homicide scenes in that time. The expressions on the faces and in the eyes of these attending officers matched the look that he had once turned upon the grieving relatives in those cases. Sympathy formed part of it, but also a simmering suspicion that persisted even after a perpetrator was identified. In certain types of homicides, a family member is more likely to be involved than a stranger, and regardless of what the facts of the case appear to be, it's always wise to consider who might gain financially or be freed of an onerous responsibility by the death in question.

Paying for Laura's care had been not a burden, but the purpose of his existence. Even if these men believed him, however, he would still see the keen edge of suspicion sheathed in their sympathy.

One of the cops stepped forward as Noah followed Vasquez to the front door. 'Mr. Farrel, I've got to ask you if you're carrying.'

He had pulled on chinos and a Hawaiian shirt. The holster

was in the small of his back. 'Yeah, but I've got a permit for it.'

'Yes, sir, I know. If you'll trust me with it, I'll return it to you when you leave.'

Noah hesitated.

'You were in my shoes once, Mr. Farrel. If you think about it, you'll realize you'd do the same.'

Noah wasn't sure why he had strapped on the pistol. He didn't always carry it. He didn't *usually* carry it. When he'd left home, after Martin Vasquez's call, he hadn't been thinking clearly.

He surrendered the handgun to the young officer.

Although the lobby was deserted, Vasquez said, 'We'll have privacy in my office,' and indicated a short hallway off to the left.

Noah didn't follow him.

Directly ahead, the door stood open between the lobby and the long main corridor of the ground-floor residential wing. At the far end, more men gathered outside of Laura's room. None wore a uniform. Detectives. Specialists with the scientific-investigation division.

Returning to Noah's side, Vasquez said, 'They'll let us know when you can see your sister.'

A morgue gurney waited near her room.

'Wendy Quail,' Noah guessed, referring to the perky raven-haired nurse who had been serving ice cream sundaes a few hours ago.

On the phone, he had been given only the essence of the tragedy. Laura dead. Gone quickly. No suffering.

Now, Martin Vasquez expressed surprise. 'Who told you?'

So his instinct had been right. And he hadn't trusted it. Ice cream wasn't the answer, after all. Love was the answer. Tough love, in this case. One of the Circle of Friends had indulged in a little tough love, teaching Noah what happens to the sisters of men who think they're too good to accept airsickness bags full of cash.

In his mind's eye, Noah imagined himself squeezing the trigger and the congressman contorting in agony around a gut wound.

He could do it, too. He was without a purpose now. A man needed worthwhile work to occupy his time. In the absence of anything more meaningful, maybe revenge would suffice.

Receiving no answer to his question, Vasquez said, 'Her resume was impressive. And her commitment to nursing. Several excellent letters of recommendation. She said she wanted to work in a less stressful atmosphere than a hospital.'

For seventeen years, since Laura was beaten out of this world but not all the way into the next, Noah had pretended that he wasn't a Farrel, that he was an outsider in his criminal family, just as Laura had been an outsider, that he was cleaner of heart than those who had conceived him, capable of being redeemed. But with his sister twice lost and beyond recovery, he could see no reason to resist embracing his true dark nature.

'But caught,' said Vasquez, 'she admitted everything. She's been a nurse in neonatal-care units at three hospitals. Each time, just when someone might begin to wonder if all the infant deaths pointed to something worse than just nature's work, she changed jobs.'

Killing the congressman wouldn't give Noah a new cup from which to drink, but the pleasure of that murder might be sweet enough to mask, for a while, the bitterness here at the bottom of his life.

'She admits to sixteen babies. She doesn't think what she's done is wrong. She calls those murders her "little mercies."'

He had been listening to Vasquez but hardly hearing what was said. At last a measure of the man's meaning penetrated. 'Mercies?'

'She chose infants with health problems. Or sometimes just those who looked weak. Or whose parents seemed dirt poor and ignorant. She says she was sparing them from lives of suffering.'

Noah's instinct had been half right. The nurse was bent, but not by the Circle of Friends. Yet their roots grew from the same swamp of self-importance and excess self-esteem. He knew their kind too well.

'Between the third neonatal unit and here,' Vasquez said, 'she worked at a nursing home. Euthanized five elderly patients without arousing suspicion. She's . . . proud of those, too. Not only no remorse, but also no shame at all. She seems to expect us to admire her for . . . for her compassion, she would call it.'

The congressman's evil was born of greed, envy, and a lust for power, which was a logical wickedness that Noah understood. That was the evil of his old man, of Uncle Crank.

The nurse's irrational idealism, on the other hand, incited only cold contempt and disgust, not a raging desire for revenge. Without a banquet of vengeance to sustain him, Noah felt starved of purpose once more.

'Another member of the staff walked in on Nurse Quail when she was . . . finishing with your sister. Otherwise, we wouldn't have known.'

At the far end of the long corridor, a guy wheeled the gurney into Laura's room.

Rolling through Noah's head came a sound like distant thunder or the faraway roar of a great cataract, soft though charged with power.

He passed through the door between the lobby and the residential hallway. Martin Vasquez called to him, reminding him that the police had restricted access to this area.

Approaching the nurses' station, Noah was met by a uniformed officer who attempted to turn him back.

'I'm family.'

'I know that, sir. Won't be much longer.'

'Yeah. It'll be now.'

When Noah tried to move past him, the cop put a hand on his shoulder. Noah wrenched loose, didn't take a swing, but kept going.

The young officer followed, grabbed him again, and they would have gotten physical then, because the cop had no choice, but mainly because Noah wanted to hit someone. Or maybe he wanted to *be* hit, hard and repeatedly, because physical pain might distract him from an anguish for which there was neither numbing medication nor any prospect of healing.

Before any punches were thrown, one of the detectives farther along the hall said, 'Let him through.'

The roar of five Niagaras still echoed from a distance in Noah's mind, and though this internal sound was no louder than before, the voices of the men around him were muffled by it.

'I can't let you alone with her,' the detective said. 'There's an autopsy gotta be done, and you know I'll have to show we've had continuous possession of the evidence.'

The corpse was evidence. Like a spent bullet or a bloody hammer. Laura had ceased to be a person. She was an object now, a thing.

The detective said, 'Don't want to give that crazy bitch's attorney any chance to say someone tampered with the remains before we got toxicology back.'

Crazy bitch instead of *defendant*, instead of *the accused*. No need to be politically correct here, as later in court.

If the attorney could sell the *crazy* without the *bitch*, however, then the nurse might do light time in a progressive mental facility with a swimming pool, TVs in every room, classes in arts and crafts, and sessions with a therapist not to analyze her homicidal compulsion but to ensure that she maintained high self-esteem.

Juries were stupid. Maybe they hadn't always been, but they were stupid these days. Kids killed their parents, resorted to the orphan defense, and a reliable percentage of jurors grew teary-eyed.

Noah couldn't rekindle his fury either with the prospect of the nurse remanded to a country-club sanitarium or with the possibility that she would be entirely acquitted.

The distant roar in his head wasn't the sound of building rage. He didn't know what it was, but he couldn't shut it off, and it scared him.

Laura on the bed. In yellow pajamas. Either she had come out of her cataleptic trance sufficiently to dress for sleep or perhaps the nurse had changed her, brushed her hair, and arranged her artfully as a courtesy before the killing.

The detective said, 'Quail figured, given the patient's brain damage, death would be attributed to natural causes without a full autopsy. She didn't bother using a substance that would be hard to trace. It was a massive injection of Haldol, a tranquilizer.'

By the time Laura turned eight, she understood that her family wasn't like others. A conscience had never been nurtured in her, not in the Farrel house, but nature had given her a strong moral sense. Shame came easily to her, and everything about her family mortified her more deeply year by year. She kept to herself, taking refuge in books and daydreams. She wanted only to grow up, to get out, and to make a life that would be 'clean, quiet, not a harm to anyone.'

The detective tried to console Noah with a final revelation: 'The overdose was so large, death was immediate. That crap just shut down the central nervous system like a switch.'

By the time she was eleven, Laura wanted to be a doctor, as if she no longer felt able to cut free of her roots merely by doing the world no harm. She needed to give to other people, perhaps through medicine, in order to ransom her soul from her family.

When she was twelve, she morphed in her daydreams from physician to veterinarian. Animals made better patients. Most people, she said, could never be cured of their worst sicknesses, only of their body's ailments. No one should have to learn that much about the human condition by the tender age of twelve.

Twelve years of striving to shape the future with dreams and seventeen more years of dreaming without purpose ended here, in this bed, where no more dreams waited beneath the pillows.

The detectives and the medical-examiner's people had stepped back, leaving Noah alone at the bedside, although they continued to watch in their capacity as guardians of the mortal evidence.

Laura rested on her back, arms at her sides. The palm of her left hand lay flat against the sheets, but her right hand was turned up and closed in a three-quarter fist, as if in the final instant, she had tried to hold fast to life.

Both the porcelain-smooth half and the ruined half of her face were revealed, God's work and Crank's.

To Noah, now that he would never see her again, both sides of her face were beautiful. They touched his heart in different ways.

We bring beauty with us into this world, as we bring innocence, and the ugliness that we take with us when we leave is what we've made of ourselves instead of what we should have made. Laura had moved on from this life with no ugliness at all. Only the soul leaves here; and hers was without stain or scar, as innocent at departure as it had been upon arrival.

Noah had lived longer and more fully than his sister, but not as well. He knew that when his time came to go, unlike her, he wouldn't be able to leave behind all his ugliness with his blood and bone.

He almost began to talk to her, as he had talked so often over the years, hour after hour, with the hope that she heard him and was comforted. But now that his sister had traveled beyond hearing,

Noah discovered he had nothing to say anymore – not to her, not to anyone.

He had hoped that the distant thunder in his head would stop rolling when he saw Laura and confirmed beyond doubt that she was gone. Instead, the roar gradually grew louder.

He turned from the bed and walked away. The air thickened and resisted him at the threshold, but only for an instant.

Across the hallway, the door opposite Laura's was closed. On his last few visits, that room – also a single – had stood open for airing because no patient currently occupied it.

Although a new resident might have been admitted in the past few hours, instinct carried Noah boldly across the hall. He threw open the door and took one step past the threshold before men seized him from behind, restraining him.

Nurse Quail sat in an armchair, so petite that her feet barely touched the floor. Twinkling blue eyes, pink complexion, pert and pretty: as Noah remembered her.

Two men and one woman were with the murderess. At least one of them would be a homicide detective and at least one would be from the D. A.'s office. The three were tough professionals, skilled at psychological manipulation, not likely to allow any suspect to hijack an interrogation.

Yet Wendy Quail clearly controlled the situation, most likely because she was too deluded to understand the real nature of her situation. Her posture and her expression weren't those of a suspect facing a hard inquisition. She appeared to be as poised as royalty, like a queen granting an audience to admirers.

She didn't shrink from Noah, but smiled at him in recognition. She held out a hand toward him as might a queen who saw before her a grateful subject who had come to kneel abjectly and to offer effusive appreciation for some grace that earlier she had bestowed on him.

Now he knew why he'd been required to check his pistol at the front door: just in case an unexpected encounter like this occurred.

Maybe he would have shot her if he'd had the handgun; but he didn't think so. He had the capacity to kill her, the nerve and the ruthlessness, but he didn't have the requisite rage.

Curiously, Wendy Quail failed to arouse his anger. In spite of the self-satisfaction that virtually oozed from her, and although her peaches-and-cream cheeks pinked with the warmth generated by a well-banked and well-tended moral superiority, she lacked the substance to excite anyone's hatred. She was a hollow creature into whose head had been poured evil philosophies that she couldn't have brewed in the cauldron of her own intellect; and if in her formative years she had been exposed to a gentler and humbler school of thought, she might have been the committed healer that now she only pretended to be. She was plates and platters of plights and pickles; she was ice cream therapy; but although she was worthy of being loathed and even of being abhorred, she was too pathetic to merit hatred.

Noah allowed himself to be drawn backward out of the room before the nurse could speak some witless platitude. Someone closed the door between them.

Wise enough to offer no commiseration or advice, two detectives escorted him along the corridor toward the lobby. Noah had never been a member of their department; his three years of service had been in another of the county's many cities, which interlocked like puzzle pieces in a jigsaw of jurisdictions. Nevertheless, they were his age or older, and they knew why he no longer wore a uniform. They surely understood why he had done what he'd done, ten years ago, and they might even sympathize with him. But they had never straddled the line that he had crossed with both feet, and to them he was to be treated as politely as any citizen but with more wariness, regardless of the fact that at one time he had worn the tin and done the job just as they did. They spoke to him only to report how long the body would be held by the medical examiner and to describe the process by which it could be claimed and be transferred to a mortuary.

The care home's residents had been asked to remain in their rooms with the doors closed, and had been issued sleep aids when they requested them. But Richard Velnod stood in his open doorway, as though waiting for Noah.

Rickster's unnaturally sloped brow seemed to recede from his eyes at a more severe angle than previously, and gravity exerted a greater than ordinary pull on his heavy features. His mouth moved, but his thick tongue, always a barrier to clear speech, failed him entirely this time; no sound came from him. Although usually his eyes were windows to his thoughts, they were paled now by tears, and he seemed to be holding back some question that he was afraid to ask.

The detectives would have preferred that Noah leave directly, but he stopped here and said, 'It's all right, son. She didn't have any pain.'

Rickster's hands moved restlessly, pulling at each other, at the buttons on his pajama top, at his low-set ears, at his wispy brown hair, and at the air as though he might pluck understanding from it. 'Mr. Noah, wha . . . wha . . . ?' His mouth went soft, twisted with anguish.

Assuming that the question had been *Why?*, Noah could provide no answer other than a platitude worthy of Nurse Quail: 'It was just Laura's time to go.'

Rickster shook his head. He wiped at his flooded eyes, swabbed wet hands across damp cheeks, and gathered his troubled face into an expression so affectingly earnest, so miserable, so desperate that Noah could hardly bear to look at it. Rickster's mouth firmed, and his malformed tongue found the shape of the words that had a moment ago eluded it, and he asked not *Why?*, but a question more to the point and yet even more difficult to answer: 'What's wrong with people?'

Noah shook his head.

'What's *wrong* with people?' Rickster implored.

His eyes fixed so beseechingly on Noah that it was impossible to turn away from him without responding, and yet impossible to lie even though, to this hard question, lies were the only answers that would soothe.

Noah knew that he should have put an arm around the boy and walked him back to his bed, where the framed photographs of his dead parents stood on the nightstand. He should have tucked him in and talked to him about anything that came to mind, or about nothing at all, as he had talked for so many years to his sister. More than a need to know what was wrong with people, loneliness plagued this boy, and although Noah had no insight into the source of human cruelty, he could medicate loneliness with a gift of his time and company.

He felt burnt out, however, and doubted that he had anything within him worth giving. Not anymore. Not after Laura.

He had no idea what was wrong with people, but he knew that whatever might have broken in the soul of humanity was manifestly broken in him.

'I don't know,' he told this cast-away boy with the castaway face. 'I don't know.'

By the time that he retrieved his pistol and reached his car in the parking lot, the previously faraway roar in his head grew louder and acquired a more distinctive character. No longer like thunder, it might have been the angry chanting of the whole mad crowd of humankind – or still the rumble of water tumbling from a high cliff into an abyss.

On the way to Cielo Vista, he'd broken every law of the highway; but he exceeded no speed limits on the way home, ran no stop signs. He drove with the exaggerated care of a cautious drunk because, mile by mile, the surging sound within him was accompanied by a deepening flood of darkness, and those black torrents seemed to spill from him into the California night. Block by block, streetlamps appeared to grow dimmer, and previously well-lighted avenues seemed to be drowned in murk. By the time he parked at his apartment, the river that might have been hope finished draining entirely into the abyss, and Noah was borne to a bottle of brandy and to his bed on the currents of a bleaker emotion.

32

Boy, dog, and grizzled grump arrive at the barn-what-ain't-a-barn, but to Curtis it appears to be a barn and nothing more. In fact, it looks like merely the ruins of a barn.

The structure stands by itself, two hundred yards northwest of the town, past clumps of stunted sage and bristles of wild sorrel and foot-snaring tendrils of creeping sandbur. At a surprisingly sharp line of demarcation, all forms of desert scrub and weeds and cactus surrender to the saline soil, and the inhospitable desert gives way to the utterly barren salt flats – which seems to be a curious place to have built a barn.

Even in the dark-drenched night, where shadows drip off shadows, the building's decrepit condition is obvious. Instead of describing a straight line, the steeply pitched roof swags from peak to eave. The walls are a little catawampus to the foundation, time-tweaked and weather-warped at the corners.

Unless the ramshackle barn is actually a secret armory stocked with futuristic weapons – plasma swords, laser-pulse rifles, neutron grenades – Curtis can't imagine what hope it offers them. No shelter will be safe in this storm.

In the strife-torn town behind them, the tempest already rages. Much of the screaming and the shouting fails to carry across the intervening desert, but a few faint cries are chilling enough to plate his spine with ice. Gunfire, familiar to this territory for a century and a half, is answered by battle sounds never heard before in the Old West or the New: an ominous tolling that shivers the air and shudders the earth, a high-pitched oscillating whistle, a pulsing bleat, a tortured metallic groan.

As Gabby wrenches open a man-size door next to the larger doors of the barn, a hard flat *crump* draws Curtis's attention to the town just in time to see one of the larger structures – perhaps the saloon and gambling hall – implode upon itself, as if collapsing into a black hole. The reverse-pressure wave pulls eddies of salt from the dry bed of the ancient ocean, sucking them toward the town, and Curtis rocks on the balls of his feet.

A second *crump*, following close after the first, is accompanied by a whirlpool of fiery orange light where the saloon had stood. In that churning blaze, the imploded structure seems to disgorge itself: Planks and shingles, posts and balcony railings, doors, cocked window frames – plus two flights of stairs like a portion of a brontosaurus spine – erupt from the darkness that had swallowed them, spinning in midair, in tornadolike suspension, silhouetted by the flames. As a pressure wave casts back the eddies of salt and chases them with showers of sand, nearly rocking Curtis off his feet once more, it's possible to believe that the whirling rubble of the saloon will magically reassemble into a historic structure once more.

Gabby has no time for the spectacle, and Curtis should have none, either. He follows the caretaker and the dog into the barn.

The door isn't as rickety as he expects. Rough wood on the exterior but steel on the inside, heavy, solid, it swings smoothly shut behind him on well-oiled hinges.

Inside lies a short shadowy corridor with light beyond an open doorway at the end. Not the light of an oil lamp, but a constant fluorescent glow.

The air contains neither the faint cindery scent of the desert nor the alkali breath of the salt flats. And it's cool.

Pine trees, pine trees, close to the floor, pine on the floor. Pine-scented wax on the vinyl tiles. Cinnamon and sugar, crumbs of a cookie, butter and sugar and cinnamon and flour. Good, good.

The fluorescent light arises in a windowless office with two desks and filing cabinets. And a refrigerator. Chilled air floods out of a ventilation duct near the ceiling.

Barely detectable vibrations in the floor suggest a subterranean vault containing a gasoline-powered generator. This is a barn worthy of Disneyland: entirely new, but crafted to resemble the battered remains of a homesteader's farm. The building provides office and work space for the support staff that oversees maintenance of the ghost town, without introducing either contemporary structures or visible utilities that would detract from the otherwise meticulously maintained period ambience.

On the nearest of the desks stands a cup of coffee and a large thermos bottle. Beside the cup lies a paperback romance novel by Nora Roberts. Unless the official night-shift support staff includes a ghost or two, the coffee and the book belong to Gabby.

Although they are on the run, with the prospect of heavily armed searchers bursting into this building behind them at any second, the caretaker pauses to sweep the paperback off the desk. He shoves it under a sheaf of papers in one of the drawers.

He glances sheepishly at Curtis. His deeply tanned face acquires a rubescent-bronze tint.

The dilapidated barn isn't at all what it appears to be from outside, and Gabby isn't entirely what he appears to be, either. The not-entirely-what-he-or-she-or-it-appears-to-be club has an enormous membership.

'Judas jump to hellfire, boy, we're in dangerous territory here! Don't just stand there till you're growed over with clockface an' cow's-tongue! Let's go, let's go!'

Curtis stopped at the desk only because Gabby stopped there first, and he realizes that the caretaker is shouting at him merely to distract his attention from the incident with the romance novel.

As he follows Gabby across the room to another door, however, Curtis wonders what sort of plants clockface and cow's-tongue might be and whether in this territory they really grow so fast that you could be completely overtaken by them if you stand too still even for a few seconds. He wonders, too, whether these are carnivorous plants that not only cocoon you, but then also feed on you while you're still alive.

The sooner he gets out of Utah, the better.

Beyond the first office lies a second and larger office. The four doors leading from this space suggest additional rooms beyond.

Gimping like a dog with two short legs on the left side, Gabby leads Old Yeller and Curtis to the farthest door, snares a set of keys off a pegboard, and proceeds into a garage with bays for four vehicles. Three spaces are empty, and an SUV waits in the fourth, facing toward the roll-up door: a white Mercury Mountaineer.

As Curtis hurries around to the passenger's side, Gabby pulls open the driver's door and says, 'That dog, she broke?'

'She fixed, sir.'

'Say what?'

'Say *fixed*, sir,' says Curtis as he frantically jerks open the front door on the passenger's side.

Levering himself in behind the steering wheel, Gabby shouts at him, 'Tarnation, I ain't havin' no biscuit-eater pissin' in my new Mercury!'

'All we had was frankfurters, sir, and then some orange juice,' Curtis replies reassuringly as, not without difficulty, he clambers into the passenger's seat with the dog in his arms.

'Spinnin' syphilitic sheep! What for you bringin' her in the front seat, boy?'

'What for shouldn't I, sir?'

As he pushes a button on a remote-control unit to put up the garage door, and starts the engine, the caretaker says, 'Iffen God made little fishes, then passengers what has a tail ought to load up through the *tail*gate!'

Pulling shut the passenger's door, Curtis says, 'God made little fishes, sure enough, sir, but I don't see what one has to do with the other.'

'You got about as much common sense as a bucket. Better hold tight to your mongrel 'less you want she should wind up bug-spattered on the wrong side of the windshield.'

Old Yeller perches in Curtis's lap, facing front, and he locks his arms around the dog to hold her in place.

'We gonna burn the wind haulin' ass outta here!' Gabby loudly declares as he shifts the Mountaineer out of park.

Curtis takes this to be a warning against the likelihood that they're going to experience flatulence, but he can't imagine why that will happen.

Gabby tramps on the accelerator, and the Mountaineer shoots out of the garage, under the still rising door.

First pinned back in his seat, then jammed against the door when the caretaker turns west-southwest almost sharply enough to roll the SUV, Curtis remembers the applicable law and raises his voice over the racing engine: 'Law says we have to wear seat belts, sir!'

Even in the weak light from the instrument panel, the boy can see Gabby's face darken as though someone from the gov'ment were throttling him at this very moment, and the old man proves that he can rant and drive at the same time. 'Whole passel of politicians between 'em ain't got a brain worth bug dust! No scaly-assed, wart-necked, fly-eatin', toad-brained politician an' no twelve-toed, fat-assed, pointy-headed bureaucrat ain't goin' to tell *me* iffen I got to wear a seat belt nor iffen I *don't* got to wear one, as far as that goes! Iffen I want to stand on these brakes an' bust through the windshield with my face, damn if I won't, an' no one can tell me I ain't got the right! Next thing them power-crazy bastards be tellin' us the law says wear a jockstrap when you drive!'

While the caretaker continues in this vein, Curtis turns in his seat as best he can, still holding on to Old Yeller, and looks back, to the east and north, toward the embattled ghost town. It's a light show back there, violent enough to make even Wyatt Earp hide in the church. When the shootout ends, whatever historical society oversees this site is going to be hard pressed to restore the town from the splinters, bent nails, and ashes that will be left.

He remains amazed that the FBI is aware of him and of the forces pursuing him, that they have intervened in this matter, and that they actually think they have a chance of locating him and taking him into protective custody before his enemies can find and destroy him. They must know how outgunned they are, but they've plunged in nonetheless. He can't help but admire their kick-butt attitude and their courage, even though they would eventually subject him to experiments if they had custody of him long enough.

Gabby can drive even faster than he can talk. They are *rocketing* across the salt flats.

To avoid drawing unwanted attention, they're traveling without headlights.

Failure to employ headlights between dusk and dawn is against the law, of course, but he decides that to broach this subject with Gabby would qualify as poor socializing. Besides, Curtis has, after all, broken the law himself more than once during his flight for freedom, though he's not proud of his criminality.

The clouded sky casts down no light whatsoever, but the natural fluorescence of the land ensures that they aren't driving blind, and fortunately Gabby is familiar with this territory. He avoids whatever roads might cross this desolate valley and stays on the open land, so there's no risk of turning a bend and ramming head-on into innocent motorists, with all the unfortunate physical and moral consequences that would ensue.

The salt flats glow white, and the Mercury Mountaineer is white, so the vehicle shouldn't be easily visible from a distance. The tires spin up a white plume behind them, but this is a wispy telltale, not a thick billowing cloud, and it quickly settles.

If FBI agents or the worse scalawags are using motion-detection gear to sweep the flats either from a point atop the valley crest or from an aerial platform, then Gabby might as well not just turn on the headlights but fire off flares, as well, because this white-on-white strategy won't be clever enough to save them from being turned into buzzard grub like the man who had come tumbling in flaming ruin between the buildings.

'. . . hogtie 'em with one of their aggravatin' seat belts, douse 'em with some bacon grease, throw 'em in a root cellar with maybe ten thousand half-starved *STINK BUGS*, an' just see how all-fired safe the God-mockin' bastards feel then!' Gabby concludes.

Seizing this opportunity to change the subject, Curtis says, 'Speakin' of stink, sir, I ain't farted, and I don't think I'm goin' to, neither.'

Though he doesn't reduce their speed and might even accelerate a little, the old caretaker shifts his attention away from the salt flats hurtling toward them. He fixes Curtis with a look of such open-mouthed bewilderment that for a moment it prevents him from talking.

But only for a moment, whereafter he smacks his lips together and gets his tongue working again: 'Judas humpin' hacksaws in Hell! Boy, what the blazes did you just say an' why'd you say it?'

Disconcerted that his well-meaning attempt at small talk has excited something like outrage from the caretaker, Curtis says, 'Sir, no offense meant, but *you're* the one who first said about burnin' the wind and haulin' ass.'

'Here's that spit-in-the-eye-malefactor side of you what ain't a pretty thing to see.'

'No offense, sir, but you *did* say it, and I was just observin' that I ain't farted, like you expected, and you ain't neither, and neither ain't my dog.'

'You keep sayin' *no offense*, boy, but I'm tellin' you right now,

I'm bound to take some offense iffen your dog starts fartin' in my new Mercury.'

This conversation is going so badly and they are tearing across the salt flats at such a scary speed that changing the subject seems to be a matter of life and death, so Curtis figures the time has come to compliment Gabby on his celebrity lineage. 'Sir, I dearly loved *Helldorado, Heart of the Golden West*, and *Roll on Texas Moon*.'

'What in tarnation's wrong with you, boy?'

The dog whines and twitches in Curtis's lap.

'Look ahead, sir!' the boy exclaims.

Gabby glances at the onrushing salt flats. 'Just tumbleweed,' he says dismissively as an enormous prickly ball bounces off the front fender, rolls across the hood, over the windshield, and spins front to back across the roof with a clitter-click like skeleton fingers clawing at the underside of a coffin lid.

Nervously but valiantly making another effort to establish better rapport with the caretaker, Curtis says, '*Along the Navajo Trail* was really a fine movie, and *The Lights of Old Santa Fe*. But maybe the best of them was *Sons of the Pioneers*.'

'You say movies?'

'I say movies, sir.'

Even as Gabby presses the Mountaineer still faster, faster, he disregards the land ahead, as though confident that he can perceive oncoming catastrophe through a sixth sense, and he focuses on Curtis with disconcerting intensity. 'With gov'ment maniacs blowin' up the world behind us, what in the name of the beheaded baptist are you talkin' *movies* for?'

''Cause they're your grandfather's movies, sir.'

'My grandpa's movies? Criminy spit an' call it wine, an' give me two bottles! What are you babblin' about? My grandpa was a mercantile porch-squatter, sellin' Bibles an' useless 'cyclopedias if you was crazy enough to open your door to him.'

'But if your grandpa was a porch-squatter, then what about Roy Rogers?' Curtis pleads.

Gabby's wiry beard, eyebrows, and ear hairs bristle with either exasperation or static electricity generated by a combination of high speed and dry desert air. 'Roy Rogers?' He's shouting again. He holds the steering wheel with one hand and pounds it with the other. 'What in the blue blazes does a fancy-boots, picture-show, singin', dead cowboy got to do with you or me, or the price of beans?'

Curtis doesn't know the price of beans or why the price is of sudden importance to the caretaker at this particular time, but he knows that they are going far too fast – and still gaining speed. The more perturbed that Gabby becomes, the heavier his foot grows on the accelerator, and everything that Curtis says perturbs him further. The floor of the valley is remarkably flat, but at this reckless velocity, even the smallest runnel or bump rattles the Mountaineer. If they encounter a deep rut or a rock, or one of those sun-bleached cow skulls that so often show up in Western movies, the best Detroit engineering won't save them, and the SUV will roll like, well, like Judas strapped to a log and tumbled down the mill chute to Hell.

Curtis is afraid to say anything, but Gabby appears to be ready to thump the steering wheel again if he doesn't say *something*. So without any desire to argue, intending only to express an alternative opinion, and by engaging in some pleasant conversation to reduce the caretaker's agitation and also the speed of the Mountaineer, he says, 'No offense, sir, but Roy Rogers's boots didn't seem to me to be all that fancy.'

Gabby glances at the land ahead, which is a relief to Curtis, but immediately he looks at Curtis once more, and yet again the SUV accelerates. 'Boy, you 'member way to hell back there at the pump, when I asked was you stupid or somethin'?'

'Yes, sir, I 'member.'

'An' you 'member what you said?'

'Yes, sir, I said I guessed I was somethin'.'

'Ever any fool was to ask you that question again, boy, you'd be better advised to tell 'em *stupid*!' Pounding the steering wheel again, he's off on another rant. 'Shove a bottle rocket in my butt an' call me Yankee Doodle! Here I put myself at war with the whole egg-suckin' gov'ment, with their bombs an' tanks an' tax collectors, all 'cause you claim they done killed your folks, an' now I see you're liable to say anythin' what makes no more sense than chicken gabble, and maybe the gov'ment never done killed your folks at all.'

Appalled to discover this misunderstanding, fighting back tears, Curtis hastens to correct the caretaker: 'Sir, I never done said the government done killed my folks.'

Flabbergasted and outraged, Gabby roars, 'Cut off my co-jones an' call me a princess, but don't you *ever* tell me that ain't what you claimed!'

'Sir, I claimed it was the *worse* scalawags what done killed my folks, not the government.'

'*Ain't* no worse scalawags than the gov'ment!'

'Oh, big-time worse, sir.'

Old Yeller fidgets in Curtis's lap. She whimpers nervously, and icy sweat drips rapidly from her black nose onto his hands, and he senses that she wants to relieve herself. Through their special boy-dog bond, he encourages her to keep control of her bladder, but now he's reminded that their relationship is dog-boy as well as boy-dog, that it can work both ways if he isn't careful, and her need to pee is rapidly becoming *his* need to pee. He can too easily imagine the catastrophe that would ensue if he and the dog both peed in Gabby's new Mercury, causing the caretaker to have a stroke and lose control of the vehicle at high speed.

For the first time since the truck-stop restaurant, the boy is losing confidence in his ability to be Curtis Hammond. Lacking adequate self-assurance, no fugitive can maintain a credible deception. Perfect poise is the key to survival. There you have Mother's wisdom as pure as it gets.

Gabby is ranting again, and the Mercury Mountaineer shudders and groans like a space shuttle blasting into orbit, and in spite of all the uproar, something that the caretaker said a moment ago makes a connection in Curtis's mind to *another* misunderstanding earlier in the evening. A small illumination follows, and Curtis desperately seizes upon his sudden insight to try to change the direction of the conversation and to reestablish the far-friendlier tone that existed between them such a short while ago.

According to the movies, most Americans strive always to better their lives and to improve themselves, and because movies provide reliable information, Curtis interrupts Gabby's blustering with the intention of offering a vocabulary lesson for which the caretaker will no doubt be grateful. 'Sir, the reason I was confused is you weren't pronouncing it properly. You meant *testicles*!'

Every look of surprise that heretofore made such dramatic use of the caretaker's highly expressive face is as nothing to the brow-corrugating, eyebrow-steepling, eye-popping, wrinkle-stretching, beard-frizzling astonishment that now possesses his features.

Gabby's expression is such an obvious precursor to another rant that Curtis hurries on, frantic to explain himself: 'Sir, you said "co-jones," when what you meant to say was "kah-ho-nays." *Cojones.* That's the English pronunciation, which is slightly different from the way you would say it in Spanish. If you—'

'*Blast all the devils from Hell to Abilene!*' Gabby bellows, and he looks away from Curtis with obvious disgust, which is good in one way and bad in another. Good because he's at last staring at the salt flats ahead of them. Bad because sooner or later, trembling from the offense that he's taken, he's going to look at Curtis again, and *that* look will peel the wet off water.

Like wet on water.

Another small enlightenment blossoms in Curtis, but he resists sharing it with the fuming caretaker. He has lost all confidence in his ability to socialize. Shaken, he is convinced that anything he says, even a wordless grunt delivered in the most inoffensive tone, will be misinterpreted and will trigger another furious oath from Gabby that will be loud enough to shatter all the windows in the Mountaineer.

The boy's failure even to attempt to hold up his end of the conversation results in only a brief silence. The caretaker splutters in exasperation after saying 'Abilene,' inhales with a rattling snort worthy of a horse, and blows out another gust of words: 'You sassy-assed, spit-in-the-eye, ungrateful, snot-nosed little punk! Maybe I ain't been to no Harvard College, an' maybe I ain't had the better advantages of some what was born with silver spoons in their mouths, but from the time I worn diapers, I knowed it was pure bad manners criticizin' your elders. You don't got no call tellin' me how to say *co-jones* when the pathetic pair of co-jones *you* have ain't no bigger than two chickpeas!'

As Gabby continues to rave, he finally eases up on the gas pedal and lets the Mountaineer's speed fall. Maybe he's considering pulling to a stop and ordering Curtis to get out and fend for himself.

Right now, if they were in a boat in the middle of a stormy sea, the boy would go overboard without a protest; therefore, he won't argue about being left afoot on these salt flats. In fact, he'll welcome it. The stress of being a desperate fugitive, maintaining a credible false identity, resisting the urge to go a little dog wild, *and* socializing in a challenging dialect is more than he's able to handle. He feels as though his head is going to explode or that something even worse and more embarrassing will occur.

Apparently having vented enough anger to look at his snot-nosed passenger without risking cardiac infarction, Gabby at last turns his attention away from the flats. Maybe the old man is surprised that Curtis hasn't already thrown himself out of the Mountaineer or maybe he's surprised by the boy's tears, or maybe he's just surprised that this sassy-assed punk dares to look him in the eye. Whatever the reason, instead of the withering display of scorn and contempt that Curtis expects, the caretaker inflates his face into an expression of astonishment that so exceeds his *previous* look of astonishment that it seems more suitable to a cartoon character than to a human being.

And he stomps on the brake pedal.

Fortunately, their speed has fallen from in excess of a hundred miles an hour to under fifty. Shrieking brakes and screaming tires sound pretty much the same on hard-packed salt as on blacktop, though the combined odors of hot rubber and churning salt produce a smell that is unique to these conditions and strangely like ham sizzling in a skillet.

If Curtis hadn't been jammed down firmly in his seat, pinching the upholstery with his tailbone, and pressing his feet into the floorboard nearly hard enough to buckle it, he and Old Yeller might indeed have splattered like bugs on the wrong side of the windshield. Instead, the poor dog's life flashes through her mind, from whelping to puppyhood to the frankfurters in the motor home, and Curtis's life flashes through his mind, too, which leaves both him and the mutt a little confused. But when the Mountaineer slides to a full stop, rocking on its springs, neither boy nor dog is hurt.

By surviving the sudden stop unscathed, Gabby, too, has proved that the miserable scaly-assed, wart-necked, fly-eatin', toad-brained politicians don't know everything. You might think that this small triumph of rugged individualism over the government and the laws of physics would inspire a mood change for the better.

On the contrary, with an astounding rush of words referring to biological waste and sexual relations, the caretaker rams the gearshift into park, throws open his door, and exits the SUV in a state of such high agitation that he tangles in his own legs and falls out of sight.

'Criminy!' Curtis exclaims.

He slides out from under Old Yeller and across the console, leaving the dog in the passenger's seat, slipping behind the wheel.

Beyond the open door, in the fall of pale light from the SUV's ceiling lamp, Gabby lies on his back, on the ground. His rumpled and sweat-stained cowboy hat rests upside down next to him, as though he will produce that banjo at last and play for quarters. His white hair bristles as it might if he'd been the conduit for a lightning bolt, and grains of salt glitter in this postelectrocution coiffure. He looks dazed, perhaps having tested the firmness of the salt bed with a rap or two of his head.

'Holy howlin' saints alive!' Curtis declares. 'Sir, are you all right?'

This question so alarms the caretaker that you would think he had just been threatened with decapitation. He scoots backward, away from the Mountaineer, thoroughly salting the seat of his pants, and he takes the time to scramble to his feet only after he has put some distance between himself and the vehicle.

To this point, Curtis has assumed that much of what seems odd about this man's behavior is not in fact peculiar, but is simply a matter of poor communication, resulting in a series of unfortunate misunderstandings. Now he isn't so sure about that. Maybe Gabby is not cranky-but-lovable, not cranky-but-tender-hearted, not cranky-but-well-meaning, but just plain cranky. Maybe he's even somewhat unbalanced. Maybe he's been chewing on loco-weed. He's probably not a serial killer, like the tooth fetishists in the motor home, unless serial killers are even a greater per-centage of the population than the movies imply, which is a scary thought.

On the ground between Gabby and the Mountaineer are two objects: the hat and the 9-mm pistol. Frantically scuttling backward a moment ago, he now reverses course and tentatively approaches. Although Curtis would like to believe Gabby is a genuine amigo, cantankerous but compassionate, the caretaker's attention is *not* focused on the hat.

The handgun is close to Curtis. He hops out of the SUV to get the weapon.

The unpredictable caretaker doesn't try to beat him to the gun. He doesn't just halt or back off, either, but turns away and runs across the salt flats in his singular hitching gait, as fast as he can go.

Bewildered, Curtis watches the receding figure until it's clear the man won't attempt to sneak back. Gabby doesn't once look over his shoulder, but lights out for the eastern side of the valley as though he believes that all the devils between Hell and Abilene, which he had previously cursed, are now in vengeful pursuit of him. He fades into the darkness and the eerie fluorescence until he appears to be the mere mirage of a man.

How strange. The entire encounter with Gabby will require a lot of thoughtful analysis later, when Curtis has outlasted his enemies and can afford the leisure for contemplation.

When he has outlasted them, not *if*. Now that the obligation to socialize has been lifted from him for a while, Curtis feels his confidence returning.

A few miles to the north, where hard-bitten gunfighters once faced off in the dusty street, a fierier and noisier confrontation is still underway, and while it doesn't look like Armageddon or the War of the Worlds, the level of combat remains impressive. Curtis expected the conflict to be over long ago; and he doesn't anticipate that these mismatched forces will be dueling much longer.

Besides, sooner rather than later, they may begin to suspect that the boy over whom they're battling has slipped out of town during the uproar and is riding the range once more. Then the two armies will disengage, rather than fight to the finish, and both the scalawags and the worse scalawags will return to the urgent boy-dog search that brought them into the same town at the same time in the first place.

Better move.

Leaving the pistol on the ground now that there's no need to worry about Gabby getting possession of it, Curtis climbs into the Mountaineer once more. He has never driven a vehicle like this. But the principles of its operation are obvious, and he's sure that he can handle it reasonably well, though most likely not with the skill of Steve McQueen in *Bullitt* or with the aplomb of Burt Reynolds in *Smokey and the Bandit.*

He is about to move from petty crimes to the commission of a major felony. Car theft. That's how the authorities will view it.

From his perspective, however, it's actually the unauthorized *borrowing* of a vehicle, because he has no intention of keeping the Mountaineer. If eventually he abandons it in as good a condition as he found it, his moral obligation will largely consist of making an apology to Gabby and compensating him for gasoline, time, and inconvenience. Because he doesn't relish coming face-to-face with the caretaker again, he hopes that his soul won't be tarnished too much if he makes both the apology and the payment by mail.

Height proves to be a problem. Curtis Hammond, a bit on the shorter side for a ten-year-old boy, can command a clear view of the terrain ahead or exercise full and easy control of the brakes and the accelerator, but not both at the same time. By slouching a little and stretching his right foot as might a leaping ballet dancer reaching for an on-point landing, he's able to proceed with a half-obstructed view and with compromised pedal control.

This slows him, however, and establishes a pace that seems more suitable to a funeral procession than to a run for freedom.

While he wants to put as much territory as possible between himself and his pursuers, he must remember that time, not distance, is his primary ally. Only by faithfully being Curtis Hammond hour after hour, day after day, is he likely to escape detection forever. Certain adjustments would allow him to handle the Mountaineer more easily, but if he were to indulge in them, he'd be more visible to his enemies the next time they came scanning in his vicinity. Which will be soon.

Mom's wisdom. The longer that you wear a disguise, the more completely you *become* the disguise. To maintain a credible deception, a fugitive must never slip out of character, not even for a moment. Establishing a new identity isn't merely a matter of acquiring a convincing set of ID documents; you aren't safe from discovery just because you look, talk, walk, and act in character. Establishing a new identity with total success requires you to *become* this new person with your every fiber, every cell – and for every minute of the day, when observed and unobserved.

Even in death, Mom remains the ultimate authority on this stuff, as well as a universal symbol of courage and freedom. She will be honored long after her passing. Even if she hadn't been his mom, he would conduct himself according to her advice; but as her son, he has a special obligation not just to survive but also to live by her teachings and eventually to pass them along to others.

Grief comes to him once more, and for a while he travels in its company.

He dares not continue southwest, for eventually the valley must bring him to the interstate, which will be patrolled. He came out of the east. The ghost town lies north. Therefore, he has little choice but to cross the width of the valley, heading due west.

Although he's in no danger of setting a land-speed record, and although he sometimes progresses in fits and starts as he cranes his neck to see over the steering wheel or ducks his head to peek between it and the top of the dashboard, he discovers that the salt flats are negotiable terrain. When he reaches the slope of the western valley wall, however, he realizes that he can't go farther in this fashion.

Here, the saltless land doesn't have an accommodating natural glow. Visibility already limited by the boy's height immediately declines to a condition not much better than blindness. Switching on the SUV headlights will provide no solution – unless he wants to call attention to himself and thereby commit suicide.

Furthermore, the rising land will be rocky and uneven. Curtis will need to react to conditions more quickly with both the brake pedal and the accelerator than he's been able to do thus far.

He shifts into park and sits high, gazing at the route ahead, stymied by the challenge.

His sister-becoming provides the solution. During the slow ride across the last of the salt flats, Old Yeller sat in the passenger's seat, decorating the side window with a pattern of nose prints. Now she stands in her seat and gives Curtis a meaningful look.

Maybe because grief is weighing on his mind, maybe because he's still rattled by his strange encounter with the caretaker, Curtis is embarrassingly slow on the uptake. At first he thinks that she simply wants to be scratched gently behind the ears.

Because she will never object to being scratched gently behind the ears or virtually anywhere else, Old Yeller accepts a minute of this pleasantness before she turns away from Curtis and, still with hind legs on the seat, places her forepaws on the dashboard. This puts her in a perfect position to see the route ahead.

This boy-dog relationship would be worthless if Curtis still failed to get her drift, but he understands what she has in mind. He will operate the controls of the SUV, and she will be his eyes.

Good pup!

He slides far enough down in his seat to plant his right foot firmly on the accelerator and to be able to shift it quickly and easily to the brake pedal. He is also in a satisfactory position to steer. He just can't see out of the windshield.

Their bonding is not complete. She is still his sister-becoming rather than his sister-become; however, their special relationship grew considerably in that scary moment when each of them saw both of their lives flashing before their eyes.

Curtis shifts the SUV out of park, presses the accelerator, and steers up the relatively easy slope of the valley wall with the eyes of his dog to guide him. Together they gain confidence during the ascent, and they function in perfect harmony by the time they reach the top.

He halts on the ridge, sits up, and through his own eyes looks northeast. The fighting at the ghost town seems to have ceased. The scalawags and the worse scalawags have realized that neither of them has captured their quarry. No longer battling each other, they are turning their attention once more to the search for boy and dog.

The running lights of *two* helicopters float in the sky. A third is approaching from farther in the east. Reinforcements.

Slouching in his seat once more, Curtis drives down off the ridge, heading farther west into unknown territory that Old Yeller scouts for him with unwavering diligence.

He drives as fast as seems prudent, keeping in mind that his sister-becoming could be hurt if he hits the brakes suddenly at too high a speed.

They need to make good time, however, because he can't expect the dog to be his eyes as long as he would like. Curtis requires no rest. Old Yeller will eventually need to sleep, but Curtis has never slept in his life.

After all, he must remember that he and his sister-becoming are not merely members of different species with far different physical abilities and limitations. More significantly, they were born on different worlds.

33

Thursday's child has far to go, according to the old nursery rhyme, and Micky Bellsong was born on a Thursday in May, more than twenty-eight years ago. On this Thursday in August, however, she was too hungover to go as far as she'd planned.

Lemon vodka diminishes mathematical ability. Sometime during the night, she must have counted the fourth double shot as a second, the fifth as a third.

Staring at the bathroom mirror, she said, 'Damn lemon flavoring screws up your memory.' She couldn't tweak a smile from herself.

She had overslept her first job interview and had risen too late to keep the second. Both were for positions as a waitress.

Although she had experience in food service and liked that work, she hoped to get a computer-related position, customizing software applications. She had compressed three years of instruction into the past sixteen months and had discovered that she possessed the ability and the interest to do well in this work.

In fact, the image of herself as a software-applications mensch was so radically in opposition to the way she'd led her life to date that it formed the center of her vision of a better future. Through the worst year of her existence, this vision had sustained her.

Thus far, seeking to make the dream real, she'd been thwarted by the perception among employers that the economy was sliding, dipping, stalling, coming under a shadow, cooling, taking a breather before the next boom. They had a limitless supply of words and phrases to convey the same rejection.

She hadn't begun to despair yet. Long ago, life had taught her that the world didn't exist to fulfill Michelina Bellsong's dreams or even to encourage them. She expected to have to struggle.

If the job hunt took weeks, however, her resolution to build a new life might prove to be no match for her weaknesses. She had no illusions about herself. She *could* change. But given an excuse, she herself would be the greatest obstacle to that change.

Now the face in the mirror displeased her, before and after she applied the little makeup she used. She looked good, but she took no pleasure in her appearance. Identity lay in accomplishment, not in mirrors. And she was afraid that before she accomplished anything, she'd again seek solace in the attention her looks could win her.

Which would mean men again.

She had nothing against men. Those who destroyed her childhood weren't typical. She didn't hold the entire male gender responsible for the perversions of a few, any more than she would judge all women by Sinsemilla's example . . . or by the example she herself had set.

Actually, she liked men more than she should, considering the lessons learned from her experiences with them. She hoped one day to have a rewarding relationship with a good man – perhaps even marriage.

The trick lay in the word *good*. Her taste in men was not much better than her mother's. Committing herself to the dead-wrong type of man, more than once, had led to her current circumstances, which seemed to her like the burnt-out bottom of a ruined life.

After dressing for a three o'clock job interview – the only one of the day that she would be able to keep and the only one related to her computer training – Micky ate a hangover-curing breakfast at eleven o'clock, while standing at the kitchen sink. She washed down B-complex vitamins and aspirin with Coke, and finished the Coke with two chocolate-covered doughnuts. Her hangovers never involved a sick stomach, and a blast of sugar cleared her booze-fuzzed thoughts.

Leilani was right when she guessed that Micky had a metabolism tuned like a space-shuttle gyroscope. She weighed only one pound more than she had weighed on her sixteenth birthday.

While she stood at the sink, eating, she watched Geneva through the open window. With a garden hose, Aunt Gen hand-watered the lawn against the depredations of the August heat. She wore a straw hat with a wide brim to protect her face from the sun. Sometimes her entire body swayed as she moved the hose back and forth, as though she might be remembering a dance that she had attended in her youth, and as Micky ate the second doughnut, Geneva began to sing softly the love theme from *Love in the Afternoon*, one of her favorite movies.

Maybe she was thinking about Vernon, the husband whom she'd lost too young. Or maybe she was remembering her affair with Gary Cooper, when she'd been young and French and adored – and Audrey Hepburn.

What a wonderfully unpredictable world it is when being shot in the head can have an up side.

That was Geneva's line, not Micky's, an argument for optimism when Micky grew pessimistic. *What a wonderfully unpredictable world it is, Micky, when being shot in the head can have an up side. In spite of an embarrassing moment of confusion now and then, it's delightful to have so many glamorous and romantic memories to draw upon in my old age! I'm not recommending brain damage, mind you, but without my quirky little short circuit, I would never have loved and been loved by Cary Grant or Jimmy Stewart, and I'd certainly never have had that wonderful experience in Ireland with John Wayne!*

Leaving Aunt Gen to her fond memories of John Wayne or Humphrey Bogart, or possibly even of Uncle Vernon, Micky left by the front door. She didn't call 'good morning' through the open window, because she was embarrassed to face her aunt. Although Geneva knew that her niece had missed two job interviews, she would never mention this new failure. Gen's bottomless tolerance only sharpened Micky's guilt.

Last evening, she'd left the Camaro's windows open two inches; nevertheless, the interior was sweltering. The air conditioning didn't work, so she drove with the windows all the way down.

She switched on the radio, only to hear a newsman describing, in excited tones, a government-enforced blockade affecting a third of Utah, related to an urgent search for some drug lords and their teams of heavily armed bodyguards. Thirty powerful figures in the illegal drug trade had gathered secretly in Utah to negotiate territorial boundaries as Mafia families had done decades ago, to plan a war against smaller operators, and to devise strategies to overcome importation problems created by a recent tightening of the country's borders. Having learned of this criminal conclave, the

FBI moved in to make mass arrests. They were met with an unusual level of violence instead of with the usual volleys of attorneys; the battle had been as fearsome as a clash of military factions. Perhaps a dozen of these drug kingpins were now on the run with highly sophisticated weaponry and with nothing to lose, and they posed a serious threat to the citizenry. Most of these details had not been released by the FBI but had been obtained from unnamed sources. *Crisis*, the reporter said, using the word repeatedly and pronouncing it as if he found those two syllables as delectable as a lover's breast.

When it wasn't about natural disasters and lunatics shooting up post offices, the news was an endless series of crises, most of which were either wildly exaggerated or entirely imaginary. If ten percent of the crises that the media sold were real, civilization would have collapsed long ago, the planet would be an airless cinder, and Micky would have no need to look for a job or worry about Leilani Klonk.

She punched a preset button, changing stations, found more of the same news story, punched another button, and got the Backstreet Boys. This wasn't exactly her style of music, but the Boys were fun and likely to facilitate her hangover cure.

No news is good news – which is true no matter which of the two possible interpretations you choose to make of those five words.

Cruising up the freeway ramp, remembering Leilani's term from their conversation the previous evening, Micky said, 'Proud to be one of the twelve-percenters,' and found her first smile of the day.

She had three and a half hours before her interview, and she intended to use this time to get Child Protective Services involved in the girl's case. Last night, when she and Geneva had discussed Leilani, the girl's predicament seemed irresolvable. This morning, either because time brought a better perspective or because too much lemon vodka followed by chocolate doughnuts inspired a measure of optimism, the situation seemed difficult, but not beyond hope.

34

Leilani Klonk, dangerous young mutant, decided that few things were more inspiring than the bonding that occurred when an American family gathered around the breakfast table. Only the night before, Mom and Dad and daughter might have been fussing at one another over who had left the lid off the peanut-butter jar, might have been in disagreement about weightier issues such as whether to watch *Touched by an Angel* or an episode of *Miracle Pets*, might even have been setting snakes loose on one another and killing young women; but here at the start of a new day – well, eleven o'clock – the differences of the past could be set aside, and new harmony could be built on the old discord. Here they could plan together for the future, share new dreams, and reaffirm their mutual devotion.

Old Sinsemilla made her breakfast from twenty-seven tablets and capsules of vitamin supplements, a bottle of sparkling water, a small tub of tofu sprinkled with toasted coconut, and a banana. After slicing the unpeeled banana in half-inch circlets, she ate the peel and all, for she believed that good health could be achieved only by the consumption of whole foods as often as possible. Considering her understanding of the term *whole foods*, dear *Mater* was well advised never to touch red meat; if she prepared a hamburger, she would also have to whip up a side dish of hoof, horn, and hide.

Dr. Doom breakfasted on chamomile tea, two coddled eggs, and English muffins spread with orange marmalade. Not sharing his wife's preference for whole foods, he failed to eat the tea bags, the egg shells, and the cardboard container in which the muffins had been packaged. He was such a supernaturally neat eater that in his hands the toasted muffins left not one crumb on table or plate. He took small bites and chewed his food thoroughly, ensuring against the possibility that he would choke to death on a honking big piece of something. The best that his optimistic stepdaughter could hope for seemed to be salmonella contamination of the undercooked egg yolks.

Leilani enjoyed a dish of Shredded Wheat garnished with a sliced banana (peeled) and doused in chocolate milk. The doctor of doom had purchased this forbidden beverage without the tofu-eater's knowledge. Though Leilani would have preferred regular milk, she used chocolate on the cereal to see if her mother would have a cerebral aneurysm at the sight of her child ingesting this hideous poison.

The taunt was wasted on Sinsemilla. Crimson-eyed, gray-faced, she languished in the morning-after slough of despond. Whatever drug she'd taken as an eye-opener had not yet delivered her into the Mary Poppins mood that she desired. She probably wouldn't be flying around under a magic umbrella, singing 'Supercalifragilisticexpialidocious,' until late afternoon.

Meanwhile, as she ate, she read a tattered copy of Richard Brautigan's *In Watermelon Sugar*. She had read this slim volume twice every month since she was fifteen. With each reading, the book had a different meaning for her, although to date none of the meanings had been entirely coherent. Sinsemilla believed, however, that the author represented a new step in human evolution, that he was a prophet with an urgent message to those who were further evolved than the human society that had produced them. Old Sinsemilla sensed that she was a further-evolved human, but in all modesty, she wasn't prepared to make this claim until she fully understood Brautigan's message and, in understanding, achieved her superhuman potential.

While immersed in the book, Sinsemilla was no more communicative than the tofu that quivered on her spoon, yet Dr. Doom frequently addressed her. He didn't expect a response, but seemed to be certain that his comments reached his wife on a subconscious level.

Sometimes he spoke of Tetsy, the young woman whose heart he had 'burst' with a massive injection of digitoxin less than twelve hours ago and whose fate he had shared with Leilani upon returning home in the dead hours of the night. At other times he relayed to Sinsemilla and to Leilani the latest gossip and news circulating on the various Internet sites maintained by the large international community of UFO believers, which he monitored on the laptop computer that rested on the table beside his breakfast plate.

Details of the Tetsy snuff were mercifully less vivid than had been the case with other killings in the past, and the latest saucer stories were no weirder than usual. Consequently, the creepy quality of the conversation – and there was always a creepy quality to the most casual chats in this family – was provided by Dr. Doom's coy references to the passion that he had visited upon Sinsemilla during the night.

Over dinner with Micky and Mrs. D the previous evening, Leilani had said that the doom doctor was asexual. This wasn't strictly true.

He didn't chase women, ogle them, or seem to have any interest in the secondary sex characteristics that preoccupied most men and made them such endearingly manipulable creatures. If a total babe in a thong bikini walked past Preston, he wouldn't notice her unless she happened to be a UFO abductee who also carried an alien-human hybrid baby spawned during a steamy weekend of extraterrestrial lust aboard the mother ship.

Under certain circumstances, however, the doom doctor did have a passion for Sinsemilla that he – and these were the perfect words for the act – *visited upon* her. In a motor home, even in a large one, when a family lives on the road all year, an inevitable intimacy arises that would be stressful even if every member of the family were a saint; and the Maddoc family currently fell three saints short of that ideal composition. Even if you could avoid seeing things that you didn't want to see, you couldn't always avoid hearing them, and even if you clamped pillows over your ears at night and created an acceptable deafness, you couldn't escape *knowing* all sorts of things that you didn't want to know, including that Preston Maddoc could get romantically inspired only when Sinsemilla was so deeply unconscious that she might as well have been dead.

Leilani had shared a hundred nightmares' worth of creepy stuff with Micky and Mrs. D, but she hadn't been able to bring herself to mention *this* creepiness. Sure, old Preston qualified as a nutball's nutball. But he was tall, good-looking, well groomed, and financially independent, which was exactly three qualities more than required to attract women younger and even prettier than Sinsemilla; financial independence alone ought to have ensured that he would never have to settle for a drug-gobbling, electro-shocked, road-kill-obsessed, moon-dancing freak who had sim-ultaneously too much past and none at all, and who came with two disabled children. Clearly one thing that won Preston's heart was old Sinsemilla's frequent drug-induced near-comas and her willingness to allow him to use her while she lay inert and insensate and as unaware as mud – which was an arrangement you didn't want to think too much about, considering his fascination with death.

Something else also attracted Preston to Sinsemilla, a quality that no other woman could – or might want to – offer, but Leilani was not quite able to put a name to it. In truth, though she sensed the existence of this mystery at the heart of their strange relationship, she didn't often wonder about it, because she already knew too much of what bonded them and was afraid of knowing more.

So while Sinsemilla read *In Watermelon Sugar*, while Dr. Doom surfed the Net for the latest saucer news, while all three of them ate breakfast, and while no one mentioned the snake, Leilani made notes in her journal, using a modified form of shorthand that she'd invented and that only she could read. She wanted to complete her account of the incident with the snake while the details were still fresh in memory, but at the same time, she recorded observations about their family breakfast, including most of what Preston said.

Recently she'd been thinking about being a writer when she grew up, assuming that on the eve of her upcoming tenth birthday she was able to avoid the gift of eternal life as a nine-year-old. She hadn't given up on her plan to grow or purchase a set of fabulous hooters with which to bedazzle a nice man, but a girl couldn't rely entirely on her chest, her face, and one pretty leg. Writing fiction remained reputable work, in spite of some of the peculiar people who practiced the art. She'd read that one of the difficulties of being a writer was finding fresh material, and she'd realized that her mother and her stepfather might be a writer's gold mine if you were fortunate enough to survive them.

'This situation in Utah,' Preston said, scowling at the screen of his laptop, 'is highly suspicious.'

On and off, he'd been talking about the blockades on all highways leading into southern Utah and the manhunt for the band of drug lords who were said to be armed like sovereign states.

'Let's never forget how in *Close Encounters of the Third Kind*, the government kept people away from the alien-contact zone with a false story about a nerve-gas spill.'

To Preston, *Close Encounters of the Third Kind* wasn't a science-fiction film, but a thinly disguised documentary. He believed that Steven Spielberg had been abducted by ETs as a child and was being used as an instrument to prepare human society for the imminent arrival of emissaries from the Galactic Congress.

As the doom doctor continued to mutter about the government's history of UFO cover-ups, which he believed explained the *true* reason for the war in Vietnam, Leilani suspected that when their motor home was repaired, they would be hitting the road for Utah. Already, UFO researchers and full-time close-encounter pilgrims like Preston were gathering at a site in Nevada, near the Utah border, in anticipation of an alien advent so spectacular that the government, even with all its resources, wouldn't be able to pass the event off as swamp gas or weather balloons, or as tobacco-industry skullduggery.

She was surprised, therefore, when a few minutes later, Preston looked up from his laptop, flushed with excitement, and declared, 'Idaho. That's where it's happening, Lani. There's been a *healing* in Idaho. Sinsemilla, did you hear? There's been a *healing* in Idaho.'

Old Sinsemilla either didn't hear or heard but wasn't intrigued. *In Watermelon Sugar* utterly enthralled her. Her lips didn't move as she read, but her delicate nostrils flared as if she detected the scent of enlightenment, and her jaw muscles clenched and unclenched as she ground her teeth on some wisdom that needed chewing.

Leilani didn't like the prospect of Idaho. It was next door to Montana, where Lukipela had 'gone to the stars.'

She expected that Preston would haul them to Montana when her birthday approached, next February. After all, if aliens had beamed Luki up to glory in Montana, logic would require a visit to the point of his ascension on the eve of Leilani's tenth, if she had not been miraculously made whole before then.

Besides, the symmetry of it would appeal to Dr. Doom: Leilani and Luki together in death as in life, Lucifer and Heavenly Flower feeding the same worms, one grave for two siblings, brother and sister bonded for eternity in a braiding of bones. Preston, after all, had a sentimental side.

If Montana was six months away, she might have time to prepare an escape or a defense. But if they were in Idaho next week, and if old Sinsemilla wanted to cross into Montana to see where Luki had supposedly met the aliens, Preston might be tempted to bring brother and sister together ahead of schedule. She didn't have an escape plan yet. Or a strategy to defend herself. And she wasn't ready to die.

35

The reception area made no concessions to comfort, and in fact the bleakness of the Department of Motor Vehicles would have seemed cheerful by comparison. Only five people waited to see caseworkers, but the lounge offered just four chairs. Because the other four women present were either older than Micky or pregnant, she remained on her feet. In recognition of the power crisis, the air was cooled only to seventy-eight degrees. Except for the smell, which included no trace of vomit, she felt as though she were in a holding pen at a jail.

With a faint note of disapproval, the receptionist explained to Micky that complaints were usually initiated over the telephone and that it was particularly unwise to arrive without an appointment, as this would necessitate a long wait. Micky assured the woman that she was prepared to wait – and reassured her twice again when, during the next forty minutes, the receptionist returned to the subject.

Unlike doctors' offices, this place offered no turn-of-the-century magazines. Reading material consisted of government pamphlets as engagingly written as computer manuals composed in Latin.

When she came out to greet Micky, the first available caseworker introduced herself as F. Bronson. The use of an initial seemed odd, and in F's office, the plaque on her desk proved only slightly more revealing: F. W. BRONSON.

In her late thirties, attractive, F wore black slacks and a black blouse, as though in denial of the season and the heat. She'd hastily pinned up her long brown hair to get it off her neck, and from this impromptu do, a few stray locks dangled limp and damp.

The posters in her oven-warm office made the small room seem even warmer: pictures of cats and kittens, black and calico, Siamese and Angora and cute whiskery specimens of no clear breed, scampering and lounging languorously. These furry images lent a claustrophobic feeling to the space and seemed to pour feline warmth into the air.

Seeing her visitor's interest in the posters, F said, 'In this work, I deal with so many ignorant, cruel, stupid people . . . sometimes I need to be reminded the world is full of creatures better than us.'

'I certainly understand that,' said Micky, although she didn't half understand. 'I guess for me it would be dog posters.'

'My father liked dogs,' said F, indicating that Micky should sit in one of the two client chairs in front of the desk. 'He was a loud-mouthed, self-centered skirt-chaser. I'll go with cats every time.'

If dogs as an entire species earned F's undying distrust because her old man liked them, how easy would it be to get on her wrong side with even an innocent remark? Micky counseled herself to adopt the deferent demeanor she'd learned – not easily – to use with authorities.

Settling into the chair behind her desk, F said, 'If you'd made an appointment, you wouldn't have had to wait so long.'

Pretending she'd heard courteous concern in the woman's remark, Micky said, 'No problem. I have a job interview at three, nothing till then, so I have plenty of time.'

'What kind of work do you do?'

'Customizing software applications.'

'Computers are ruining the world,' said F, not contentiously, but with a note of resignation. 'People spend more time interacting with machines, less time with other people, and year by year we're losing what little humanity we have left.'

Sensing that it was always best to agree with F, which would require Micky to explain her work with demon machines, she sighed, feigned regret, and nodded. 'But it's where the jobs are.'

F's face pinched with disapproval, but instantly cleared.

Although the expression had been subtle and brief, Micky read into it the opinion that defendants at the Nuremberg trials had made similar excuses for working the gas chambers at Dachau and Auschwitz.

'You're concerned about a child?' F asked.

'Yeah. Yes. The little girl who lives next door to my aunt. She's in a terrible situation. She—'

'Why isn't your aunt making the complaint?'

'Well, I'm here for both of us. Aunt Gen isn't—'

'I can't approve an inquiry on hearsay,' F said, not harshly, almost regretfully. 'If your aunt has seen things that cause her to be concerned about this girl, she'll need to speak to me directly.'

'Sure, of course, I understand. But, see, I live with my aunt. I know the girl, too.'

'You've seen her being abused – struck or shaken?'

'No. I haven't seen any physical abuse taking place. I've—'

'But you've seen evidence? Bruises, that sort of thing?'

'No, no. It isn't like that. No one's beating her. It's—'

'Sexual abuse?'

'No, thank God, Leilani says that's not the case.'

'Leilani?'

'That's her name. The girl.'

'They usually say it's not the case. They're ashamed. The truth comes out only through counseling.'

'I know that's often the way it goes. But she's different, this kid. She's tough, very smart. She speaks her mind. She'd tell me if there were sexual abuse. She says there isn't . . . and I believe her.'

'Do you see her regularly? Do you speak to her?'

'She came to our place for dinner last night. She was—'

'So she's not being confined? We're not talking about abuse by cruel restraint?'

'Restraint? Well, maybe we are, in a way.'

'In what way?'

The room was insufferably warm. As in many modern highrises, for reasons of efficient ventilation and energy conservation, windows did not open. The system fan was on, but it produced more noise than air circulation. 'She doesn't want to be in that family. No one would.'

'None of us gets to choose our family, Ms. Bellsong. If that alone constituted child abuse, my caseload would quadruple. By *cruel restraint*, I mean has she been shackled, locked in a room, locked in a closet, tied to a bed?'

'No, nothing like that. But—'

'Criminal neglect? For instance, is the girl suffering from an untreated chronic illness? Is she underweight, starved?'

'She's not starved, no, but I doubt her nutrition's the best. Her mother's apparently not much of a cook.'

Leaning back, raising her eyebrows, F said, 'Not much of a cook? What am I missing here, Ms. Bellsong?'

Having slid forward on her chair, Micky sat in a supplicatory posture that felt wrong, that made it seem as though she were trying to *sell* her story to the caseworker. She straightened up, eased back. 'Look, Ms. Bronson, I'm sorry, I'm not going about this at all well, but I'm really not wasting your time. This is a unique case, and the standard questions just don't get to the heart of it.'

Disconcertingly, while Micky was still talking, F turned to the computer on her desk, as if impatient, and began to type. Judging by the speed at which her fingers flew over the keys, she was familiar with this satanic technology. 'All right, let's open a case file, get the basic facts. Then you can tell me the story in your own words, if that'll be easier, and I'll condense it for the report. Your name is Bellsong, Micky?'

'Bellsong, Michelina Teresa.' Micky spelled all three names.

F asked for an address and telephone number. 'We don't disclose any information about the complainant – that's you – to the family we're investigating, but we've got to have it for our records.'

When the caseworker requested it, Micky also presented her social-security card.

After entering the number from the card, F worked with the computer for a few minutes, pausing repeatedly to study the screen, entirely involved with the data she summoned, as if she'd forgotten that she had company.

Here was the dehumanizing influence of technology, which she'd so recently decried.

Micky couldn't see the screen. Consequently, she was surprised when F, still focused on the computer, said, 'So you were convicted of the possession of stolen property, aiding and abetting document forgery, and possession of forged documents with the intention to sell – including phony driver's licenses, social-security cards . . . .'

F's words did what too much lemon vodka and chocolate doughnuts had failed to accomplish: caused a tremor of nausea to slide through Micky's stomach. 'I'm . . . I mean . . . I'm sorry, but I don't think you have a right to ask me about this.'

Still gazing at the screen, F said, 'I didn't ask. Just ran an ID check. Says you were sentenced to eighteen months.'

'None of that has anything to do with Leilani.'

F didn't reply. Her slender fingers stroked the keys, no longer hammering, as though she were *finessing* information from the system.

'I didn't do anything,' Micky said, despising the defensiveness in her voice, and the meekness. 'The guy I was with at the time, he was into stuff I didn't know about.'

F remained more interested in what the computer told her about Micky than what Micky had to say about herself.

The less that F asked, the more Micky felt obliged to explain. 'I just happened to be in the car when the cops took him down. I didn't know what was in the trunk – not the phony paper, the stolen coin collection, not any of it.'

As though she hadn't heard a word of Micky's reply, F said, 'You were sent to the Northern California Women's Facility. That's south of Stockton, isn't it? I went to the asparagus festival in Stockton once. One of the booths offered dishes created by Women's Facility inmates involved in a culinary vocational program. Far as I remember, none of them was particularly tasty. This says you're still there.'

'Yeah, well, that's so wrong. I've never been to the asparagus festival.' When Micky saw F's face tighten, she bit the tartness out of her voice, tried to sound contrite: 'I was released last week. I came to live with my aunt until I get on my feet.'

'Says here you're still at NCWF. Two more months.'

'I was granted early release.'

'Doesn't mention parole here.'

'I'm not a parolee. I served my time, minus good behavior.'

'Be right back.' F rose from her desk and, without making eye contact, went to the door.

36

Across the badlands, through the night, as the clouds move east and the sky purifies, the boy drives westward to the dog's direction.

Gradually the desert withers away. A grassy prairie grows under the rolling tires.

Dawn comes pink and turquoise, painting a sky now as clear as distilled water. A hawk, gliding on high thermals, seems to float like the mere reflection of a bird on the surface of a still pool.

The engine dies for lack of fuel, requiring them to proceed afoot in more fertile land than any they have seen since Colorado. By the time the Mountaineer coughs out the fumes from its dry tank, they're finished with the prairie, as well. They are now in a shallow valley where cottonwood and other trees shade a swift-slipping stream and where green meadows roll away from the banks of the watercourse.

Throughout the long drive, no one shot at them, and no more charred cadavers tumbled out of the night. Mile after mile, the only lights in the sky were stars, and at dawn, the great constellations conceded the stage to the one and nearest star that warms this world.

Now, when Curtis gets out of the SUV, the only sounds in the morning are the muted pings and ticks of the cooling engine.

Old Yeller is exhausted, as she ought to be, good scout and stalwart navigator. She totters to the edge of the brook and laps noisily at the cool clear current.

Kneeling upstream of the dog, Curtis slakes his thirst, too.

He sees no fish, but he's sure that the brook must contain them.

If he were Huckleberry Finn, he'd know how to catch breakfast. Of course, if he were a bear, he'd catch even more fish than Huck.

He can't be Huck because Huck is just a fictional character, and he can't be a bear because he's Curtis Hammond. Even if there were a bear around here somewhere, to provide him with a detailed example of bear structure and bear behavior, he wouldn't dare get naked and try to be a bear and wade into the stream after fish, because later when he was Curtis once more and put on his clothes, he'd be starting all over in this new identity that remains his best hope of survival, and therefore he would be easier to spot if the worse scalawags showed up again, searching for him with their tracking scopes.

'Maybe I *am* stupid,' he tells the dog. 'Maybe Gabby was right. He sure seemed smart. He knew *everything* about the government, and he got us out of that trouble. Maybe he was right about me, too.'

The dog thinks otherwise. With typical doggy devotion, she grins and wags her tail.

'Good pup. But I promised to take care of you, and now here we are without food.'

Relying on his survival training, the boy could find wild tubers and legumes and fungi to sustain him. The dog won't want to eat those things, however, and won't be properly nourished by them.

Old Yeller calls his attention to the Mountaineer by trotting to it and standing at the closed passenger's-side door.

When Curtis opens the SUV for the dog, she springs onto the seat and paws at the closed glove box.

Curtis opens the box and discovers that Gabby travels prepared for the munchies. Three packets of snack crackers, a package of beef jerky, turkey jerky, two bags of peanuts, and a candy bar.

The box also contains the motor-vehicle registration for the SUV, which reveals that the owner's name is Cliff Mooney. Obviously, if he's related to the immortal Gabby Hayes, it must be through his mother's side of the family. Curtis memorizes Cliff's address, which he will one day need in order to properly compensate the man.

With the glove-box vittles, boy and dog settle by the silvery stream, under the wide-spreading branches of a seventy-foot *Populus candican,* also known as the balm-of-Gilead or the Ontario poplar.

Curtis knows more than movies: He knows local botany as

well as local animal biology. He knows local physics, also complete physics, chemistry, higher mathematics, twenty-five local languages, and how to make a delicious apple pandowdy, among many other things.

Regardless of how much you know, however, you can never know everything. Curtis is aware of the limitations of his knowledge and of the abyssal ignorance that lies beneath what he knows.

Sitting with his back against the trunk of the tree, he tears the beef jerky into pieces and feeds it to the dog, morsel by morsel.

Anyway, knowledge isn't wisdom, and we aren't here just to stuff ourselves with facts and figures. We are given this life so we might earn the next; the gift is a chance to grow in spirit, and knowledge is one of many nutrients that facilitate our growth. Mom's wisdom.

As the sun climbs higher, it cooks the night dew, and a low mist shimmers just above the meadow, as though the earth breathes out the dreams of the vanished generations buried in its breast.

The dog watches the mist with such interest that she exhibits no impatience when Curtis takes a while to strip off the stubborn wrapping from the second jerky. Ears pricked, head cocked, she focuses not on the treat, but on the mystery that is the meadow.

Her species has been granted limited but significant intellect, also emotions and hope. What most separates her from humankind and from other higher life forms isn't her mental capacity, however, but her innocence. The dog's self-interest expresses only in matters of survival, never degenerating into the selfishness that is expressed in an infinite variety of ways by those who consider themselves her betters. This innocence carries with it a clarity of perception that allows her to glory in the wonder of creation in even the most humble scene and quiet moment, to be aware of it every minute of every hour, while most human beings pass days or even weeks – and too often whole lives – with their sense of wonder drowned in their sense of self.

Unwrapped jerky, of course, takes precedence over the meadow and the mist. She eats with a sense of wonder, too, with pure delight.

Curtis opens one of the packets of crackers. He allows the dog two of the six little sandwiches with peanut-butter filling.

She's had all she needs now, and he doesn't want her to be sick.

Eventually, he'll provide more balanced nutrition for her – but a better diet will have to wait until they are no longer in imminent danger of being gutted, beheaded, shredded, broken, blasted, burned, and worse. Running in desperate fear for your life is pretty much a righteous justification for eating junk food.

Old Yeller takes another drink from the stream, then returns to Curtis and lies with her spine pressed snugly against the length of his left leg. Eating cracker sandwiches, he strokes her side with his left hand – slowly, comfortingly. Soon she is asleep.

Commotion contributes to concealment, and motion is commotion. He would be safer if he remained on the move, and safer still if he reached a populous area and mingled with a great many people.

The dog, however, doesn't have his stamina. He can't ask her to exhaust herself from lack of sleep and risk running herself to death.

He finishes the four cracker sandwiches in the first pack, eats all six in the second pack, follows the crackers with the candy bar, and concludes breakfast with a bag of peanuts. Life is good.

As he eats, his thoughts are drawn to Gabby's abandonment of the Mercury Mountaineer in the middle of the salt flats. The caretaker's conduct was at best eccentric and at worst psychotic.

Gabby's personality and behavior have been the most alien that Curtis has encountered on this adventure. Although many things about the cantankerous desert rat puzzle the boy, the explosive exit from the SUV, punctuated by a storm of foul language, and the flight on foot across the fluorescent plain are the most baffling. He can't quite believe that his well-meant criticism of Gabby's pronunciation of *cojones* could have caused the old man to hightail it into the barrens in an uncontrolled emotional fit of rage and/or humiliation.

Another possibility teases at the back of Curtis's mind, but he can't quite haul it out in the light for inspection. As he's puzzling over the matter, he's distracted when the dog begins to dream.

She signals her dreaming with a whimper: not a cry of fear, but a wistful sound. Her forepaws twitch, and from the movement of her hind legs, Curtis infers that she is running in her dream.

He puts his hand on her flank, which rises and falls rapidly with her breathing. He feels her heartbeat: strong and quick.

Unlike the boy for whom he named himself, this Curtis never sleeps. Therefore he never dreams. Curiosity compels him to employ the special boy-dog bond that synchronizes his mind to that of his sister-becoming. Thus he enters the secret world of her dreams.

A puppy among puppies, she suckles at a teat, enraptured by the throb of her mother's heart, which pulses through the nipple into her greedy lips, and then she submits to her mother's licking, the great warm tongue, the black nuzzling nose icy with affection . . . scrambles clumsily over Mother's furry flank, climbing eagerly as though some mystery lies beyond the curve of her mother's ribs, an astonishment that she must see, must see . . . and then fur fades into meadow, cicadas singing, their music shivering in her blood . . . and now she's an older dog racing through succulent grass in pursuit of an orange butterfly bright as a fluttering flame, burning mysteriously in the air . . . from meadow into woods, shadows and the scent of hemlock, the fragrance of decaying leaves and needles, here the butterfly as bright as the sun in a shaft of light but now eclipsed and lost . . . around her the croaks of woodland toads, as she follows the scent of deer along trails overhung by ferns, unafraid in the deepening shadows because the playful Presence runs with her here, as always elsewhere . . . .

One dream flows swiftly into another, lacking a connective narrative. Joy is the only thread on which these images are strung: joy the thread, and memories like bright beads.

Sitting against the balm-of-Gilead, Curtis shivers, first with exhilaration and delight.

This meadow becomes less real to him than the fields in the dog's mind, the chuckle of this brook less convincing than the croak of toads in her clear and vivid dreams.

Spates of shivers build into continuous trembling as Curtis more clearly experiences the dog's profound joy. This isn't simply the joy of running, of springing agilely from log to mossy rock; this isn't just the joy of freedom or of being fully *alive*, but the piercing joy that comes with the awareness of that holy, playful Presence.

Running with her in the dreams, Curtis seeks a glimpse of

their constant companion, expecting suddenly to see an awesome countenance looking out from the layered fronds of the ferns or gazing down from the cathedral trees. Then the dog's ultimate wisdom, arising from her perfect innocence, is shared with Curtis, and he receives the truth that is simultaneously a revelation and a mystery, both a euphoric exaltation and a profound humbling. The boy recognizes the Presence everywhere around him, not confined to one bosk of ferns or one pool of shadows, but resonant in all things. He feels what otherwise he has only known through faith and common sense, *feels* for one sweet devastating moment what only the innocent can feel: the exquisite *rightness* of creation from shore to shore across the sea of stars, a clear ringing in the heart that chases out all fears and every anger, a sense of belonging, purpose, hope, an awareness of being loved.

Mere joy gives way to rapture, and the boy's awe grows deeper, an awe lacking any quality of terror, but so filled with wonder and with liberating humility that his trembling swells into shakes that seem to clang his heart against the bell of his ribs. At the moment when rapture becomes peals of bliss, his shaking wakes the dog.

The dream ends and with it the connection to eternity, the joy-inducing nearness of the playful Presence. A sense of loss shudders through Curtis.

In her innocence, waking or sleeping, the dog lives always with the awareness of her Maker's presence. But when she's awake, Curtis's psychic bond with her isn't as profound as when she sleeps, and now he cannot share her special awareness as he did in her dreams.

The iridescent blues of summer sky shimmer down, becoming golden currents as they descend, greening in meadow grass, sparkling silver in the purling brook – as though the day takes inspiration from one of those 1940s jukeboxes that phases ceaselessly through a custom rainbow, silently waiting for the next nickel to be dropped.

Nature never seemed this vivid before; wherever he looks, the day is electrified, radiant, shocking in its beauty and complexity.

He wipes his face repeatedly, and each time that he lowers his hands, the dog licks his fingers, partly in consolation, partly with affection, but also because she likes the taste of his salty tears.

The boy is left with a memory of transcendence, but not with the *feeling* of it, which is the core of the experience – yet he doesn't mourn the loss. Indeed, life would be unlivable if at every moment he felt the full intimacy of his spiritual bond with his Maker.

The dog was born in that state of grace. She is accustomed to it, and she is comfortable with her awareness because her innocence leaves her unfettered by self-consciousness.

For Curtis, as for humankind, such spiritual intensity must be reserved for a life beyond this one, or for many lives beyond, when deep peace has been earned, when innocence has been recaptured.

When he can stand, he stands. When he can move, he leaves behind the shade of the tree.

His cheeks are stiff with dried tears. He wipes his face on his shirt sleeves and takes a deep breath filtered by the cotton cloth, relishing the faint lemony fragrance of the fabric softener used in Mrs. Hammond's laundry and the patina of scents laid down by hundreds of miles of experience since Colorado.

The apex of the sky lies east of the sun, for noon has come and gone while they have been at rest under the tree.

Refreshed, Old Yeller ambles along the stream bank, sniffing yellow and pink wildflowers that nod their bright heavy heads as if conferring on a matter of importance to flowers everywhere.

A vagrant breeze, seeming to spring first from one quarter of the compass and then from another, lazily wanders the meadow.

Suddenly Curtis finds the scene to be dangerously lulling. This is no ordinary day, after all, but day three of the hunt. And this is no ordinary meadow. Like all fields between birth and death, this is potentially a field of battle.

As before, the threat will approach from the east, trailing the sun. If sanctuary can ever be found, it lies in the west, and they must at once ford the stream and move on.

He whistles the dog to his side. She is no longer his sister-becoming. Call her sister-become.

37

Leaving without explanation, F. Bronson closed the office door behind her.

From every side, feline stares fixed Micky with the intensity of security cameras. She felt as if the absent F still watched her magically through the unblinking eyes of these photo familiars.

The issue had become not the danger to Leilani, but Micky's reliability, her integrity or lack of it.

Now the heat wasn't just a condition, but a presence, like a clumsy man too eager in his passion, all moist hands and hot breath, pressing and persistent, suffocating in his need.

She would have sworn the sultry air was thick with the scent of fur, a musky redolence. Maybe F had cats at home, real cats, not just posters. Maybe she carried their dander on her clothes, in her hair.

Micky sat with her hands tightly clutching the purse in her lap, and when a minute had passed, she closed her eyes against the stares of the cats. She closed them also against the false yet convincing perception that the office was rapidly growing smaller, that it had become correctional in design, with the sterility and the restrictive proportions known to inspire either rehabilitation or suicide.

Claustrophobia, nausea, and humiliation steeped Micky with more debilitating effect than did the heat, the humidity, and the scent of cats. But what distressed her more than all these things was an anger cooking in her heart, as bitter as any brew concocted in a cauldron full of goat blood, eye of newt, and tongue of bat.

Anger was a reliable defense, but one that allowed no chance of final victory. Anger was a medicine but never a cure, briefly numbing the pain without extracting the thorn that caused the agony.

Now she could afford anger less than ever. If she answered F's bureaucratic arrogance and insults with the double-barreled blast of sarcasm and ridicule that she had used to cut down formidable targets in the past, her petty satisfaction would come at Leilani's expense.

F had left the room most likely to instruct the receptionist to call the police to check out Micky's story of an early release from prison. After all, she might be a dangerous fugitive who had come here, dressed in a coral-pink suit and pleated white shell and white high-heeled shoes, to steal the office coffee fund or to abscond with an entire carton of that electrifyingly well-written pamphlet about the link between secondhand cigarette smoke and the alarming rise in the number of child werewolves.

Trying to dampen her anger, Micky reminded herself that her choices – and hers alone – had landed her in prison and had led to the humiliation that now both humbled and galled her. F. Bronson hadn't hooked her up with the deadbeat document forger who had taken her down with him. Nor was F responsible for Micky's bullheaded refusal to turn state's evidence on that useless man in return for probation instead of hard time. She alone had made the decision not to rat out the bastard and to trust that the jury would see in her the misguided but innocent woman that she really was.

The door opened, and F entered the office.

At once Micky raised her head and opened her eyes, loath to be seen in a humbled posture.

Offering no explanation for her absence, F returned to her desk and settled in her chair without making eye contact. She *did* glance at Micky's small purse as if nervously wondering whether it contained semi-automatic weapons, spare ammunition, and supplies necessary to endure a long standoff with the police.

'What's the child's name?' F asked.

'Leilani Klonk.' Micky spelled both names – and decided not to explain that the surname had evidently been invented by the girl's deranged mother. Leilani's story was complicated enough even when condensed to the bare essentials.

'Do you know her age?'

'She's nine.'

'Parents' names?'

'She lives with her mother and stepfather. The mother calls herself Sinsemilla.' Micky spelled it.

'What do you mean – "calls herself"?'

'Well, it can't be her real name.'

'Why not?' F asked, staring at the keyboard on which her poised fingers waited to dance.

'It's the name of a really potent type of weed.'

F seemed baffled. 'Weed?'

'You know – pot, grass, marijuana.'

'No.' F plucked a Kleenex from a box, blotted her sweat-damped neck. 'No, I don't know. I wouldn't. My worst addiction is coffee.'

Feeling as though she had just been judged and convicted again, Micky strove to keep her voice calm and her response measured: 'I don't do drugs. I never have.' Which was true.

'I'm not a policeman, Ms. Bellsong. You don't have to worry about me. I'm only interested in the welfare of this girl.'

For F to bring to the case a crusader's determination, she had to believe Micky, and to believe Micky, she had to feel a connection between them. At the moment, they seemed to have nothing in common except that they were women, but shared gender alone didn't generate even the most feeble current of sisterhood.

In prison she had learned that the subject in which dissimilar women most easily found common ground was *men*. And with some women, sympathy could be earned most quickly when you mocked men and their pretension. So Micky said, 'A lot of guys have told me dope expands your consciousness, but judging by them, it just makes you stupid.'

Finally F looked away from the computer. 'Leilani must know her mother's real name.'

F's face and eyes were as unreadable as those of a mannequin. This studied vacancy and refusal to be charmed conveyed more contempt than might have been seen in the most vivid expression of disdain.

'No,' Micky said. 'Leilani never heard her called anything but Sinsemilla. The woman's superstitious about names. She thinks knowing someone's true name gives you power over them.'

'She told you this herself?'

'Leilani told me, yeah.'

'I mean the mother.'

'I've never exactly spoken to the mother.'

'Since you're here to report her for child endangerment of one kind or another, may I assume you've at least met her?'

Quickly plugging the dam of anger that sprung a leak in response to F's rebuke, Micky said, 'Met her once, yeah. She was real strange, doped to the eyeballs. But I think there's also—'

'Do you have a last name for the mother,' F asked, returning her attention to the computer, 'or is it just Sinsemilla?'

'Her married name is Maddoc. M-a-d-d-o-c.'

Flatly, absent the slightest note of accusation, F asked, 'Do you have a history with her?'

'Excuse me? History?'

'Are you related to her, perhaps by marriage?'

A bead of sweat slid down Micky's left temple. She blotted it with her hand. 'Like I said, I just met her once.'

'Ever dated anyone she's dated, fought over a boyfriend, been involved with an ex-spouse of hers – any prior history she'd be sure to bring up when I talk to her? Because everything comes out in the open sooner or later, I assure you, Ms. Bellsong.'

The cats watched Micky, and Micky stared at F, and F appeared to be prepared to gaze forever at her computer.

The ignorant, cruel, and stupid people to whom F had referred earlier, the rabble that motivated her to paper her walls with cat posters, now included Micky. Maybe it was the prison record that put Micky in this category. Maybe it was an offense she had given without intention. Maybe it was just a matter of bad chemistry. Whatever the reason, she was on F's list now, and she knew the woman well enough to suspect that F made her list with a pencil that had no eraser.

Finally, Micky said, 'No. Nothing personal between Leilani's mother and me. I'm just worried about the girl, that's all.'

'The father's name?'

'Preston.'

F's face at last became marginally more expressive than the screen in front of her, and she looked at Micky again. 'You don't mean *the* Preston Maddoc.'

'I guess he is. I'd never heard of him until last night.'

Eyebrows arched, F said, 'You'd never heard of Preston Maddoc?'

'I haven't had a chance to read up on him yet. According to Leilani . . . well, I don't know, but I guess he must've been accused of murdering some people, but he got away with it somehow.'

The light texture of surprise in F's face quickly smoothed away under the trowel of bureaucratic neutrality, but the caseworker was not entirely able to soften her voice, which cut with a honed edge of disapproval: 'He was acquitted, Ms. Bellsong. Not guilty in two separate trials. That isn't the same as "getting away with it."'

Micky found herself on the edge of her seat again, hunched in that supplicatory posture once more, but she didn't straighten her shoulders this time or slide back on the chair. She licked her lips, discovered they were salty from perspiration. She felt as if she'd been *busted*. 'Ms. Bronson, I don't know about him being acquitted, but I do know there's a little girl who's been through a lot in her life, and now she's stuck in this godawful situation, and someone *has* to help. Whatever Maddoc was supposed to have done, maybe he didn't do it, all right, but Leilani had an older brother, and he's gone missing. And if she's right, if Preston Maddoc killed her brother, then her life is on the line, too. And I believe her, Ms. Bronson. I think you'd believe her, too.'

'Killed her brother?'

'Yes, ma'am. That's what she says.'

'So she's a witness to a murder?'

'No, she didn't actually see it. She—'

'If she didn't *actually* see it, how does she *actually* know it happened?'

Counting on patience to prevail, Micky said, 'Maddoc took the boy away and then came back without him. He—'

'Took him away where?'

'Into the woods. They were—'

'Woods? Not very much in the way of woods around here.'

'Leilani says this was in Montana. Some UFO contact site—'

'UFO?' Like a nest-building bird worrying threads from a scrap of fabric, F seemed determined to pick relentlessly at Micky's story, though not with the intention of building anything, seemingly for the sheer pleasure of reducing it to a scattering of scrambled fibers. In the service of this goal, she seized upon the mention of UFOs. Her eyes sharpened a hawk glare fit to pin a mouse from a thousand feet; and if she'd had slightly less self-control, her next two words would have come out as a birdy screak of cold delight. 'Flying saucers?'

'Mr. Maddoc is a UFO buff. Alien contact, that weird stuff—'

'Since when? Seems if this were true, the media would've made a lot out of it. Don't you think? They're pretty merciless, the press.'

'According to Leilani, he was into this UFO stuff since at least back when he married her mother. Leilani says—'

'Have you asked Mr. Maddoc directly about the boy?'

'No. What would be the point?'

'So you're operating entirely on the word of a child, are you?'

'Don't you often do the same in your line of work? Anyway, I've never met him.'

'You've never met Mr. Maddoc? Never met him or the mother—'

'Like I told you, I met the mother once. She was so high, she was bumping her head on the moon. She probably wouldn't even remember meeting me.'

'You saw her actually taking drugs?'

'I didn't have to see her *take* them. She was *saturated*. They were virtually squirting out her pores. You ought to remove Leilani from that home if only because her mother's wrecked half the time.'

On F's phone, the intercom beeped, but the receptionist didn't say anything. Another beep. Like an oven timer: The goose is cooked.

'Be right back,' F promised, and again she left the room.

Micky wanted to tear the cat posters off the walls.

Instead, she hooked a finger in the scooped neck of her pleated shell, pulled it away from her body, and blew down the front of her blouse, on her breasts. She wanted to take off her suit jacket, but somehow it seemed that to remove it would put her at an even greater disadvantage with F. Bronson. The caseworker's black outfit, in this heat, seemed to be an endurance challenge to visitors.

This time F was out of the office only briefly. Returning to her desk, she said, 'So tell me about the missing brother.'

Warning herself to check her anger but not able entirely to

heed her own counsel, Micky said, 'So did you call off the SWAT team?'

'Excuse me?'

'You checked to see if I'm an escapee.'

Unruffled, not in the least embarrassed, F met her eyes. 'You'd have done the same in my position. There was no offense intended.'

'That's not how it looks from my perspective,' Micky replied, dismayed to hear herself pressing for an unnecessary confrontation.

'With all due respect, Ms. Bellsong, I don't live from your perspective.'

A slap in the face couldn't have been more to the point. Micky burned with humiliation.

If F had been gazing at the computer, Micky might have snapped back at her. But in the woman's eyes, she saw a chilly contempt that was a match for her hot anger, obstinacy as unyielding as cold stone.

Of all the caseworkers she might have drawn, she'd been brought head-to-head with this one, as though the Fates were amused by the prospect of two women butting like a pair of rams.

Leilani. She had a duty to Leilani.

Swallowing enough anger and pride to ensure that she would still have no appetite by dinnertime, Micky pleaded, 'Let me tell you about the girl's situation. And the brother. Straight through, beginning to end, instead of questions and answers.'

'Give it a try,' F said curtly.

Micky condensed Leilani's story but also censored from it the most outrageous details that might give F an excuse to dismiss the whole tale as fiction.

Even as she listened to this *Reader's Digest* version, F grew restive. She expressed her impatience by shifting constantly in her chair, by repeatedly picking up a legal pad as though she intended to make notes but replacing it on her desk without writing a word.

Each time that Preston Maddoc was mentioned, F's brow pleated. Delicate lines tightened as though they were threads tugged by a needle, forming plicated fans of skin at the corners of her eyes, sewing her lips together as if with fine-draw stitches.

Evidently she disapproved of the suggestion that Maddoc might be a murderer, and her disapproval was a subtle seamstress at work in her face.

Her dislike of Micky couldn't entirely explain her attitude. She seemed to hold some brief for Maddoc, and though she didn't argue on his behalf, her opinion of him appeared to be beyond reconsideration.

When Micky finished, F said, 'If you believe there's been a murder, why would you come here instead of going to the police?'

The truth was complicated. For one thing, two cops had stretched the facts in her arrest, suggesting she'd been more than a companion to the document forger, that she'd been an accomplice, and the public defender appointed to her case by the court had been too overworked or too incompetent to correct this misrepresentation before the jury. She'd had enough of the police for a while. And she didn't entirely trust the system. Furthermore, she knew that the local authorities would not be eager to investigate a report of a murder in a far jurisdiction when they had plenty of homegrown crime to keep them busy. She couldn't claim to have known Lukipela. Her accusation was based on her faith in Leilani, and though she was convinced the cops also would find the girl credible, her own testimony was hearsay.

She kept her reply succinct: 'Luki's disappearance has to be investigated eventually, sure, but right now the issue is Leilani, her safety. You don't have to wait for the cops to prove Luki was murdered before you can protect Leilani. She's alive now, in trouble now, so it seems to me that her situation has to be addressed first.'

Eschewing comment, turning to her computer once more, F typed for two or three minutes. She might have been entering a version of Micky's statement or she might have been composing an official report and closing out the file without further action.

Beyond the window, the day looked fiery. A nearby palm tree wore a ruffled collar of dead brown fronds. California burning.

When she stopped typing and turned to Micky again, F said, 'One more question, if you don't mind. You may consider it too personal to answer, and of course you're under no obligation.'

Wary, applying a smile no more sincere than lipstick, Micky hoped that the machinery of Child Protective Services would get the job done in spite of how badly this interview had gone. 'What is it?'

'Did you find Jesus in jail?'

'Jesus?'

'Jesus, Allah, Buddha, Vishnu, L. Ron Hubbard. Lots of people find religion behind bars.'

'What I hope I found there was direction, Ms. Bronson. And more common sense than I went in with.'

'People take up lots of things in prison that are pretty much religions, even if they aren't recognized as such,' the caseworker said. 'Extreme political movements, left-wing and right-wing, some of them race-based, most with a grudge against the world.'

'I don't have a grudge against anyone.'

'I'm sure you realize why I'm curious.'

'Frankly, no.'

F clearly doubted Micky's denial. 'We both know Preston Maddoc inspires hatred from various factions, both religious and political.'

'Actually I *don't* know. I really don't know who he is.'

F ignored this protestation. 'Lots of people who're usually at odds with one another are united on Maddoc. They want to destroy him just because they disagree with him philosophically.'

Even with her bottomless reservoir of anger to draw upon, Micky wasn't able to pump up any rage at the accusation that philosophical motives drove her to character assassination. She almost laughed. 'Hey, my philosophy is to make as few waves as possible, get through the day, and maybe find a little happiness in something that won't land you in a mess of trouble. That's as deep as I get.'

'All right then,' said F. 'Thank you for coming in.'

The caseworker turned to the computer.

A long moment passed before Micky realized that she'd been dismissed. She didn't get up. 'You'll send someone out there?'

'It's got a case number now. There has to be follow-through.'

'Today?'

F looked up from the computer, not at Micky but at one of the posters: a fluffy white cat wearing a red Santa hat and sitting in snow. 'Not today, no. There's no physical or sexual abuse involved. The child isn't at immediate risk.'

Feeling as though she had failed completely to be understood, Micky said, 'But he's going to kill her.'

Gazing wistfully at the cat, as if she wished she could crawl into the poster with it, trading the California meltdown for a white Christmas, F said, 'Assuming the girl's story isn't a fantasy, you said he'll kill her on her birthday, which isn't until February.'

'*By* her birthday,' Micky corrected. 'Maybe next February – maybe next week. Tomorrow's Friday. I mean, you don't work on weekends, and if you don't get out there today or tomorrow, they might be gone.'

F's stare was so fixed, her eyes so glazed, that she appeared to be meditating on the image of the cat.

The caseworker was a psychic black hole. In her vicinity, you could feel your emotional energy being sucked away.

'Their motor home is being overhauled,' Micky persisted, though she felt drained, enervated. 'The mechanic might finish at any time.'

With a sigh, F snatched two Kleenex from the box and blotted her forehead carefully, trying to spare her makeup. When she threw the tissues in the waste can, she seemed surprised to see that Micky hadn't left. 'What time did you say you had a job interview?'

Short of sitting here until security was called to remove her, which wouldn't accomplish anything, Micky had no choice but to get up and move toward the door. 'Three o'clock. I can make it easily.'

'Was it in prison you learned all about software applications?'

Although the caseworker looked harmless behind a heretofore unseen smile, Micky expected that the question had been prelude to another insult. 'Yeah. They have a good program up there.'

'How're you finding the job market these days?'

This appeared to be the first genuine woman-to-woman contact since Micky entered the office. 'They all say the economy's sliding.'

'People suck in the best of times,' said F.

Micky had no idea how she ought to respond to that.

'In this market,' F said with something that sounded vaguely like sisterly concern, 'you have to go into a job interview perfect – all pluses, no minuses. If I were you, I'd take another look at the way you're dressing for it. The clothes don't do what you want.'

This coral-pink suit with the pleated white shell was the nicest outfit in Micky's closet.

As though she'd read that thought, F said, 'It's not because the suit's from Kmart, or wherever it's from. That doesn't matter. But the skirt's too short, too tight, and with all the cleavage you've got, don't wear a scoop-necked blouse. Honey, this country's full of greedy trial lawyers, which makes you look like you're trying to sucker some executive into making a pass so you can slam his company with a sexual-harassment suit. When personnel directors see you, it doesn't matter if they're men or women, what they see is trouble, and they're full up on trouble these days. If you have time to change before that interview, I'd recommend it. Don't look so . . . obvious.'

F's black-hole gravity drew Micky toward oblivion.

Maybe the advice about clothes was well meant. Maybe it wasn't. Maybe she thanked F for her counsel. Maybe she didn't. One moment she was in the office, and an instant later she stood outside; the door was closed, yet she had no memory of having crossed the threshold.

Whatever she'd said or not said as she'd left the room, she was sure she'd done nothing to alienate F further or to harm Leilani's chances of getting help. Nothing else mattered. Not her own dreams, not her pride, at least not here, not now.

As before, just four chairs in the reception lounge. Seven people waiting instead of the previous five.

The corridor seemed hotter than the office.

Hotter than hot, the elevator broiled. Pressure built during the descent, as though Micky were aboard a bathysphere, dropping into an oceanic trench. She placed one hand against the wall, half expecting to feel the metal panel buckling beneath her palm.

She almost wished that her quenched anger would flare up again, raw and hot, balancing the summer heat with that inner fire, because what took its place was a quiet desperation too much like despair.

On the ground floor, she located the public restrooms. Warm, oily nausea crawled the walls of her stomach, and she feared that she might throw up.

The stall doors stood open. The room was deserted. Privacy.

Harsh fluorescent light bounced off white surfaces, ricocheted from the mirrors. The icy impression couldn't chill the hot reality.

She turned on the cold water at one of the sinks and held her upturned wrists under the flow. Closed her eyes. Took slow, deep breaths. The water wasn't cold enough, but it helped.

When at last she'd dried her hands, she turned to a full-length mirror on the wall next to the paper-towel dispenser. Leaving home, she'd thought that she was dressed to make the right impression, that she appeared businesslike, efficient. She'd thought she looked *nice*.

Now her reflection mocked her. The skirt *was* too short. And too tight. Though not shockingly low-cut, the blouse nevertheless looked inappropriate for a job interview. Maybe the heels on her white shoes were too high, as well.

She *did* look obvious. Cheap. She looked like the woman she had been, not like the woman she wanted to be. She wasn't dressing for herself or for work, but for men, and for the type of men who never treated her with respect, for the type of men who ruined her life. Somehow the mirror at home hadn't shown her what she needed to see.

This pill was bitter, but more bitter still was the way that it had been administered. By F. Bronson.

Though difficult, taking such advice from someone who respected you and cared for you would be like swallowing medicine with honey. This dosage came with vinegar. And if F. Bronson had thought of it as medicine, instead of poison, she might not have given it.

For years, in mirrors Micky had seen the good looks and the sexual magnetism that could get anything she desired. But now that she no longer wanted those things, now that parties and thrills and the attention of bad men held no appeal, now that she harbored higher aspirations, the mirror revealed cheap flash, awkwardness, naivete – and a desperate yearning, the sight of which made her cringe.

She'd thought that she had merely grown beyond the need to

use her beauty as either a tool or a weapon, but something more profound had happened. Her concept of beauty had changed entirely; and when she looked in the mirror, she saw frighteningly little that matched her new definition. This might be maturity, but it scared her; always before, her confidence in her physical beauty was something to fall back on, an ultimate consolation in bad times. Now that confidence was gone.

An urge to shatter the mirror overcame her. But the past could not be broken as easily as glass. It was the past that stood before her, the stubborn past, relentless.

38

Boy and dog – the former better able to tolerate the August sun than is the latter, the latter somewhat better smelling than is the former, the former thinking again about Gabby's strangely hysterical exit from the Mountaineer, the latter thinking about frankfurters, the former marveling at the beauty of an azure-blue bird perched on a section of badly weathered and half-broken rail fence, the latter smelling the bird's droppings and thereby deducing its recent history in significant detail – are grateful for each other's company as they seek their future, first across open land and then along a lonely country road that, around a bend, is suddenly lonely no more.

Thirty or forty motor homes, about half that many pickup trucks with camper shells, and a lot of SUVs are gathered along the side of the two-lane blacktop and in the adjacent meadow. Attached to some of the motor homes, canvas awnings create shaded areas for socializing. At least a dozen colorful tents have been pitched, as well.

The only permanent structures in sight are in the distance: a ranch house, a barn, stables.

A green John Deere tractor connected to a hay wagon serves as the rental office, manned by a rancher in jeans, T-shirt, and straw sombrero. A hand-lettered sign states that meadow spaces cost twenty dollars per day. It's also emblazoned with one disclaimer and one condition: NO SERVICES PROVIDED, LIABILITY WAIVER REQUIRED.

Encountering this bustling encampment, Curtis is disposed to pass quickly and with caution. So many motor homes in one location worry him. For all he knows, this is a convention of serial killers.

Here might be where the murderous tooth fetishists were bound. That white-haired couple could be nearby, proudly displaying their dental trophies while admiring the even more hideous collections of other homicidal psychopaths in this summer festival of the damned.

Old Yeller, however, smells no trouble. Her natural sociability is engaged, and she wants to explore the scene.

Curtis trusts her instincts. Besides, a crowd offers him some camouflage if the wrong scalawags come prowling with electronics, searching for the unique energy signature that the boy produces.

The meadow is enclosed by a ranch fence of whitewashed boards needing repair and fresh whitening. The tractor guards the open gate.

A tarp on four tall poles shields the hay wagon from the direct sun, and under the tarp, merchandise awaits sale. From a series of picnic coolers filled with crushed ice, the rancher and a teenage boy dispense cans of beer and soft drinks. They offer packaged snack foods like potato chips, as well as homemade cookies, brownies, and jars of 'Grandma's locally famous' black-bean-and-corn salsa, which a sign promises is 'hot enough to blow your head clean off.'

Curtis can conceive of no way in which anyone's head could be blown off cleanly. Decapitation by any means is a messy event.

He has no difficulty understanding why Grandma's deadly salsa is locally famous, but he can't comprehend why anyone would buy it. Yet several jars are missing from the geometric display, and as he watches, two more are sold.

This seems to indicate that a portion of those gathering in the meadow are suicidal. The dog has discounted the theory of a serial-killer convention, since she detects none of the telltale pheromones of full-blown psychosis, but Curtis is equally unenthusiastic about a gathering of the suicide-prone, regardless of their reasons for considering self-destruction.

In addition to beverages, snacks, and the infamous salsa, the hay wagon also offers T-shirts bearing strange messages. NEARY RANCH, one declares, STARPORT USA. Another shirt features the picture of a cow and the words CLARA, FIRST COW IN SPACE. Yet another states WE ARE NOT ALONE – NEARY RANCH. And a fourth insists THE DAY DRAWS NEAR and also features the name of the ranch.

Curtis is interested in Clara. Although he's familiar with the entire history of NASA and with the space program of the former Soviet Union, he's unaware of any attempt to place a cow in orbit or to send one to the moon. No other country possesses the capability to orbit a cow and to bring it back alive. Furthermore, the *purpose* of sending a bovine astronaut into space completely eludes the boy.

A book is displayed for sale beside the T-shirts: *Night on the Neary Ranch: Close Encounters of the Fourth Kind.* From the title and the cover illustration – a flying saucer hovering over a farmhouse – Curtis begins to understand that the Neary Ranch is the origin of a modern folk tale similar to those told about Roswell, New Mexico.

Intrigued but still concerned about the suicidal types that are at least a portion of this gathering, he again trusts Old Yeller's judgment. She smells no prospect of exploding heads, and she's eager to sniff her way through the fragrant throng.

Boy and dog enter the meadow without being challenged at the open gate. Evidently they are thought to be with attendees who rented a space and legitimately established camp.

In a holiday mood, carrying drinks, eating homemade cookies, lightly dressed for the heat, people stroll the close-cropped grass in the aisles between campsites, making new friends, greeting old acquaintances. Others gather in the shade under the awnings, playing cards and board games, listening to radios – and talking, talking.

Everywhere, people are engaged in conversation, some quiet and earnest, others noisy and enthusiastic. From the scraps that Curtis hears as he and Old Yeller amble through the field, he concludes that all these folks are UFO buffs. They gather here twice a year, around the dates of two famous saucer visitations, but this assemblage is related to some new and recent event that has excited them.

The campsites are organized like spokes on a wheel, and at the hub is a perfectly circular patch of bare earth about twelve feet in diameter. The meadow grows all around this circle, but the earth within is chalky and hard-packed, not softened by so much as a single weed or blade of grass.

A tall, thickset man, about sixty years of age, stands in the center of this barren plot. Wearing bushman's boots with rolled white socks, khaki shorts that expose knees as rough and hairy as coconuts, and a short-sleeve khaki shirt with epaulets, he looks as though he will soon embark on an expedition to Africa, to search for the fabled elephants' graveyard.

Eighteen or twenty people have gathered around this man. All appear reluctant to venture into the dead zone where he stands.

As Curtis joins the group, one of the new arrivals explains to another: 'That's old man Neary himself. He's been up.'

Mr. Neary is talking about Clara, the first cow in space. 'She was a good cow, old Clara. She produced a tanker truck of milk with low butterfat content, and she never caused no trouble.'

The concept of troublemaking cows is a new one for Curtis, but he resists the urge to ask what offenses cows are likely to commit when they're not as amiable as Clara. His mother always said that you'd never learn anything if you couldn't listen; and Curtis is always in the mood to learn.

'Holsteins as a breed are a stupid bunch,' says Mr. Neary. 'That is my opinion. Some would argue Holsteins are as smart as Jerseys or Herefords. Frankly, anyone who'd take that position just don't know his cows.'

'Alderneys and Galloways are the smartest breeds,' says one of those gathered around the dead zone.

'We could stand here all day arguin' cow smartness,' says Mr. Neary, 'and be no closer to Heaven. Anyway, my Clara wasn't your typical Holstein, in that she was smart. Not smart like you or me, probably not even as smart as that dog there' – he points at Old Yeller – 'but she was the one always led the others from barn to pasture in the mornin' and back at the end of the day.'

'Lincolnshire reds are smart cows,' says a stocky, pipe-smoking woman whose hair is tied in twin ponytails with yellow ribbons.

Mr. Neary gives this rather formidable lady an impatient look. 'Well, these aliens didn't go huntin' for no Lincolnshire reds, now did they? They come here and took Clara – and my theory is they knew she was the smartest cow in the field. Anyway, as I was sayin', this vehicle like whirlin' liquid metal hovered over my Clara as she was standin' exactly where I'm standin' now.'

Most of those around the circle look up at the afternoon sky, some wary, some with a sense of wonder.

A young woman as pale as Clara's low-butterfat milk says, 'Was there any sound? Patterns of harmonic tones?'

'If you mean did me and them play pipe organs at each other like in the movie, no ma'am. The abduction was done in dead silence. This red beam of light come out of the vehicle, like a spotlight, but it was a levitation beam of some type. Clara lifted off the ground in a column of red light, twelve feet in diameter.'

'That is a *big* levitation beam!' exclaims a long-haired young man in jeans and T-shirt that announces FRODO LIVES.

'The good old girl let out just one startled bleat,' says Mr. Neary, 'and then she went up with no protest, turnin' slowly around, this way and that, end-over-end, like she weighed no more than a feather.' He looks pointedly at the pipe-smoking, ponytailed woman. 'Had she been a Lincolnshire red, she'd probably have kicked up a hell of a fuss and choked to death on her own cud.'

After blowing a smoke ring, the woman replies, 'It's next thing to impossible for a ruminant animal to choke on its own cud.'

'Ordinarily, I'd agree,' concedes Mr. Neary, 'but when you're talkin' a fake-smart breed like Lincolnshire reds, I wouldn't be surprised by *any* dumbness they committed.'

Listening, Curtis is learning a great deal about cows, although he can't say to what purpose.

'Why would they want a cow anyway?' asks the Frodo believer.

'Milk,' suggests the pale young woman. 'Perhaps their planet has suffered a partial ecological breakdown entirely from natural causes, a collapse in some segments of the food chain.'

'No, no, they'd be technologically advanced enough to clone their native species,' says a professorial man with a larger pipe than the one the woman smokes, 'whatever's equivalent to a cow on their planet. They'd repopulate their herds that way. They would never introduce an off-planet species.'

'Maybe they're just hungry for a good cheeseburger,' says a florid-faced man with a can of beer in one hand and a half-finished hot dog in the other.

A few people laugh; however, the pale young woman, who is pretty in a tragic-dying-heroine way, takes deep offense and glowers the smile right off the florid man's face. 'If they can travel across the galaxy, they're an *advanced* intelligence, which means vegetarians.'

Summoning what socializing skills he possesses, Curtis says, 'Or they might use the cow as a host for biologically engineered weapons. They could implant eight or ten embryos in the cow's body cavity, return her to the meadow, and while the embryos mature into viable specimens, no one would realize what was inside Clara. Then one day, the cow would experience an Ebola-virus type biological meltdown, and out of the disintegrating carcass would come eight or ten insectile-form soldiers, each as big as a German shepherd, which would be a large enough force to wipe out a town of one thousand people in less than twelve hours.'

Everyone stares at Curtis.

He realizes at once that he has strayed from the spirit of the conversation or has violated a protocol of behavior among UFO buffs, but he doesn't grasp the nature of his offense. Struggling to recover from this faux pas, he says, 'Well, okay, maybe they would be reptile form instead of insectile form, in which case they would need *sixteen* hours to wipe out a town of one thousand, because the reptile form is a less efficient killing machine than the insectile form.'

This refinement of his point fails to win any friends among those gathered in the circle. Their expressions still range between puzzlement and annoyance.

In fact, the pale young woman turns on him with a glower as severe as the one with which she silenced the man holding the hot dog. '*Advanced* intelligences don't have our flaws. They don't destroy their ecologies. They don't wage war or eat the flesh of animals.' She directs her liquid-nitrogen stare on the pipe smokers. 'They do not use tobacco-type products.' She focuses again on Curtis, her eyes so cold that he feels as if he might go into cryogenic suspension if she keeps him in her sights too long. 'They have no prejudices based on race or gender, or anything else. They never despoil their bodies with high-fat foods, refined sugar, and caffeine. They don't lie and cheat, they don't wage war, as I've said, and they certainly don't incubate giant killer insects inside cows.'

'Well, it's a big universe,' says Curtis in what he imagines to be a conciliatory tone, 'and fortunately most of the worst types I'm talking about haven't gotten around to this end of it.'

The young woman's face pales further and her eyes become icier, as if additional refrigeration coils have activated in her head.

'Of course, I'm only speculating,' Curtis quickly adds. 'I don't know for a fact any more than the rest of you.'

Before Curtis can be frozen solid by the snakeless Medusa, Mr. Neary intervenes. 'Son, you ought to spend a bunch less time playin' those violent sci-fi video games. They've stuffed your head full of sick nonsense. We're talkin' reality here, not those blood-soaked fantasies Hollywood spews out to pollute young minds like yours.'

Those gathered around the dead zone express their agreement, and one of them asks, 'Mr. Neary, were you scared when the ETs came back for you?'

'Sir, I was naturally concerned, but not truly scared. That was six months after Clara floated away, which is why we have two contact vigils here each year, on the anniversaries. By the way, some folks say they would come here just for my wife's homemade cookies, so be sure you try 'em. Of course, this year, it's three vigils – this one impromptu because of what's going on right this minute, over there.' Standing taller, wearing his African-explorer clothes with even greater authority, he points east, past the end of the meadow, toward the land that rises beyond a scattering of trees. 'The uproar across the border in Utah, which you and I know has nothin' whatsoever to do with no drug lords, regardless what the government says.'

Neary's statement gives rise to expressions of a mutual distrust of the government from many in the growing crowd gathered around the dead zone.

Curtis seizes upon this shared sentiment as a way to redeem himself with these people and to polish his inadequate socializing skills. He steps off the grass onto the barren chalky earth and raises his voice to declare, '*Gov'ment!* Rule-makin', power-crazy, know-nothin' bunch of lily-livered skunks in bald-faced shirts!'

He senses that his declaration fails to win for him the immediate embrace of the assemblage.

His words *have* caused the group to fall silent again.

Assuming that their silence arises from their need to digest his words rather than from any disagreement with what he's said, he gives them more reason to welcome him into their community.

'Call me a hog an' butcher me for bacon, but don't you *ever* tell me the gov'ment ain't a land-crazy, dirt-grabbin' tyrant!'

Old Yeller drops to the ground and rolls onto her back, exposing her belly to the crowd, because she thinks that Curtis's socializing requires an expression of submission to avoid violence.

He's quite sure that Old Yeller misapprehends the mood of these people. The dog's senses and preternatural perceptions are reliable in many matters, but human social interaction is far too complex for accurate analysis merely by scent and instinct. Admittedly, the pale young woman's face hardens into an ice sculpture at the mention of bacon, but the others appear to have the open-mouthed expression of people absorbing a well-spoken truth.

Consequently, even as Old Yeller timidly exposes her belly, Curtis spouts more of what these folks want to hear, while hitching himself in a circle, mimicking the gimpy movement that made Gabby so endearing: 'Gov'ment! Tax collectors, land grabbers, nosey do-gooders more self-righteous than any Bible-poundin' preacher ever born! Stink-bug-lovin' gov'ment bastards!'

The dog is whimpering now.

Surveying the encircling ufologists, Curtis sees not one smile, but several looks of astonishment and numerous frowns, and even what seem to be a few expressions of pity.

'Son,' says Mr. Neary, 'I figure your folks aren't amongst this group, or they'd be whuppin' your butt for this performance. Now you go find 'em and you stay with 'em the rest of the time you're here, or I'll have to insist that you and your family accept a refund and vacate the meadow.'

Oh, Lord, maybe he's never going to get the hang of being Curtis Hammond. He blinks back tears, as much because he has embarrassed his sister-become as because he's somehow made a fool of himself.

'Mr. Neary, sir,' he pleads with utmost sincerity, 'I am not some sassy-assed, spit-in-the-eye malefactor.'

This assurance, although it could not be more truthful or more well-intentioned, inexplicably causes Mr. Neary's face to redden into a dark and ominous mask. 'That's enough, young man.'

In one last desperate effort to make amends, Curtis says, 'Mr. Neary, sir, I'm not quite right. I've been told by a beautiful immensity of a lady that I'm too sweet for this world. If you asked me whether I was stupid or somethin', I'd have to say I was stupid. I'm a not-quite-right, too-sweet, stupid Gump, is what I am.'

Old Yeller virtually *spins* off her back, onto all fours, judging the situation too dangerous to expose her belly any longer, and she sprints away from the dead zone even as Mr. Neary takes his first step toward Curtis.

Trusting the dog's instincts at last, Curtis bolts after her. Fugitives again.

39

If libraries in southern California had ever been like those portrayed in books and movies – mahogany-dark millwork, shelves rising to the ceiling, cozy little reading nooks tucked into odd corners in labyrinthine stacks – they weren't that way anymore. All surfaces here were easy-clean paint or Formica. Shelves didn't rise to the ceiling because the ceiling was a suspended grid of acoustic tiles punctuated by fluorescent panels that shed too much light to foster any sense of the romance of books. The shelves stood in predictable ranks, metal instead of wood, bolted to the floor for safety in an earthquake.

To Micky, the atmosphere seemed like that in a medical facility: bleak in spite of the brightness, antiseptic, marked not by the quiet of diligent study but by the silence of stoic suffering.

A significant area had been set aside for computers. All offered Internet access.

The chairs were uncomfortable. Harsh light glared off the desk. She felt at home: reminded not of the trailer she shared with Geneva, but of the home provided by the California Department of Corrections.

Other library patrons were busy at half the work stations, but Micky ignored them. She was self-conscious in the coral-pink suit that had so recently made her feel professional, fresh, and self-confident. Besides, after F. Bronson, she'd had enough of people for the day; machines would be more helpful, and better company.

On-line, feeling like a detective, she sought Preston Maddoc, but little in the way of a manhunt was required. The villain came to her on so many linked sites, she was overwhelmed with information.

From a pay phone, she'd canceled the job interview at three

o'clock. So she spent the afternoon learning about Dr. Doom, and what she discovered suggested that Leilani was penned in an even darker and more escape-proof death cell than the girl had described.

The essence of Maddoc's story was as simple as the details were outrageous. And the implications were terrifying not just for Leilani but for anyone who currently lived and breathed.

Preston Maddoc's doctorate was in philosophy. Ten years ago, he declared himself a 'bioethicist,' accepting a position with an Ivy League university, teaching ethics to future doctors.

That breed of bioethicists who call themselves 'utilitarians' seek what they believe to be ethical distribution of supposedly limited medical resources by establishing standards for determining who should receive treatment and who should not. Scorning the belief in the sanctity of all human life that has guided Western medicine since Hippocrates, they argue that some human lives have greater moral and social value than others and that the authority to set these comparative values belongs rightfully to their elite group.

Once, a small but significant minority of bioethicists had rejected the utilitarians' cold approach, but the utilitarians had won the battle and now ruled their departments in academia.

Preston Maddoc, as did most bioethicists, believed in denying medical care to the elderly – defined as over sixty – if their illness would impact the quality of their lives, even if patients believed their lives were still worth living or in fact enjoyable. If they could be fully cured, but if the rate of cure was below, say, thirty percent, many bioethicists agreed the elderly should be allowed to die anyway, without treatment, because in utilitarian terms, their age ensured they would contribute less to society than they'd take.

Incredulous, Micky read that nearly all bioethicists believed disabled infants, even those mildly disabled, should be neglected until they died. If the babies developed an infection, they should not be treated. If they developed temporary respiratory problems, breathing should not be assisted; they should suffocate. If disabled babies have trouble eating, let 'em starve. Disabled people were said to be burdens to society even when they could care for themselves.

Micky felt an anger brewing different from her usual destructive rage. This had nothing to do with abuses and slights that she had suffered. Her ego wasn't involved; this anger had a cleansing purity.

She read an excerpt from the book *Practical Ethics*, in which Peter Singer, of Princeton University, justified killing newborns with disabilities no more severe than hemophilia: *'When the death of a disabled infant will lead to the birth of another infant with better prospects of a happy life, the total amount of happiness will be greater if the disabled infant is killed. The loss of the happy life for the first infant is outweighed by the gain of a happier life for the second. Therefore, if the killing of the hemophiliac infant has no adverse effect on others it would be . . . right to kill him.'*

Micky had to get up, turn away from this. Outrage had energized her. She couldn't sit still. She walked back and forth, repeatedly flexing her hands, working off energy, trying to calm herself.

Like a child frightened by and yet morbidly drawn to stories of ghouls and monsters, she soon returned to the computer.

Singer had once suggested that if infanticide at the request of the parents will promote the interests of the family and society, then killing the child would be ethical. Further, he had stated that an infant doesn't become a person until sometime during the first year of life, thus opening the door, on a case-by-case basis, to the idea that infanticide could be ethical long after birth.

Preston Maddoc believed that killing children was ethical up to the first indications that they were developing language skills. Say *Dada* or die.

Most bioethicists supported 'supervised' medical experimentation on mentally disabled subjects, on the comatose, and even on unwanted infants in place of animals, arguing that self-aware animals can know anguish, while the mentally disabled, the comatose, and infants cannot.

Asking the mentally disabled what they think is, of course, not necessary, according to this philosophy, because they, like infants and certain other 'minimally cognizant people,' are 'nonpersons' who have no moral claim to a place in the world.

Micky wanted to start a crusade to have bioethicists declared 'minimally cognizant,' for it seemed clear that they were exhibiting no human characteristics and were more obviously nonpersons than the small, the weak, and the elderly whom they would kill.

Maddoc was a leader – but only one of several – in the movement who wanted to use 'cutting-edge bioethics debate and scientific research' to establish a minimum IQ necessary to lead a quality life and to be useful to society. He thought that this threshold would be 'well above a Down's Syndrome IQ,' but he was quick to assure the squeamish that the establishment of a minimum IQ wasn't intended to suggest that society should be culled of the slow-witted currently alive. Rather, it was 'an exercise in clarifying our understanding of what constitutes a quality life,' toward the day when scientific advances would allow IQ to be accurately predicted in infancy.

Yeah. Sure. And the extermination camps at Dachau and Auschwitz had never been constructed with the intention of *using* them, only to see if they could be built, if they were architecturally viable.

At first, as she wandered through the bioethics websites, Micky thought this culture of death wasn't serious. It must be a game in which participants competed to see who could be the most outrageous, who could pretend to be the most inhumanly practical, the coldest of mind and heart. Surely this was nothing more than a playful exercise in make-believe evil.

When eventually she acknowledged that these people lived and acted on their philosophy, she felt certain that they were not taken seriously outside their lunatic tower at some far corner of academia. Instead, she soon realized they were at the center of the academic community. Most medical schools required bioethics instruction. More than thirty major universities offered degrees in bioethics. Numerous state and federal laws, crafted by bioethicists, had been enacted with the intention of making contemporary bioethics the moral and legal arbiter of whose life has value.

The disabled are so costly, don't you agree? And the elderly. And the weak. And the dumb. Costly, but also often disturbing to sensitive people, frequently unsightly to look at, icky to interact with, not like *us*. The poor dear things would be so much happier if they shuffled off; indeed, if they've had the temerity to be born or the bad judgment to suffer a disfiguring accident, then dying is the least that they can do if they have a proper social conscience.

When had the world become a madhouse?

Micky was beginning to understand her enemy.

Preston Maddoc had seemed half threatening and half a joke.

Not anymore. He was now pure threat. Formidable, frightening. *Alien.*

Nazi Germany (in addition to trying to eradicate the Jewish people), the Soviet Union, and Mao's China had previously solved the 'social problem' posed by the weak and the imperfect, but when utilitarian bioethicists were asked if they had the stomach for such final solutions, they dodged the question by making the astonishing claim that the Nazis and their ilk killed the weak and the infirm for, as Preston put it in one interview, 'all the wrong reasons.'

Not that the killing itself was wrong, you see, but the thinking behind the Nazis' and the Soviets' actions was unfortunate. We wish to kill them now not out of hatred or prejudice, but because killing a disabled child makes a place for one who is whole, who will please his family more, who will be happier, who will be useful to society and increase 'the total amount of happiness.' This is not the same, they say, as killing the child to make way for another who is more representative of his *Volk*, who is more blond, who is more likely to make his nation proud and please his *Führer*.

'Give me a microscope,' Micky muttered, 'and maybe in a few centuries, I'll be able to tell the difference.'

These people were taken seriously because they operated in the name of compassion, of ecological responsibility, and even of animal rights. Who could argue with compassion for the afflicted, with a professed intention to use natural resources wisely, with the desire to treat all animals with dignity? If the world is our Fatherland, and if it is the only world we have, and if we believe this world is fragile, then the worth of each weak child or aged grandmother must be measured against the loss of the whole world. And dare you argue then for one crippled girl?

Maddoc and other famous American and British bioethicists – the two nations in which this madness seemed most deeply rooted – were welcomed as experts on television programs, received approving press, and counseled politicians on progressive legislation dealing with medical care. None of them could safely speak in Germany, however, where crowds jeered them and threatened them with violence. There was nothing like a holocaust to inoculate a society against such savagery.

Micky wondered grimly if a holocaust would be required here, too, before sanity could be restored. Minute by minute, exploring the world of bioethics in general and Preston Maddoc in particular, she became increasingly afraid for her country and for the future.

Worse awaited her discovery.

As she did her research, the library remained bathed in bright fluorescent glare, but she felt darkness steadily rising beneath the light.

40

Avoiding the long lengths of open grassy aisles across which the ranks of vehicles face one another, the dog leads the boy between a motor home and a pickup with a camper shell, runs *across* an aisle, between two other motor homes, kicking up plumes of dust and bits of dead dry grass, thus in and around the wheel of campsites, through the area of brightly colored tents, eventually back among mechanized campers, dodging grownups and kids and a barbecue and a sunbathing woman in a lounger and a terrified Lhasa apso that squeals away from them. When Curtis at last glances back, he sees that their pursuers, if ever there were any, have given up, proving that he's better at adventuring than he is at socializing.

He remains mortified and shaken.

For a while at least, he doesn't want to leave the commotion and cover of the crowd at this contact vigil. Tonight or tomorrow, maybe he can hitch a ride with someone headed for a more populous area that will provide even better concealment, but right now this is as good as it gets, better than the lonely country road. As long as he avoids another encounter with Mr. Neary, he should be able to hang out in the meadow safely enough – assuming that Clara the smart cow doesn't suddenly drop out of the sky and crush him to death.

Old Yeller whimpers, sits next to a huge Fleetwood motor home, and tilts her head up in the posture of a dog howling at the moon, although no moon rides the sky this afternoon. She's not howling, either, but searching the heavens for a plummeting cow.

Curtis crouches beside her, scratches her ears, and explains as best he can that there's no danger of a Holstein flattening them, whereupon she grins and leans her head into his ministering hands.

'Curtis?'

The boy looks up to discover that an astonishingly glamorous woman looms over him.

Her toenails are painted azure-blue, so it seems as though they are mirrored to reflect the sky. Indeed, she's such a magical-looking person and the color on her toenails has such lustrous depth that Curtis can easily imagine he is looking at ten mystical entry points to the sky of another world. He is half convinced that if he drops a tiny pebble on one of her toenails, it will not bounce off, but will disappear into the blue, falling through into that other sky.

He can see her perfectly formed toes, for she wears minimalist white sandals. These have high heels made of clear acrylic, so she appears to be standing effortlessly on point, her feet as unsupported as those of a ballerina.

In tight white toreador pants, her legs look impossibly long. Curtis is sure that this must be an illusion fostered by the woman's dramatic appearance and by the severe angle from which he gazes up at her. When he rises from beside the dog, however, he discovers that no trick of perspective is involved. If H. G. Wells's Dr. Moreau, on his mysterious island, had been a success at his genetic experiments, he couldn't have produced a human-gazelle hybrid with more elegant legs than these.

The low-rider pants expose her tanned tummy, which serves as the taut setting for an oval-shaped, bezel-faceted opal the exact same shade of blue as the toenail polish. This gemstone is held securely in her navel by either glue or a cleverly concealed tension device of unimaginable design, or by sorcery.

Her bosoms are of the size that cameras linger on in the movies, brimming the cups of a white halter top. This top is made from such thin and pliant fabric, and supported by such fine-gauge spaghetti straps – capellini straps, actually – that as a wonder of the man-made world, it rivals the Golden Gate Bridge. Scores of engineers and architects might require weeks to study and adequately analyze the design of this astonishingly supportive garment.

Honey-gold hair frames a centerfold face with eyes that match the color of the opal. Her mouth, the ripe centerpiece of a lipstick advertisement, is a frosted red like the petals of the last rose on a November bush.

If the boy had been Curtis Hammond for more than two days, say for two weeks or two months, he might have been so completely adapted to the human biological condition that he would have felt the stir of male interest that apparently had begun to tease the original Curtis into adding Britney Spears to the big posters of movie monsters that papered his bedroom. Nevertheless, although he's largely still a work in progress, he undeniably feels *something*, a dryness of the mouth that has nothing to do with thirst, a peculiar tingle along the nerves of his limbs, and a tremble short of weakness in his knees.

'Curtis?' she asks again.

'Yes, ma'am,' he says, and realizes as he speaks that he hasn't told anyone his name since he chatted with Donella in the restaurant at the truck stop the previous evening.

Warily she surveys their surroundings, as if to be certain they are not observed or overheard. A few men in the vicinity, staring at her while she's focused on Curtis, look away when she turns toward them. Perhaps she notices this suspicious behavior, for she leans closer to the boy and whispers: 'Curtis *Hammond*?'

Except for Donella and poor dumb Burt Hooper, the waffle-eating trucker, and the man in the DRIVING MACHINE cap, no one but Curtis's enemies could know his name.

As defenseless as any mere mortal standing before a shining angel of death, Curtis is paralyzed in expectation of being gutted, beheaded, shredded, broken, blasted, burned, and worse, though never did he imagine that Death would arrive in dangling silver earrings, *two* silver-and-turquoise necklaces, three diamond rings, a silver-and-turquoise bracelet on each wrist, and navel decoration.

He could deny that he is either the original or the current Curtis Hammond, but if this is one of the hunters that wiped out his family and Curtis's family in Colorado two nights ago, he has already been identified by his singular energy signature. In that case, every attempt at deception will prove useless.

'Yes, ma'am, that's me,' he says, polite to the end, and steels himself to be slaughtered, perhaps to the delight of Mr. Neary and others whom he has offended with no intention of doing so.

Her whisper grows yet softer. 'You're supposed to be dead.'

Resistance is as pointless as deception, for if she is one of the worse scalawags, she has the strength of ten men and the speed of a Ferrari Testarossa, so Curtis is road kill waiting to happen.

Trembling, he says, 'Dead. Yes, ma'am. I guess I am.'

'You poor child,' she says with none of the sarcasm you might expect from a killer intending to decapitate you, but with concern.

Surprised by her sympathy, he seizes upon this uncharacteristic suggestion of a potential for mercy, which her kind supposedly does not possess: 'Ma'am, I'll freely admit that my dog here knows too much, considering that we've bonded. I won't pretend otherwise. But she can't talk, so she can't tell anyone what she knows. Whether my bones ought to be stripped out of this body and crushed like glass is something we're sure to disagree about, but I sincerely believe there's no good reason for her to be killed, too.'

The expression that overcomes the woman is one that Curtis has learned to recognize on faces as diverse as the round physiognomy of smiling Donella and the grizzled visage of grumpy Gabby. He supposes that it implies befuddlement, even bewilderment, though not complete mystification.

'Sweetie,' she whispers, 'why do I get the feeling that some awesomely bad people must be looking for you?'

Old Yeller has not assumed a submissive posture, but has risen to her feet. She grins at the woman in white, tail wagging with the wide sweep of expectancy, pleased to make this new acquaintance.

'We better get you out of sight,' whispers the angel, who now seems less likely to be assigned to the Death Division. 'Safer to sort this out in privacy. Come with me, okay?'

'Okay,' Curtis agrees, because the woman has been given the Old Yeller seal of approval.

She leads them to the door of the nearby Fleetwood American Heritage. Forty-five feet long, twelve feet high, eight to nine feet wide, the motor home is so immense and so solid in appearance that – except for its cheerful white, silver, and red paint job – it might be an armored military-command vehicle.

In her acrylic heels, with her golden hair, the woman reminds Curtis of Cinderella, though these are sandals rather than slippers. Cinderella most likely wouldn't have worn toreador pants, either, at least not a pair that so clearly defined the buttocks. Likewise, if Cinderella's bosoms had been as large as these, she wouldn't have displayed them so prominently, because she had lived in a more modest age than this. But if your fairy godmother is going to turn a pumpkin into stylish equipage to transport you to the royal ball, you want her to dispense with the mice-into-horses bit and use her magic wand to whack the pumpkin into a new Fleetwood American Heritage, which is cooler than any coach drawn by enchanted vermin.

The instant the door is opened, the dog leaps up the steps and into the motor home, as though she has always belonged here. At the suggestion of his hostess, Curtis follows Old Yeller.

Entry is directly into the cockpit. As he steps between the well-separated passenger's and driver's seats, into a lounge with flanking sofas, he hears the door shut behind him.

Suddenly this fairy tale becomes a horror story. Looking across the lounge, into the open kitchen, Curtis sees at the sink the last person that he might expect to find there. Cinderella.

He turns in shock, looking behind him, and Cinderella is there, as well, standing between the driver's and passenger's seats, smiling and even more dramatic-looking in this confined space than she had been out in the sun.

The Cinderella at the sink is identical to the first Cinderella, from the silky honey-gold hair to the opal-blue eyes, to the opal in the navel, to the long legs in low-rider white toreador pants, to the sandals with acrylic heels, to the azure toenails.

Clones.

Oh, Lord, *clones*.

Clones are usually trouble, and there's no prejudice in this opinion, because most clones are born to be bad.

'Clones,' Curtis mutters.

The first Cinderella smiles. 'What'd you say, sweetie?'

The second Cinderella turns away from the sink and takes a step toward Curtis. She's also smiling. And she's holding a large knife.

41

Sitting in the fluorescent-flooded brick-and-mortar library but also outbound through cyberspace with its infinite avenues of radiant circuitry and light pipes, traveling the world on the swift wheels of electric current and microwaves, exploring virtual libraries that are always open, ever bright, poring through paperless books of glowing data, Micky found the primitive self-interest and darkest materialism of humanity everywhere in these palaces of technological genius.

Bioethicists reject the existence of objective truths. Preston Maddoc had written, 'There is no right or wrong, no moral or immoral conduct. Bioethics is about efficiency, about establishing a set of rules that will do the most good for the most people.'

For one thing, this efficiency means assisting suicide in every case where a suffering person considers it, not merely assisting the suicides of the terminally ill, not just of the chronically ill, but assisting even those who could be cured but are at times depressed.

In fact, Preston and many others considered depressed people as candidates not only for suicide assistance but also for 'positive suicide counseling' to ensure they self-destructed. After all, a depressed person has an inadequate quality of life, and even if his depression can be alleviated with drugs, he isn't 'normal' when on mood-altering medication and therefore is incapable of leading a life of quality.

An increase in the suicide rate is, they believe, a benefit to society, for in a well-managed medical system, the organs of assisted suicides should be harvested for transplantation. Micky read many bioethicists who were gleeful at the prospect of alleviating organ shortages through managed-care suicide programs; in their enthusiasm, it was clear they would work aggressively to *increase* the number of suicides if given all the laws for which they relentlessly pressed.

If we are all just meat, having no soul, then why shouldn't some of us join together to butcher others for our benefit? There will be an immediate gain and no long-term consequences.

Micky snatched her right hand away from the mouse, her left hand off the keyboard. To save electricity, the library was almost as warm as the day outside, but a chill slithered into her from the Internet, as though someone at a computer in Dr. Frankenstein's castle had crossed paths with her in cyberspace, reaching out of the ether to trace her spine with a virtual finger colder than ice.

She looked around at the other library patrons, wondering how many of them would be as shocked as she was by what she'd read, how many would be indifferent – and how many would agree with Preston Maddoc and his colleagues. She had often brooded about the fragility of life, but for the first time, she realized with sobering acuity that civilization itself was as fragile as any human being. Any of the many hells that humankind had created throughout history, in one corner of the world or another, could be re-created here – or a new hell could be built, more efficient and more thoroughly reasoned.

Back to the mouse, the keys, the World Wide Web, and back to Preston Maddoc, the spider, out there spinning . . . .

The organs of the suicidal and the disabled were coveted, but Maddoc and others in the bioethics community expressed great sympathy for the harvesting of organs from the healthy and the happy, as well.

In *The Elimination of Morality*, by Anne Maclean, Micky read of a program proposed by John Harris, a British bioethicist, in which everyone would be given a lottery number. Then 'whenever doctors have two or more dying patients who could be saved by transplants, and no suitable organs have come to hand through "natural deaths," they can ask a central computer to supply a suitable donor. The computer will then pick the number of a suitable donor at random and he will be killed so that the lives of two or more others may be saved.'

Kill a thousand to save three thousand. Kill a million to save three million. Kill the weak to save the stronger. Kill the disabled to provide a higher quality of life to the firm of limb. Kill those with lower IQs to provide more resources to those judged smarter.

Great universities like Harvard and Yale, like Princeton, once citadels of knowledge where truth might be pursued, had become well-oiled machines of death, instructing medical students that killing should be viewed as a form of healing, that only selected people who meet a series of criteria have a right to exist, that there is no right or wrong, that death is life. We are all Darwinians now, are we not? The strong survive longer, the weak die sooner, and since this is the plan of Nature, shouldn't we help the old green gal in her work? Accept your expensive diploma, toss your mortarboard in the air to celebrate, and then go kill a weakling for Mother Nature.

Somewhere Hitler smiles. They say that he killed the disabled and the sick (not to mention the Jews) for all the wrong reasons, but if in fact there is no wrong or right, no objective truth, then all that really matters is that he *did* kill them, which by the standards of contemporary ethics, makes him a visionary.

Photographs of Preston Maddoc, as they appeared on the screen, revealed a good-looking if not handsome man with longish brown hair, a mustache, and an appealing smile. Contrary to Micky's expectations, he didn't sport a Universal Product Code on his forehead with the numerals 666 rendered in bar code.

His short-form bio revealed a man on whom Lady Luck smiled. He was the sole heir to a considerable fortune. He didn't need to work in order to travel in style from one end of the country to the other in search of extraterrestrials who might have a healing gift.

Micky could find no story in the media exploring Maddoc's belief that UFOs were real and that ETs walked among us. If it was a genuine long-held belief, he had never spoken publicly about it.

Four and a half years ago, he resigned his university position to 'devote more time to bioethic philosophy, rather than teaching,' and to unspecified personal interests.

He was known to have assisted in eight suicides.

Leilani claimed he had killed eleven people. Evidently she knew of three who were not part of the public record.

A few elderly women, a thirty-year-old mother with cancer, a seventeen-year-old high-school football star who suffered a spinal injury . . . In Micky's mind, as she read of Maddoc's kills, she heard Leilani's voice reciting the same list.

Twice Maddoc had been prosecuted for murder, in two different cases and jurisdictions. Both times, juries had acquitted him because they felt that his intentions had been noble and that his compassion had been admirable, unimpeachable.

The husband of the thirty-year-old cancer victim, though present during the assisted suicide, subsequently filed a civil suit seeking damages from Maddoc when an autopsy discovered that his wife had been misdiagnosed, that she didn't have cancer, and that her condition had been curable. The jurors sided with Maddoc, nevertheless, because of his good intentions and because they felt the true fault resided with the doctor who had delivered the wrong diagnosis.

A year after the death of her son, the mother of the six-year-old wheelchair-bound boy filed suit, too, claiming that Maddoc, in conspiracy with her husband, subjected her to 'relentless mental and emotional intimidation using techniques of psychological warfare and brainwashing,' until in a state of physical and mental exhaustion, she agreed to terminate her son's life, for which she was remorseful. She dropped all legal action prior to trial, maybe because she didn't have the heart for the media circus that began to pitch its tents or because Maddoc reached an undisclosed settlement with her.

Luck undeniably favored Preston Maddoc, but you couldn't lightly regard the importance of the powerhouse legal-defense team that his fortune provided or the effect of the $20,000-per-month public-relations firm that for years worked tirelessly to polish his image.

He kept a lower profile these days. Indeed, since he had become Sinsemilla's devoted husband and deep-pocket pharmacy, he'd steadily moved farther off the public stage, allowing other true believers to man the barricades on behalf of their vision of a brave new world of greater happiness through useful killing.

Curiously, Micky could find no reference to Maddoc's marriage. According to every thumbnail biography to be found on the Internet, he was single.

When a figure as controversial as Preston Maddoc took a wife, the wedding should be news. Whether he'd drawn a marriage license in busy Manhattan or in a sleepy backwater in Kansas, the media would have learned of the event and would have reported it widely, even if the ceremony had been conducted and the bride had been kissed before journalists could fly to the scene with cameras. Yet . . . not a word.

Leilani had called it an amazing wedding, though it lacked a carved-ice swan. By now, Micky believed that no matter how outrageous the girl's stories seemed, Leilani never lied. Somewhere, a wedding had been held, without either the carved-ice swan or the breathless attention of the media.

Understandably, when your bride was a woman like Sinsemilla, you might not want your publicist to seek a three-page spread in *People* or to arrange for the two of you to do a TV interview with Larry King in celebration of your nuptials.

Most likely, however, the reason for this singular degree of discretion had been the groom's intention to kill his stepson and stepdaughter if his expectation of extraterrestrial healers wasn't fulfilled. Fewer questions will be asked about your missing children if no one knows they existed in the first place.

Micky remembered Leilani saying that Maddoc didn't use his own name at campgrounds when they traveled in their motor home and that he affected a different appearance these days. Judging by copyright dates, the most recent photos of him were at least four years old.

Staring at Dr. Doom's blithe face on the computer, she suspected that his murderous intent toward Lukipela and Leilani wasn't the only reason he kept his marriage secret. A mystery awaited revelation.

She logged off. The resources on the Internet were exhaustive, but Micky could learn nothing more of use from them. The real world always trumped the virtual, and it always would. The next step was to meet Preston Maddoc face-to-face and take his measure.

Leaving the library, she was no longer self-conscious about her too-short, too-tight skirt. If she hadn't canceled, she could have gone to the job interview with confidence.

In the past couple hours, she'd changed in some fundamental way. She felt this difference profoundly, but she couldn't yet define it.

Brooding about bioethics, Micky arrived at her Camaro without quite realizing that she'd crossed the parking lot, as though she had teleported from the library to the car in an instant.

Behind the wheel, she didn't switch on the radio. She *always* drove by radio. Silences made her edgy, and music was a caulking that filled every jagged chink. But not today.

The real world trumped the virtual . . . .

Bioethicists were dangerous because they devised their rules and schemes not for the real world but for a virtual reality in which human beings have no heart, no capacity to love, and where everyone is as convinced of the meaninglessness of life as are the ethicists themselves, where everyone believes that humanity is just meat.

On her way home, the highways were as clogged as an aging sumo wrestler's arteries. Usually she chafed at the stop-and-go traffic. But not today.

Maddoc and his fellow bioethicists ceased to be merely dangerous and became bloody tyrants when they obtained the power to try to make the world conform to their abstract model of it, a model that was in conflict with human nature and no more representative of reality than an idiot savant's math tricks are representative of true genius.

Stop, go. Stop, go.

She remembered reading that California had halted freeway construction for eight years in the 1970s and '80s. The governor back then believed automobiles would no longer be in wide use by 1995. Public transit would take over. Alternate technology. Miracles.

In all the years that she'd railed at bumper-to-bumper traffic, during so many frustrating two-hour drives that should have taken thirty minutes, she had never before connected that idiotic public policy to the current mess. Suddenly she felt that by her own choice she'd been living entirely in the current moment, in a bubble that separated her from the past and the future, from cause and effect.

Stop, go. Stop, go.

How many millions of gallons of gasoline were wasted in traffic like this, how much unnecessary pollution generated by the unintended consequence of that moratorium on highway construction?

And yet the current governor had announced his own ban on freeway construction.

If she let Leilani die, how could she live with herself other than by embracing the we're-just-meat philosophy of Maddoc's crowd? In her own way, she'd been living by that empty faith for years – and look where it had gotten her.

One new thought led to another. Stop, go. Stop, go.

Micky felt as if she were waking from a twenty-eight-year dream.

42

With the swiftness of a genie's spirit rising from the prison of his lamp, the sweet oily fragrance of vanilla magically spread through the humid air to every corner of Mrs. D's kitchen the moment that she opened the bottle.

'Mmmmm. That's the best smell in the world, don't you think?'

Putting ice cubes in the two tall glasses, Leilani drew a deep breath. 'Wonderful. Unfortunately, it reminds me of old Sinsemilla's bath water.'

'Good heavens. Your mother bathes in vanilla?'

As she watched Geneva dribble vanilla extract over the ice in the glasses, as she carried the glasses to the table, and as Geneva followed with cans of Coke, Leilani explained Sinsemilla's passion for purging toxins through reverse osmosis in hot baths.

'Then it must be a little like belling the cat,' said Mrs. D, handing Leilani one of the Cokes.

'Mrs. D, you've lost me again. I'm afraid I'm hampered in conversation by a need to grasp how each comment springs logically from the one preceding it.'

'How sad for you, dear. I meant you always know when your mom's coming because she's preceded by clouds of wonderful fragrances.'

'Not so wonderful when she's had a bath seasoned with garlic, condensed cabbage juice, and stinkweed extract.'

They sat at the table and sampled their vanilla Cokes.

'This is fabulous,' Leilani enthused.

'I can't believe you've never mixed one before.'

'Well, we rarely have cola in the fridge. Old Sinsemilla says caffeine inhibits development of your natural telepathic ability.'

'Then you must be a terrific little mind reader.'

'Scarily good. Right now you're trying to remember the names of all the singers who've ever been in the group Destiny's Child, and you can only recall four.'

'Uncanny, dear. What I'm actually thinking is how this vanilla Coke would go perfectly with a big fat sugar cookie.'

'I like the way you think, Mrs. D, even if your mind is too complex to be read accurately.'

'Leilani, would you like a big fat sugar cookie?'

'Yes, thank you.'

'So would I. Very much. Unfortunately, we don't have any. Some nice crisp cinnamon cookies would be good, too. How about cinnamon cookies with vanilla Cokes?'

'You've talked me into it.'

'We don't have any of those, either, I'm afraid.' Geneva sipped her drink, pondered a moment. 'Do you think chocolate-almond cookies would go with vanilla Cokes?'

'I'm reluctant to have an opinion, Mrs. D.'

'Really? Why's that, dear?'

'It seems pointless somehow.'

'Too bad. Not to brag, but my chocolate-almond cookies are quite wonderful.'

'Do you have any?'

'Six dozen.'

'More than enough, thank you.'

Geneva brought a plate of the treats to the table.

Leilani sampled a cookie. 'Phenomenal. And they go with vanilla Cokes just fine. But these aren't almonds. They're pecans.'

'Yes, I know. I don't particularly care for almonds, so when I make chocolate-almond cookies, I use pecans instead.'

'There's something I'm dying to ask, Mrs. D, but I don't want you to think I'm being disrespectful.'

Geneva's eyes widened. 'You couldn't be if you tried. You're an absolute, no-doubt-about-it . . .' Geneva frowned. 'What is the term?'

'Absolute, no-doubt-about-it, fine young mutant.'

'If you say so, dear.'

'I ask this with great affection, Mrs. D, but do you *work* at being a charming screwball, or does it just come naturally?'

Delighted, Geneva said, 'Am I a charming screwball?'

'In my estimation, yes.'

'Why, you sweet child, I can't imagine anything better to be! As to your question . . . let me think. Well, if I *am* a charming screwball, I'm not sure whether I always was, or maybe only since being shot in the head. Either way, no, I don't work at it. I wouldn't know how.'

Munching, Leilani said, 'Dr. Doom is going to haul us to Idaho.'

A quiver of alarm rang the smile off Geneva's face. 'Idaho? When?'

'I don't know. When the mechanic's finished with the motor home. Next week sometime, I guess.'

'Why Idaho? I mean, I'm sure they're nice people in Idaho, with all their potatoes, but that's an awful long way from here.'

'Some guy lives near Nun's Lake, Idaho, claims he was taken aboard an alien spacecraft and healed.'

'Healed of what?'

'Of the desire to live in Nun's Lake. That's my guess. The guy probably figures a really wild story will get him a book deal, a TV movie, and enough money to move to Malibu.'

'We can't let you go to Idaho.'

'Heck, Mrs. D, I've been to North Dakota.'

'We'll keep you here, hide you in Micky's room.'

'That's kidnapping.'

'Not if you're agreeable to it.'

'Yeah, even if I'm agreeable to it. That's the law.'

'Then the law's silly.'

'The silly-law defense never works in court, Mrs. D. You'll wind up sucking down all the free lethal gas you want, courtesy of the state of California. May I have a second cookie?'

'Of course, dear. But this Idaho thing is so distressing.'

'Eat, eat,' Leilani advised. 'Your cookies are so good, they'd make prisoners tap dance in the torture chambers of Torquemada.'

'Then I should bake up a batch and we'll send them some.'

'Torquemada lived during the Spanish Inquisition, Mrs. D, back in the fourteen hundreds.'

'I wasn't baking cookies then. But it's always given me so much pleasure that people enjoy my cooking. And even back when I had the restaurant, the baked goods drew the most compliments.'

'You had a restaurant?'

'I was a waitress, then I owned my own restaurant, and in fact it developed into a prosperous little chain. Oh, and I met this lovely man, Zachary Scott. Success, passion . . . Everything would've been wonderful, except my own daughter began coming on to him.'

'I didn't know you had a daughter, Mrs. D.'

Geneva nibbled thoughtfully at her cookie. 'Actually, she was Joan Crawford's daughter.'

'Joan Crawford's daughter came on to your boyfriend?'

'In fact, the restaurants belonged to Joan Crawford, too. I guess this stuff happened in *Mildred Pierce*, not in my life at all – but that doesn't change the fact that Zachary Scott was a lovely man.'

'Maybe tomorrow I could come over, and we could bake a bunch of cookies for Torquemada's prisoners, after all.'

Geneva laughed. 'And I'll bet George Washington and the boys at Valley Forge would enjoy a batch, too. You're a peach, a pip, and a corker, Leilani. Can't wait to see what you'll be like all grown up.'

'For one thing, I'll have boobs, one way or the other. Not that having them is the be-all and end-all of my existence.'

'I particularly liked my breasts when I was Sophia Loren.'

'You're pretty funny yourself, Mrs. D, and you're already all grown up. In my experience, not too many grown-up people are funny.'

'Why don't you call me Aunt Gen, like Micky does.'

This particular expression of affection almost undid Leilani. She tried to cover her inability to speak by quickly taking a swig of her vanilla Coke.

Geneva saw through the clever vanilla-Coke ruse, and her eyes misted. She seized a cookie as an instrument of distraction, but that didn't work because there wasn't any logical reason for her to hold a cookie in such a way as to block Leilani's view of her teary eyes.

From Leilani's perspective, the worst thing that could happen would be for the two of them to start sobbing at each other as if this were an episode of *Oprah* titled 'Little Crippled Girls Marked for Murder and the Charming Screwball Shot-in-the-Head Surrogate Aunts Who Love Them.' Just as the way of the Ninja was not the way of the Klonk, so the way of the weepy was not the way of the Klonk, either, at least not *this* Klonk.

Time for the penguin.

She fished it out of one pocket of her shorts and put it on the table, among the candleholders that were still arranged as they had been at dinner the previous night. 'I was wondering if you could do me a favor and help get this back to the person who should have it.'

'How cute!' Geneva put aside the cookie that she neither wanted to eat nor wanted to plaster over her eyes. She plucked the figurine off the table. 'Why, it's adorable, isn't it?'

The two-inch-tall penguin – sculpted from clay, kiln-fired, and hand-painted – was indeed so adorable that Leilani would have kept it if not for its creepy provenance.

'It belonged to a girl who died last night.'

Geneva's smile first froze and then melted away.

Leilani said, 'Her name was Tetsy. I don't know her last name. But I think she's local, here in the county.'

'What's this all about, sweetie?'

'If you'd buy a newspaper tomorrow and Saturday, an obituary should be published one day or the other. It'll have the last name.'

'You're spooking me, dear.'

'Sorry. I don't mean to. Tetsy collected penguins, and this was one of hers. Preston might have asked to have it, but he might have taken it without asking. Anyway, I don't want it.'

They stared across the table at each other because Geneva's eyes were no longer misty and because Leilani was functioning unshakably in the way of the Klonk, no longer in danger of flushing the kitchen furniture out of the back door on a tide of tears.

Geneva said, 'Leilani, should I be calling the police?'

'Wouldn't do any good. They pumped a huge dose of digitoxin into her, which caused a massive heart attack. Preston's used this trick before. Digitoxin would show up in an autopsy, so they must have been sure there wouldn't be one. Most likely, she's already cremated.'

Geneva looked at the penguin. She looked at Leilani. She looked at her vanilla Coke. She said, 'This is bizarre stuff.'

'Isn't it? Anyway, Preston gave this penguin to me because he said it reminded him of Lukipela.'

Geneva's voice bit with a venom that Leilani had not imagined she contained: *'The rotten bastard.'*

'It's cute, Luki was cute. It leans to one side, same as Luki. But it doesn't look like Luki because, of course, it's a *penguin*.'

'I have a sister-in-law who lives out in Hemet.'

Although this seemed to have nothing to do with dead girls and penguins, Leilani leaned forward with interest. 'So is this a real sister-in-law or possibly Gwyneth Paltrow?'

'Real. Her name's Clarissa, and she's a good person – as long as you have some tolerance for parrots.'

'I like parrots. Do hers talk?'

'Oh, constantly. She has over sixty.'

'I'm pretty much a one-parrot-at-a-time person.'

'I'm thinking, maybe when you disappear, the police would come looking here, but they wouldn't know about Clarissa in Hemet.'

Leilani pretended to consider it. Then: 'Out of sixty talking parrots, at least one will be a fink and turn us in.'

'She'd love your companionship, dear. And there's always work to be done, filling seed trays and water cups.'

'Why does this feel like a Hitchcock movie? And I don't just mean *The Birds*. I suspect somewhere in the situation, there's a guy who dresses up like his mother and has an obsession with big knives. Anyway, if Clarissa went to jail for kidnapping, what would happen to the parrots?'

Geneva looked around as though assessing the accommodations. 'I could take them in here, I suppose.'

'Holy smokes, we'd want twenty-four/seven video of *that!*'

'But they'd never send Clarissa to prison. She's sixty-seven years old, weighs two hundred fifty pounds even though she's just five feet three – and, of course, there's the goiter.'

Leilani didn't ask the obvious question.

Geneva answered it anyway. 'Strictly speaking, it's not really a goiter. It's a tumor, and because it's benign, she won't have it removed. Clarissa doesn't trust doctors, and given her history with them, who can blame her? But she just lets it hang there, getting bigger. Even if they could cope with her age and weight, prison officials would worry about that goiter scaring the other inmates.'

Leilani drained the last of the vanilla Coke from her glass. 'Okay, so when the obituary appears, if you'd track down an address for

Tetsy's parents and mail the penguin back to them, that would be swell. I'd do it myself, but Preston doesn't let me have money, not even enough for a few stamps. He buys me anything I want, but I think he figures that if I had an allowance, I'd ramp it up with shrewd investments until I had enough to afford a hit man.'

'You've still got half the Coke in the can, dear. Would you like me to add some fresh ice and vanilla to your glass?'

'Yes, thank you.'

After Geneva had built a second serving for each of them, she sat opposite Leilani once more. Worry drew connecting lines through her constellations of coppery freckles, and her green eyes clouded. 'Micky will think of something we can do.'

'I'll be okay, Aunt Gen.'

'Honey, you're *not* going to Idaho.'

'Just how big is the goiter?'

'Can you come for dinner this evening?'

'Great! Dr. Doom is supposed to be out again, so he won't know. He'd stop me, but old Sinsemilla's too self-involved to notice.'

'I'm sure Micky will have some strategy by then.'

'Is it, say, bigger than a plum?'

'I'll turn on the air conditioning this evening, so we'll be able to think clearly. You can bet the *governor* never does without.'

'Bigger than an orange?'

43

Resplendent in acrylic-heeled sandals and navel opals, these two Cinderellas have no need of a fairy godmother, for they are magical in their own right. Their laughter is musical, infectious, and Curtis can't help but smile even though they're laughing at his ridiculous and shakily expressed fear that they might be clones.

They are, of course, identical twins. The one he met outside is named Castoria. The one he encountered second is Polluxia.

'Call me Cass.'

'And call me Polly.'

Polly puts down the big knife with which she was chopping vegetables. Dropping to her knees on the galley floor, with squeaky baby talk and vigorous ear scratching, she reduces Old Yeller at once to licking, tail-lashing adulation.

Placing a hand gently on Curtis's shoulder, Cass brings him out of the lounge and into the galley.

'In Greek mythology,' says Curtis, 'Castor and Pollux were the sons of Leda, fathered by Jupiter disguised as a swan. They're the patron deities of seamen and voyagers. They're famous warriors, too.'

This knowledgeable recitation surprises the women. They regard him with evident curiosity.

Old Yeller turns to stare at him as well, though accusingly, because Polly has stopped the baby talk and the ear scratching.

'They tell us half the kids graduating from high school can't read,' says Cass, 'but you're mythology savvy in grade school?'

'My mother was big on organic brain augmentation and direct-to-brain megadata downloading,' he explains.

Their expressions cause Curtis to review what he has just said, and he's chagrined to realize that he revealed more about his true nature and his origins than he ever intended to share with anyone. These two dazzle him, and as with Donella and Gabby, dazzlement seems to evoke in him either a looseness of the tongue or a tangling of the same potentially treacherous organ.

In a lame attempt to distract them from what he revealed, Curtis continues with a harmless lie: 'Plus we had a Bible and a useless 'cyclopedia sold to us by a mercantile porch-squatter.'

Cass plucks a newspaper from the table in the dining nook and hands it to Polly.

Polly's sparkling eyes widen, and blue beams seem to flash at Curtis as she says, 'I didn't recognize you, sweetie.'

She turns the newspaper so Curtis can see three photos under the headline SAVAGE COLORADO MURDERS TIED TO FUGITIVE DRUG LORDS IN UTAH.

The photos are of the members of the Hammond family. Mr. and Mrs. Hammond, shown here, are surely the people who were asleep in their bed, in the quiet farmhouse, when the fugitive boy shamefully took twenty-four dollars from the wallet on the dresser.

The third picture is of Curtis Hammond.

'You're not dead,' Cass says.

'No,' Curtis replies, which is true as far as it goes.

'You escaped.'

'Not quite yet.'

'Who're you here with?'

'Nobody but my dog. We've pretty much hitched across Utah.'

Polly asks, 'Whatever happened at your family's farm in Colorado – is that all tied to this hullabaloo in Utah?'

He nods. 'Yeah.'

Castoria and Polluxia make eye contact, and their connection is as precise as that between a surgical laser and the calculated terminus of its beam, so that Curtis can almost see the scintillant trace of thought passing from one to the other. They share their next question in a duologue that does nothing to diminish his dazzlement:

'It's not just—'

'– a bunch of—'

'– crazy drug lords—'

'– behind all this—'

'– like the government says—'

'– is it, Curtis?'

His attention bounces from one to the other as he answers the question twice, 'No. No.'

When these twins exchange a meaningful look, which they now do again, they seem not to convey just a quick single thought, but whole paragraphs of complex data and opinion. In the womb, fed by the same susurrous river of blood, soothed by the two-note lullaby of the same mother's heart, gazing eye to eye in dreamy anticipation of the world to come, they had perfected the telemetric stare.

'Over there in Utah—'

'– is the government—'

'– trying to cover up—'

'– contact with—'

'– extraterrestrials?'

'Yes,' Curtis says, because this is the answer they expect and the only one they will believe. If he lies and says that no aliens are involved, they will either know that he is dissembling or will think that he's merely stupid and that he's as bamboozled by the government spinmeisters as is everyone else. He's drawn to Cass and Polly; he likes them partly because Old Yeller likes them, partly because the genes of Curtis Hammond ensure that he likes them, but also because there is a tenderness about them, quite apart from their beauty, that he finds appealing. He doesn't want them to think that he is either stupid or disposed to lie. 'Yes, aliens.'

Cass to Polly, Polly to Cass, blue lasers transmitting unspoken volumes. Then Polly says, 'Where are your folks, really?'

'They're really dead.' His vision blurs with tears of guilt and remorse. Sooner or later, he'd have been forced to stop somewhere, if not at the Hammond farm, then at another, to find clothes and money and a suitable identity. But if he had realized just how close on his tail the hunters had been, he wouldn't have chosen the Hammond place. 'Dead. The newspaper's right about that.'

To his tears the sisters fly as birds to a nest in a storm. In an instant he's being hugged and kissed and comforted by Polly, then by Cass, by Polly, by Cass, caught in a spin cycle of sympathy and motherly affection.

In a swoon short of an outright faint, Curtis is conveyed, as if by spirit handlers, into the dining nook, and with what seems to him to be a miraculousness equal to the sun spinning off spangles in the sky over Fatima, a divine refreshment appears in front of him – a tall glass of cold root beer in which floats a scoop of vanilla ice cream.

Not forgotten, Old Yeller is served a plate piled with the cubed white meat of chicken, and ice water in a bowl. After cleaning the chicken off the plate nearly as fast as it could have been sucked up by an industrial vacuum cleaner, the dog chews the ice with delight, grinning as she crunches it.

As though image and reflection exist magically side by side, Cass and Polly sit across the table from Curtis in the nook. Four silver earrings dangle, four silver-and-turquoise necklaces shine, four silver bracelets gleam – and four flushed breasts, as smooth as cream, swell with sympathy and concern.

Playing cards are fanned on the table, and Polly gathers them up as she says, 'I don't mean to salt your grief, sweetie, but if we're going to help, we need to know the situation. Were your folks killed in a cover-up because they saw too much, something like that?'

'Yes, ma'am. Something like that.'

Slipping the deck of cards into a pack bearing the Bicycle logo and setting the pack aside, Polly says, 'And evidently you also saw too much.'

'Yes, ma'am. Something like that, ma'am.'

'Please call me Polly, but *never* ask me if I want a cracker.'

'Okay, ma'— Okay, Polly. But I like crackers, so I'll eat any you don't want.'

As Curtis noisily sucks root beer and melting ice cream through a straw, Cass leans forward conspiratorially and whispers ominously, '*Did you see an alien spacecraft, Curtis?*'

He licks his lips and whispers, '*More than one, ma'am.*'

'*Call me Cass,*' she whispers, and now their conversation is firmly established in this sotto-voce mode. '*Castoria sounds too much like a bowel medication.*'

'*I think it's pretty, Cass.*'

'*Should I call you Curtis?*'

'*Sure. That's who I'm being . . . who I am.*'

'So you saw more than one alien ship. And did you see . . . honest-to-God aliens?'

'Lots of 'em. And some not so honest.'

Electrified by this revelation, she leans even farther over the table, and a greater urgency informs her whisper. *'You saw aliens, and so the government wants to kill you to keep you from talking.'*

Curtis is utterly beguiled by her twinkly-eyed look of childlike excitement, and he doesn't want to disappoint her. Leaning past his root beer, not quite nose-to-nose with Cass, but close enough to feel her exhilaration, he whispers, *'The government would probably lock me away to study me, which might be worse than killing.'*

'Because you had contact with aliens?'

'Something like that.'

Polly, who has not leaned over the table and who does not speak in a whisper, looks worriedly at the nearby window. She reaches over her sister's head, grabs the draw cord, and shuts the short drape as she says, 'Curtis, did your parents have an alien encounter, too?'

Although he continues to lean toward Cass, when Curtis shifts his eyes toward Polly, he answers her in a normal tone of voice, as she has spoken to him: 'Yes, they did.'

'Of the third kind?' whispers Cass.

'Of the worst kind,' he whispers.

Polly says, 'Why didn't the government want to study them, like they want to study you? Why were they killed?'

'Government didn't kill them,' Curtis explains.

'Who did?' whispers Cass.

'Alien assassins,' Curtis hisses. *'Aliens killed everyone in the house.'*

Cass's eyes are bluer than robin's eggs and seemingly as big as those in a hen's nest. She's briefly breathless. Then: *'So . . . they don't come in peace to serve mankind.'*

'Some do. But not these scalawags.'

'And they're still after you, aren't they?' Polly asks.

'From Colorado and clear across Utah,' Curtis admits. 'Both them and the FBI. But I'm getting harder to detect all the time.'

'You poor kid,' Cass whispers. *'All alone, on the run.'*

'I've got my dog.'

Getting up from the booth, Polly says, 'Now you've got us, too. Come on, Cass, let's pull stakes and hit the road.'

'We haven't heard his whole story yet,' Cass protests. 'There's aliens and all sorts of spooky stuff.' Still leaning toward Curtis, she drops her voice to a whisper: '*All sorts of spooky stuff, right?*'

'*Spooky stuff,*' he confirms, thrilled to see the delight that he has given her with this confirmation.

Polly is adamant. 'They're hunting for him right across the state line. They're sure to come nosing around here soon. We've got to get moving.'

'*She's the alpha twin,*' Cass whispers solemnly. '*We've got to listen to her, or there'll be hell to pay.*'

'I'm not the alpha twin,' Polly disagrees. 'I'm just practical. Curtis, while we get the rig ready to roll, you take a shower. You're just a little too fragrant. We'll throw your clothes in the washer.'

He's reluctant to endanger these sisters, but he accepts their hospitality for three reasons. First, motion is commotion, which makes it harder for his enemies to detect him. Second, but for the big windshield, the motor home is more enclosed than most vehicles; the other windows are small, and the metal shell largely screens his special biological-energy signature from the electronic devices that can detect it. Third, he has been Curtis Hammond for approximately two days, and the longer that he settles into this new life, the harder he is to find, so he probably poses little danger to them.

'My dog could use a bath, too.'

'We'll give her a good scrubbing later,' Polly promises.

Past the galley, a door stands open to a water closet on the right, which is separate from the rest of the bathroom. On the left, a vertically stacked washer-dryer combination.

Directly ahead is the bathroom door, and beyond it lies the last eighteen feet or so of the motor home. The sole bedroom is accessed through the bathroom.

Old Yeller stays behind with Polly, and Cass shows Curtis how to work the shower controls. She unwraps a fresh cake of soap and lays out spare towels. 'After you've undressed, just toss your clothes out the bathroom door, and I'll wash them.'

'This is very nice of you, ma'am. I mean Cass.'

'Sweetie, don't be silly. You've brought us just what we've been needing. We're girls who like adventure, and you've seen *aliens*.'

How her eyes sparkle on the word *adventure*, only to sparkle even more bewitchingly on the word *aliens*. Her face glows with excitement. She all but quivers with expectation, and her body strains against her clothes just as the powerful body of Wonder Woman forever strains against every stitch of her superhero costume.

Alone, Curtis removes his small treasury from his pockets and puts the cash aside on the vanity. He slides open the bathroom door just far enough to toss his clothes out in front of the washer, then slides it firmly shut again.

He is Curtis Hammond enough to blush at being naked here in the sisters' bathroom. At first this seems to indicate that he's well settled in his new identity, already more Curtis than he is himself, and becoming more Curtis all the time.

Peering in the mirror, however, he watches his face darken to a shade of scarlet that he's never noticed in other people, suddenly causing him to question whether he's fully in control of himself. A blush this fierce is surely beyond the range of human physiological response. He seems to be as red as a lobster cooking in a pot, and he's convinced that anyone, seeing him like this, would suspect that he's not who he pretends to be. Furthermore, he looks so sheepish that his expression alone would fill any policeman with suspicion and predispose any jury to convict.

Heart beating fast and hard, counseling himself to remain calm, he steps into the shower before turning on the water, which Cass advised him *not* to do. It's immediately so hot that he cries out in pain, stifles the cry, mistakenly cranks the water hotter still, but then overcompensates, and stands in a freezing spray. He's lobster-bright from top to bottom, and his teeth chatter so hard he could crack walnuts, if he had walnuts, and it's just as well he doesn't have walnuts, because the shells would make a mess, and then he'd have *that* to clean up. Listening to himself babble to himself about walnuts, he's amazed that he has survived this long. Once more he tells himself to be calm – not that it did much good the last time.

He remembers that Cass advised a quick shower because the motor home isn't connected to utilities; the system is operating off the vehicle's storage tanks and the gasoline-powered generator. Because he failed to obtain a precise definition of *quick*, he's certain that he's already used more water than is prudent, so he soaps up as fast as possible, rinses down, remembers his hair, pours shampoo straight from the bottle onto his head, realizes at once that he has seriously overused the product, and stands in rising masses of suds that threaten to fill the shower stall.

To dissolve the suds as quickly as possible, he cranks the water to cold again, and by the time that he finally shuts the spray off, his teeth are rattling like an electric-powered nutcracker once more. He's sure that he has so drained the motor home's water system that the vehicle will topple sideways out of balance or suffer some catastrophic failure resulting in great financial loss and possibly even the destruction of human life.

Out of the shower, on the bath mat, vigorously drying himself, he realizes that personal grooming is related to socializing, and he has proven time and again that he's a lousy socializer. Yet he can't go through life without a bath, because walking around filthy and stinky is not good socializing, either.

In addition to those worries and woes, he's still embarrassed about being naked in the sisters' bathroom, and now he realizes that he will have to wear nothing but a large towel until his clothes are laundered. He turns to the mirror, anxious to see if his face remains an unnatural shade of lobster, and he discovers something far worse than expected in his reflection.

He isn't being Curtis Hammond.

'Holy howlin' saints alive.'

In shock, he drops the towel.

More accurately: He is being Curtis Hammond but not entirely, not well, certainly not convincingly enough to pass for human.

Oh, Lord.

The face in the mirror isn't hideous, but it is stranger than any face in any carnival freak show that ever welcomed gawking rubes into its sawdust-carpeted chambers.

In Colorado, in the farmhouse, beyond the bedroom door with the plaque announcing STARSHIP COMMAND CENTER, this motherless boy had found the used Band-Aid discarded on the nightstand, and the dried blood on the gauze pad had provided him with a perfect opportunity to fashion a disguise. Touching the blood, absorbing it, he'd added Curtis Hammond's DNA to his repertoire. While the original Curtis continued sleeping, his namesake had fled out of the bedroom window, onto the porch roof, and then here to Castoria and Polluxia's bathroom, though not directly.

Being Curtis Hammond – in fact, being anyone or anything other than himself – requires a constant biological tension, which produces a unique energy signature that identifies him to those equipped with the proper scanning technology. Day by day, however, as he adjusts to a new identity, sustaining the adopted physical form becomes easier, until after a few weeks or months, his energy signature is virtually indistinguishable from those of other members of the population that he has joined. In this case, that population is humanity.

Stepping closer to the mirror, he wills himself to be Curtis Hammond, not in the half-assed fashion revealed by the mirror, but with conviction and attention to detail.

In the reflection of his face, he watches several peculiar changes occur, but the flesh resists his command.

One slip-up like this can be disastrous. If Cass and Polly were to see him in this condition, they would know that he isn't Curtis Hammond, that he isn't of this earth. Then he could probably kiss their generous assistance and their root-beer floats goodbye.

As good as his motives are, he might nevertheless wind up like the stitched-together brute who escaped Dr. Frankenstein's lab only to be pursued by torch-bearing villagers with zero tolerance for dead bodies revived in creative new formats. He couldn't imagine Cass and Polly hunting him with torches high, howling for his blood, but there would be no shortage of others eager to take up the chase.

Worse, even a brief lapse in the maintenance of his new identity reestablishes the original biological tension and makes his unique energy signature as visible to his enemies as it would have been in the minutes immediately following his original transformation into Curtis Hammond, back in Colorado. In essence, with this lapse, he has reset the clock; therefore, he remains highly vulnerable to detection if his savage pursuers cross his path again in the next couple days.

He worriedly studies the mirror as the pleasant features of Curtis Hammond reassert possession of his face, but they return gradually and with stubborn errors of proportion.

As his mother always told him, confidence is the key to the

successful maintenance of a new identity. Self-consciousness and self-doubt fade the disguise.

The mystery of Gabby's panicky exit from the Mercury Mountaineer is solved. Racing across the salt flats, rattled by his inability to calm the ever more offended and loudly blustering caretaker, the boy had suffered a crisis of confidence and for a moment had been less Curtis Hammond than he'd needed to be.

Physical danger doesn't shake his equanimity. Adventuring, he is comfortable in his new skin. He's able to be Curtis Hammond with aplomb even in great jeopardy.

Although remaining poised in peril, he is seriously unnerved by socializing. The simple act of showering, with all the complications that arose, reduced him to this imperfect Curtis.

With deep chagrin, he decides that he is the Lucille Ball of shapechangers: physically agile, admirably determined, and recklessly courageous in the pursuit of his goals – but socially inept enough to entertain demanding audiences and to exasperate any Cuban-American bandleader crazy enough to marry him.

Okay. Good. He is being Curtis Hammond once more.

He finishes drying himself, all the while inspecting his body for weirdnesses, but finding none.

A beach towel has been provided as a sarong. He wraps himself in it but feels nonetheless immodest.

Until his clothes are washed and dried, he must stay with Cass and Polly; but as soon as he's outfitted once more, he'll slip away with Old Yeller. Now that he can be easily detected by his family's killers – and perhaps by the FBI, as well, if they have developed the necessary tracking technology – he can't any longer justify putting the sisters at risk.

No more people should die just because fate brings them into his life at the wrong time.

The hunters are surely coming. Heavily armed. Grimly determined. Thoroughly pissed.

44

The sun worked past quitting time, and the long summer afternoon blazed far beyond the hour when bats would have taken wing in cooler seasons. At six o'clock, the sky still burned gas-flame blue, gas-flame bright, and southern California broiled.

Risking economic ruin, Aunt Gen set the thermostat at seventy-six degrees, which didn't qualify as chilly anywhere other than in Hell. Compared to the furnace beyond the closed windows and doors, however, the kitchen was luxuriously comfortable.

While Micky brewed a large pitcher of peach-flavored iced tea and set the table for dinner, she told Geneva about Preston Maddoc, about bioethics, about killing as healing, killing as compassion, killing to increase 'the total amount of happiness,' killing in the name of sound environmental management.

'Good thing I was shot in the head eighteen years ago. These days, I'd be environmentally managed into a hole in the ground.'

'Or they'd harvest your organs, make lampshades out of your skin, and feed your remains to wild animals to avoid despoiling the earth with another grave. Iced tea?'

When Leilani hadn't arrived by 6:15, Micky was certain that something was wrong, but Geneva counseled patience. By 6:30, Geneva was concerned, too, and Micky heaped chocolate-almond cookies – sans almonds, plus pecans – on a gift plate, providing an excuse to pay a visit to the Maddocs.

The blue ceramic curve of sky, firing in a fierce kiln, offered a receptive bowl if the earth, as seemed likely, melted quick away. A long day's interment of heat shimmered out of the ground as though spirits were fleeing up through the open gates of perdition, and the air had a scorched smell.

Perched on fence pickets at the back of Geneva's property, near the bloomless rosebush, crows shrieked at Micky. Perhaps they were familiars of the dark witch Sinsemilla, posted to warn her of the approach of anyone who might be armed with the knowledge of her name.

At the fallen fence between properties, Geneva's green lawn gave way to the withered brown mat that had served as Sinsemilla's dance floor. Micky's nerves wound tight at the prospect of coming face-to-face with either the moon dancer or the philosophical murderer.

She didn't actually expect to meet Preston Maddoc. Leilani had told Aunt Gen that Dr. Doom would be out all evening.

The drapes were shut, the windows bright with the dragon glare of the westering sun.

Standing on the concrete steps, she knocked, waited, and raised her hand to knock again, but took the cookie plate in both hands when suddenly the knob rattled and the door opened.

Preston Maddoc stood before her, smiling, barely recognizable. His longish hair had been shorn; he wore it now in a short punkish bristle, which didn't lend him an edgy quality, as it might have given most men, but made him look like a tousled boy. He'd shaved off his mustache, too.

'Can I help you?' he asked pleasantly.

'Uh, hi, we're your neighbors. Me and Aunt Gen. Geneva. Geneva Davis. And I'm Micky Bellsong. Just wanted to say hello, bring you some homemade cookies, welcome you to the neighborhood.'

'That's so kind of you.' He accepted the plate. 'These look delicious. My mother, God rest her soul, made more varieties of pecan cookies than you could shake a stick at. Her maiden name was Hickory, so she took an interest in the tree that shared her family name. The pecan tree, you know, is a variety of the hickory.'

Micky hadn't been prepared for his exceptional voice, which was full of the quiet confidence that money can buy, but which also had an appealing masculine timbre and a warmth as inviting as maple syrup spilling over golden waffles. That voice, plus his pleasant looks, made him a disarming advocate for death. She could understand how he might paint a gloss of idealism over the meanest cruelties, charm the gullible, convert well-meaning people into apologists who applauded the executioner and smiled at the musical ring of the blade meeting the chopping block in a busy guillotine.

'My name's Jordan Banks,' he lied, as Leilani had said he would. 'Everyone calls me Jorry.'

Maddoc offered his hand. Micky almost cringed as she shook it.

She had come here knowing she couldn't mention Leilani's failure to keep a dinner invitation. The girl's best interests would not be served by revealing that she'd made friends next door.

Micky had hoped to see Leilani, to suggest by one indirection or another that she wouldn't go to bed tonight until the girl could sneak out to rendezvous after Maddoc and Sinsemilla were asleep.

'I'm sorry, it's not terribly considerate of me, keeping you here on the doorstep,' Maddoc apologized. 'I'd invite you in, but my wife's suffering a migraine, and the slightest noise in the house pierces her like a spike through the skull. During migraines, we have to whisper and pussyfoot around as if the floor's actually a drum.'

'Oh, don't worry about it. That's fine. I just wanted to say hello, and welcome. I hope she's feeling better soon.'

'She can't eat when she's got a migraine – but she's starved when it passes. She'll love these cookies. Very kind. See you soon.'

Micky backed down the steps as the door closed, hesitated on the dead lawn, trying to think of another ploy to let Leilani know that she'd come here. Then she worried that Maddoc might be watching her.

Returning home, eliciting a new round of shrieks from the crows that stood sentinel on the back fence, Micky heard his mellifluous voice in her mind: *My mother, God rest her soul, made more varieties of pecan cookies than you could shake a stick at.*

How smoothly the words *God rest her soul* had flowed off his tongue, how natural and convincing they had sounded – when in fact he believed in neither God nor the existence of the soul.

Hands wrapped around a glass of iced tea, Geneva waited at the kitchen table.

Micky sat, poured tea, and told her about Maddoc. 'Leilani won't be here for dinner. But I know she'll come to see me after they've gone to sleep. I'll wait for her no matter how late it gets.'

'I wondered . . . could she stay with Clarissa?' Aunt Gen suggested.

'And the parrots?'

'At least they're not crocodiles.'

'If I find the public record of Maddoc's marriage, I can get a reporter interested. He's kept a low profile for four years, but the press would still be curious. The mystery ought to intrigue them. Why hide the marriage? Was the marriage why he left the public stage?'

'Sinsemilla – she's a media circus all by herself,' Geneva said.

'If the press gives it some play, someone'll come forward who knows Lukipela existed. The boy wasn't hidden away his whole life. Even if his nutcase mother never settled in one place for long, *she's memorable*. People who knew her even briefly are likely to remember her. Some will remember Luki, too. Then Maddoc will have to explain where the boy is.'

'How are you going to find a record of the marriage?'

'I'm brooding on it.'

'What if a lot of reporters respect Maddoc and think you just have a grudge against him? Like that Bronson woman?'

'They probably will. He gets mostly good press. But reporters have to have some curiosity, don't they? Isn't that their *job*?'

'You sound determined to *make* it their job.'

Micky picked up the penguin figurine, which earlier Aunt Gen had explained to her. 'I won't let him hurt Leilani. I won't.'

'I've never heard you like this before, little mouse.'

Micky met Geneva's eyes. 'Like what?'

'So determined.'

'It's not just Leilani's life hanging by a thread, Aunt Gen. It's mine, too.'

'I know.'

45

Crackerless, Polly drives with an open bag of cheese-flavored popcorn in her lap and a cold can of beer in the built-in cupholder on her customized command chair.

Having an open container of any alcoholic beverage in a moving vehicle is against the law, but Curtis refrains from advising Polly about this infraction. He doesn't want to repeat the errors that he made with Gabby, who had taken extreme offense at being reminded that the law requires seat belts to be worn at all times.

Cleaving prairie, a lonely two-lane blacktop highway runs north-northwest from Neary Ranch. According to the twins, the south-bound lane, not taken, leads eventually to a cruel desert and ultimately to the even crueler games of Las Vegas.

They have no destination in mind yet, no plan to ensure justice for the Hammond family, no idea of what future Curtis might expect or with whom he might live. Until the situation clarifies and they have time to think, the twins' only concern is keeping him free and alive.

Curtis approves of this scheme. Flexibility is any fugitive's greatest strength, and a fugitive burdened by a rigid plan makes easy quarry of himself. Mom's wisdom. Anyway, he will leave the sisters soon, so planning beyond the next few hours would be pointless.

Polly drives fast. The Fleetwood rushes across the prairie, like a nuclear-powered battle wagon on a medium-gravity moon.

In the lounge, Cass relaxes on a sofa that backs up to the port flank of the motor home, directly behind the driver's seat. The dog lies beside her, chin resting on her thigh, blissfully assuming a right of continuous cuddling, and having that assumption rewarded.

At the sisters' gentle insistence, Curtis occupies the co-pilot's chair, which boasts various power features, including one that turns it away from the road, toward the driver. Having powered the seat to port, he can see both women.

Although wearing only the beach-towel sarong, he's no longer self-conscious. He feels quite Polynesian, like Bing Crosby in *The Road to Bali*.

Instead of chunks of coconut or a bowl of poi, instead of the shredded flesh of a wild pig spiced with eel tongue, he has his own bag of cheese-flavored popcorn and a can of Orange Crush, though he had asked for a beer.

Better still, he's blessed by the company of the Spelkenfelter sisters, Castoria and Polluxia. He finds the details of their lives to be unlike anything he knows from films or books.

They were born and raised in a bucolic town in Indiana, which Polly calls 'a long yawn of bricks and boards.' According to Cass, the most exciting pastimes the area offers are watching cows graze, watching chickens peck, and watching hogs sleep, although Curtis can perceive no entertainment value in two of these three activities.

Their father, Sidney Spelkenfelter, is a professor of Greek and Roman history at a private college, and his wife, Imogene, teaches art history. Sidney and Imogene are kind and loving parents, but they are also, says Cass, 'as naive as goldfish who think the world ends at the bowl.' Because *their* parents were academics, too, Sidney and Imogene have resided ever in tenured security, explaining life to others but living a pale version of it.

Co-valedictorians of their high-school class, Cass and Polly skipped college in favor of Las Vegas. Within a month, they were the centerpiece feathered-and-sequined nudes in a major hotel's showroom extravaganza with a cast of seventy-four dancers, twelve showgirls, nine specialty acts, two elephants, four chimps, six dogs, and a python.

Because of a mutual lifelong interest in juggling and trapeze acrobatics, within a year they were elevated to Las Vegas stardom in a ten-million-dollar stage-musical spectacular featuring a theme of extraterrestrial contact. They played acrobatic alien queens plotting to turn all human males into love slaves.

'That was when we first got interested in UFOs,' Cass reveals.

'In the opening dance number,' Polly reminisces, 'we descended these neon stairs from a giant flying saucer. It was awesome.'

'And this time we didn't have to be naked the whole show,' says Cass. 'We came out of the saucer nude, of course—'

'Like any alien love queens would,' adds Polly, and they reveal delicious giggles that remind Curtis of the immortal Goldie Hawn.

Curtis laughs, too, amused by their irony and self-mockery.

'After the first nine minutes,' Cass says, 'we wore lots of cool costumes better suited to juggling and acrobatic trapeze work.'

'Trying to juggle honeydews while nude,' Polly explains, 'you risk grabbing the wrong melons and ruining the act.'

They both giggle again, but this time the joke eludes Curtis.

'Then we were nude in the last number,' Polly says, 'except for the feathered headdress, sequined G-string, and stiletto-heeled ankle boots. The producer insisted this was "authentic" love-queen attire.'

Cass says, 'Tell me, Curtis, how many alien love queens have you seen wearing gold-lame, stiletto-heeled ankle boots?'

'None,' he answers truthfully.

'That was our argument exactly. They look stupid. Not queenly in *any* corner of the universe. We didn't mind the feathered headdresses, but how many alien love queens have you met who wear those, either?'

'None.'

'To be fair, you can't disprove our producer's contention,' says Polly. 'After all, how *many* alien love queens have you really seen?'

'Only two,' Curtis admits, 'but neither of them was a juggler.'

For some reason, the twins find this highly amusing.

'But I guess you could say one of them was something of an acrobat,' Curtis elaborates, 'because she could bend over backward until she was able to lick the heels of her own feet.'

This statement only rings new peals of laughter and more silvery giggles from the Spelkenfelter girls.

'It isn't an erotic thing,' he hastens to clarify. 'She bends backward for the reason a rattlesnake coils. From that position, she can spring twenty feet and snap your head off with her mandibles.'

'Try to turn *that* into a Vegas musical number!' Cass suggests, joining her sister in yet more laughter.

'Well, I don't know everything about Las Vegas stage shows,' Curtis says, 'but you'd probably have to leave out the part where she injects her eggs into the severed head.'

Through genuinely explosive laughter, Polly says, 'Not if you did it with enough glitter, sweetie.'

'You're a pistol, Curtis Hammond,' says Cass.

'You're a hoot,' agrees Polly.

Listening to the twins giggle, watching Polly drive with one hand and wipe tears of laughter off her face with the other, Curtis decides that he must be wittier than he has heretofore realized.

Maybe he's getting better at socializing.

Speeding northwest over a seemingly infinite stretch of two-lane blacktop as beautiful and mysterious as any view of classic American highway in any movie, speeding also toward a setting sun that fires the prairie into molten red-and-gold glass, as the mighty engine of the Fleetwood rumbles reassuringly, in the company of the fabulous Castoria and the fabulous Polluxia and the God-connected Old Yeller, with cheese popcorn and Orange Crush, showered and fully in control of his biological identity, feeling more confident than at any time in recent memory, Curtis believes he must be the luckiest boy alive.

When Cass excuses herself to take Curtis's clothes out of the dryer, the dog follows her, and the boy turns his chair to face the road ahead. Co-pilot in name only, he nevertheless feels empowered by Polly's fast and expert driving.

For a while they talk about the Fleetwood. Polly knows every detail of the big vehicle's construction and operation. This is a 44,500-pound, 45-foot-long behemoth with a Cummins diesel engine, an Allison Automatic 4000 MH transmission, a 150-gallon fuel tank, a 160-gallon water tank, and a GPS navigation system. She speaks of it as lovingly as young men in the movies speak of their hot rods.

He's surprised to hear that this customized version cost seven hundred thousand dollars, and when he makes the assumption that the twins' wealth resulted from their success in Vegas, Polly corrects his misapprehension. They became financially independent – but not truly wealthy – following marriage to the Flackberg brothers. 'But that's a tragic story, sweetie, and I'm in too good a mood to tell it now.'

Because of a mutual lifelong interest in the mechanical design and repair of motor vehicles, Polly and Cass are well suited to the continuous travel that marks this phase of their lives. Regardless of what breaks or wears out, they can fix it, given the necessary spare parts, a basic supply of which they carry with them.

'There's nothing better in this world,' declares Polly, 'than getting dirty, oily, greasy, and sweaty while working on your wheels – and in the end putting wrong right with your own hands.'

These women are the cleanest, most well-groomed, most spark-ling, sweetest-smelling people whom Curtis has ever seen, and though he's hugely enamored of them in their current condition, he is intrigued by the prospect of seeing them dirty, oily, greasy, sweaty, wielding wrenches and power tools, confronting a recal-citrant 44,500-pound mechanical beast and, with their skill and determination, returning it to full operation.

Indeed, a mental image of Castoria and Polluxia, in the throes of engine-repair delight, pulses so persistently through his thoughts that he wonders why it has such great appeal. Odd.

Trailed by Old Yeller, Cass returns to report that she has finished ironing Curtis's clothes.

Retreating to the bathroom to trade sarong for proper dress, he's saddened that his time with the Spelkenfelter twins is drawing to an end. For their safety, he must leave at the first opportunity.

By the time he returns, fully clothed, to the co-pilot's seat, the last sullen red light of sunset constricts in a low arc along a portion of the western horizon, like the upper curve of a bloodshot eye belonging to a murderous giant watching from just beyond the edge of the earth. Curtis is settling into his seat when the arc dims from mordant red to brooding purple; soon the purple fades as if the eye has fallen shut in sleep, but still the night seems to be watching.

If farms or ranches exist out in this lonely vastness, they are set so far back from the highway that even from the elevated cockpit of the Fleetwood, their lights are screened by wild grass, by widely scattered copses of trees, and primarily by sheer distance.

Rare southbound vehicles approach, rocketing by at velocities that suggest they are fleeing from something. Even fewer north-bound vehicles pass them, not because the northbound lane is less busy, but because Polly demands performance from the motor home; only the most determined speeders overtake her, including someone in a silver 1970 Corvette that elicits admiring whistles from the car-savvy sisters.

Because of mutual interests in extreme skiing, skydiving, hard-boiled detective fiction, competitive rodeo bronc-busting, ghosts and poltergeists, big-band music, wilderness-survival techniques, and the art of scrimshaw (among many other things), the twins are fascinating conversationalists, as much fun to listen to as they are to look at.

Curtis is most interested, however, in their wealth of UFO lore, their rococo speculations about life on other worlds, and their dark suspicions regarding the motives of extraterrestrials on Earth. In his experience, humankind is the only species ever to concoct visions of what might lie in the unknown universe that are even stranger than what's really out there.

A glow appears in the distance, not the headlamps of approaching traffic, but a more settled light alongside the highway.

They arrive at a rural crossroads where a combination service station and convenience store stands on the northwest corner. This isn't a shiny, plasticized, standard unit allied with a nation-wide chain, but a mom-and-pop operation in a slightly sagging clapboard building with weathered white paint and dust-frosted windows.

In movies, places like this are frequently occupied by crazies of one kind or another. In such lonely environs, monstrous crimes are easily concealed.

Since motion is commotion, Curtis wants to keep moving until they reach a well-populated town. The twins, however, prefer not to let the on-board fuel supply drop below fifty gallons, and they are currently running with less than sixty.

Polly drives off the blacktop onto the unpaved service apron in front of the building. Gravel raps the Fleetwood undercarriage.

The three pumps – two dispensing gasoline, one diesel fuel – are not sheltered under a sun-and-rain pavilion, as in modern operations, but stand exposed to the elements. Strung between two poles, red and amber Christmas lights, out of season, hang over the service island. These are taller than contemporary service-station pumps, perhaps seven feet, and each is crowned by what appears to be a large crystal ball.

'Fantastic. Those probably date back to the thirties,' Polly says. 'You rarely see them anymore. When you pump the fuel, you can watch it swirl through the globe.'

'Why?' Curtis asks.

She shrugs. 'It's the way they work.'

A faint exhalation of wind lazily stirs the string of Christmas lights, and reflections of the red and amber bulbs glimmer and circle and twinkle within the gas-pump glass, as though fairy spirits dance inside each sphere.

Entranced by this magical machinery, Curtis wonders: 'Does it also tell your fortune or something?'

'No. It's just cool to look at.'

'They went to all the trouble of incorporating that big glass globe in the design just because it's cool to look at?' He shakes his head with admiration for this species that makes art even of daily commerce. With affection, he says, 'This is a wonderful planet.'

The twins disembark first – Cass with a large purse slung from one shoulder – intent on conducting a service-stop routine that is military in its thoroughness and precision: All ten tires must be inspected with a flashlight, the oil and the transmission fluid must be checked, the window-washing reservoir must be filled . . . .

Old Yeller's mission is more prosaic: She needs to toilet. And Curtis goes along to keep her company.

He and the dog stand at the foot of the steps and listen to a mere whisper of a breeze that travels to them out of the moonlit plains in the northwest, from beyond the service station that is now blocked from sight by the Fleetwood. Apparently the night air carries a disturbing scent that inspires Old Yeller to raise her talented nose, to flare her nostrils, and to ponder the source of the smell.

The antique pumps are on the farther side of the motor home. As the twins disappear around the bow in search of service, the sniffing dog trots toward the back, not with typically wayward doggy curiosity, but with focus, purpose. Curtis follows his sister-become.

When they round the stern of the Fleetwood to the port side, they come into sight of the weather-beaten store about forty feet away, past the pumps. The door stands half open on hinges stiff enough to resist the breeze.

The dog halts. Backs up a step. Perhaps because the fantastical pumps disconcert her.

On closer consideration, Curtis finds them to be no less magical but less Tinkerbellish than they appeared from inside the vehicle. As he stares up at the globes, which are currently filled with darkness instead of with churning fuel, reflections of the red and amber Christmas lights shimmer on the surface of the glass but appear to swarm within it, and suddenly this display has an air of malevolence. Something needful and malign seems to be pent up in the spheres.

Near the bow of the motor home, a tall bald man is talking to the twins. His back is toward Curtis, and he's forty feet away, but something seems wrong with him.

The dog's hackles rise, and the boy suspects that the uneasiness he feels is actually her distrust transmitted to him through their special bond.

Although Old Yeller growls low in her throat and clearly has no use for the station attendant, her primary interest lies elsewhere. She scampers away from the motor home, almost running, toward the west side of the building, and Curtis hurries after her.

He's pretty sure this isn't about toileting anymore.

The store sets cater-corner on the lot, facing the crossroads rather than fronting one highway, and all the lights are at its most public face. Night finds a firmer purchase along the flank of the building. And behind the place, where the clapboard wall offers one door but no windows, the darkness is deeper still, relieved only by a parsimonious moon carefully spending its silver coins.

A Ford Explorer stands in this gloom, its contours barely traced by the lunar light. Curtis supposes that the SUV belongs to the man who's out front talking to the twins.

The silver Corvette, which passed them on the highway earlier in the night, waits here, as well. Intently studying this vehicle, Old Yeller whimpers.

The moon favors the sports car over the SUV, plating its chrome and paint to a sterling standard.

Even as Curtis takes a step toward the Corvette, however, the dog dashes to the back of the Explorer. She stands on her hind legs, forepaws on the rear bumper, gazing up at the tailgate window, which is too high to provide her with a view inside.

She looks at Curtis, dark eyes moon-brightened.

When the boy doesn't go to her at once, she paws insistently at the tailgate.

In this murk, he can't see the dog shuddering, but through the psychic umbilical linking them, he senses the depth of her anxiety.

Fear like a slinking cat has found a way into Curtis's heart, and from his heart into the whole of him, and now it whets its claws upon his bones.

Joining Old Yeller behind the Explorer, he squints through the rear window. He isn't able to discern whether the SUV carries a cargo or is loaded only with shadows.

The dog continues to paw at the vehicle.

Curtis tries the door handle, lifts the tailgate.

Disengagement of the latch activates a soft light in the SUV, revealing two corpses in the cargo space. They have been tumbled together in such a way as to suggest that they were heaved in here as if they were bags of garbage.

His heart, a sudden stutterer, spasms on the *l* in *lub*, and on the *d* in *dub*.

He would run if he were not his mother's son, but he'd rather die than, by his actions, cast shame upon her memory.

Pity and revulsion would turn him away had he not been taught to react to every horror like this as though it were a survival text, to read it quickly but closely for clues that might save his life and the lives of others.

Others, in this case, means Cass and Polly.

Tall, bald, and male, the first of these cadavers appears to be a physical match for the station attendant who'd been talking to the twins a moment ago. Curtis didn't see that guy's face; nevertheless, he's convinced that it will prove to be identical to this one, though not wrenched by terror.

Billowy, glossy, chestnut hair surrounds and softens the dead woman's features. Her wide-open hazel eyes stare with startlement at the first glimpse of eternity that she received in the instant when her soul fled this world.

Neither victim bears a visible wound, but each appears to have a broken neck. Heads loll at such unnatural angles that the cervical vertebrae must have been shattered. For these hunters, who thrill to the administration of terror and who revel in murder, such kills are unusually clean and merciful.

Necessity rather than mercy explains the simple wounds. Each corpse has been stripped of its shoes and outer layer of clothing. To masquerade as their victims, the killers needed costumes without rips or stains.

If the combination service station and convenience store is a mom-and-pop operation, then here lie mom and pop. Their business *and* their identities have been subjected to a hostile takeover.

The dog's attention is directed once more at the Corvette. Her interest, though intense, isn't strong enough to draw her toward the sports car, which she regards with obvious dread. She appears to be as puzzled as she is apprehensive, cocking her head left, and then right, blinking, turning half away from the vehicle but then snapping her head toward it as if she'd seen it start to move.

Perhaps in the Corvette waits something worse than what he found in the Explorer, in which case he'll keep his distance, too. Instead, seeking to learn what he can by sharing the dog's perceptions, Curtis opens himself more completely to their bond, and looks at the 'Vette through her eyes.

At first his sister-become seems to see nothing more than Curtis sees – but then for just a second, no longer, the moonlit car shimmers like a mirage. Dream car in more ways than one, internal-combustion illusion, it is merely the *suggestion* of a 1970 Corvette, masking a fearsome reality. The dog blinks, blinks, but the sports car remains apparently solid, so she turns her head away from it, and out of the corner of her eye, for two seconds or three, she glimpses what Curtis can't perceive from the corner of his: a transport not of this earth, sleeker even than the sharklike Corvette, like a beast born to *stalk* sharks with a vengeance. So mighty-looking is this vehicle that you can't think of it in the language of designers or engineers, but must resort to the vocabulary of military architecture, because in spite of its sleekness, it seems to be a fortress on wheels: all compact buttresses, ramparts, terrepleins, scarps, counterscarps, bastions made aerodynamic, condensed and adapted to rolling stock.

With this evidence before him, no doubt can linger any longer. The worse scalawags have arrived.

His nerves feel as taut as high-tuned violin strings, and his dark imagination plucks them with dire possibilities.

Death is here now, as always it is here, but it is not always as engaged and *attentive* as it is at this moment, waiting for a third course in its supper of bones.

The hunters must suspect that Curtis is in the motor home. Kind fate and his clever sister-become brought him out of the Fleetwood and around the building to this moonlit killing ground without being detected. He won't remain undiscovered for long: perhaps two minutes, maybe three if his luck holds.

The instant that he shows himself, he will be known.

In his place, therefore, he sends the dog to Polly.

Fearful but obedient, she trots away, retracing the route along which she led him.

Curtis has no illusions that he'll survive this encounter. The enemy is too near, too powerful, too remorseless to be defeated by one as small and defenseless as this motherless boy.

He harbors some hope, however, that he might be able to warn off Cass and Polly, that they might escape with the dog rather than be slaughtered with him.

Old Yeller disappears around the corner of the building. Beloved familiar, companion spirit, she walks always with an awareness of her Maker – and she will need Him now as never before.

46

The penitentiary walls crumbled away from her, but she re-stacked the stones around herself, and when the bars fell out of the windows, she repaired them with a welder's torch and fresh mortar.

From this dream of a self-made prison – not a nightmare, scary only because she labored so *cheerfully* to rebuild her cell – Micky woke, instantly aware that something was wrong.

Life had taught her to recognize danger at a distance. Now even in sleep, she'd sensed a threat in the waking world that called her back from that faraway, comfortable incarceration.

On the living-room sofa, lying on her side, eyes closed, head raised slightly upon a throw pillow, chin tucked down and resting against her clasped hands, she remained perfectly still, breathing softly like a sleeper, listening. Listening.

The house lay enfolded by a shroud of quiet as deep as that in a mortuary after viewing hours, the mourners gone.

Deaf to the threat, she was nonetheless able to sense it, feel it, as she could feel the change in atmospheric pressure when the air thickened just before a thunderstorm flashed and cracked and broke.

Micky had settled on the sofa to read a magazine while waiting for Leilani. The evening waned, and Geneva eventually retreated to her bedroom, leaving instructions to be awakened at once if the girl paid a visit. With Aunt Gen gone, with the contents of the magazine exhausted, Micky stretched out merely to rest her eyes, not to nap. The cumulative weight of the difficult day, the heat, the humidity, and a growing despair had pressed her down into that dream prison.

Instinctively, she hadn't opened her eyes when she woke. Now she kept them closed, operating on the theory – so dear to every child and sometimes resurgent in adulthood – that the boogeyman could not hurt her until she looked him in the eye and acknowledged his existence.

Frequently, in prison, she had learned that a pretense of sleep, of stupidity, of naivete, of cataleptic indifference, a pretense of deafness to an obscene invitation and of blindness to an insult, were all wiser responses than confrontation. Childhood can be remarkably similar to prison; the theory of the boogeyman's eye offers guidance to child and inmate alike.

Someone moved nearby. The soft scuff of shoes on carpet and the creak of floorboards argued against the possibility that the intruder was either a figment of her imagination or a trailer-park ghost.

The footsteps approached. Stopped.

She sensed a looming presence. Someone stood over her, watching as she pretended to sleep.

Not Geneva. Even in one of her movie moments, she wouldn't be furtive or unnervingly strange like this. Gen remembered being Carole Lombard in *My Man Godfrey*, Ingrid Bergman in *Casablanca*, Goldie Hawn in *Foul Play*, but she shared no darker experiences than those of *Mildred Pierce*. Her secondhand lives were romantic, even if sometimes tragic, and you didn't have to worry that she would ever be in the grip of a Bette Davis psychosis per *Whatever Happened to Baby Jane* or Glenn Close per *Fatal Attraction*.

Micky's sense of smell seemed heightened by her meditative stillness and her defensive blindness. She detected the faint astringent scent of strange soap. A crisp aftershave.

He stirred, betrayed once more by the protesting floorboards. Even over the thump of her bass-drum heart, Micky could tell that he was moving away from her.

Through a fringe of eyelashes, she sought him, saw him. He passed the low buffet divider that separated the living room from the kitchen.

One small lamp, the three-way bulb set at the lowest wattage, didn't reject the shadows in the living room, but romanced them, and in the kitchen, only the small light under the range hood staved off the full embrace of darkness.

Even seen from behind, and then glimpsed only briefly in profile as he turned in the kitchen gloom to approach the back door, he could be mistaken for no one else. Uninvited, Preston Maddoc had paid a visit.

Micky had left the back door ajar for Leilani if she came. Now Maddoc left it standing wide open when he departed.

Warily she got off the sofa and approached the kitchen. She half expected to find him waiting beyond the threshold, facing inside, amused to have caught her faking sleep.

He wasn't there.

She dared to step outside. No one lurked in the backyard. Maddoc had gone home.

Retreating into the kitchen, she shut out the night. Engaged the deadbolt lock.

Fear drained away, leaving a feeling of violation. Before she could work up a proper sense of outrage, however, she thought of Geneva, and fear flooded back.

She had no idea how long Maddoc was in the house. He might have gone elsewhere before entering the living room to watch her sleep.

Micky hurried out of the kitchen, into the short hall. As she passed her own room, she noticed light bleeding under the door. She was certain that she hadn't left a lamp on.

End of the hall. Last door. Standing ajar.

The luminous numerals and the lighted tuning bands on the clock radio provided the only relief from a clutching darkness that seemed jagged with menace. When Micky reached the bed, this ghostly radiance revealed only the one thing that she wanted to see: Aunt Gen's face against a pillow, eyes shut, peaceful in sleep.

Micky held one trembling hand before Geneva's face and felt the gentle breath against her palm.

A knot pulled loose in her breast, freeing her bound breath.

In the hall once more, she soundlessly drew Geneva's door shut and went directly to her own room.

Scattered across the bedspread were her purse and everything it had contained. Her wallet had been emptied, though no money had been stolen; the currency lay discarded with her social-security card, her driver's license, lipstick, compact, comb, car keys . . . .

The closet was open. The dresser had been searched, as well, and the contents of each drawer had been left in disarray.

On the floor lay her prison-discharge papers. She'd left them in the nightstand, under the Bible that Aunt Gen had provided.

Regardless of the initial purpose of Maddoc's visit, he'd taken brazen advantage of the situation when he found the kitchen door ajar and Micky asleep on the sofa. From what she'd learned at the library, she knew that he was a calculating man rather than a reckless one, so she attributed his shameless prowling not to impetuosity, but to arrogance.

Evidently he knew more about her relationship with Leilani than she'd thought he did, perhaps more than Leilani realized, too. The contrived welcome with the plate of cookies either had not fooled him or had sharpened his suspicion.

Now he'd learned enough about Micky's recent past and about her weakness to make her uneasy.

She wondered what he might have done if she'd awakened and found him in her room.

The Bible lay open on the nightstand, in the lamplight. Maddoc had used the felt-tip pen from her purse to circle a passage. *Joel*, chapter 1, verse 5: *Awake, ye drunkards, and weep.*

She was unnerved that he knew the Bible well enough to recall such an apt but obscure passage. This erudition suggested that he might be an adversary even more clever and resourceful than she'd expected. Also, clearly, she impressed him as being such a negligible threat that he believed he could mock her with impunity.

Flushed with humiliation, Micky went to the dresser, confirming that Maddoc had turned back the concealing yellow sweater and had found the two bottles of lemon-flavored vodka.

She removed the bottles from the drawer. One was full, the seal unbroken. The sight of it gave her a sense of power, of control; to an impoverished and improvident spirit, an untapped bottle seemed to be a bottomless fortune, but it was really fortune's ruin. After her binge the previous night, little remained in the second container.

In the kitchen, Micky switched on the light above the sink and emptied both bottles into the drain. The fumes – not the lemony aroma, but the quasi-aphrodisiacal scent of alcohol – enflamed more than one appetite: for drink, for oblivion, for self-destruction.

After she dropped the two empties in the trash can, her hands shook uncontrollably. They were damp, too, with vodka.

She breathed the evaporating spirits rising from her skin, and then pressed her cool hands to her burning face.

Into her mind came an image of the brandy that Aunt Gen kept in a kitchen cupboard. Following the image came the taste, as real as if she'd taken a sip from a full snifter.

'No.'

She understood too well that the brandy wasn't what she wanted, nor the vodka; what she really sought was an excuse to fail Leilani, a reason to turn inward, to retreat beyond the familiar drawbridge, up to the ramparts, behind the battlements of her emotional fortress, where her damaged heart wouldn't be at risk of further wounds, where she could live once more and forever in the comparatively comfortable suffering of isolation. Brandy would give her that excuse and spare her the pain of caring.

When she turned away from the cupboard where the brandy waited, leaving the door unopened, she went to the refrigerator, hoping to satisfy her thirst with a Coca-Cola. But this was less a thirst than a hunger, a ravenous clawing in the gut, so she plucked a cookie from the ceramic bear whose head was a lid and whose plump body was a jar. On further consideration, she carried the bear and all its contents to the table.

Sitting down to Coke and cookies, feeling like an eight-year-old girl, confused and afraid as she had so often been back then, seeking solace from the sugar demon, the first unsettling thing she noticed was the plate beside the candleholders. The gift plate that she had piled with cookies and taken next door earlier in the evening. Maddoc had returned it empty, washed.

Arrogance again. If Micky hadn't awakened in time to see him leave, she might have guessed who had searched her dresser drawers and turned out the contents of her purse, but she couldn't have been certain that her guess was correct. By leaving the plate, Maddoc had made it clear that he *wanted* her to know who the intruder had been. This was a challenge and an act of intimidation.

More disturbing than the plate returned was the penguin taken. The two-inch figurine, from the collection of a dead woman, had been standing on the kitchen table, among the small colored glasses that held half-melted candles. Maddoc must have seen it when he put down the plate.

Whatever suspicions he'd harbored about Leilani's relationships with Micky and with Aunt Gen had been confirmed and had surely grown darker when he'd discovered the penguin.

The dropping sensation in the stomach, the tightening in the chest, the lightheadedness familiar from the sudden speedy plunge of a roller coaster afflicted her now, as she sat dead still on the kitchen chair.

47

Although Polly wasn't a Pollyanna, she liked most people she met, made friends easily, and seldom made enemies, but when the service-station attendant came up to her, grinning like a jack-in-the-box jester with a ticklish spring up its butt, saying, 'Hi, my name's Earl Bockman and my wife's Maureen, we own this place, been here twenty years,' she made an immediate judgment that he wasn't going to be one of the people she liked.

Tall, pleasant in appearance, his breath smelling of spearmint, looking freshly scrubbed and shaved, in neatly laundered clothes, he possessed many of the fundamentals necessary to make a good first impression, and though a tragic Pagliacci-smiling-through-heartbreak expression might have provided him a certain additional melancholy appeal, *this* toothy display was classic mad-clown grin from molar to molar.

'I'm originally from Wyoming,' Earl said, 'but Maureen is from around these parts, and now I've been here so long, it seems like I'm a native, too. Every last man, woman, and child in the county knows Earl and Maureen Bockman.' He seemed to feel that he had to convince them of his bona fides before they would trust the purity of the fuel that he was selling. 'Just say the names Earl and Maureen, and anyone will tell you that's the folks who own the little pump-and-grocery out at the federal-highway crossroads. And they'll probably tell you Maureen is a peach, too, because she's just as sweet as they come, and what *I'll* tell you is I'm the luckiest man ever stood before an altar and took the vows, and never regretted it one minute since.'

He babbled half this astonishing speech *through* his toothpaste-advertisement smile, wrapping the grin in and around the rest of it when punctuation gave him pause, and Polly was ready to bet

$10,000 against a pack of Hostess cup cakes that poor Maureen lay dead inside the store, perhaps strangled by Earl's bare hands, perhaps bludgeoned with an economy-size can of pork and beans, perhaps staked through the heart with a fossilized Slim Jim sausage that had hung neglected on a snack rack for fifteen years.

The insistent smile and the inappropriate deluge of personal chatter was enough to win Earl a place in Polly's let-him-vote-but-don't-let-him-run-for-President file, but there was also the matter of his wristwatch. The face of this unusual timepiece was black and blank: no hour numbers, no minute checks, no hands. It might have been one of those inconvenient digital chronometers that gave you the time in a luminous read-out only when you pushed a button on the casing; but she suspected that it wasn't a watch at all. From the moment that he arrived at the service island, Earl contrived to turn his body and his right arm to direct the numberless black face toward Cass, then toward Polly, and then toward Cass again, back and forth, while further contriving to glance repeatedly and furtively at the gadget in the inadequate light of the red and amber Christmas bulbs. If he'd ever taken a home-correspondence course in successful furtive behavior, he had wasted his money. Polly first thought that the thing on his wrist must be a camera, that he must be some brand of pervert who secretly took pictures of women for whatever sick purpose, but though his nervous folksiness definitely screamed *PERVERT*, she didn't believe that anyone had yet invented a camera that could see through women's clothing.

Cass liked more people than Polly did, and if she had popped out of Mom's oven with a twin whose personality had been identical to her own, she *would* have been a Pollyanna, trusting implicitly and equally in nuns and convicted murderers. During the twenty-seven years that they had lived together this side of the placenta, however, Cass's optimism had been tempered by Polly's more-reasoned expectations of people and fate. Indeed, Cass had grown so street-smart that by the time Earl had spoken only a single sentence, she cocked an eyebrow and tweaked her mouth in a *Freak alert!* expression that Polly had no difficulty reading.

Earl might have chattered at them until either he or one of them fell dead from natural causes, all the while not-so-secretly aiming his curious wristwatch at them – which suddenly seemed reminiscent of the way airport-security personnel sometimes used a handheld metal-detection wand to scan a traveler who had more than once failed to pass through the standard gate without setting off an alarm. But as Earl babbled, Cass examined the antique pump marked DIESEL, and when she found its workings to be more arcane than any she had previously encountered, she asked for assistance.

When Earl turned to the pump, Polly thought he looked baffled, as though he were no more familiar with its operation than was Cass. Frowning, he stepped to the pump, put one hand on it, stood as if in profound thought, almost as if through some sixth sense he were divining the workings of the machinery, soon broke again into that crackbrained-clown grin, and said cheerily, 'Fill 'er up?' Assured that they wanted the tank topped off, he cranked a handle on the pump, disengaged the hose spout from the nozzle boot, and turned toward the Fleetwood, whereupon both he and his smile froze.

As it became clear that this seasoned pump jockey wasn't sure where to service the big motor home, Cass telegraphed *What's wrong with this bozo?* by way of a glance at her sister. She took the hose from Earl with the polite explanation that she, being a fussbudget loath to get a scratch on the paint around the fuel port, would be happier if she could tend to the task herself.

Polly flipped open the hinged lid of the port, twisted the cap off the tank, and stepped back as her sister jammed the spout into the Fleetwood, all the while surreptitiously keeping an eye on Earl, who, thinking that she was preoccupied, boldly aimed his trick watch at two windows of the motor home, twice glancing at the face of the timepiece as though reading something in its glossy black surface – which made him unique among men, who invariably checked out Polly's ass when they thought she wasn't looking, even gay men burning not with desire but with envy.

She might have judged him to be a harmless crank, a once-proud gasoline merchant made dotty by the vast open spaces of Nevada, by the frighteningly huge sky that hung so fiercely starred over the black land, by too little human contact or by too much contact with too many prairie rustics, or even by Maureen, that sweet peach. But even cranks, eccentrics, and certifiably insane men checked out her butt when they had a chance, and the more often she saw that teeth-drying grin of his, the less it reminded her of a clown, psychopathic or otherwise, and the more she flashed to the velociraptors in those *Jurassic Park* movies. The thought had formed, however odd, that Earl was something she had never before encountered.

Out of the night came Old Yeller, running, agitated as she had never been before, straight to Polly or rather straight to Polly's left sandal, which she seized by the acrylic heel and which she tried to shake as a terrier might shake a rat. Polly blurted out the name of a famous movie star she'd known when married to the film producer Julian Flackberg; the star was a dreadful actor as well as a deeply vile human being, and sometimes Polly used his famous name in place of an obscenity, usually in place of a four-letter word meaning 'dung.' Startled, Cass called to the dog, Polly tried to pull her foot away without hurting either the animal or herself, Old Yeller likewise seemed to be trying to avoid causing injury as she vigorously chewed on the footwear without even the softest of growls, and Smilin' Earl Bockman, believing himself to be unobserved in this uproar, aimed the wristwatch at the pooch and peered anxiously at the timepiece, as if it were an analytic device that could tell him whether or not the animal was rabid.

In trying to yank her foot away from Old Yeller, Polly pulled it out of the sandal, and the dog at once made off with the prize, stopping at the front corner of the motor home to look back and to adjust her grip until the shoe dangled from her mouth by one thin strap. The dog swung the sandal teasingly back and forth. Cass said, 'She's inviting you to play,' and Polly said, 'Yeah, well, the way I interpret it, even cute as she is, she's asking me to drop-kick her over that string of Christmas lights,' and for once Earl's maniacal smile almost seemed appropriate.

With the hose nozzle set securely in the fuel port and with at least five minutes required to fill the big tank, Cass's hands were free, and Polly had complete confidence in her sister's ability to deal with the likes of Earl Bockman, even if he might have this day received word from the *Guinness Book of World Records* that he had displaced the late Jeffrey Dahmer in the category of Most Severed Heads Kept in a Single Refrigerator. Hobbling, she pursued Old Yeller around the front of the Fleetwood, to the starboard flank, where the dog bounded through the open door and up the steps, into the motor home.

By the time Polly got inside, the sandal lay discarded on the floor of the lounge, directly under the only interior light that had been left burning, while in the kitchen area just beyond the lounge, the dog sprang onto the dining-nook booth, craned her neck across the table, and snatched the packet of playing cards in her teeth. As Polly picked up the sandal, Old Yeller returned to the lounge, shook the packet until the lid flap came untucked, and scattered the cards across the carpeted floor.

As one who had been raised in a rural community where cows and hogs and chickens provided examples of deportment and dignity seldom matched by human beings, as one who'd worked in a multimillion-dollar stage show where the two elephants, four chimps, six dogs, and even the python had been more amenable than sixty-six of the seventy-four dancers in the cast, Polly considered herself an animal lover, and she also qualified as an astute enough observer of animal conduct to know that Old Yeller was acting out of character and that something uncanny was happening. She didn't scold, therefore, and didn't begin at once to clean up the mess, as ordinarily she would have done, but gave the dog room and dropped to her knees to watch.

Half the cards had spilled faceup on the floor, and Old Yeller began to paw through these, making selections frantically and yet with clear deliberation, until she sorted out two clubs, two hearts, and one spade. The suits of the chosen cards were of no consequence, but the numbers on them were meaningful, because using her nose and her paws, the dog lined them up side by side in correct numerical order – 3 of spades, 4 of clubs, 5 of hearts, 6 of clubs, 7 of hearts – and then grinned at Polly expectantly.

Gymnastic dogs balancing on rolling beachballs and walking on parallel bars, pyrophilic dogs leaping through flaming hoops, tiny dogs riding the backs of big dogs as those mounts raced and leaped through obstacle courses, mortified dogs in pink tutus dancing on their hind feet: In Vegas, Polly had seen trained dogs do impressive stunts, but she had never until now seen any mutt exhibit advanced numerical aptitude, so even as she watched Old Yeller paw the 6 of clubs into place and nose the 7 of hearts in line immediately after it, she muttered the name of the loathsome movie star not once but twice, made eye contact with this furry mathematician, shivered with a delicious sense of wonder, and said what Lassie must have been sick to death of hearing during her long years with Timmy on the farm, 'You're trying to tell me something, aren't you, girl?'

$\sim$ $\sim$ $\sim$

Intending no offense to Romulus, Tarzan, and HAL 9000, Cass judged Earl Bockman's social skills to be worse than those of a child nursed in infancy by wolves, subsequently adopted by a tribe of apes, and later educated entirely by machines.

He was stiff. Self-conscious. Fidgety. His facial expressions were seldom appropriate to what he happened to be saying, and every time he appeared to recognize an instance of this inappropriateness, he resorted to the same cartoon-cat-caught-at-the-canary-cage smile that he seemed to think was folksy and reassuring.

Worse yet, Earl was a droner. Each pause in conversation longer than two seconds made him nervous. He rushed to fill every brief silence with the first thing that came into his head, which reliably proved to be something tedious.

Cass decided that Maureen, Earl's wife and reputed peach, must be either a saint or as dumb as a carrot. No woman would stay with this man unless she was a religiosity who hoped to purify her soul through suffering or had no detectable cerebral function.

Leaning against the motor home, waiting for the tank to fill, Cass felt as if she were a condemned prisoner with her back pressed to the executioner's wall. Earl was a one-man firing squad, the bullets were his words, and boredom the method of execution.

And what was the story with the watch? No better skilled at surreptitious action than at conversation, Earl aimed the gadget at various points in the night around them. He even dropped to one knee to tie a shoelace that appeared to be tied perfectly well before he decided to tend to it, obviously as an excuse to direct the face of the wristwatch toward the space under the Fleetwood.

Maybe he suffered from obsessive-compulsive disorder. Maybe he was compelled to aim his wristwatch ceaselessly at people and things, just as some obsessives washed their hands four hundred times a day, and just as others counted the socks in their dresser drawers or the plates in the kitchen cupboards once every hour.

At first he'd been a little bit of a sad case, but then quickly he'd become amusing.

He wasn't amusing anymore.

Increasingly, he gave Cass the creeps.

During the three years she'd been married to Don Flackberg – film producer, younger brother of Julian – Cass moved in the highest levels of Hollywood society, where she had eventually calculated that of the entire pool of successful actors, directors, studio executives, and producers, 6.5% were sane and good, 4.5% were sane and evil, and 89% were insane and evil. In accumulating the experience to make this assessment, she had learned to recognize a series of eye expressions, facial ticks, and body-language quirks, as well as other physical and behavioral tells that unfailingly alerted her to the maddest of the mad and to the most monstrously wicked of the wicked before she fell prey to them. Following three minutes of observation, she believed that Earl Bockman, a simple pump jockey and grocer, was every bit as insane and evil as any of the richest and most highly honored members of the film community whom she had ever known.

In the darkness behind the crossroads store, between the moon-drizzled faux Corvette and the Explorer stuffed with corpses, Curtis keeps a watch on the back door of the building and on both the north and the south corners, around either of which epic trouble might come at any moment.

Most of his attention, however, is reserved for the boy-dog bond that he's exploiting now more intensely than ever before. He is here with a dry breeze whispering through the prairie grass at his back, but he is also – and more completely – with his sister-become inside the motor home, dazzling Polly with canine arithmetic and then with an instrument more complicated than playing cards.

When he's sure that Polly understands his message, that she is alarmed, and that she'll act to save herself and her sister, Curtis retreats from the dog and from the motor home. Now he lives only here in the warm breath of the prairie, in the cold light of the moon.

These hunters always travel in pairs or squads, never alone. The fact that both of the mom-and-pop cadavers in the SUV were stripped of clothes indicates that in addition to the man out at the pumps, a killer masquerading as the chestnut-haired woman waits in the store.

The Corvette-what-ain't-a-Corvette is roomier than the sports car that it pretends to be. The vehicle can comfortably accommodate four passengers.

Ever hopeful, as he was raised to be, Curtis will operate under the assumption that only two assassins are present at the crossroads. Anyway, if there are four, he has no chance whatsoever of surviving a confrontation. And in that event, he wouldn't know *how* to fight a quartet of these vicious predators; consequently, faced with four, his only sensible strategy would be to run into the prairie in search of a high cliff or a drowning river, or in pursuit of some other death that might be easier than the one that the killers plan to measure out to him.

Although usually he would avoid a clash with even just two of these hunters – or with one! – he doesn't have the luxury of flight in this case, because he has an obligation to Cass and Polly. He's told them to run, but they might not be permitted to leave if they are thought to harbor him. In that case, he can only distract the enemy from the twins by revealing himself.

Quickly now, into the thick of it, between the meat-wagon Ford Explorer and the extraterrestrial road-burner, to the back door of the building. Try the knob carefully, quietly.

Locked.

Curtis challenges the door, willpower against matter, on the micro scale where will should win – as it won at the back door of the Hammond farmhouse in Colorado, as it won at the door of the SUV on the auto carrier in Utah, and elsewhere.

He has no sixth sense, no superpowers that would make him prime material for a series of comic books portraying him in color-ful cape and tights. His main difference lies in his understanding of quantum mechanics, not as it is half understood on this world, but as it is more fully understood on others.

At the fundamental structural level of the universe, matter is energy; everything is energy expressed in myriad forms. Consciousness is the marshaling force that builds all things from this infinite sea of energy, primarily the all-encompassing consciousness of the Creator, the playful Presence in the dog's dreams. But even a mere mortal, having been granted intelligence and consciousness, possesses the power to affect the form and function of matter by a sheer act of will. This isn't the great world-making, galaxy-creating power of the playful Presence, but a humble power with which we can achieve only limited effects.

Even on this world, at its current early stage of development, scientists specializing in quantum mechanics are aware that at the subatomic level, the universe seems to be more like *thought* than like matter. They also know that their expectations, their thoughts, can affect the outcome of some experiments with elemental particles like electrons and photons. They understand that the universe is not as mechanistic as they once believed, and they have begun to suspect that it exists as an act of will, that this willpower – the awesomely creative consciousness of the playful Presence – is the organizing force within the physical universe, and that this power is reflected in the freedom that each mortal possesses to shape his or her destiny through the exercise of free will.

Curtis is already hip to all this.

Nevertheless, he remains afraid.

Fear is an unavoidable element of the mortal condition. Creation in all its ravishing beauty, with its infinite baroque embellishments and subtle charms, with all the wonders that it offers from both the Maker and the made, with all its velvet mystery and with all the joy we receive from those we love here, so enchants us that we lack the imagination, less than the faith, to envision an even more dazzling world beyond, and therefore even if we believe, we cling tenaciously to this existence, to sweet familiarity, fearful that all conceivable paradises will prove wanting by comparison.

Locked. The back door of the crossroads store is locked.

Then it isn't.

Beyond lies a small storeroom, revealed not by the single bare bulb dangling on a cord at ceiling center, but only by the light that sifts in from another room, around an inner door standing ajar, and dusts this chamber as if with a fine-ground fluorescent powder.

Curtis steps inside. He quietly closes the outer door behind him to prevent the breeze from shutting it with a bang.

Some silences soothe, but this one unnerves. This is the cold steel silence of the guillotine blade poised at the top of its track, with the target neck already inserted through the lunette below, the harvesting basket waiting for the head.

Ever hopeful even in his fear, Curtis eases toward the door that stands two inches ajar.

～　～　～

In the bedroom of the motor home, Polly grabbed the pump-action, pistol-grip, 12-gauge shotgun from the mounting brackets at the back of the closet, where it was stored behind the hanging clothes.

The dog watched.

Polly yanked open a dresser drawer and seized a box of shells. She inserted one in the breech, three more in the tube-type magazine.

The dog lost interest in weaponry and began to sniff curiously at the shoes on the closet floor.

In the interest of a snug fit that was flattering to the figure, her white toreador pants had no pockets. Polly tucked three spare shells into her halter top, between her breasts, grateful that nature had given her sufficient cleavage to serve as an ammunition depot.

The dog followed from the bedroom, through the bath, into the kitchen, but then was distracted by a whiff of some tasty treat in the food cupboard.

As Old Yeller sniffed inquisitively at the narrow gap between the cabinet doors, Polly stepped into the lounge and stared down at the laptop computer on the floor. On her return from the bedroom, she'd been half convinced that she'd imagined the business with the dog and the computer; but the proof remained before her, glowing on the screen.

The laptop had been stored on a shelf in the entertainment center, under the TV. After the trick with the cards, the dog had stood on her hind feet, pawing at the shelf, until Polly moved the laptop to the floor, opened it, and switched it on.

Bewildered but game, her sense of wonder surprisingly intact after three years in the wonder-crushing upper echelons of the film-industry, Polly had quickly set up the computer, while the dog had raced into the bathroom. Following a clatter, the pooch had returned with Cass's toothbrush. Using the brush as a stylus, Old Yeller then tapped out a message on the keyboard.

RUM, the dog had typed, whereupon Polly had decided that any dog able to differentiate one playing card from another and possessed of advanced numerical skills ought to be allowed to indulge in an adult beverage if it wanted one, assuming that it could hold its booze and exhibited no tendency to alcoholism. Polly would have prepared Old Yeller a pina colada right then, or a mai tai, though she suspected that she had lost her mind and that paramedics with psychiatric training, medevacked to the prairie from the nearest metropolitan center, were even now approaching the Fleetwood with a straitjacket and a drawn dose of Thorazine in a syringe of a size usually employed to treat horses. Unfortunately, she had no rum, only beer and a small collection of fine wines, a fact that she conveyed to the dog along with an apology for being an inadequate hostess.

RUM had proved to be not the wanted word, but an error resulting from the understandable clumsiness of a dog gripping a toothbrush in its mouth as a stylus with which to type on a keyboard. With a whine of frustration but with admirable determination, Old Yeller had tried again: RUN!

So here and now, but a minute after the dog had finished typing, Polly stood staring down at the laptop, on which continued to burn the entire six-line message that had motivated her to race to the bedroom and load the shotgun:

RUM
RUN!
MAN EVIL
ALIEN
EVIL ALIEN
RUM!

On the face of it, the message was absurd, one level of order above meaningless gibberish, and if it had shown up on the screen as if resolving out of the ether or even if it had been typed by a preliterate child, Polly wouldn't have acted upon it so quickly and might not have gone directly to the shotgun, but she felt justified in taking immediate and drastic action *because the message had been typed by a dog with a toothbrush in its mouth!* She'd never gone to college, and no doubt she'd lost a fearsome number of brain cells during the three years she spent in Hollywood, and she had no difficulty acknowledging that she was woefully ignorant about a long list of subjects, but she knew a miracle when she saw one, and if a dog typing messages with a toothbrush wasn't a miracle, then neither was Moses parting the Red Sea nor Lazarus rising from the dead.

Besides, considering his peculiarities, Earl Bockman made more sense as an evil alien than as the bumpkin proprietor of a crossroads store and service station in the great Nevada lonesome. This was one of those seemingly impossible things that you intuitively knew were true the moment that you heard them: such as the recent report that none of the members of the hit rap-music group calling itself Shot Cop Ho Busters could read a note of music.

She wasn't going to rush outside and blow Earl's head off, if only because even in her fear and excitement, she could appreciate the difficulty of explaining this action in a court of law. She did not, in fact, know quite *what* she was going to do now that she had the shotgun, but she felt better with the weapon in hand.

A crackling noise caused her to spin around and bring up the 12-gauge, but Old Yeller was the source of the sound. The dog had gotten her head stuck in the empty cheese-popcorn bag that Curtis had left on the floor by the co-pilot's chair.

Polly plucked the cellophane trap off the dog's head, revealing a foolish grin, a wildly active tongue, and a popcorn-speckled face that she couldn't easily relate to the determined messenger of alien doom that had labored so ingeniously over the keyboard. She turned to the computer once more, expecting the screen to be blank, but the exhortation to RUM! still burned in white letters on a blue field with five other lines of urgently conveyed information.

Old Yeller swabbed her snout with a propeller-action tongue that cleaned nose to chin to nose again, and Polly decided not to question miracles, not to dismiss the message because of the unlikely nature of the messenger, but to act, God help her, as the situation appeared to require.

And suddenly she realized: 'Where's Curtis?'

The dog pricked her ears and whined.

Carrying the shotgun, Polly went to the door, took a deep breath as she'd always taken just before she had disembarked, nude, from the flying saucer and had descended the neon stairs in that Las Vegas extravaganza, and she stepped into a prairie night turned as strange as any land reached by rabbit hole.

~ ~ ~

Curtis Hammond in commando mode, as acutely aware as ever that he's more poet than warrior, concentrates on silence as he silently eases open the storeroom door, concentrates on stealth as stealthily he enters the store itself, concentrates on not screaming and running in terror as, not screaming and running in terror, he proceeds in a crouch along the first aisle, seeking the false mom of mom-and-pop.

The shelves of merchandise follow the rectangular shape of the store; therefore, the aisles are long, and the displays prevent him from seeing the front windows.

Apparently, prairie folk have little concern for a balanced diet, because no fresh fruits or vegetables seem to be sold here, only a variety of packaged goods. Along the back wall stand glass-door coolers stocked with beer, soft drinks, milk, and fruit juice.

At the end of the first aisle, Curtis hesitates, listening for any sound that might reveal the mom's position, but this killer seems to be concentrating on silence as assiduously as is Curtis himself.

Finally he leans forward and peers around the corner, past a display of batteries and butane lighters. This end aisle is short, leading directly to the front of the store, which in total offers only three long aisles formed by two islands of tall shelves.

He can see a portion of one dust-filmed window, but to determine if Cass and Polly have both boarded the Fleetwood, he would have to stand. The banks of shelves are taller than he is, which means if the bad mom is lingering near the front of the store, she won't see him; nevertheless, he remains in a crouch.

Soon he'll announce his presence to distract the pair of hunters and thus give the twins a chance to flee. Success, however, depends on choosing exactly the right moment to stand and reveal himself.

Moving past the batteries and the cigarette lighters, Curtis peeks warily into the middle aisle. Deserted.

He continues to the next aisle-end display – razor blades, nail clippers, penknives, regrettably no serious weaponry – and pauses again to listen.

The pooled silence is too deep, immeasurable fathoms beyond a mere stillness, deeper even than a hush. This deathly quiet makes Curtis want to shout just to prove that he remains among the living.

A sudden chill on the nape of the neck. Looking behind himself, toward the fearful expectation of a creeping assassin, he almost cries out with relief when he sees that nothing stalks him. Yet.

He leans past packages of razor blades dangling from display hooks, and surveys the aisle nearest the front of the store, spotting the bad mom at once. She stands a few feet inside the open door, staring toward the pumps outside, and as far as he can tell, she's a ringer for the dead woman tumbled with her husband in the SUV.

More likely than not, these hunters are part of the pack that has been after him since Colorado, although it is possible that they are new to the mission. Because they aren't traveling in the stolen saddlery truck, aren't using local transport of any kind, he doubts that they are the two who, posing as cowboys, tracked him to the truck stop on Wednesday night.

Whether new to the hunt or members of the original pack, they are as violent and as dangerous as all the others, not individuals but members of a killing swarm. Their name is legion.

Drawn by activity at the pumps, the bad mom steps closer to the open door, and then moves all the way onto the threshold. She is now as much out of the store as in it, and she's no longer in a position to catch a glimpse of Curtis from her peripheral vision.

Between Curtis and the front door, on the counter near the cashier's station, a pistol lies in plain sight. Perhaps either the man or the woman now dead in the SUV had time to draw the handgun from under the counter but not enough time to use it. And the bad pop left it behind when he stepped outside to greet the Fleetwood.

The twins are no less endangered just because the hunter went to them unarmed. These are cruel assassins, as quick as vipers striking, more savage than crocodiles two days past their last good meal. They *prefer* to kill barehanded, though seldom with anything as prosaic as hands, to wade in the wet of death. The twins' beauty, kindness, wit, and high spirits will gain them not one split second of additional life if one of these hunters chooses to destroy them.

Gazing at the weapon on the counter, perhaps forty feet away, Curtis recognizes opportunity when he sees it. He doesn't even need to review his mother's numerous admonitions about the importance of seizing the moment, but sets out at once along the aisle, toward the cashier's station, proceeding in a crouch but otherwise as bold as any death-marked fool in battle who sees incoming tracers in the sky and assumes they are fireworks celebrating his impending triumph. He is halfway to the cash register when he wonders if he has mistaken bait for opportunity.

The bad mom could step backward off the threshold, whip toward him, and peel him like an orange before he could say *Oh, Lord.*

Curtis is undaunted, however, because he is Roy Rogers without the singing, Indiana Jones without the fedora, James Bond without the shaken martini, steeped in heroism as defined in 9,658 films enjoyed over two days of an intense three-week cultural-preparation program, all 9,658 viewed by direct-to-brain megadata downloading prior to planetfall. In truth, he has been made just a smidgin crazy by all those movies, which he hasn't quite yet assimilated, and he isn't at all times able to sort out the truth from the fiction in what he has seen on his mental silver screen. But because movies have inspired in him such a glorious sense of freedom and such a passion for this strange world, he happily accepts the consequences of a temporary mental imbalance if that is the necessary price for those two days of unparalleled entertainment, education, and uplift.

Indeed, the examples set by film heroes prove to be what he needs, because he reaches the cashier's station and rises to his full height without alerting the bad mom. She still stands in the doorway, costumed in the dead woman's clothes, facing the pumps.

The window behind the cashier's station is clouded by dust, but Curtis can see the Fleetwood. Cass leans against it, facing the bad pop, and appears not to have been alerted to their danger.

Two minutes have passed since Polly received the message through the dog. She no doubt will act soon. The time has come for Curtis to provide the necessary distraction.

When he picks up the pistol from the counter, he notices beside it a paperback romance by Gabby's favorite novelist, Nora Roberts. Evidently, everyone reads her, but he assumes that this copy belongs to one of the dead people out back rather than to one of the killers, and that Ms. Roberts's popularity is not yet multiplanetary.

The external safety on the pistol isn't engaged. He holds the weapon with his right hand, steadies his right with his left, and dares to inch toward the open door, angling for a clearer shot.

The killer remains unaware of him.

Nine feet from the door. Eight feet.

He halts. This line of fire is ideal.

Standing with feet apart for maximum balance, his right foot ahead of the left, leaning forward from the waist to prepare for the recoil, he hesitates because the target in the doorway looks so much like an ordinary woman, appears so vulnerable. Curtis is ninety-nine percent certain that she is only slightly less vulnerable than an armored tank and that she's not a woman at all, let alone an ordinary one, yet he can't quite bring himself to apply the final increment of killing pressure to the trigger.

That one percent of doubt inhibits him, though his mother always said that nothing in this life is absolutely certain and that refusal to act on anything less than a hundred percent certainty is in fact an act of moral cowardice, an excuse never to take a stand. He thinks of Cass and Polly, and lost in a vast wasteland of one percent doubt, he wonders if the dead woman in the SUV might have an identical twin who stands now before him. This worry is ridiculous, considering the off-world transport disguised as a Corvette, considering the broken-necked victims. Yet the boy stands in this purgatory of indecision because although he is his mother's son and although, in her company, he has endured heated battles and has seen terrible violence, he's never before killed, has trained with various weapons but has never fired upon another living creature, and here in this small crossroads store, he discovers that killing, even for heroic purpose, is harder than his mother warned him that it could be and much harder than ever it appears to be in movies.

Alerted by scent or by intuition, the woman in the open doorway turns her head so quickly, so sharply that a snap should be audible, and on sight she knows Curtis. Her eyes flare wide, as any startled woman's would, and she raises one hand defensively as though to ward off bullets, as any frightened woman might, but in the same instant, she is betrayed by her smile, which is as inappropriate here as would be a sudden burst of song: a predatory smile of serpent cracking wide to swallow mouse, of leopard poised to make a deadly pounce.

In the telling moment, when you either have the right stuff or you don't, Curtis discovers he has it, and in abundance. He squeezes the trigger once, twice, rocked by the recoils, and he neither falls back in the face of the assassin's fierce shriek nor merely holds his ground, but takes a step forward and fires again, again, again.

Any fear that this woman might be the legitimate twin of the one lying dead in the SUV is put to rest even as the first round from the pistol shreds through her torso. Although the human form serves well the wars of this world, it isn't the ideal physiology for a warrior species, and even before the first bullet leaves the barrel, the bad mom begins to morph into something that Curtis would rather not have seen this soon after consuming an entire large bag of cheese popcorn washed down with Orange Crush.

In the first instant, the killer launches itself at him, but it is mortal, not supernatural, and though its rage would drive it into the teeth of death, its cunning overcomes blind fury. Even in the act of springing at Curtis, it kicks off the corner of the cashier's station and launches itself in a new trajectory, toward the tall shelves of packaged goods.

Of the four additional shots that Curtis fires, three find their mark, jolting the shrieking assassin, which scrambles quickly up the shelves as an acrobat might swarm a ladder with leaps and flourishes. Hampered by a cascade of cans and bottles and boxes, the killer is in fact scaling an avalanche, yet it blitzes past all tumbling obstacles to reach the summit even as the fourth shot strikes and the fifth misses.

During this lightning-swift ascent, the killer morphs toward more than a single shape, simultaneously sampling a menagerie of murderous species, bristling with talons and beaks, with horns and spikes and scapulae. Hands grasp, pedipalpi quiver, spiracles ripple, pincers snap like scissors, and other ill-defined extrusions appear and at once vanish in a roiling tumult of glistening carapaces that melt into whipping tails, in snarls of coarse hair that smooth into scaly flanks, expressing a biological chaos that makes Curtis's confusion in the twins' bathroom seem, by comparison, merely an amusing faux pas. Clinging for but a fraction of a second to the crest of the shelves, hunched under the fluorescent lights, all shapes and none, and every shape a lie, the churning beast might be the Beast himself, recognizable to the poet Milton as the ruling prince of the 'darkness visible' in Hell – and then it's gone into the next aisle.

Although mortal, the assassin will not die as easily as Curtis would have perished if it had reached him. The spirit of every evil is resilient, and in this case, so is its flesh. Its wounds won't heal miraculously, but those it has might not be sufficient to put it down permanently.

Curtis is loath to turn his back on this crippled but dangerous adversary; however, Cass and Polly are outside with the second killer and helpless against its savagery. With at most five rounds left in the pistol, he's committed to further distracting the remaining assassin in order to give the twins a chance to flee.

Frantic, clambering across the treacherously shifting drift of merchandise that has crashed from shelves to floor, he makes his way to the open door, praying that his two beautiful benefactors, glass-shod Cinderellas, fragile flowers of Indiana, will not have their kindness to him repaid by bloody death.

While diesel fuel fed the hungry belly of the Fleetwood, Earl Bockman droned on about the varieties of packaged macaroni dishes, frozen and not, that he and Maureen stocked in the store. He held forth not in the tone and manner of a merchant trying to drum up a few bucks' worth of business, but with the chatty enthusiasm of a pathetic social misfit who believed that sparkling conversation could be made from any subject short of the raw lists of names in the telephone directory, although perhaps he would get around to those, as well, before the cap was back on the tank.

If Cass had been a criminal type or a rabid activist committed to the elimination of sound pollution, she might have shot Earl and put an end to her misery and his. Instead, she watched the gallons mount up in the tabulation windows on the antique pump and thanked God that she had developed such a high tolerance for boredom during her childhood and adolescence in rural Indiana and in a family whose friends were all college academics.

The gunfire in the store immediately enlivened the night – not merely of itself, but by the effect it had on Earl. Cass wasn't surprised that he reacted with alarm, as she did, but *surprise* was inadequate to describe her further reaction when she saw the changes occurring in his face during the four shots that followed the first. Unless Earl happened to be a werewolf out of phase with the moon, he wasn't in fact Earl the packaged-macaroni-aficionado at all, but something that Cass might not have been prepared to cope with if she hadn't pursued an eight-year fascination with ufology.

She'd been leaning against the motor home, her left hand in the roomy purse slung from her shoulder, and on the sound of the first shot, she had stood up straight. By the time the flat crack of the fifth round split the air and echoed off the side of the Fleetwood, as Earl grew weary of his old dull personality and began to set loose the party animal within, Cass knew what to do, and did it.

When her left hand came out of the purse, it held a 9-mm pistol, which she conveyed to her right hand with a cross-body toss. As she opened fire on an Earl Bockman grown uglier than he had been boring, she thrust her left hand into the purse once more, withdrew a second pistol identical to the first, and opened fire with it, too, hoping that no round would hit a gasoline pump, sever a fuel line, and turn her into a dancing human torch more spectacular than any fabulously costumed role she had ever played on a Vegas stage.

As she stepped out of the motor home with the 12-gauge, Polly heard the gunfire and knew at once that it didn't originate from the other side of the Fleetwood but came from a point somewhat farther away, perhaps from the store.

Because of a mutual lifelong interest in firearms inspired by Castor and Pollux, the mythological Greek warriors after whom they had been named, and because of a more recent mutual interest in self-defense and martial arts inspired by the three years that they had spent in the higher social echelons of the film industry, Polly and Cass traveled the lonely highways of America with confidence that they could handle any threat that might arise.

Rounding the front of the motor home, Polly heard a fusillade that originated nearer than the first. She recognized the distinct sound of Cass's twin pistols, which she had heard often enough on firing ranges over the years.

When she arrived on scene, shotgun at the ready, she discovered that her sister was dealing with one lonely-highway threat that, in all honesty, they had not foreseen. The evil alien of Old Yeller's succinct laptop message, bursting out of Earl Bockman's ripped and wrenched clothing, pitched violently backward between two gasoline pumps, reeling under the impact of hollow-point 9-mm slugs, twitching and squealing in pain and rage, flopping like a beached fish on the graveled ground between the pumps and the station.

'Got this covered,' Cass said, though her face was ghastly pale even in the flattering amber-and-red glow of the Christmas lights, and though her eyes bulged like those of someone suffering from a wildly overactive thyroid gland, and though her hair was seriously in need of a comb. 'Curtis must be inside,' she added, before following the unpredictable Mr. Bockman between the pumps.

Fearful for Curtis, hurrying toward the building, Polly got a better look at the apparently terminal station proprietor, and she decided that she much preferred Earl when he'd been tall, bald, and boring. Writhing, spasming, coiling, flailing, hissing, snapping – and now shrieking even more furiously when Cass opened fire on him again – he resembled something (in fact, a hideous tangled mass of several somethings) that you might call a pest-control company to deal with, assuming you knew a pest-control company that armed its exterminators with semiautomatic weapons and flamethrowers.

The dog sure knew what she was talking about.

≈ ≈ ≈

Using a log-rolling technique to get across all the fallen cans of fruit and vegetables, Curtis reaches the front door just in time to see the second killer driven backward between two pumps by a noisy barrage of gunfire. Cass – identifiable by the large purse slung from one shoulder – follows with two pistols, flames spurting from both muzzles. Even in a ten-million-dollar Vegas stage production, surely she had never cut a more dramatic figure than this, not even when she had been nude with a feathered headdress. The boy wishes, however, that he could have had the experience of one of those performances – and at once blushes at this wish, even though it seems to indicate that in spite of his recent problems being Curtis Hammond to fullest effect, he is nonetheless steadily becoming human on a deep emotional level, which is a good thing.

Here comes Polly with a shotgun, looking no less dramatic than her sister, even though also fully clothed. When she sees Curtis in the open door, she calls out his name with evident relief.

Maybe he hears relief where he should hear an angrier quality, because as Polly arrives, she levels the pistol-grip 12-gauge at his head and shouts at him. She has every right to be furious with him, of course, for bringing a pair of otherworldly assassins into her life, and he won't blame her if she shoots him down right here and now, though he might have expected her to be more understanding and though he *will* be sorry to go.

Then he realizes that she's shouting 'Down, down, down,' and finally the word computes. He drops flat to the ground, and she fires at once into the store. She pumps four thunderous rounds before the bad mom, which he had previously wounded, stops shrieking behind him.

Scrambling to his feet, Curtis is so fascinated by the sight of Polly plucking shotgun shells from her cleavage with the flair of a magician producing live doves from silk scarves that he turns almost as an afterthought to peer into the store. Something that will strain the county coroner's powers of description lies just inside the door, midst the wreckage of a snack-food display rack, and a golden-orange blizzard of shotgun-blasted potato chips, Doritos, and Cheez Doodles slowly settles in salty drifts upon the carcass.

'Are there more of these damn things?' Polly asks breathlessly, having already reloaded the 12-gauge.

'Plenty more,' says Curtis. 'But not here, not now – not yet.'

Cass has at last dispatched the second killer. She joins her sister, looking disarranged as Curtis has never seen her.

'The fuel tank's probably just about full,' Cass says, staring strangely at Curtis.

'Probably,' he agrees.

'We should probably be getting out of here real fast,' Polly says.

'Probably,' Curtis agrees, because although he doesn't want to further endanger them, he's even more averse to the idea of heading out from here alone, on foot into the night. 'And real fast isn't fast enough.'

'Once we hit the road,' Cass says, 'you've got some explaining to do, Curtis Hammond.'

Hoping he doesn't sound like a sassy-assed, spit-in-the-eye, ungrateful, snot-nosed little punk, Curtis says, 'You, too.'

48

Caffeine and sugar, in quantity and in tandem, were supposed to be twin wrecking balls of human health in general and destructive to sleep in particular, but Coke and cookies marginally improved Micky's low spirits and didn't prevent her eyes from growing heavy.

She sat at the kitchen table, dealing out game after game of solitaire, waiting for Leilani. She remained convinced that the girl would find a way to visit before dawn, even though her stepfather had now been alerted to their relationship.

Without delay, immediately upon Leilani's arrival, Micky would drive the girl to Clarissa's in Hemet, in spite of all the parrots and the risk. No time remained for strategy, only for action. And if Hemet proved to be but the first stop on a journey of uncertainty and hardship, Micky was prepared to pay whatever ticket price might be demanded of her.

When eventually even worry, anger, caffeine, and sugar could not stave off drowsiness, and when her neck began to ache from resting her head on her crossed arms upon the table, she carried the seat cushions from the living-room sofa into the kitchen and put them on the floor. She needed to be near enough to the door to be awakened at once by the girl's knock.

She doubted that Maddoc would return, but she didn't dare fall asleep with the door unlocked for Leilani, because if the doom doctor *did* pay another visit, surely he'd come with syringes of digitoxin, or the equivalent, with the compassionate intention of administering a little mercy.

At 2:30 in the morning, Micky stretched out upon the cushions, head next to the door, expecting to lie awake, and fell instantly asleep.

Her dream began in a hospital where she lay abed and paralyzed, alone and afraid of being alone, because she expected Preston Maddoc to appear, to have his way with her as she lay helpless, and then to kill her. She called to nurses passing in the hall, but all were deaf, and every nurse wore the face of Micky's mother. She called to passing doctors, who came to the open door to peer at her, but they only smiled and went away; none looked like another, but each was one of her mother's men who, in her childhood, had known her in ways that she hadn't wished to be known. The only sounds were her cries and the soft clatter and the mournful whistle of a passing train, as she had heard night after night in her prison cell. With the fluid transition of a dream, she was out of the hospital, aboard the train, paralyzed but sitting up, alone in a long coach car. The clatter of wheels and rails grew louder, the periodic whistle sounded no longer mournful but like a groan of misery, and the train picked up speed, rocking on the tracks. Journeying through blackness of night into darkness of a different quality, she was delivered to the platform of a deserted train station, where Preston Maddoc, at last appearing, arrived with a wheelchair in which she sat in quadriplegic submission as he took custody of her. He wore a necklace of Leilani's teeth, and held a veil made from the girl's blond hair. When Maddoc fitted this veil to Micky's head, Leilani's tresses draped her ears as well as her face, and she lost all use of the senses thus covered: Struck deaf, mute, blind, denied the faintest of scents, she was left with no perception of her surroundings other than the rolling motion of the wheelchair and the bump of irregularities in the pavement. Maddoc conveyed her toward her fate while she sat unrespited, unpitied, unreprieved.

Micky woke into a warm morning, bone-cold from the repeating dream. The quality of light at the window and then the clock revealed that dawn had come thirty or forty minutes ago.

Having slept with her head against the bolted door, she would have heard even a timid knock. Leilani hadn't come.

Micky got up from the three sofa cushions, stacked them in a pile, and pushed the pile aside.

With sunrise had arrived the courage to open the door, Maddoc or no Maddoc. She crossed the threshold and stood on the yard-square concrete stoop at the head of the three steps.

Quiet reigned at the house next door. No madwoman waltzed in the backyard. No spacecraft hovered in fulfillment of Maddoc's vision.

Single file, three crows flew westward, feathered commuters heading toward a morning's work in the bowers of fig trees or among gnarled olive branches, but none shrieked at Micky from the pickets of the rear fence, as they had harassed her the previous evening.

At that fence, the snarled skeins of thorny rosebush trailers prickled the skin of the morning, and a sparse distribution of sickly leaves mocked Geneva's gardening. But among these familiar barren brambles, three enormous white roses, tinted peach along each petal edge by the ascending sun, greeted the day with slow, heavy nods.

Micky went down the steps and crossed the yard, amazed.

For years, the bush had failed to bloom. The previous afternoon, not one bud, let alone three, could have been found anywhere within this punk-stubborn mass of unruly thorns.

Closer inspection revealed that the three big roses had been snipped from another garden, no doubt elsewhere in the trailer park. With green ribbon, each flower had been secured to this Little Shop of Horrors plant.

Leilani.

The girl had managed to sneak out of the house, after all, but she hadn't knocked, which meant that she'd given up all hope of help and that she was reluctant to risk focusing Maddoc's wrath on Micky and Geneva more than she'd already done.

These three roses, each a perfect specimen and obviously chosen with care, were more than a gift: They were a message. In their white sun-kissed splendor, they said *goodbye*.

Feeling as though she'd been pierced by every thorn on the bush, Micky turned away from a message that she was emotionally unable to accept, and stared at the house trailer next door. The place appeared to be deserted.

She had crossed the lawn to the fallen fence between properties before she quite realized that she'd begun to move. She was running by the time she reached the neighbors' back door.

Impetuously, even though she hadn't composed an excuse for the visit if Maddoc or Sinsemilla responded, Micky knocked with an urgency that she couldn't quell. She rapped too long, too hard, and when she paused to rub her stinging knuckles against the palm of her other hand, the silence in the house abided as though she had never knocked at all.

As before, drapes shrouded the windows. Micky looked left and right, hoping to see a fold of fabric stir, any indication that she was being watched, that someone still resided here.

When she pounded on the door again and failed once more to draw a response, she tried the knob. Unlocked. The door opened.

Morning hadn't fully arrived in the Maddoc kitchen, where heavy curtains filtered the early daylight. Even with the door open and sunshine streaming past Micky, shadows dominated.

The illuminated clock, brightest point in the room, seemed to float supernaturally upon the wall, as if it were the clock of fate counting down to death. She could hear nothing but the purr of its cat-quiet mechanism.

She shouted into the house: 'Hello? Is anyone here? Is anyone home? Hello?'

Unanswered, she crossed the threshold.

The possibility of a trap occurred to her. She didn't think that Maddoc would scheme to lure her farther by silence, and then bludgeon her with a hammer. She was undeniably a trespasser, however; and she could be easily framed for theft if, in answer to Maddoc's call, the police suddenly arrived and found her here. With her prison record, any trumped-up charge might stick.

Dropping all pretense that she was looking for anyone but the girl, she called only Leilani's name as, nervously, she moved deeper into the narrow house. The greasy drapes, the sagging furniture, the matted shag carpet absorbed her voice as effectively as would have the draped walls and the plush surfaces of a funeral home, and step by step she found herself in the steadily constricting embrace of claustrophobia.

As furnished rentals went, this was at the desperation end of the financial spectrum, leased by the week to tenants who more often than not were still scrambling to put together every Friday's rent payment even after Friday had dawned. The contents, aside from being worn to the point of collapse, were utterly impersonal: no souvenirs or knickknacks, no family photographs, not even any ten-dollar artworks on the walls.

In the kitchen and living room, Micky saw no possession that hadn't come with the house, no indication that the Maddocs were in residence. Born to wealth, raised with fine things, the doom doctor could have paid for the presidential suite at the Ritz-Carlton, and surely would have preferred those accommodations. The fact that he had rented this place for the week, using the name Jordan Banks, seemed to prove that he not only wanted to keep a low profile these days but that, when eventually he was finished with Leilani and with her mother, he intended to have left behind little or no proof that he had ever traveled in their company.

The depressing nature of these digs and the lack of concern about his bride's comfort, when better could so easily have been afforded, argued that Preston Maddoc's reasons for marrying had nothing to do with love and affection, or with the desire to have a family of his own. Some mysterious need drove him, and not even all of Leilani's colorful observations and bizarre speculations had come close to casting light upon his scabrous motives.

Venturing into the bedrooms and the bathroom required a greater degree of courage – or perhaps reckless stupidity – than she had needed to enter the back door. Night shadows, having fled here to escape the dawn, waited in a conclave for the sunset that would return the world to them, more numerous in these rooms than in the first two. Although she switched on the lights as she went, every lamp seemed fitted with a weak bulb, and gloom clung to every corner.

The shabby bathroom contained no toothbrushes, no shaving kit, no bottles of medicine, nothing to indicate the presence of tenants.

In the smaller of the two bedrooms, the closet was empty, as were the nightstand and the dresser. The bedclothes had been left in disarray.

In the larger bedroom, the closet stood open, and the rod held only empty wire hangers.

On the floor, visible from the doorway, stood a bottle of lemon-flavored vodka. Full. The seal unbroken.

At the sight of the booze, Micky began to shake uncontrollably, but not out of any desire for a drink.

Having seen Leilani's gift of roses, Maddoc somehow knew that Micky would be drawn here immediately when she, too, saw the blooms. He'd left the back door unlocked for her.

He must have gone to an all-night market to purchase this gift of spirits, confident that Micky would venture to the last room in the house and discover what he'd left for her. The mocking bastard had attached a fancy stick-on bow to the neck of the bottle.

In one brief conversation, and after just a few minutes spent ransacking her bedroom, Maddoc understood her uncannily well.

As Micky considered his preternatural insight, she knew that Maddoc was a Goliath impervious to slingshots. The shakes that seized her at the sight of the bottle grew worse as she thought of Leilani on the road with this man, traveling faster than justice could move, speeding ever farther from hope, toward a death that would be called *healing*, toward an unmarked grave in which her small body would soon be rotting even if her spirit went to the stars.

By leaving the bottle, Maddoc was saying that he harbored no fear of Micky, that he trusted her to be weak, ineffectual, entirely predictable. Having appointed himself as her suicide counselor, he believed that she needed no more assistance than the simple direction provided by this bottle – and enough years – to destroy herself by degrees.

She left the house without touching the vodka.

Outside, the too-bright morning stung her eyes, sharp as grief, and everything in the August day looked hard, brittle, breakable, everything from the porcelain sky to the ground beneath her feet, in which quakes were stored as surely as the vodka in the bottle. Given time enough, all things passed away: the sky and the earth and the people caught between. She didn't unduly fear the death that she had been born to meet, but now as never previously, she feared that she would keep her rendezvous with death before she had a chance to do what she had been put here to do, what she realized now that everyone had been put here to do – bring hope, grace, and love into the lives of others.

What twenty-eight years of suffering had never taught her, what she had stubbornly refused to learn from even the hardest knocks of life, had suddenly been taught to her in less than three days by one disabled girl whose articles of instruction were only these two: her great joy in Creation, her *inextinguishable* joy, and her unshakable faith that her small challenged life, however chaotic, nevertheless possessed meaning and an important purpose in the infinite scheme of things. The lesson Micky had learned from this dangerous young mutant, though plain and simple, rocked her now as she stood on the dead brown lawn where Sinsemilla had danced with the moon: None of us can ever save himself; we are the instruments of one another's salvation, and only by the hope that we give to others do we lift ourselves out of the darkness into light.

Aunt Gen, in pajamas and slippers, stood in her backyard. She had found the goodbye roses.

Micky ran to her.

While untying the knot in a length of green ribbon, freeing one of the white blooms, Geneva had been pricked repeatedly by brambles. Her hands were liberally spotted with blood. She appeared to be oblivious of her wounds, however, and the glaze on her face was inspired not by thorns, but by the farewell message that she, too, had read in the roses.

When their eyes met, they had to look at once away, Aunt Gen to the perfect rose, Micky to the section of fallen fence between this property and the next, then to the slip of discarded ribbon, green on the green grass, and finally to her own palsied hands.

She was able to speak sooner than she had expected: 'What was the name of that town?'

'What town?' Aunt Gen asked.

'In Idaho. Where the guy claimed to have been healed by aliens.'

'Nun's Lake,' Aunt Gen replied without hesitation. 'Leilani said he was up there in Nun's Lake, Idaho.'

49

Hula girls, hula girls, hips rotating, swished their skirts of polyester grass. Ever smiling, black eyes shining, arms extended in perpetual invitation, they would dance their hip joints to dust if bone were the issue; however, their femurs and acetabulums were made not of bone, but of extremely durable, high-impact plastic.

The word *acetabulum* appealed to Leilani not merely because of its magical resonance, but because it didn't sound like what it was. You might expect acetabulum to be a substance that old Sinsemilla smoked, sniffed, popped in pill form, shot into her veins with huge veterinary hypodermic needles, baked into brownies and ate by the dozen, or ingested by more exotic means and through orifices best left unmentioned. The acetabulum was instead the rounded concavity in the innominate bone that formed the hip joint in conjunction with the femur, which sounded like a jungle cat but was another bone. Since Leilani had no intention of becoming a medical doctor, this information was largely useless to her. But her head had long ago been filled with useless information, anyway, which she believed helped to keep out more useful but depressing and scary information that would otherwise preoccupy her.

The dinette table, at which she sat reading a paperback fantasy novel, provided a dance floor to three plastic hula girls that ranged between four and six inches in height. They wore similar skirts, but their tube tops were different colors and patterns. Two had modest breasts, but the third was a busty little wahine with the proportions that Leilani intended to acquire by the age of sixteen, through the power of positive thinking. All three were constructed and weighted in such a fashion that even the most subtle road vibrations passing through the motor home were sufficient to keep them gyrating.

Two more hula girls danced on the small table between the two armchairs in the lounge, another three on the table beside the sofabed that faced the chairs. Counter space in the kitchen was at a premium, but ten additional figurines danced there, as well. Still others were performing in the bathroom and bedroom.

Although simple counterweight systems kept many of the dancers moving, others operated on batteries to ensure that when the motor home stopped to refuel or when it dropped anchor for the night, the hula-hula celebration would continue unabated. Sinsemilla believed that these ever-swiveling dolls generated beneficial electromagnetic waves, and that these waves protected their vehicle from collisions, breakdowns, hijackings, and from being sucked into another dimension in an open-highway version of the Bermuda Triangle. She insisted that never fewer than two dancers be in motion in every room at all times.

On the sofabed in the lounge at night, Leilani was occasionally lulled to sleep by the faint rhythmic whisper of hula hips and tiny swirling skirts. But as often as not, she clamped a pillow around her ears to block out the sound and to resist the urge to jam the little dancers into a pot, put the pot on the cooktop, and smelt them down in a dramatic production that she'd already written in her head and had titled *Dangerous Young Mutant Hawaiian Volcano Goddess*.

On those not infrequent occasions when the incessant sound of hula dolls in the night irritated Leilani, the seven-foot-diameter face painted on the ceiling of the lounge, over her fold-out bed, sometimes soothed her to sleep. This kindly countenance of the Hawaiian sun god, faintly phosphorescent in the dark, gazed down with a sleepy-eyed, stone-temple smile.

Their motor home, which featured other Hawaiian motifs in its interior design, was a high-end luxury custom coach converted from a Prevost bus. Old Sinsemilla christened it *Makani 'olu'olu* – Hawaiian for 'Fair Wind' – which seemed no more appropriate for a vehicle with a gross weight of over fifty-two thousand pounds than *Fluffy* would have been the right name for an elephant. With slide-out bedroom and galley-lounge extensions, it reliably proved to be the biggest vehicle in any campground, so large that children gaped in awe. Retiree vagabonds of a certain age, already worried about turning radiuses and tricky angles of approach to their campsite hookups, turned as pale as Milk of Magnesia if they were unfortunate enough to be required to slot-park their humbler Winnebagos and Airstreams in this beast's shadow, and most regarded the leviathan with resentment or paranoid terror.

It sure rode well, however, as stable and solid as a bank vault on wheels. The motion-triggered hula dolls danced steadily, but in pleasantly lazy swivels, never with spasmodic abandon. And while in transit, Leilani could read her novel about evil pigmen from another dimension with no risk of motion sickness.

She was so accustomed to the dolls that they didn't distract her from her book, and the same could be said of the colorful Hawaiian-shirt fabrics in which the dinette chairs were uphol-stered. Plenty of distraction was continually provided, however, by old Sinsemilla and Dr. Doom, who occupied the pilot's and co-pilot's chairs.

They were up to something. Of course, being *up to something* was the natural condition of these two, as sure as bees were born to make honey and beavers to build dams.

Conspiratorial, they kept their voices low. Since Leilani was the only other person aboard *Fair Wind*, she was inclined to suspect that they were conspiring against *her*.

They wouldn't be scheming up a simple game of find-the-brace or its equivalent. Such mean fun was impromptu by nature, dependent on opportunity and on what chemicals dear Mater had recently ingested. Besides, petty cruelties had no appeal for Dr. Doom, whose interest was excited only by cruelty on an operatic scale.

From time to time, Sinsemilla looked sneakily over her shoulder at Leilani or peeked around the wing of the co-pilot's chair. Leilani pretended to be unaware of this surreptitious monitoring. Her mother might interpret even fleeting eye contact as an invitation to wreak a little torment.

More than anything else, the giggling unnerved her. Sinsemilla was a frequent giggler, and perhaps seventy or eighty percent of the time, this indicated that she was in an effervescent girls-just-want-to-have-fun frame of mind, but sometimes it served the same purpose as a rattlesnake's rattle, warning of a strike. Worse, more than once during this long conversation, between whispers and murmurs, Dr. Doom giggled, as well, which was a first; his giggle had the artery-icing effect of Charles Manson merry-eyed and tittering with delight.

They were eastbound on Interstate 15, nearing the Nevada border, deep in the blazing Mojave Desert, when Sinsemilla left the cockpit and joined Leilani at the dinette table.

'What're you reading, baby?'

'A fantasy thing,' she replied without looking up from the page.

'What's it about?'

'Evil pigmen.'

'Piggies aren't evil,' Sinsemilla corrected. 'Piggies are sweet, gentle creatures.'

'Well, these aren't pigs as we know them. These are from another dimension.'

'People are evil, not piggies.'

'Not all people are evil,' Leilani countered in defense of her species, finally looking up from the book. 'Mother Teresa wasn't evil.'

'Evil,' Sinsemilla insisted.

'Haley Joel Osment isn't evil. He's cute.'

'The actor kid? Evil. All of us are evil, baby. We're a cancer on the planet,' Sinsemilla said with a smile that was probably like the one that she had worn when the doctors shot enough megawatts of electricity through her brain to fry bacon on her forehead.

'Anyway, these are pig*men*. Not just pigs.'

'Baby, Lani, trust me. If you combined a piggy and a man, the natural goodness of the piggy would overcome the evil of the man. Pigmen would never be evil. They'd be good.'

'Well, these pigmen are total bastards,' Leilani said, wondering if anyone, anywhere, in the history of the world, had ever engaged in philosophical discussions like those that her mother inspired. As far as she was aware, Plato and Socrates hadn't conducted a dialogue on the morality and the motives of pigmen from other dimensions. 'These particular pigmen,' she said, tapping the book, 'would gut you with their tusks as soon as look at you.'

'Tusks? They sound more like boars than piggies.'

'They're pigs,' Leilani assured her. 'Pigmen. Evil, nasty, rude, obnoxious, filthy pigmen.'

'Boarmen,' Sinsemilla said with a serious expression that most people reserved for news of untimely deaths, 'would never be evil, either. Piggymen and boarmen would both be good. So would monkeymen, chickenmen, dogmen, or any type of animal-man crossbreed.'

Leilani wished that she could fetch her journal and record this conversation in her invented form of shorthand without making her mother suspicious as to the true nature of the diary. 'There aren't any chickenmen in this story, Mother. This is *literature*.'

'Smart as you are, you should be reading something enlightening, not piggymen books. Maybe you're old enough to read Brautigan.'

'I've already read him.'

Sinsemilla looked surprised. 'You have? When?'

'Before birth. You were reading him even back then, over and over again, and I just absorbed it all through the placenta.'

Sinsemilla took this declaration seriously and was delighted. Her expression brightened. 'Cool. That's so cool.' Then a sly look found fox features in her face and brought them to the fore as if she were undergoing a moon-driven transformation. She leaned across the table and whispered, '*You want to know a secret?*'

This question alarmed Leilani. The impending revelation surely involved whatever the mother and the pseudofather had been murmuring and whispering about all the way from Santa Ana to San Bernardino, to sun-baked Barstow, to Baker and beyond. Anything that tickled them could not be good news for Leilani.

'*I'm making a little piggy* right now,' Sinsemilla whispered.

On some level, perhaps Leilani knew immediately what her mother meant but simply couldn't bear to contemplate it.

Reading her daughter's blank expression, Sinsemilla gave up the whisper and spoke slowly, as though Leilani were thickheaded. 'I'm making . . . a little piggy . . . *right now*.'

Leilani couldn't keep the revulsion out of her voice. 'Oh, God.'

'This time, I'm going to do it right,' Sinsemilla assured her.

'You're pregnant.'

'I used a home-pregnancy test two days ago. That's why I bought thingy, my little snaky fella.' She indicated her left hand, where the bite was now covered by a large Band-Aid. 'He was my gift to me for being preggers.'

Leilani knew that she was dead already, still breathing but as good as dead, not on her birthday next February, but much sooner. She didn't know why this should be true, why her mother's pregnancy meant that she herself was facing an earlier execution date, but she had no doubt that her instinct could be trusted.

'When you were such a baby about poor thingy,' Sinsemilla said, 'I thought you brought bad luck. Killing thingy, maybe you jinxed me, and maybe I wasn't knocked up anymore. But I gave myself another test yesterday and' – she patted her belly – 'piggy's still in the pen.'

Nausea brought a sudden flood of saliva to Leilani's mouth, and she swallowed hard.

'Your daddy, Preston, he's wanted this for a long time, but I wasn't ready till now.'

Leilani looked toward the driver's seat, toward Preston Maddoc.

'See, baby, I needed time to figure out why you and Luki never developed psychic powers even though I gave you, like, a magic bus full of truly fine psychedelics from my blood to yours while you were in the mommy oven.'

The back of the pull-down sun visor featured a makeup mirror. Even at a distance of sixteen or eighteen feet, Leilani was able to discern Maddoc's eyes repeatedly shifting focus from the highway to the mirror in which he could see her and Sinsemilla.

'And then it just hit me – I have to stay *natural*! Sure, I was doing peyote, you know, cactus buttons, and I was doing psilocybin, from mushrooms. But I also did some DMT and plenty of LSD, and that shit is *synthetic*, Lani baby, it's man-made.'

Pain throbbed in Leilani's deformed hand. She realized that with both hands she was twisting the paperback that she'd been reading.

'Psychic power comes from Gaea, see, from Earth herself, she's alive, and if you *resonate* with her, baby, she gives you a gift.

Without realizing what she'd been doing, Leilani had broken the spine of the book, crumpled the cover, and wadded some of the pages. She put the book aside and held her aching left hand in her right.

'But, baby, how can you resonate when you're being strummed with both the good natural hallucinogens like peyote but also hammered by chem-lab crap like LSD? That's where I went wrong.'

Maddoc wanted to make a baby with Sinsemilla, knowing full

well that throughout pregnancy she'd be heavily consuming hallucinogens, resulting in a high likelihood of yet another infant with severe birth defects.

'Yeah, went way wrong with the synthetic crap. I'm enlightened now. This time, I'm going to use nothing but pot, peyote, psilocybin – all natural, wholesome. And this time, I'm going to get myself a miracle child.'

Dr. Doom wasn't also Mr. Sentimentality. He didn't get weepy on anniversaries or while watching sad movies. You couldn't imagine him playing with children, reading fairy tales to children, relating to children. The desire to have a child with anyone, let alone with this woman under these circumstances, was out of character for him. His motives were as mysterious as his furtive eyes glimpsed in the mirror on the sun visor.

Sinsemilla drew the damaged paperback across the table and began to smooth the rumpled pages as she talked. 'So if Gaea smiles on us, we'll have more than one miracle baby. Two, three, maybe a litter.' She grinned mischievously and winked. 'Maybe I'll just curl up on a blanket in the corner, like a true bitch, with all my little puppies squirming against me, so many tiny hungry mouths competing for just two tits.'

All of her life, Leilani had lived in the cold tides of this deep strange sea called Sinsemilla, struggling against its drowning currents, riding out daily squalls and storms, as though she were a shipwrecked sailor clinging to a floating length of shattered deck plank, grimly aware of dark and murderous shapes circling hungrily in the fathoms under her. During these nine years, as far back as she could remember, she had coped with every surprise and every writhing horror this sea threw at her. Although she hadn't lost respect for the deadly power of the elemental force called Sinsemilla, although she remained wary and always prepared for hurricanes, her ability to cope had gradually freed her from most of the fear that had plagued her as a younger child. When strangeness is the fundamental substance of your existence, it loses its power to terrorize, and when you tread weirdness like water for nine years, you gain the confidence to face the unexpected, and even the unknown, with equanimity.

For only the second time in years and for the first time since Preston had driven away in the Durango with Lukipela into the late-afternoon dreariness of the Montana mountains, Leilani was seized by a fear that she couldn't cast off, not a passing terror such as the snake had aroused in her, but an abiding dread with many hands that clutched her throat, her heart, the pit of her stomach. This new strangeness, this irrational and sick scheme to make psychic miracle babies, shook her confidence that she would be able to understand her mother, to predict the upcoming patterns in Sinsemilla's madness, and to cope as she had always coped before.

'Litter?' Leilani said. 'All your puppies? What're you talking about?'

Still smoothing the rumpled pages in the paperback, looking down at her hands, Sinsemilla said, 'I've been taking fertility drugs. Not that I need 'em to make just one fat little piggy.' She smiled. 'I'm as fertile as a rabbit. But sometimes with fertility drugs, you know, lots of eggs plop in the basket all at once, you get twins, you get triplets, maybe more. So harmonizing with Mother Earth through peyote and magic mushrooms, plus other healthy highs, maybe I'll persuade old Gaea to help me pop out three or four wizard babies all at once, a whole nestful of pink little squirming superbabies.'

Although Leilani had long known the true nature of this woman, she had never been able to admit that one word above all others best described her. She had lived in denial, calling her mother *weak* and *selfish*, excusing her as an *addict*, resorting to evasive words like *troubled*, like *damaged*, even *crazy*. Sinsemilla was undeniably all those things, but she was something worse, something far less worthy of pity than was any addict or a merely troubled woman. Beautiful, blessed with clear blue eyes that met yours as directly as might the eyes of an angel with no reason for guile or shame, flashing a smile warm enough to enchant the sourest cynic, she was defined by one word more than any other, and the word was *evil*.

For many reasons, until now Leilani had found it hard to admit that her mother wasn't just misguided, but also wretched, vile, and rotten in the heart. All these years, she'd longed for Sinsemilla's redemption, for a day when they might be at least a normal mother and a mutant daughter; but genuine evil, the pure cold stuff, couldn't be redeemed. And if you acknowledged that you'd come from evil, that you were its spawn, what were you to think about yourself, about your own dark potential, about your chances of one day leading a good, decent, useful life? What were you to think?

As when she'd lost Luki, Leilani sat in the tortuous duel grip of fear and anguish. She trembled in recognition of the thread by which her life hung, but she also struggled to hold back tears of grief. Here, now, she surrendered forever all hope that her mother might one day be clean and straight, all hope that old Sinsemilla, once reformed, might eventually provide a mother's love. She felt stupid for having harbored that naive, impossible little dream. In the instant, a termitic loneliness ate away the core of Leilani's heart and left her hollow, shaking not only with fear, but also with a chill of utter isolation. She felt abandoned, deserted, forsaken.

She detested the weakness in herself revealed by a tremor in her voice: 'Why? Why babies, why babies at all? Just because *he* wants them?'

Her mother looked up from the book, slid it across the table to Leilani, and repeated the interminable mantra that she had composed to express her satisfaction with herself when she was in a good mood: 'I am a sly cat, I am a summer wind, I am birds in flight, I am the sun, I am the sea, I am *me!*'

'What does that even *mean*?' Leilani asked.

'It means – who else but your own mama is cool enough to bring a new human race into the world, a psychic humanity bonded to Gaea? I'll be the mother of the future, Lani, the new Eve.'

Sinsemilla believed this nonsense. Her belief imbued her face with a beatific radiance and brought a sparkle of wonder to her eyes.

Maddoc surely wouldn't put any credence in this garbage, however, because the doom doctor wasn't moronic. Evil, yes, he had earned the right to have his towels monogrammed with that word, and he loved himself no less than Sinsemilla loved herself. But he wasn't stupid. He didn't believe that fetuses carried to term in a bath of hallucinogens were likely to be the superhuman forerunners of a new humanity. He wanted babies for his own reasons, for some enigmatic purpose that had nothing to do with being the new Adam or with a yearning for fatherhood.

'Wizard babies by late April, early May,' said Sinsemilla. 'I've been knocked up close a month. I'm already a brood bitch, filled up with wizard babies that'll change the world. Their time's coming, but first *you*.'

'Me what?'

'Healed, you ninny,' said Sinsemilla, getting to her feet. 'Made good, made right, made pretty. The only reason we've been haulin' ass from Texas to Maine to shitcan towns in Arkansas all these past four years.'

'Yeah, healed, just like Luki.'

Sinsemilla didn't hear the sarcasm. She smiled and nodded, as though she expected Luki, fully remade, to be beamed back to them at their next rest stop. 'Your daddy says it'll happen soon, baby. He's got a feeling maybe in Idaho we'll meet some ETs ready for a laying-on of hands. North of a hunch, he says, and south of a vision, a real strong feeling that you'll get your healing soon.'

The brood bitch went to the refrigerator and got a beer to wash down whatever baby-shaping cactus or mushroom snacks were medically appropriate for midmorning.

On her way back to the co-pilot's chair, she ruffled Leilani's hair. 'Soon, baby, you'll go from pumpkin to princess.'

As usual, Sinsemilla got her fairy tales screwed up. The pumpkin had been transformed into Cinderella's coach. Mater was remembering the story of the frog that became a prince, not a princess.

Hula-hula, grass skirts swishing.

Sun god on the ceiling.

Sinsemilla giggling in the co-pilot's chair.

The mirror. Preston's twitchy eyes.

Beyond the panoramic windshield, the vast Mojave blazed, and sunshine seemed to gather in molten pools upon the desert plains.

In Nun's Lake, Idaho, a man claimed to have had contact with extraterrestrial physicians.

In the Montana woods, Lukipela waited for his sister at the bottom of a hole. He was no longer her precious brother, but just a worm farm, gone not to the stars but gone forever.

When she and Preston were alone in a deepness of forest, as he and Luki had been alone, when they were beyond observation, beyond the reach of justice, would he kill her with compassion? Would he press a chloroform-soaked rag against her face to anesthetize her quickly and then finish the job with a lethal injection while she slept, sparing her as much terror as possible? Or in the lonely cloisters of ancient evergreens, where civilizing sunlight barely reached, would Preston be a different man than the one he played in public, perhaps less man than beast, free to admit that he took pleasure not from the administration of mercy, as he called it, but from the killing itself?

Leilani read the answer in the predator's eyes, as he kept a watch on her by angled mirror. The quiet deaths that were arranged with genteel rituals as complex as tea ceremonies – like that of penguin-collecting Tetsy – didn't fully slake Preston's thirst for violence, but in the solitudinous woods, he could drink his fill. Leilani knew that if ever she were alone with the pseudofather in any remote place, her death, like Lukipela's, would be hard, brutal, and prolonged.

He married Sinsemilla in part because in her deepest drug stupors, she seemed dead, and death stirred Preston as beauty stirred other men. Furthermore, she'd come with two children who, by his philosophy, needed to die, and he had been attracted to her because he possessed the desire to fulfill her children's need. So was his purpose in breeding new babies really so enigmatic? Preston was fond of saying that death was never truly a tragedy but always a natural event, because we are all born to die, sooner or later. From his perspective, could any significant difference exist between children being born to die, as are we all, and children *bred* to die?

50

Elsewhere, the California dream might still have a glowing tan; but here it had blistered, peeled, and faded. Once a good residential street, the neighborhood had been rezoned for mixed use. Depression-era bungalows and two-story Spanish houses – never grand, but at one time graceful and well maintained – now wanted paint, stucco patches, and repairs to crumbling porch steps. Some sagging residences had been torn down decades ago, replaced by fast-food outlets and corner minimalls. These commercial properties, too, were beyond their best days: bottom-feeding burger franchises you'd never see advertised on television; shabby beauty salons, themselves in need of makeovers; a thrift shop selling all things used.

Micky parked at the curb and locked her car. Ordinarily, she wouldn't have worried that her aging Camaro might be boosted, but the low quality of the other iron on the block suggested that her tired wheels might present a temptation.

In the windows that flanked the front door of the narrow house, a blue neon sign in the left pane announced PALM READER, and in the right glowed an orange neon outline of a hand, bright even on a sunny morning. The cracked and hoved walkway led to a blue door featuring a painting of a mystic eye, but it also branched toward a flight of exterior stairs, most likely not originally part of the house, at the south side of the structure, where a discreet sign indicated that the detective's offices were on the second floor.

The house stood among enormous phoenix palms, one of which shaded the stairs with its great green crown. The tree hadn't been trimmed in years; a densely layered, twenty-foot-long collar of dead fronds drooped over one another and encircled the bole, creating a fire danger and an ideal home for tree rats.

Ascending toward the covered landing, Micky heard the rustle of busy rodents scurrying along vertical tunnels in the thatchwork of dry brown fronds, as though they were pacing her, keeping her under observation.

When no one responded to the doorbell, she knocked. When the knock was ignored, she leaned on the bell again.

The man who finally responded to her insistent summons was big, good-looking in a rough sort of way, with melancholy eyes. He wore tattered sneakers, chinos, and a Hawaiian shirt. He had skipped his morning shave.

'You,' he said, without preamble, 'are a woman in some kind of trouble, but I'm not in that line of work anymore.'

'Maybe I'm just from County Vector Control, want to talk to you about the rat farm in this tree right here.'

'That would sure be a waste of talent.'

Expecting a nasty crack in the tradition of F. Bronson, Micky bristled. 'Yeah? What's that supposed to mean?'

'It wasn't an insult, if that's how you took it.'

'Wasn't it? Talent, huh? You think I should be turning tricks or something?'

'That's never been your type of trouble. I just meant I think you could kick something way bigger than a rat's ass.'

'You're the PI, the detective?'

'Used to be. Like I said. Closed up shop.'

She hadn't called ahead because she'd been afraid that he would obtain a quick financial report on her before she got here. Now, having seen the place, she figured most of his clients weren't the type that American Express pursued with offers of platinum cards.

'I'm Micky Bellsong. I'm not with Vector Control, but you've got a rat problem.'

'Everybody does,' he said, and somehow managed to convey that he wasn't talking about long-tailed rodents. He started to shut her out.

She planted one foot on the threshold. 'I'm not leaving till you either hear me all the way through – or snap my neck and throw me down the stairs.'

He seemed to consider the second option, studying her throat. 'You ought to sell Jesus door-to-door. The whole world would be saved by Tuesday.'

'You did good work for a woman I knew once. She was desperate, she couldn't pay much, but you did good work anyway.'

'I take it you can't pay much, either.'

'Part cash, part IOU. Might take me a while to pay you off, but if I don't, I'll break my own legs and save you the trouble.'

'Wouldn't be any trouble. I might enjoy it. But the fact still is, I've gone out of business.'

'The woman you helped was Wynette Jenkins. She was in prison at the time. That's where I met her.'

'Sure. I remember.'

Wynette had arranged for her six-year-old son, Danny, to live with his maternal grandparents while she did her time. She'd been in the can less than a week when her ex-husband, Vin, had taken the boy to live with him. The law refused to intervene because Vin was the child's legal father. He was also a mean drunk and a wife abuser who had frequently knocked Danny around, and Wynette knew that he would terrorize the boy on a daily basis and eventually scar him for life, if not kill him. She heard about Farrel through another prisoner and persuaded her parents to approach him. Within two months, Farrel had provided the police with evidence of Vin's criminal activities that got the man arrested, indicted, and separated from his son. They returned the boy to the custody of Wynette's parents. Her folks said they suspected Farrel had taken the case, even at a loss, because it involved a child in trouble, and that he had a soft spot for kids.

Still employing her right foot as a doorstop, Micky said, 'A little girl's going to be killed if I don't help her. And I can't help her alone.'

This dramatic claim had an effect opposite of the one that she expected. The detective's expression of weary indifference hardened into a glower, although his sudden anger seemed not to be directed at her. 'Lady, I'm exactly who you *don't* need. You want real cops.'

'They're not going to believe me. It's a strange case. And this girl . . . she's special.'

'They're all special.' Farrel's voice was flat, almost cold; and perhaps Micky should have heard a dismissive platitude in those three words, or even callousness. But in his eyes, she thought she saw pain instead of genuine anger, and suddenly his glower seemed to be a mask that concealed an anguish he'd long kept private. 'Cops are who you want. I know. I used to be one.'

'I'm an ex-con. The girl's sonofabitch stepfather is rich and well connected. And he's highly regarded, mainly by a bunch of fools, but they're fools whose opinion matters. Even if I could get the cops to take me seriously, I couldn't make them move fast enough to help this girl.'

'There's nothing I can do for you,' he insisted.

'You know the deal,' Micky said stubbornly. 'Either hear me out – or throw me down the stairs. And if you try throwin', for starters you'll need Bactine, Band-Aids, and a sitz bath for your balls.'

He sighed. 'Pushing me like this is a mile past desperation, lady.'

'I never claimed I wasn't desperate. But I'm glad to hear you think I'm a lady.'

'Can't figure why the hell I answered the door,' he said sourly.

'In your heart, you were hoping for a flower delivery.'

He moved backward. 'Whatever your story is, just spit it out plain and simple. Don't bother strumming on the heartstrings.'

'Can't strum what I can't find.'

His living room also served as his office. To the left stood a desk, two client chairs, one file cabinet. To the right a single armchair was aimed at a television set; a small table and a floorlamp flanked the chair. Bare walls. Books piled in the corners.

The drab furniture had probably been purchased in the thrift shop on the corner. The carpet looked as cheap as any loom could weave it. Everything appeared to be scrubbed and polished, however, and the air smelled like lemon-scented furniture wax and pine-scented disinfectant. The place might have been the austere cell of a monk with a cleaning obsession.

A cramped kitchen lay visible beyond one of two interior doors. The other door, closed now, evidently led to a bedroom and bath.

As Farrel sat behind the desk, Micky settled in an unpadded, rail-backed chair provided for clients, which was uncomfortable enough to serve as dungeon furniture.

The detective had been working at his desk, on the computer, when Micky had rung the doorbell. The printer fan hummed softly. She couldn't see the screen.

At a few minutes past ten in the morning, Farrel had also been working on a can of Budweiser. Now he picked it up, took a swallow.

'Early lunch or late breakfast?' Micky wondered.

'Breakfast. If it makes me look any more like a responsible citizen, I also had a Pop-Tart.'

'I'm familiar with that diet.'

'If it's all the same to you, let's can the chitchat. Just tell me your sad story if you really have to, and then let me get back to my retirement.'

Micky hesitated, wanting to start her story well, and remembered Aunt Gen's prophetic words from Monday evening, not yet four days past. She said, 'Sometimes a person's life can change for the better in one moment of grace, like a miracle almost. Someone so special can come along, all unexpected, and pivot you in a new direction, change you forever. You ever had that experience, Mr. Farrel?'

He grimaced. 'You *are* peddling Jesus door-to-door.'

As succinctly as possible, Micky told him about Leilani Klonk, old Sinsemilla, and the pseudofather on the hunt for extraterrestrial healers. She told him about Lukipela gone to the stars.

She withheld Preston Maddoc's identity, however, afraid that Farrel shared F. Bronson's admiration for the killer. If he heard the name, he might never give her the opportunity to win his involvement.

More than once as Micky talked, Farrel gazed at the computer, as though her story wasn't sufficiently involving to keep him from being distracted by whatever was on the screen.

He asked no questions and gave no reliable signs of interest. At times he leaned back in his chair, eyes closed, so still and so lacking in expression that he might have been asleep. At other times, his features once again seemed as hard as mortared stone, and he made eye contact of such discomfiting intensity that Micky thought he had lost patience and would throw her down the stairs regardless of her threat to put up a fight.

Breaking off a nail-you-to-the-wall stare, he abruptly rose to his feet. 'The more I hear, the more I know I'm not right for this. Never would have been right, even when I was in business. I don't even see what you could want from me.'

'I'm getting there.'

'And I suppose you *insist* on getting there. So to lubricate my way through this meeting, I'll need another beer. You want one?'

'No thanks.'

'I thought you were familiar with this diet.'

'I'm not on it anymore.'

'Hooray for you.'

'I've already lost all the years I can afford to lose.'

'Yeah, well, not me.'

Farrel went into the kitchen, and a fog of gray discouragement crept into Micky as she watched him through the open door. After taking a beer from the refrigerator, he pulled off the tab, drained a couple ounces in one swallow, set the can on a counter, and spiked the remaining Budweiser with a shot of whiskey.

Returning to the desk but not to his chair, Farrel seemed to vibrate with a barely throttled fury that Micky had said nothing to evoke. As he stood there staring down at her, his voice remained low, weary rather than angry, but also tight with a tension that he couldn't conceal. 'You're wasting my time and yours, Ms. Bellsong. But mine isn't worth much. So if you want to wait while I use the john, that's fine. Or are you ready to leave now?'

She almost left. Noah Farrel appeared to be as worthless as he was indifferent to her problem.

She remained in the rail-backed chair, however, because the anguish in his eyes belied his apparent indifference. On some level, she had reached him even though he didn't want to become involved. 'You still haven't heard me out.'

'By the time I *have* heard you out, I'm going to need eardrum transplants.'

When he left the room, he closed the door to the bedroom-bath. And he took the spiked Budweiser with him.

He probably didn't need to use the john, and he certainly didn't need another breakfast beer. These were excuses to interrupt Micky's story and thus dilute its impact. Leilani's predicament had affected him, sure enough; but Farrel was determined not to be affected to the extent that he would feel obligated to help her.

410

From bitter experience, Micky knew how useful alcohol could be when making a morally bankrupt decision didn't come naturally and when you needed to numb your conscience a little in order to do the wrong thing. She recognized the strategy.

Farrel wouldn't return until he'd drunk the fortified Budweiser. More likely than not, he would visit the kitchen for a third serving before at last sitting down at his desk again. Tuning Micky out would be easier by then, and he would be able to convince himself that the wrong thing was the right move.

If she hadn't known the great kindness he'd done for Wynette, she might not have hung in here as long as this.

But she also held on to a thread of hope because Noah Farrel clearly didn't have long-term experience with morning drinking or perhaps with drinking binges at any hour. Evidence of his nouveau-drunk status was evident in the self-conscious way he handled the can, first pushing it aside as if shunning it, but a moment later turning it nervously in his hands, tracing the rim with one thumb, clicking a fingernail against the aluminum as if to assess by sound how much brew remained, utterly lacking the casualness of a seasoned lush's relationship with his poison.

Micky's history with drink convinced her that pressing Farrel harder, right now, would fail to move him and that this was one of those times when retreat – and special tactics – would prove to be the wiser course. She needed him for his expertise, because she couldn't afford another detective; she was depending on the kindness that he had shown Wynette and on his rumored weakness for cases involving children at risk.

A lined yellow legal pad and a pen lay among other items on the detective's desk. The moment Farrel left the room, Micky snatched up the pen and pad to write a message:

Leilani's stepfather is Preston Maddoc. Look him up. He's killed 11 people. Uses the name Jordan Banks, but was married under his real name. Where were they married? Proof? Who is Sinsemilla, really? How do we prove she had a disabled son? Time running out. Gut feeling – the girl dead in a week. Reach me through my aunt, Geneva Davis.

She concluded the message with Aunt Gen's phone number and put the legal pad on the desk.

From her purse, she withdrew three hundred dollars in twenties. This was the most she could afford to pay him. In fact, she couldn't afford this much, but she calculated that it was a sum sufficient to make him feel obligated to do *something*.

She hesitated. He might spend this retainer on beer, of course. She had too little money to risk ten bucks on a gamble, let alone three hundred.

One thing about him, above all else, convinced her to put the cash atop the legal pad and weight it with the pen. Nouveau drunk or not, he was obviously a haunted man, and by Micky's reckoning, that counted as a point in his favor. She didn't know what loss or what failure haunted him, but her own journey had taught her that haunted people are not dissolute by nature and that they will try to exorcise their demons if a caring hand is extended to them at the right time.

Before leaving, she stepped around the desk to take a quick look at his computer. He was on-line. Skimming the displayed text, she discovered that it was part of an article exposing an epidemic of supposedly compassionate killing by nurses who considered themselves angels of death.

A shudder, less fear than wonder, traced the architecture of Micky's spine as she sensed a strange synchronicity linking her life to Farrel's. Gen often said that what we perceive to be coincidences are in fact carefully placed tiles in a mosaic pattern the rest of which we can't apprehend. Now Micky sensed that intricate mosaic, vast and panoramic, and mysterious.

Leaving the apartment, she quietly closed the door behind her, as though she were a burglar making off with a treasure of jewels while her victim dozed unaware.

Hurriedly, she descended the palm-shaded stairs.

The rising heat of late morning had made the rats lethargic. Silent and unseen, they hung like foul fruit among the layers of collapsed brown fronds.

51

Thanks to direct-to-brain megadata downloading, Curtis knows that whereas New Jersey has a population density of nearly eleven hundred people per square mile, Nevada has fewer than fifteen per square mile, most of whom are located in and around the gambling meccas of Las Vegas and Reno. Tens of thousands of the state's 110,000 square miles are all but devoid of people, from the desert barrens in the south to the mountains in the north. Principal products include slot machines, other gaming devices, aerospace technology, gold, silver, potatoes, onions, and topless dancers. In *Carson City Kid*, Mr. Roy Rogers – with the courageous aid of the indispensable Mr. Gabby Hayes – successfully pursues a murderous Nevada gambler; however, this is a 1940 film, shot in a more innocent time, and it involves no bare-breasted women. If Mr. Rogers and Mr. Hayes were still engaged upon heroic deeds, they would no doubt these days be uncovering nefarious activity at Area 51, the famous Nevada military site widely believed to house extraterrestrials either alive or dead, or both, as well as spacecraft from other worlds, but which is in fact involved in far stranger and more disturbing business. Anyway, vast regions of Nevada are lonely, mysterious, forbidding, and particularly spooky at night.

From the crossroads store and service station – where the real mom and pop lie dead in the SUV, and where two tangled and bullet-riddled masses of preposterous physiology lie waiting to scare the living hell out of whoever finds them – Highway 93 leads north and isn't intersected by a paved road until it meets Highway 50. This occurs thirty miles south of Ely.

Piloting the Fleetwood with jet-jockey skill, coaxing more speed out of it than seems probable, Polly decides against turning east on Highway 50, which leads to the Utah state line.

Boasting a population in excess of 150,000, Reno lies to the west. Plenty of motion and commotion in Reno. But between here and there, Highway 50 crosses 330 miles of semiarid mountains, just the type of desolate landscape in which one boy and two showgirls – even two heavily armed showgirls – might vanish forever.

As the moon sets and the night deepens, Polly continues north on Highway 93 another 140 miles, until they intersect Interstate 80. One hundred seventy-seven miles to the west lies Winnemucca, where in 1900, Butch Cassidy and the Sundance Kid robbed the First National Bank. One hundred eighty-five miles to the east stands Salt Lake City, where Curtis would enjoy hearing the Mormon Tabernacle Choir perform under the world's largest domed roof without center supports.

Cass, relieving Polly at the wheel, proceeds north on Highway 93, because neither sister is in a touristy mood. Sixty-eight miles ahead lies Jackpot, Nevada, just this side of the Idaho state line.

'When we get there, we'll tank up and keep moving,' says Cass.

From the co-pilot's chair, Curtis admits to a gap in his mission preparation: 'I don't have any info about the town of Jackpot.'

'It's not much of a town,' Cass declares. 'It's a wide place in the road where people throw away all their money.'

'Does this have religious significance?' he wonders.

'Only if you worship a roulette wheel,' Polly explains from the lounge, where she's resting on the sofa with Old Yeller. Though she's gotten no answers, she's been whispering questions to the dog. She speaks in a normal voice to Curtis: 'Jackpot's got like five hundred hotel rooms and two casinos, with a couple of first-rate buffets for six bucks, surrounded by thousands of empty acres. After a satisfying dinner and bankruptcy, you can drive to a nice barren place, commune with nature, and blow your brains out in private.'

'Maybe,' Curtis theorizes, 'that's why so many people back at the Neary Ranch were buying Grandma's locally famous black-bean-and-corn salsa. Maybe they were going to use it in Jackpot.'

Polly and Cass are quiet. Then Cass says, 'Things don't often go over my head, Curtis, but that one cleared my scalp by six inches.'

'It was so far over mine,' Polly admits, 'I didn't even feel the breeze when it passed.'

'They were selling cold drinks and T-shirts and stuff off the hay wagon,' Curtis explains. 'The sign for Grandma's salsa said it was hot enough to blow your head clean off, though I personally doubt that any method of decapitation could be clean.'

The twins are silent again, this time for a quarter of a mile.

Then Polly says, 'You're a strange lad, Curtis Hammond.'

'I've been told that I'm not quite right, too sweet for this world, and a stupid Gump,' Curtis acknowledges, 'but I sure would like to fit in someday.'

'I've been thinking sort of *Rain Man*,' says Cass.

'Good movie!' Curtis exclaims. 'Dustin Hoffman and Tom Cruise. Did you know that Tom Cruise is friends with a serial killer?'

'I didn't know that,' Polly confesses.

'A guy named Vern Tuttle, old enough to be your grandfather, collects the teeth of his victims. I heard him talking to Tom Cruise in a mirror, though I was so scared, I didn't register whether the mirror was a communications device linking him to Mr. Cruise, like the mirror the evil queen uses in *Snow White and the Seven Dwarfs*, or just an ordinary mirror. Anyway, I'm sure Mr. Cruise doesn't know Vern Tuttle is a serial killer, cause if he did, he'd bring him to justice. What's your favorite Tom Cruise movie?'

'*Jerry Maguire*,' says Cass.

'*Top Gun*,' says Polly.

'What's your favorite Humphrey Bogart movie?' Curtis asks.

'*Casablanca*,' the twins say simultaneously.

'Mine too,' Curtis confirms. 'Favorite Katherine Hepburn movie?'

Polly says, '*Woman of the Year*,' Cass says, '*The Philadelphia Story*,' but they change their minds in unison: '*Bringing Up Baby*.'

And so they proceed north through the night, socializing with the ease of old friends, never once discussing the shootout at the crossroads store, the shapechanging assassins, or the dog's use of the laptop computer to warn Polly of the presence of evil aliens.

Curtis doesn't deceive himself that his rapidly developing ability to socialize and his conversational legerdemain will distract the sisters from these subjects forever. Castoria and Polluxia aren't fools, and sooner or later, they are going to request explanations.

In fact, recalling the aplomb with which they handled themselves at the crossroads, they are likely to *demand* explanations when they are ready to broach the subject. Then he'll have to decide how much truth to tell them. They are his friends, and he is loath to lie to friends; the more they know, however, the more they'll be endangered.

After topping off the fuel tank in Jackpot, pausing neither for one of the buffets nor to observe a suicide, they cross the state line into Idaho and continue north to the city of Twin Falls, which is surrounded by five hundred thousand acres of ideal farmland irrigated by the Snake River. Curtis knows a great many facts about the geological and human history of the city, the 'Magic Valley' area, and the vast lava beds north of the Snake River, and he dazzles the sisters by sharing this wealth of knowledge.

With a population of more than twenty-seven thousand Twin Falls offers some cover, making the boy less easily detectable than he's been since he arrived in Colorado and first became Curtis Hammond. He is safer here, but not reliably safe.

Dawn is not yet two hours old when Cass parks the Fleetwood in an RV campground. A night without rest and the long drive have taken a toll, though the sisters still look so glamorous and so desirable that the campground attendant, assisting with the utility hookups, seems in danger of polishing his shoes with his tongue.

Curtis doesn't need to sleep, but he fakes a yawn as the twins extend the sofabed in the lounge and dress it with sheets. Old Yeller has recently learned more about the dark side of the universe than any dog needs to know, and has been a bit edgy since the shootout. She'll benefit from sleep, and Curtis will share her dreams for a while before spending the rest of the day planning his future.

While the sisters prepare the bed, they switch on the TV. Every major network is offering exhaustive coverage of the manhunt for the drug lords who may possess military weapons. At last the government has confirmed that three FBI agents died in a gun battle at the truck stop in Utah; three others were wounded.

Reports are circulating of a more violent confrontation in a restored ghost town, west of the truck stop. But FBI and military spokesmen decline to comment on these rumors.

In fact, the government is providing so few details about the crisis that the TV reporters have insufficient information to fill the ample air time given to this story. Inanely, they interview one another on their opinions, fears, and speculations.

Authorities haven't provided photographs or even police-artist sketches of the men they're hunting, which convinces some reporters that the government doesn't know all the identities of their quarry.

'Idiots,' says Polly, 'There aren't any drug lords, only evil aliens. Right, Curtis?'

'Right.'

Cass says, 'Are the feds searching just for you—'

'Right.'

'— because you saw these ETs and know too much—'

'Yeah, exactly.'

'— or are they also after the aliens?'

'Uh, well, both of us, I guess.'

'If they know you're alive, why have they put out the story that you were killed by drug lords in Colorado?' Polly wonders.

'I don't know.' Mom had counseled that eventually every cover story develops contradictions and that instead of devising elaborate explanations to patch over those holes, which will only create new contradictions, you should instead simply express bafflement whenever possible. Liars are expected to be slick, whereas bafflement usually sounds sincere. 'I just don't know. It doesn't make sense, does it?'

Cass says, 'If they said you'd survived, they could plaster your face all over the media, and everyone would help them look for you.'

'I'm baffled.' Curtis is remorseful about this deceit, but also proud of the smoothness with which he applies his mother's advice, controlling a situation that might have aroused suspicion. 'I really am baffled. I don't know why they haven't done that. Strange, huh?'

The sisters exchange one of those blue-laser glances that seem to transmit encyclopedias of information between them.

They resort to one of their mesmerizing duologues that cause Curtis's eyes to shift metronomically from one perfect frosted-red mouth to the other. Tucking in a sheet, Polly starts with: 'Well, this isn't—'

'– the time,' Cass continues.

'– to get into all that—'

'– UFO stuff—'

'– and what happened—'

'– back at the service station.' Cass stuffs a pillow into a case. 'We're too tired—'

'– too fuzzy-headed—'

'– to think straight—'

'– and when we do sit down to talk—'

'– we want to be sharp—'

'– because we have a lot—'

'– of questions. This whole thing is—'

'– mondo weird,' Polly concludes.

And Cass picks up with: 'We haven't wanted—'

'– to talk about it—'

'– during the drive—'

'– because we need to think—'

'– to absorb what happened.'

Sister to sister, by telemetric stare, volumes are communicated without a word, and then all four blue eyes fix on Curtis. He feels as though he is being subjected to an electron-beam CT scan of such a sophisticated nature that it not only reveals the condition of his arteries and internal organs, but also maps his secrets and the true condition of his soul.

'We'll catch eight hours of sleep,' says Polly, 'and discuss the situation over an early dinner.'

'Maybe by then,' says Cass, 'some things won't seem quite so . . . baffling as they seem now.'

'Maybe,' Curtis says, 'but maybe not. When things are baffling they usually don't unbaffle themselves. There's just, you know, a certain amount of baffling stuff that always, like, really baffles you, and I've found that it's best to accept bafflement whenever it comes along, and then move on.'

Paralyzed by the intensity of the double blue stares, Curtis is motivated to review what he has just said, and as he hears his words replaying in his mind, they no longer seem as smooth and convincing as they did when he spoke them. He smiles, because according to Mom, a smile can sell what words alone cannot.

Even if he were selling dollars for dimes, the sisters might not be buying. His smile doesn't elicit return smiles from them.

Polly says, 'Better sleep, Curtis. God knows what might be coming, but whatever it is, we'll need to be rested to deal with it.'

'And don't open the door,' Cass warns. 'The burglar alarm can't distinguish whether someone's coming in or going out.'

They are too tired to discuss recent events with him now, but they're ensuring that he won't slip away before they have a chance to make a lot of chin music with him later.

The sisters retire to the bedroom.

In the lounge, Curtis slips under a sheet and a thin blanket. The dog has yet to receive a bath, but the boy welcomes her onto the sofabed, where she curls atop the covers.

Applying will against matter, on the micro level where will can win, he might disengage the burglar alarm. But he owes the twins some honest answers, and he doesn't want to leave them entirely mystified.

Besides, after a difficult and tumultuous journey, he has at last found friends. His socializing skills might not be as smooth as he had briefly believed they were, but he has made two fine chums in the dazzling Spelkenfelters, and he is loath to face the world alone again, with just his sister-become. The dog is a cherished companion, but she isn't all the company that he needs. Though praised by nature poets, solitude is just isolation, and loneliness curls in the heart like a worm in an apple, eating hope and leaving a hollow structure.

Furthermore, the twins remind him of his lost mother. Not in their appearance. For all her virtues, Mom wasn't born to be a Las Vegas showgirl. The twins' spirit, their high intelligence, their toughness, and their tenderness are all qualities that his mother possessed in abundance, and in their company, he feels the blessed sense of belonging that arises from being among family.

The weary dog sleeps.

Placing one hand upon her flank, feeling the slow thump of her noble heart, Curtis enters her dreams and grows aware of the playful Presence, from which simple creatures like the dog have not distanced themselves. Worlds away from any place that he has ever called *home*, the orphaned boy quietly cries, less with grief for his loss than with happiness for his mother; she has crossed the great divide into the light, and now in God's presence she knows a joy similar to the one that her son had always known in *her* presence. He can't sleep, but for a while, he finds a little peace this side of Heaven.

52

The sun burned a bright hole in the western sky, still a few hours above the quenching sea, and the breeze that swept through the trailer park seemed to blow down out of that hole, hot and dry and seasoned with a scent of scorched metal.

Friday afternoon, only five hours after Micky met with Noah Farrel, she loaded a single suitcase in the trunk of her Camaro.

She'd sprung for an oil change, new filters, new fan belts, a lubrication, and four new tires. Counting the money that she had advanced to the detective, more than half her bankroll was gone.

She dared not fail to connect with Leilani in Nun's Lake, Idaho. Even if she discovered where Maddoc intended to go from there, she probably wouldn't have enough cash left to chase him down and then get all the way back to California with the girl.

When Micky returned to the house, Aunt Gen was in the kitchen, fitting two Ziploc bags full of ice into a picnic cooler already packed with sandwiches, cookies, apples, and cans of Diet Coke. With these provisions, Micky wouldn't have to waste time stopping for meals through lunch tomorrow, and she would save money, as well.

'Don't you try to drive all night,' Aunt Gen cautioned.

'Not to worry.'

'They don't even have a full day's head start, so you'll catch up with them easy enough.'

'I should make Sacramento by midnight. I'll get a motel there, zonk out for six hours, and try to reach Seattle by tomorrow evening. Then Nun's Lake, Idaho, late Sunday.'

'Things can happen to women alone on the road,' Geneva worried.

'True. But things can happen to women alone in their own homes.'

Putting the lid on the insulated picnic cooler, Geneva said, 'Honey, if the motel clerk looks like Anthony Perkins or if some guy at a service station looks like Anthony Hopkins, or if you meet a man *anywhere* and he looks like Alec Baldwin, you kick him in the crotch before he has a chance to say two words, and you run.'

'I thought you shot Alec Baldwin in New Orleans.'

'You know, that man's been pushed off a tall building, drowned, stabbed, mauled by a bear, shot – but he just keeps coming back.'

'I'll be on the lookout for him,' Micky promised, lifting the picnic cooler off the table. 'As for Anthony Hopkins – Hannibal Lecter or not, he looks like a Huggy Bear.'

'Maybe I should go along with you, dear, ride shotgun,' Geneva said, following Micky to the front door.

'Maybe that would be a good idea if we *had* a shotgun.' Outside, she squinted into the hard sunlight that flared off the white Camaro. 'Anyway, you've got to stay here to take Noah Farrel's call.'

'What if he never calls?'

At the car, Micky opened the passenger's door. 'He will.'

'What if he can't find the proof you need?'

'He will,' Micky said, setting the cooler on the passenger's seat. 'Listen, what's happened to my aunt Sunshine all of a sudden?'

'Maybe we should call the police.'

Micky closed the car door. 'Which police would we call? Here in Santa Ana? Maddoc's not in their jurisdiction anymore. Call the cops in whatever town he might be passing through in California or Oregon, or Nevada, depending on the route he's taken? Hitler could be passing through, and as long as he kept moving, they wouldn't care. Call the FBI? Me an ex-con, and them busy chasing drug lords?'

'Maybe by the time you get to Idaho, this Mr. Farrel will have your proof, and you can go to the police up there.'

'Maybe. But it's a different world from the one you see in those old black-and-white movies, Aunt Gen. Cops cared more in those days. *People* cared more. Something happened. Everything changed. The whole world feels . . . broken. More and more, we're on our own.'

'And you think I've lost *my* sunshine,' said Geneva.

Micky smiled. 'Well, I've never been exactly jolly. But you know, even with this damn hard thing to get done, I feel better than I've felt in . . . maybe better than I've ever felt.'

A shadow seemed to pass through Gen's green eyes, between the lens and an inner light, darkening her stare. 'I'm scared.'

'Me too. But I'd be more scared if I *wasn't* doing this.'

Geneva nodded. 'I packed a little jar of sweet pickles.'

'I like sweet pickles.'

'And a little jar of green olives.'

'You're the best.'

'I didn't have any pepperoncinis.'

'Oh. Well, then, I guess the trip is off.'

They hugged each other. For a while, Micky thought Gen wasn't going to release her, and then she herself couldn't let go.

Gen's words came as hushed as a prayer: *'Bring her back.'*

'I will,' Micky whispered, half convinced that making the pledge in a louder voice would seem like bragging and would tempt fate.

After Micky got in the car and started the engine, Gen kept one hand on the sill of the open window. 'I packed three bags of M&M's.'

'After this trip, I'll be on a strict lettuce diet.'

'And, dear, there's a special treat in a small green jar. Be sure you try it with your dinner tonight.'

'I love you, Aunt Gen.'

Blotting her eyes with a Kleenex, Geneva let go of the door and stepped back from the Camaro.

Then, as Micky pulled away, Geneva hurried after her, waving the tear-dampened tissue.

Micky braked to a full stop, and Gen leaned down to the window again. 'Little mouse, do you remember a riddle that I used to puzzle you with when you were just a girl?'

Micky shook her head. 'Riddle?'

'What will you find behind the door—'

'– that is one door away from Heaven,' Micky completed.

'You *do* remember. And can you remember how you gave me answer after answer, so many answers, and none of them the right one?'

Micky nodded to avoid speaking.

The shadowed green of Geneva's eyes shimmered beneath

brimming emotion. 'I should have known from your answers that something was so wrong in your life.'

Micky managed to say, 'I'm okay, Gen. None of that is dragging me down anymore.'

'What will you find behind the door that is one door away from Heaven? Do you remember the *right* answer?'

'Yes.'

'And do you believe it's true?'

'You told me the right answer when I couldn't get it, so it must be true, Aunt Gen. You told me the right answer . . . and you never lie.'

In the afternoon sun, Geneva's shadow lay longer than she was, thinner than she was, blacker than the blacktop on which it reclined, and the gentle breeze stirred her gold-and-silver hair into a lazily shifting nimbus, with the result that a supernatural quality settled upon her. 'Honey, remember the lesson of that riddle. This is a great good thing you're doing, a crazy-reckless good thing, but if maybe it doesn't work out, there's always that door and what's beyond it.'

'It's going to work out, Aunt Gen.'

'You come home.'

'Where else am I gonna get free rent and such good cookin'?'

'You come *home*,' Geneva insisted with an edge of desperation.

'I will.'

Geneva radiant in the sunshine, as though she were as much a source of light as the sun itself. Geneva reaching through the open window to touch Micky's cheek. Reluctantly withdrawing her hand. No cheerful movie memory softened the anguish of the moment. Then Geneva in the rearview mirror, waving goodbye. Geneva dwindling, shining in the sun, waving, waving. A corner turned, Geneva gone. Micky alone and Nun's Lake over sixteen hundred miles away.

53

Packed full of wizard babies, the hive queen rode into Nevada beside the scorpion who had serviced her, their already inscrutable eyes concealed by sunglasses, a pair of celebrity insects abroad in the royal coach.

They continued to conspire with each other, speaking in lowered voices. Their conversation was punctuated by twitters of laughter and by the queen's squeals of manic delight.

Considering what old Sinsemilla had already revealed, Leilani couldn't logically deduce even the general shape of the additional secrets that these two might still share. As a would-be writer, she didn't worry about her failure of imagination, for no one this side of Hell could be expected to conceive of the horrors that squirmed in the deeper recesses of either her mother's mind or Dr. Doom's.

West of Las Vegas, they stopped for lunch in the coffee shop at a hotel-casino surrounded by miles of barren sand and rock. The establishment had been erected in this wasteland not because the natural setting was ideal for a resort, but because a significant percentage of the multitudes who traveled to Vegas would stop here first, impatient to skin Lady Luck, and would themselves be fleeced.

This gaudy dream palace provided cheap drinks to boozehounds, induced compulsive gamblers to bankrupt themselves at games of chance in which the rules gave the main chance to the house, satisfied self-destructive impulses ranging between a lust to consume mountains of rich desserts from an all-you-can-eat buffet to the sweaty desire to be punished by sadistic prostitutes with whips. Yet even *here*, the hotel coffee shop offered a cholesterol-free egg-white omelet with fat-free tofu cheese and blanched broccoli.

Trapping Leilani between herself and Preston in a semicircular red leatherette booth, old Sinsemilla ordered two of those flavorless constructions, one for herself and one for her daughter, with dry toast and two fresh-fruit plates. The doom doctor ate a cheeseburger and fries – grinning, licking his lips, being insufferable.

Their waitress was a teenage girl with oily blond hair worn in a shaggy chop that apparently resulted from the risky application of a lawn mower. The name tag on her uniform announced HELLO, MY NAME IS DARVEY. Darvey's gray eyes were as blank as tarnished spoons. Bored and not inclined to conceal it, she yawned frequently while serving her customers, spoke in a disinterested mumble, moved in a foot-sliding slouch, and got their orders mixed up. When any mistake was called to her attention, she sighed as wearily as a waiting soul in Limbo who had been playing solitaire with an imaginary deck of cards since before three wise-men carried gifts to Bethlehem by camel.

Calculating that someone as terminally bored as Darvey might welcome a colorful encounter to relieve the tedium of her day, might actually *listen*, and might enjoy involvement in a real-life drama, Leilani spoke up when, at the end of lunch, the waitress arrived with the check: 'They're going to take me up to Idaho, smash my skull with a hammer, and bury me in the woods.'

Darvey blinked as slowly as a lizard sunning on a rock.

To Leilani, Preston Maddoc said, 'Now, sweetie, be honest with the young lady. Your mother and I aren't hammer maniacs. We're *ax* maniacs. We aren't going to club you to death. It's our plan to chop you to pieces and feed you to the bears.'

'I'm entirely serious,' Leilani told Darvey. 'He killed my older brother and buried him in Montana.'

'Fed him to bears,' Preston assured the waitress. 'As we always do with difficult children.'

Sinsemilla affectionately ruffled her daughter's hair. 'Oh, Lani baby, you are such a morbid child sometimes.'

The slowly, slowly blinking Darvey seemed to wait with coiled tongue for an unwary fly to buzz by.

To this blond gecko, dear Mater said, 'Her brother was actually abducted by aliens and is undergoing rehabilitation at their secret base on the dark side of the moon.'

'My mother really believes the alien crap,' Leilani told Darvey, ''cause she's a totally wrecked junkie who's had like a billion volts shot through her brain in electroshock therapy.'

Her mother rolled her eyes and made an electrical sound, 'Zzzt, zzzt,' and laughed, and made it again, 'Zzzt, zzzt!'

Playing the stern but loving father, Preston Maddoc said, 'Lani, enough already. This isn't funny.'

Sinsemilla frowned disapprovingly at the pseudofather. 'Oh, now, honey, it's all right. She's exercising her imagination. That's good. It's *healthy*. I don't believe in repressing children's creativity.'

To the waitress, Leilani said, 'If you call the cops and swear you saw these two hit me, that'll start an investigation, and when it's all over, you'll be a hero. You'll be praised on *America's Most Wanted* and maybe even hugged on *Oprah.*'

Putting the lunch check on the table, Darvey said, 'This is one of like a million reasons why I'm never having kids.'

'Oh, no, don't say that,' Sinsemilla objected with deep feeling. 'Darvey, don't deny yourself motherhood. It's such a natural high, and making a baby bonds you to the living earth like nothing else.'

'Yeah,' the waitress said with yet another yawn, 'it looks just totally fabulous.'

After Darvey shuffled away, as Preston put an extravagant tip on the table, Sinsemilla said, 'Lani baby, this morbid thinking is what you get when you read too many trashy nonsense books about evil pigmen. You need some real literature to clear your head out.'

Here was advice from the matriarch of the new psychic humanity. And she was serious: Books that lied about the nobility of pigs, and portrayed these good animals as evil, corrupted Leilani's mind and spawned morbid, paranoid notions about what had happened to Lukipela.

'You're amazing, Mother.'

Old Sinsemilla put an arm around Leilani and drew her close, squeezing too tightly with what passed, in her dementia, for motherly affection. 'Sometimes you worry me, little Klonkinator.' Of Preston, she inquired, 'Do you think she might be a candidate for therapy?'

'When the time comes, they'll heal her mind and her body both,' he predicted. 'To a superior extraterrestrial intelligence, the mind and the body are one entity.'

Appealing to Darvey for help had been a fiasco, not primarily because the waitress's skull bone was too thick to allow truth to resonate through it, but because for the first time, Leilani had revealed to Preston that she didn't believe his story about Lukipela being beamed up into the gentle caring hands of medicine men from Mars or Andromeda, and that she suspected him of committing murder. He might previously have sensed her suspicion, but now he *knew*.

As she followed her mother out of the booth, Leilani dared to glance at Preston. He winked.

She could have run for freedom then. In spite of the leg brace, she was able to move with speed and surprising grace for a hundred yards, and then with speed but with less grace; however, if she raced between the tables and out of the restaurant, if she ran along the shopping arcade and into the casino, screaming *He's going to kill me*, the casino personnel and the gamblers were likely to do nothing more than make bets on how far the malfunctioning girl cyborg would get before colliding disastrously with either a cocktail waitress or a slot-machine-playing grandma in a jackpot-seeking frenzy.

Therefore to the *Fair Wind* Leilani went, with an ill wind at her back. By the time Darvey was yawning over the tip that she'd received and was thinking that the crazy-rude little crippled kid was lucky to have such a generous father, the motor home returned fully fueled to Interstate 15, once more speeding northeast toward Vegas.

In the co-pilot's seat again, following a morning of relative sobriety, and now fortified by lunch, old Sinsemilla prepared to embark upon the course of mind-expanding medications that any genuinely committed breeder of psychic superhumans must follow. She held a pharmacist's ceramic mortar between her knees and employed a matching pestle to grind three tablets into powder.

Leilani had no idea what this substance might be, except that she confidently ruled out aspirin.

When the hive queen finished grinding, she pinched her right nostril around the stem of a sterling-silver straw and inhaled a portion of this psychoactive farina. Then she switched nostrils in an effort to balance the inevitable long-term damage to nasal cartilage that resulted from being a vacuum cleaner for toxic substances.

Let the party begin, and feel the superbabies mutate.

At Las Vegas, they switched to Federal Highway 95, which struck north along the western edge of Nevada. For a hundred fifty miles, they paralleled the Death Valley National Monument, which lay just across the state line in California. The desolate terrain got no less forbidding past Death Valley, nor later past the town of Goldfield, nor when they angled northwest from Tonopah.

This route kept them far from eastern Nevada where federal forces had blockaded highways and cordoned off thousands of square miles, searching for drug lords that Preston continued to insist must be ETs. 'It's typical government disinformation,' he groused.

Seated in the dining nook, Leilani had no interest in drug lords or aliens from another world, and she also had difficulty maintaining an interest in the evil pigmen from another dimension that previously had captured her fancy. This was book three in a six-book pigmen series, and her frustrating inability to concentrate on the story wasn't because the bacony bad guys had grown less mesmerizingly evil or because the amusing heroes had grown less amusing or less heroic. Since her situation with Preston had deteriorated so dramatically, she could no longer easily thrill to the menacing schemes of the pork-bellied villains. A real-world equivalent of a pigman sat behind the wheel of the *Fair Wind*, wearing sunglasses, crafting wicked plans that made even the hammiest wrongdoers seem utterly unimaginative and unthreatening by comparison.

Eventually she closed the novel and opened her journal, wherein she recorded the scene at the coffee shop. Later, as the converted Prevost bus laid down a continuous peal of thunder through the arid mountain passes and across the high plains, Leilani preserved her observations of her mother's descent through increasingly disturbing states of altered consciousness. These were brought about by at least two drugs in addition to the pestle-pulverized tablets that Mater had snorted while passing Las Vegas.

Nearing Tonopah, two hundred miles from Vegas, Sinsemilla sat at the dinette with Leilani and prepared to mutilate herself. She laid her 'carving towel,' on the table: a blue bath towel folded to make padding for her left arm and to catch messy drips. Organized in a Christmas-cookie tin with capering snowmen on the lid, her mutilation kit included rubbing alcohol, cotton balls, gauze pads, adhesive tape, Neosporin, razorblades, three surgical-steel scalpels different in shape from one another, and a fourth scalpel with an exceptionally keen ruby blade intended for eye surgeries in which sufficiently delicate incisions could not be executed with a steel cutting edge.

Resting her arm on the towel, Sinsemilla smiled at the six-inch-long, two-inch-wide, intricate snowflake pattern of scars on her forearm. For long minutes she meditated on this disfiguring lacework.

Leilani ardently wished not to be a witness to this insanity. She wanted to hide from her mother, but the motor home provided no escape. She wasn't permitted in the bedroom that Sinsemilla shared with Preston; and the sofabed in the lounge wasn't far enough away, still within sight. If she retreated to the bathroom and closed the door, her mother might come after her.

Indeed, she'd learned that by showing the slightest revulsion or even mild disapproval, she would precipitate her mother's wrath, a storm not easily ridden out. Conversely, if Leilani expressed an interest in any of her mother's activities, Sinsemilla might accuse her of being nosy or patronizing, whereupon torment of one kind or another would follow.

Indifference remained the safest attitude, even if it might be a pretense that masked disgust. Therefore, as Sinsemilla set out the instruments of self-mutilation, Leilani focused on her journal and wrote busily, without interruption.

This time, indifference provided an inadequate defense. Leilani applied her left hand to most tasks in hope of keeping the deformed joints as flexible as possible, and also to expand the function of the fused digits; consequently, she was an ambidextrous writer. Now, as she penned her journal entry left-handed, her mother watched with growing interest from across the table. Leilani first assumed that Sinsemilla was curious about what was being written, but her interest proved to be that of a back-porch country whittler with a taste for butchery.

'I could make it pretty,' Sinsemilla said.

Leilani replied while continuing to write: 'Make what pretty?'

'The gnarly hand, the pigman paw that wants to be a hand and a cloven hoof at the same time, that stumpy little, twisty little, half-baked muffin lump at the end of your arm – that's what. I could make it pretty, and more than pretty. I could make it beautiful, make it art, and you wouldn't ever be ashamed of it again.'

Leilani considered herself too well armored to be hurt by her mother. Sometimes, however, the thrust came from such an unexpected direction that the blade found the chink in her defenses, slipped past the ribs, and scored her heart: a quick hot piercing.

'I'm not ashamed of it,' she said, dismayed by the tightness in her voice because it revealed that she'd been wounded, even if just lightly pricked. She didn't want to give her mother the satisfaction of knowing that the point had made its pain.

'Brave baby Lani, doin' her nothin'-can-stop-me number, doin' her I-ain't-a-pumpkin-I'm-a-princess routine. Me here talkin' plain truth, while you're the type says Frankenstein's ugly old neck bolts were really jewelry from Tiffany's. I'm not afraid to say *cripple*, and what you need is a dose of reality, girl. You need to get rid of the idea that thinkin' normal *makes* you normal, which is gonna only leave you disappointed all your life. You can't ever be normal, but you can be close normal. You hear me?'

'Yes.' Leilani wrote faster, determined to record her mother's every word, with notations as to the rhythms and inflections of her speech. By treating this mean monologue as an exercise in dictation, she could distance herself from the cruelty of it, and if she kept her mother at arm's length emotionally, she couldn't be wounded again. You could be hurt only by real people, by real people about whom you cared or at least about whom you wished you *could* care. So call her 'old Sinsemilla' and 'hive queen' and 'dear Mater,' regard her as an object of amusement, a lurching slapstick figure, and then you won't care what she does to herself or what she says about you, because she's just a clown whose gibberish means nothing except that it might be useful in a book if you live long enough to write novels.

'To be close to normal,' said old Sinsemilla the hive queen, the electroshocked snakehandler, the wizard-baby breeder, 'you've got to *face* up to what's *screwed* up. You've got to look at your lobster-claw hand, got to truly *see* your scare-the-shit-out-of-little-babies hand, and when you can truly *see* it instead of pretending it's like anyone else's hand, when you can *face* up to what's *screwed* up, then you can improve it. And you know how you can improve it?'

'No,' said Leilani, writing furiously.

'Look.'

Leilani raised her eyes from the journal.

Sinsemilla slid one fingertip across her forearm, tracing the snowflake scars. 'Put your pigman hoof-hand right here on the carving towel, and I'll make it beautiful like me.'

Having fed on egg-white omelets with tofu cheese, also having feasted on a banquet of illegal chemicals, Sinsemilla still harbored appetites that perhaps could never be satisfied. Her face was drawn by hunger, and her gaze had teeth.

Eye to eye, Leilani felt as though her mother's stare would gnaw her blind. She looked down at her left hand. Sensing Sinsemilla's attention settle upon those deformed fingers, Leilani expected to see bite marks appear upon her skin, psychic-vampire stigmata.

If she bluntly rejected the offer to have her hand carved to 'make it pretty,' she might anger her mother. Then the risk was that Sinsemilla's desire to sculpt some skin would soon darken into an obsession and that Leilani would be hectored ceaselessly for days.

During this trip to Idaho and, possibly, to that quiet corner of Montana where Luki waited, Leilani needed to keep a clear mind, to be alert for the first sign that Preston Maddoc was soon to act upon his murderous intent, and to recognize an opportunity to save herself if one arose.

She couldn't do any of those things if her mother bullied her relentlessly. Peace wasn't easy to come by in the Maddoc household, but she needed to negotiate a truce in the matter of mutilation if she were to have any chance of staying clearheaded enough to save herself from worse than a little hand carving.

'It's beautiful,' Leilani lied, 'but doesn't it hurt?'

Sinsemilla withdrew another item from the Christmas-cookie tin: a bottle of topical anesthetic. 'Swab this on your skin, it gives you the numbies, takes away the worst sting. The rest of the pain is just the price you pay for beauty. All the great writers and artists know beauty *only* comes from pain.'

'Put some on my finger,' Leilani said, extending her right hand, withholding the deformed hand that her mother wanted to whittle.

A ball of spongy material attached by a stiff wire to the lid served as a swab. The fluid had a peppery scent and felt cool against the soft pad of Leilani's index finger. Her skin tingled and then grew numb, strangely rubbery.

As old Sinsemilla watched with the red-eyed, squint-eyed, hard-eyed hunger of a ferret watching an unsuspecting rabbit, Leilani put down the pen and, not in the least unsuspecting, raised her deformed hand, pretending to examine it thoughtfully. 'Your snowflakes are pretty, but I want my own pattern.'

'Every child's got to be a rebel, even baby Lani, even little Miss Puritan, she wouldn't eat a slice of rum cake 'cause maybe it would turn her into a gutter-livin' drunkie, wrinkles her nose at her own mother's most harmless pleasures, but even little Miss Tight-ass has to be a rebel sometime, has to have her own *pattern*. But that's good, Lani, that's just like it ought to be. What a useless suck-up sort of kid would ever want to wear homemade tattoos exactly like her mother's? I don't want that, either. Shit, next thing you know, we'd be dressin' alike, doin' our hair the same, goin' to afternoon tea parties, makin' cakes for some stupid church bake sale, and then Preston would have to shoot us quick and put us out of our misery. What pattern do you have in mind?'

Still studying her hand, Leilani strove to match the tropes and rhythms of her mother's drug-shaped speech, hoping to encourage the hive queen to believe that they were bonding as never before and that many tender hours of shared mutilation were indeed in their future. 'I don't know. Somethin' as unique as the cracked-glass patterns on a horsefly's wings, somethin' awesomely cool, that everyone thinks is bitchin', kind of beautiful but edgy, scary, the way your road-kill pictures are beautiful, somethin' that says *Screw you, I'm a mutant and proud of it.*'

Ferret fierce, storms in her eyes and pent-up thunder waiting to break in her voice, old Sinsemilla did a mood turn on a dime of flattery, caged the ferret, pressed the looming storms back beyond the mountains of her madness, and became kittenish, filled with a girlish sunniness. '*Yes!* Give the world the finger before the world gives it to you, and in this case, *decorate* the finger! Maybe there's a little bit of me in you, after all, sweet Leilani, maybe there's rich blood in your veins, just when it looked like there was nothin' but water.'

At sixty miles an hour, as the Nevada sky boiled to a pale blue and as the white-hot sun slowly described a glowing forge-hammer arc toward the anvil mountains in the west, with hula-hula girls swiveling their hips to the rhythm of tire rotation, Leilani and her mother huddled at the table, like pajama-party teenagers gossiping about boys or swapping makeup and fashion tips, but in fact circling around various schemes for engraving one already odd hand.

Her mother favored a multiyear project: obscenities carved in intricate and clever juxtapositions, descending every finger, curling in lettered whorls across the palm, fanning in offensive rays across the opisthenar, which is the name for the back of the hand, a word that Leilani knew because she had studied the structure of the human hand in detail, the better to understand her difference.

While pretending to entertain the concept of transforming her hand into a living billboard for depraved and demonic ravings, Leilani suggested alternatives: floral designs, leaf patterns, Egyptian hieroglyphics, a series of numbers with magical properties culled from Sinsemilla's books on numerology . . . .

After nearly forty minutes, they agreed that the unique canvas represented by Leilani's 'freak-show hand' (as dear Mater put it) must not be misused. As much fun as it would have been to drench a finger in topical anesthetic and slash at it vigorously with scalpels and razorblades right now, without delay, they both acknowledged that great art required not only a price of pain but also contemplation. If Richard Brautigan had conceived and written *In Watermelon Sugar* on one summer afternoon, it would have been so simple that Sinsemilla would have understood its message in a single reading and would not have been wonderfully involved in its mysteries through so many rewarding perusals. For a few days, they would mull over approaches to the project and meet again to consult further on design.

Leilani gave the art form a name, *bio-etching*, which rang more pleasantly on the ear than did *self-mutilation*. The artist in old Sinsemilla thrilled to the avant-garde quality of the term.

So successfully had the danger of a major Sinsemilla storm

been averted that dear Mater repacked her mutilation kit without either taking a scalpel to Leilani's hand or elaborating upon the snowflake frieze on her arm. For the time being, her need to cut had passed.

Her need to fly, however, drove her to the produce drawer of the refrigerator, from which she withdrew a Ziploc bag packed with exotic dried mushrooms of a potency not recommended for salads.

By the time that they were hooked up to utilities at a campsite associated with a motel-casino in Hawthorne, Nevada, the hive queen had worked up a hallucinogenic buzz. This buzz was of such intensity that if focused as tightly as the laser weapon of Darth Vader's Death Star, it would vaporize the moon.

She lay on the floor of the lounge, gazing at the smiling sun god on the ceiling, communing with that provider of island heat and surf-gilding rays, speaking to him sometimes in English, sometimes in Hawaiian. In addition to mystical and spiritual matters, the subjects that she chose to discuss with this plump deity included her opinions of the newest boy bands, whether her daily intake of selenium was sufficient, recipes for tofu, what hair styles were likely to be the most flattering to the shape of her face, and whether Pooh of Pooh Corner was a secret opium smoker with a secondary Prozac habit.

With sundown coming, Dr. Doom stepped over his wife, who might not have been aware of him if he had tramped on her, and he went out to get dinner for the three of them, leaving Leilani in the company of her murmuring, muttering, giggling mother and of those battery-powered hula girls who remained in perpetual sway.

54

Friday evening in Twin Falls, Idaho, is not likely to be much different from Saturday or Monday or Wednesday in Twin Falls, Idaho. Idahoans call their territory the Gem State, possibly because it is a major source of star garnets; the primary product, by tonnage, is potatoes, but no one with a sense of civic pride and PR savvy wants to call his home the Potato State, if only because Idahoans would risk being referred to as Potatoheads. Perhaps the most breathtaking mountain scenery in the United States is located in Idaho, though not around Twin Falls, but even the prospect of gorgeous alpine vistas could not induce Curtis Hammond to play tourist this evening, for he prefers the comforts of hearth and home as manufactured by Fleetwood.

Besides, no show produced by humankind or nature could equal the beauty and the wonder of Castoria and Polluxia preparing dinner.

In matching Chinese-red silk pajamas with billowy bell-bottom sleeves and pants, standing tall on platform sandals that glitter with midnight-blue rhinestones, their fingernails and toenails no longer azure-blue but crimson, their glossy golden hair swept up in chignons with long spiral curls framing their faces, they glide and turn and twist around the cramped galley with an uncanny awareness of each other's position at all times, exhibiting choreography that might please Busby Berkeley as they whip up a feast of Mandarin and Szechwan specialties.

A mutual interest in the culinary arts and in the flamboyant use of knives in the manner of certain Japanese chefs, a mutual interest in novelty acts involving tomahawks and cleavers thrown at brightly costumed assistants strapped to spinning target wheels, and a mutual interest in personal defense employing a variety of sharp-edged and pointed weapons have enabled the twins to prepare dinner with enough entertainment value to ensure that, given their own program, they would be a huge hit on the Food Network. Blades flash, steel points wink, serrated edges shimmer with serpentine light as they slice celery, chop onions, dice chicken, shave beef, shred lettuce . . . .

Curtis and Old Yeller sit side by side at the back of the U-shaped dining nook, enchanted by the sisters' style of full-tilt cooking, eyes wide as they track the scintillant blades, which are handled with flourishes that invite the expectation of mortal injury. The finest scimitar dancers, whirling and leaping among flashing swords, would be humbled by the twins' performance. Soon it's clear that a delicious dinner will be served, and that no fingers will be severed and no one decapitated in its preparation.

Sister-become merits a place at the table for many reasons, including that she helped to save their lives, but also because she has been bathed. Earlier, rising from seven hours of sleep, before taking their own showers, Polly and Cass scrubbed the dog in the bathtub, styled her with a pair of 1600-watt blow-dryers, brushed and combed her with an imposing collection of hair-grooming instruments, and atomized two light puffs of Elizabeth Taylor's White Diamonds perfume on her coat. Old Yeller sits proudly at Curtis's side: fluffy and grinning, smelling just as the glamorous movie star must smell.

Like crimson butterflies, like fire billowing, but really like nothing so much as themselves, the twins bring forth so many fragrant and delicious dishes that the table won't entirely hold them; some remain on the kitchen counter to be fetched as appetites demand. They also bring to the dining nook one 12-gauge, pistol-grip, pump-action shotgun and a 9-mm pistol, because since the crossroads in Nevada, they have gone nowhere, not even to the bathroom, without weapons.

The sisters pop open bottles of Tsingtao beer for themselves and a bottle of nonalcoholic beer for Curtis, so that he might have some appreciation for the exquisite combination of good Chinese food and cold beer. Plates are piled high, and the sisters prove to have appetites more prodigious than Curtis's, even though the boy must eat not only to sustain himself but also to produce the additional energy that is necessary to control his biological structure and continue being Curtis Hammond, an identity that isn't yet natural to him.

Old Yeller is served strips of beef and chicken on a plate, as though she is like any other guest. Curtis is able to use the boy-dog bond to ensure she refrains from wolfing down the food, as programmed in her canine nature, and to ensure she eats the meat one piece at a time, savoring each morsel. She finds this dining pace to be odd at first, but soon she recognizes the greater pleasure to be had from a meal when it isn't consumed in forty-six seconds flat. Even if she had been able to use silverware, hold a porcelain teacup in one paw with her dew claw raised like a pinkie, and converse in the flawless English of an heiress who had attended a first-rate finishing school, Old Yeller could not have conducted herself more like a lady than she did at this Chinese feast.

Throughout dinner, the sisters prove to be vastly entertaining, recounting adventures they have had while skydiving, bronco-busting, hunting sharks with spear guns, skiing down the faces of 70-degree cliffs, parachuting off high-rise buildings in several major cities, and defending their honor at chichi Hollywood parties attended by, in Polly's words, 'rodent hordes of grasping, horny, drug-crazed, dimwitted, sleazebag movie stars and famous directors.'

'Some of them were nice,' Cass says.

Polly demurs: 'With all respect and affection, Cassie, you would find *someone* to like even at a convention of cannibal Nazi kitten killers.'

To Curtis, Cass says, 'After we left Hollywood, I performed an exhaustive analysis of our experiences and determined that six and one-half percent of people in the film business are both sane and good. I will admit that the rest of them are evil, even if another four and one half percent are sane. But it's not fair to condemn the *entire* community, even if the vast majority of them are mad swine.'

When they have all eaten to excess and then have eaten just a little more, the table is cleared, two fresh bottles of Tsingtao and one of nonalcoholic beer are opened, a dish of water is provided for Old Yeller, candles are lit, the electric lights are turned off, and after Cass has determined that the ambience is 'deliciously spooky,' the twins return to the dining nook, clasp their hands around their bottles of Tsingtao, lean over the table, and focus intently on their guests, both boy and dog. Cass says, 'You're an alien, aren't you, Curtis?' Polly says, 'You're an alien, too, aren't you, Old Yeller?' And they both say, 'Dish us the dirt, ET.'

55

Waiting for Dr. Doom to return with dinner, trying not to listen to her mother's headcase monologue in the lounge, Leilani sat in the co-pilot's seat, at the panoramic windshield, watching the sunset. Hawthorne was a true desert town established on a broad plain, rimmed by rugged mountains. The sun, as orange as a dragon's egg, cracked on the western peaks and spilled a crimson yolk. Against this fiery backlight, the mountains wore king's gold for a while, then gradually took off their shining crowns and drew royal-blue nightclothes up their slopes.

Preston now knew that Leilani believed he'd murdered Lukipela. If he hadn't previously been planning to rid himself of her in Idaho or during a subsequent side trip to Montana, he had begun making such plans since lunch.

The scarlet twilight drained into the west, washed away by the incoming tides of east-born darkness. Curtains of stored heat rose from the desert plain, causing the purple mountains to shimmer as might a landscape in one of dear Mater's hallucinatory fantasies.

As dusk faded at the windows and the motor home fell into gloom relieved only by the glow of one lamp in the lounge, old Sinsemilla ceased muttering, stopped giggling, and began to whisper to the sun god or to other spirits not represented on the ceiling.

The idea of bio-etching her daughter's hand had been planted in the fertile swamp of her mind. That seed would sprout, and the sprout would grow.

Leilani worried that her mother, in possession of an extensive pharmacopoeia, would drug her milk or orange juice, slip her a Mickey Finn, a blackjack in a glass. She could imagine waking, groggy and disoriented, to discover that Sinsemilla had been busily carving.

She shuddered as the last light died in the west. Although the desert night was warm, chill chased chill up and down the ladder of her spine.

If the motherthing was in a sour mood, perhaps inspired by a bad mushroom or by an ill-conceived mix of chemicals, she might decide that prettifying Leilani's hand would fail to bring balance to her appearance, that it would be easier and more interesting and more *creative* to carve the normal parts of her to match the deformed hand, the twisted leg. Then Leilani might awake in agony, with obscenities cut into her *face*.

This was why she made a joke of everything, why wisecracks and prayers were equally important to her. If she couldn't find a silver laugh, bright and sparkling, then she would find a dark one, cold but comforting, because if ever she failed to find a laugh of any kind, then she would be crushed by dread, by hopelessness, and it wouldn't matter if she was technically still alive, for she'd be dead in her heart.

Laughs of any variety were getting harder to find.

As the dream-racked hive queen whispered, whispered, no longer lying on her back, no longer face-to-face with the smiling sun god, but curled in the fetal position on the lounge floor, she seemed to be speaking in two distinct voices, though both were as hushed as lovers sharing intimacies. One whisper remained recognizably her own, but the other sounded deeper, rougher, strange, as though she were conversing with a demon that possessed her and spoke through her.

Sitting in the co-pilot's chair with her back to the lounge, Leilani couldn't quite hear what old Sinsemilla said either in her whisper or in that of her alter ego. Only two words, repeated from time to time, rose out of the susurrant flow of dialogue and became distinguishable, although in truth Leilani was probably imagining them, translating meaningless babble to feed her growing paranoia. *The girl,* Sinsemilla seemed to whisper, and later the demon said it, too, with a hungry guttural longing, *the girl.*

These words were surely just fumes of fantasy, for when Leilani listened, head cocked either left or right, or when she turned in the swiveling chair to face her mother's jackknifed form, she heard only meaningless murmurs, as though the hive queen had reverted to insect speech or, under the influence of the mushroom god, talked only in tongues impossible to interpret. Yet when she faced front again, when her thoughts sped forward to Idaho and to means of self-defense, when she didn't actively listen to old Sinsemilla, she either imagined or heard again what she dreaded hearing: *the girl . . . the girl . . . .*

She needed her knife.

Lukipela had gone with Preston Maddoc into a Montana twilight, never to return, and in the first night that followed her brother's disappearance, Leilani had crept into the kitchen of the motor home to steal a paring knife from the cutlery drawer. Sharp and pointed, the blade measured three and a half inches from the haft to the tip. As a weapon, it rated less desirable than either a .38 revolver or a flamethrower, but unlike those more formidable armaments, it was available and easy to conceal.

A few nights later, she had realized that Preston wouldn't send her to the stars anytime soon, perhaps not until the eve of her tenth birthday in February. If she tried to keep the knife hidden on her person for fifteen months, she would inadvertently drop it or be caught with it in one way or another, revealing that she expected eventually to have to fight for her life.

Without the advantage of surprise, the paring knife would be only a slightly more effective weapon than bare but determined hands.

She'd considered returning the blade to the kitchen. But she'd been worried that in a crisis, under suspicion and closely watched, she might not be allowed to get near the cutlery drawer.

Instead, she'd hidden the knife in the mattress of the foldaway sofabed on which she slept each night. She lifted one corner of the mattress, and on the underside made a three-inch slit in the ticking. After inserting the weapon in the mattress, she had repaired the slit with two pieces of electrician's tape.

Changing bed linens and doing laundry were her responsibilities. Consequently, no one but Leilani herself was likely to see the tape-mended tear.

In the dead hours of the oncoming night, while Preston and old Sinsemilla were asleep, Leilani would turn up the corner of the mattress again, peel back the tape that she had applied nine months ago, and extract the paring knife. From here through Idaho

– and into the Montana woods with Preston, if it came to that – she would carry the blade taped to her body.

She sickened at the thought of stabbing anyone, even Dr. Doom, whose fellow high-school classmates had surely voted him 'Most Likely to Be Stabbed' only because there had been no category titled 'Most Deserving of Being Stabbed.' Leilani could act as tough as anyone, and if real toughness could be measured by how much adversity you endured, then she figured that her cup of toughness was more than half full. But the type of toughness that involved violent action, that required a capacity for savagery, might be beyond her.

She would tape the knife to her body anyway.

Eventually the time would come to act, and Leilani would do what she could to defend herself. Her disabilities were less severe than Luki's; she'd always been stronger than her brother. When at last she arrived at her unwanted moment alone with the pseudofather, when he cast aside the mask behind which he lived, revealing his true booger face, she might die as horribly as sweet Luki had died, but she would not go easily. Whether or not she had the stomach to use the knife, she would put up a fight that Preston Maddoc would remember.

A groan from old Sinsemilla caused Leilani to turn her powered chair away from the windshield, toward the lounge.

In the soft lamplight, Sinsemilla rolled off her side. She lay prone, head raised, peering into the shadowy kitchen. Then, as though she'd been brought here in a ventilated pet-store box, she crawled on her belly toward the back of the motor home.

Leilani sat watching until her mother reached the galley and, still prostrate, pulled open the refrigerator door. Sinsemilla didn't want anything in the fridge, but she wasn't able to get to her feet to reach the switches that turned on the central ceiling fixture and the downspot over the sink. In the wedge of icy light, which narrowed as the door slowly swung shut, she crawled to a cabinet behind which the liquor supply was stored conveniently at floor level.

Something in Leilani held her back as she rose from the co-pilot's chair and followed her mother into the galley. Her braced leg didn't respond as fluidly as usual, and she clumped through the motor home in an ungainly gait rather like the one she used when she wanted to exaggerate her disability in order to enhance a joke.

By the time that Leilani reached the galley, the refrigerator closed. She switched on the sink light.

Old Sinsemilla had gotten a liter of tequila from the liquor supply. She was sitting on the floor, her back against a cabinet door. She held the bottle between her thighs, struggling to open it, as though the twist-off cap were complex futuristic technology that challenged her twenty-first-century skills.

Leilani took a plastic tumbler from an upper cabinet. All the drinking vessels aboard the *Fair Wind* were in fact plastic, precisely because of the danger that Sinsemilla would injure herself with real glassware when she descended to this condition.

She added ice and a slice of lime to the tumbler.

Although the motherthing would happily pour down tequila warm, without a drinking glass and condiments, the consequences of allowing her to do so were unpleasant. Swigging from the bottle, she always drank too fast and too much. Then what went down came up, and Leilani was left with the mess.

Until Leilani stooped to take the bottle from her mother, old Sinsemilla seemed unaware that she had company. She relinquished the tequila without resistance, but she cringed into a corner formed by the cabinets, holding her hands protectively in front of her face. Tears suddenly washed her cheeks, and her mouth softened in these salt tides.

'It's only me,' Leilani said, assuming that her mother was still operating from an altered state and was less here in the galley than in some tweaked version of the real world.

With her wrenched face and tortured voice, Sinsemilla made an anguished plea for understanding. 'Don't, wait, don't, don't . . . I only wanted some buttered cornbread.'

Pouring the tequila, Leilani nervously rattled the neck of the bottle against the plastic tumbler when she heard the word *cornbread*.

On those occasions when Leilani had awakened to find her steel support missing, when she had been forced to endure a difficult and humiliating game of find-the-brace, her mother had been highly amused by her struggle but had also insisted that the game would teach her self-reliance and remind her that life 'throws more stones at you than *buttered cornbread*.'

That peculiar admonition had always seemed to be of a piece

with old Sinsemilla's general kookiness. Leilani had assumed that *buttered cornbread* had no special significance, that the words *oatmeal cookies* or *toasted marshmallows*, or *long-stemmed roses*, would serve as well.

Huddled on the floor, peeking out between the knuckled staves of her palisade of fingers, apparently expecting an assault, Sinsemilla pleaded, 'Don't. Please don't.'

'It's only me.'

'Please, please don't.'

'Mother, it's Leilani. Just Leilani.'

She didn't want to consider that her mother might not be in some drug-painted fantasy, that she might instead be trapped in the canvas of her past, because this would suggest that at one time she had been afraid, had suffered, and had begged for mercy that perhaps had never been given. It would suggest also that she deserved not just contempt but at least some small measure of sympathy. Leilani had often pitied her mother. Pity allowed her to keep a safe emotional distance, but sympathy implied an equality of suffering, a kindred experience, and she would not, could not, ever excuse her mother to the extent that sympathy seemed to require.

A-shudder, Sinsemilla's body rattled the cabinet doors against which she leaned, and each clatter seemed to crack the rhythm of her breathing, so that she inhaled and exhaled in short erratic gasps, blowing out bursts of words with breathless urgency. *'Please please please. I just wanted cornbread. Buttered cornbread. Some buttered cornbread.'*

Holding the tumbler of tequila with ice and lime, the way dear Mater preferred it, Leilani knelt on her one good knee. 'Here's what you wanted. Take it. Here.'

Two fans of trembling fingers visored Sinsemilla's face. Her eyes, glimpsed between overlapping digits, were as blue as ever but were tinted by a vulnerability and by a terror not like anything she had shown before. This wasn't the extravagant fear of the never-were monsters that sometimes stalked her head trips, but a grittier fear that the passage of years could not allay, that corroded the heart and bent the mind, a fear of some monster that, if not still abroad in the world, had once been real.

'Just buttered. Just cornbread.'

'Take this, Mama, tequila, for you,' Leilani urged, and her own voice was as shaky as her mother's.

'Don't hurt me. Don't don't don't.'

Insistently Leilani pressed the tumbler against her mother's face-shielding hands. 'Here it is, the damn cornbread, the buttered cornbread, Mama, take it. *For God's sake, take it!'*

Never before had she shouted at her mother. Those last five words, screamed in frustration, shocked and scared Leilani because they revealed an inner torment more acute than anything she'd ever been able to admit to herself, but the shock was insufficient to bring Sinsemilla out of memory into the moment.

The girl placed the tumbler between her mother's thighs, where the bottle of tequila had been. 'Here. Hold it. Hold it. If you knock it over, *you* clean it up.'

Then her cyborg leg went on the fritz, or maybe panic short-circuited her memory of how to move the encumbered limb, but in either case, Leilani was locked in genuflection to the failed god of mother love, as Sinsemilla sobbed behind her screen of hands. The galley shrank until it was as confining as a confessional, until claustrophobic pressure seemed certain to wring unwanted revelations from Sinsemilla and to compel Leilani to acknowledge a bitterness so deep and so viscid that it would swallow her as sure as quicksand and destroy her if ever she dared to dwell on it.

Frantic to be out of her mother's suffocating aura, the girl clawed at the nearest countertop, at the refrigerator handle, and pulled herself erect. She pivoted on her bad leg, pushed away from the refrigerator, and lurched toward the front of the *Fair Wind* as though she were on the deck of a pitching ship.

In the cockpit, she half climbed and half fell into a seat, and fisted her hands in her lap, and clenched her teeth, biting down on the urge to cry, biting it in half, swallowing hard, holding back the tears that might dissolve all the defenses she so desperately needed, drawing hot staccato breaths, then breathing just as hard but deeper and more slowly, then more slowly still, getting a grip on herself, as always she'd been able to do, regardless of the provocation or the disappointment.

Only after a few minutes did she realize that she had sat in the driver's seat, that she had chosen it unconsciously for the illusion of control that it provided. She would not in fact start the engine and drive away. She had no key. She was just nine years old, in need of a pillow to see over the wheel. Although she wasn't a child in any sense other than the chronological, though she'd never been *permitted* the chance to be a child, she had chosen this seat in the manner of a child pretending to be in charge. If a pretense of control was the only control you had, if a pretense of freedom was the only freedom you might ever know, then you better have a rich imagination, and you better take some satisfaction from make-believe, because maybe it was the only satisfaction that you would ever get. She opened her fists and clutched the steering wheel so tightly that her hands almost at once began to ache, but she did not relax her grip.

Leilani would endure old Sinsemilla, clean up after her, obey her to the extent that obedience caused no harm to herself or to others, pity her, treat her with compassion, and even pray for her, but she would not pour out *sympathy* for her. If there were reasons to sympathize, she didn't want to know them. Because to sympathize would be to surrender the distance between them that made survival possible in these close confines. Because to sympathize with her would be to risk being pulled into the whirlpool of chaos and rage and narcissism and despair that *was* Sinsemilla. Because, damn it, even if the old motherthing had suffered as a child herself, or later, and even if her suffering had driven her to seek escape in drugs, nevertheless she had the same free will as anyone else, the same power to resist bad choices and easy fixes for her pain. And if she didn't think that she owed it to herself to clean up her act, then she must know that she owed it to her kids, who never asked to be born wizards or to be born at all. No one would ever see Leilani Klonk strung out on dope, stinking drunk, lying in her own vomit, in her own piss, by God, no way, no how, not ever. She would be a mutant, all right, but not a spectacle. Sympathy for her mother was too much, dear God, too much to ask, too much, and she would not give it when the cost of giving it would be to surrender that precious sanctuary in her heart, that small place of peace to which she could retreat in the most difficult times, that inner corner where her mother could not reach, did not exist, and where, therefore, hope dwelled.

Besides, if she gave the sympathy wanted, she wouldn't be able to mete it out in drops; she knew herself well enough to know that she would open the faucet wide. Furthermore, if she lavished sympathy on the motherthing, she would no longer be as vigilant as she needed to be. She would lose her edge. And then she would not be alert to the possibility of the Mickey Finn. She would wake from a sleep deep enough to accommodate surgery, and discover that her hand had been richly carved with obscenities or that her face had been deformed to match the hand. Even rivers of sympathy wouldn't wash her mother clean of her addictions, her delusions, her self-infatuation, and a pathetic monster was a monster nonetheless.

Leilani sat high in the driver's seat and held fast to the steering wheel, going nowhere, but at least not slipping down into the chasm that for so long had threatened to swallow her.

She needed the knife. She needed to be strong for whatever might be coming, stronger than she had ever been before. She needed God, God's love and guidance, and she asked now for the help of her Maker, and she held on to the wheel, held on, held on.

56

So here sits Curtis Hammond in a moral dilemma where he never expected to be faced with one: in a Fleetwood motor home in Twin Falls, Idaho. Considering all the exotic, spectacular, dangerous, and outright improbable places in the universe that he has been, this seems to be a disappointingly mundane setting for perhaps the greatest ethical crisis of his life. *Mundane*, of course, does not refer to the Spelkenfelter twins, only to the venue.

His mother had been an agent of hope and freedom in a struggle spanning not merely worlds but galaxies. She had faced down assassins of immeasurably more fierce breeds than the false mom and pop at the crossroads store, had brought the light of liberty and desperately needed hope to countless souls, had dedicated her life to rolling back the darkness of ignorance and hate. Curtis wants more than anything to continue her work, and he knows that his best chance of success lies in following her rules and respecting her hard-won wisdom.

One of his mother's most frequently repeated axioms instructs that regardless of the world you visit, regardless of the precarious state of civilization on that world, you can accomplish nothing if you reveal your true extraterrestrial nature. If people know you come from another planet, then alien contact becomes the story; indeed, it is such a huge story that it obscures your message and ensures that you will never accomplish your mission.

You must fit in. You must *become* one of those whose world you hope to save.

Although eventually the time might arrive for revelation, most of the work must be done in anonymity.

Furthermore, a civilization spiraling into an abyss often finds the spiral thrilling, and sometimes loves the promise of the depths below. People often see the romance of darkness but cannot see the ultimate terror that waits at the bottom, in the deepest blackness. Consequently, they resist the hand of truth extended, regardless of the goodwill with which it's offered, and have been known to kill their would-be benefactors.

In this work, at least initially, secrecy is the key to success.

So when Cass leans over the table in the spooky candlelight and asks if Curtis is an alien, and when Polly suggests that Old Yeller might be an alien as well, and when together the perspicacious twins say, 'Dish us the dirt, ET,' Curtis meets the piercing blue eyes of one sister, gazes into the piercing blue eyes of the other, takes a swallow of nonalcoholic beer, reminds himself of all his mother's teachings – which he didn't learn from megadata downloading, but from ten years of daily instruction – takes a deep breath, and says, 'Yes, I'm an alien,' and then he tells them the whole truth and nothing but the truth.

After all, his mom also taught that extraordinary circumstances arise in which any rule can wisely be broken. And she often said that from time to time someone so special comes along that upon meeting him or her, the direction of your life shifts unexpectedly, and you are therewith changed forever and for the better.

Gabby, the night caretaker of the restored ghost town in Utah, had manifestly *not* been such a force for positive change.

The Spelkenfelter twins, however, with their dazzling variety of mutual interests, with their great appetite for life, with their good hearts and with their tenderness, are absolutely the magical beings of whom his mother had spoken.

Their delight in his revelations thrills the motherless boy. A childlike wonder so overcomes them that he can see what they had been like and what they must have looked like when they were little girls in Indiana. Now, in a different way from Old Yeller, Castoria and Polluxia also have become his sisters.

57

Maybe Preston stopped to play blackjack in Hawthorne's small casino, or maybe he found a good point of observation from which to study the spectacular panoply of stars that brightened the desert sky, hoping to spot a majestic extraterrestrial cruise ship on an aerial tour of jerkwater towns. Or maybe he took so long to return with dinner because he paused to kill some poor wretch who had ugly thumbs and therefore was fated to lead a life of substandard quality.

When at last he arrived, he brought paper bags from which arose ravishing aromas. Submarine sandwiches packed with meat and cheese and onions and peppers, drenched in dressing. Pints of fabulous potato salad, macaroni salad. Rice pudding, pineapple cheesecake.

For old Sinsemilla, her ever thoughtful husband had provided a tomato-and-zucchini sandwich, with bean paste and mustard, on a whole-wheat roll, a side order of pickled squash seasoned with sea salt, and carob-flavored tofu pudding.

Due to the long day on the highway, all the wicked scheming, the drugs snorted, the drugs smoked, the drugs eaten, and the chasers of tequila, dear Mater was unfortunately too unconscious to eat dinner with her family.

Valiant Preston proved himself to be as much of an athlete as he was an academic. He muscled the motherthing's limp body off the galley floor and carried her into their bedroom at the back of the motor home, where she could more discreetly lie in a disreputable sprawl. As she was borne away, old Sinsemilla made no more sound and exhibited no more proof of life than would have a sack of cement.

Dr. Doom remained in their boudoir for a while, and although the door stood open, Leilani didn't venture one step toward that ominous threshold to see what might be up. She assumed he would be turning down the bedclothes, lighting a stick of strawberry-kiwi incense, undressing his enchantingly comatose bride, and in general setting the stage for a session of connubial bliss utterly unlike anything that the late Dame Barbara Cartland, prolific writer of romance novels, had ever imagined in the more than one thousand love stories that she had produced.

Leilani took advantage of Preston's absence to open the sofabed in the lounge, which was already fitted with sheets and a blanket, and to poke through the bags of sandwich-shop food, taking her fair share of the tastiest stuff. She retreated to her bed with dinner and with the novel about evil pigmen from another dimension, eating and pretending to read with great absorption in order to avoid having to sit with the pseudofather at the table.

Her worries about being forced to share a menacing little dinner for two with Preston Maddoc, alias Jordan Banks, possibly with black candles and a bleached skull on the table, proved to be unfounded. He opened a bottle of Guinness and settled down alone at the dinette, extending no invitation to join him.

He sat facing her, perhaps twelve feet away.

Relying on peripheral vision, Leilani knew that from time to time, he looked at her, perhaps even stared for extended periods; however, he said not a single word. In fact, he hadn't spoken to her since lunch in the coffee shop west of Vegas. Because she had openly claimed that he killed her brother, Dr. Doom was pouting.

You might think that homicidal maniacs wouldn't be thin-skinned. Considering their crimes against their fellow human beings, against humanity itself, you might suppose that they would *expect* to have their motives questioned and even to be insulted on occasion. Over the years, however, Leilani's experience with Preston indicated that homicidal maniacs had feelings more tender and more easily bruised than those of girls in early adolescence. She could almost *feel* the hurt and the sense of injustice radiating from him.

He knew, of course, that he *had* killed Lukipela. He didn't suffer from amnesia. He hadn't murdered and buried Luki while in a fugue state. Yet he seemed to feel that Leilani had shown woefully bad manners by referring to this sad, gruesome business at lunch and in front of a stranger, and by calling into question his veracity in the matter of the extraterrestrial healers and their Luki-lifting levitation beam.

She was certain that if she looked up from her pigmen book and apologized, Preston would smile and say something like, *Hey, that's all right, pumpkin, everybody makes mistakes*, which was too creepy to contemplate, although she couldn't seem to *stop* contemplating it.

At this very moment, his inamorata awaited him, as slack as sludge, as aware and alert as a block of cheese. The sweet prospect of romance cheered him sufficiently that he didn't sit brooding like a mad Russian over dinner. The doom doctor ate quickly and returned to the bedroom, closing the door behind him this time, leaving the dinette littered with bags, deli containers, and dirty plastic spoons, confident that Leilani would clean up after him.

Immediately, she hopped out of bed, fetched the TV remote, and switched on a humorless sitcom. She turned the sound up only as loud as she was permitted to have it at night; but the volume, although low, would be sufficient to screen any expressions of passion that she might otherwise be able to hear from the room at the far end of the motor home.

While the wizard-baby breeder lay insensate and while Preston remained preoccupied with unthinkable acts back there in the love nest of the damned, Leilani lifted the foot of her mattress, at the right-hand corner, pulled the two strips of tape off the ticking, and gingerly felt inside the hole. She located the small plastic bag in which, months ago, she'd stowed the knife to ensure that it wouldn't gradually work deeper into the padding.

The package didn't feel as it should. The size, the shape, and the weight were all wrong.

The plastic bag was clear. Extracting it from beneath the mattress, she saw at once that it contained not the knife that she had hidden, not a knife at all, but the penguin figurine that had belonged to Tetsy, that Preston had brought home because it reminded him of Luki, and that Leilani had left in the care of Geneva Davis.

58

Midnight in Sacramento: Those three words would never be the title of a romance novel or a major Broadway musical.

Like every place, this city had its special beauty and its share of charm. But to a worried and weary traveler, arriving at a dismal hour, seeking only cheap lodgings, the state capital appeared to huddle miserably under a mantle of gloom.

A freeway ramp deposited Micky in an eerily deserted commercial zone: no one in sight, her Camaro the only car on the street. Acres of concrete, poured horizontal and vertical, oppressed her in spite of a brightness of garish electric signs. The hard lights honed sharp shadows, and the atmosphere was so oddly medieval that she mistook a cluster of brown leaves in a gutter for a pile of dead rats. She half expected to find that everyone here lay dead or dying of the plague.

In spite of the lonely streets, her uneasiness had no external cause, but only an inner source. During the long drive north, she'd had too much time to think about all the ways she might fail Leilani.

She located a motel within her budget, and the desk clerk was both alive and of this century. His T-shirt insisted LOVE IS THE ANSWER! A small green heart formed the dot in the exclamation point.

She carried her suitcase and the picnic cooler to her ground-floor unit. She'd eaten an apple while driving, but nothing more.

The motel room was a flung palette of colors, a fashion seminar on the disorienting effects of clashing patterns, bleak in spite of its aggressive cheeriness. The place wasn't entirely filthy: maybe just clean enough to ensure that the cockroaches would be polite.

She sat in bed with the cooler. The ice cubes in the Ziploc bags hadn't half melted. The cans of Coke were still cold.

While she ate a chicken sandwich and a cookie, she watched TV, switching from one late-night talk show to another. The hosts were funny, but the cynicism that informed every joke soon depressed her, and under all the yuks, she perceived an unacknowledged despair.

Increasingly since the 1960s, being hip in America had meant being nihilistic. How strange this would seem to the jazz musicians of the 1920s and '30s, who invented hip. Back then hipness had been a celebration of individual freedom; now it required surrendering to groupthink, and a belief in the meaninglessness of human life.

Between the freeway and the motel, Micky had passed a packaged-liquor store. Closing her eyes, she could see in memory the ranks of gleaming bottles on the shelves glimpsed through the windows.

She searched the cooler for the special treat that Geneva had mentioned. The one-pint Mason jar, with a green cast to the glass, was sealed airtight by a clamp and a rubber gasket.

The treat was a roll of ten- and twenty-dollar bills wrapped with a rubber band. Aunt Gen had hidden the money at the bottom of the cooler and had mentioned the jar at the last minute, calculating that Micky wouldn't have accepted it if it had been offered directly.

Four hundred thirty bucks. This was more than Gen could afford to contribute to the cause.

After counting the cash, Micky rolled it tightly and sealed it in the Mason jar once more. She put the cooler on the dresser.

This gift came as no surprise. Aunt Gen gave as reliably as she breathed.

In the bathroom, washing her face, Micky thought of another gift that had come in the form of a riddle, when she'd been six: *What will you find behind the door that is one door away from Heaven?*

The door to Hell, Micky had replied, but Aunt Gen had said that her response was incorrect. Although the answer seemed logical and right to young Micky, this was, after all, Gen's riddle.

Death, that long-ago Micky had said. *Death is behind the door because you have to die before you can go to Heaven. Dead people . . . they're all cold and smell funny, so Heaven must be gross.*

Bodies don't go to Heaven, Geneva explained. *Only souls go, and souls don't rot.*

After a few more wrong answers, a day or two later, Micky had said, *What I'd find behind the door is someone waiting to stop me from getting to the next door, someone to keep me out of Heaven.*

What a peculiar thing to say, little mouse. Who would want to keep an angel like you out of Heaven?

Lots of people.

Like who?

They keep you out by making you do bad things.

Well, they'd fail. Because you couldn't be bad if you tried.

I can be bad, Micky had assured her, *I can be real bad.*

This claim had struck Aunt Gen as adorable, the tough posing of a pure-hearted innocent. *Well, dear, I'll admit I haven't checked the FBI's most-wanted list recently, but I suspect you're not on it. Tell me one thing you've done that would keep you out of Heaven.*

This request had at once reduced Micky to tears. *If I tell, then you won't like me anymore.*

Little mouse, hush now, hush, come here, give Aunt Gen a hug. Easy now, little mouse, I'm always going to love you, always, always.

Tears had led to cuddling, cuddling had led to baking, and by the time the cookies were ready, that potentially revealing train of conversation had been derailed and had remained derailed for twenty-two years, until two nights ago, when Micky had finally spoken of her mother's romantic preference for bad boys.

What will you find behind the door that is one door away from Heaven?

Aunt Gen's revelation of the correct answer made the question less of a riddle than it was the prelude to a statement of faith.

Here, now, as she finished brushing her teeth and studied her face in the bathroom mirror, Micky recalled the correct answer – and wondered if she could ever believe it as her aunt seemed genuinely to believe it.

She returned to bed. Switched off the lamp. Seattle tomorrow. Nun's Lake on Sunday.

And if Preston Maddoc never showed up?

She was so exhausted that even with all her worries, she slept – and dreamed. Of prison bars. Of mournfully whistling trains in the night. A deserted station, strangely lighted. Maddoc waiting with a wheelchair. Quadriplegic, helpless, she watched him take custody of her, unable to resist. *We'll harvest most of your organs to give to more-deserving people, he said, but one thing is mine. I'll open your chest and eat your heart while you're still alive.*

59

Upon finding the penguin in place of the paring knife, Leilani shot to her feet faster than her cumbersome leg brace had previously allowed. Suddenly, Preston seemed to be all-seeing, all-knowing. She looked toward the galley, half expecting to discover him there, to see him smiling as if to say *boo*.

The TV-sitcom characters became instant mimes, and no less funny, when Leilani pressed the MUTE button on the remote control.

A suspicious silence welled from the bedroom, as though Preston might be biding his time, trying to judge the moment when he would be most likely to catch her in the discovery of the penguin – not with a confrontation in mind, but strictly for the amusement value.

Leilani moved to the transition point between the lounge and the galley. She peered warily toward the back of the motor home.

The door to the bathroom-laundry stood open. Beyond that shadowy space was the bedroom door: closed.

A thin warm luminous amber line defined the narrow gap between the door and the threshold. And that was wrong. The amorous side of Preston Maddoc took no inspiration from the romantic glow of a silk-shaded lamp or from the sinuous throb of candle flames. Sometimes he wanted darkness for the deed, perhaps the better to imagine that the bedroom was a mortuary, the bed a casket. At other times—

The amber light winked out. Darkness married door to threshold. Then in that gap, Leilani detected the faint yet telltale flicker of a television: the pulse of phantoms moving through dreamscapes on the screen, casting their ghost light on the walls of the bedroom.

She heard familiar strains, the theme music of *Faces of Death*.

This repulsive videotape documentary collected rare film of violent death and its aftermath, lingering on human suffering and on cadavers in all stages of ravagement and corruption.

Preston had watched this demented production so often that he'd memorized every hideous image to the same extent that a stone-serious fan of *Star Trek III: The Search for Spock* could recite its dialogue word for word. Occasionally Sinsemilla enjoyed the gorefest with him; admiration for this documentary had been the animating spirit behind her road-kill photography.

After being compelled to watch a few minutes of *Faces of Death*, Leilani had struggled free of Sinsemilla's arms and thereafter had refused even to glance at it again. What fascinated the pseudofather and the hive queen only sickened Leilani. More than nausea, however, the video inspired such pity for the real dead and dying people shown on screen that after viewing but three or four minutes of it, she'd taken refuge in the water closet, muffling her sobs in her hands.

Sometimes Preston called *Faces of Death* a profound intellectual stimulant. Sometimes he referred to it as avant-garde entertainment, insisting that he wasn't titillated by its content but was creatively intrigued by the high art with which it explored its grisly subject.

In truth, even if you were only nine going on ten, you didn't have to be a prodigy to understand that this video did for the doom doctor exactly what the racy videos produced by the Playboy empire did for most men. You understood it, all right, but you didn't want to think about it often or deeply.

The theme music quieted as Preston adjusted the volume. He liked it low, for he was more attuned to images than to cries of pain and anguish.

Leilani waited.

Ghost light under the door, pale spirits fluttering.

She shuddered when at last she became convinced that this wasn't merely a trick to catch her unaware. Love – or what passed for love aboard the *Fair Wind* – was in full bloom.

Boldly Leilani went into the galley, switched on the sink light that earlier Preston had switched off, and opened the cutlery drawer. After extracting the paring knife from inside her mattress, he hadn't returned it to the collection. Gone also were the butcher knife, the carving knife, the bread knife – in fact, all the knives. Gone.

She opened the drawer that contained their flatware. Teaspoons, tablespoons, and serving spoons were arrayed as always they had been. The steak knives were gone. Though too dull to be effective weapons, the table knives had been removed, as well. The forks were missing.

Drawer to drawer, door to door, around the small galley, no longer caring if Preston caught her in the search, Leilani sought something that she could use to defend herself.

Oh, yes, of course, with a rasp or a file, as per a thousand prison movies, you could reshape the handle of an ordinary teaspoon until it acquired a killing point, until one edge gleamed as sharp as a knife. Maybe you could do the work secretly even in the confines of a motor home, and do it although your left hand was a stumpy little, twisty little, half-baked muffin lump. But you couldn't do it if you didn't *have* a rasp or a file.

By the time she opened the last drawer, checked the final cabinet, and inspected the dishwasher, she knew that Preston had removed every object that might serve as a weapon. He had also purged the galley of every tool – equivalent to a rasp or file – that might be employed to transform an ordinary object into a lethal instrument.

He was preparing for the end game.

Maybe they would cross into Montana after visiting the alien-healed fruitcake in Nun's Lake. Or maybe Preston would forego the satisfying symmetry of burying her with Luki, and would simply kill her in Idaho.

After years in these close quarters, the galley was as familiar to her as any place on earth, and yet she felt as lost as she might have felt if she'd abruptly found herself in the depths of a primeval forest. She turned slowly in a circle, as though bewildered by a dark forbidding wood, seeking a promising path, finding none.

For so long, she had been operating under the belief that she wouldn't be in serious jeopardy until her tenth birthday drew near, that she had time to plan an escape. Consequently, her mental file of survival schemes was thin, although not empty.

Even before Leilani's appeal to the waitress at lunch, Preston had changed his timetable. The proof was in the missing knives, which he must have removed from the motor home during the night, before he had driven Leilani and Sinsemilla to the garage early this morning and had brought them aboard the *Fair Wind*.

She wasn't ready to make a break for freedom. But she'd better be ready by the time they reached Nun's Lake on Sunday.

Until then, the best thing she could do would be to encourage Preston to believe that she hadn't yet discovered the trade of the penguin for the paring knife or the removal of all the sharp-edged utensils from the kitchen. He was taunting her for the sheer pleasure of it, and she was determined not to let him see the intensity of her fear, not to let him feed on her dread.

Besides, the moment he knew that *she* knew about the penguin, he might further advance his killing schedule. He might not wait for Idaho.

So she cleaned up the dinner table as usual. Put the leftovers in the refrigerator. Rinsed the plastic utensils from the sandwich shop – all spoons – and dropped them in the trash compactor.

At the sofabed again, she inserted the penguin in the mattress and resealed the slashed ticking with the two strips of tape.

Using the remote control, she restored the sound to the TV, blocking the faint music and the voices from *Faces of Death*.

She climbed onto her bed, where she'd left dinner unfinished. Although she had no appetite, she ate.

Later, lying alone with only the glow of the TV to relieve the darkness, as ghostly light pulsed across the features of the sun god on the ceiling, she wondered what had happened to Mrs. D and Micky. She'd left the penguin figurine in their care, and somehow Preston had recovered it. Neither Mrs. D nor Micky would have given it to him voluntarily.

She desperately wanted to phone them.

Preston had a digital telephone providing worldwide service, but when he wasn't carrying it with him, clipped to his belt, he left it in the bedroom, where Leilani was forbidden to go.

Over the months, she had secreted three quarters in three places within the motor home. She filched each coin from Sinsemilla's purse on occasions when the two of them were alone aboard the *Fair Wind* and when her mother was in one state of drugged detachment or another.

In an emergency, with just a quarter, if she could get to a pay phone, she could call 911. She could also place a collect call to anyone who might accept it – though Mrs. D and Micky were the only people who *would* accept a collect call from her.

The nearby motel-casino surely had pay phones, but getting to them would be tricky. In fact, reaching a phone before morning wasn't possible because Preston armed the security alarm after he arrived with dinner, using a keypad by the door. Only he and Sinsemilla knew the code that would disarm it. If Leilani opened the door, she would trigger a siren and switch on all the lights from one end of the vehicle to the other.

When she closed her eyes, she saw in her mind Mrs. D and Micky at the kitchen table, by candlelight, laughing, on the night that they invited her to dinner. She prayed that they were safe.

When you've got this I-survived-the-nuclear-holocaust left hand and this kick-ass-cyborg left leg, you expect people to be especially aware of you, to stare, to gawk, to blanch in terror and scurry for cover if you hiss at them and roll your eyes. But instead, even when you're wearing your best smile and you've shampooed your hair and you think you're quite presentable, even pretty, they look away from you or *through* you, maybe because they're embarrassed for you, as if they believe that your disabilities are your fault and that you are – or ought to be – filled with shame. Or, to give them the benefit of the doubt, maybe most people look through you because they don't trust themselves to look *at* you without staring, or to speak to you without unintentionally saying something that will be hurtful. Or maybe they think you're self-conscious, that therefore you *want* to be ignored. Or maybe the percentage of human beings who are hopeless assholes is just fantastically higher than you might want to believe. When you speak to them, most only half listen; and if in their half-listening mode, they realize that you're smart, some people go into denial and nevertheless resort to a style of speech hardly more sophisticated than baby talk, because ignorantly they associate physical deformity with dumbness. In addition to having the freak-show hand and the Frankenstein-monster walk, if you are also a kid and if you are rootless, always hitting the road in search of Obi-Wan Kenobi and the bright side of the Force, you are *invisible*.

Aunt Gen and Micky, however, had seen Leilani. They had

looked *at* her. They had listened. She was *real* to them, and she loved them for seeing her.

If they had been hurt because of her . . .

Lying awake until the TV timer went off, and then closing her eyes to block out the faintly luminous sun god's sleepy smile, she worried up numerous possible deaths for them. If Preston had killed Gen and Micky, then Leilani would kill him somehow, and it wouldn't matter if she had to sacrifice herself to get him, because life would not be worth living anymore, anyway.

60

'Your work is so exciting. If I could live my life again, I'd be a private investigator, too. You call yourselves *dicks*, don't you?'

'Maybe some do, ma'am,' Noah Farrel said, 'but I call myself a PI. Or used to.'

Even in the morning, two hours before noon, the August heat prowled the kitchen, as though it were a living presence, a great cat with sun-warmed fur, slinking among the table legs and chairs. Noah felt a prickle of sweat forming on his brow.

'In my twenties,' said Geneva Davis, 'I fell passionately in love with a PI. Though I must admit I wasn't worthy of him.'

'I find that hard to believe. You would've been quite a catch.'

'You're sweet, dear. But the truth is, I was something of a bad girl in those days, and like all his kind, he had a code of ethics that wouldn't bend for me. But you know about PI ethics.'

'Mine are tied in knots.'

'I sincerely doubt that. How do you like my cookies?'

'They're delicious. But these aren't almonds, ma'am.'

'Exactly. They're pecans. How's your vanilla Coke?'

'I think it's a cherry Coke.'

'Yes, I used cherry syrup instead of vanilla. I've had vanilla Cokes with vanilla two days in a row. This seemed a nice change.'

'I haven't had a cherry Coke since I was a kid. I'd forgotten how good they taste.'

Smiling, indicating his glass with a nod of her head, she said, 'And what about your vanilla Coke?'

Having sat at Geneva Davis's kitchen table for fifteen minutes, Noah had adapted to the spirit of her conversation. He raised his glass as if in a toast. 'Delicious. You said your niece phoned you?'

'Seven this morning, yes, from Sacramento. I worried about her staying there overnight. A pretty girl isn't safe in a town where there's so many politicians. But she's on the road now, hoping to make Seattle by tonight.'

'Why didn't she fly to Idaho?'

'She might not be able to grab Leilani right away. Might have to follow them somewhere else, maybe for days. She preferred her own car for that. Plus her budget's too tight for planes and rental cars.'

'Do you have her cell-phone number?'

'We aren't people who have cell phones, dear. We're church-mouse poor.'

'I don't think what she's doing is advisable, Mrs. Davis.'

'Oh, good Lord, of course it's not advisable, dear. It's just what she had to do.'

'Preston Maddoc is a formidable opponent.'

'He's a vicious, sick sonofabitch, dear, which is exactly why we can't leave Leilani with him.'

'Even if your niece doesn't wind up in physical danger up there, even if she gets the girl and brings her back here, do you realize what trouble she's in?'

Mrs. Davis nodded, sipped her drink, and said, 'As I understand it, the governor will make her suck down a lot of lethal gas. And me, too, no doubt. He's not a very nice man, the governor. You'd think he would let us alone after already tripling our electricity bills.'

Mopping his brow with a paper napkin, Noah said, 'Mrs. Davis—'

'Please call me Geneva. That's a lovely Hawaiian shirt.'

'Geneva, even with the very best of motives, kidnapping is still kidnapping. A federal offense. The FBI will get involved.'

'We're thinking of hiding Leilani with all the parrots,' Geneva confided. 'They'll never find her.'

'What parrots?'

'My sister-in-law, Clarissa, is a sweet tub of a woman with a goiter and sixty parrots. She lives out in Hemet. Who goes to Hemet? Nobody. Certainly not the FBI.'

'They'll go to Hemet,' he solemnly assured her.

'One of the parrots has a huge vocabulary of obscenities, but none of the others is foul-mouthed. The garbage-talking bird used to be owned by a policeman. Sad, isn't it? A *police officer*. Clarissa's been trying to clean up its act, but without much success.'

'Geneva, even if the girl isn't making up all this stuff, even if she's in real danger, you can't take the law into your hands—'

'There's lots of law these days,' she interrupted, 'but not much justice. Celebrities murder their wives and go free. A mother kills her children, and the news people on TV say *she's* the victim and want you to send money to her lawyers. When everything's upside down like this, what fool just sits back and thinks justice will prevail?'

This was a different woman from the one with whom he had been speaking a moment ago. Her green eyes were flinty now. Her sweet face hardened as he wouldn't have thought possible.

'If Micky doesn't do this,' she continued, 'that sick bastard will kill Leilani, and it'll be as if she never existed, *and no one but me and Micky will care what the world lost*. You better believe it'll be a loss, too, because this girl is the right stuff, she's a shining soul. These days people make heroes out of actors, singers, power-mad politicians. How screwed up are things when that's what *hero* has come to mean? I'd trade the whole self-important lot of 'em for this girl. She's got more steel in her spine and more true heart than a thousand of those so-called heroes. Have another cookie?'

Lately, Noah's preferred sources of sugar were all liquid and came with an alcohol component, but he felt the need for a metabolic kick-start to hold his own with this woman and to get his most urgent point across to her. He took another cookie from the plate.

Geneva said, 'Have you found any record of Maddoc's marriage to Leilani's mother?'

'No. Even with Internet resources, it's a big country. In a few states, if you have a convincing reason and some friends in the right places, you could arrange an in-camera marriage, in the privacy of a judge's chambers, with the license issued and properly filed but not published. That's not easy to track. More likely, they were hitched in another country that'll marry foreign nationals. Maybe Mexico. Or Guatemala's a good bet. A lot of resources could be saved if Leilani would tell us where the wedding took place.'

'We were going to ask exactly that when she came to dinner the second time. But we didn't see her again. I guess the mother's real name and proof that the brother existed aren't any easier to track than the marriage license.'

'Not impossible. But, again, it would help if I could speak to Leilani.' Frustrated, he put down the unbitten second cookie. 'I'm sitting here listening to myself talk like I'm completely on-board for this, and that's not the case, Geneva.'

'I know it'll be expensive, and Micky didn't give you much—'

'That's not the problem.'

'– but I have a little equity in this house that I could borrow against, and Micky's going to get a good job soon, I know she is.'

'It's hard to get a good job and keep it when you're on the run from the FBI. Listen, that's the point. If I do any work for you, knowing that your niece intends to snatch this girl from her legal parents, then I'm aiding and abetting a kidnapping.'

'That's ridiculous, dear.'

'I'd be an accessory to a felony. It's the law.'

'The law is ridiculous.'

'In fact, to protect myself from any chance of being charged as an accessory, once I've given back your three hundred bucks, which I've brought with me, I have to go directly to the authorities and warn them what your niece is intending to do up there in Idaho.'

Geneva cocked her head and favored him with a look of amused disbelief. 'Don't tease me, dear.'

'Tease? I'm dead serious here.'

She winked at him. 'No, you're not.'

'Yes, I am.'

'No, you're not.' She punctuated her words with another wink. 'You won't go to the police. And even if you give back the money, you'll still be on the case.'

'I will *not* be on the case.'

'I know how this works, dear. You've got to establish – what do they call it? – plausible deniability. If everything goes bad, you can claim you weren't working on the case because you took no money.'

Withdrawing the three hundred from a pocket of his chinos, he placed the cash on the table. 'I'm not establishing anything. All I'm doing is quitting.'

'No, you're not,' she said.

'I never took the job in the first place.'

She wagged one finger at him. 'Yes, you did.'

'I did not.'

'Yes, you did, dear. Otherwise, where did the three hundred dollars come from?'

'I,' he said firmly, 'quit. Q-U-I-T. I'm resigning, I'm walking, I'm splitting this gig, gone, finito, out of here.'

Geneva smiled broadly and winked at him again. This time it was a great, exaggerated wink of comic conspiracy. 'Oh, whatever you say, Mr. Farrel, sir. If ever I have to testify in a court of ridiculous law, you can count on me telling the judge that you Q-U-I-T in no uncertain terms.'

This woman had a smile that could charm birds out of the sky and into a cage. One of Noah's grandmothers had died before he was born, and his grandmother on the Farrel side had looked nothing like Geneva Davis; she had been a chisel-faced, chain-smoking, ferret-eyed crone with a voice burnt raw by a lifelong thirst for whiskey, and during the years that she and Grandfather Farrel had operated a pawnshop that fronted a bookie operation, she had routinely terrified even the toughest young punks with a mere look and a few snarled words in Gaelic, even though the punks didn't speak the language. Yet he felt that he was sitting here having cookies with his grandmother, his ideal grandmother rather than the real one, and beneath his frustration quivered a warm and fuzzy feeling that he had never known before, which had to be a *dangerous* feeling under the circumstances.

'Don't wink at me again, Geneva. You're trying to pretend we're in some sort of little conspiracy here, and we're not.'

'Oh, dear, I know we're not. You have Q-U-I-T, resigned, finito, and that's perfectly clear to me.' She smiled broadly and refrained from winking – but gave him a vigorous thumbs-up sign with both hands.

Noah picked up his unbitten second cookie and bit it. Twice. The cookie was big, but with just two bites, he crammed more than half of it in his mouth. Chewing ferociously, he glared across the table at Geneva Davis.

'More vanilla Coke, dear?' she asked.

He tried to say no, but his mouth was too full to permit speech, so he found himself nodding yes.

She refreshed his vanilla Coke with a drizzle of cherry syrup, more cola, and a couple ice cubes.

When Geneva sat at the table again, Noah said, 'Let me try this one more time.'

'Try what, sweetie?'

'Explaining the situation to you.'

'Good heavens, I'm not *dense*, dear. I understand the situation perfectly. You've got your plausible deniability, and in court I'll testify that you didn't help us, even though you did. Or will.' She scooped up the three hundred dollars. 'And if everything goes well and no one ends up in court, then I'll give this back to you, and we'll pay anything else you bill us. We may need some time, may need to make monthly payments, but we honor our debts, Micky and me. And none of us will end up in court, anyway. I mean no disrespect, dear, but I'm sure your understanding of the law is weak in this instance.'

'I was a police officer before I became a PI.'

'Then you really should have a better grasp of the law,' she admonished with one of those your-grandmother-thinks-you're-adorable smiles that exacerbated his case of the warm fuzzies.

Scowling, leaning across the kitchen table, resorting to a display of his dark side, he tried to jolt her out of this stubborn refusal to face facts. 'I had a perfect grasp of the law, but I was stripped of my badge anyway because I severely beat a suspect. *I beat the crap out of him.*'

She clucked her tongue. 'That's nothing to be proud of, dear.'

'I'm not proud of it. I'm lucky I didn't end up in prison.'

'You certainly sounded proud of it.'

Staring unblinkingly at her, he consumed the last third of the cookie. He washed it down with cherry-flavored vanilla Coke.

She wasn't intimidated by his stare. She smiled as though she took pleasure from the sight of him enjoying her baked goods.

He said, 'Actually, I am half proud of it. Shouldn't be, not even considering the circumstances. But I am. I was answering a domestic-disturbance call. This guy had really pounded on his wife. She's a mess when I get there, and now he's beating his daughter, just a little girl, like eight years old. He's knocked out some of her teeth. When he sees me, he lets her go, he doesn't resist arrest. I lost it anyway. Seeing that girl, I lost it.'

Reaching across the table, Geneva squeezed his hand. 'Good for you.'

'No, it wasn't good. I would've kept going until I killed him – except the girl stopped me. In my report, I lied, claimed the creep resisted arrest. In the hearing, the wife testified against me . . . but the girl lied for me, and they believed the girl. Or pretended to. I made a deal to leave the force, and they agreed to give me severance pay and support my application for a PI license.'

'What happened to the child?' Geneva asked.

'Turns out the abuse was long-term. The court removed her from her mother's custody, put her with her maternal grandparents. She'll graduate high school soon. She's okay. She's a good kid.'

Geneva squeezed his hand again and then leaned back in her chair, beaming. 'You're just like my gumshoe.'

'What gumshoe?'

'The one I was in love with back when I was in my twenties. If I hadn't hidden my murdered husband's body in an oil-field sump, Philip might not have rejected me.'

Noah didn't quite know how to respond to this. He blotted his damp brow again. Finally he said, 'You killed your husband?'

'No, my sister, Carmen, shot him. I hid the body to protect her and to spare our father from the scandal. General Sternwood – that was our daddy – wasn't in good health. And he . . .'

Puzzlement crossed Geneva's face as her voice trailed away.

Noah encouraged her to continue: 'And he . . . ?'

'Well, of course, that wasn't me, that was Lauren Bacall in *The Big Sleep*. The gumshoe was Humphrey Bogart playing Philip Marlowe.'

Geneva clapped her hands and let out a musical laugh of delight.

Although he didn't know *why* he was smiling, Noah smiled.

Geneva said, 'Well, it's a delicious memory even if it's a false memory. Honestly, I must admit, I'm something of a wimp when it comes to being naughty. I've never had it in me to be a bad girl, so if I hadn't been shot in the head, I'd never have had a memory like that.'

The sugar content of cookies and cola provided sufficient mental lift to deal with a wide spectrum of intellectual challenges, but, by God, for some things you needed a beer. He didn't have a beer, so instead of making an attempt to deduce logically the meaning of what she'd said, he asked another question: 'You were shot in the head?'

'A polite and well-dressed bandit held up our convenience store, killed my husband, shot me, and disappeared. I won't tell you that I tracked him to New Orleans and blew him away myself, because that was Alec Baldwin and not a part of my real life. But even wimp that I am, I'd have been *capable* of shooting him if I'd known how to track him down. I'd have shot him repeatedly, I think. Once in each leg, let him suffer, then twice in the gut, then once in the head. Do I sound terribly savage, dear?'

'Not savage. But more vindictive than I would have expected.'

'That's a good honest answer. I'm impressed with you, Noah.'

She turned on one of those ice-melting smiles.

He found himself smiling, too.

'I'm enjoying our little get-together,' she said.

'Me too.'

61

Saturday: Hawthorne, Nevada, to Boise, Idaho. Four hundred forty-nine miles. Mostly wasteland, bright sun, but an easy haul.

A cloud of vultures circled something dead in the desert half an hour south of Lovelock, Nevada. Though intrigued, Preston Maddoc decided against a side trip to investigate.

They stopped for lunch at a diner in Winnemucca.

On the sidewalk outside the restaurant, swarms of ants were feeding on the oozing body of a fat, crushed beetle. The bug juice had an interesting iridescent quality similar to oil on water.

Taking the Hand into a public place was risky these days. Her performance on Friday, in the coffee shop west of Vegas, had been unnerving. She might have gotten what she wanted if the waitress hadn't been stupid.

Most people were stupid. Preston Maddoc had made this judgment of humanity when he'd been eleven. In the past thirty-four years, he'd seen no reason to change his mind.

The diner smelled of sizzling hamburger patties. French fries roiling in hot oil. Bacon.

He wondered what the beetle ooze smelled like.

Several men were sitting side by side on stools at the lunch counter. Most were overweight. Chowing down jowl to jowl. Disgusting.

Maybe one of them would have a stroke or heart attack during lunch. The odds were good.

The Hand led them to a booth. She sat next to the window.

The Black Hole settled beside her daughter.

Preston sat across the table from them. His fair ladies.

The Hand was grotesque, of course, but the Black Hole actually was fair. After so many drugs, she ought to have been a withered hag.

When her looks finally started to go, they would slide away fast. Probably in two or three years.

Maybe he could squeeze two litters out of her before she'd be too repulsive to touch.

On the windowsill lay a dead fly. Ambience.

He consulted his menu. The owners ought to change the name of the establishment. Call it the Palace of Grease.

Naturally the Black Hole couldn't find many dishes to her taste. At least she didn't whine. The Hole was in a cheerful mood. Coherent, too, because she seldom used heavy chemicals before the afternoon.

The waitress arrived. An ugly wretch. The wall-eyed, pouchy-cheeked face of a fish.

She wore a neatly pressed pink uniform. Elaborately coiffed hair the color of rat fur, with a pink bow to match the uniform. Carefully applied makeup, eyeliner, lipstick. Fingernails manicured but clear-coated, as if they were something sweet to look at, as if her fingers weren't as stubby and ugly as the rest of her.

She was trying too hard to look nice. A hopeless cause.

Bridges were made for people like her. Bridges and high ledges. Car tailpipes and gas ovens. If she ever phoned a suicide hot line and some counselor talked her out of sucking on a shotgun, she'd have been done a disservice.

They ordered lunch.

Preston expected the Hand to appeal to Fish Face for help. She didn't. She seemed subdued.

Her performance the previous day had been unnerving, but he was disappointed that she didn't try again. He enjoyed the challenge posed by her recent rebellious mood.

While they waited for their food, the Hole chattered as inanely as always she did.

She was the Black Hole partly because her psychotic energy and her mindless babble together spun a powerful gravity that could pull you toward oblivion if you weren't a strong person.

He was strong. He never shied from any task. Never flinched from any truth.

Although he conversed with the Hole, he remained less than

half involved with her. He always lived more inside himself than not.

He was thinking about the Gimp, brother to the Hand. He had been thinking about the Gimp a lot lately.

Considering the risks that he had taken, he'd not gotten enough satisfaction from his last visit with the boy in the Montana woods. Everything had happened far too quickly. Such memories needed to be rich. They sustained him.

Preston had more elaborate plans for the Hand.

Speaking of whom: Nonchalantly, almost surreptitiously, she slowly swept the diner with her gaze, obviously looking for something specific.

He noticed her spot the restroom sign.

A moment later she announced that she needed to use the toilet. She said *toilet* because she knew the term displeased Preston.

He'd been raised in a refined family that never resorted to such vulgarities. He far preferred *lavatory*. He could endure either *powder room* or *restroom*.

The Hole stood, allowing her daughter to slide out of the booth.

As the Hand got clumsily to her feet, she whispered, 'I really gotta pee.'

This, too, was a slap at Preston. The Hand knew that he was repulsed by any discussion of bodily functions.

He didn't like to watch her walk. Her deformed fingers were sickening enough. He continued exchanging stupidities with the Hole, thinking about Montana, tracking the Hand with his peripheral vision.

Abruptly he realized that under the RESTROOMS sign, another had indicated the location of what she might really be seeking: PHONE.

Excusing himself, he got out of the booth and followed the girl.

She had disappeared into a short hall at the end of the diner.

When he reached that same hall, he discovered the men's lavatory to the right, the women's to the left. A pay phone on the end wall.

She stood at the phone, her back to him. As she reached for the receiver with her warped hand, she sensed him and turned.

Looming over her, Preston saw the quarter in her good hand.

'Did you find that in the coin return?' he asked.

'Yeah,' she lied. 'I always check.'

'Then it belongs to someone else,' he admonished. 'We'll turn it in to the cashier when we leave.'

He held out his hand, palm up.

Reluctant to give him the quarter, she hesitated.

He rarely touched her. Contact gave him the creeps.

Fortunately, she held the coin in her normal hand. If it had been in the left, he would still have been able to take it, but then he wouldn't have been able to eat lunch.

Pretending that she had come here to use the lavatory, she went through the door marked GALS.

Maintaining a similar pretense, Preston entered the men's lav. He was grateful it wasn't in use. He waited inside, near the door.

He wondered who she'd intended to phone. The police?

As soon as he heard her exit the women's restroom, he returned to the hall, as well.

He led her back to the booth. If he had followed her, he would have had to watch her walk.

Lunch arrived immediately after they were seated.

Fish Face, the ugly waitress, had a mole on the side of her nose. He thought it looked like melanoma.

If it *was* melanoma and she remained unaware of it even for a week or so, her nose would eventually rot away. Surgery would leave her with a crater in the center of her face.

Maybe then, if the malignancy hadn't gotten into her brain and killed her, maybe *then* she would at last do the right thing with a tailpipe or a gas oven, or a shotgun.

The food was pretty good.

As usual, he didn't look at his companions' mouths while they were eating. He focused on their eyes or looked slightly past them, studiously avoiding the sight of their tongues, teeth, lips, and masticating jaws.

Preston assumed that occasionally someone might look at his mouth while he chewed or at his throat as he swallowed, but he forced himself not to dwell on this. If he dared think much about it, he would have to eat in private.

During meals, he lived even more inside himself than he did at other times. Defensively.

This posed no problem for him, required no special effort. His major at Yale and then at Harvard, through his bachelor's and master's and doctoral degrees, had been philosophy. By nature, philosophers lived more inside themselves than did ordinary people.

Intellectuals in general, and philosophers in particular, needed the world less than the world needed them.

Throughout lunch, he upheld his end of a conversation with the Hole while he recalled Montana.

The sound of the boy's neck snapping . . .

The way the terror in his eyes darkened into bleak resignation and then had clarified into peace . . .

The rare smell of the final fitful exhalation that produced the death rattle in the Gimp's throat . . .

Preston left a thirty-percent tip, but he didn't surrender the quarter to the cashier. He was certain that the Hand hadn't found the money in the pay phone. The coin was his to keep, ethically.

To avoid the government-enforced blockade of eastern Nevada, where the FBI was officially searching for drug lords but was – in his opinion – probably covering up some UFO-related event, Preston turned north from Winnemucca, toward the state of Oregon, using Federal Highway 95, an undivided two-lane road.

Fifty-six miles inside Oregon, Highway 95 swung east toward Idaho. They crossed the Owyhee River, and then the state line.

By six o'clock, they arrived at a campground north of Boise, Idaho, where they hooked up to utilities.

Preston bought takeout for dinner. Mediocre Chinese this time.

The Black Hole loved rice. And though she was wired again, she was nevertheless still compos mentis enough to eat.

As usual, the Hole directed the conversation according to her interests. She required always to be the center of attention.

When she mentioned new design ideas for carving her daughter's deformed hand, he encouraged her. He found the subject of decorative mutilation stupid enough to be amusing – as long as he avoided looking at the girl's twisted appendage.

In addition, he knew that this talk terrified the Hand, though she hid her fear well. Good. Fear might eventually burn away her delusion that she had any hope of a normal life.

She had chosen to thwart her mother by shrewdly playing along with this demented game. Listening to the Black Hole enthuse about going at her with scalpels, however, she might begin to realize that she had not been born to win any game, least of all this one.

She had come out of her mother broken, imperfect. She was a loser from the moment that the physician slapped her butt to start her breathing instead of mercifully, discreetly smothering her.

When the time arrived for him to take this girl into the forest, perhaps she would have come to the conclusion that death was best for her. She should choose death before her mother could carve her. Because sooner or later, her mother *would*.

Death was her only possible deliverance. Otherwise, she would have to endure more years as an outsider. Life could hold nothing but disappointment for someone so damaged as she.

Of course, Preston didn't want her to be *entirely* pliable and eager to die. A measure of resistance made for memories.

Dinner finished, leaving the Hand to clean the table, he and the Hole took evening showers, separately, and retired to the bedroom.

Eventually, reading *In Watermelon Sugar*, the Hole passed out.

Preston wanted to use her. But he couldn't discern whether she'd been hammered by drugs into deep unconsciousness or whether she was just sleeping soundly.

If she were merely sleeping, she might awaken in the middle of the action. Her awareness would ruin his mood.

Waking, she would be enthusiastic. She *knew* that the deal they had made didn't permit her active participation in physical intimacy. Yet she would be enthusiastic nonetheless.

The deal: The Hole received everything that she needed in return for this one thing that Preston wanted.

He was mildly nauseated by the thought of her enthusiasm, her participation. He had no desire to witness the more intimate bodily functions of anyone.

And he was loath to *be* observed.

When suffering from a head cold, he unfailingly excused himself to blow his nose in private. He didn't want anyone to hear his mucus draining.

Consequently, the prospect of having an orgasm in the presence of an interested partner was distressing if not unthinkable.

Discretion was underrated in contemporary society.

Uncertain as to the nature and reliability of the Hole's current state of unconsciousness, he turned off the light and settled on his own side of the bed.

He contemplated the babies that she would bring into the world. Little twisted wizards. Ethical dilemmas awaiting firm resolutions.

≈ ≈ ≈

Sunday: Boise to Nun's Lake. Three hundred fifty-one miles. More-demanding terrain than what Nevada had offered.

Usually he didn't hit the road until nine or ten o'clock, with the Black Hole still abed, the Hand awake. Although they were seeking a close encounter, their mission wasn't as urgent as it was dramatic.

This morning, however, he hauled the Prevost out of Twin Falls at 6:15 A.M.

Already the Hand was dressed, eating a granola bar.

He wondered if she had discovered that all the knives and sharp utensils had been removed from the galley.

He remained convinced that she lacked the guts to stab him in the back while he drove the motor home. In fact he didn't believe that she would prove capable of making a serious effort to defend herself when the two of them were alone in the moment of judgment.

Nevertheless, he was a careful man.

North out of the broad chest of Idaho into the narrow neck, they passed through spectacular scenery. Soaring mountains, vast forests, eagles in flight.

Every encounter with Nature at her most radiant gave rise to the same thought: *Humanity is a pestilence. Humanity doesn't belong here.*

He could not be counted as one of the radical environmentalists who dreamed of a day when a virulent plague could be engineered to scour every human being from the earth. He had ethical problems with the systematic extermination of an entire species, even humanity.

On the other hand, using public policy to halve the number of human beings on the planet was a laudable goal. Benign neglect of famines would delete millions. Cease the exportation of all life-extending drugs to Third World countries where AIDS raged epidemic, and additional millions would pass in a more timely fashion.

Let Nature purge the excess. Let Nature decide how many human beings she wished to tolerate. Unobstructed, she would solve the problem soon enough.

Small wars unlikely to escalate into worldwide clashes should be viewed not as horrors to be avoided, but as sensible prunings.

Indeed, where large totalitarian governments wished to expunge dissidents by the hundreds of thousands or even by the millions, no sanctions should be brought against them. Dissidents were usually people who rebelled against sensible resource management.

Besides, sanctions could lead to the foment of rebellion, to clandestine military actions, which might grow into major wars, even spiral into a nuclear conflict, damaging not just human civilization but the natural world.

No human being could do anything whatsoever to improve upon the natural world – which, without people, was perfect.

Few contributed anything positive to human civilization, either. By the tenets of utilitarian ethics, only those useful to the state or to society had a legitimate claim on life. Most people were too flawed to be of use to anyone.

Soaring mountains, vast forests, eagles flying.

Out there beyond the windshield: The splendor of nature.

In here, behind his eyes, inside where he most fully lived, waited a grandeur different from but equal to that of nature, a private landscape that he found endlessly fascinating.

Yet Preston Claudius Maddoc prided himself that he possessed the honesty and the principle to acknowledge his own short-comings. He was as flawed as anyone, more deeply flawed than some, and he never indulged in self-delusion in this matter.

By any measure, his most serious fault must be his frequent homicidal urges. And the pleasure he took from killing.

To his credit, at an early age, he recognized that this lust for killing was an imperfection in his character and that it must not be lightly excused. Even as a young boy, he sought to channel his murderous impulses into responsible activities.

First he tortured and killed insects. Ants, beetles, spiders, flies, caterpillars . . .

Back then, everyone seemed to agree that bugs of all kinds were largely a scourge. Perhaps the ultimate grace is to find one's bliss in useful work. His bliss was killing, and his useful work was the eradication of anything that creeped or crawled.

Preston hadn't been environmentally aware in those days. His subsequent education left him mortified at the assault he had waged on nature when he'd been a boy. Bugs do enormously useful work.

To this day, he remained haunted by the possibility that he *had* known on some deep level that his activities were unethical. Otherwise, why had he been so secretive when pursuing his bliss?

He'd never bragged about the spiders crushed. The caterpillars dusted with salt. The beetles set afire.

And without quite thinking about it, all but unconsciously, he had escalated from insects to small animals. Mice, gerbils, guinea pigs, birds, rabbits, cats . . .

The family's thirty-acre estate in Delaware provided a plenitude of wildlife that could be trapped for his purposes. In less fruitful seasons, his generous allowance permitted him to get what he needed from pet stores.

He seemed to spend his twelfth and thirteenth years in a semi-trance. So much secretive killing. Often, when he made an effort at recollection, those years blurred.

No justification existed for the wanton destruction of animals. They belonged on this world more surely than people did.

In retrospect, Preston wondered if he hadn't been perilously close to losing control of himself in those days. That period held little nostalgic value for him. He chose to remember better times.

On the night following Preston's fourteenth birthday, life changed for the better with the visit of Cousin Brandon, who arrived for a long weekend in the company of his parents.

A lifelong paraplegic, Brandon depended on a wheelchair.

In Preston's inner world, where he lived far more than not, he called his cousin the Dirtbag because, for almost two years between the ages of seven and eight, Brandon had required a colostomy bag until a series of complex surgeries ultimately resolved a bowel problem.

Because the mansion boasted an elevator, all three floors were accessible to the disabled boy. He slept in Preston's room, which had long been furnished with a second bed for friends on sleepovers.

They had a lot of fun. The Dirtbag, thirteen, possessed a singular talent for impersonation, uncannily reproducing the voices of family members and employees on the estate. Preston had never laughed so much as he had laughed that night.

The Dirtbag fell asleep around one o'clock in the morning.

At two o'clock, Preston killed him. He smothered the boy with a pillow.

Only the Dirtbag's legs were paralyzed, but he suffered from other conditions that resulted in somewhat diminished upper-body strength. He tried to resist, but not effectively.

Having recently recovered from a protracted bout with a severe bronchial infection, the Dirtbag's lung capacity might not have been at its peak. He died much too quickly to please Preston.

Hoping to prolong the experience, Preston had relented a few times with the pillow, giving the Dirtbag an opportunity to draw a breath but not to cry out. Nevertheless, the end came too soon.

The bedclothes had been slightly disarranged by the boy's feeble struggle. Preston smoothed them.

He brushed his dead cousin's hair, making him more presentable.

Because the Dirtbag died on his back, as he always slept, there was no need to reposition the body. Preston adjusted the arms and the hands to convey the impression of a quiet passing.

The mouth hung open. Preston firmly closed it, held it, waited for it to lock in place.

The eyes were wide, staring in what might have been surprise. He drew the lids shut and weighted them with quarters.

After a couple hours, he removed the coins. The lids remained closed.

Preston switched off the lamp and returned to his bed, burying his face in the same pillow with which he had smothered his cousin.

He felt that he had done a fine thing.

During the remainder of the night, he was too excited to sleep soundly, although he dozed on and off.

He was awake but pretending to oversleep when at eight o'clock, the Dirtbag's mother, Aunt Janice – also known as the Tits – rapped softly on the bedroom door. When her second knock wasn't answered, she entered anyway, for she was bringing her son's morning medicines.

Planning to fake a startled awakening the instant that the Tits screamed, Preston was denied his dramatic moment when she made only a strangled sound of grief and sagged against the Dirtbag's bed, sobbing as softly as she had knocked.

At the funeral, Preston heard numerous relatives and family friends say that perhaps this was for the best, that Brandon had gone to a better place now, that his lifelong suffering had been relieved, that perhaps the parents' heavy grief was more than balanced by the weight of responsibility that had been lifted from their shoulders.

This confirmed his perception that he had done a fine thing.

His endeavors with insects were finished.

His misguided adventures with small animals were at an end.

He had found his work, and it was his bliss, as well.

A brilliant boy and superb student, the top of his class, he naturally turned to education to seek a greater understanding of his special role in life. In school and books he found every answer that he wanted.

While he learned, he practiced. As a young man of great wealth and privilege, he was much admired for the unpaid work he performed in nursing homes, which he modestly called 'just giving back a little to society in return for all my blessings.'

By the time that he went to university, Preston determined that philosophy would be his field, his chosen community.

Introduced to a forest of philosophers and philosophies, he was taught that every tree stood equal to the others, that each deserved respect, that no view of life and life's purpose was superior to any other. This meant no absolutes existed, no certainties, no universal right or wrong, merely different points of view. Before him were millions of board feet of ideas, from which he'd been invited to construct any dwelling that pleased him.

Some philosophies placed a greater value on human life than did others. Those were not for him.

Soon he discovered that if philosophy was his community, then contemporary ethics was the street on which he most desired to live. Eventually, the relatively new field of bioethics became a cozy house in which he felt at home as never before in his life.

Thus he had arrived at his current eminence. And to this place, this time.

Soaring mountains, vast forests, eagles flying.

North, north to Nun's Lake.

The Black Hole had resurrected herself. She settled in the co-pilot's chair.

Preston conversed with her, charmed her, made her laugh, drove with his usual expertise, drove north to Nun's Lake, but still he lived more richly within himself.

He reviewed in memory his most beautiful killings. He had many more to remember than the world realized. The assisted suicides known to the media were but a fraction of his career achievements.

Being one of the most controversial *and* one of the most highly regarded bioethicists of his day, Preston had a responsibility to his profession not to be immodest. Consequently he'd never brag of the true number of mercies that he'd granted to those in need of dying.

As they sped farther north, the sky steadily gathered clouds upon itself: thin gray shrouds and later thick thunderheads of a darker material.

Before the day waned, Preston intended to locate and visit Leonard Teelroy, the man who claimed to have been healed by aliens. He hoped that the weather wouldn't interfere with his plans.

He expected to find that Teelroy was a fraud. A dismayingly high percentage of claimed close encounters appeared to be obvious hoaxes.

Nevertheless, Preston ardently believed that extraterrestrials had been visiting Earth for millennia. In fact, he was pretty sure that he knew what they were doing here.

Suppose Leonard Teelroy had told the truth. Even suppose the alien activity at the Teelroy farm was ongoing. Preston still didn't believe the ETs would heal the Hand and send her away dancing.

His 'vision' of the Hand and the Gimp being healed had never occurred. He'd invented it to explain to the Black Hole why he wanted to ricochet around the country in search of a close encounter.

Now, still chatting with the Hole, he checked the mirror on the visor. The Hand sat at the dinette table. Reading.

What was it they called a condemned man in prison? *Dead man walking*. Yes, that was it.

See here: Dead girl reading.

His real reasons for tracking down ETs and making contact were personal. They had nothing to do with the Hand. He knew, however, that the Black Hole would not be inspired by his true motives.

Every activity must somehow revolve around the Hole. Otherwise, she would not cooperate in the pursuit of it.

He had figured that this healing-aliens story would be one that she would buy. Likewise, he had been confident that when at last he killed her children and claimed they had been beamed up to the stars, the Hole would accept their disappearance with wonder and delight – and would fail to recognize her own danger.

This had proved to be the case. If nature had given her a good mind, she had methodically destroyed it. She was a reliable dimwit.

The Hand was another matter. Too smart by half.

Preston could no longer risk waiting until her tenth birthday.

After he visited the Teelroy farm and assessed the situation there, if he saw no likelihood of making contact with ETs, he would drive east into Montana first thing in the morning. By three o'clock in the afternoon, he would take the girl to the remote and deeply shaded glen in which her brother waited for her.

He would open the grave and force her to look at what remained of the Gimp.

That would be cruel. He recognized the meanness of it.

As always, Preston forthrightly acknowledged his faults. He made no claim to perfection. *No* human could honestly make such a claim.

In addition to his passion for homicide, he had over the years gradually become aware of a taste for cruelty. Killing mercifully – quickly and in a manner that caused little pain – had at first been immensely satisfying, but less so over time.

He took no pride in this character defect, but neither did it shame him. Like every person on the planet, he was what he was – and had to make the best of it.

All that mattered, however, was that he remained *useful* in a true and profound sense, that what he contributed to this troubled society continued to outweigh the resources he consumed to sustain himself. In the finest spirit of utilitarian ethics, he had put his faults to good use for humanity and had behaved responsibly.

He reserved his cruelty strictly for those who needed to die anyway, and tormented them only immediately before killing them.

Otherwise, he quite admirably controlled every impulse to be vicious. He treated all people – those he had not marked for death – with kindness, respect, and generosity.

In truth, more like him were needed: men – and women! – who acted within a code of ethics to rid an overpopulated world of the takers, of the worthless ones who, if left alive, would drag down not merely civilization with all their endless needs, but nature as well.

There were so many of the worthless. Legions.

He wanted to subject the Hand to the exquisite cruelty of seeing her brother's remains, because he was annoyed by her pious certainty that God had made her for a purpose, that her life had meaning she would one day discover.

Let her look for meaning in the biological sludge and bristling bones of her brother's decomposed body. Let her search hopelessly for any sign of any god in that reeking grave.

North to Nun's Lake under a darkening sky.

Soaring mountains, vast forests. Eagles gone to roost.

Dead girl reading.

62

According to the inset chart of estimated driving times on the AAA map, Micky should have required eight hours and ten minutes to travel the 381 miles between Seattle and Nun's Lake. Speed limits and rest stops were factored into this estimate, as were the conditions of the narrower state and county roads that she had to use after she exited Interstate 90 southeast of Coeur d'Alene.

After leaving Seattle promptly at 5:30 A.M., she reached her destination at 12:20 P.M., one hour and twenty minutes ahead of schedule. Light traffic, a disregard for speed limits, and a lack of interest in rest stops served her well.

Nun's Lake proved to be true to its name. A large lake lay immediately south of it, and an imposing convent, built of native stone in the 1930s, stood on a high hill to the north. An order of Carmelite nuns occupied the convent, while fish of many denominations meditated in the deeps of the lake, bracketing the community between a monument to the power of the spirit and a flourishing recreational enterprise.

Evergreen forests embraced the town. Under a threatening sky, great pines sentineled the looming storm, orders upon orders of symbolic sisters in green wimples and guimpes and habits, needled garments so dark in this somber light that at a distance, they looked almost as black as the vestments of the real nuns in the convent.

Although the town had fewer than two thousand residents in the off season, a steady influx of fishermen, boaters, campers, hikers, and jet-ski enthusiasts doubled the population during the summer.

At a busy sportsman's store that sold everything from earthworms by the pint to six-packs of beer, Micky learned that three facilities in the area provided campsites with power-and-water hookups to motor homes and travel trailers. Favoring tenters, the state park dedicated only twenty percent of its sites to campers requiring utilities. Two privately owned RV campgrounds were a better bet for those roughing it in style.

Within an hour, she visited all three places, inquiring whether the Jordan Banks family had checked in, certain that Maddoc would not be traveling under his real name. They were in residence at none of the campgrounds, nor did they have a reservation at one.

Because the stagnant economy had crimped some people's vacation plans and because even in better times the area had a surplus of RV campsites, reservations weren't always required, and space was likely to be available at all three facilities when Maddoc pulled into town.

She asked each of the registration clerks not to mention her inquiry to the Banks family when eventually they showed up. 'I'm Jordan's sister. He doesn't know I'm here. I want to surprise him. It's his birthday.'

If Maddoc had false ID supporting his Jordan Banks identity, he probably had identification in other names, as well. He might already be in one of these campgrounds, using a name that she didn't know.

Leilani had described the motor home as a luxurious converted Prevost bus: 'When people see it rolling along the highway, they get all excited 'cause they assume Godzilla is on vacation.' Furthermore, Micky had seen the midnight-blue Dodge Durango parked at the house trailer next door to Gen's place, and she knew Maddoc towed it behind the Prevost. Consequently, if he was registered under a third name, she'd be able to find him anyway during a tour of the campgrounds.

The problem was that at each facility, she needed to know a registered guest in order to obtain a visitor's pass. Until Maddoc either checked in under the Banks name or until she learned what other identity he might be using, she wasn't able to undertake such a search.

She could have rented a site at each campground, which would have allowed her to come and go as she pleased. But she had no tent or other camping gear. While you could sleep in a van and pass as RV royalty, sleeping in a car branded you as half a step up the social ladder from a homeless person, and you were not welcome.

Besides, her budget was so tight that if she plucked it, the resulting note would be heard only by dogs. If she connected with Maddoc here but was unable to find an opportunity to grab Leilani, she might have to follow them elsewhere. Because she didn't know where this quest might lead, she needed to conserve every dollar.

Short of returning to all three campgrounds at one- or two-hour intervals, making a nuisance of herself, Micky could see only one course of action likely to lead her to Maddoc soon after he finally arrived in Nun's Lake. He had come all this way to talk to a man who claimed to have experienced a close encounter with extraterrestrials. If she could run surveillance on that man's home, she would spot her quarry when he paid a visit.

At the busy sportsman's store where previously she had inquired about RV-friendly campgrounds, she'd also asked about the local UFO celebrity, eliciting a weary laugh from the clerk. The man's name was Leonard Teelroy, and he lived on a farm three miles east of the town limits.

The directions proved easy to follow, and the narrow county road was well marked, but when she arrived at the Teelroy place, she found that it qualified as a farm only because of the work that had once been done there, not because it currently produced anything. Broken-down fences surrounded fields long ago gone to waist-high weeds.

The weathered barn had not been painted in decades. Wind and rain, rot and termites, and the power of neglect had stripped fully a third of the boards from the flanks of this building, as though it were a fallen behemoth from the ribs of which carrion eaters had torn away the meat. The swaybacked ridgeline of the roof suggested that it might collapse if so much as a blackbird came to rest upon it.

An ancient John Deere tractor, trademark corn-green paint faded to a silver-teal, lay on its side, entwined by rambling weeds along the oiled-dirt driveway that led to the house, as if in some distant age, the angry earth had rebelled at ceaseless cultivation and, loosing a sudden ravel of green brambles from its bosom, had snared the busy tractor, tipped it off its tires, and strangled the driver.

Micky had not originally intended to visit Teelroy, only to keep a watch on the house until Maddoc arrived. She drove past the farm, and immediately east of it, she saw that the north shoulder of the county road lay at the same elevation as surrounding land; she had her choice of several places where she could back the car among the trees to maintain surveillance from a relatively concealed position.

Before she could pick her spot, she began to worry that Maddoc might already have been here and gone. If she'd come after him, she would be maintaining surveillance while he and Sinsemilla headed out of Nun's Lake with Leilani for points unknown, untraceable.

She'd chosen a route around Nevada, fearing that the government quarantine of the eastern portion of the state might widen to include the entire territory, trapping her within its boundaries. If Maddoc had taken the Nevada route and had encountered no roadblocks, he had traveled fewer miles to get here than she did.

Each day, she had driven long hours, surely much longer than Maddoc would have wanted to sit behind the wheel of a more-difficult-to-handle vehicle like the motor home. And she was confident that her Camaro had throughout the trip maintained a much higher average speed than his lumbering bus.

Nevertheless . . .

At the first opportunity, she swung the car around and returned to the Teelroy farm. Entering the driveway, passing the rusting hulk of the overturned tractor, she slowed and took a closer look. She half expected to glimpse the sun-bleached bones of the bramble-strangled driver that she had previously imagined, because on second view the farm appeared to be an even grimmer place – and stranger – than it had been at first sight.

If Norman Bates, psycho of psychos, having escaped from the asylum and fearing that an immediate return to the motel business might make him easier for the police to find, decided to apply his knowledge of the hospitality industry to a simple bed-and-breakfast, this old house would have delighted him when he found it. Sun, rain, snow, and wind were the only painters these walls had seen in twenty years. Teelroy had done barely enough maintenance to spare himself from grisly death in a spontaneous structural implosion.

Between the Camaro and the porch steps, Micky crossed what

remained of a front lawn: bare dirt and scraggly clumps of bunch-grass. The wooden steps popped and creaked. The porch floor groaned.

After knocking, she stepped back a few feet. By standing too close to the threshold, she seemed to be inviting a Jack the Ripper moment.

The air could not have been stiller if the entire farm had been covered by a bell jar.

The bruised and swollen sky looked angry, as though momentarily it would take hard revenge on everything below it.

Micky didn't hear anyone approaching the door, but abruptly it was yanked inward. Into the doorway hove a formidable bulk that smelled rather like sour milk, had a face as round and as red as a party balloon, and wore a beard so bristly that it looked less like hair than like tumbleweed. Bib overalls and a short-sleeve white T-shirt suggested this was a person standing before her, but the impression could be confirmed only by what she saw above a squash-shaped nose aglow and webbed with burst capillaries. Between that nose and a head as utterly hairless as a tomato, two fat-swaddled brown eyes confirmed his humanity, for they were filled nearly to overflowing with suspicion, misery, hope, and need.

'Mr. Teelroy?' she asked.

'Yes – who else? – nobody here but me.' From out of that bulk and beard and bad body odor had come a voice as sweet as a choirboy's.

'You're the Leonard Teelroy who had the close encounter?'

'What outfit are you from?' he asked pleasantly.

'Outfit?'

He looked her over from head to foot and back up again. 'Real people don't look as good as you, missy. You're dressed down, tryin' to hide it, but you've got Hollywood written all over you.'

'Hollywood? I'm afraid I don't follow you.'

He peered past her at the Camaro in the driveway. 'The junk heap's a nice touch.'

'It's not a *touch*. It's my car.'

'People like me are born to cars like that. Someone looks as actress-pretty as you – she's born with a Mercedes key in one hand.'

He wasn't gruff or argumentative. But he had his opinions and, in spite of his dulcet tones, an attitude.

He seemed to be expecting someone else. Because he appeared to have mistaken her for that person, she tried to start over.

'Mr. Teelroy, I've just come to hear about your UFO experience and to ask—'

'Of course you've come to ask, because it's one of *the* great stories ever. It's a blockbuster, what happened to me. And I'm willin' to give you everythin' you need – *after* the deal is made.'

'Deal?'

'But I expect honesty from anyone I do business with. You should have driven up in your real Mercedes, wearin' your real clothes, and straight out told me what studio or network you're with. You haven't even told me your own name.'

Now she understood. He believed his UFO experience would be the next Spielberg epic, with Mel Gibson in the Leonard Teelroy role.

She didn't have any interest in his close encounter; however, she saw a way to use his misapprehension to get the information that she really needed. 'You're a shrewd man, Mr. Teelroy.'

He beamed and seemed to swell in response to this compliment. His unnaturally red complexion brightened further, as boilers always brighten in cartoons just prior to exploding. 'I know what's fair. That's all I'm asking – just what's fair for a story this big.'

'I can't reach my boss on a Sunday. Tomorrow, I'll call him at the studio, discuss the situation, and come back with an offer in an entirely professional manner.'

He nodded slowly twice, as a courtly gentleman might acknowledge agreement with a lady's kind proposal. 'I'd be gratified.'

'One question, Mr. Teelroy. Do we have competition?' When he raised one eyebrow, she said, 'Has a representative from another studio been here already this morning?'

'No one's been here till you.' Suddenly and visibly, he realized that he ought to leave her with the impression that enormous sums had already been dangled before him. 'One fella visited yesterday' – he hesitated – 'from one of the big studios.' Poor Leonard didn't lie well; his boyish voice thickened with embarrassment at his boldness.

Even if someone had been here on Saturday, inquiring about the

UFO, he couldn't have been Maddoc. At most, the Prevost might have rolled into Nun's Lake a few hours ahead of Micky.

'I won't say *which* studio,' Teelroy added.

'I understand.'

'And not thirty minutes ago I had a call about all this. Man says he came here from California to see me, so I'm sure he's one of you people.' The hesitancy and the thickness had gone out of his voice. This was no lie. 'We have an appointment shortly.'

'Well, Mr. Teelroy, I'm sure you've heard of Paramount Pictures – haven't you?'

'They're big-time,'

'Way big-time. My name's Janet Hitchcock – no relation – and I'm an executive with Paramount Pictures.'

If Maddoc proved to be the man with an appointment, she hoped to prevent Teelroy from mentioning her in such a way that the doom doctor would realize who'd been here before him. Now there would be no reference to a nameless 'actress-pretty' woman in a dusty old Camaro. Teelroy would instead be eager to drop the name Janet Hitchcock of Paramount Pictures.

'Pleased to meet you, Miss Hitchcock.'

He held out his hand, and she shook it before she had time to think about where it might have been recently. 'I'll give you a call tomorrow,' she lied. 'We'll set up a meeting for the afternoon.'

Although the man was a grotesque, though he was trying to work a scam, though he might be delusional, possibly dangerous, Micky regretted lying to him. He'd shed all suspicion, but his eyes still brimmed with misery and need. He was more pathetic than offensive.

The world held too many people who couldn't wait to shoot the wounded. She didn't want to be one of them.

63

Curtis sits in the co-pilot's chair of the parked Fleetwood, gazing through the windshield, wondering if the nuns will risk water-skiing with a storm soon to break.

He had arrived here in Nun's Lake Saturday afternoon, in the protection of the Spelkenfelter sisters. They settled in a campground on a site that offered them a view of the lake through framing trees.

During the past twenty-four hours, Curtis has spotted no nuns either on the lake or engaged in activities on its shores. This disappoints him because he has seen so many wonderful caring nuns in movies – Ingrid Bergman! Audrey Hepburn! – but has yet to glimpse a real live one since his arrival on this world.

The twins have assured him that if he is patient and watchful, he will see scores of fully habited nuns water-skiing, parasailing, and jet-boat racing. They have made these assurances with such delightful giggles that he infers that nuns at play must be one of the most charming sights this planet offers.

After Curtis revealed his true nature on Friday evening in Twin Falls, Cass and Polly volunteered to be his royal guard. He had tried to explain that he descended from no imperial lineage, that he was an ordinary person just like them. Well, not *just* like them, considering that he possesses the ability to control his biological structure and to change shape to imitate any organism that has a reasonably high level of intelligence, but *otherwise* pretty much like them, except that he has no talent as a juggler and would be paralyzingly self-conscious if he had to perform nude on a Las Vegas stage.

They, however, apply a *Star Wars* template to the situation. They insist on seeing him as Princess Leia without either ample breasts or elaborate hairdo. The transmission for their sense of wonder has been engaged, shifted into high gear, and set racing. They say that they have long dreamed of this moment, and they are ready to dedicate the rest of their lives to helping him perform the work that his mother and her followers came here to do.

He has explained his mission to them, and they understand what he can do for humanity. He has not yet given them the Gift, but soon he will, and they are excited by the prospect of receiving it.

Because they have been so kind to him and because he has come to think of them as his sisters, Curtis was at first reluctant to remain with them and thus put them at risk. Since his lapse on Thursday, he has been Curtis Hammond without fail, in full and fine detail. He is less easily detected by his enemies now than he has been at any time since he arrived on this world, and hour by hour he blends better with the human population. Yet even when he can no longer be detected at all by the biological scanners that he has spent so much time and effort dodging, both human and extraterrestrial hunters will continue to search for him. And if the wrong scalawags ever find him, those who are aligned with him in his work – like Cass and Polly – will be marked for death as certainly as he himself is.

During his six frantic days on Earth, however, he has grown up; his terrible losses and his isolation from his own kind have forced him to the understanding that he must not merely survive, must not simply *hope* to advance his mother's mission, but must seize the day and do the work. *Do the work.* This requires the strong assistance of a circle of friends, a reliable cadre of committed souls who are good of heart, quick of mind, and courageous. Much as he dreads having to assume responsibility for putting the lives of others at risk, he has no choice if he is to prove himself worthy of being his mother's son.

Changing a world, as he must change this one to save it, comes at a cost, sometimes a terrible price.

If he must assemble a force for change, then Cass and Polly are the ideal recruits. The goodness of their hearts cannot be doubted, nor the quickness of their minds, and between them, they have enough courage to sustain a platoon of marines. Furthermore, their years in Hollywood have sharpened their survival skills and motivated them to become masters of weaponry, which has already proved useful.

They have brought Curtis to Nun's Lake because they would have come here anyway if they'd never met him. It had been the next stop on their UFO pilgrimage, and they'd taken a detour to the Neary Ranch when the government cordoned off part of Utah in search of the crazed drug lords that all clear-thinking people knew must actually be ETs.

Besides, after the violent encounter at the crossroads store, they believed it would be wise to get farther from the Nevada border than Twin Falls, Idaho.

Now, after a much needed day of rest, as the twins confer in the dining nook, studying maps and deciding where best to go next, Curtis watches the lake for nuns at play. And he occupies his mind with such big plans for a world-changing campaign that his ten-year-old brain, though organically augmented more than once at his beloved mother's insistence, feels as if it might explode.

Even when plans are being busily spun to save a world, dogs must pee. Old Yeller makes her urgent need known by pawing at the door and by rolling her eyes at her brother-become.

When Curtis goes to the door to let the dog out, Polly rises from the dining nook and warns him to stay inside, where he will be less easily detected if agents of the evil empire are in the vicinity with scanners.

He's told them that there is no empire aligned against him. The true situation is in some ways simpler and in other ways more complex than standard political entities. The twins are staying with the *Star Wars* template nonetheless, perhaps hoping that Han Solo and a Wookie will show up in an Airstream travel trailer to add to the fun.

'I'll take her out,' says Polly.

'No one needs to go along,' Curtis explains. 'I'll let her out by herself, but I'll stay with her in spirit.'

'The boy-dog bond,' Polly says.

'Yeah. I can have a look around the campground through little sister here.'

'This is so Art Bell,' Polly says, referring to a radio talk-show host who deals in UFO reports and stories of alien contact. She shivers with the thrill of it.

Old Yeller jumps from the motor home to the ground, the sisters reconvene over the maps, and Curtis returns to the co-pilot's seat.

His bond with little sister is at all times established, twenty-four hours a day, whether he is focused on it or not. Now he focuses.

The cockpit of the Fleetwood, the trees beyond the windshield, and the nunless lake beyond the trees all fade from his awareness, and Curtis is both inside the motor home and afoot in the world with Old Yeller.

She pees but not all at once. Padding among the motor homes and the travel trailers, she happily explores this new territory, and when she finds something particularly to her liking, she marks the spot with a quick squat and a brief stream.

The warm afternoon is gradually cooling as the clouds pour out of the west, roll down the rocky peaks, and, trapped between the mountains, condense into ever darker shades of gray.

The day smells of the sheltering pines, of the forest mast, of rain brewing.

Death-still, the air is also heavy with expectancy, as if in an instant, the eerily deep calm might whip itself into a raging tumult.

Everywhere, campers prepare for the storm. Extendable canvas awnings are cranked shut and locked down. Women fold lawn furniture and stow it in motor homes. A man leads two children back from the lakeshore, all in swimsuits and carrying beach toys. People gather up magazines, books, blankets, anything that shouldn't get wet.

Old Yeller receives unsolicited coos and compliments, and she rewards every expression of delight with a grin and the brisk wagging of her tail, although she cannot be distracted from her explorations, which she finds ceaselessly intriguing. The world is an infinite sea of odors and every scent is a current that either brings fresh life to complex memories or teases with mystery and a promise of wondrous discoveries.

Curiosity and the measured payout of a full bladder lead Old Yeller through a maze of recreational vehicles and trees and picnic benches to a motor home that looms like a juggernaut poised to crush battalions in a great war that is straining toward eruption at any moment. Even compared to the twins' impressive Fleetwood American Heritage, this behemoth is a daunting machine.

Sister-become is drawn to this caravan fit for Zeus, not because of its tremendous size or because of its formidable appearance, but because the scents associated with it both fascinate and disturb her. She approaches warily, sniffs the tires, peers cautiously into the shadows beneath the vehicle, and at last arrives at the closed door, where she sniffs still more aggressively.

Aboard the Fleetwood, physically far removed from Old Yeller, Curtis nonetheless is disquieted and overcome by a sense of danger. His first thought is that this juggernaut, like the Corvette behind the crossroads store, might be more than it appears to be, a machine not of this world.

The dog had penetrated the illusion of the sports car and had perceived the alien conveyance beneath. Here, however, she sees only what anyone can see – which strikes her as plenty strange enough.

At the motor-home door, one sharp smell suggests bitterness, while another is the essence of rot. Not the bitterness of quassia or quinine; the bitterness of a soul in despair. Not the stench of flesh decomposing, but of a spirit hideously corrupted in a body still alive. To the dog, everyone's body emits pheromones that reveal much about the true condition of the spirit within. And here, too, is a twist of an odor suggesting sourness; not the sourness of lemons or spoiled milk, but of fear so long endured and purely distilled that sister-become whimpers in sympathy with the heart that lives in such constant anxiety.

She has not a dram of sympathy, however, for the vicious beast whose malodor underlies all other scents. Someone who lives in this vehicle is a sulfurous volcano of repressed rage, a steaming cesspool of hatred so dark and thick that even though the monster currently is not present, its singularly caustic spoor burns like toxic fumes in sister-become's sensitive nose. If Death truly stalks the world in living form, with or without hooded robe and scythe, its pheromones can be no more fearsome than these. The dog sneezes to clear her nostrils of the stinging effluvium, growls low in her throat, and backs away from the door.

Old Yeller sneezes twice again as she rounds the front of the enormous motor home, and when, at Curtis's instruction, she looks up toward the panoramic windshield, she sees – as thus does he – neither a goblin nor a ghoul, but a pretty young girl of nine or ten. This girl stands beside the unoccupied driver's seat, leaning on it, bent forward, peering toward the lake and at the steadily hardening sky, probably trying to judge how long until the tension in the clouds will crack and the storm spill out.

Hers might be the bitter despair and the long-distilled sourness of fear that in part drew sister-become to investigate this ominous motor home.

Surely the girl isn't the source of the rotten fetor that, for the dog, identifies a deeply corrupted soul. She is too young to have allowed worms so completely to infest her spirit.

Neither can she be the monster whose heart is a machine of rage and whose blood is hatred flowing.

She notices sister-become and looks down. The dog – and Curtis unseen in his Fleetwood redoubt – gaze up from the severe angle that is the canine point of view on all the world above two feet.

Yeller's wagging tail renders a judgment without need of words. The girl is radiant.

In her home on wheels, where evidently she belongs, she appears nevertheless to be lost. And haunted. More than merely haunted, she half seems to be a ghost herself, and the big windshield lies between her and the dog as though it is a cold membrane between the land of the living and the land of the dead.

The radiant girl turns away and moves deeper into the motor home, evanescing into the dim beyond.

64

Nature had all but reclaimed the land that had been the Teelroy farm. Deer roamed where horses had once plowed. Weeds ruled.

Undoubtedly handsome in its day, the rambling Victorian house had been remodeled into Gothic by time, weather, and neglect.

The resident was a repulsive toad. He had the sweet voice of a young prince, but he looked like a source of warts and worse.

At first sight of the Toad, Preston almost returned to his SUV. He almost drove away without a question.

He found it difficult to believe that this odious bumpkin's fantastic story of alien healing would be convincing. The man was at best a bad joke, and more likely he was the mentally disordered consequence of generations of white-trash incest.

Yet . . .

During the past five years, among the hundreds of people to whom Preston had patiently listened recount their tales of UFO sightings and alien abductions, occasionally the least likely specimens proved to be the most convincing.

He reminded himself that pigs were used to hunt for truffles. Even a toad in bib overalls might once in a while know a truth worth learning.

Invited inside, Preston accepted. The threshold proved to lie between ordinary Idaho and a kingdom of the surreal.

In the entry hall, he found himself among a tribe of Indians. Some smiled, some struck noble poses, but most looked as inscrutable as any dreamy-faced Buddha or Easter Island stone head. All appeared peaceable.

Decades ago, when the country had been more innocent, these life-size, hand-carved, intricately hand-painted statues had stood at the entrances to cigar stores. Many held faux boxes of cigars as if offering a smoke.

Most were chiefs crowned by elaborate feathered headdresses, which were also carved out of wood and were hand-painted like the rest of their costumes. A few ordinary braves attended the chiefs, wearing headbands featuring one or two wooden feathers.

Of those not holding cigar boxes, some stood with a hand raised perpetually in a sign of peace. One of the smiling chiefs made the okay sign with thumb and forefinger.

Two – a chief, a brave – gripped raised tomahawks. They weren't threatening in demeanor, but they looked sterner than the others: early advocates of aggressive tobacco marketing.

Two chiefs held peace pipes.

The hall was perhaps forty feet long. Cigar-store Indians lined both sides. At least two dozen of them.

A majority stood with their backs to the walls, facing one another across the narrow walk space. Only four figures stood out of alignment, angled to monitor the front door, as if they were guardians of the Teelroy homestead.

More Indians loomed on alternating risers of the ascending stairs, against the wall opposite the railing. All faced the lower floor, as though descending to join the powwow.

'Pa collected Indians.' The Toad didn't often trim his mustache. This fringe drooped over his lips and almost entirely concealed them. When he spoke, his lilting voice penetrated this concealing hair, with the mystery of a spirit at a seance speaking through the veiled face of a medium. Because he barely moved his hair-draped lips when he spoke, you could almost believe that he himself wasn't speaking at all, but was an organic radio receiving a broadcast signal from another entity. 'They're worth a bunch, these Indians, but I can't sell 'em. They're the most thing I've got left of my daddy.'

Preston supposed that the statues might indeed have value as folk art. But they were of no interest to him.

A lot of art, folk art in particular, celebrated life. Preston did not.

'Come on in the livin' room,' said his flushed and bristling host. 'We'll talk this out.'

With all the grace of a tottering hog, the Toad moved toward an archway to the left.

The arch, once generous, had been reduced to a narrow opening by magazines tied with string in bundles of ten and twenty, and then stacked in tight, mutually supportive columns.

The Toad appeared to be too gross to fit through that pinched entry.

Surprisingly, he slipped between the columns of compressed paper without a hitch or hesitation. During years of daily passage, the human greaseball had probably lubricated the encroaching magazines with his natural body oils.

The living room was no longer truly a room. The space had been transformed into a maze of narrow passageways.

'Ma saved magazines,' explained the Toad. 'So do I.'

Seven- and eight-foot stacks of magazines and newspapers formed the partitions of the maze. Some were bundled with twine. Others were stored in cardboard boxes on which, in block letters, had been hand-printed the names of publications.

Wedged between flanking buttresses of magazines and cartons, tall wooden bookshelves stood packed with paperbacks. Issues of *National Geographic*. Yellowing piles of pulp magazines from the 1920s and '30s.

Cramped niches in these eccentric palisades harbored small pieces of furniture. A needlepoint chair had been squeezed between columns of magazines; more ragged-edged pulps were stacked on its threadbare cushion. Here, a small end table with a lamp. And here, a hat tree with eight hooks upon which hung a collection of at least twice that many moth-eaten fedoras.

More life-size wooden Indians were incorporated into the walls, wedged between the junk. Two were female. Indian princesses. Both fetching. One stared at some far horizon, solemn and mystical. The other looked bewildered.

No daylight penetrated from the windows to the center of the labyrinth. Veils of shadow hung everywhere, and a deeper gloom was held off only by the central ceiling fixture and occasional niche lamps with stained and tasseled shades.

Overall, the acidic odor of browning newsprint and yellowing paperbacks dominated. In pockets: the pungent stink of mouse urine. Underneath: a whiff of mildew, traces of powdered insecticide – and the subtle perfume of decomposing flesh, possibly a rodent that had died long ago and that was now but a scrap of leather and gray fur wrapped around papery bones.

Preston disliked the filth but found the ambience appealing. Life wasn't lived here: This was a house of death.

The incorporation of cigar-store Indians into the walls of the maze lent a quality of the Catacombs to the house, as though these figures were mummified corpses.

Following the Toad through the twists and turns of this three-dimensional webwork, Preston expected to find Ma Toad and Pa Toad, though dead, sitting in junk-flanked niches of their own. Funeral clothes hanging loose and largely empty on their dry skeletal frames. Eyes and lips sewn shut with mortuary thread. Ears shriveled into gristly knots. Mottled skin shrink-wrapped to their skulls. Nostrils trailing spiders' silk like plumes of cold breath.

When the Toad ultimately led him to a small clearing in the maze, where they could sit and talk, Preston was disappointed not to find any family cadavers lovingly preserved.

This parlor at the hub of the labyrinth barely measured large enough to accommodate him and the Toad at once. An armchair, flanked by a floorlamp and a small table, faced a television. To the side stood an ancient brocade-upholstered sofa with a tassel-fringed skirt.

The Toad sat in the armchair.

Preston squeezed past him and settled on the end of the sofa farthest from his host. Had he sat any closer, they would have been brought together in an intolerably intimate tete-a-tete.

They were surrounded by maze walls constructed of magazines, newspapers, books, old 78-rpm phonograph records stored in plastic milk crates, stacks of used coffee cans that might contain anything from nuts and bolts to severed human fingers, boxy floor-model radios from the 1930s balanced atop one another, and an array of other items too numerous to catalog, all interlocked, held together by weight and mold and inertia, braced by strategically placed planks and wedges.

The Toad, like his loon-mad ma and pa before him, was a world-class obsessive. Packrat royalty.

Ensconced in his armchair, the Toad said, 'So what's your deal?'

'As I explained on the phone earlier, I've come to hear about your close encounter.'

'Here's the thing, Mr. Banks. After all these many years, the government went and cut off my disability checks.'

'I'm sorry to hear that.'

'Said I'd been fakin' twenty years, which I flatly did not.'

'I'm sure you didn't.'

'Maybe the doctor who certified me made a true racket of it, like they say, and maybe I was the only *for-real* sufferin' soul ever crossed his doorstep, but I have been a genuine half-cripple, damn if I weren't.'

'And this relates to your close encounter – how?' Preston asked.

A small glistening pink animal poked its head out of the Toad's great tangled beard.

Preston leaned forward, fascinated until he realized that the pink animal was the man's tongue. It slid back and forth between lips no doubt best left unrevealed, perhaps to lubricate them in order to facilitate the passage of his lies.

'I'm grateful,' said the Toad, 'that some three-eyed starmen come along and healed me. They were a weird crew, no two ways about it, and plenty scary enough to please the big audience you need, but in spite of their bein' so scary, I acknowledge they committed a good deed on me. The problem is, now I'm *not* the pitiful half-cripple that I always used to be, so there's no way to get back on disability.'

'A dilemma,' Preston said.

'I made a promise to the starmen – and a solemn promise, it was – not to reveal them to the world for what they done here. I feel most bad about breakin' that promise, but the hard fact is I've got to eat and pay bills.'

Preston nodded at the bibbed and bearded moron. 'I'm sure the starmen will understand.'

'Don't mean to say I'm not for-sure grateful about havin' the cripple takin' right out of me with that blue-light thing of theirs. But all-powerful like they were, it seems queer they wouldn't also thought to give me some skill or talent I could put to use makin' a livin'. Like mind readin' or seein' the future.'

'Or the ability to turn lead into gold,' Preston suggested.

'*There* would be a good one!' the Toad declared, slapping his armchair with one hand. 'And I wouldn't abuse the privilege, neither. I'd make me just as little gold as I needed to get by.'

'You strike me as responsible in that respect,' said Preston.

'Thank you, Mr. Banks. I do appreciate the sentiment. But this is all just jabber, 'cause the spacemen didn't think to bless me in that regard. So . . . though it shames me to break my solemn promise, I can't see any damn way out of this dilemma, as you called it, except to sell my story of bein' de-crippled by aliens.'

Although the Toad gave even deeper meaning to the word fraud than had any politician of recent memory, and though Preston had no intention of reaching for his wallet and fishing out a twenty-dollar bill, curiosity compelled him to ask, 'How much do you want?'

What might have been a shrewd expression furrowed the Toad's blotchy red brow, pinched the corners of his eyes, and further puckered his boiled-dumpling nose. Or it might have been a mini seizure.

'Now, sir, we're both smart businessmen here, and I have a world of respect for you, just as I'm sure you have for me. When it comes to business matters between such as us, I don't believe it's my place to set a final price. More like it's your place to start the dealin' with a fair offer to which, with due consideration, I'll reply. But seein' as how you have been a gentleman to me, I will give you the special courtesy of sayin' that I know what's fair and that what's fair is somewhere north of a million dollars.'

The man was a complete lunatic.

Preston said, 'I'm sure it's fair, but I don't think I've got that much in my wallet.'

The choirboy voice produced a silvery, almost girlish laugh, and the Toad slapped his armchair with both hands. He seemed never to have heard a funnier quip.

Leaning forward in his chair, clearly confident of his ability to be amusing in return, the Toad winked and said, 'When the time comes, I'll accept your check, and no driver's license necessary.'

Preston smiled and nodded.

In his quest for extraterrestrial contact, he had tolerated uncounted fools and frauds over the years. This was the price he had to pay for the hope of one day finding truth and transcendence.

ETs were real. He badly wanted them to be real, though not for the same reasons that the Toad or average UFO buffs wanted them to be real. Preston *needed* them to be real in order to make sense of his life.

The Toad grew serious. 'Mr. Banks, you haven't told me your outfit yet.'

'Outfit?'

'In a true spirit of fair dealin', I'm obliged to tell you that just earlier this very day, Miss Janet Hitchcock herself of Paramount Pictures paid me a visit. She'll be makin' an offer tomorrow. I told her straight out about your interest, though I couldn't tell her your outfit, bein' as I didn't know it.'

If Paramount Pictures ever sent an executive to Nun's Lake to buy the Toad's tale of being de-crippled by aliens, their purchase of screen rights could be reliably taken as an omen that the universe would at any moment suddenly implode, instantly compacting itself into a dense ball of matter the size of a pea.

'I'm afraid there's been a misunderstanding,' said Preston.

The Toad didn't want to hear about misunderstandings, only about seven-figure bank drafts. 'I'm not pitchforkin' moo crap at you, sir. Our mutual respect is too large for moo crap. I can prove every word I'm sayin' just by showin' you one thing, *one thing*, and you'll know it's all real, every bit of it.' He rolled up and out of the armchair as though he were a hog rising from its slough, and he waddled out of the hub of the maze by a route different from the one that they had followed here from the front hall. 'Come on, you'll see, Mr. Banks!'

Preston had no fear of the Toad, and he was pretty sure the man lived alone. Nevertheless, although additional members of this inbred clan might be lurking around and might prove ferociously psychotic, he wasn't put off by the prospect of meeting them, if they existed.

The atmosphere of decline and dissolution in this house was from Preston's perspective a romantic ambience. To a man so in love with death, this was the equivalent of a starlit beach in Hawaii. He wished to explore more of it.

Besides, although the Toad had thus far seemed to be a flagrant fraud, his sweet clear voice had resonated with what had sounded like sincerity when he'd claimed that he could show Preston one thing to prove that his story was 'all real, every bit of it.'

Into tunnels of paper and Indians and stacked furniture, Preston followed his host. Into a warren of glossy fashion, pulp fiction, and yellowing news compacted into building blocks.

Out of angular and intersecting passageways as oddly scented as the deepest galleries of ancient Egyptian tombs, around a shadowy cochlear spiral where the Toad's open-mouthed breathing whispered off every surface with a sound like scarabs scuttling in the walls, they progressed through two more large rooms, identifiable as separate spaces only by the intervening doorways. The doors had been removed, evidently to facilitate movement through the labyrinth. The remaining jambs and headers were embedded like mine-shaft supports in the tightly packed materials that formed these funhouse corridors.

All windows had been blocked off. Maze partitions often rose until the overhead plaster allowed no higher stacks; therefore, the ceiling transitions from chamber to chamber were difficult to detect. The oak floors remained consistent: worn to bare wood by shuffling traffic, darkened here and there by curious stains that resembled Rorschach patterns.

'You'll see, Mr. Banks,' the Toad wheezed while through his snaky warrens he hurried like a Hobbit gone to seed. 'Oh, you'll see the proof, all right!'

Just when Preston began half seriously to speculate that this bizarre house was a tesseract bridging dimensions, existing in many parallel worlds, and that it might go on forever, the Toad led him out of the labyrinth into a kitchen.

Not an ordinary kitchen.

The usual appliances were here. An old white-enameled range – yellowed and chipped – with side-by-side ovens under a cooktop. One humming and shuddering refrigerator that appeared to date from the days when people still called them iceboxes. Toaster, microwave. But with these appliances, the ordinary ended.

Every countertop, from the Formica surface to the underside of the upper cabinets, was packed to capacity with empty beer and soda bottles stacked horizontally like the stock of a wine cellar. A few cabinet doors stood open; within were more empty bottles. A pyramid of bottles occupied the kitchen table. The window above the sink provided a view of an enclosed back porch that appeared to contain thousands of additional bottles.

The Toad apparently prepared all his meals on the butcher-block top of the large center island. The condition of that work surface was unspeakable.

A door opened on a set of back stairs too narrow for the storage of Indians. Here, with glue, empty beer bottles – most of them green, some clear – had been fixed to the flanking walls and to the ceiling, hundreds upon hundreds of them, like three-dimensional wallpaper.

Although the malty residue in all the containers had years ago evaporated, the stairwell still smelled of stale beer.

'Come along, Mr. Banks! Not much farther. You'll see why north of a million is a fair price.'

Preston followed the Toad to the top of the glass-lined stairs. The upper hall had been narrowed by an accumulation of junk similar to the collection on the lower floor.

They passed rooms from which the doors had been removed. Annexes of the primary first-floor maze appeared to have been established in these spaces.

The Toad's bedroom still featured a door. The chamber past this threshold had not been transformed into an anthill of tunnels as had so much of the house. Two nightstands with lamps flanked the large unmade bed. A dresser, a chiffonier, and a chifforobe provided the Toad with ample storage space for his bib overalls.

The threat of normalcy was held at bay, however, by a collection of straw hats that hung on nails from every wall, ceiling to floor. Straw hats for men, women, and children. Straw hats in every known style, for every need from that of the working farmhand to that of a lady wanting a suitable chapeau to attend church on a hot summer Sunday. Straw hats in natural hues and in pastel tints, in various stages of deterioration, hung in overlapping layers, until Preston almost began to forget they were hats, to see the repetitive shapes of the crowns as a sort of wraparound upholstery like the acoustic-friendly walls of a recording studio or radio station.

A second collection cluttered the room: scores upon scores of both plain and fancy walking sticks. Simple walnut canes with rubber tips and sleek curved handles. Hickory canes with straight shafts but with braided-wood handles. Oak, mahogany, maple, cherry, and stainless-steel models, some with plain handles, others graced by figured grips of cast brass or carved wood. Lacquered black canes with silvery tips, the perfect thing for a tuxedoed Fred Astaire, hung next to those white canes that were reserved for the blind.

The canes were stored in groups in several umbrella stands, but they also hung from the sides of the dresser, the chiffonier, and the chifforobe. Instead of cloth panels, curtains of canes dangled from the drapery rods.

At one window, the Toad had previously unhooked a dozen canes from the rod, revealing a portion of the pane. He'd also rubbed the glass half clean with his hand.

He led Preston to this view and pointed northeast across a weedy field, toward the two-lane road. A little winded from the journey, he said, 'Mr. Banks, you see the woods yonder, past the county blacktop? Now look seventy yards easterly of the entrance here to my farm, and you'll damn well see a car pulled in among the trees over there.'

Preston was confused and disappointed, having hoped that the Toad's proof of a healing close encounter might be an alien artifact obviously not manufactured on this world or snapshots of strange three-eyed beings – or, if the evidence was obviously fake, then something worth a good laugh.

'That's the sneaky junk car she used to disguise herself when first she come here, pretendin' not to be big-time movie people.'

Preston frowned. 'She?'

'Miss Janet Hitchcock, like I told you, all the way here from Paramount Pictures down in California, your stompin' grounds. She's watchin' my place so she can see *who her competition is!*'

A pair of high-power binoculars rested on the windowsill. The Toad handed them to Preston.

The binoculars felt greasy. He winced and almost cast them aside in disgust.

'Proof, sir,' said the Toad. 'Proof I'm not inventin' all this whoop-de-do about Paramount Pictures, proof I'm bein' foursquare fair with you, businessman to businessman, with full respect. It's just a speck of brightness in among the pines, but you'll see.'

Curious, Preston raised the field glasses and focused on the car in the woods. Even though the vehicle was white, it was tucked among the high-skirted trees, shrouded by shadows, and not easy to see in any useful detail.

The Toad said, 'She was leanin' against the front of it earlier, watchin' to where my driveway meets the county road, hopin' she'd see who you might be.'

The woman no longer leaned against the car.

Maybe she had gotten into the vehicle. The interior was dark. He couldn't tell whether someone sat behind the wheel.

'Whatever outfit you're with down there in California, I'm sure you're well connected to the movie world entire, you go to all the same parties as the stars, so you'll recognize a true big wheel like Miss Janet Hitchcock of Paramount Pictures.'

When he located the woman, Preston recognized her, all right. She stood apart from the car, not as deep in the shadows as it was, leaning now against a tree, identifiable even in the drowned light of the pending storm. Michelina Teresa Bellsong – ex-con, apprentice alcoholic, job-seeker without hope, niece to senile old Aunt Gen, cheap slut trying to reform, guilt-racked wretch looking for meaning in her stupid sorry little life, self-appointed savior of Leilani, would-be exhumer of Lukipela, self-deluded dragonslayer, useless nosy meddlesome *bitch*.

Still watching Micky Bellsong, Preston said, 'Yes, it's Janet Hitchcock, sure enough. Looks like I'm not going to be able to avoid a bidding war, Mr.' – and he almost said *Mr. Toad* – 'Mr. Teelroy.'

'Wasn't ever the case I was schemin' toward that, Mr. Banks. I just wanted you to know fair enough that you had competition. I'm not lookin' for more than my story's rightly worth.'

'I understand, of course. I'd like to make you an offer before I leave today, but it's my preference, in these cases, to present the deal in the presence of the whole family, since this much money will affect all of you profoundly. Is there a wife, sir, and children? And what of your parents?'

'Ma and Pa, they're both long gone, Mr. Banks.'

'I'm sorry to hear that.'

'And I never did marry, not that I was wholly without some good opportunities.'

Still focused on the distant woman, Preston said, 'So it's just you here alone in this rambling house.'

'Just me,' said the Toad. 'And much as I surely am a committed bachelor, I must admit . . . it gets awful lonely sometimes.' He sighed. 'Just me.'

'Good,' said Preston, turning away from the window and, with savage force, smashing the heavy binoculars into the Toad's face.

The blow produced a wet crunch, a strangled sob, and the man's immediate collapse.

Preston threw the binoculars on the disheveled bed, where he would be able to find them later.

Hooked on the windowsill were several canes. He seized one that featured a bronze wolf's head for a handle.

On his back, flat on the floor, the Toad gazed up, his hideous nose now shattered and more repulsive than before, his unkempt beard bejeweled with blood, his blotchy face suddenly every bit as pale as it had previously been flushed.

Holding the cane by the wrong end, Preston raised it overhead.

The Toad lay stunned, perhaps disoriented, but then his eyes cleared, and when he saw what was coming, he spoke with tremulous emotion and with obvious relief: 'Thank you.'

'You're welcome,' Preston assured him, and hammered the wolf's head into the center of the man's brow. More than once. Maybe half a dozen times. The cane cracked but didn't come apart.

When he was certain that he had killed the Toad, he threw the damaged walking stick on the bed beside the binoculars. Later, he would wipe both objects clean of fingerprints.

He intended ultimately to burn down this great pile of tinder. No evidence would be likely to survive the flames. But he was a careful man.

Quickly, Preston selected another cane. A polished-brass serpent formed the handle, inset with faceted red-glass eyes.

He suppressed the madcap urge to select a jaunty straw hat in which to court the lady of the hour. In addition to being a service to humanity and to Mother Earth, killing was fun, but one must never lose sight of the fact that it was also serious business, fraught with risk and frowned upon by many.

Out of the dead toad's boudoir, along the trash-packed upstairs hall, to the bottle-decorated back stairs and down. Through the foul kitchen, onto the enclosed porch where a thousand and yet a thousand bottles glimmered darkly as if the coming storm were pent up in them and soon to be uncorked.

Outside, he hurried across a backyard that was more dirt than scattered bunch-grass, careful to keep the house between him and the position in the woods from which the entirely useless Ms. Bellsong maintained surveillance.

Most likely she expected to follow him into Nun's Lake, staying at a distance to avoid being spotted. Once she'd found where he had parked the motor home, she evidently intended to watch and wait – and seize the first opportunity to spirit Leilani away, out of Idaho, to Clarissa the Goiter and her sixty parrots in Hemet.

The stupid slut. Fools, the lot of them. They thought that he knew nothing, but he knew all.

Beyond the barren yard lay a thriving field of shoulder-high weeds. He had to stoop only slightly to disappear among them.

Heading east, he plunged through wild grass, milkweed. Cover was provided, too, by scattered cornstalks that had been cultivated long in the past and that had gone wild generations ago, but that still raggedly, stubbornly ruled the field.

He hurried parallel to the distant road, intending eventually to turn north, cross the road beyond her view, and then turn west. He would circle behind the useless Micky Bellsong and club her to the ground with the serpent cane.

The glowering sky pressed lower by the minute, black clouds like knotted fists, full of cruel power. No thunder yet, but thunder soon. And eventually lightning would score the sky and cast hot reflections on the brass serpent, perhaps even as it struck – and struck. But in spite of the dazzling flash and rumble soon to descend, Preston Maddoc knew that the halls of Heaven were deserted, and that no one occupied those heights to look down on what he did, or to care.

65

The motherless boy is troubled, and he doesn't trouble easily. He sits on one of the sofas in the lounge of the Fleetwood, petting Old Yeller, who lies across his lap, while the twins continue to brood over maps in the dining nook.

Advance preparation had left Curtis with considerable knowledge regarding most of the Earth species he would be likely to encounter on his mission. Consequently he knows a great deal about dogs, not solely what he absorbed from the astonishing number of canines that he's seen in 9,658 movies, but from specific flash-feed instruction he has received regarding the flora and fauna of this planet.

Sister-become has numerous admirable qualities, not the least of which is her nose. Its shape, pebbly texture, and shiny blackness contribute to her beauty, but more important, her sense of smell is perhaps twenty thousand times more sensitive than that of any human being.

If the enormous motor home in which he saw the radiant girl also contained hunters of the kind that were encountered at the crossroads store in Nevada, the dog would have detected their unique scent, would have recognized it instantly, and would have reacted either ferociously or with greater fear than she had shown. Bonded with his sister-become, Curtis would have been aware of her memories from the crossroads, flurries of mental images triggered by this exotic smell, as he is aware of such images when the dog encounters other familiar odors.

The vicious beast whose malodor Old Yeller smelled around that motor home is not one she has met before. It is something or someone of her world.

This is not entirely reassuring. He remembers her reaction to

Vern Tuttle, the teeth-collecting serial killer, when they had been watching him from the bedroom in the Windchaser as he had conversed with his bathroom mirror. She had wagged her tail a little. If such a fiend as Tuttle hadn't put her hackles up, how much worse must the human monster be in this new motor home, this ominous juggernaut? It has, after all, elicited a growl from her.

Since he is confident that their mysterious campground neighbors are not hostile extraterrestrials and, therefore, do not require any action from him, evasive or otherwise, the prudent course would be to stay safely inside the Fleetwood. He finds it difficult, however, to be entirely judicious or even cautious as long as the memory of the radiant girl continues to haunt him.

He cannot put her out of his mind.

When he closes his eyes, he can see her standing beside the driver's seat, leaning forward, peering out of the windshield. Her expression of profound loneliness and loss resonates with him because it expresses emotions he knows too well, feelings that rise anew in him each time he dares to dwell upon what happened in the Colorado mountains before he ever was Curtis Hammond.

At last he realizes that he would not be his mother's son if he could turn away from this wounded-looking girl. The prudent course is not always the course that the heart demands.

He is here, after all, to change the world. And as always, this task begins with the rescue of one soul, and then the next, and then the next, with patience and commitment.

When he moves from lounge to nook and interrupts Cass and Polly at their maps, explaining what he intends to do, they are opposed to his plan. They prefer that he remain safely in the Fleetwood until, come morning, they can pull up stakes and head for Seattle. There, the large population will provide adequate commotion and give him cover until he is confidently Curtis Hammond, is at last producing an ordinary energy signature, and is beyond detection.

Their adamant resistance to his leaving the motor home is for a moment frustrating. Then, using the template through which they are most comfortable regarding these recent events, he reminds them that they are his royal guards and that while valuing their valiant service and respecting their sage advice, he cannot allow his guards to dictate what an heir to the throne may or may not do. 'That's no more a choice for me than it would be for Princess Leia.'

Perhaps they realize that he's using their own rope to tie their hands, so to speak, because he's previously denied being ET royalty, but this strategy nevertheless flummoxes them. They continue to be in such awe of his off-world origins and so thrilled to be a part of his mission that they can't long resist him. As much as they might like to deal with him sometimes as the sovereign majesty of a far planet and sometimes as just a ten-year-old boy, they cannot have it both ways. Realizing this, they beam megadata at each other with one of their Spelkenfelter glances, sigh prettily, as only they can sigh, and prepare to provide him with an armed escort.

Although they would prefer that Curtis remain indoors, they reveal a quiet enthusiasm at the prospect of accompanying him now that he's pulled rank on them. After all, as they themselves have said, they are girls who like adventure.

They are dressed this afternoon in carved-leather cowboy boots, blue jeans, and blue-checkered Western shirts with bolo ties. This seems to be a suitable costume for bodyguards, though it lacks the dazzle of low-cut toreador pants, halter tops, and navel opals.

Each of the twins slings a purse over her right shoulder. Each purse contains a 9-mm pistol.

'You stay between us, sweetie,' Polly cautions Curtis, which seems an odd form of address if she insists on viewing him as alien royalty, though he sure likes it.

Cass leaves the Fleetwood first, keeping her right hand inside the purse that is slung over her shoulder.

Sister-become follows Cass. Curtis follows the dog, and Polly comes last, right hand firmly on the pistol in her purse, too.

At only a few minutes past three o'clock on a summer afternoon, the day looks more like a winter twilight, and in spite of the warm air, the gray light imposes a chilly impression on everything that it touches, emphasizing the trace of frosty silver in each evergreen needle, plating the lake with a mirage of ice.

Outside, Old Yeller assumes the lead, following her previous route to the juggernaut, though with no pee stops this time.

Few campers are out and about. Having finished battening down for the storm, most are inside.

The radiant girl hasn't returned to the front of the motor home. Curtis can see nothing more than a dim light farther back in the big vehicle, filtered by the tinted windshield, and reflections of pine branches and sullen clouds on the surface of the glass.

Cass intends to knock on the door, but Curtis halts her with a softly spoken 'No.'

As before, the dog senses not only that a vicious beast of the human variety frequents this motor home, but also that it is, as before, not in residence at this time. Once more, she detects two presences, the first producing both the bitter odor of a soul in despair and the pheromonal stench of a spirit profoundly corrupted. The second is one who, having so long endured fear, is steeped in chronic anxiety, although utterly free of despair.

Curtis infers that the fear-troubled heart is that of the girl whom earlier he saw through the windshield.

The corrupted presence is so unappealing that the dog skins her teeth back from her lips, producing an expression as close to one of disgust as the form of her face allows. If sister-become could pucker her muzzle sufficiently to spit, she would do so.

Curtis can't be certain if the object of this disgust poses a threat. Perhaps it is revealing, however, that this person seems not to be troubled by any of the fear that is a yoke upon the girl.

While the twins, bracketing him, keep a watch on the surrounding campground, Curtis places both hands on the door of the motor home. On the micro level, where will can prevail over matter, he senses a low-voltage electrical circuit and recognizes that it is similar to the alarm-system circuit on the Fleetwood, which the twins engage each night.

Every circuit has a switch. The low-voltage flow is energy, but the switch is mechanical and therefore vulnerable to the power of the will. Curtis has a strong will. The alarm is engaged – and then not.

The door is securely locked. And then unlocked. Quietly, he opens it and peers into the cockpit, which is deserted.

Two steps up, and in.

He hears one of the twins hiss in disapproval, but he doesn't turn back.

A single lamp lights the lounge. One of the sofas has been folded out to form a bed.

She is sitting on the bed, writing rapidly in a journal. One leg is bent, the other stuck straight out in the grip of a steel brace.

The radiant girl.

Intently focused on her composition, she doesn't hear the door open and doesn't at first realize that someone has entered and is standing at the head of the steps.

Sister-become follows Curtis, pushes halfway between his legs to get a clear look at this steel-braced vision.

This movement attracts the girl's attention, and she looks up.

Curtis says, 'You shine.'

66

After reversing the Camaro into the cover of the trees, Micky stood for a while, leaning against the car, watching the turnoff to the Teelroy farm from a distance of about seventy yards. Three vehicles passed during the next ten minutes, giving her a chance to determine that from this far away she wouldn't be able to discern if Maddoc had come alone in the Durango, even if she could positively identify the vehicle itself. She moved fifty yards farther west.

Less than twenty minutes later, positioned behind a tree, she saw the Durango approaching from the direction of Nun's Lake. When the SUV slowed for the right turn into the Teelroy driveway, Micky could see that the driver was alone: Preston Maddoc.

She hurried east, back the way that she had come, and took up a new position in the shelter of a pine near the Camaro. From here, she couldn't see the front porch of the farmhouse clearly enough to watch Leonard Teelroy greet Maddoc. She was able to see the parked Durango, however; and when it began to move again, she would have time to get into her car, ease out from among the trees, and follow him back to Nun's Lake at such a distance that she wouldn't raise his suspicion.

Her irrational hope had been that he might bring Leilani with him, in which case she would have crept to the farmhouse with the intention of disabling the Durango and with the hope that in the subsequent confusion, she might have an opportunity to spirit the girl away, before Maddoc could know that she had gone.

The irrational hope had not been fulfilled. She could choose between waiting here to follow Maddoc or returning to Nun's Lake to inquire after him – or Jordan Banks – at all three campgrounds.

She feared that if she returned to town, she might not receive accurate information at the campground offices. Or Maddoc could have used a name that she didn't know. Or perhaps he never registered his motor home at any campground, but temporarily parked it in a public place, having no intention of staying in this place overnight. Then, as she went from one registration clerk to the next, in search of him, he might cut short his pursuit of extraterrestrials at the Teelroy farm, hook the Durango to the Prevost, and hit the highway. Returning to Nun's Lake ahead of Maddoc, Micky risked losing him, and even if the risk might be small, she didn't intend to take it.

Given her own brief encounter with Leonard Teelroy, Micky didn't expect Maddoc to spend much time with him. Teelroy was an eccentric, a transparent fraud looking to make a buck, and more than a few slices short of a full loaf. His tale of alien healers wasn't likely to beguile the doom doctor for any length of time, regardless of what had motivated Maddoc to start following the UFO trail more than four and a half years ago.

Yet five minutes passed, then five more, and the SUV remained at the farmhouse.

Time on her hands gave Micky time to think, and she realized that she hadn't phoned Aunt Gen. Having left Seattle at an ungodly hour, she would have awakened Geneva if she'd called from the motel. She'd intended to use a public phone in Nun's Lake, but as soon as she arrived, she'd plunged into the search for Maddoc and forgotten everything else. Gen would be worried. But if everything went well, maybe Micky could call Gen later today from some roadside restaurant in Washington State, with Leilani at her side waiting to say hello and to make some wise-ass remark about Alex Baldwin.

As dark as iron in places, the sky at last grew heavy enough to press an anxious breath from the still afternoon. The pleasantly warm day began to cool. All around Micky, trees shivered, and whispered to the wind.

Birds like black arrows, singly and in volleys, returned to their quivers in the pine branches, with flap and flutter, vanishing among the layered boughs: a reliable prediction that the storm would soon break.

Turning to follow a cry of sparrows, Micky discovered Preston Maddoc, and a club descending.

518

Then she was on the ground with no awareness of falling, with pine needles and dirt in her mouth, lacking sufficient energy to spit them out.

She watched a beetle crawling a few inches in front of her nose, busy on its journey, disinterested in her. The bug appeared huge from this perspective, and just beyond it loomed a pine cone as large as a mountain.

Her vision blurred. She blinked to clear it. The blink knocked loose a keystone in the arch of her skull, and great blocks of pain tumbled in upon her. And darkness.

67

Curtis Hammond sees the girl first through his own eyes, and he doesn't perceive the previous radiance seen when she'd stood gazing out the windshield.

Then sister-become climbs the steps and pushes between his legs. Through the eyes of the innocent dog, eyes that also are peripherally aware at all times of the playful Presence, the girl is radiant indeed, softly aglow, lit from within.

The dog at once adores her but hangs back shyly, almost as she might hang back in awe if ever the playful Presence called her closer to smooth her fur or to scratch under her chin.

'You shine,' Curtis declares.

'You don't win points with girls,' she admonishes, 'by telling them they're sweaty.'

She speaks softly, and as she speaks, she glances toward the rear of the motor home.

Being a boy who has been engaged in clandestine operations on more than one world, Curtis is quick on the uptake with clues like this, and he lowers his voice further. 'I didn't mean sweat.'

'Then was it a rude reference to this?' she asks, patting her stainless-steel brace.

Oh, Lord, he's put his foot in a cow pie again, metaphorically speaking. Recently, he'd begun to think that he was getting pretty good at socializing, not as good as Cary Grant in virtually any Cary Grant movie, but better than, say, Jim Carrey in *Dumb and Dumber* or in *The Grinch Who Stole Christmas*. Now this.

Striving to recover from this misstep, he assures her: 'I'm not really a Gump.'

'I didn't think you were,' she says, and smiles.

The smile warms him, and it all but melts sister-become, who would go closer to the radiant girl, roll on her back, and put all four paws in the air as an expression of complete submission if shyness did not restrain her.

When the girl's eyebrows lift and she looks past Curtis, he glances over his shoulder to see that Polly has come onto the steps behind him and, even though still one step below, is able to look over his head. She is no less formidable in appearance than she is lovely, even with her gun concealed. Her gas-flame eyes have gone ice-blue, and judging by the flintiness with which she surveys the interior of the motor home and then regards the girl, her time in Hollywood has either inspired in her a useful ruthlessness or has taught her how to act hard-assed with conviction.

In the lounge wall opposite the girl's bed is a window, to which movement draws her and Curtis's attention. Cass has found something to stand upon outside, perhaps an overturned trash barrel or a picnic table, which she has dragged near the motor home. Her head is framed in that window, and like her sister, she looks as redoubtable as Clint Eastwood in a full go-ahead-make-my-day squint.

'Wow,' the girl exclaims softly, putting aside her journal and turning her attention to Curtis once more, 'you travel with Amazons.'

'Just two,' he says.

'Who are you?'

Because he can see the girl shine when he looks through the eyes of the perceptive dog, and because he knows what this radiance means, he decides that he must be as immediately straightforward with this person as, ultimately, he was with the twins. And thus he answers: 'I'm being Curtis Hammond.'

'I'm being Leilani Klonk,' she replies, swinging her braced leg like a counterweight that pulls her to a seated position on the edge of the sofabed. 'How did you turn off the alarm and unlock the door, Curtis?'

He shrugs. 'Willpower over matter, on the micro level where will can prevail.'

'That's exactly how I'm growing breasts.'

'It's not working,' he replies.

'I think maybe it is. I was positively concave before. At least now I'm just flat. Why'd you come here?'

'To change the world,' Curtis says.

Polly lays a warning hand upon his shoulder.

'It's all right,' he tells his royal guard.

'To change the world,' Leilani repeats, glancing again toward the back of the motor home before pushing off the bed to a standing position. 'Have you had any luck so far?'

'Well, I'm just starting, and it's a long job.'

With a rather different-looking hand, Leilani points to a happy face painted on the ceiling and then to hula dolls swiveling their hips on nearby tables. 'You're changing the world starting *here*?'

'According to my mother, all the truths of life and all the answers to its mysteries are present to be seen and understood in every incident in our lives, in every place, regardless of how grand or humble it may be.'

Again indicating the ceiling and the swiveling dolls, Leilani says, 'And regardless of how tacky?'

'My mother has wisdom to sustain us through any situation, crisis, or loss. But she never said anything about tackiness, pro or con.'

'Is this your mother?' Leilani asks, referring to Polly.

'No. This is Polly, and never ask her if she wants a cracker. I've agreed to eat them for her. Looking in the window there is Cass. As for my mother . . . well, have you ever been to Utah?'

'These past four years, I've been everywhere but Mars.'

'You wouldn't like Mars. It's airless, cold, and boring. But in Utah, at a truck stop, did you ever meet a waitress named Donella?'

'Not that I recall.'

'Oh, you'd recall, all right. Donella doesn't look anything like my mother, since they're not the same species, although Mother could have looked exactly like her if she were *being* Donella.'

'Of course,' says Leilani.

'As far as that goes, I could look like Donella, too, except that I don't have enough mass.'

'Mass.' Leilani nods sympathetically. 'It's always a problem, isn't it?'

'Not always. But what I'm trying to say is that in her way, Donella reminds me of my mother. The fine hulking shoulders, a neck made to burst restraining collars, the proud chins of a fattened bull. Majestic. Magnificent.'

'Already I like your mom better than mine,' says Leilani.

'I'd be honored to meet your mother.'

'Trust me,' the radiant girl advises, 'you wouldn't. That's why we're all but whispering. She's a terror.'

'I realized we were having a clandestine conversation,' Curtis replies, 'but how sad to think your mother is the reason. You know, I don't believe I've told you I'm an extraterrestrial.'

'That is news,' Leilani agrees. 'Tell me something else . . . .'

'Anything,' he promises, because she shines.

'Are you related to a woman named Geneva Davis?'

'Not if she's of this planet.'

'Well, she is more than not, I guess. But I'd swear you were at least a nephew.'

'Should I be honored to meet *her*?' Curtis asks.

'Yes, you should. And if you ever do, I sure would like to be a fly on the wall.'

They are socializing so well, and suddenly this last statement of hers confuses him. 'Fly on the wall? Are you a shapechanger, too?'

68

Circling from the Teelroy place to the Slut Queen's car in the woods, Preston had time to think and to modify his initial plan.

For one thing, when he first headed east through the field of weeds and scattered corn plants behind the farmhouse, he'd begun to think of her as the Drunk. But that didn't resonate satisfactorily. Lady Liver Rot and Miss Shitfaced were both more fun, but still not right. He couldn't call her the Tits, even though it was applicable, because he'd already used that one for Aunt Janice, the mother of his first kill, Cousin Dirtbag. Over the years, he had employed all the most interesting parts of female anatomy as his private names for other women. While he was willing to reuse a name if he could couple it with a fresh and pleasing adjective, he had also exhausted most of those in conjunction with anatomical terms. Finally he had settled on the Slut Queen, based on what little but telling details he knew about her weakness for men who used her and about the likelihood that she had been used against her will at a young age: Queens, after all, are born to their station in life.

The importance of selecting the right name couldn't be exaggerated. It must be amusing, of course, but yet it must also be an accurately descriptive sobriquet and must diminish the person sufficiently to dehumanize him or, in this case, her. These last two requirements were a matter of good ethics. To fulfill his obligation to thin the human herd and thereby preserve the world, a utilitarian bioethicist must cease to think about most of the herd as being people like he himself. In Preston's inner world, only *useful* people, people with something of substance to offer humanity and with a high quality of life, had the same names as they did in the outer world.

So, kill the Slut Queen. That was his mission when he left the farmhouse, and that remained his mission when he crept up behind her through the trees. Along the way from there to here, however, he had changed his mind about how the killing should be done.

Finished with the serpent-head cane, Preston tossed it on the backseat of the Camaro.

The Slut Queen's keys were in the ignition. He used them to open the trunk of the Camaro.

He dragged her across the woodland carpet of pine needles and dead vegetation, to the back of the car.

Overlooking these deeds, the sky darkened further. A dam's breast of stacked thunderheads seemed about to crack and tumble.

Wind, a clever mimic, stampeded an invisible herd of snorting bulls through the trees, and then chased them with phantom packs of panting hounds in heat.

All the bluster and the smell of an impending storm excited Preston. The Slut Queen – so attractive and limp and still warm – tempted him.

The wildwood offered a savage bed. And the hooting wind spoke to a cruel brute in his heart.

With an honesty in which he took pride, he fully acknowledged that he harbored this brute. Like everyone born of man and woman, he couldn't claim perfection. This admission was part of the penetrating self-analysis that each ethicist must undergo to have the credibility and the authority to establish rules for others to live by.

Seldom did he have the opportunity to deal in violence without restraint. Mostly, to avoid imprisonment, he had been limited in his killing to massive injections of digitoxin, genteel smothering, the administration of air-bubble embolisms . . . .

These recent exertions with the Toad and with the Slut Queen had been hugely revitalizing, invigorating. Indeed, Preston Maddoc was *aroused*.

Unfortunately, he didn't have time for passion. He had left his SUV in front of the farmhouse. A cane-clubbed body sprawled in that hat-lined bedroom, awaiting discovery. Although only the mentally impaired and carnival freaks were likely to visit the Toad for Sunday supper, Preston had to eliminate all incriminating evidence as soon as possible.

The Slut Queen qualified as yet more evidence. He lifted her and tumbled her into the trunk of the Camaro.

Some wet blood stained his hands. He scooped a wad of dry pine needles from the ground. He rolled them gently back and forth between palms and fingers, to remove the worst of the stains and to dry what would not easily wipe off.

Then behind the steering wheel, out of the woods, onto the road, to the driveway, and past the old canted tractor.

He parked beside the Durango, in front of the farmhouse.

Hauling the Slut Queen out of the trunk proved much harder than dumping her into it.

Blood glistened on the carpet where she'd rested. For an instant the sight of those stains paralyzed Preston.

He had intended to stage things to make it appear as though the woman had burned to death in the farmhouse with the Toad. Packed wall to wall with stacked paper and wooden Indians and other dry tinder, accelerated with a gallon of judiciously placed gasoline, the blaze would be so intense that not much would remain of the bodies; even bones might be largely consumed, leaving little or no evidence that it hadn't been the fire that had killed them. Jerkwater towns like Nun's Lake didn't possess the police and forensics capabilities to detect murders this thoroughly concealed.

He would have to deal with the bloodstains in the trunk. Later. He would also need to wipe down portions of the car to eliminate his fingerprints. In time.

Now, as the wind whipped up dust devils that capered in advance of him, he carried the Slut Queen in his arms: across the lawn, onto the porch, through the front door, into the lower hall, where Indians stood sentinel and offered cigars, past the wooden chiefs, smiling at the one that gave him the okay sign, and onward into the labyrinth.

In these catacombs, he chose the place. He made the necessary preparations.

Within a few minutes, he sat once more behind the wheel of the Durango.

On his return trip to Nun's Lake, wind buffeted the SUV as though urging it along, huffed and hooted at the window beside him as though offering its enthusiastic approval of the deeds that he had done and its counsel regarding what remained to be accomplished.

Considering these developments, he could no longer wait for the Hand's tenth birthday to deal with her. He couldn't even delay until they returned to the site of the Gimp's grave in Montana, though the moldering boy lay less than half a day away.

The Teelroy farmhouse offered an excellent alternative stage for the final act in the sad and useless life of the Hand. Of course, he wouldn't be able to force her to confront, to touch, to kiss, and to settle down with her brother's decomposing remains before he killed her, as he'd dreamed of doing for several months. He regretted being denied that delicious and sustaining memory. On the bright side, the maze offered the privacy that was necessary to torment the Hand at length, without much fear of interruption. And the very architecture of the Toad's bizarre construction provided an ideal home for terror. Preston's time alone in the Montana forest with the Gimp had been bliss. Admittedly, the bliss of a flawed man, but bliss nonetheless. This game with the Hand would be bliss doubled, tripled. And when it was over, as cruel as his pleasure would have been, he still would be able to take satisfaction – and even a measure of quiet pride – from the fact that in one day he had terminated three pathetic and useless drudges, preserving the resources that they would have consumed in the years ahead, sparing all useful people from the sight of their misery, and thereby increasing the total amount of happiness in the world.

69

The alien shapechanger, come to save the world, looked like a nice boy. Although not as dreamy as Haley Joel Osment, he had a sweet face and an appealing sprinkle of freckles.

'In the entire known universe, there are only two species of shapechangers,' he earnestly informed her, 'and mine is one of them.'

'Congratulations,' Leilani said.

'Thank you, ma'am.'

'Call me Leilani.'

He beamed. 'Call me . . . well, you wouldn't be able to pronounce it, considering the way the human tongue works, so just call me Curtis. Anyway, these are also the two most ancient species in the known universe.'

'How much of the universe *is* known?' she asked.

'Some say forty percent, others think closer to sixty.'

'Gee, I thought it would be no more than fourteen to sixteen percent. Okay, so are you here to change the world for the better or to pretty much destroy it?'

'Oh, Lord, no, my people aren't destroyers. That's the *other* species of shapechangers. They're evil, and they seek only to serve entropy. They love chaos, destruction, death.'

'So being the two most ancient species . . . it's sort of like angels and demons.'

'More than sort of,' he said, with a smile as enigmatic as that of the sun god on the ceiling. 'Not to say we're perfect. Good Lord, no. I myself have stolen money, orange juice, frankfurters, and a Mercury Mountaineer, although I hope and intend to make restitution. I have picked locks and entered premises not my own, driven a motor vehicle at night without headlights, failed to wear my seat belt, and lied on numerous occasions, though I'm not lying now.'

The funny thing was, she believed him. She didn't know exactly *why* she believed him, but he seemed credible. Having spent her entire life in the company of deceivers, she'd developed perfect pitch when it came to differentiating the sour notes of lies from the music of the truth. Besides, she'd spent half her life being hauled around in search of ETs, and as bogus as the vast majority of the chased-down reports had proved to be, she had nevertheless been steeped in the concept of otherworldly visitors, and unconsciously she had come to accept that, even if elusive, they were real.

Here she stood face-to-face with a genuine space cadet and, for once, not one born on this world.

'I've come here,' the boy said, 'because my dog told me you were in great distress and danger.'

'This keeps getting better.'

Shy, peering out from between Curtis's legs, head slightly bowed and eyes rolled up to gaze at Leilani, the cute mutt slaps its tail against the floor.

'But I'm also here,' the boy said, 'because you're radiant.'

Second by second, Curtis appeared to be more the equal of Haley Joel Osment.

'Do you need help?' he asked.

'God, yes.'

'What's wrong?'

Listening to herself, Leilani realized that what she was telling him – and what remained to be told – was nearly as incredible as his declaration of his extraterrestrial origin, and she hoped that he, too, possessed the perfect pitch to separate lies from truth. 'My stepfather's a murderer who's going to kill me soon, my druggie mother doesn't care, and I don't have anywhere to go.'

'Now you do,' said Curtis.

'I do? Where? I'm not too keen on interstellar travel.'

From the bedroom at the back of the *Fair Wind*, with an unfailing instinct for spoiling a good mood, old Sinsemilla called, 'LaniLani-LaniLaniLaniLani!' in an ululant squeal. 'Come here, hurry! Lani, come, I *neeeeeeed* you!'

So shrill and eerie was dear Mater's voice that Polly, the Amazon behind Curtis, pulled a gun from her purse and held it with the muzzle pointed at the ceiling, alert and ready.

'Coming!' Leilani shouted, desperate to forestall her mother's appearance. More softly to the alien delegation, she said: 'Wait here. I'll handle this. Bullets probably wouldn't work even if they were silver.'

Suddenly Leilani was scared, and this wasn't the dull grinding anxiety with which she lived every day of her life, but a fear as sharp as the scalpel with the ruby blade that her mother sometimes used for self-mutilation. She was afraid Sinsemilla would burst out of the bedroom and be among them in a wicked-witch whirl, or pursue them in a shrieking fit, all the stored-up flash of electroshock therapy sizzling back out of her in a fury, and that in an instant she would put an end to all hope – or otherwise get herself shot by an alien blond bombshell, which Leilani didn't want to see happen, either.

She took three swift steps past the foot of the sofabed, and then an amazing thought struck her nearly hard enough to knock her down. Halting, she looked at Cass beyond the window, at Curtis, at Polly behind him, and at Curtis again, before she found the breath to say, 'Do you know Lukipela?'

The boy's eyebrows arched. 'That's Hawaiian for Satan.'

Heart racing, she said, 'My brother. That's his name, too. Luki. Do you know him?'

Curtis shook his head. 'No. Should I?'

The timely arrival of aliens, even without whirling saucer and levitation beam, ought to be miracle enough. She shouldn't expect to discover that the greatest loss in her hard nine years would prove to be no loss at all. Though she saw divine grace and mercy at work in the world every day, and felt its power, and survived always on the strength she drew from it, she knew that not all suffering would be relieved in this life, for here people had the free will to lift one another but also to smash one another down. Evil was as real as wind and water, and Preston Maddoc served it, and all the fervent hope in one girl's heart could not undo what he had done.

'LANILANILANILANI! Lani, I *neeeeeed* you!'

'Wait,' she whispered to Curtis Hammond. 'Please wait.'

She moved as fast as ever her inhibiting left leg had allowed her to move, to the back of the *Fair Wind*, through the half-open door into the bedroom.

70

Along the county road, lush meadows trembled in the wind, but no crop circles or elaborate designs formed in the grass as Preston passed.

The sky lowered steadily, as portentous as those in numerous films about alien contact, but no mother ship materialized out of the ominous clouds.

Preston's quest for a close encounter would not end here in Idaho, as he had hoped. Indeed, he might spend the remaining years of his life traveling in search of that transcendent experience, seeking the affirmation that he believed ETs would give him.

He was patient. And in the meantime, he had useful work – which continued now with the Hand.

Aware that the clock was ticking off her last days, the Hand had begun to seek a way out of her trap. She had developed an unexpected bond with the Slut Queen and the ditzy aunt, had extracted the knife in her mattress only to find Tetsy's penguin, and had then developed strategies to fight or evade Preston when he came for her.

He knew all this because he could read her journal.

The coded shorthand that she had invented for her writings was clever, especially for one so young. If she had been dealing with someone other than Preston Maddoc, her secrets would not have been plumbed.

Being a highly respected intellectual with friends and admirers in many academic disciplines, in several major universities, he had connected with a mathematician named Trevor Kingsley, who specialized in cryptography. More than a year ago, that codemaker – and breaker – had employed sophisticated encryption-analysis software to decipher the Hand's journal.

Having been provided with a transcription of one full page from the journal, Trevor expected to get the job done in fifteen minutes, because that was the average time required to crack any simple code devised by anyone lacking significant education in various branches of higher mathematics; by comparison, more ingeniously composed systems of encryption required days, weeks, even months to penetrate. Instead of fifteen minutes, using his best software, Trevor required twenty-six, which impressed him; he wanted to know the codemaker's identity.

Preston couldn't understand what was so impressive about the code having resisted analysis for just an additional eleven minutes. He withheld the Hand's name and made no mention of her relationship to him. He professed to have found the journal on a park bench and to have developed a keen curiosity about it because of its mysterious-looking contents.

Trevor also said that the text on the sample page was 'amusing, acerbic but full of gentle humor.' Preston had read it several times, and although he was relieved to discover that nothing in it required him to paste patches on his original park-bench story, he hadn't been able to find anything to smile about. In fact, using the translation bible that Trevor provided, Preston secretly studied the entire journal – a few pages every morning when Leilani showered, odd bits and pieces as other opportunities arose – and found not one amusing line, cover to cover. In the year since, continuing to sneak peeks at the girl's self-important scribblings, he'd not been charmed into even a faint smile by any of her observations in subsequent entries. In fact, she'd revealed herself to be a disrespectful, mean-spirited, ignorant little smart-ass who was as ugly inside as out. Evidently, Trevor Kingsley had a degenerate sense of humor.

These past few days, as the journal entries revealed that the Hand was scheming to save herself, Preston made careful preparations to overcome her resistance with ease when he was ready to take her to a suitably secluded killing ground. He didn't know when and in what circumstances he might need to overpower her, and while he hadn't any concern that she could effectively resist him, he didn't want to give her a chance to scream and perhaps draw the attention of someone who would intervene on her behalf.

Since Friday, when they had driven east from California, he'd been carrying a folded, one-quart Hefty OneZip plastic bag in the left back pocket of his pants. The bag could be closed airtight by means of a small plastic slide-seal device built into it. Inside the OneZip was a washcloth saturated in a homemade anesthetic that he had produced by combining carefully measured quantities of ammonia and three other household chemicals. In his life's work, he had used this concoction to assist in a few suicides. When inhaled, it caused instantaneous collapse into unconsciousness; sustained application resulted in respiratory failure and in the rapid destruction of the liver. He intended to use this anesthetic only to ensure against resistance and induce unconsciousness, because as a killing weapon, it was too merciful to excite him.

Nun's Lake lay one mile ahead.

71

Old Sinsemilla, wearing a sarong in a bright Hawaiian pattern, sat among the disheveled bedclothes, leaning back against mounds of pillows. She'd torn the pages out of her worn copy of *In Watermelon Sugar* and scattered this enlightening confetti across the bed and floor.

She wept but with fury, red-faced and tear-streaked and shaking. 'Somebody, some bastard, some sick *freak* screwed around with my book, screwed it all up, and it's not right, it's not *fair.*'

Leilani cautiously approached the bed, looking for pet-shop boxes and the equivalent. 'Mother, what's wrong?'

With a snarled curse that tied her face in red knots of anger, Sinsemilla snatched handfuls of torn pages off the rumpled sheets and threw them in the air. 'They didn't print it right, they got it all wrong, all backwards, they did it *just to mess with me.* This page where that page should be, paragraphs switched around and sentences backwards. They took a beautiful thing, and they turned it into just a bunch of *shit*, because they didn't want me to *understand*, they didn't want me to *get the message.*' Mere tears gave way to wretched sobs and with her fists she pounded her thighs, struck herself again and again, hard enough to bruise. And maybe she hit herself because on some level she understood that the problem wasn't the book, that the problem was her stubborn insistence to find the meaning of life in this one slim volume, to demand that broth be stew, to acquire enlightenment as easily as she daily attained escape through pills, powders, and injections.

In ordinary times – or as ordinary as any time could be aboard the *Fair Wind* – Leilani would have been patient with her mother, would have assumed the bitter role always expected of her in these dramas, providing sympathy and reassurance and attentive concern, drawing out the woman's anguish as a poultice draws upon a wound. But this moment was extraordinary, for lost hope had been restored by means fantastic and perhaps even mystical; therefore, she dared not squander this chance by being once more entangled either by her mother's emotional demands or by her own yearning for a mother-daughter reconciliation that could never happen.

Leilani didn't sit on the bed, but remained standing, didn't offer commiseration, but said, 'What do you want? What do you need? What can I get for you?' She kept repeating these simple questions as Sinsemilla wallowed in self-pity and in perceived victimization. 'What do you need? What can I get for you?' She kept her tone of voice cool, and she persisted, because she knew that in the end no amount of sympathy or attentive concern would in fact bring peace to her mother and that Sinsemilla would, as always, finally turn for solace to her drugs. 'What do you need? What can I get for you?'

Persistence paid off when Sinsemilla – still crying, but trading anger for a good pout – slumped back against the pillows, head hung, and said, 'My numbies. Need my numbies. Took some stuff already, but wasn't numbies. Weirded me. Must've been bad shit. Supposed to take me after Alice down the rabbit hole, but it weirded me into some snake hole instead.'

'What numbies do you want? Where are they?'

Her mother pointed toward the built-in dresser. 'Bottom drawer. Blue bottle. Numbies to chase the head snakes out.'

Leilani found the pills. 'How many do you want? One? Two? Ten?'

'One numbie now. One for later. Later's gonna come. Mommy's got a bad day goin', Lani. Snaky day goin' here. You don't know trouble till you've been your mommy.'

A bottle of vanilla-flavored soy milk stood on the nightstand. Sinsemilla sat up and used the milk to chase the first pill. She put the second on the nightstand with the bottle.

'Do you want anything else?' Leilani asked.

'A new book.'

'He'll buy you one.'

'Not that damn book.'

'No. Something else.'

'Some book makes sense.'
'All right.'
'Not one of your stupid pigmen books.'
'No. Not one of them.'
'You'll get stupid reading those stupid books.'
'I won't read them anymore.'
'You can't afford to be ugly *and* stupid.'
'No. No, I can't.'
'You've got to *face* up to bein' *screwed* up.'
'I will. I'll face up to it.'
'Ah, shit, leave me alone. Go read your stupid book. What does it matter? Nothing matters anyway.' Sinsemilla rolled onto her side and drew her knees up in the fetal position.

Leilani hesitated, wondering if this might be the last time that she saw her mother. After what she had endured, after growing all these grim years in the harsh desert of Sinsemilla, she should have felt nothing less than relief, if not joy. But it wasn't easy to cut yourself loose of what few roots still held you down, even if they were rotten. The prospect of freedom thrilled her, but life as a tumbleweed, blown here and there and to oblivion by the capricious winds of fate, wasn't a much better future than this.

Leilani murmured too softly for her mother to hear, *'Who will take care of you?'*

She had never imagined that such a concern would cross her mind when the longed-for chance to escape at last arrived. How peculiar that so many years of cruelty had not hardened Leilani's heart, as she had so long believed to be the case, but proved now to have made it tender, leaving her capable of compassion even for this pitiable beast. Her throat thickened with something not quite grief, and her chest tightened in a Gordian knot of pain the causes of which were so complex that she would need a long, long time to untie it.

She retreated from the bedroom. Into the bath. Into the galley.

Holding her breath. Expecting Curtis and Polly to be gone.

They were waiting. And the dog, tail whisking the floor.

72

Micky had not driven more than sixteen hundred miles just to die. She could have died at home with a bottle and enough time, or by compacting her Camaro against a bridge abutment at high speed if she'd been in a hurry to check out.

When she had regained consciousness, she'd first thought that she *was* dead. Strange walls enclosed her, like nothing she'd ever seen either waking or in nightmares: structures neither plumb nor plaster-smooth, curving to enfold the space, appearing organic to her blurred vision, as if she were Jonah in the belly of the whale, already beyond the stomach of the leviathan and trapped now within a turn of its intestine. The foul air smelled of mold and mildew, of rodent urine, vaguely of vomit, of floorboards cured with layers of spilled beer dating back beyond Micky's birth, of cigarette smoke condensed into a sour residue, and underlying all that – and more – was the faint but acidic scent of decomposition. For a breath, for five or six rapid heartbeats, she thought she might be dead because this was what Hell could be like if it turned out not to be as operatic as always portrayed in books and movies, if instead Hell were less about fire than about futility, less about brimstone than about isolation, less about physical torture than about despair.

Then her vision cleared in her left eye. Realizing that these walls were formed of trash and bundled publications, she knew where she must be. Not Hell. Inside the Teelroy house.

She couldn't have intuited this interior when earlier she'd been standing on the front porch, talking to Leonard Teelroy, but now she could infer the identity of the inhabitant from the evidence.

In addition to all the other aromas in this rich stew of odors, she smelled blood. Tasted it, too, when she licked her lips.

She was having difficulty opening her right eye, because the lashes were stuck together by a wad of congealed blood.

When she tried to wipe the blood away, she discovered that her hands were bound tightly at the wrists, in front of her.

She was lying on her side, on a matted musty brocade-upholstered sofa. Crowded in front of the sofa were a TV and an armchair.

A pulse of tolerable pain beat, beat, beat along the right side of her skull, but when she raised her head, the pulse became a throb, the pain became an agony, and she thought for a moment that she would pass out. Then the torment subsided to a level she could endure.

When she tried to sit up, she discovered that her ankles were bound as securely as her wrists and that a yard-long tether, which connected the wrist and ankle restraints, would not permit her either to stretch out or stand to full height. She swung both legs as one, planted her feet on the floor, and perched on the edge of the sofa.

This maneuver triggered another paroxysm of head pain that made her feel as though one side of her skull were repeatedly swelling and deflating like a balloon. This was familiar to her; call it party head, morning-after head, just worse than she'd ever experienced it before, not accompanied by the usual remorse, but by cold anger. And this wasn't the irrational anger she'd so long nurtured as an excuse to isolate herself, but was a rage tightly focused on Preston Maddoc.

He had become for her the devil incarnate, and perhaps not for her alone, and maybe not merely metaphorically speaking, but in fact. In the past few days, a new perception of evil had settled on Micky, and it seemed to her that the evil of men and women was – as she would once have ardently denied – a reflection of a greater and purer Evil that walked the world and worked upon it in ways devious and subtle.

When the pain subsided once more, she leaned forward and wiped her blood-plastered right eye against her right knee, swabbing the glutinous clots from lashes to blue jeans. Her vision proved to be fine; the blood hadn't come from the eye but from a gash on her head, which might still be oozing but was no longer bleeding freely.

She listened to the house. The silence seemed to grow deeper the longer that she waited for it to be broken.

Logic suggested that Leonard Teelroy had been killed. That he had lived here alone. And that now the house was Maddoc's playpen.

She didn't cry out for help. The farmhouse sat on a lot of open land and far back from the county road. There were no neighbors to hear a scream.

The doctor of doom had gone somewhere. He would be back. And sooner rather than later.

She didn't know exactly what he planned to do with her, why he hadn't killed her in the woods, but she didn't intend to wait around for the chance to ask him.

He had fashioned impromptu bonds from lamp cords. Copper wires encased in soft plastic.

Considering the material with which they were formed, the knots shouldn't have been as tight as they were. Looking closely, Micky saw that these makeshift shackles were cleverly and strongly interwoven, employing as few knots as possible – and that each knot had been fused by heat. The plastic had melted, encasing the knots into hard lumps, foiling any attempt to untie them, and making it impossible to loosen the cords by persistently stretching and relaxing them.

Her attention returned to the armchair. On the table beside the chair, an ashtray brimmed with cigarette butts.

Maddoc had probably used Teelroy's butane lighter to melt the cords. Maybe he'd left it behind. What had been fused with heat might be entirely melted away, freeing her, if she approached the task with caution.

Her wrists were too tightly bound to allow her to hold a lighter in such a way as to apply the flame to the knots between her wrists without also burning herself. The knots between her ankles, however, could be more safely attacked.

She slid off the sofa and, limited by the tether between ankles and wrists, stood hunched, knees slightly bent. The play in the cord that linked her ankles was insufficient to allow her to walk or even shuffle, and when she tried to hop, she lost her balance and fell, nearly striking her head on the table beside the armchair, meeting the floor with teeth jarring impact.

Had she not avoided the table, she might easily have broken her neck.

Remaining on the floor, lying on her side, Micky squirmed like a snake, searching for the butane lighter beside the chair, behind it.

Close to the floor, the pervading stink pooled thicker than it had been higher up, so thick that she could actually taste it. She had to struggle to repress her gag reflex.

A crack-boom-crash, loud enough to shake the house, caused her to cry out in alarm, because for an instant she thought that she had heard a door being slammed, slammed hard, announcing the return of the demon himself. Then she realized that the sound was a peal of thunder.

The pending storm had broken.

In his rental car, entering Nun's Lake after having driven south from the airport in Coeur d'Alene, Noah Farrel used his cell phone to ring Geneva Davis. When Micky had called her aunt this morning before leaving Seattle, Geneva would have told her that her nervy three-hundred-dollar ploy to rope the hapless PI into this game had worked and that he was on his way to Idaho. He wanted Micky to wait for him, instead of going off half-cocked. Geneva would have told her niece, per Noah's instructions, to call home again from Nun's Lake to leave the name of a local diner or other landmark where he could meet her as soon as he arrived. Now, when he got Geneva on the line to find out where this rendezvous had been set, he discovered that Micky hadn't called this morning from Seattle and had not rung from Nun's Lake, either.

'She has to be there by now,' Geneva fretted. 'I don't know whether to be just worried or worried sick.'

The radiant girl is surprisingly quick to trust strangers. Curtis suspects that anyone who shines like she does must possess exceptional insight that allows her to perceive, to some depth, whether those people whom she encounters have largely good or bad intentions.

She takes with her no suitcase, no personal effects, as though she has nothing in this world but what she wears, as if she needs no mementos and wishes to walk out of her past entirely and forever – though she does remember the journal on the bed. She retrieves it before coming so close to Curtis and Old Yeller that, through the dog, he can *feel* the warmth of her glorious shine.

'Mother's giving a great performance as a wasted acidhead. She's really into the role,' Leilani says softly. 'She might not know I'm gone until I've published maybe twenty novels and won the Nobel prize for literature.'

Curtis is impressed. 'Really? Is that what you foresee happening to you?'

'If you're going to foresee anything at all, then you might as well foresee something big. That's what I always say. So tell me, Batman, have you saved *other* worlds?'

Curtis is tickled to be called Batman, especially if she is thinking of Michael Keaton's interpretation, which is the only really *great* Batman, but he must be honest: 'Not me. Though my mother saved quite a few.'

'It figures our world would get a novice. But I'm sure you'll be good at it.'

The girl's confidence in him, although unearned, makes Curtis blush with pride. 'I'm going to try my best.'

Old Yeller moves from between Curtis's legs to Leilani, and the girl reaches down to stroke her furry head.

By virtue of the boy-dog bond, Curtis almost swoons to the ground when he is swept by the powerful tidal wash of sister-become's emotional reaction to Leilani. She is as enchanted as any dog ever could be – which is saying a lot, considering that dogs are born to be enchanted every bit as much as they are born to enchant.

'How do you know that a world needs saving?' Leilani asks.

Avoiding a swoon, Curtis says, 'It's obvious. Lots of signs.'

'Are we getting out of here this week or next?' asks Polly, who has climbed all the way into the motor home.

She steps aside to let sister-become, then Leilani and Curtis, precede her to the door. The dog bounds out of the motor home, but the radiant girl descends the steps with caution, planting her good leg on the ground first, then swinging the braced leg down beside it, wobbling, but at once regaining balance.

Descending to Leilani's side, feeling the dog shiver anew at the spoor of evil that lingers around the motor home, Curtis wonders, 'Where's your stepfather, the murderer?'

'He went to see a man about an alien,' Leilani says.

'Alien?'

'It's a long story.'

'Will he be back soon?'

Suddenly her fine face darkened from within as she surveyed the shaded campground, where a wind had risen to shake showers of loose needles out of the high boughs of the overarching evergreens. 'Maybe any minute.'

Having abandoned her post on the overturned trash can beside the motor home, Cass joins them in time to hear this exchange, which she clearly finds disturbing. 'Honey,' she says to the girl, 'can you run with that thing weighing you down?'

'I can hurry, but not as fast as you. How far?'

'The other end of the campground,' Cass says, pointing past the dozens of intervening motor homes and travel trailers, all battened down for bad weather, warm lights glowing in their windows.

'I can make it easy,' Leilani assures them, starting to limp in a quick hitching gate, in the direction that Cass pointed. 'But I can't hurry at top speed all the way.'

'Okay,' Polly says, moving with Leilani, 'if we're going to do this crazy thing—'

Cass grabs Curtis by one hand and pulls him with her as though he might otherwise roam off in the wrong direction like a Rain Man or a Gump, and as she heads eastward, she continues Polly's speech in one of their fractured duologues: '– *if we're really* going to do it, and risk being chased down—'

'– as kidnappers—'

'– then let's—'

'– move ass.'

'Curtis, you run ahead with me,' Cass directs, now treating him less like alien royalty than like an ordinary boy. 'Help me pull up stakes. We'll have to hit the road as quick as we can, storm or no storm, and head for the state line.'

'I'll stay with you, Leilani,' Polly says.

Reluctant to leave the girl's side, Curtis digs in his heels and holds Cass back, but only long enough to say, 'Don't worry, you'll like the Spelkenfelters.'

'Oh,' Leilani assures him, 'I like nothing better than a good Spelkenfelter.'

This eccentric answer spawns in Curtis several questions.

Cass denies him further socializing when she hisses, '*Curtis!*' Her tone of voice is not unlike the one that his mother had used on the three occasions when he'd displeased her.

Lightning spears the sky. The prickly shadows of the evergreens leap, leap across the brightened ground, over the walls of the ranked motor homes and trailers, as though running from those hot celestial forks or from the roar of thunder that after two seconds chases them.

The dog sprints for the Fleetwood, Cass sets a pace that argues for the proposition that she has some canine blood in her veins, too, and Curtis follows where duty calls.

He looks back once, and the radiant girl is rocking along on her braced leg faster than he had expected. This world is as vivid as any Curtis has ever seen, and more dazzling than many, but even among the uncountable glories of this place and even with the fabulous Polluxia at her side, Leilani Klonk is the focus of this scene and seems to trail the whole world behind her as if it were but a cloak.

≈   ≈   ≈

A private investigator's license reliably received a snappy response anywhere in the country, regardless of the state in which it had been issued. As often as not, women who had a moment earlier looked *through* you suddenly found you to be a man of dark mystery and magnetic power. Thousands upon thousands of detective novels, episodes of television programs, and suspense films were a magic brush that painted a romantic veneer over many a wart and wattle.

The male registration clerk at the campground office didn't flutter his eyelashes with desire when Noah Farrel flashed his PI license, but the guy responded, as did most men, with acute interest and a sort of friendly envy. Fiftyish, he had a pale face wider at the bottom than at the top, and a body that matched the proportions of the face, as though the dullness of his life had distorted him and pulled him down more effectively than gravity could ever manage. He wanted all the vicarious thrills he could get from Noah. Convincing him that cows could sing opera would be easier than getting him to believe that a private detective's work amounted to a boring parade of faithless-husband and disloyal-employee investigations. He *knew* that it must be a whirl of hot babes, cool gunplay, fast cars, and fat envelopes full of cash money. He asked more questions than Noah, not only about the current case, but also about the Life. Noah lied baldly in response, portraying this investigation as a grindingly tedious hunt for potentially key claimants in a class-action suit against a major corporation, with a legal filing deadline looming so near that he had to track people on their vacations, and he fabricated glamorous details about his prior adventures.

The helpful clerk confirmed that Jordan Banks had rented a prime campsite earlier in the afternoon. The license number and description of the motor home – a converted Prevost bus – matched the information that Noah had obtained, through police contacts, from the California Department of Motor Vehicles. Bingo.

The clerk also recognized Micky when Noah presented a photograph that he'd obtained from her aunt. 'Oh, yeah, absolutely, she come around earlier today, before Mr. Banks arrived, asking had he checked in yet.'

Alarm stiffened Noah's bones and drew him up from a slump to full height. If Maddoc knew that she had come looking for him . . . .

'She's his sister,' said the clerk. 'Pullin' a surprise for his birthday, so I didn't say word one to him when he checked in later.' His eyes narrowed. 'Say, she *is* his sister, you think?'

'Yes. Yes, she is. Has she been back since Mr. Banks arrived?'

'Nope. Hope she comes around 'fore my shift ends. She's a tonic to the eyes, that girl.'

'Do I need a visitor's pass?' Noah asked.

'Don't work that easy. If he didn't leave your name, which he didn't, I have to send one of my grounds boys down there to campsite sixty-two and ask if I should put you through. Problem is, one of 'em is off sick today, and the other's run half-crazy doin' two jobs. I got to go down there myself and do the askin' while you wait here.'

The first lightning of the coming storm flared beyond the office windows, and a hammerfall of thunder rattled every pane, sparing Noah the expense of fishing a C-note from his wallet and playing out one of the most cliched scenes in all of detective fiction.

The clerk winced and said, 'Don't like to leave my station in a storm. Got responsibilities here. Hell, anyway, you're next thing to the cops, aren't you?'

'Next thing,' Noah agreed.

'Go on, then. Pull your car up, and I'll raise the gate.'

~ ~ ~

The first bolt of lightning, thrown open with a crash, had not unlocked the rain. The longer part of a minute passed before another bolt, brighter than the first, slammed out of the hasp of the heavens and opened a door to the storm.

Scattered drops of rain, as fat as grapes, snapped into the oiled lane that served the many campsites, striking with such force that sprays of smaller droplets bounced a foot high from each point of impact.

Leilani's best speed was behind her. The cyborg leg might appear to be ass-kicking fearsome, but it cramped sooner than she expected, perhaps because she'd done so little walking these past few days when they had been on the road. She lost the smooth hip action necessary to keep swinging along, and she couldn't reestablish the rhythm.

The prelude to the symphony of rain lasted only seconds before a Niagara cascaded onto the campground, a concert composed entirely of furious drums. The downpour came so hard that even where the trees arched across the lane, the instantly sodden boughs provided little protection.

She tried to shield her journal against her body, but the wind whipped sheets of rain against her, and she saw the pressboard cover darkening as it sucked up the water. She was already soaked to the skin, as wet as if she'd gone swimming fully clothed, and clutching the notebook against her chest provided it no protection whatsoever.

Putting a hand on Leilani's shoulder and leaning close to be heard over the roar of the rain and over thunder that now came in volleys, Polly said, 'Not far! That Fleetwood, thirty yards!'

Pushing the journal into Polly's hands, Leilani said, 'Take this! Go ahead! I'll catch up!'

Polly insisted they were close, and Leilani *knew* they were close, but she couldn't move as fast as Polly because the cramps in her leg had grown painful, and because she was unable to recover the correct hip rhythm no matter how hard she tried, and because the dirt service lane – generously oiled to suppress the dust – proved slippery when wet, adding to her balance problems. No matter how aggressively she insisted on being a dangerous young mutant every day of her life, she was undeniably a disabled little girl in a situation like this, regardless of how much that galled her. She pushed the journal into Polly's hands, gut-wrenched by the thought that rain was seeping through the pages, smearing the ink, making her elaborate code hard if not impossible to read, gut-wrenched because between these covers were years of her suffering, not merely tales of Sinsemilla and Dr. Doom, but so many memories of Lukipela in detail that she might not be able to perfectly recall. On these pages were the observations and the ideas that would help her to become a writer, to become *someone*, to take her shapeless life and to impress meaning and purpose upon it, and it seemed to her that if she lost these four hundred pages of tightly written, highly condensed experience, if she allowed them to be reduced to meaningless blurs and smears, then her life would be meaningless, as well. On one level, she knew this fear was unfounded, but *that* wasn't the level on which she was operating, so she shoved the journal into Polly's hands and screamed, '*Take it, keep it dry, it's my life, it's my LIFE!*' Maybe this seemed crazy to Polly, and in fact it was crazy, absolutely loony, but she must have seen something in Leilani's face or eyes that scared her, shook her, moved her, because maybe twenty-five yards from the Fleetwood, she accepted the journal and tried to jam it in her purse, and when it wouldn't fit, she ran with it. The sky, an ocean coming down; the wind, a banshee whirling. Leilani slipped and slid, staggered and stumbled, but kept hitching forward, propelling herself toward the Fleetwood, relying as much on the power of positive thinking as on her legs. Polly sprinted ten yards, slowed, looked back, still fifteen yards from the trailer, no longer the vivid figure that she had been, but merely a gray phantom of an Amazon, faded by curtain upon curtain of rain. Leilani waved her onward – 'Go, go!'

– until Polly turned away and continued running. Polly closed to within ten yards of the motor home, Leilani within twenty, every yard a gazelle leap for the woman and every yard a struggle for the girl, until she wondered why she hadn't applied the power of positive thinking as determinedly to the healing of her twisted leg as she had to the growth of her breasts.

~ ~ ~

Down on the floor, Micky was half convinced she could *see* the rank stench like a faint green-yellow fog eddying in the first few inches above the floorboards.

She sought the butane lighter but couldn't find it. After less than a minute spent in the search, she took another and longer look at the bizarre walls towering over her, and realized that using fire to undo the knots in her bonds presented a greater danger than a minor skin burn. Shackled and fettered, able to squirm along hardly more efficiently than an inchworm, she dared not risk unintentionally igniting a major blaze.

As a second blast of thunder rocked the day and as the *tramp-tramp-tramp* of rain marched across the roof, she scanned the walls, seeking some item in the trash that might serve her. Only the coffee cans held promise.

Maxwell House. Four rows of large four-pound cans, each row measuring six cans wide, were wedged between columns of twine-bundled newspapers, with more papers stacked under and atop them. A plastic lid capped each can.

No one would keep twenty-four *unopened* cans of Maxwell House here instead of in a pantry. People saved empty coffee containers to store things in. Teelroy, who apparently had never thrown out anything in his life, who seemed to have filled his home with an eccentric collection worthy of a chapter in a psychology textbook, surely would not have left any of these twenty-four empty.

Micky inched away from the chair, passed the TV, arrived at the Maxwell House display, rose onto her knees with more than a little effort, and got a firm grip on one of the cans in the topmost of the four rows. She hesitated to wrench the container out of the stacks, fearful that she would trigger a sudden collapse of the entire wall, burying herself in a ton of moldering trash.

After studying the structure, assessing its stability, she opted for action, realizing that she had no other choice. At first the can seemed to be as immovable as a stone mortared in a rampart. Then it wiggled a little between the compressed block of newsprint above it and the second row of cans below. Wiggled, slid, and came loose.

Still on her knees, bracing the can between her thighs, Micky pried at the stubborn lid. Over the years, the plastic had pressure bonded to the aluminum. Micky clawed at in frustration, but at last tore it off.

At least a hundred small pale crescents, varying in color from white to dirty yellow, spilled out of the can, onto the floor at her knees, before she corrected its tilt. Thousands of little quarter-moons filled the container, and Micky stared in bafflement for a second, not because she failed to identify the contents, but because she couldn't wrap her mind around the scope of Teelroy's obsessive hoarding. Fingernail and toenail clippings: *years'* worth.

Not all had come from the same two hands. Some were smaller than others and bright with nail polish: a woman's trimmings. Maybe the whole family had contributed in years past when there had been more people living here than just poor Leonard with his needful, desperate eyes. Multigenerational obsession.

She set the can aside, worked loose another one. Too light. Not likely to contain anything of use to her. She clawed it open anyway.

Hair. Oily hair clippings.

When Micky popped the lid off a third can, a clean calcium scent wafted up, a sort of seashell smell. Peering inside, she cried out and let the container drop from between her thighs.

The can rolled across the floor, spilling the tiny white skeletons of six or eight birds, all as fragile as sugar lace. They were too small to have been anything but canaries or parakeets. The Teelroys evidently had kept parakeets, and every time one of their little birds had died, they had somehow separated feathers and flesh from the bones, saving those blanched and brittle remains for . . . For what? Sentimental reasons? The papery bones crumbled as the skeletons rattled across the floor, and the skulls, none bigger than a cherry tomato, bounced and tumbled and rattled like misshapen dice.

Maybe she had too quickly dismissed the idea that she was dead and in Hell. This place had surely been a hell of sorts for Leonard Teelroy and evidently for other Teelroys before him.

These coffee cans weren't going to yield anything of use.

This foul room didn't contain a clock, but she could hear one ticking nonetheless, counting down to Preston Maddoc's return.

~ ~ ~

Clutching the rain-soaked journal, Polly reached the Fleetwood, opened the door, climbed inside, paused on the steps, turned to urge Leilani to hurry – and saw that the girl had vanished.

Having disconnected the utility hookups, Curtis appeared around the front of the motor home just as Cass, ensconced in the driver's seat, started the engine.

'Trouble!' Polly shouted, tossing the journal into the lounge and then plunging out of the Fleetwood, once more into the downpour.

She surveyed the rain-washed campgrounds, numb with disbelief. The girl had been right behind her. Polly had looked back, and the girl had been trailing by no more than fifteen feet, and Polly had sprinted the rest of the way to the Fleetwood in maybe *five seconds*, for God's sake; and yet the girl was *gone*.

~ ~ ~

The windshield wipers were barely able to cope with the torrents that streamed down the glass, but Noah piloted his rental car through the campgrounds and located site 62 with little difficulty, though he wondered if he should have made arrangements for an ark instead of a coupe.

He gaped in amazement at Maddoc's motor home, a behemoth that appeared to be almost as big as the average roadside diner. It rose in the deluge as a galleon might loom out of the mists on a storm-tossed sea, and Noah's Mazda seemed like a rowboat riding a deep trough windward of the great ship's starboard hull.

His intention had been to scout site 62 and find a place from which he could maintain surveillance on it at least for fifteen or twenty minutes, until he had gained a better sense of the situation.

That plan had to be discarded, however, when he saw that the door to the Prevost stood wide open in the tempest.

The wind pinned the door against the wall of the vehicle. Rain slashed into the cockpit, and during the minute that Noah watched, no one appeared to close up.

Something was wrong.

≈   ≈   ≈

Lightning bared its bright teeth in the sky, and its reflection gnashed in the mirrored blacktop surface of the county road.

Nun's Lake lay two miles behind Preston, the farmhouse just a mile ahead.

In spite of having been washed thoroughly by the rain, he felt dirty. The desperate nature of the moment had required that he touch the Hand, including the most deformed parts of her, without a chance to pull on a pair of gloves.

Unless he could find work gloves at the Teelroy house, he would have to touch her again, more than once, before the afternoon drew to a close, if only to carry her into the filthy heart of the living-room portion of the maze, where he had left the Slut Queen. There, he would secure her to the armchair, which would allow her a front-row seat for the murder of her friend.

She herself would die in that armchair, after he had indulged the brute within and had done a satisfying number of hurtful things to her. He had been born for this, and so had she. Both of them were broken spokes in the dumb grinding wheel of nature.

Those tortures could be conducted without touching the Hand directly, using imaginative instruments. Therefore, the moment that he had secured her, he would vigorously wash his hands with a strong soap and lots of water nearly hot enough to scald. He would feel clean then, and the coiling nausea in his stomach would relent, and he would be able to enjoy his necessary work.

He worried at the possibility that the Toad might not have soap, and then he let out a short sharp bark of laughter. Even as slovenly as that bearded geek had been, it was more likely that he would have *thousands* of slivers of soap-bar remains, carefully stored and maybe even cataloged, than that he would have no soap at all.

Slowly regaining consciousness, the Hand groaned softly on the seat beside him. She was sitting up, restrained by the belt, her head slumped against the window in the passenger's door.

The plastic Hefty OneZip bag lay on the console, folded but not sealed. Driving with one hand, he fished the anesthetic-saturated washcloth out of the bag and spread it over the girl's face.

He didn't want to apply it continuously, for fear of killing her too soon and too mercifully.

Her groaning subsided to an anxious murmur, and her hideous hand stopped twitching in her lap, but she didn't grow as still as she had been previously. Once exposed to the air, the homemade anesthetic in the cloth had begun to evaporate, and the rain had further diluted the chemical, even though he had quickly returned the cloth to the bag after initially felling her with the fumes.

Repeatedly, he checked the rearview mirror, expecting to see the shimmer of headlights through the silver skeins of rain.

He remained confident that the storm had adequately screened him from observers when he had captured the Hand. Even if other campers, at their windows, had been able to glimpse anything of significance in the bleak light and the occluding cloudburst, they would be likely to interpret what they'd seen as nothing more sinister than a father scooping up his errant child and carrying her through thunderclaps and thunderbolts to safety.

As for the two women and the boy from that Fleetwood, he had no clue who they were or what they had been doing in his motor home. He doubted that they were associates of the Slut Queen, because if she'd come to Nun's Lake with backup, she probably wouldn't have stationed herself alone in the woods to watch the farmhouse.

Whoever they were, they could not have gotten past the alarm system unless the Black Hole had let them inside. When Preston had left for the Teelroy farm, he'd told the stupid bitch to keep the *Fair Wind* buttoned up tight. In the past, she'd always done what he required of her. That was the deal. She knew the deal well, all the paragraphs and subparagraphs and clauses, knew it as well as if it actually existed in a written form that she could study. It was a good deal for her, a dream contract, providing a fortune in drugs and a quality of life she couldn't otherwise have known, guaranteeing the aggressive and unrelenting disso-lution for which she hungered. In spite of how crazy she was –

crazy and venal and sick – she'd always upheld her end of the bargain.

Occasionally, of course, the Hole stuffed herself with so many contraindicated chemicals that she didn't remember the deal any more than she remembered who she was. Those depths of indulgence rarely occurred this early in the day, but nearly always at night, when he usually arranged to be present to manage her with a whiff of this same homemade anesthetic if she could not be calmed by words or by a little physical force.

He removed the cloth from the girl's face and threw it on the floor instead of bothering to return it to the plastic bag. She still groaned and rolled her head against the back of the seat, but the job was done: They had reached the turnoff to the Teelroy farm.

The driving wind gave way to hard shifting gusts that blew from more than one point of the compass, causing the door to rattle and bang against the side of the big Prevost, but still no one rushed to secure it.

Drenched during the few seconds that he was exposed while racing from the car to the motor home, Noah Farrel entered cautiously but without pausing to knock. He ascended the steps, stood beside the co-pilot's seat. He listened to the door thumping behind him and to the mad drumming of the rain on the metal roof, seeking other sounds that might help him to analyze the situation, hearing nothing useful.

An unfolded sofabed occupied most of the lounge. One lamp cast light down upon three hula dolls, two motionless and one rotating its hips, and sprayed light up on a dreamily smiling painted face that filled most of the ceiling.

Disregarding the daylight, which settled as gray as a coat of wet ashes on the windows, the only additional illumination issued from the rear of the vehicle, past the open door to the bedroom. The light back there was subdued and red.

Saturday afternoon, when he'd left Geneva Davis's place to do some final research on Maddoc and to pack a suitcase, and again this morning during his flight to Coeur d'Alene and then during his drive to Nun's Lake, Noah mulled over numerous approaches to the problem, each depending on different circumstances that he might encounter when he arrived here. None of his scenarios included *this* situation, however, and after all his mulling, he was forced to wing it.

The first choice was whether to proceed silently or to announce his presence. He decided on the latter course. Affecting a jolly-fellow-camper voice, he called out, 'Hello! Anybody home?' And when he got no reply, he eased past the sofabed, toward the galley. 'Saw your door open in the rain. Thought something was wrong.'

More hula dolls on the dining-nook table. On the galley counter.

He glanced toward the front of the Prevost. No one had entered behind him.

Lightning flared repeatedly, and every window flickered like a television screen afflicted by inconstant reception. Ghostly faces, formed of shadows, swarmed the rain-smeared panes and peered into the motor home as though spirits strove to channel themselves from their plane of existence to this one through the transmitting power of the storm. Thunder boomed, and after the last peal had tolled to the far end of the sky, a tinny vibration lingered in the metal shell of the motor home, like the faint screaky voices of haunting entities.

Proceeding toward the back, he called out once more, 'You okay, neighbor? Does anybody need help here?'

In the bathroom, hula dolls flanked the sink.

At the open bedroom door, Noah hesitated. He called out again, but received no answer.

He stepped across the threshold, out of the shadowy bath, into the crimson glow, which had been achieved by draping the lamps with red blouses.

Beside the rumpled bed, she waited, standing straight, head held high on a graceful neck, as though she were a titled lady who'd risen to grant an audience to an inferior. She wore a brightly patterned sarong. Her hair appeared windblown, but she had not been out in the storm, for she was dry.

Her bare arms hung slackly at her sides, and although her face was a mask of serenity, like the peaceful countenance of a Buddhist meditating, her eyes were as twitchy as those of a rabid animal. He'd seen this contrast before, and often in his youth. Though she didn't appear to be amped out on meth, she was operating on a substance more potent than caffeine.

'Are you Hawaiian?' she asked.

'No, ma'am.'

'Why the shirt?'

'Comfort,' he said.

'Are you Lukipela?'

'No, ma'am.'

'Did they beam you up?'

On his long trip to Nun's Lake, during all his planning, Noah had not anticipated, under *any* circumstances, that he would boldly reveal his intentions either to this woman or to Preston Maddoc. But Sinsemilla – easily identifiable from Geneva's description – reminded him of Wendy Quail, the nurse who had killed Laura. Sinsemilla didn't resemble Quail, but in her serene face and her bird-bright busy eyes, he detected a smugness, a self-satisfaction, a self-*adoration* that the nurse, too, had worn as though it were the aura of a saint. Her attitude, the atmosphere in this place, the sound of the front door banging in the wind, cranked up the heat under the stew pot of his instinct, and he suspected that Micky and Leilani were someplace beyond mere trouble. He said, 'Where's your daughter?'

She took a step toward him, swayed, stopped. 'Luki baby, your mommy's glad you got healed all righteous and then got fast-grown into a whole new incarnation, been out there to the stars and seen cool stuff. Mommy's glad, but it scares her, you comin' back here like this.'

'Where's Leilani,' he persisted.

'See, Mommy's got new babies comin', pretty babies different only in their heads, not like you used to be different, all screwed up in your hips. Mommy's movin' on, Luki baby, Mommy's movin' on and don't want her new pretty babies hangin' with her old gnarly babies.'

'Has Maddoc taken her somewhere?'

'Maybe you been to Jupiter and got healed up, but you still got the gnarly inside you, the little crip you used to be is still like a worm inside your spirit, and my new pretty babies will see all the sad gnarly in you 'cause they're gonna be *true wizard* babies, got themselves total psychic powers.'

Until now loosely cupped at her side, Sinsemilla's right hand tightened into a fist, and Noah knew that she held a weapon.

When he backed off a step, she rushed him. Her right arm came up, and she slashed at his face with what might have been a scalpel.

Past his eyes the keen blade arced, glimmering with red light, two inches short of a blinding cut.

He leaned away from the attack, then came in under it and seized her right wrist.

The scalpel in her left hand, unanticipated, punctured his right shoulder, which was a stroke of luck, pure good luck. She could have slashed instead of jabbed, opening his throat and one or both of his carotid arteries.

The wound registered more as pressure than as pain. Rather than struggle to disarm her, when suddenly she was spitting and screaming like a Tasmanian devil, he kicked her legs out from under her and simultaneously pushed her backward.

As she fell away, she held fast to the scalpel with which she'd scored, yanking it out of him. *That* was all pain, no pressure.

She landed on the bed and virtually bounced to her feet, not with any grace, but with the jerky energy of a jack-in-the-box.

Noah drew the snub-nosed .38 out of the belt-clipped holster in the small of his back, from beneath his shirt. Loath to use the revolver, he was even less enthusiastic about being carved like Christmas turkey.

He expected only more of what she'd given him thus far, more irrational ranting and an even more determined effort to remake his face and anatomy, but she surprised him by tossing aside the blades and turning away from him. She went to the dresser, and he stepped farther into the room rather than retreat from it, because he feared that she was going for a handgun. She came up with bottles of pills instead, muttering over them, letting some drop out of her hands, throwing others aside angrily, ransacking the drawer for still more bottles, until at last she found what she wanted.

As though she had forgotten Noah, she returned to the bed and settled down on the tossed sheets, amid the torn and crumpled pages of a book. She crossed her legs and sat like a young girl waiting for her friends to arrive for a pajama party, tossed her head, and laughed insouciantly. As she popped open the bottle of pills, she chanted in a singsong voice: 'I am a sly cat, I am a summer wind, I am birds in flight, I am the sun, I am the sea, I am *me*!' With one of the wanted pills in hand, she allowed the others to spill among the bedclothes. At last looking up at Noah, she said, 'Go, go, Luki baby, you don't have a place here anymore.' And then, as if never she had drawn his blood, she began to rock her head back and forth, shaking her tangled locks, and she sang again: 'I am a sly cat, I am a summer wind, I am birds in flight . . . .'

Noah retreated, backing across the bathroom, keeping a watch on the red-lit bedroom, holding fast to the gun in his right hand, using his left hand to test the wound in his shoulder. The pain was sharp but not intolerable, and though blood had spread across the front of his shirt, the bleeding wasn't arterial. She hadn't severed any major blood vessels or punctured a vital organ. His biggest problem would be the risk of infection – assuming he got out of here alive.

As Noah backed into the galley, the woman continued her singsong chant, celebrating her wonderfulness, which reassured him that she remained on the bed where he had left her.

When he reached the dinette, Noah turned, intending to flee with no regard for pride.

A young boy, a statuesque blonde, and a dog stood in the lounge, and as much as that sounded like the opening line of one of those a-priest-a-rabbi-and-a-minister jokes, Noah didn't have a smile in him. The boy had freckles, the blonde had a 9-mm pistol, and the dog had a bushy tail that, after a moment, began to wag so vigorously that its burden of rain spattered opposite walls of the motor home.

Eternally waiting Indians, guardians without power, watched him bring the Hand into the house. He dumped her on the hall floor at the entrance to the maze.

The door had bounced open when he kicked it shut after himself. He closed it and engaged the lock.

With his hands, he pressed some of the water out of his hair, slicking it back from his face.

The girl lay in a sopping mound. The shiny braced leg stuck out at a severe angle from the shapeless rest of her. The runt hadn't fully regained consciousness. She muttered and sighed – and belched, which disgusted Preston no less than if she'd urinated on herself.

He could feel the microscopic filth of this useless little cripple crawling on his hands, squirming in the webs of his fingers.

Reluctantly, carrying her in from the Durango, he had reached the conclusion that he wasn't going to be able to spend the time with her that he had allotted. The women and the boy in the Fleetwood were a wild card. He could no longer assume that he would have a long period of privacy here in the Mad Kingdom of Teelroy.

Now he would have to kill the Slut Queen with less finesse than planned. He no longer had the leisure for exquisitely protracted violence. In front of the girl, he would finish her friend as quickly as he might crush the skull of a rat with a shovel.

The runt would try to avoid watching. Therefore, in addition to binding her to the armchair, he would have to fix her head immovable and tape open her eyes.

Preston could risk a few minutes, only a very few, to torment the girl. Then he would leave her bound and would set fire to the maze as he backed out of the hub where she would be left to die with the TV off. No episode of *Touched by an Angel* to buck her up in her last minutes.

As he left, he would tell her how her brother suffered. He'd ask her where her loving God was now when she needed Him, ask her whether God was maybe off playing golf with angels or taking a snooze. Leave her to the smoke and the flames. Leave her screaming with no one to hear but cigar-store Indians.

Over the years, assisting unto death many who were suicidal and some who were not, he had discovered first that a brute in him took pleasure in extreme violence, and second that killing the young was more thrilling than dispatching the old. Nursing homes were drab playgrounds compared to nurseries. He didn't know why this should be so; he only knew that it was true. True for him, and thus as true as anything could be. Objective truths don't exist, after all, only personal ones. As most ethicists agree, no philosophy is superior to that of any other. Morality is not simply relative. Morality doesn't exist. *Experience* is relative, and you cannot judge the choice of experiences that others undertake if you have chosen a different path through life. You approve my pleasure in killing the young, and I'll politely grant you the validity of your peculiar passion for bowling.

He would not have the private hours with the Hand that he had so long anticipated, which was a grievous disappointment, although a disappointment that he could bear in light of the Hole's pregnancy and considering the likelihood that she was carrying two, three, or even additional brats more twisted than the Hand and the Gimp, all needing more from the world than they could ever hope to give back. For the coming year, his work had been secured, his entertainment brilliantly arranged; and bliss would be his.

The Hand blinked blearily, regaining consciousness. While the girl remained groggy and disoriented, Preston steeled himself for the unpleasant task of carrying her to the hub of the living-room maze. He touched the runt, shuddered, plucked her off the floor, and bore her into the labyrinth, through the lobes and the binding corpus callosum of the Teelroy family's group brain as modeled here in trash and mold and mouse droppings.

Where the TV stood and the armchair waited, the floor appeared to have been the site of a voodoo ceremony: bird bones scattered in what might have been a meaningful pattern before it had been kicked apart; distributions of human hair; fingernail and toenail clippings cast like bridal rice over all else.

The Slut Queen was gone.

Tied securely, left unconscious, alone for only the twenty minutes – *twenty minutes*! – that Preston required to drive into Nun's Lake and return with the Hand, this vodka-sucking wad of human debris had nevertheless managed to screw things up. But then screwing things up was the only talent her useless kind possessed.

She couldn't have gone far. Her car still stood in the driveway, and the keys jingled softly in Preston's pocket. She probably lay nearby in the maze, still bound and unable to move fast.

He deposited the Hand in the armchair. Cringing with disgust, he uncoupled her brace and stripped it off her leg. If she regained her wits before he returned, she wouldn't be able to move any faster than the Slut Queen.

Preston took the brace away with him. It made a good club.

~   ~   ~

An Indian in a red-and-white headdress, standing proud between towering stacks of *The Saturday Evening Post*, offered no cigars, but brandished a tomahawk.

Clutching at the Indian, Micky pulled herself to her feet. Her ankles were so tightly bound, with less than two inches of play in the cord between them, that she could shuffle each foot no more than a fraction of an inch at a time. But she didn't have far to go.

Directly across the passageway from the chief, a bay in the maze wall featured a two-foot-diameter round table on which stood a lamp with a bell-shaped yellow glass shade. An ornate bronze finial in the form of a smiling cherub's head fixed the shade to the lamp rod. Being not merely shackled and fettered, but also hogtied, Micky initially intended to set the lamp carefully on the floor, where she could more easily work with it. On second thought, she knocked it off the table with a sweep of her arm.

The shade smashed, and the bulb, as well, casting this length of the labyrinth into deeper gloom. Shards of glass clinked and rattled as they spun across the floor.

For a moment, Micky froze, listening intently. The breaking lamp had been unnervingly loud in the tomb-still house. She half expected to hear heavy and ominous footsteps, to be set upon by a mazekeeper straight out of *Tales from the Crypt*, a livid-eyed undead bureaucrat dressed in ragged gravecloth and displeased about being interrupted in its dinner of dead beetles. But if a mazekeeper arrived, he would exceed in grisliness the darkest imaginative efforts of those writers who created the *Crypt*, for he would be Preston Maddoc, not shudder-evoking in appearance, but harboring the father of all monsters under his skin.

She stooped in the shadows, cautiously explored the floor, found a few large shards, gingerly tested them against her thumb, and found one sharp enough. When she sat on the table, it held her weight.

Sawing with the glass edge, Micky worked first on the length of cord that connected her wrist restraints to those that bound her ankles. The plastic cut easily, and because copper was a soft metal, the twist of wires at the heart of the cord offered only slightly little more resistance than did the coating.

Thankful that she had remained limber by faithfully adhering to an exercise regimen while in prison, she pulled her feet up onto the small table and set to work on the loops of cord that trammeled her. In a few minutes, her feet were free.

As she puzzled over how to hold the cutting edge of the glass to best apply it to her shackles without slicing her wrists, she heard faint noises elsewhere in the house. Then a loud thud was followed by a slamming door.

Maddoc had returned.

≈   ≈   ≈

Slumped in a grungy armchair, Leilani didn't know where she was or how she had gotten here, but though her thought processes remained frayed at the edges, she had no illusions that a maid would appear at any moment with a pot of Earl Grey and a tray of tea cakes.

Wherever she might be, the place reeked more nauseatingly than the worst of old Sinsemilla's toxin-purging baths. In fact, the stink was so offensive that perhaps this was where the years and years of dear Mater's extracted toxins had been shipped for disposal. Maybe this foul miasma was what the wizard-baby breeder would smell like if she hadn't soaked away her sins on a regular basis.

Leilani slid to the edge of the chair, stood up – and fell down. The stench at floor level motivated her to get a grip on herself and concentrate to expel the haze that clouded her thoughts.

Her brace had been taken. She'd been mere steps from freedom, from a Fleetwood full of aliens. Boy, dog, Amazons, and the prospect of great adventures *without* evil pigmen. Now this. The work of the doom doctor was evident. Tiny bird skulls staring with empty sockets.

≈   ≈   ≈

The Hand's useless nature, her pathetic dependency, her deep genetic corruption, squirmed across every plane and curve and crook of the steel brace as surely as bacteria swarmed the surfaces of a public toilet.

A highly educated man, Preston *knew* that her uselessness and her dependency were abstract qualities that left no residue on things she touched, and he knew that her genetic corruption could not be passed along like a viral disease. Nevertheless, his right hand, in which he held the brace, grew sticky with sweat, and as he roamed the maze in search of the Slut Queen, he became convinced that the girl's hideous residues were dissolving in his perspiration and that they would seep deep into him through his traitorous pores. In the best of times, his sweat distressed him no less than did the urine and the mucus and the other offensive products of his metabolism, but in this instance, as his hand grew slimier, his antipathy to the girl swelled into a ripe disgust, disgust into a bile-black hatred that should have been beneath an ethical man like him. With each step that he took into the stinking bowels of the labyrinth, however, what he *knew* became less important than what he *felt*.

≈ ≈ ≈

Hands still bound, holding the wicked shard of glass in front of her as though it were a halberd, Micky eased to an intersection of passageways, keeping her back against one wall of the maze, her head raised to detect faint telltale sounds. She moved as silently as fog, practicing a stealth that she had learned in childhood, when preventing further assaults on her dignity meant avoiding one of her mother's bad boys by making of herself a living ghost, silent and unseen.

She didn't pause to saw at the wrist bindings, because that tricky task would take time, at least a few minutes, and would inevitably distract her. She was St. George in the lair, and the awakened dragon prowled.

At the corner, she paused. The next passageway, meeting this one at right angles, continued both to the left and the right. She didn't want to stick her head out there and find Maddoc watching, listening. She remembered how furtively, how fox-smooth, and with what boldness he had invaded Geneva's home only a few nights ago, and she did not underestimate him.

Her assessment of him immediately proved accurate when suddenly he cursed, his voice arising no more than a few feet from her, around the corner to the left, where he had been standing without so much as a revealing inhalation. But then, in an apparent fit of uncontrolled anger, he threw down something that hit the wood floor with a hard clatter, tumbled, and came to rest in front of the termination point of the passage in which Micky sheltered, only inches from her feet: Leilani's leg brace.

If he followed the steel contraption, they would be at once face-to-face, and her survival would hinge on her ability to thrust the shard of glass into one of his eyes in the instant of his surprise. Miss, cut only his cheek or his brow, and he would take advantage of her shackled hands to finish her with brutal dispatch.

Micky held her breath. Waited. Shifted her body without moving her feet, turning to face the intersection more directly, glass at the ready.

She wore a cheap and classic Timex. No digital components. Old-fashioned watchworks in the case. She swore she could hear the *tick-tick-tick* of gear teeth biting time between them. She'd never heard them before, but she detected them now, so acutely heightened were her senses.

Nothing followed the clatter of the tossed leg brace. No sound of Maddoc approaching or departing. Just the expectant silence of a coiled snake, sans rattle.

Loud, her rampant heart stampeded. Her body resonated just as hard ground would vibrate with the thunder of a herd of drumming hooves.

Yet somehow she heard *through* the tumult of her heart, filtered it, and filtered out also the regiments of rain tramping across the roof, so she could still perceive the silence that otherwise ruled, and would perceive any sound that, however faintly, disturbed it.

Wait here another minute? Two minutes? Can't wait forever. When you stand still too long, they find you. Ghosts, living and not, must be elusive, in constant drift.

She leaned forward, exposing as little as possible, just the side of her head, one wary eye.

Maddoc had moved on. The next passageway, to the left and right, was deserted.

The brace meant Leilani had been brought here. And she must

not be dead yet, because Maddoc wouldn't have removed the brace from her corpse, only from the living girl with the cold intention of further incapacitating her.

A tough choice here. Leave the brace or try to take it? Getting Leilani out alive would be easier if the girl had two legs to stand on. But the contraption might make noise when Micky tried to gather it off the floor. Besides, with her hands tied, she couldn't easily carry the brace and also effectively wield the shard of glass as a weapon.

Micky stooped and gripped the appliance anyway, because Leilani would be not only faster and more surefooted with the brace, but also less afraid. She lifted it slowly, carefully. A faint clink and a tick. She held the brace against her body, cushioning it to prevent further noise, and rose to her feet.

Because Maddoc was rain-soaked, Micky could see which way he had gone and where he'd come from. The bare wood floor, its finish long worn away, left no water standing on the surface, but sopped up each of the man's wet steps, resulting in dark footprints.

She was sure that he must have left the girl in the space with the television, where he had bound Micky herself earlier. Indeed, the trail led to that very place, but Leilani wasn't there.

Bottles, bottles everywhere, and not one genie in them, nor any message meant to be tossed overboard at sea. They contained only the dried residue of soft drinks and beer, which in spite of its age lent a nose-wrinkling scent to the enclosed back porch.

Stabbed but not disabled, Noah had hurried around the house with Cass and found the porch door unlocked. Guns drawn, they entered.

The three-mile drive from Nun's Lake had not provided suffi cient time for Noah to get a grip on the complete background of the twins. Although he knew that they were ex-showgirls fascinated with UFOs, he remained more mystified than not by their game attitude and by their armaments.

He hadn't seen either of them fire a weapon, but from the wholly professional way they handled guns, Noah felt as comfortable having Cass for a partner as he'd ever felt about any cop with whom he had partnered during his years in uniform.

The floor of the porch groaned under the weight of a bottle collection that would, redeemed at a nickle apiece, purchase a fine automobile for the owners to put up on blocks in the front yard. When Noah led the way through a narrow walk space, the bottles made fairy music.

The door between the porch and the kitchen was double-locked. One lock could easily be loided with a credit card, but the other was a deadbolt that would not succumb to a slip of plastic.

They had to assume that Maddoc had either heard them drive up, in spite of the wind and rain and thunder, or that he had seen them arrive. Stealth might matter inside, but it didn't matter when they were *getting* in.

The bottles encroaching on both sides didn't allow him a full range of motion, but he kicked the door hard. The shock of the impact expressed itself all the way into the wound in his shoulder, but he kicked again, and then a third time. Half eaten away by dry rot, the jamb crumbled around the lock, and the door flew inward.

≈ ≈ ≈

Three blows shook the house, and Preston knew at once that his hope of having more than the briefest pleasure with the Hand had in this instant evaporated.

The Slut Queen wouldn't have made that noise. She was in the farmhouse, seeking an exit, but striving *not* to draw attention to herself. In the unlikely event that she'd already found a route through the maze, she wouldn't have needed to hammer her way out of the house.

Preston hadn't heard sirens, and no one had yelled *police*. Yet he didn't delude himself that a burglar would, by chance, have chosen precisely this point in time to force entry. Someone had come to stop him.

He abandoned his search for the Slut Queen hardly before it had begun, and turned back on his trail, eager to get to the armchair in which he'd left the Hand. He might still have time to choke the ugly little bitch to death, although such intimate contact would make his stomach churn, and then use the maze to slip away. He couldn't allow her to fall under the protection of others, after all, because if at last she was able to convince anyone to listen to her, she would be the only witness against him.

~ ~ ~

Polly wants Curtis to remain in Noah's rental car, but galactic royalty will always have its way.

Curtis wants Old Yeller to remain in the car, and he easily wins the issue that Polly lost, because sister-become is a good, good dog.

The grassless yard has turned to mud that sucks at their shoes. They splash through deep puddles as lightning strikes a pine tree in a nearby field, about a hundred feet away, causing a banner of flame to flutter briefly through the boughs before the downpour quenches the fire, and thunder loud enough to announce the Apocalypse shakes the day. It's all so *wonderful*.

On the front porch, when she tries the door and finds it locked, Polly draws the pistol from her purse and tells Curtis to stand back.

'It'd be cool to blow down the door,' the boy says, 'but my way is easier, and Mother always says the simplest strategy is usually the best.'

He places both hands lightly on the door, wills it to open, and down on the micro level, where it matters, the brass molecules of the deadbolt suddenly prefer to be *there* rather than *here*, to be in the lock's disengaged position.

'Can I learn that?' Polly asks.

'Nope,' he says, pushing the door inward.

'Got to be a spaceboy like you, huh?'

'Every species has its talents,' he says, allowing her to enter first, with her gun drawn, because in fact she edges him aside and gives him no choice.

Mummies line the downstairs hall. Indian mummies, embalmed in standing positions and clothed in their ceremonial best.

At the back of the big house, Noah or Cass is kicking down the door, and seconds later, they appear at the far end of the hallway, gaping in amazement at the mummies.

Polly signals them to check out the rooms on their end, and to Curtis, she says, 'This way, sweetie.'

He follows her into chambers more interesting than any he has seen since arriving on this world, but – Oh, Lord – it sure does seem to be the kind of place where serial killers would hang out by the dozen to reminisce about the atrocities they have committed.

Leilani wasn't in the chamber with the television, but her wet footprints lingered there, with the older, fading prints of Preston Maddoc. Micky could also see where the girl had faltered, fallen, and gotten up again, leaving the damp imprint of her sodden clothes.

Micky followed this trail from one short passageway into another, then around a second blind corner, moving far faster than prudence allowed, terrified that the girl would blunder into Maddoc.

Clearly, the bastard had brought her here to kill her, just as he'd brought Micky for that purpose. Couldn't wait for Montana. Not with the complications that Micky had brought to his plans.

The house shook with three loud, rapid knocks, not peals of thunder, but hard blows, as though someone had struck the building with a great hammer.

The noise scared Micky, because she had no idea what caused it. A death blow of some kind? Maddoc triumphant? Leilani dead?

Then Micky turned another corner, and the girl was six feet ahead, bracing herself with one hand against the maze wall, limping but making determined progress, such a small figure and yet somehow towering at the same time, her head held high, shoulders thrown back in a posture of absolute resolution.

Sensing a presence, Leilani looked over her shoulder, and her expression at the sight of a faithful friend was a joy that Micky would never forget if she lived to be five hundred and if God chose to take all other memories from her in old age. All other memories, He could have if that day came, but she would never give Him the sight of Leilani's face at this moment, for this alone would sustain her even in the hour of her death.

When he discovered that the Hand wasn't in the armchair where he'd left her, wasn't anywhere in the television annex, Preston began to set the maze on fire.

Ultimately, following what pain he'd wished to put her through, he'd always intended to leave the girl still alive so that she could live her last minutes in terror as the flames encircled her, and as the smoke stole the breath from her lungs. The former cruelty had been denied him; but he might still have the pleasure of standing in the rain outside and hearing her screams as she staggered and crawled helplessly through the baffling, burning labyrinth.

Bundled newspapers and magazines offered the best fuel. The kiss of the butane lighter ignited an immediate passionate response. The publications were so tightly compacted in the lower portions of the walls that, almost as dense as bricks, they would burn fiercely and for hours.

He circled the cramped space, bringing flame to paper in half a dozen places. He had never killed with fire before, except when as a boy he tortured bugs by dropping matches on them in a jar. Licking flames, lavishing bright tongues upon the walls, thrilled him.

When he first found the armchair empty, Preston had noticed the runt's damp footprints made patterns with his own. Now he followed them, pausing briefly every few steps to apply the lighter to the tinder-dry walls.

Neither of them had time to be weepy, but they wept anyway, even though tough babes like Micky B and dangerous young mutants were both averse to giving anyone the satisfaction of their tears.

Crying didn't slow Leilani as she used the fragment of yellow glass to cut the loops of lamp cord that shackled Micky's wrists. She needed perhaps a half minute to do the job, less than a half minute to clamp the brace around her leg.

When they were ready to move again, flames bloomed elsewhere in the maze. Leilani couldn't yet see the fire itself, but its reflected light crawled the ceiling, like swarms of bright chameleons whipping lizardy tails across the plaster.

Fear nothing. That's what the surfers said. Yeah, sure, but how long since the last time that any of those dudes had to worry about being burned to death while they were catching a honking big wave?

They started back the way they had come, but simultaneously they noticed the damp footprints, and without discussing the matter, they reached the same conclusion: Preston would follow the spoor as surely as Micky had followed it.

In truth, finding their way out was no harder if they went one direction instead of another. No easier, either.

Already, on the ceiling, slithering salamanders of firelight faded behind rising masses of smoke that were first carried on the updraft but that would soon pour down through the labyrinth in thick, choking clouds.

Micky put one arm around Leilani, lending support, and together they hurried as fast as the cyborg leg would allow. At intersection after intersection, they turned left or right, or continued straight ahead if that option existed, basing every choice on instinct – which brought them eventually to a dead end.

Two of Preston's three university degrees were in philosophy; consequently, he had taken numerous logic courses. He remembered one class that, in part, had dealt with the logic of mazes. When these three-dimensional puzzles were designed by educated mathematicians or logicians, who drew upon all their learned cunning to deceive, the result was usually a labyrinth that few could find their way through in a timely manner, and from which a certain percentage of frustrated challengers had to be rescued by guides. On the other hand, when the maze was designed by anyone other than a mathematician or a logician – by ordinary folk, that is – these more mundane mazemakers followed a startlingly predictable pattern, because the design flowed from instinct rather than from intelligent planning; evidently, embedded in every human psyche was an affinity for a basic pattern that rarely failed to be asserted in the designing of a maze. Perhaps this was the pattern of the network of caves and tunnels in which the first extended family of mankind had dwelled; perhaps the map of that earliest of all human homes had been imprinted in our genes, and represented comfort and security when we re-created it. The mystery intrigued psychologists as well as philosophers, though Preston had never spent much time brooding on the subject.

The Toad of Teelroy Farm might not have been ordinary by the standard definition of the word, but when his thought processes were compared to those of a Harvard-educated mathematician, he must be judged ordinary beyond argument. Having followed the Toad through this labyrinth once, without giving a thought to whether it conformed to the classic design, Preston suspected in retrospect that it did.

Following the scheme as he remembered it from that long-ago class, he repeatedly set fire to the stacks behind him, essentially barring his retreat. In this fashion, as the first thin gray smoke settled into the tunnels of the warren, with a heavier black soot soon to press after it, and as waves of heat began to wring noxious sweat from him, he arrived at the dead end in which the Hand and the Slut Queen had trapped themselves.

He would not have turned into that passageway, but he did hurry *past* it, catching sight of them peripherally. When he reversed course and blocked their retreat, the woman and the girl cowered together in their blind alley, coughing, squinting at him through the descending veil of smoke, clearly fearful of what he would do next.

What he did next was step into the passage, forcing them to retreat further to the end of it. Then from the midpoint, he backed out, setting fire to the walls at several places on both sides.

This seemed like old times. Bugs in a jar.

When fire suddenly appears and grows with explosive speed, Polly wants to plunge at once deeper into the maze, perhaps having bought her own image too completely, seeing herself as a superhero without cape.

Curtis restrains her.

'The girl's in there,' she reminds him, as if he's such a Gump that he's forgotten why they are here. 'And Cass, Noah – they might have gone too far in from the other end to reverse out.'

'You head back the way we came before the smoke gets too thick to see the signs we left.' At every turn, he had marked the walls with Polly's lipstick: STRAWBERRY FROST said the label on the tube. 'I'll find the others.'

'*You*,' Polly says, disbelieving, because though she knows that he is an ET, she also knows that he's a boy, and in spite of all he's told her, she can think of a boy as having but one basic form, and a vulnerable form at that. 'Sweetie, you're not going in there alone. Hey, you're not going in there *at all*.'

'I can't imagine a Spelkenfelter turning spooky on me,' Curtis assures her, 'but promise you won't.'

'What're you talking about,' she demands, shifting her attention between him and the fire ahead.

He shows her what he's talking about by ceasing to be Curtis Hammond, reverting not to any of the many forms in his repertoire, but to the shape in which he was born, an incarnation that allows him to move faster than he can move as Curtis, and with senses more acute. This is quite a performance, even if he does say so himself.

He would not be surprised if Polly fainted. But after all, she is a Spelkenfelter, and though she sways, she does not fall. Indeed, flashing back on part of the story that he told them after their Chinese dinner in Twin Falls, she says, '*Holy howlin' saints alive!*'

Micky, at the back of the dead end, didn't want to confront Preston Maddoc in part because of his greater strength and in part because of his lighter. He would probably use it to set their clothes afire.

Flames seethed over the walls along the forward half of the passageway. In a minute, the hungrily feeding fires would join from side to side, creating an impassable wall of death.

The haze of smoke thickened second by second. She and Leilani were coughing. Already, a rawness burned in her throat. Soon they wouldn't be able to breathe unless they dropped to the floor. The moment they were forced to the floor in search of clean air, however, they were as good as dead.

She turned to the back wall of this blind alley and tried to claw newspapers and magazines out of the construction, hoping to burrow through to another passageway where the flames had not yet reached. The bundled publications were so tightly packed that she couldn't pry them loose.

Okay. All right. Topple the damn thing. All this crap was just piled here, wasn't it? No one had cemented it in place. No one had reinforced it with rebar.

When she pushed against the palisade, however, it felt every bit as solid as anything the pharaohs had built. At the end caps of some passages, she'd been able to see that the maze walls were always at least two and sometimes three stacks thick, with sheets of Masonite and plyboard between layers. Perhaps more support structure existed than met the eye. She put everything she had into a shove, without effect, and then tried to rock the wall, attacked it with rhythm, pressing and relenting and pressing again, hoping to start the trash swaying, but it wouldn't sway.

Turning to face Maddoc beyond the flames, she pulled Leilani to her side and gathered her courage. She saw no option now but to rush the entrance, get out before the flames closed the way, and try to take Maddoc down before he could harm them. Bowl him over, try to kick his head if he fell – because if *she* fell, he would be trying to kick hers.

~ ~ ~

Paper whispered when it burned in great volume, crackled and popped and hissed, as well, but *whispered*, as if divulging secrets printed on it, naming names, citing sources.

Preston realized that he had lingered too long in the smoke and heat when the burning paper began to whisper the names of those whom he had killed.

The foul air remained breathable. Yet even before the smoke grew dense enough to clog the lungs, the air assailed with lethal toxins spewed out by burning materials, gases that were invisible compared to the roiling soot, but no less dangerous. The manufacture of paper required numerous chemicals, which fire liberated and transformed into even more effective poisons.

If he were hearing the names of those he killed, he had inhaled enough toxins to half unscrew his mind. He'd better get out of here before he became disoriented.

He hesitated, however, because the sight of the Hand and the

Slut Queen, trapped in the blind alley, thrilled him. He hoped they would run the fiery gauntlet before their sole escape route closed forever. Maybe they'd misjudge the moment, be caught by the shifting flames, and go up like torches – a spectacle he was loath to miss.

The vodka-sucking whore pulled the girl against her. She seemed to be trying to work out a way to use her body to shield the kid when they made their run for it, as if a few burn scars could possibly render the Hand any uglier than she already looked.

Abruptly, a section of the stacks on one side of their passage collapsed onto the floor between them and Preston, releasing clouds of sparks like fireflies and great black moths of paper ash. They could no longer exit without wading through knee-deep, furiously blazing debris.

Fate sealed, the woman and the girl retreated to the back of the cul-de-sac.

They would live another three minutes, five at most, before smoke flooded through here in smothering tides, before they became a pair of animate candles. Preston dared not wait for the final act, lest he be trapped in the house with them.

A heavy weight of disappointment lay on his heart. Their final throes, witnessed firsthand, would have given him much pleasure and thus would have added to the total amount of happiness in the world. Now their deaths would be nearly as useless as their lives.

He consoled himself with the thought that the Black Hole's first batch of lumpy cupcakes was baking in her oven.

As Preston turned away, leaving these two wads of living tallow to the mercy of the fire, the woman began to cry out for help at the top of her voice. Excited by the note of desperation in her pleas, he lingered a moment longer.

An answering shout, arising elsewhere in the maze, startled him. He had forgotten the three loud blows, likely the sounds of someone breaking down a door – further proof that the polluted air was already affecting his thinking, clouding his judgment.

Heartened, the woman cried out again, again, making a beacon of her voice.

Another answering shout rang above the rapidly rising chant of a million tongues of flame, and to Preston's left, about ten feet away, a big man in a colorful Hawaiian shirt appeared out of the mouth of another passageway. He carried a revolver.

With a shocking disregard for ethical conduct, the sonofabitch shot Preston. They were strangers; neither of them had the informed perspective necessary to judge the other's usefulness to the world; yet the ruthless bastard squeezed the trigger without hesitation.

When he saw the stranger raising the gun, Preston realized that he should fling himself backward and to the right, but he was more a man of thought than action, and before he could move, the impact of the slug punished his hesitation. He staggered, fell, rolled onto his stomach, and scrambled away from the shooter, away from the cul-de-sac in which the woman and the girl awaited burning, around a corner, into another run of the maze, shocked by the intensity of his pain, which was worse than anything he'd experienced before or had expected to be forced to endure.

~ ~ ~

'We're here!' Noah shouted to Micky and the girl. 'Hold on, we'll get you out!'

Only a few minutes old, the blaze had grown astonishingly fast throughout the front of the house. Not a man who had often – or ever – suspected that uncanny forces were afoot in the world, never having gotten so much as a single nape-hair bristle at a scary movie, Noah Farrel couldn't shake the feeling that this fire was *different*, that it was somehow alive, aware, cunning. Prowling the maze with strange purpose. Seeking more than just fuel to feed its bottomless appetite. He knew that firefighters sometimes felt this way, that they called it the Beast. When flames hissed at him, when from more distant and fully involved corridors rose what sounded like grumbling, snarling, and thick-throated cackling, Beast seemed a fitting name.

The door to the enclosed porch and the back door between porch and kitchen had been left open when he and Cass broke in. Interior doors had been removed a long time ago. Now the superheated air in the house sought the cool day beyond the bottle collection, and the accelerating draft drew smoke and ashes and hot embers through the labyrinth, and coaxed the conflagration toward a richer supply of oxygen.

Largely, the fire remained confined to the front half of the house. That wouldn't be the case much longer.

With smears of wet blood from his oozing scalpel wound, Noah had left markers on the stacked-paper walls along the route they'd followed. He was afraid that if they didn't begin to retrace their path soon, smoke would blind them to those crimson signs.

He squinted into the mouth of the dead-end passage where but a moment ago Maddoc had been posted. About ten feet long. The first four feet of both walls were afire. On the floor, a deep threshold of burning debris barred entrance. Micky and the girl, visible beyond shimmering curtains of fire, couldn't be reached from here.

Grabbing a fistful of Hawaiian shirt, Cass pulled Noah to one side and pointed out that only one of the cul-de-sac's flanking walls towered all the way to the nine-foot ceiling. The other wall, shared with the parallel corridor that she and Noah had recently followed, was two feet shorter.

Returning to that passage, out of which he had stepped before shooting Maddoc, Noah holstered his revolver and allowed Cass to give him a boost. She was tall and strong, and with an assist from her, he levered himself onto the top of the barrier that separated them from the dead end where Micky and the girl were trapped.

Going up, acutely sensitive to the stability of the stacks, Noah prepared to drop away at the first indication that his ascent might cause the trash to collapse upon the very people he hoped to rescue. The construction wasn't as supportive as a concrete-block wall, but it didn't shift under him.

At the summit, in the narrow space between the stacks and the ceiling, with his feet sticking out in the aisle where Cass waited, with his chest flat on the top of the wall, he was in thicker – though far from blinding – smoke that irritated his eyes and pricked tears from them. Better hold each breath as long possible. Minimize the amount of crap he sucked in. He couldn't, however, perform the entire operation on a single inhalation.

In the Valley of the Shadow. Every second, a tick closer to Death.

A coiled bramble of pain twisted its thorns back and forth in the scalpel wound. He almost welcomed the pain, hoping it would help compensate for the sense-dulling effect of the fumes, keeping him alert.

Gingerly but quickly, he eased forward until he could peer down into the dead-end passage. One yard to his right, seething fire ate at the floor and fed all the way up the vertical surface of the cul-de-sac. He flinched from the heat, and felt the sweat stiffen on the skin of his right forearm as it flash-dried in an instant.

The portion of the seven-foot-high wall directly below him had not yet caught fire. As Noah appeared and at once reached down with both arms, Micky looked up. Wheezing. Her face less than two feet from his. Right profile stained with thick dried blood, hair matted with blood along that side of her head.

Without hesitation, Micky boosted Leilani, and Noah could see from the woman's wrenched expression that the effort unleashed tribes of tiny devils that jabbed their pitchforks in her scalp wound.

He grabbed the girl. Muscled her up toward him. She helped as much as she could, seizing his left shoulder as though it were a ladder rung, clutching at the top of the partition. Pulled from above, pushed from below, she squeezed between Noah and the corner of the cul-de-sac, up and into the smoky crawlspace between the stacks and the ceiling.

As he felt Leilani squirm past him toward the passageway where Cass waited to lift her down, Noah hooked his hands under Micky's arms, and she followed the girl's example. She was heavier than the child, and no one pushed her from below. She gave herself as much of a boost as she could by toeing off the wall once, twice, then again, and each time she did so, Noah felt the stacks shudder under them.

Now he held his breath not merely to minimize smoke inhalation, but in expectation that the wall would shift and collapse, either burying Micky in the burning cul-de-sac or crushing him, Cass, and Leilani in the passage that they were trying to reach.

Aware of the danger, she eased quickly but judiciously past him, eeling across the two-foot-wide top of the palisade.

To his right, bright teeth of fire chewed through the stacks, almost a foot closer than when he'd first come up here. The hairs on that forearm, stiff with dried sweat, bristled like hundreds of tiny torches waiting to be lit.

Edging backward, Noah rapped his head against the ceiling. He froze as the compacted mass trembled under him. Remained frozen until it grew still once more. Then he dropped into the safe passageway, joining the others.

Safe like the *Titanic*. Safe like Hiroshima, 1945. Safe: like Hell.

The rescue operation had taken at most a minute and a half, but conditions had worsened noticeably in the meantime. Night seemed to have arrived toward the front of the maze, though it wasn't night: more like a tsunami of black water, suspended by the magical stoppage of time, powerful and roiling within itself, but not yet advancing. Veins of red fire opened in that thick blackness, bled for a moment, closed up, and new veins ruptured elsewhere. And here, the cloying air pressed upon him, heavier with portent than with smoke, pregnant with a sense of tremendous forces rapidly building beyond restraint. Blackened pages of old magazines, little more than large flakes of ash, glided lazily toward them through the air, like stingrays seeking prey, and great schools of tiny lanternfish swam overhead in sinuous parades, sometimes extinguishing themselves when they collided with the maze walls, but in other places sparking small new fires, not yet attracted downward to the hair and clothes that they would eventually find so tasty. The heat demanded a toll of greasy sweat, but then parched Noah's mouth and cracked his lips and seared the linings of his nostrils.

They were all coughing and clearing their throats, sneezing and wheezing, hawking black spit and gray phlegm.

Cass declared, 'Outta here, *now!*' and led the way, followed by Leilani and Micky.

Last man in line, .38 revolver drawn in case Maddoc still had something to prove, Noah saw the throb of firelight toward the back of the house, where they had encountered none on the way in. Maybe there would be a path around it.

Turn by turn, through the convolutions of the labyrinth, as if exploring the gyri and the sulci on the surface of a brain, Preston chose his route according to his understanding of the classic maze pattern imprinted in the human racial memory, to which all ordinary mazemakers unfailingly resorted. Maybe the Toad, in spite of bib and bristle, wasn't ordinary, after all – subhuman seemed more likely – or maybe Preston's recollection of what he'd learned in that long-ago logic class was flawed, because he seemed to be getting nowhere, and he suspected that more than once he had doubled back and crossed his path.

Blame might best be placed on the bullet wound, which steadily drained him, or on the quality of the air, rather than on faulty memory or on the Toad's failure to get in touch with his inner primitive. The Black Hole worried frequently about the ever worsening quality of the planet's air, which was under continuous assault by barbecue grills and flatulent cows and SUVs and bathroom deodorizing cakes and, oh, so many things, so many. The air in here had gotten more disgusting than the air in a vomitorium. It probably contained more psychoactive chemical toxins than the Hole kept in her entire drug supply. The Hole, the good old Hole, mess that she might be, she sometimes got a thing or two right. Preston had a buzz on, a paper-chemical buzz, exacerbated by heat and by the thin haze of smoke that lent these wooden-Indian catacombs some of the atmosphere of an opium den, though the smell was not as pleasant, and no bunks were provided for those who had toked the pipe and felt wasted, as he felt ever more wasted, step by step.

He attempted to determine which of these coral-reef accretions of trash might be piled against an outer wall of the house, because windows lay behind those stacks, windows offering escape and clean air, or as clean as air ever got in a world full of barbecue grills. Unfortunately, he couldn't stay focused on the task. One moment he would be searching urgently for concealed windows, and the next thing he knew, he'd find himself standing at a bafflingly complex juncture of passages, muttering, spitting on his shoes. Spit. Disgusting. So many fluids in the human body. Noxious fluids. He felt sick. He felt sick . . . but then he found himself peering warily around corners, searching not for windows but for the mysterious damn, sneaky damn extraterrestrials that had been eluding him for years.

For most of his life, he hadn't needed to believe in a superior intelligence. His own intelligence seemed, to him, to be as superior as anyone could expect. But he was a profound thinker, a philosopher, and a respected academic whose view of the world had been shaped – and could be reshaped – by other academics, the elite of the elite, whose value to society (in his estimation and generally in theirs, too) was of unparalleled importance. Five years ago, when he discovered that some quantum physicists and some molecular biologists had begun to believe that the universe offered profuse and even incontrovertible evidence of intelligent design, and that their numbers were slowly growing, his comfortable worldview had been shaken, had been too deeply disturbed to allow him to shrug off this information and blithely go on with his killing. He continued killing, yes, but not blithely. He could not accept any God hypothesis whatsoever because it was too limiting; it resurrected the whole business of right and wrong, of morality, which the enlightened community of utilitarian ethicists had largely succeeded in purging from society. A world created by a superior intelligence, who had imbued human life with purpose and meaning, was a world in which Preston Maddoc didn't want to exist; it was a world he rejected, for he had always been and forever would be the only master of his fate, the only judge of his behavior.

Fortunately, in the midst of his intellectual crisis, Preston had come across a most useful quote by Francis Crick, one of the two scientists who won the Nobel prize for the discovery of the double-helix structure of DNA. In a crisis of his own, Crick had reached a point at which he no longer believed that a sound scientific case could be made for evolution through natural selection. All life at even a molecular level was so irreducibly complex that it argued for intelligent design, which convinced Crick (who also wasn't too keen on this God business) that every form of life on Earth – all flora and fauna, the entire ecosystem – had been created not by God, but by an alien race of incomprehensibly vast intelligence and powers, a race that might also have created this universe itself, and others.

Extraterrestrials.

Extraterrestrial worldmakers.

Mysterious extraterrestrial worldmakers.

If that theory satisfied Francis Crick, Nobel laureate, it was plenty damn good enough for Preston Claudius Maddoc. Extraterrestrial worldmakers were no more likely to care what their creations did with their lives, in a moral sense, than any nerdy kid with an ant farm cared whether the ants inhabiting it were behaving their itty-bitty selves according to a posted set of rules.

In fact, Preston had a theory to explain why an alien race of incomprehensibly vast intelligence and powers might skip across the universe making worlds and seeding them with infinite varieties of life, intelligent and otherwise. It was a good theory, a fine theory, a *brilliant* theory.

He knew it was brilliant, pure genius, but as he stood here spitting on his shoes, he could not remember his splendid theory, not a word of it.

Spitting on his shoes? Disgusting.

He shouldn't be standing around, spitting on his shoes, when he hadn't found a window yet. The windows of any house were arranged in certain classic patterns dating back to the Stone Age and seeded in the human racial memory, so they ought to be easy to find even in this bizarre and rambling opium den.

Windows. Hidden windows. Find one of the mysterious hidden windows. Most likely, an extraterrestrial will be behind the damn thing, big grin on its worldmaker face.

He had their number. He knew what they were about. Perverse bunch of incomprehensibly intelligent and vastly powerful old farts.

His theory – yes, he remembered it now – his *brilliant* theory was that they built worlds and seeded life on them because they *got off* on the suffering of the species that they created. Not necessarily got off on in the sense of *experienced orgasms*. This was a brilliant theory, not a tacky one. But they built us to die, to die by the tens of billions over the centuries, because our deaths did something for them, provided them with something of value. Maybe there was a form of energy released every time a creature perished, an energy beyond the human ability to detect, which they employed to power their starships and toasters, or which they personally absorbed in order to guarantee themselves eternal life. Oh, they were the ultimate utilitarians, ethical in all their undertakings, creating us to be of use to them and using every one of us fully, wasting none of us.

Move over, Francis Crick. Move over, all you other lame Nobel laureates. The academy would award him not just the coveted prize, but all of Sweden, if he could prove what he had theorized.

Seeking to confirm his theory, Preston had spent the past four and a half years ricocheting around the country, from one UFO siting to another, meeting with gaggles of alien abductees, everywhere from Arkansas backwaters to Seattle, to purple mountain majesties, across the fruited plain, yearning to be beamed up and to have a chance to present his theory to the incomprehensibly intelligent worldmakers themselves in their bib overalls and straw hats, which is why he came here to Nun's Lake, only to be disappointed again, only to wind up in want of a window, spitting in his lap.

Spitting in his lap? What a repulsive act. Next thing you knew, he'd be pissing his pants. Maybe he already had.

Yet in spite of his fastidiousness, it was true: Here he sat in a peculiar corner of an odd sort of place, repeatedly and vigorously hawking up clots of vile black phlegm and spitting them in his lap. He was also ranting aloud about his theory. Deeply humiliated to hear himself raving like a booze-addled street person, he nevertheless could not shut up because, after all, deep intellectual analysis and philosophical rumination were the essence of his work. That's what he *did*. That's who he *was*. Analyzer, ruminator, killer. The only thing that perhaps he needed to be embarrassed about was that he had been talking aloud to himself . . . but then he realized that he wasn't alone, after all.

He had company.

The pall of smoke retreated like a gray tide, and the air in the immediate vicinity grew clean, and into this sudden clarity came a visitor of extraordinary appearance. It was about the size of the Hand, but not the Hand, not anything that Preston had ever previously seen or dreamed about. Feline, but not like a cat. Canine, but not like a dog. Covered in lustrous white fur, glossy as ermine, but fur that sometimes appeared to be feathers, yes, that certainly was *both* fur and feathers – and yet neither. Round and golden eyes, as large as teacups, pellucid and luminous eyes that in spite of their beauty struck fear in him, even though he understood that the visitor meant him no harm.

When it spoke, he was not surprised, though its voice – that of a young boy, mellifluous enough for the Vienna choir – was not what he expected. Evidently it had listened to his ranting, for it said, 'One problem with the theory. If incomprehensibly intelligent aliens made this world and everything in it – who made the aliens?'

An answer eluded Preston, and he could come up with nothing but another glutinous wad of black phlegm.

The gray tide flooded over him again, and the visitor retreated into the gloom, dissolved into a white blur, moving away, and then a final glimmer of luminous gold as just once it glanced back.

He felt an inexpressible loss at its departure.

The thing had been a figment of his imagination, of course, born of blood loss and toxic fumes. Figments seldom spoke. This one had spoken, though Preston couldn't remember what it had said.

The firelight dimmed as thickening haze screened it. Evidently, too many pipes were being smoked here in the old opium den.

From a far corner came a peculiar sound, a protracted *thuuuuuuud*. Then again: *thuuuuuuud*. And yet a third time: *thuuuuuuud*. Like giant dominoes toppling into one another in slow motion. Ominous.

He felt death coming. A wave. Sudden darkness, absolute. And no air, only soot that his lungs sought to store up by the pound.

Preston Maddoc screamed into a black pillow, screamed in terror at the realization that his time had come to provide a little power for the starship.

≈ ≈ ≈

Thuuuuuuud . . .

Last in line, moving toward the rear of the house, toward fire where fire had not been earlier, Noah worriedly looked back in the direction that they had come, back into air where blackened magazine pages glided like stingrays, back into the schools of lanternfish, and he saw the suspended black tsunami abruptly pour forward through the maze, and he cried out much as he had cried out when his aunt Lilly shot him so many years ago.

Thuuuuuuud . . .

Maze walls were collapsing, stacks of bundled newspapers and other trash falling into the walls beside them, triggering further collapses.

Thuuuuuuud . . . .

The floor shook with the third crash, which proved to be the last one for the time being, but the tsunami kept coming, racing toward them, a smothering tide of smoke, so dense that as it came, it muffled the voice of the fire that continued to rage behind it.

'Down!' Noah shouted.

They couldn't outrun this. They could only hit the floor, press their faces to the well-worn tongue-and-groove, and hope that an inch of sustaining air might be compressed beneath the black cloud.

Here, now. Oh, God. Darkness as deep as caves and crypts. And only a thin sour air even at the floor. Then thinner and more sour. And then no air at all, and then—

The black tide relented, dissolved away from them, until they huddled together in a miraculous clearing, where the air tasted as sweet as that in a primeval forest, lacking the slightest scent of soot. The tsunami of smoke still rushed at them, over them, and past them, providing this impossible refuge, this saving eye of calm in the tumult.

And unto them, out of the blinding masses, came a creature of such heart-stopping beauty that Noah might have fallen to his knees before it if he had not already been on the floor. As white as a fresh winter mantle in a pristine wilderness, the entity arrived utterly unsoiled by the storm of filth through which it had passed. The huge luminous golden eyes, which should have terrified Noah by virtue of their strangeness and by the directness of their regard, did not instill terror, however, but fostered a sense of peace. He was overcome by the humbling perception that this visitor saw him as no one previously had ever seen him, gazed into the secret heart of him, and was not offended by what it discovered there. No terror, no fear troubled him except the reverential fear called *awe*; instead, set loose was a joy that he hadn't been aware he contained, that all his life had been caged in his breast, and now flew free.

Rising slowly to his feet, he looked wonderingly at Cass . . . Micky . . . Leilani. They were in the grip of the same emotions by which he himself had been overwhelmed. Magic was the moment, as when doves are delivered from thin air, but these wings were Noah's, the wings of pure elation.

The enchanted being had arrived like a leopard, but it rose now and stood like a man, barely taller than Leilani, whom it approached and to whom it spoke, incredibly, in the voice of a young boy. In fact, this was perhaps the voice of Curtis Hammond: 'You still shine, Leilani Klonk.'

'You too,' said the girl.

'You can't be broken.'

'I came broken.'

'Not in the heart.'

Tears overwhelmed the girl, and Noah – with Micky and Cass – moved to her. He didn't know what was happening here, didn't understand how this magical entity and Curtis Hammond could be one and the same, but his long-worn yoke of despair had lifted, and for the moment, he did not need to understand more than that the world had changed for him, forever. He touched Leilani's shoulder, Cass touched Noah's arm, and Micky took the girl's withered hand in hers.

The golden eyes regarded each of them before lowering to Leilani once more. 'Not in the heart,' the apparition repeated. 'Suffering can't crack you. Evil can't turn you. You're going to do great things in your life, Leilani Klonk, great and wonderful things. And I ain't just shovelin' horseshit at you, neither.'

Leilani laughed through her tears. Self-consciously, as though embarrassed by what had been said of her, she looked away from her enchanted rescuer, blinked up at the sea of soot and fumes churning across the top of their protective bubble, and said, 'Hey, spaceboy, this sure is some neat trick with the smoke.'

'Smoke is just fine particles of matter. On the micro level, where will can win, I can move some of the particles from where they are to where I want them to be. It's really fewer molecules than in a deadbolt. It's a little trick. I only have three tricks, really, and they're all little ones, but useful.'

'Better than Batman,' Leilani said.

The apparition's smile proved to be as luminous as his eyes. 'Gee, thanks. But it's an energy-intensive trick, uses up a lot of frankfurters and moo goo gai pan, so we better get out of here.'

Through a tempest of smoke and fire, they traveled in cool clean air, following the signs in blood that Noah had left to mark the true path.

Along angular passageways, around a cochlear spiral, into the kitchen, through the vault of empty bottles . . .

Breathtaking gray sky, the beautiful shades of silver polished and of silver patinated. Rain, rain falling less forcefully than when they'd gone inside, rain as Noah had never felt it before: pure, fresh, exhilarating.

Polly waited in the backyard, holding Curtis Hammond's soaked clothes and shoes. Soaked herself, mud-spattered, bedraggled, she grinned like a holy fool oblivious of the storm.

As graceful as water flowing, his white fur appearing to repel the rain, the golden-eyed apparition went to Polly, recovered the boy's clothes from her, and then turned to meet the stares of all assembled until they took the hint and, as one, turned their backs to grant him privacy.

For a moment they stood in silence, still stunned, struggling to wrap their minds around the enormity of their experience, and then Leilani giggled. Her mirth infected the twins, Micky, and even Noah.

'What's so funny?' asked the apparition.

'We already saw you naked,' Leilani said through her laughter.

'Not when I'm being Curtis Hammond, you didn't.'

'It's sure nice to know,' Leilani said, 'you're not the kind of tacky alien, come to save the world, who has to shake his booty at everybody.'

As they leave the Teelroy farm in their two cars, only wisps of smoke escape from under the eaves, as well as from a few chinks here and there. Then the firestorm in the house begins to blow out windows, and great black plumes churn upward through the rain.

They reach the county road and head toward Nun's Lake without encountering any traffic.

By stepping out of his human disguise and then returning to it, the motherless boy has reestablished the original biological tension that made him easier to trace during his first few eventful days of being Curtis Hammond. For a while, if worse scalawags come scanning for him, his unique energy signal will be detectable and quickly recognized.

Immediately upon their return to the Fleetwood, they must break camp and roll out, keep moving. Motion is commotion, and all that, but he will regret departing Nun's Lake without having seen any nuns water-skiing, parasailing, or jet-boat racing. Perhaps when the world is saved, they can return here to visit, for in those better days to come, the nuns are more likely to be lighthearted and in a mood for recreation.

He looks through the back window of the Camaro to be sure that Polly and Cass are still following in Noah's rental car. Yes, Polly is behind the wheel, and Cass is riding shotgun. No doubt they have their purses on the seat beside them, open for easy access.

If ever he loses the twins, his fabulous sisters, he will be heartbroken beyond endurance, and therefore he must never lose them. Never. He has lost too much already.

Micky drives the Camaro, and Noah rides up front beside her. Leilani shares the backseat with Curtis, and Old Yeller lies between them. Exhausted from an eventful day, the dog dozes.

They ride in silence, each occupied with their thoughts, which Curtis entirely understands. Sometimes socializing is easy, sometimes hard, and sometimes socializing does not require words.

By the time they arrive at the campground, the rain stops. The washed pine trees are an enthralling green; the graceful boughs have been diamond-strung; saturated trunks and limbs as dark as chocolate shed singing birds and inquisitive squirrels into the aftermath of the storm. This is an exquisite world, and the motherless boy loves it desperately.

To reach the Fleetwood, they must pass the Prevost, and as they approach that vehicle, which had been Leilani's prison, Curtis sees emergency vehicles parked near it. The swiveling, roof-racked beacons on a police car cannot chase off the beauty of the overarching trees, but they do remind him that, although exquisite, this world turns in turbulence and is not at peace.

A uniformed police officer, standing by his cruiser, motions for Micky to drive past, to keep moving.

An ambulance stands ready, its back door open.

Two paramedics, flanking a gurney, guide it along the oiled lane, through puddles, to the ambulance.

On the stretcher lies a woman. Though Curtis has never seen her, he knows who she must be.

For her own safety and most likely for the safety of those who want to help her, Leilani's mother is strapped to the gurney. She rages against her restraints, strains furiously to slip free of them. Wildly tossing her head, she curses the paramedics, curses onlookers, and screams at the sky.

Leilani looks away, lowers her head, and stares at her hands, which are folded in her lap.

On the seat between them, sister-become has not been roused from her nap by the scene at the Prevost. Her damp flank rises and falls with her slow breathing.

As the Camaro rolls past the ambulance, Curtis reaches out and lifts the girl's deformed hand from her lap.

She looks up, and misery clouds her eyes.

He says, 'Shhhhhh,' and he gently places her palm against the sleeping dog, covering her hand with his.

Every world has dogs or their equivalent, creatures that thrive on companionship, creatures that are of a high order of intelligence although not of the highest, and that therefore are simple enough in their wants and needs to remain innocent. The combination of their innocence and their intelligence allows them to serve as a bridge between what is transient and what is eternal, between the finite and the infinite.

Of the three little tricks that Curtis can do, the first is the ability to exert his will on the micro level, where will can win. The second is the lovely ability to form the boy-dog bond. The third is the ability to teach the second trick to anyone he meets, and it is this third trick with which he can save a world.

'Shhhhh,' he repeats, and as Leilani's eyes widen, he takes her with him into the dog's dreams.

For those who despair that their lives are without meaning and without purpose, for those who dwell in a loneliness so terrible that it has withered their hearts, for those who hate because they have no recognition of the destiny they share with all humanity, for those who would squander their lives in self-pity and in self-destruction because they have lost the saving wisdom with which they were born, for all these and many more, hope waits in the dreams of a dog, where the sacred nature of life may be clearly experienced without the all but blinding filter of human need, desire, greed, envy, and endless fear. And here, in dream woods and fields, along the shores of dream seas, with a profound awareness of the playful Presence abiding in all things, Curtis is able to prove to Leilani what she has thus far only dared to hope is true: that although her mother never loved her, there is One who always has.

73

Old Yeller sprints past the open double doors of the study, gripping a brightly colored tug toy in her teeth. In close pursuit are a pair of golden retrievers named Rosencrantz and Guildenstern, or Rosie and Jilly for short.

Here in her study, Constance Veronica Tavenall, soon to be the former wife of Congressman Jonathan Sharmer, sits behind a wonderful Chinese Chippendale desk decorated with intricate chinoiserie. She is writing in her checkbook.

The lady reminds Curtis of Grace Kelly in movies like *To Catch a Thief*. She manages to be glamorous yet dignified, regal yet warm, with the gracefulness of a swan. She is not as immense, majestic, and magnificent as Donella, the truck-stop waitress, but then virtually no one is.

Noah stoops to pick up the cards that have been left on the floor near the sofa, but Ms. Tavenall says, 'No, no. Leave them the way they are. Just the way they are for a while.'

Earlier, operating under Curtis's direction, sister-become had separated from a shuffled deck all the cards in the suit of hearts. With nose and paws, she had ordered them from deuce to ace.

Rosie backs along the hall and through the study door, pulling on the tug toy – which is made of braided red and yellow ropes with a large tasseled knot at each end – and here comes Old Yeller, attached to the being-dragged end of the rope. They are growling at each other and trying to shake each other loose, but their tails wag, wag.

Ms. Tavenall tears a check out of the book and slides it across the desk to Curtis. Her handwriting is as precise and pleasing to the eye as calligraphy.

When Curtis reads the number on the check, he whistles softly.

'Oh, Lord, Ms. Tavenall, are you sure you can afford this?'

'That's for the two motor homes,' she says. 'They should be top-of-the-line because, after all, you're going to be spending a lot of time in them.'

The first motor home will be for Micky, Leilani, and Aunt Gen. The second will be for Noah, Curtis – and for Richard, whom he has not yet met.

Polly and Cass already have their wheels, courtesy of Hollywood divorces, which they had insisted upon after their producer husbands – Julian and Don Flackberg – had killed a screenwriter. The Flackberg brothers, renowned screamers, ruled their employees by terror – though they never screamed at movie stars, at critics, or at the twins. Cass says that the brothers were always sweet to her and Polly, while even Polly agrees they were Huggy Bears at home. Julian and Don had never killed a screenwriter previously, and in this case they resorted to violence only after the writer had successfully sued them for breach of contract. Over the years, Julian and Don had breached hundreds of contracts, perhaps thousands, always with impunity, and in their defense, they had tearfully claimed temporary insanity resulting from the shock of having their entire business model stood on its head.

Curtis wonders if the place to start saving the world might be in Hollywood.

At the doorway, Old Yeller finds new determination and, with the tug toy, drags Rosie away into the hall. The contract between them is one in which fun is given in return for fun, and neither would think of breaching it.

For several weeks, Curtis and his new family will be constantly on the move, until he has fully become the Curtis that he wants to be, until he can't any longer be identified by the unique biological-energy signature for which his extraterrestrial enemies – and possibly the FBI – are able to scan.

Thereafter, the worse scalawags will continue to search for him, though by less effective means. They have been at work on this world for a while, and they do not welcome interference with their plans, which are the antithesis of those that Curtis has inherited from his mother. The battle has been engaged.

He and his four new sisters, his aunt Gen, his brother Noah, his brother Richard yet unmet, and his sister-become will be Gypsies for a long time, because even when he's no longer detectable by scanners, he will be safest if he stays in motion and works in secret. Besides, the job requires extensive travel: You can't save the whole world from an office in Cleveland.

From time to time, not often but dependably, as he gives the Gift of a dog's dreams, he will encounter people who, once having received this power from him, will be able to pass it along, as he can. Each will go forth in a caravan of his or her own, sharing the Gift with still others all across the world, in every vale and peak of every continent.

The first of these is Leilani. She will not be going out on her own for many years, but the time will come. She shines.

Ms. Tavenall passes three more checks across the desk, and this time Noah whistles.

'I've postdated them at one-month intervals,' Ms. Tavenall says. 'Use them as you need the money for ongoing expenses.'

She glances at the computer on her desk and smiles.

From where he sits, Curtis isn't able to see the screen, but he knows what's on it. Earlier, following the card trick, perched upon the lady's chair and holding a stylus in her teeth, Old Yeller, under Curtis's influence, had typed: I AM A GOOD DOG. I HAVE A PLAN, BUT I NEED FUNDING.

'By the time you've used those three checks,' says Ms. Tavenall, 'we'll have worked out an entire funding scheme for the long term.'

'I don't know how to thank you,' Noah says.

'I'm the one who needs to say thank you,' Ms. Tavenall insists. 'You've changed my life twice now . . . and this time in a way I never imagined it could be changed.'

Her eyes fill with those beautiful human tears that express not anguish or grief, but joy. She blots her eyes, her cheeks, and blows her nose in a Kleenex.

Curtis is hoping for a huge funny horn-honk of a blow, like Meg Ryan cut loose with in *When Harry Met Sally*, but Ms. Tavenall hardly makes any sound. She's so discreet, genteel. He wonders if it would be good socializing if he asked for a Kleenex and then faked a huge funny horn-honk of a blow to amuse her.

Before Curtis can decide this thorny question, Ms. Tavenall throws her tissue in a waste can, rises from her chair, blinks back her tears as best she can, and says to Noah, 'The other issue may be more difficult. It's not simply a matter of writing a check.'

'His aunt and uncle have legal guardianship,' Noah says, 'but I'm pretty sure they'd be willing to relinquish it. They parked him in that care home after his parents died, and they never see him. He embarrasses them. I think the issue will be . . . financial.'

'Bastards,' she says.

This somewhat shocks Curtis because he has until now been under the impression that she is too much of a lady to know the meaning of such words.

'Well,' she continues, 'I've got good attorneys. And maybe I can pour a little charm on these people.'

'You?' Curtis says. 'Oh, Ms. Tavenall, call me a hog and butcher me for bacon if you couldn't *drown* them in charm anytime you wanted.'

She laughs, if a little oddly, and tells him that he's a lovely boy, and he's just about to reply to the effect that he never was the sassy-assed, spit-in-the-eye malefactor that some have accused him of being, when Jilly races into the study with a white rag in his teeth, pursued by Rosie and Old Yeller.

Apparently, Jilly felt left out when the game was tug-rope-for-two. He's found this rag and has somehow convinced his playmates that it is a better toy. Now they must have it, must have it, must, must, must.

'Jilly, here!' Ms. Tavenhall commands, and Jilly at once obeys, wiggling with delight as he approaches his mistress. 'Give me that, you silly pooch.'

Denied their must-have, the three dogs plop onto the carpet, panting from their play, grinning at one another.

'Since the congressman proved to be what he proved to be,' Ms. Tavenall explains to Noah, 'I've been throwing out a lot of things. I certainly don't want any mementos. Jilly must have snatched this from the trash.'

The rag isn't a rag, after all, but a T-shirt. On it are printed four words and an exclamation point. The dot of the exclamation point is in the form of a small green heart.

Reading the words on the T-shirt, remembering the man from

whom Old Yeller had stolen a sandal along the interstate highway in Utah, Curtis says, '"Love is the answer."'

'It's true, I suppose,' Ms. Tavenall says, 'even when it's said by people who don't mean it.'

Rising from his chair, Curtis Hammond shakes his head. 'No, ma'am. If we're talking about *the* answer, then that's not it. *The* answer, the whole big enchilada, is a lot more complex than that. Love alone is an easy answer, and easy answers are what usually lead whole worlds into ruin. Love is *part* of the answer, sure, but just part. Hope is another part, and courage, and charity, and laughter, and really *seeing* things like how green pine trees look after a rain and how the setting sun can turn a prairie into molten gold glass. There are so many parts to the answer that you couldn't possibly squeeze them all onto a T-shirt.'

Time passes as always time does, and the caravan settles one late-spring afternoon in a campground near a lazy river, where willow trees stencil filigrees of shadow on the purling water.

As dinnertime approaches, they bring blankets, hampers loaded with delicious things, and numerous dog toys to a grassy bank, where frogs sing and butterflies dance in sunlight as ochery as old brass.

Polly brings her Diana, a beautiful black Labrador. Cass has her Apollo in tow; he's a handsome yellow Lab.

Here is Noah with a big old goofy mutt named Norman, and the cocker spaniel, Ladybug, is the sister-become of Richard Velnod, alias Rickster.

Aunt Gen, Micky, and Leilani are accompanied by Larry, Curly, and Moe. These three golden retrievers are actually female dogs, but Aunt Gen chose the names.

Larry, Curly, and Moe were all obtained through golden-retriever rescue organizations. In the past, all three were abused, neglected, abandoned, but they are happy dogs now, with lustrous coats and quick tails and soulful eyes.

The other dogs were all rescued from pounds, and their pasts are filled with suffering, too, though you wouldn't know it to watch them chase balls, leap for Frisbees, and wriggle-wriggle-wriggle on their backs in the grass with all four paws in the air in absolute joyous celebration of the playful Presence.

Curtis, of course, has sister-become. And though all these dogs could tell enthralling stories if they could talk, Old Yeller's story surely is and most likely always will be more enthralling than any of theirs.

Games without dogs are played, as well, though Leilani insists there will be no three-legged races. Rickster and Curtis play a few rounds of *Who's the Gump?*, a game of their invention. The object is to reveal an act of supreme dumbness that you have committed; the winner is the player who, by the judgment of a third party, has done the dumbest thing. Sometimes Leilani and Curtis play *Who's the Gump?*, and Rickster judges. Sometimes Micky and Curtis play, while Aunt Gen serves as judge. Everyone likes to play the game, but they seldom play with each other; they all want to go head-to-head with Curtis. What fascinates Rickster, not just as a contestant but also as co-inventor of the game, is that Curtis usually wins, even though he is an ET, has had the benefit of massive direct-to-brain megadata downloading, and is arguably smarter than all of them.

Here under the willows by the river, after dinner, when night has fallen, when butterflies have retired for the day and flickering fireflies have come on duty to replace them, the family gathers around a campfire to share their lives, as they do more nights than not, for every one of them has seen and done and felt so much that the others have not. This is in part also the point of *Who's the Gump?* – to better know one another. Curtis's mother always said that the better you know others, the better you will know yourself, and that in the fullest sharing of experience, we learn the wisdom of a world. More important still, from the sharing of experience, we learn that every life is unique and precious, that no one is expendable; and with this discovery, we acquire the humility that we must have to live our lives well, with grace, and with gratitude for the gift of breath.

He misses his mother terribly, and the loss of her will leave a hole in his heart for the rest of his time in this life, though she will be with him in memory all his days. When those days end and he joins her again . . . oh, Lord, will they have a lot to share.

Among others, Aunt Gen speaks this evening, looking as young as a girl in the firelight. On other evenings she has told stories about her life with her beloved husband, gone now nineteen years; but on this occasion, she tells them something of her childhood lived along a river not dissimilar to this willow-shaded, moonlit water slipping past them in the night. The story is quite dramatic, involving her evil stepfather, a preacher who killed her mother and tried also to kill Geneva and her brother, for their inheritance. Most of those gathered here soon realize that this is not anything that happened to Aunt Gen, but is the story line of *The Night of the Hunter*, starring Robert Mitchum. No one raises this point, because Aunt Gen tells the story so well and with such feeling. In time, when she realizes that this is a shot-in-the-head story, not a real one, she gets sly with them and, rather than correct the record, begins to layer in elements from *The Rainmaker*, starring Burt Lancaster, and then characters and plot twists from *Kindergarten Cop*, starring Arnold Schwarzenegger. Soon they are having a grand good time.

Laughter and the presence of so many wonderful dogs inevitably encourages a visit now and then from other folks whose rigs and tents are tied down in this campground. After hard play, many of the dogs are sleeping. Although the family is not at work right now, they will always take advantage of an opportunity to pass along the Gift. And so before they all retire, long after midnight, the number of people who have gathered around the campfire has grown by seven, and there have been tears, though only tears of joy, and seven lives have been changed forever, but only for the better.

For the newcomers, after they have known the dreams of the dogs, Micky poses the riddle that she learned from Aunt Gen. *What will you find behind the door that is one door away from Heaven?*

To date, Curtis is the only one who has answered it correctly on the first try, and this evening, the seven newcomers eventually puzzle their way close to the true response, but none earns a cigar.

Leilani gives the answer according to Geneva, which everyone in the family can recite to the word. 'If your heart is closed, then you will find behind that door nothing to light your way. But if your heart is open, you will find behind that door people who, like you, are searching, and you will find the *right* door together with them. None of us can ever save himself; we are the instruments

594

of one another's salvation, and only by the hope that we give to others do we lift ourselves out of the darkness into light.'

Time passes as time does, and the campfire subsides to a mound of glowing coals. People and dogs drift home to bed.

Other than Curtis, the last two to leave are Micky and Leilani. Larry, Curly, and Moe have gone home with Aunt Gen. The campsites are about two hundred yards from these picnic grounds, and Micky lights the way with a Coleman lantern, held high. Woman and girl walk hand in hand, into a darkness that holds no fear for them. The murmur of their voices and their gentle laughter drifts back to him, all the music anyone could ever need. If this were a movie, and if Curtis were a film director, he would make this the final scene: woman and girl, saviors of each other, walking away from the camera into a future that together they have redeemed. Indeed, the movie would be called *Redemption*. Having seen 9,658 films and then some, he knows that in this final scene, as they walk away, the screen would fade to black; however, this is reality, and neither Micky nor Leilani will ever fade to black but will go on forever.

Curtis remains behind to extinguish the hot coals with river water and to stir the ashes, although he doesn't do so at once. He sits with sister-become at his side, just the two of them enthralled by the mystery of the stars and by the pearl-perfect moon, together enjoying the *rightness* of all things.

He is no longer being Curtis Hammond, for he has *become* Curtis Hammond. This world is his destiny, and he can't imagine a finer home or one more beautiful. Oh, Lord, he is a Gump, all right, but he's finding his way well enough in spite of that.

A sudden whirl of wind spins up a twist of fallen leaves, sends them dancing slowly, slowly around the perimeter of the smoldering campfire until they reach Curtis, whereupon the wind expires in a puff, casting the greenery in his face. Leaves stick in his hair, dangle from his ears. He spits one out of his mouth.

Dogs laugh. At least most of them do, and *this* one is always ready to be amused. The playful Presence must love her even more than He loves others of her kind, and He sees in Curtis not merely one who will save a world, but also a perfect foil for His jokes.

One door away from Heaven,
We live each day and hour.
One door away from Heaven,
But it lies beyond our power
To open the door to Heaven
And enter when we choose.
One door away from Heaven,
And the key is ours to lose.
One door away from Heaven,
But, oh, the entry dues.

—*The Book of Counted Sorrows*

AUTHOR'S NOTE

Utilitarian bioethics as portrayed in *One Door Away from Heaven* is unfortunately not a figment of my imagination, but a real threat to you and to everyone whom you love. This philosophy embodies the antihuman essence of fascism, expresses the contempt for individual freedom and for the disabled and the frail that has in the past marked every form of totalitarianism. One day our great universities will be required to redeem themselves from the shame of having honored and promulgated ethicists who would excuse and facilitate the killing of the disabled, the weak, and the elderly.

Serendipitously, as I was finishing this novel, Encounter Books published a nonfiction work offering the best survey of utilitarian bioethics, written for a general audience, that I have yet seen. If, for your own protection and for the sake of those you love, you want to know more about the subject than I've covered herein, I highly recommend *Culture of Death: The Assault on Medical Ethics in America* by Wesley J. Smith. You will find it more hair-raising than any novel you've ever read.

For the second time (the first having been as I worked on *From the Corner of His Eye*), I have written a novel while listening to the singular and beautiful music of the late Israel Kamakawiwo'ole. When I mentioned Bruddah Iz in that previous book, a couple thousand of you wrote to share your enthusiasm for his life affirming music. Of his six CDs, my personal favorites are *Facing Future*, *In Dis Life*, and *E Ala É*. Israel's work is available from The Mountain Apple Company, P.O. Box 22373, Honolulu, Hawaii 96823. Or visit them on the Web at www.mountainapplecompany.com.